By Tad Williams

Memory, Sorrow and Thorn
The Dragonbone Chair
Stone of Farewell
To Green Angel Tower: Siege
To Green Angel Tower: Storm

Otherland
City of Golden Shadow
River of Blue Fire
Mountain of Black Glass
Sea of Silver Light

Tailchaser's Song
Child of an Ancient City (with Nina Kiriki Hoffman)
Caliban's Hour

The War of the Flowers

Shadowmarch
Shadowplay

TAD WILLIAMS

Shadowplay

Volume Two of Shadowmarch

www.orbitbooks.net

ORBIT

First published in the United States in 2007 by Daw Books, Inc.
First published in Great Britain in 2007 by Orbit
This edition published in 2008 by Orbit
Reprinted 2009

A CIP catalogue record for this book
is available from the British Library.

ISBN: 978-1-84149-294-0

YA

Typeset in Bembo by M Rules
Printed and bound in Great Britain by
CPI Mackays, Chatham, ME5 8TD

Papers used by Orbit are natural, renewable and recyclable
products sourced from well-managed forests and certified in
accordance with the rules of the Forest Stewardship Council.

Mixed Sources
Product group from well-managed
forests and other controlled sources
www.fsc.org Cert no. SGS-COC-004081
© 1996 Forest Stewardship Council

FSC

Orbit
An imprint of
Little, Brown Book Group
100 Victoria Embankment
London EC4Y 0DY

An Hachette Livre UK Company
www.hachettelivre.co.uk

www.orbitbooks.net

This book like the first volume, is dedicated to our children Connor Williams and Devon Beale—who, since that first dedication, are a couple of years older and louder, but still quite fabulous. I flinch with love every time they shriek at me.

Acknowledgements

Those wishing the full story of my gratitude should inspect the "thank-you-all" page in *Shadowmarch*. Nothing much has changed with the second volume.

Or those who don't have Volume One to hand:

As always, many thanks to my editors Betsy Wollheim and Sheila Gilbert and everyone else at DAW Books, my wife Deborah Beale and our assistant Dena Chavez, and my agent Matt Bialer, and also my pets and children, who make every day a challenge and an adventure. (And whoever did good work without being challenged?)

Last of all, another shout-out to the folks at Shadowmarch.com. You are welcome to join us there. You don't even have to bring booze or anything. (It's a virtual community, after all.)

Irisian Ocean

MARCH KINGDOMS

Southmarch   Blueshore

Landers Port   Oscastle

Kertewall   Marrinswalk

           Silverside

Whitewood   Elusine River

Great Kertish Road

                              Weeping Moors

                          N

                    W   E

                          S

           Esterian River

Upper SYAN

        The Heartwood   TW 2006

Author's Note

For those who wish to feel securely grounded in the Who, What, and Where of things, there are several maps and, at the end of the book, indexes of characters and places and other important materials.

The maps have been compiled from an exhaustive array of traveler's tales, nearly illegible old documents, transcripts of oracular utterances, and the murmurings of dying hermits, not to mention the contents of an ancient box of land-office records discovered at a Syannese flea market. A similarly arcane and wearying process was responsible for the creation of the indexes. Use them well, remembering that many have died, or at least seriously damaged their vision and scholarly reputations, to make these aids available to you, the reader.

Contents

PART THREE: MACHINES

Prelude

THE OLDER ONES IN THE HOUSEHOLD had hunted the missing boy for an hour without result, but his sister knew where to look.

"Surprise," she said. "It's me."

His dark hose and velvet tunic gray with dust and his face streaked with grime, he looked like a very sad goblin. "Auntie 'Lanna and the other women are all making a great fuss, searching for you," she said. "I can't believe they didn't look here. Don't they remember anything?"

"Go away."

"I can't, now, stupid. Lady Simeon and two of the maids were just behind me—I heard them coming up the corridor." She set the candle between two paving stones in the floor. "If I go out now they'll know where you're hiding." She grinned, pleased with her maneuver. "So I'm staying, and you can't make me go."

"Then be quiet."

"No. Not unless I want to be. I'm a princess and you can't give me orders. Only Father's allowed to do that." She settled in beside her brother, staring up at the shelves, seldom used now that the new kitchens had been built closer to the great hall. Only a few cracked pots and bowls had been left behind, as well as a half-dozen stoppered jars whose contents were so old that opening them, as Briony had once said, would be an experiment dangerous enough for Chaven of Ulos. (The children had been thrilled to learn that the household's new physician was a man of many strange and fascinating interests.) "So why are you hiding?"

"I'm not hiding. I'm thinking."

"You're a liar, Barrick Eddon. When you want to think you go walking on the walls, or you go to Father's library, or . . . or you stay in your room like a temple-mantis saying prayers. You come here when you want to hide."

"Oh? And what makes you so clever, strawhead?"

It was a term he used often when he was irritated with her, as though the differing color of their hair, hers golden-fair, his red as a fox's back, made some difference—as though it made them any less twins. "I just am. Come, tell me." Briony waited, then shrugged and changed the subject. "One of the ducks in the moat has just hatched out her eggs. The ducklings are ever so sweet. They go *peep-peep-peep* and follow their mother everywhere in a little line, as though they were tied to her."

"You and your ducks." He scowled as he rubbed his wrist. His left hand was like a claw, the fingers curled and crabbed.

"Does your arm hurt?"

"No! Lady Simeon must be gone by now—why don't you go play with your ducks or dolls or something?"

"Because I'm not leaving until you tell me what's wrong." Briony was on firm ground now. She knew this negotiation as well as she knew her morning and evening prayers, as well as she knew the story of Zoria's flight from the cruel Moonlord's keep—her favorite tale from *The Book of the Trigon*. It might last a while, but in the end it would go her way. "Tell me."

"Nothing's wrong." He draped his bad arm across his lap with the same care Briony lavished on lambs and fat-bellied puppies, but his expression was closer to that of a father dragging an unwanted idiot child. "Stop looking at my hand."

"You know you're going to tell me, redling," she teased him. "So why fight?"

His answer was more silence—an unusual ploy at this stage of the old, familiar dance.

The silence and the struggle both continued for some time. Briony had moments of real anger as Barrick resisted her every attempt to get him to talk, but she also became more and more puzzled. Eight years old, born in the same hour, they had lived always in each other's company, but she had seldom seen him so upset outside of the small hours of the night, when he often cried out in the grip of evil dreams.

"Very well," he said at last. "If you're not going to leave me alone, you have to swear not to tell."

"Me? Swear? You pig! I *never* told on you for anything!" And that was true. They had each suffered several punishments for things the other twin had done without ever breaking faith. It was a pact between them so deep and natural that it had never been spoken of before now.

But the boy was adamant. He waited out his sister's gust of anger, his pale little face set in an unhappy smirk. She surrendered at last: principle could only stretch so far, and now she was painfully curious. "So, then, pig. What do you want me to do? What shall I swear to?"

"A blood oath. It has to be a blood oath."

"By the heads of the gods, are you mad?" She blushed at her own strong language and could not help looking around, although of course they were alone in the pantry. "Blood? What blood?"

Barrick drew a poniard from the vent of his sleeve. He extended his finger and, with only the smallest wince, made a cut on the tip. Briony stared in sickened fascination.

"You're not supposed to carry a knife except for public ceremonies," she said. Shaso, the master of arms, had forbidden it, fearing that Briony's angry, headstrong brother might hurt himself or someone else.

"Oh? And what am I supposed to do if someone tries to kill me and there are no guards around? I'm a prince, after all. Should I just slap them with my glove and tell them to go away?"

"Nobody wants to kill you." She watched the blood form a

droplet, then run down into the crease of his finger. "Why would anyone want to kill you?"

He shook his head and sighed at her innocence. "Are you just going to sit there while I bleed to death?"

She stared. "You want me to do that, too? Just so you'll tell me some stupid secret?"

"So, then." He sucked off the blood, wiped his finger on his sleeve. "I won't tell you. Go away and leave me alone."

"Don't be mean." She watched him carefully—she could see he would not change his mind—he could be as stubborn as a bent nail. "Very well, let me do it."

He hesitated, clearly unwilling to do something as unmanly as surrender his blade to his sister, but at last let her take it. She held the sharp edge over her finger for long moments, biting her lip.

"Hurry!"

When she did not immediately comply, he shot out his good arm, seized her hand, and forced her skin against the knife blade. It cut, but not too deeply; by the time she had finished cursing him the worst of the sting was over. A red pearl appeared on her fingertip. Barrick took her hand, far more gently now, and brought her finger against his.

It was a strange moment, not because of the sensation itself, which was nothing more noteworthy than the girl would have expected from rubbing a still-sore finger against her brother's, smearing a little blood across the whorled fingertips, but because of the intensity in Barrick's eyes, the way he watched that daub of red with the avidity of someone witnessing something far more arresting: lovemaking or a hanging, nakedness or death.

He glanced up and saw her staring. "Don't look at me like that. Do you swear you'll never reveal what I tell you? That the gods can punish you horribly if you do?"

"Barrick! What a thing to say. I'm not going to tell anyone, you know that."

"We've shared blood, now. You can't change your mind."

She shook her head. Only a boy could think that a ceremony with knives and finger cutting was a stronger bond than having shared the warm darkness of a mother's womb. "I won't change my mind." She paused to find the words to convey her certainty. "You know that, don't you?"

"Very well. I'll show you."

He stood up, and to his sister's surprise, clambered onto a block of wood that had been used as a pantry stool since before either of them could remember, then scrabbled in the back of one of the upper shelves before pulling out a bundle wrapped in a cleaning-rag. He took it down and sat again, holding it carefully, as though it were something alive and potentially dangerous. The girl was caught between wanting to lean forward and wanting to scramble away, in case anything might jump out at her. When the stained cloth had been folded back, she stared.

"It's a statue," she said at last, almost disappointed. It was about the size of one of the privy garden's red squirrels sitting up on its hind legs, but there the resemblance to anything ordinary ended: the hooded figure, face almost entirely hidden, was made of cloud-chip crystal, gray-white and murky as frost in some places, clear and bright as cathedral glass in others, with colors ranging from the palest blue to pinks like flesh or watered blood. The squat, powerful figure held a shepherd's crook; an owl crouched on its shoulder like a second head. "It's Kernios." She had seen it somewhere before, and reached out her hand to touch it.

"Don't!" Barrick pulled it back, wrapped the cloth around it again. "It's . . . it's bad."

"What do you mean?"

"I don't know. I just . . . I hate it."

She looked at him curiously for a moment, then suddenly remembered. "Oh, no! Barrick, is that . . . is that the statue from the Erivor Chapel? The one Father Timoid was so angry about when it went missing?"

"When someone *stole* it. That's what he said, over and over." Barrick flushed, a bold burst of red on his pale cheeks. "He was right."

"Zoria's mercy, did you . . . ?" He did not speak, but that was an answer in itself. "Oh, Barrick, why?"

"I don't know. I told you, I hate it. I hate the way it looks, so blind and quiet, just . . . thinking. Waiting. And I can feel it all the time, but it's even worse when I'm in the chapel. Can't you *feel* it?"

"Feel what?"

"It . . . I don't know. It's hot. It makes a hot feeling in my head. No, that's not right. I can't say. But I hate it." His little face was determined again, pale and stern. "I'm going to throw it into the moat."

"You can't! It's valuable! It's been in the family for . . . for a long time."

"I don't care. It's not going to be in the family any longer. I can't even bear to look at it." He stared at her. "Remember, you promised, so you can't tell anyone. You swore an oath—we shared blood."

"Of course I won't tell. But I still don't think you should do it."

He shook his head. "I don't care. And you can't stop me."

She sighed. "I know. No one can stop you doing anything, redling, no matter how foolish. I was just going to tell you not to throw it in the moat."

He stared at her from beneath a furious brow. "Why?"

"Because they drain it. Don't you remember when they did it the summer before last and they found those bones of that woman who drowned?"

He nodded slowly. "Merolanna wouldn't let us go see—like we were babies! I was so angry." He seemed to regard her for the first time as a true collaborator rather than an antagonist. "So if I throw it in the moat, someone will find it someday. And put it back in the chapel."

"That's right." She considered. "It should go into the ocean. Off the outwall behind the East Lagoon. The water comes up right under the wall there."

"But how can I do it without the guards noticing?"

"I'll tell you how, but you have to promise me something."

"What?"

"Just promise."

He scowled, but she had obviously caught his curiosity. "So be it, I promise. Well, how do I throw it over without the guards seeing me do it?"

"I'll go with you. We'll say we want to go up and count the seagulls or something. They all think we're children, anyway—they don't pay any attention to what we do."

"We *are* children. But why does you coming along help? I can throw it off myself, you know." He looked down quickly at his clenched left hand. "I can get it into the water easily. It's not very heavy."

"Because I'm going to fall down just when we get to the top. You'll be just in front of me and the guards will stop to help me—they'll be terrified I've broken my leg or something—and you just step to the wall and . . . do it."

He stared at her with admiration. "You're clever, strawhead."

"And you need someone like me to keep you out of trouble, redling. Now what about that promise?"

"Well?"

"I want you to swear on our blood oath that the next time you think of something like stealing a valuable statue out of the chapel, you'll talk to me first."

"I'm not your little brother, you know . . . !"

"Swear. Or the oath I made doesn't count anymore."

"Oh, very well. I swear." He smiled a little. "I feel better."

"I don't. For one thing, think of all those servants who were stripped and searched and even beaten when Father Timoid was looking for the statue. It wasn't their fault at all!"

"It never is. They're used to it." But he at least had the good sense to appear a little troubled.

"And what about Kernios? How is he going to feel about having his statue stolen and thrown into the sea?"

Barrick's open expression shuttered again. "I don't care about that. He's my enemy."

"Barrick! Don't say such things about the gods!"

He shrugged. "Let's go. Lady Simeon must have given up by now. We'll come back and get the statue later. We can take it up to the wall tomorrow morning." He stood, then reached down his good hand to help his sister, who was struggling with her long skirts. "We'd better clean this blood off our hands before we get back to the Residence or they'll be wanting to know where we've been."

"It's not very much blood."

"It's enough to cause questions. They love to ask questions—and everyone pays attention to blood."

Briony opened the pantry door and they slipped back out into the corridor, quiet as phantoms. The throne hall was also oddly quiet—tomb-silent, as though the immense old building had been holding its breath while it listened to the whispering voices in the pantry.

PART ONE

MASKS

1

Exiles

If, as many of the Deep Voices believe, the darkness is just as much a something as is the light, then which came first after Nothing—the dark or the light?

The songs of the oldest voices claim that without a listener there can be no first word: the darkness was until the light became. The lonely Void gave birth to the Light of love, and afterward they made all that would be—the good and bad, the living and unliving, the found and lost.

—from *One Hundred Considerations,*
out of the Qar's *Book of Regret*

IT WAS A TERRIBLE DREAM. The young poet Matt Tinwright was declaiming a funeral ode for Barrick, full of high-flown nonsense about the loving arms of Kernios and the warm embrace of the earth, but Briony watched in horror as her twin brother's casket rocked and shook. Something inside was struggling to escape, and the old jester Puzzle was doing his best to hold down the lid, clinging with all the strength of his scrawny arms as the lid creaked and the box shuddered beneath him.

Let him out, she wanted to cry, but could not—the veil she wore was so tight that words could not pass her lips. *His arm, his poor crippled arm!* How it must pain him, her poor dead Barrick, having to struggle like that in such a confined place.

Others at the funeral, courtiers and royal guards, helped the jester hold the lid down, then together they hustled the box out of the chapel. Briony hurried after them, but instead of the grass and sun of the graveyard, the chapel doorway led directly downward into a warren of dark stone tunnels. Tangled in her cumbersome mourning garments, she could not keep up with the hurrying mourners and quickly lost sight of them; soon all she could hear were the muffled gasps of her twin, the coffined prisoner, the beloved corpse—but even those noises were growing fainter and fainter and fainter . . .

Briony sat up, heart fluttering in her chest, and discovered herself in a chilly darkness pierced by the bright, distant eyes of stars. The boat rocked under her, the oars creaking quietly in their locks as the Skimmer girl Ena slipped them in and out of the water with the smooth delicacy of an otter sporting in a quiet cove.

Only a dream! Zoria be praised! Barrick is still alive, then—I would know it if he wasn't, I'm sure of it. But although the rest of the terrible fancy had melted like fog, the rasping of labored breath hadn't. She turned to find Shaso dan-Heza slumped over in the boat behind her, eyes closed, teeth clenched so that they gleamed with reflected starlight in his shadowed face. Air scraped slowly in and out; the old Tuani warrior sounded near death.

"Shaso? Can you talk to me?" When he did not reply, Briony grabbed at the thin, hard shoulder of the Skimmer girl. "He's ill, curse you! Can't you hear him?"

"Of course I can hear him, my lady." The girl's voice was surprisingly hard. "Do you think I am deaf?"

"Do something! He's dying!"

"What do you want me to do, Princess Briony? I cleaned and bound his wounds before we left my father's house, and gave him good tangle-herb for physick, but he is still fevered. He needs rest and a warm fire, and even then it may not do him any good."

"Then we need to get ashore! How far to the Marrinswalk coast?"

"Half the night more, my lady, at the best. That is why I have turned back."

"*Turned back?* Have you lost your mind? We are fleeing assassins! The castle is held by my enemies now."

"Yes, enemies who will hear you if you shout too loudly, my lady."

Briony could barely make out the face beneath the hooded cloak, but she didn't need to see to know she was being mocked. Still, Ena was right in at least one thing: "All right, I'll talk more quietly—and *you* will speak to the point! What are you doing? We cannot go to the castle. Shaso will die there more surely than if we were to push him into the water this moment. And I'll be killed, too."

"I know, my lady. I did not say I was going to take you back to the castle, I only said I had turned back. We need shelter and a fire as soon as possible. I am taking you to a place in the bay to the east of the castle—*Skean Egye-Var* my people call it—'Erivor's Shoulder' in your tongue."

"Erivor's Shoulder? There is no such place . . . !"

"There is, and there is a house upon it—your family's house."

"There is no such place!" For a moment Briony, faced with Shaso dying in her arms, was so full of rage and terror that she almost hit the girl. Then she suddenly understood. "M'Helan's Rock! You mean the lodge on M'Helan's Rock."

"Yes. And there it is." The Skimmer girl stilled her oars and pointed at a dark bulk on the near horizon. "Praise the Deep Ones, it looks empty."

"It ought to be—we did not use it this summer, with Father away and all else that has happened. Can you land there?"

"Yes, if you'll let me think about what I am doing, my lady. The currents are sharp at this hour of the night, just before morning."

Briony fell into anxious silence while the Skimmer girl, moving her oars as deftly as if they were an extension of her own arms, directed the pitching boat in a maddeningly slow circle around the island, searching for the inlet between the rocks.

Always before Briony had come to the island on the royal barge, standing at the rail far above the water as the king's sailors leaped smartly from place to place to make sure the passage would be smooth, and so she had never realized just how difficult a landing it was. Now, with the rocks looming over her head like giants and the waves lifting and dropping Ena's little craft as though it were a bit of froth in a sloshing bucket, she found herself hanging on in silent dread, one hand clamped on the railing, the other clutching a fold of the thick, plain shirt the Skimmers had given Shaso, doing her best to keep the old man upright.

Just as it seemed the Skimmer girl had misjudged the rocks, that their boat must be shattered like bird bones in a wolf's jaws, the oars dug hard into the dark water and they slid past a barnacled stone so closely that Briony had to snatch back her hand to save her fingers. The wooden hull scraped ever so briefly, just enough to send a single thrill of vibration through the tiny boat, and then they were past and into the comparatively quiet inlet.

"You did it!"

Ena nodded, studiously calm as she rowed them across the inlet to the floating dock shackled to the rock wall. Just a few yards away, on the ocean side, the waves thumped and roared like a thwarted predator, but here the swell was gentled. When the boat was tied, they dragged Shaso's limp weight out of the boat and managed to haul him up the short ladder and onto the salt-crusted dock where they had to let him drop.

Ena slumped down into a crouch beside Shaso's limp form. "I must rest . . . just for a bit . . ." she said, her head sagging.

Briony thought about how hard and how long the Skimmer girl had worked, rowing for hours to get them away from the castle to the safety of this inlet. "I've been ungrateful and rude," she told the girl. "Please forgive me. Without your help, Shaso and I both would have been dead long ago."

Ena said nothing, but nodded. It was possible that, in the depths of her hooded cloak she might have smiled a little, but the night was too dark for Briony to be sure.

"While you two rest, I'm going to go up to the lodge and see what I can find. Stay here." Briony draped her own cloak over Shaso, then climbed the stairway cut into the stone of the inlet wall. It was wide, and even though the worn steps were slippery with spray and the dewy mists of night, it was so familiar that she could have climbed it in her sleep. For the first time she began to feel hopeful. She knew this place well and she knew its comforts. She had been resigned to spending her first exiled night in a cave on a Marrinswalk beach, or sleeping in the undergrowth on the lee side of a sea-cliff—at least here she would find a bed.

The lodge on M'Helan's Rock had been built for one of Briony's ancestors, Ealga Flaxen-Hair, by her husband King Aduan—a love-tribute some said; a sort of prison others claimed. Whatever the truth, it was only fading family gossip now, the principals dead for a hundred years or more. In Briony's childhood the Eddons had spent at least a tennight on the island each summer, and sometimes much longer than that. Her father Olin had liked the seclusion and quiet of the place, and that he could keep a much smaller court there, often bringing only Avin Brone for counsel, a dozen or so servants, and a skeleton force of guards. As children, Briony and Barrick had discovered a slender, difficult hillside path down to a sea-meadow (as many other royal offspring had doubtless done before them) and had loved having a place where they could often spend an entire afternoon on their own, without guards or any other adults at all. To children who spent nearly every moment of their lives surrounded by servants and soldiers and courtiers, the sea-meadow was a paradise and the summer lodge a place of almost entirely happy memories.

Briony found it very strange to be walking up the front steps alone under the stars. The familiar house, which should be spilling welcoming light from each window, was so deep in darkness she could scarcely make out its shape against the sky. As with so much else this year, and especially these last weeks, here was another treasured part of her life turned higgle-piggle, another memory stolen and mishandled by the Eddon family's enemies.

The memory of Hendon Tolly's mocking face came to her with a stab of cold fury, his amusement at her helplessness as he told her how he was going to steal her family's throne. *You may not be the only one responsible for what's happened to our family, you Summerfield scum, but you're the one I know, the one I can reach.* In that moment she felt as chill and hard as the stones of the bay. *Not tonight—but someday. And when that day comes, I'll take the heart out of you the way you've taken mine. Only yours won't be beating when I'm done.*

She did not bother with the massive front door, knowing it would be locked, but walked around to the kitchen, which had a bad bolt that could be wiggled loose. As expected, a few good thumps and the door swung open, but it was shockingly dark inside. Briony had never been in the place at night without at least a few lamps glowing, but now it was as lightless as a cave, and for a terrified moment she could not make herself enter. Only the thought of Shaso lying on the chilly dock, suffering, perhaps dying, finally forced her through the open doorway.

Locked in a cell for months, and it was my fault—mine and Barrick's. She frowned. *Yes, and a bit of blame on his own cursed stiff neck as well. . . .*

She managed to find her way by touch to the kitchen fireplace, although not without a few unpleasant encounters with cobwebs. Things skittered in the darkness around her—just mice, she promised herself. After some searching, and many more cobwebs, she located the leather-wrapped flint and fire-iron in its niche in the stone chimney with a handful of oil-soaked firestarters beside it. After a little work Briony struck a spark, and soon a small blaze caught in the firestarters, which gave her the courage to knock over a spidery pile of logs and throw on a few of the smaller branches so the fire could begin growing into something useful. She considered setting a fire in the main hall fireplace as well. The thought made her ache with the memory of her lost father, who had always insisted on lighting that fire as his own personal task, but she knew it would be foolish to show light at the front of the house, on the side facing Southmarch Castle. Briony doubted anyone would see it without looking through a spyglass, even from the castle walls, but if there were any night that Hendon Tolly and his men might be on the walls doing just that, it would be tonight. The kitchen would be refuge enough.

The front of the summer house was still darkly unfamiliar as she went back down the steep path, but the knowledge that a fire now burned in the kitchen made it a friendlier place, and this time she had a shuttered lantern in her hand so she could see where she was putting her feet.

So, we've lived through the first day—unless someone saw the boat and they're coming after us. Startled by the thought, she looked toward the castle, but although she saw a few lights moving on the walls, there was no obvious sign of pursuit by water. And if someone came to search M'Helan's Rock before she and Shaso could depart? Well, she knew the island and its hiding places better than almost anyone else. *But, what am I doing?* she asked herself. *I shouldn't tempt the gods by even thinking such things. . . .*

Shaso was able to walk a little, but the two young women had to do most of the work getting him up the stairway; it was a mark of how weak he was, how close to utter collapse, that he did not protest.

When they reached the lodge Briony found blankets to wrap around the old man, then sat him in a corner near the kitchen fireplace, propped on cushions she had pilfered from the over-furnished sitting room known as the Queen's Withdrawing Chamber. The girl Ena had already begun to search through the few odds and ends left in the cupboards in hopes of adding to the food she had brought from her house beside Skimmer's Lagoon, but Briony knew the pantries would be empty. Supper would be dried fish again.

Dried fish was a great deal better than starvation, she reminded herself, but since Briony Eddon had never in her life come any-where near starving, that was a purely academic sort of comfort.

★

After having been fed the first mouthful or two of fish broth, Shaso made it very clear he was going to feed himself. Although still too weary and ill to speak, he managed to get enough soup into his stomach that Briony felt confident for the first time that the old man would survive the night. Now she could feel her own exhaustion pulling at her. She pushed her bowl aside and stared at it, fighting to keep her head upright.

"You are tired, Highness," said Ena. Briony could not easily read the girl's expressions, but she thought she saw kindness there, and a surprising, calm strength. It made her feel a little ashamed of her own frailty. "Go and find a bed. I will look after *Shaso-na* until he falls asleep."

"But you are tired yourself. You rowed that boat all night!"

"It is something I was raised to do, like swimming and mending nets. I have worked harder—and for less cause."

Briony stared at the girl for a moment, at the huge, round dark eyes and the naked brow shiny as soapstone. Was she pretty? It was too hard to say, too many things about her were unusual, but looking at the intelligent gaze and strong, regular features, Briony guessed that among her own kind Ena might be considered pretty indeed.

"Very well," she said, surrendering at last. "You are most kind. I'll take a candle and leave you the lamp. We have bedding in the chest in the hall—I'll leave some out for you and for Shaso."

"He will sleep where he is, I think," said Ena quietly, perhaps to spare Shaso the shame of being talked about like a child. "He should be comfortable enough."

"When this is over and the Tollys are rotting on the gibbet, the Eddons will not forget their friends." The Skimmer girl showed no emotion at this, so Briony tried to make herself clear. "You and your father will be rewarded."

Now Ena definitely *did* smile, even looked as though she might be stifling laughter, which confounded Briony utterly, but she only said, "Thank you, Highness. It is my honor to do what I can."

Puzzled, but too weary to think about it, Briony felt her way to the nearest bedchamber, turned over the dusty bedcover, then stretched out. It was only as sleep dragged her down that she remembered this room had been the one that Kendrick had used.

Come back, then, she told her dead brother, dizzy with exhaustion. *Come back and haunt me, dear, dear Kendrick—I miss you so . . . !*

But the sleep into which she fell, tumbling slowly downward like a feather in a well, was impenetrably dark, empty of both dreams and ghosts.

The island was surrounded by fog, but dawn still brought enough light to make the lodge on M'Helan's Rock a familiar place once more—light that slipped in through the high windows and filled the great hall with a blue-gray glow as soft as the sheen on a pearl and made the statues of the holy *onirai* in their wall-niches look as if they were stirring into life. Even the kitchen again seemed to be the homely place Briony remembered. Things that she had been too exhausted to notice the night before, the tang of the air, the lonely cries of shearwaters and gulls, the heavy furniture scuffed by generations of Eddon children creating imaginary riding-caravans or fortresses, now made her insides twist with sorrow and longing.

Gone. Every one of them. Barrick, Father, Kendrick. She felt her eyes brim with tears and wiped them angrily. *But Barrick and Father are alive—they must be. Don't be a stupid girl. Not gone, just . . . somewhere else.*

Crouched in the heather at the front of the lodge, she stared long and hard back at the castle. A few torches seemed to be moving on the bay at the base of the castle walls—search boats checking the inlets and caves along the shore of Midlan's Mount—but none of them seemed to have ventured any farther from Southmarch. Briony felt a gleam of hope. If she herself had forgotten the summer house, there was a chance the Tollys wouldn't remember until she and Shaso were long gone.

Back in the kitchen she dutifully ate her fish soup, enlivened this time by wild rosemary which Ena had found thriving in the masterless, overgrown garden. Briony could not be certain when she would eat again, and she reminded herself that even fish soup was noble if it would give her the strength to survive so that one day she could drive something sharp through Hendon Tolly's heart.

Shaso was eating too, if not much more skillfully or swiftly than the night before. Still, his ashen pallor had improved a little and his breathing did not hiss like a fireplace bellows. But most important of all, though his eyes still lay sunken in dark-ringed flesh (which Briony thought gave him the look of an *oniron* like Iaris or Zakkas the Ragged or some other sun-scorched, wilderness-maddened prophet from *The Book of the Trigon*), his gaze was bright and intent again—that of the Shaso she knew.

"We can go nowhere today." He took one last swallow before lowering the empty bowl. "We cannot risk it."

"But surely the fog will hide us . . . ?"

His look had much of the old Shaso in it, equal parts irritation at being disputed and disappointment that she had not thought things through completely. "Perhaps here, upon the bay, Princess. But what about when we make land in the late afternoon, with the mist burned away? Even if we are not seen by enemies, do you think the local fishermen there would be likely to forget the unusual pair they saw landing?" He shook his head. "We are exiles, Highness. Everything that has gone before will mean nothing if you give yourself away to your enemies. If you are captured, Hendon Tolly will not put you on trial or lock you away in the stronghold to be a rallying flag for those loyal to the Eddons. No, he will kill you and no one will ever see your body. He will not mind a few rumors of you among the people as long as he knows that you are safely dead."

Briony thought of Hendon's grinning face and her hands twitched. "We should have stripped his family of their titles and lands long ago. We should have executed the whole traitorous lot."

"When? When did they reveal their treachery before it was too late? And Gailon, although I did not like him, was apparently an honorable servant of your family's crown—if Hendon has told the truth in this one thing, at least. As for Caradon, we also know only what Hendon says of him, so his wickedness is as much in question as Gailon's goodness. The world is strange, Briony, and it will only become stranger in the days ahead."

She looked at his leathery, stern face and was filled with shame that she had been such a fool, to have taken so little care with the most precious of her family's possessions. What must he think, her old teacher? What must he think of her and her twin, who had all but given away the Eddons' throne?

As if he understood her thoughts, Shaso shook his head. "What happened in the past remains in the past. What is before us—*that* is everything. Will you put your trust in me? Will you do just as I say, and only what I say?"

Despite all her mistakes and self-disgust, she could not help bristling. "I am not a fool, Shaso. I am not a child any longer."

For a moment his expression softened. "No. You are a fine young woman, Briony Eddon, and you have a good heart. But this is not the time for good hearts. This is the hour for suspicion and treachery and murder, and I have much experience of all those things. I ask you to put your trust in me."

"Of course I trust you—what do you mean?"

"That you will do nothing without asking me. We are exiles, with a price on our heads. As I said, all that came before—your crown, your family's history—will mean nothing if we are captured. You must swear not to act without my permission, no matter how small or unimportant the act seems. Remember, I kept my oath to your brother Kendrick even when it might have cost my life." He stopped and took a deep breath, coughed a little. "It still might. So I want you to swear the same to me." He fixed her with his dark eyes. This time it was not the imperious stare of old, the teacher's stare—there was actually something pleading in it.

"You shame me when you remind me what you did for my family, Shaso. And you don't take credit for your own stubbornness. But yes, I hear you, and yes, I understand. I'll listen to what you say. I'll do what you think is best."

"Always? No matter how you may doubt me? No matter how angry I make you by not explaining my every thought?"

A quiet hiss startled Briony, until she realized it was the girl Ena, laughing quietly as she scrubbed out the soup pot. It was humiliating, but it would be more shameful still to continue arguing like a child. "Very well. I swear on the green blood of Erivor, my family's patron. Is that good enough?"

"You should be careful when you make oaths on Egye-var, Highness," said Ena cheerfully, "especially here in the middle of the waters. He hears."

"What are you talking about? If I swear to Erivor, I mean it." She turned to Shaso. "Are you satisfied now?"

He smiled, but it was only a grim flash of teeth, an old predator's reflex. "I will not be satisfied with anything until Hendon Tolly is dead and whoever arranged Kendrick's death has joined him. But I accept your promise." He winced as he straightened his legs. Briony looked away: even though the Skimmer girl had bandaged the worst sores from the shackles, he was still covered with ugly scrapes and bruises and his limbs were disturbingly thin. "Now, tell me what has happened—everything you can remember. Little news was brought to me in my cell, and I could make small sense out of what you told me last night."

Briony proceeded as best she could, although it was difficult to summon up all that had happened in the months Shaso dan-Heza had been locked in the stronghold, let alone make a sensible tale of it. She told him of Barrick's fever and of Avin Brone's spy who claimed to have seen agents of the Autarch of Xis in the Tolly's great house at Summerfield Court. She told him about the caravan apparently attacked by the fairies, of Guard Captain Vansen's expedition and what happened to them, and of the advancing army of the Twilight People that had apparently invaded and secured the mainland city of Southmarch across Brenn's Bay, leaving only the castle free. She even told him of the strange potboy Gil and his dreams, or at least what little about them she could remember.

Although the Skimmer girl had shown no other signs of paying attention to the bizarre catalogue of events, when she heard Gil's pronouncements about Barrick, Ena put down her washing and sat up straight. "Porcupine's eye? He said to beware the Porcupine's eye?"

"Yes, what of it?"

"The Porcupine-woman is one of the most ill-named of all the Old Ones," Ena said seriously. "She is death's companion."

"What does that mean?" Briony asked. "And how would you know?"

The secretive smile stretched the girl's wide mouth again, but her eyes did not meet Briony's. "Even on Skimmer's Lagoon, we know some important things."

"Enough," said Shaso angrily. "I will sleep today—I do not like being a burden. When the sun goes down, we will leave. Girl," he said to Ena, "take us to the Marrinswalk coast and then your service will be over."

"As long as you eat something else before we leave," Ena told him. "More soup—you barely touched what I gave you. I promised my father I would keep you safe, and if you collapse again he will be angry."

Shaso looked at her as if she might be mocking him. She stared back, unfraid. "Then I will eat," he said at last.

Briony spent much of the afternoon staring out at the bay, fearful of seeing boats coming toward the island. When she got too cold at last, she went in and warmed herself at the fire.

On her way back to her sentinel perch in the heather, she walked through the lodge—a place that once, because of its small size, had been more familiar to her than Southmarch Castle itself. Even in daylight it now seemed as strange as everything else because of the way the world had changed, all the things which had been so familiar and ordinary transformed in a single night.

Right here, in this room, is where Father told us the story about Hiliometes and the manticore. A tennight ago she would have sworn she could never forget the smallest detail of what it had felt like to huddle in the blankets on their father's bed and hear the tale of the demigod's great battle for the first time, yet here she was in the very chamber and suddenly it all seemed vague. Had

Kendrick been with them, or had he gone to bed, intent on going out early in the morning with old Nynor to catch fish? Had there been a fire, or had it been one of those rare, truly hot summer nights on M'Helan's Rock when the servants were told to leave all but the kitchen fire unlit? She couldn't remember anything but the story, now, and their father's exaggeratedly solemn, bearded face as he spoke. Would she forget that one day, too? Would all her past vanish this way, bit by bit, like tracks in the dirt pelted by rain?

Briony was startled by a wriggle of movement at the edge of her vision—something moving quickly along the skirting board. A mouse? She moved toward the corner and startled something out from behind a table leg, but before she had a chance to see what it was it had vanished again behind a hanging. It seemed strangely upright for a mouse—could it be a bird, trapped in the house? But birds hopped, didn't they? She pulled back the wall hanging, strangely apprehensive, but found nothing unusual.

A mouse, she thought. *Climbed up the back of the tapestry and it's back in the roof by now. Poor thing was probably startled half to death to have someone walk into this room—the place has been empty for more than a year.*

She wondered if she dared open the shuttered doors of King Olin's bedroom balcony. She itched to look back at the castle, half-afraid that it too would have become insubstantial, but caution won out. She made her way back through the room, the bed naked of blankets, a thin powdering of dust on every surface, as if it were the tomb of some ancient prophet where no one dared touch anything. In an ordinary year the doors would have been thrown wide to air the room as the servants bustled through, sweeping and cleaning. There would have been fresh flowers in the vase on the writing desk (only yellow ragwort if it was late in the season) and water in the washing jug. Instead, her father was trapped in a room somewhere that was probably smaller than this—maybe a bleak cell like the hole in which Shaso had been imprisoned. Did Olin have a window to look out, a view—or only dark walls and fading memories of his home?

It did not bear thinking about. So many things these days did not bear thinking about.

"I thought you said he had barely eaten," Briony said, nodding toward Shaso. She held out the sack. "The dried fish is gone. Was it you? There were three pieces left when I saw last."

Ena looked in the sack, then smiled. "I think we have made a gift."

"A gift? What do you mean? To whom?"

"To the small folk—the Air Lord's children."

Briony shook her head in irritation. "Made a gift to the rats and mice, more likely. I think I just saw one." She did not hold with such silly old tales—it was what the cooks and maids said every time something went missing: *"Oh, it must have been the little folk, Highness. The Old Ones must've took it."* Briony had a sudden pang, knowing what Barrick would have said about such an idea, the familiar mockery that would have tinged his voice. She missed him so fiercely that tears welled in her eyes.

A moment later she had to admit the irony of it: she was mourning her brother, who would have poured scorn on the idea of "the small folk" . . . because he was off fighting the fairies. "It doesn't matter, I suppose," she said to Ena. "Surely we will find something to eat in Marrinswalk."

Ena nodded. "And perhaps the small folk will bring us luck in return for the food—perhaps they will call on Pyarin Ky'vos to lend us fair winds. They are his favorites after all, just as my folk belong to Egye-Var."

Briony shook her head in doubt, then caught herself. Who was she, who had fought against a murderous demon and barely survived, to make light of what others said about the gods? She herself, although she prayed carefully and sincerely to Zoria every day, had never believed Heaven to be as active in people's lives as others seemed to think—but at the moment she and her family needed all the help they could find. "You remind me, Ena. We must make an offering at the Erivor shrine before we go."

"Yes, my lady. That is right and good."

So the girl approved, did she? How kind of her! Briony grimaced, but turned away so the girl did not see. She realized for the first time that she missed being the princess regent. At least people didn't openly treat you like you were a child or a complete fool—out of fear, if nothing else! "Let's get Shaso down to the boat, first."

"I'll walk, curse it." The old man roused himself from his drowsing nap. "Is the sun down yet?"

"Soon enough." He looked better, Briony thought, but he was still frighteningly thin and clearly very weak. He was *old,* older by many years than her father—she sometimes forgot that, fooled by his strength and sharpness of mind. Would he recover, or would his time in the stronghold leave him a cripple? She sighed. "Let's get on with things. It's a long way to the Marrinswalk coast, isn't it?"

Shaso nodded slowly. "It will take all the night, and perhaps some of the morning."

Ena laughed. "If Pyarin Ky'vos sends even a small, kind wind, I will have you on shore before dawn."

"And then where?" Briony knew better than to doubt this strong-armed girl, at least about rowing a boat. "Should we not consider Blueshore? I know Tyne's wife well. She would shelter us, I'm certain—she's a good woman, if overly fond of clothes and chatter. Surely that would be safer than Marrinswalk, where . . ."

Shaso growled, a deep, warning sound that might have issued from a cave. "Did you or did you not promise to do as I say?"

"Yes, I promised, but . . ."

"Then we go to Marrinswalk. I have my reasons, Highness. None of the nobility can shield you. If we force the Tollys' hand, Duke Caradon will bring the Summerfield troops to Blueshore and throw down Aldritch Stead—they will never be able to hold off the Tollys with Tyne and all his men gone to this battle you tell me of. They will announce you were a false claimant—some serving girl I forced to play the part of the missing princess regent—and that the real Briony is already long dead. Do you see?"

"I suppose . . ."

"Do not suppose. At this moment, strength is all and the Tollys hold the whip hand. You must do what I ask and not waste time arguing. We may soon find ourselves in straits where hesitation or childish stubbornness will kill us."

"So. Marrinswalk, then." Briony stood, struggling to hold down her anger. *Calm,* she told herself. *You made a promise—besides, remember the foolishness with Hendon. You cannot afford your temper right now. You are the last of the Eddons.* Suddenly frightened, she corrected herself. *The last of the Eddons in Southmarch.* But of course, even that wasn't true—there were no true Eddons left in Southmarch anymore, only Anissa and her baby, if the child had survived his first, terrible night.

"I will attend to the sea god's shrine," she said, speaking as carefully as she could, putting on the mask of queenly distance she had supposedly left behind with the rest of the life that had been stolen from her. "Help Lord dan-Heza down to the boat, Ena. I will meet you there."

She walked out of the kitchen without looking back.

2
Drowning

In the beginning the heavens were only darkness, but Zo
came and pushed the darkness away. When it was gone all
that was left behind was Sva, the daughter of the dark. Zo
found her comely, and together they set out to rule over
everything, and make all right.

—from *The Beginnings of Things*
The Book of the Trigon

DESPITE THE RAIN hissing down all around, spattering on the mossy rocks and drizzling from the branches of the trees that leaned over them like disapproving old men, the boy made no effort to cover himself. As raindrops bounced from his forehead and ran down his face, he barely blinked. Watching him made Ferras Vansen feel more lonely than ever.

What am I doing here? No power of the gods or earth should have been able to lure me back to this mad place. But shame and desire, commingled in a most devastating way, had clearly been more powerful than any gods, because here he was behind the Shadowline again, lost in an unholy forest of crescent-leaved trees and vines sagging with heavy, dripping black blossoms, terrified that if he did lose the boy he would bring even more pain to the Eddons—and more important, to Barrick's sister, Princess Briony.

Hidden lightning glowed above them and thunder rumbled as the cold torrent grew stronger. Vansen scowled. This storm was too much, he decided: even if it meant another pitched battle with the unresponsive prince, they dared not go any farther today. If they were not struck by lightning or a deathly fever, their horses would surely stumble blindly off a crag and they would die that way—even Barrick's strange, dark fairy-horse was showing signs of distress, and Vansen's own mount was within moments of balking completely. No sane person would travel unknown roads in weather like this.

Of course, just now, Barrick Eddon was clearly far from sane; the prince showed no inclination even to slow down, and was almost out of sight.

"Highness!" Vansen called above the hiss of rain. "If we ride farther we'll kill the horses, and we won't survive without them." Time was confusing behind the Shadowline, but it seemed they had been riding through this endless gloaming for at least a day. After a terrible battle and a sleepless night spent hiding in the rocks at the edge of the battlefield, Ferras Vansen was already so exhausted he feared he would lose his balance and fall out of his saddle. How could the prince be any less weary?

"Please, Highness! I do not know where you are going but we will not reach it safely in this weather. Let us make some shelter and rest and wait for the storm to pass."

To his surprise, Barrick suddenly reined up and sat waiting in the harsh drizzle. The young man did not even resist when Vansen caught up and half yanked him, half helped him out of his saddle, then he sat quietly on a rock like an obedient child while the guard captain did his best, spluttering and cursing, to shape wet branches into some kind of shelter. It was as though only part of the prince were truly present, as though he were living deep inside his own body like an ailing man in a huge house. Barrick Eddon did not look up even when Vansen accidentally scratched his cheek with a pine bough, nor responded to the guardsman's apologies with anything more than a slow eyeblink.

During his life at the castle Vansen had often thought that the nobility lived in a different world than he and his kind, but never had it seemed more true than this moment.

What kind of lackwit are you? Vansen's tiny fire, only partly protected by the overhanging rock against which he'd set it, hissed and struggled against the horizontal rain. An animal—he prayed it was an animal—howled in the distance, a stuttering screech that made Vansen's hair stand and prickle. *Trigon guard us, will you truly give up your own life for a boy who scarcely knows you're here?*

But he wasn't doing it for Barrick, not really. He'd nothing against the youth, but it was the boy's sister that Vansen feared, whose grief if her twin were lost would break Ferras Vansen's own heart beyond repair. He had sworn to her he would treat Barrick as though he were his own family—an oath that was foolish in so many ways as to beggar the imagination.

He watched the prince eating one of their last pieces of jerked meat, chewing and staring as absently as a cow in a meadow. Barrick was not merely distracted, he seemed lost in a way Vansen couldn't quite understand. The boy could hear what Vansen said at least some of the time or he would not have stopped here, and he occasionally looked his companion in the eye as though actually seeing him. A few times he had even spoken, although saying nothing much that Vansen could understand, mostly what the guardsman had begun to think of as *elf-talk,* the same sort of babble Collum Dyer had spouted when the shadowlands had swallowed his sense. But even at his best moments, the prince was not completely there. It was as though Barrick Eddon were dying—but in the slowest, most peaceful way possible.

With a shudder, Vansen remembered something told to him by one of his Southmarch guardsmen—Geral Kelty, who had been lost in these same lands on Vansen's last, terrifying visit, vanished along with the merchant Raemon Beck and the others. Kelty had grown up a fisherman's son on Landsend, and when he was still a boy, he and his father and younger brother had been caught in a sudden violent squall where the bay met the ocean. Their boat tipped over, then was pushed under by a wave and sank with horrifying swiftness, taking their father with it. Kelty and his younger brother had clung to each other, swimming slowly toward the land for a long time, fighting wind and high waves.

Then, with the beach at Coiner's Point just a short distance away, Kelty told Vansen, his young brother had simply let go and slipped beneath the water.

"Tired, mayhap," Kelty had said, shaking his head, eyes still haunted. "Cramped. But he just looked at me, peaceful-like, and then let himself slide away like he was getting under his blanket of a night. I think he even smiled." Kelty had smiled too as he told this, as if to make up for the tears in his eyes. Vansen had been scarcely able to look at him. They had both been drinking, another payday spent in the Badger's Boots or one of those other pestholes off Market Square, and it was the time of night when strange things were said, things that were sometimes difficult to forget, although most folk did their best.

Wincing now at the rain that leaked through their pathetic shelter of woven branches and ran down the neck of his cloak, Ferras Vansen wondered if Kelty had seen the same thing in his younger brother's eyes that Vansen was seeing in Prince Barrick's, the same inexplicable remoteness. Was Briony's brother about to die, too? Was he about to surrender himself and drown in the shadowlands?

And if he does? What becomes of me? He had only barely made his way out of the shadowlands the first time, led by the touched girl, Willow. No one, he felt sure, least of all Ferras Vansen, could be that fortunate twice.

They had found an open track through the forest, a bit of clear path. Vansen jogged out ahead of the prince, trying to spy out a place where they might stop and spend a few hours of rest in the endless gray twilight. After what must have been several days' riding, the supplies in his pack had dwindled to almost nothing; if they had to hunt for food, he wanted to do it here, where the dim ghosts of the sun and moon still haunted the sky behind the mists. He could not be certain that whatever animal he caught here would be more ordinary than prey taken deeper behind the Shadowline, but it was one small thing he was determined to do.

Vansen's horse abruptly shrilled and reared, almost throwing him from the saddle. At first he thought they were being attacked, but the forest was still. His heart slowed a little. As he brought the horse under control he called back to the prince to hold up, then, as he leaned forward to stroke his mount's neck, trying to soothe the still-frightened animal, he saw the dead thing on the ground.

At first disgust and alarm were mingled with relief, because the creature was no bigger than a child of four or five years and was obviously in no state to do any harm: its head was mostly off, and black blood gleamed all over its chest and belly and on the wet grass where it lay, thinning and running away under the remorseless rain. The more Vansen looked at the corpse, though, the more disturbing he found it. It was like an ape, but with abnormally long fingers and skin like a lizard's, rough and netted with scales. Knobs of gray bone stuck out through the scaly hide at the joints and along the spine, not injuries but as much a part of it as a cow's horns or a man's fingernails. As Vansen examined the dead thing further, he saw that its face was disturbingly manlike, as brown as the rest of its studded hide but covered with smooth, leathery skin. The dark eyes were wide open in a net of wrinkled flesh, and if he had seen only them he would have been sure it was some little old man lying here, though the fanged mouth gave things a different flavor.

Vansen poked hard with his sword but the thing did not move. He guided his horse wide around the corpse, and watched as Barrick's milky-eyed mount took the same roundabout path. The prince himself did not even look down.

Within moments Vansen saw a second and a third creature, both as dead and bloodied as the first, slashed by a blade or long claws.

He reined up, wondering what sort of beast had so easily bested these unpleasant creatures. Was it one of the terrible, sticklike giants that had taken Collum Dyer? Or something worse, something . . . unimaginable? Perhaps even now it watched them from the forest shadows, eyes gleaming. . . .

"Go slowly, Highness," he told Barrick, but he might have spoken Xixian for all the notice the youth paid him.

Only a few paces ahead lay another clot of small, knobby corpses in the middle of the trail. Vansen's horse pulled up, snuffling anxiously. Clearly, it did not want to step over the things, although Barrick's shadow-bred horse showed no such compunction as it passed him. Vansen groaned and climbed down to clear the trail. He was pushing one of the bodies with his sword, hesitant to touch any of the creatures, when the thing abruptly came to life. Whistling in a horrid way that Vansen only realized later was the mortal slash across its chest sucking air, it managed to climb up his sword and sink its teeth into his arm before he could do more than grunt in shock. He had thought many times of removing his mail shirt—the damp cold had made it seem much more a burden than a benefit—but now he thanked the gods he had kept it. The creature's teeth did not pierce the Funderling-forged rings, and he was able to smash its wizened face hard enough to dislodge it from his arm. It hit the ground but did not run away, scuttling toward him again, still whistling like a hillman's pipes with the sack burst.

"Barrick!" he shouted, wondering how many more of the creatures might be still alive and lurking, "Highness, help me!"— but the prince was already out of sight down the trail.

Vansen backed away from his horse, not wanting to risk wounding it with a wild swing, and as the little monstrosity leaped up toward his throat he managed to strike it with the flat of his blade, knocking it aside. His heavy sword was not the best weapon, but he did not dare take the time to pull his dagger. Before the hissing thing could get up again he stepped forward and skewered it against the wet ground with his sword, pushing through muscle and gut and crunching bone until his hilt was almost in reach of the creature's claws, which waved feebly a few times, then curled in death.

Vansen took only a moment to catch his breath and wipe his blade on the wet grass before clambering back up into the saddle, worried about the prince but also irritated. Hadn't the boy heard him call?

He found Barrick just a short ride ahead, dismounted and staring down at a dozen or more of the hairy creatures, all apparently safely dead this time. In their midst lay a dead horse with its throat torn out and what Vansen at first thought was its equally dead rider lying facedown beside it. The black-haired body was human enough in shape, wrapped in a torn dark cloak and armor of some strange material with a blue-gray tortoiseshell-like finish. Vansen dismounted and cautiously put his hand on the back of the corpse's neck, in a gap between helmet and armor. To his surprise he could feel movement under his fingers—a slow, labored rise: the rider was breathing. When he turned the victim over and pulled off the disturbing skull helm, he got his second shock. The man had no face.

No, he realized after an instant, still sickened, *it does—but that's no human face.* He made the sign of the Three as he fought against a sudden clutch of nausea. There were eyes in that pale, membrane of flesh that stretched between scalp and narrow chin, but because they were shut they had seemed no more than creases of flesh beneath the wide brow, obscured by smears of blood from what looked like a near-mortal gash in the thing's forehead—the blood, at least, was as red as that which flowed in a godly man. But the rest of the face was as featureless as a drumskin, with no nose or mouth.

The faceless man's eyes flicked open, eyes red as his smeared blood. They struggled to fix on the guard captain and the prince, then rolled up and the waxy lids fell again.

Vansen staggered to his feet in revulsion and fear. "It is one of *them.* One of the murdering Twilight People."

"He belongs to my mistress," Barrick said calmly. "He wears her mark."

"What?"

"He is injured. See to him. We will stop here." Barrick climbed down from his horse and stood waiting, as though what he had said made perfect sense.

"Forgive me, Highness, but what are you thinking? This is one of the demons who has tried to kill us—tried to kill *you*. They have destroyed our armies and our towns." Vansen sheathed his sword and slipped his dagger from its battered sheath. "No, step back and I will slit his gorge. It is a more merciful death than many of our folk have received . . ."

"Stop." Prince Barrick moved forward as if to put his own body between the wounded creature and the killing stroke. Ferras Vansen could only stare in astonishment. Barrick's eyes were calm and intent—in fact, he seemed closer to his old self than he had since they had crossed the Shadowline—but he was still acting like a madman.

"Highness, please, I beg of you, stand away. This thing is a murderer of our people. I saw this very creature killing Aldritchmen and Kertewallers like a dog among rats. I cannot let him live."

"No, you *must* let him live," Barrick declared. "He is on a grave errand."

"What? What errand?"

"I do not know. But I know the signs upon him and I hear the voices they make in my head. If we do not help him, more of . . . our kind will die. Mortals." The young prince regent's hesitation was strange, as if for a moment he had forgotten to which side of the conflict he belonged.

"But how can you know that? And who is this 'mistress' you speak of? Not your sister, surely. Princess Briony would not want you to do any of these things."

Barrick shook his head. "Not my sister, no. The great lady who found me and commanded me. She is one of the highest. She looked at me and . . . and knew me. Now help him, please." For a moment the prince's gaze became even clearer, but a hard look of pain and loss came too, like ice forming on a shallow pond. "I do not . . . do not know what to do. How to do it. You must."

Vansen stared at Barrick. Barrick stared back. The boy would not let him kill this monster without a fight, he'd made that clear. Vansen had already tried several times to sway Barrick from these strange, spellbound moods but had found no way to do it without harming him, so fierce was his resistance. It would be bad enough to face Briony Eddon if he allowed the boy to come to harm—how much worse if it was Vansen himself who hurt the prince?

He cursed under his breath and sheathed his sword, then began to remove the creature's strange shell-like armor, which, considering the cold, wet day, was warmer to the touch than if it had been metal or anything else decent. *Cursed black magic—I should never have come here again.* Every hour, it seemed, some new and unwholesome choice was put before him. *Instead of a soldier, I should have been a king's poison-taster,* he thought bleakly. *At least then I wouldn't have survived to see the outcome of my failures.*

He had been adrift in the depths of his own being for so long that only now, as he was finally nearing the surface again, did Barrick Eddon begin to understand how completely he had been lost.

From the moment that the fairy-woman's eye had caught and held his own he had lost the sequence of everything. From that astounding instant when he had lain stunned and helpless as the giant's club had swung up but death had *not* followed, all the moments of his life, strung in ordered sequence like Kanjja pearls on a necklace, had suddenly flown apart, as if someone had broken the string and dumped those precious pearls into swirling water. His childhood, his dreams, barely recognized faces and even all the moments of Briony and his father and family, the army of Shadowline demons, a million more glittering instants, had all become discontinuous and simultaneous, and Barrick had floated among them like a drowning man watching his own last bubbles.

In fact, for a while the most clear-thinking part of him had been certain he *was* dead, that the giant's club had fallen, that the spiky porcupine woman and her fierce, all-knowing gaze had been nothing but a last momentary glimpse of the living world before it was torn from him, a glimpse which had expanded into an entire, shadowy imitation of life, another bubble to observe, another loose pearl.

Now he knew better—now he could *think* again. But even though he could feel the wind and rain on his face once more, even though he again had a sense of life unrolling moment by moment instead of surrounding him in a disordered whirl, it was all still very strange.

For one thing, although he could no longer remember the important thing the fairy-woman had told him, he knew that he could no more go against her wishes than he could sprout wings and fly away, just as he had known that her servant, the faceless one they had discovered, must be saved. But how could it be that someone could command him and he could not say the reason or remember the command?

Even the few things in his life that had once given Barrick comfort now seemed distant—his home, his family, his pastimes, the things he had clung to throughout his youth, when he had often feared he would go mad. But at this moment, of all of it, only Briony still seemed entirely real—she was in his heart and it seemed now that not even his own death would dislodge her. He felt he would carry her memory even into the darkest house, right to the foot of Kernios' throne, but all the other things that he had been taught were so important were revealed to be only beads on a fraying string.

Ferras Vansen did not notice the wounded fairy wake. For hours the creature had lain deathlike and limp, eyes shut, then he suddenly discovered the red stare burning out at him from that awful, freakish face.

Something pressed behind his eyes, a painful intrusion that buzzed in his head like a trapped hornet. He took a step back, wondering what magic this shadow-thing was using to attack him, but the scarlet eyes widened and the buzzing abruptly faded, leaving only a trace of confused inquiry like a voice heard in the last moments of sleep.

"I cannot really tell him," Prince Barrick said. "Can you?"

"Tell . . . ? What do you mean?" Vansen eyed the fairy, who still lay with his head propped on a saddlebag, looking weak and listless. If he was preparing to spring he was hiding it well.

"Didn't you hear him?" But now Barrick seemed confused, rubbing his head and grimacing as though it hurt. "He said he wants to know why we saved him, our enemy. But I don't know why we did it—I can hardly remember."

"*You* told me we had to, Highness—don't you remember?" Vansen paused. Somehow, he was being pulled into the madness as well, just when he could not afford to lose his grip on sanity—not here behind the Shadowline. "But what do you mean, 'said'? He said nothing, Prince Barrick. He has only just woken and he said nothing."

"Ah, but he did, although I could not understand all of it." Barrick leaned forward, watching the stranger intently. "Who are you? Why do I know you?"

The Twilight man stared back. Vansen again felt something pressing behind his eyes and his ears began to ache as though he had held his breath too long.

"Surely you heard that." Barrick had closed his eyes, as if listening to fascinating music.

"Highness, he said nothing! For the love of Perin Skyfather, *he has no mouth!*"

The prince's eyes popped open. "Nevertheless, he speaks and I hear him. He is called Gyir the Storm Lantern. He is on a mission to the king of his people, the ones we call the fairy folk. Lady Yasammez, his mistress, has sent him." Barrick shook his head. "I did not know her name before now, but she is my mistress, too. *Yasammez.*" For a moment his face clouded as if he remembered a terrible pain. "I should love her, but I do not."

"*Love* her? Who are you talking of? That she-dragon who led the enemy? That spiky bitch with the white sword? May the gods save us, Prince Barrick, she must have put some kind of evil spell on you!"

The red-haired boy shook his head again, forcefully this time. "No. That is not true. I do not know how I know, or . . . or even *what* I know, but I know that isn't the truth. She revealed things to me. Her eye found me and she laid a task on me." He turned to the one he had named Gyir, who was watching with the bright, sullen glare of a caged fox. For a moment, Barrick sounded like his old self. "Tell me, why has she chosen me? What does she want, your mistress?"

There was no reply that Vansen could hear, only the pressure in his head again, but more gentle this time.

"But you are high in her confidences," said Barrick, as if carrying on an ordinary conversation. "You are her right hand."

Whatever answer he thought he heard, though, it brought the young prince no happiness. He waved his hand in frustration, then turned back to the fire, refusing to speak more.

Ferras Vansen stared at the impossible creature. Gyir, if that was truly his name and not some madness of the prince's, did not seem disposed to move, let alone to try to escape. The huge welt on the creature's forehead still seeped blood, and he had other ugly wounds that Vansen felt sure were bites from the strange lizard-apes, but even so the dalesman could not imagine sleeping while this monstrosity lay just on the other side of the fire. Could the prince really talk to him? And how did a thing like that survive, with no mouth or nose? It seemed utter madness. How did it breathe, how did it eat?

I am trapped in a nightmare, he thought, *and it grows worse with each passing hour. Now we have invited a murderous enemy to share our fire.* He propped himself against an uncomfortable tree root in the hopes it would keep him awake and alert. *A waking nightmare, and all I want to do is sleep . . .*

The rain had abated when Vansen woke, but water still drizzled from the trees, pattering on the thick carpet of fallen leaves and needles like a thousand muffled footsteps. There was light, but only the usual directionless gray glow.

Vansen groaned. He hated this place. He had hoped never to see this side of the Shadowline again, but instead—as though the gods had heard his wish and decided to play a cruel joke—it seemed he could not stay out of it.

He started up suddenly, realizing he had drowsed when he had been determined not to—with one of the deadly Twilight folk in their camp! He clambered to his feet, but the strange creature known as Gyir was asleep: with most of his faceless head shrouded in his dark cloak, he looked almost like a true man.

The prince was also sleeping, but a superstitious fear made Vansen crawl across the sodden carpet of dead leaves that separated them so that he could get a closer look. All was well: Barrick's chest rose and fell. Vansen stared at the youth's pale face, the skin so white that even by firelight he could see the blue veins beneath the surface. For a moment he felt unutterably weary and defeated. How could he possibly keep one frail child—and a mad one at that—safe in the midst of so much strangeness, so much peril?

I promised his sister. I gave my word. Even here, surely, at the end of the world, a man's pledge meant something—perhaps everything. If not, the world tottered, the skies fell, the gods turned their back on meaning.

"Gyir will ride with me," Barrick announced.

The Twilight man stirred, beginning to wake, or at least beginning to show that he was awake. Vansen leaned closer to the prince so he could speak quietly. "Highness, I beg of you, think again. I do not know what magic has possessed you, but what possible reason could you have to take this enemy with us—a creature whose race is bent on destroying all our kind?"

Barrick only shook his head, almost sadly. "I cannot explain it to you, Vansen. I know what I must do, and it is something far more important than you can understand. I may not understand it all myself, but I know this is true." The prince looked more animated than he had since they had first ridden from Southmarch weeks before. "And I know just as clearly that this man Gyir must complete his task as well. He will ride with me. Now give him his armor and his sword back. These are dangerous lands."

"What? No, Highness—he will not have his sword, even if you call me traitor!"

Gyir had awakened. Vansen saw an expression on the creature's featureless face that almost seemed like amusement—a drooping of the eyelids, a slow turn away from Vansen's scrutiny. It enraged him, but also made him wonder again at how the creature lived at all, how it ate and breathed. If it could not make a recognizable expression on the curved skin of its face, how did it communicate to others? The prince certainly seemed to think he understood him.

Gyir chose to retain his thundercloud-blue breastplate and his helmet, but left the rest of his armor where it had been thrown. Already the grass seemed to be covering it over. The tall fairy sat behind Barrick on the strange dark horse the prince had brought from the battlefield. The tall Twilight demon Gyir could snap the boy's neck in an instant if he chose, but Barrick seemed undisturbed to have him so near. Together they looked like some two-headed monstrosity out of an old wall-painting, and Vansen could not help superstitiously making the sign of the Three, but if this invocation of the true gods bothered Gyir in any way, he gave no sign of it.

"Where are we going exactly, Highness?" Vansen asked wearily. He had lost command of this journey long ago—there was no sense in pretending otherwise.

"That way," Barrick said, pointing. "Toward high M'aarenol."

How the prince could claim to see some foreign landmark in this confounding eternal twilight was more than Ferras Vansen could guess. Gyir now turned his ember-red eyes toward Vansen, and for a moment he could almost hear a voice inside his skull, as though the wind had blown a handful of words there without him hearing them first—words that were not words, that were almost pictures.

A long way, the words seemed to say. *A long, dangerous way.*

Ferras Vansen could think of nothing to do but shake the reins, turn his horse, and ride out in the direction Barrick had indicated. Vansen had lost his mind to madness once before in this place, or as near to it as he could imagine. Perhaps madness was simply something he would have to learn to live in, as a fish could live in water without drowning.

3
Night Noises

O my children, listen! In the beginning all was dry and empty and fruitless. Then the light came and brought life to the nothingness, and of this light were born the gods, and all the earth's joys and sorrows. This is truth I tell you.

—from *The Revelations of Nushash*, Book One

THE FACE WAS COLD and emotionless, the skin pale and bloodless as Akaris marble, but it was the eyes that terrified Chert most: they seemed to glare with an inner fire, like red sunset knifing down through a crack in the world's ceiling.

"Who are you to meddle in the gods' affairs?" she demanded. *"You are the least of your people—less than a man. You betray the Mysteries without apology or prayer or ritual. You cannot even protect your own family. When the day comes that Urrigijag the Thousand-Eyed awakes, how will you explain yourself to him? Why should he take you before the Lord of the Hot Wet Stone to be judged and then welcomed, as the*

righteous are welcomed when their tools are at last set down? Will he not simply cast you into the void of the Stoneless Spaces to lament forever . . . ?"

And he could feel himself falling already, tumbling into that endless emptiness. He tried to scream, but no sound would come from his airless throat.

Chert sat up in bed, panting, sweat beading on his face even in the midst of a chilly night. Opal made a grumbling sound and reclaimed some of the blanket, then rolled over, putting her back to her annoying, restless husband.

Why should that face haunt his dream? Why should the grim noblewoman who had commanded the Twilight army—who in actuality had regarded Chert as though he were nothing more than a beetle on the tabletop—rail at him about the gods? She had not even really spoken to him, let alone made accusations that were so painful it felt as though they had been chiseled into his heart and could not be effaced.

I can't even protect my family—it's true. My wife cries every evening after Flint has fallen asleep—the boy who no longer recognizes us. And all because I let him go dashing off and could not find him until it was too late. At least that's what Opal thinks.

Not that she said any such thing. His wife was aware of the weapon her tongue could be, and since that strange and terrible time a tennight gone, she had never once blamed him. *Perhaps I am the only one blaming me,* he thought, *perhaps that is what the dream means.* He wished he could believe that were true.

A quiet noise suddenly caught his attention. He held his breath, listening. For the first time he realized that what had awakened him was not the fearfulness of the dream but a dim comprehension of something out of the ordinary. There it was again—a muffled scrabbling sound like a mouse in the wall. But the walls of Funderling houses were stone, and even if they had been made of wood like the big folks' flimsy dwellings, it would be a brave mouse indeed that would brave the sovereign territory of Opal Blue Quartz.

Is it the boy? Chert's heart flopped again. *Is he dying from those strange vapors we breathed in the depths?* Flint had never been well since coming back, sleeping away most days, speechless as a newborn much of the time he was awake, staring at his foster parents as though he were a trapped animal and they his captors—the single thing that tore most at Opal's heart.

Chert rolled out of bed, trying not to wake his wife. He padded into the other room, scarcely feeling the cold stone against his tough soles. The boy looked much as always, asleep with his mouth open and his arms cast wide, half on his stomach as though he were swimming, the covers kicked away. Chert paused first to lay a hand on Flint's ribs to be reassured by his breathing, then felt the boy's forehead for signs that the fever had returned. As he leaned close in the darkness he heard the noise again—a strange, slow scratching, as though some ancient Funderling ancestor from the days before burning were digging his way up toward the living.

Chert stood, his heart now beating very swiftly indeed. The sound came from the front room. An intruder? One of the burning-eyed Twilight folk, an assassin sent because the stony she-general now regretted letting him go? For a moment he felt his heart would stutter and stop, but his thoughts kept racing. The entire castle was in turmoil because of the events of Winter's Eve, and Funderling Town itself was full of mistrustful whispers—might it be someone who feared the strange child Chert and Opal had brought home? It seemed unlikely it was someone planning thievery—the crime was almost unknown in Funderling Town, a place where everyone knew everyone else, where the doors were heavy and the locks made with all the cunning that generations of stone- and metal-workers could bring to bear.

The front room was empty, nothing amiss except the supper dishes still sitting on the table, ample witness to Opal's unhappiness and lethargy. In Endekamene, the previous month, she would have dragged herself across the house on two broken legs rather than risk a morning visitor seeing the previous night's crockery still unwashed, but since Flint's disappearance and strange return his wife seemed barely able to muster the energy to do anything but sit by the child's bedside, red-eyed.

Chert heard the dry scratching again, and this time he could tell it came from outside the front door: something or someone was trying to get in.

A thousand superstitious fears hurried through his brain as he went to where his tools were hanging on the wall and took out his sharpest pick, called a shrewsnout. Surely nothing could get through that door unless he opened it—he and Opal's brother had worked days to shape the heavy oak, and the iron hinges were the finest product of Metal House craftsmen. He even considered going back to bed, leaving the problem for the morning, or for whatever other householder the scratching burglar might visit next, but he could not rid himself of a memory of little Beetledown, the Rooftopper who had almost died helping Chert look for Flint. The castle above was in chaos, with troops in Tolly livery ranging everywhere to search for any information about the astonishing kidnapping of Princess Briony. What if Beetledown was now the one who needed help? What if the little man was out there on Chert's doorstep, trying desperately to make his presence known in a world of giants?

Weapon held high, Chert Blue Quartz took a breath and opened the door. It was surprisingly dark outside—a darkness he had never seen in the night streets of Funderling Town. He squeezed the handle of his pick until his palm hurt, the tool he could wield for an hour straight without a tremor now quivering as his hand shook.

"Who is there?" Chert whispered into the darkness. "Show yourself!"

Something groaned, or even growled, and for the first time the terrified Chert could see that it was not black outside because the darklights of Funderling Town had gone out, but because a huge shape was blocking his doorway, shadowing everything. He stepped back, raising the shrewsnout to strike at this monster, but missed his blow as the thing lunged through the door and knocked him sideways. Still, even though he had failed to hit it, the intruding shape collapsed in the doorway. It groaned again, and Chert raised the pick, his heart hammering with terror. A round, pale face looked up at him, grime-smeared but quite recognizable in the light that now spilled in through the doorway.

Chaven, the royal physician, lifted hands turned into filthy paws by crusted, blackened bandages. "Chert . . . ?" he rasped. "Is that you? I'm afraid . . . I'm afraid I've left blood all over your door. . . ."

The morning was icy, the stones of Market Square slippery. The silent people gathered outside the great Trigonate temple of Southmarch seemed a single frozen mass, packed shoulder to shoulder in front of the steps, wrapped in cloaks and blankets against the bitterly cold winds off the sea.

Matty Tinwright watched the solemn-faced nobles and dignitaries as they emerged from the high-domed temple. He desperately wanted a drink. A cup of mulled wine—or better, two or three cups!—something to warm his chilled bones and heart, something to smear the hard, cold edges of the day into something more acceptable. But of course the taverns were closed and the castle kitchens had been emptied out, every lord, lady, serving maid, and scullion commanded to stand here in the cold and listen to the pronouncements of their new masters.

Mostly new, at least: Lord Constable Avin Brone stood with the others at the top of the steps, big as ever—bigger even, since the dark clothes and heavy cloak he wore made him look like something that should be on creaking wooden wheels instead of boots, some monstrous machine for knocking down the walls of besieged castles. Brone's presence, more than all else, had quelled any doubts Tinwright might have had about the astonishing events of the last days. Surely King Olin's most solid friend and most trusted servitor would not stand up beside Hendon Tolly if (as some whispered) there had been foul dealing in Princess Briony's disappearance. Tinwright had not forgotten his own encounter with Brone—surely not even the Tollys of Summerfield would dare make that man angry!

The skirl of the temple musicians' flutes died away, the last censer was swung—already the smoke was vanishing, shredded by the hard, cold breeze—and, after a ragged flourish of trumpets from the shivering heralds, Avin Brone took a few steps forward to the edge of the steps and looked down at the gathered castle folk.

"You have heard many things in these last days." His great bull-bellow of a voice carried far across the crowd. "Confused times breed confused stories, and these have been some of the most confusing times any of us have seen in our lifetimes." Brone lifted a broad hand. "Quiet! Listen well! First, it is true that Princess Briony Eddon has been taken, apparently by the criminal Shaso dan-Heza, the traitor who was once master of arms. We have searched for days, but there is no sign of either of them within the walls of Southmarch. We are praying for the princess' safe return, but I assure you we are not merely leaving it up to the gods."

The murmuring began again, louder. "Where is the prince?" someone near the front shouted. "Where is her brother?"

Brone's shoulders rose and he balled his fists. "Silence! Must you all jabber like Xandy savages? Hear my words and you will learn something. Prince Barrick was with Tyne of Blueshore and the others, fighting the invaders at Kolkan's Field. We have had no word from Tyne for days, and the survivors who have made their way back can tell us little." Several in the crowd looked out across the narrow strait toward the city, still now and apparently empty. They had all heard the singing and the drums that echoed there at night, and had seen the fires. "We hold out hope, of course, but for now we must assume our prince is lost, killed or captured. It is in the hands of the gods." Brone paused at the uprush of sound, the cries and curses which started out low but quickly began to swell. When he spoke again his voice was still loud, but not as clear and composed as it had been; that by itself helped still the crowd. "Please! Remember, Olin is still king here in Southmarch! He may be imprisoned in the south, but he is still king—and his line still survives!" He pointed to a young woman standing next to Hendon Tolly, plump, and plain—a wet nurse holding what was apparently an infant, although it could have been an empty tangle of blankets for all Matt Tinwright could make it out. "See, there is the king's youngest," Brone declared, "—a new son, born on Winter's Eve! Queen Anissa lives. The child is healthy. The Eddon line survives."

Now Brone waved his hands, imploring the crowd for quiet rather than ordering them, and Tinwright could not help wondering at how this man who had terrified him down to the soles of his feet could have changed so, as if something inside of him had torn and not been fully mended.

But why should that surprise? Briony, our gracious, wonderful princess, is gone, and young Barrick is doubtless dead, killed by those supernatural monsters. Tinwright's poetic soul could feel the romantic correctness of that, the symmetry of the lost twins, but could not work up as much sympathy for the brother. He truly, truly missed Briony, and feared for her—she had been Matt Tinwright's champion. Barrick, on the other hand, had never hidden his contempt.

Brone now gave way to Hendon Tolly, who was dressed in unusually somber attire—somber for him, anyway—black hose, gray tunic, and fur-lined black cloak, his clothes touched here and there with hints of gold and emerald. Hendon was known as one of the leading blades of fashion north of the great court at Tessis. Tinwright, who admired him without liking him, had always been sensitive to the nuances of dress among those above his own station, and thought the youngest Tolly brother seemed to be enjoying his new role as sober guardian of the populace.

Hendon raised his hand, which was mostly hidden by the long ruff on his sleeve. His thin, usually mobile face was a mask of refined sorrow. "We Tollys share the same ancient blood as the Eddons—King Olin is my uncle as well as my liegelord, and despite the bull on our shield, the wolf blood runs in our veins. We swear we will protect his young heir with every drop of that blood." Hendon lowered his head for a moment as if in prayer, or perhaps merely overcome by humility at the weight of his task. "We have all been pained by great loss this terrible winter, we Tollys most of all, because we have also lost our brother Gailon, the duke. But fear not! My other brother Caradon, the new duke of Summerfield, has sworn that the ties between our houses will become even stronger." Hendon Tolly straightened. "Many of you are frightened because of worrisome news from the battlefield and the presence of our enemy from the north—the enemy that even now waits at our doorstep, just across the bay. I have heard some speak of a siege. I say to you, what siege?" He swept his arm toward the haunted, silent city beyond the water, sleeve flaring like a crow's wing. "Not an arrow, not a stone, has passed our walls. I see no enemy—do you? It could be that someday these goblins will come against us, but it is more likely that they have seen the majesty of the walls of Southmarch and their hearts have grown faint. Otherwise, why would they give no sign of their presence?"

A murmur drifted up from the crowd, but it seemed, for the first time, to have something of hope in it. Hendon Tolly sensed it and smiled.

"And even if they did, how will they defeat us, my fellow Southmarchers? We cannot be starved, not as long as we have our harbor and good neighbors. And already my brother the duke is sending men to help protect this castle and all who dwell in it. Never fear, Olin's heir will someday sit proudly on Olin's throne!"

Now a few cheers broke out from the heartened crowd, although in the windswept square it did not make a very heroic sound. Still, even Matt Tinwright found himself reassured.

I may not like the man overmuch, but imagine the trouble we would have been in if Hendon Tolly and his soldiers had not been here! There would have been riots and all manner of madness. Still, he had not slept well ever since hearing about the supernatural creatures on their doorstep, and he noticed that Tolly, for all his confidence, had said nothing about rooting the shadow folk out of the abandoned city.

Hierarch Sisel now came forth to bless the crowd on behalf of the Trigonate gods. As the hierarch intoned the ritual of Perin's Forgiveness, Lord Tolly—the castle's new protector—fell into deep conversation with Tirnan Havemore, the new castellan. The king's old counselor Nynor had retired from his position, and Havemore, who had been Avin Brone's factor, had been the surprising choice to replace him. Tinwright could not resist looking at the man with envy. To rise so quickly, and to such importance! Brone must have been very pleased with him to give him such honor. But as Avin Brone now watched Tolly and Havemore, Tinwright could not help thinking he did not look either pleased or proud. Tinwright shrugged. There were always intrigues at court. It was the way of the world.

And perhaps there is a place for me there, too, he thought hopefully, *even without my beloved patroness. Perhaps if I make myself noticed, I too will be lifted up.*

Turning, the blessing forgotten, Matty Tinwright began to work his way out through the crowd, thinking of ways his own splendid light might be revealed to those in the new Southmarch who would recognize its gleam.

To her credit, Opal handled the discovery of a bleeding, burned man twice her size sprawling on her floor with no little grace.

"Oh!" she said, peering out from the sleeping room, "What's this? I'm not dressed. Are you well, Chert?"

"I am well, but this friend is not. He has wounds that need tending . . ."

"Don't touch him! I'll be out in a moment."

At first Chert thought she feared for her dear husband, that he might take some contagion from their wounded visitor, or that the injured man, in pain and delirium, might lash out like a dying animal. After some consideration, though, he realized that Opal didn't trust him not to make things worse.

"The boy's still asleep," she said as she emerged, still pulling her wrap around herself. "He had another poor night. What's this, then? Who is this big fellow and why is he here at this hour?"

"It is Chaven, the royal physician. I've told you about him. As to why . . ."

"Crawled." Chaven's laugh was dry and painful to hear. "Crawled across the castle in darkness . . . to here. I need help with my . . . my wounds. But I cannot stay. You are in danger if I do."

"Nobody's in anywhere near as much danger as you, looking at those burns," Opal said, scowling at the physician's pitiful, crusted hands. "Hurry, bring me some water and my herb-basket, old man, and be quiet about it. We don't need the boy underfoot as well."

Chert did as he was told.

By the time Opal had finished cleaning Chaven's burns with weak brine, covered them with poultices of moss paste, and begun to bind them with clean cloth, the wounded physician was asleep, his chin bumping against his chest every time she pulled a bandage snug.

Opal stood and looked down at her handiwork. "Is he trustworthy?" she asked quietly.

"He is the best of the big folk I know."

"That doesn't answer my question, you old fool."

Chert couldn't help smiling. "I'm glad to see the difficulties we've been through lately haven't cost you your talent for endearments, my sweet. Who can say? The whole world up there is topsy-turvy. Up there? We have a child of the big folk living in our own house who plays some part in this war with the fairy folk. Everything has gone mad both upground *and* here."

"Injured or not, I won't have the fellow in the house unless you tell me he can be trusted. We have a child to think of."

Chert sighed. "He is one of the best men I know, ordinary *or* big. And he might understand something of what's happened to Flint."

Opal nodded. "Right. He'll sleep for hours—he drank a whole cup of mossbrew, and he can't have much blood left to mix it with. We'd best get what sleep we can ourselves."

"You are a marvel," he told her as they climbed back under the blanket. "All these years and I still cannot believe my luck."

"I can't believe your luck, either." But she sounded at least a little pleased. Better than that, Chert had seen in her eyes as she tended the doctor's wounds something he had not seen there since he had brought Flint back home—purpose. It was worth a great deal of risk to see his good wife become something like herself again.

★

Chaven could barely hold the bread in his hands, but he ate like a dog who had been shut for days in an abandoned cottage. Which, as he began to tell Chert and Opal his story, was not so far from the truth.

"I have been hiding in the tunnels just outside my own house." He paused to wipe his face with his sleeve, trying to dab away some of the water that had escaped his clumsy handling of the cup. "The secret door, Chert, the one you know—there is a panel that comes out of the wall of the inside hallway and hides the door from prying eyes. I closed that behind me and went to ground in the tunnels like a hunted fox. I managed to bring a water bottle that had gone with me on my last journey, but had no time to find food."

"Eat more, then," Chert said, "—but slowly. Why should you be hiding? What has happened to the world up there? We hear stories, and even if they are only half true or less, they are still astonishing and terrifying—the fairy folk defeating our army, the princess and her brother dead or run away . . ."

"Briony has not run away," said Chaven, scowling. "I would stake my life on that. In fact, I already have."

Chert shook his head, lost. "What are you talking about?"

"It is a long tale, and as full of madness as anything you have heard about fairy armies . . ."

Opal stood abruptly as a noise came from behind them. Flint, pale and bleary-eyed, stood in the doorway. "What are you doing out of bed?" she demanded.

The boy looked at her, his face chillingly dull. With all the things that had been strange or even frightening about him before, Chert could not help thinking, this lifeless, disinterested look was worse by far. "Thirsty."

"I'll bring you in water, child. You are not ready to be out of bed yet, so soon after the fever has passed." She gave Chert and Chaven a significant glance. "Keep your voices down," she told them.

Chert had barely begun to describe the bizarre events of Winter's Eve when Opal returned from getting Flint back into bed, so he started again. His tale, which would have been an incredible one coming from the mouth of someone recently returned from exotic foreign lands, let alone the familiar precincts of Southmarch, would have been impossible to believe had it not been Chaven himself speaking, a man Chert knew to be not just honest, but rigorously careful about what he knew and did not know, about what could be proved or only surmised. *"Built on bedrock,"* as Chert's father had always said of someone trustworthy, *"not on sand, sliding this way and that with every shrug of the Elders."*

"So do you think that this Tolly villain had something to do with the southern witch, Selia?" Chert asked. "With the death of poor Prince Kendrick and the attack on the princess?" From his one brief meeting with her, Chert had a proprietorial fondness for Briony Eddon, and already loathed Hendon Tolly and his entire family with an unquenchable hatred.

"I can't say, but the snatches of conversation I heard from him and his guards made them sound just as surprised as me. But their treachery to the royal family cannot be questioned, nor their desire to murder me, a witness of what really happened."

"They truly would have killed you?" asked Opal.

"Definitely, had I remained to be killed," Chaven said with a pained smile. "As I hid from them in the Tower of Spring, I heard Hendon Tolly telling his minions that I was by no means to survive my capture—that he would reward the man who finished me."

"Elders!" breathed Opal. "The castle's in the hands of bandits and murderers!"

"For the moment, certainly. Without Princess Briony or her brother, I see no way to change things." All the talking had tired the physician; he seemed barely able to keep his head up.

"We must get you to one of the powerful lords," Chert said. "Someone still loyal to the king, who will protect you until your story is told."

"Who is left? Tyne Aldritch is dead in Kolkan's Field, Nynor retreated to his country house in fear," Chaven said flatly. "And Avin Brone seems to have made his own peace with the Tollys. I trust no one." He shook his head as if it were a heavy stone he had carried too long. "And worst of all, the Tollys have taken my house, my splendid observatory!"

"But why would they do that? Do they think you're still hiding there?"

"No. They want something, and I fear I know what. They are tearing things apart—I could hear them through the walls from my tunnel hiding-places—searching. *Searching . . .*"

"Why? For what?"

Chaven groaned. "Even if I am right about what they seek, I am not certain why they want it—but I am frightened, Chert. There is more afoot here and in the world outside than simply a struggle for the throne of the March Kingdoms."

Chert suddenly realized that Chaven did not know the story of his own adventures, about the inexplicable events surrounding the boy in the other room. "There is more," he said suddenly. "Now you must rest, but later I will tell you of our own experiences. I met the Twilight folk. And the boy got into the Mysteries."

"What? Tell me now!"

"Let the poor man sleep." Opal sounded weary, too, or perhaps just weighed down again with unhappiness. "He is weak as a weanling."

"Thank you . . ." Chaven said, barely able to form words. "But . . . I must hear this tale . . . immediately. I said once that I feared what the moving of the Shadowline might mean. But now I think I feared . . . too little." His head sagged, nodded. "Too little . . ." he sighed, ". . . and too . . . late . . ." Within a few breaths he was asleep, leaving Chert and Opal to stare at each other, eyes wide with apprehension and confusion.

4

The *Hada-d'in-Mozan*

*The greatest offspring of Void and Light was Daystar, and
by his shining all was better known and the songs had new
shapes. And in this new light Daystar found Bird Mother
and together they engendered many things, children, and
music, and ideas. But all beginnings contain their own
endings.*

*When the Song of All was much older, Daystar lost his
own song and went away into the sky to sing only of the
sun. Bird Mother did not die, though her grief was mighty,
but instead she birthed a great egg, and from it the beautiful
twins Breeze and Moisture came forth to scatter the seeds of
living thought, to bring the earth sustenance and
fruitfulness.*

—from *One Hundred Considerations*
out of the Qar's *Book of Regret*

A STORM SWEPT IN from the ocean in the wake of the setting sun, but although cold rain pelted them and the little boat pitched until Briony felt quite ill, the air was actually warmer than it had been on their first trip across Brenn's Bay. It was still, however, a chilly, miserable journey.

Winter, Briony thought ruefully. *Only a fool would lose her throne and be forced to run for her life in this fatal season. The Tollys won't need to kill me—I'll probably drown myself, or simply freeze.* She was even more worried about Shaso soaking in the cold rain so soon after his fever had broken, but as usual the old man showed less evidence of discomfort than a stone statue. That was reassuring, at least: if he was well enough for his stiff-necked pride to rule him, he had unquestionably improved.

By comparison, the Skimmer girl Ena seemed neither to be made miserable by the storm nor to bear it bravely—in fact, she hardly seemed to notice it. Her hood was back and she rowed with the ease and carelessness of someone steering a punt through the gentle waters of a summertime lake. They owed this Skimmer girl much, Briony knew: without her knowledge of the bay and its tides they would have had little hope of escape.

I shall reward her well. Of course, just now the daughter of Southmarch's royal family had nothing to give.

The worst of the storm soon passed, though the high waves lingered. The monotony of the trip, the continuous pattering of rain on Briony's hooded cloak and the rocking of the swells, kept dropping her into a dreamy near-sleep and a fantasy of the day when she would ride back into Southmarch, greeted with joy by her people and . . . and who else? Barrick was gone and she could not think too much about his absence just yet: it was as though she had sustained a dreadful wound and dared not look at it until it had been tended, for fear she would faint away and die by the roadside without reaching help. But who else was left? Her father was still a prisoner in far-off Hierosol. Her stepmother Anissa, although perhaps not an enemy if her servant's murderous treachery had been nothing to do with her, was still not really a friend, and certainly no mother. What other people did Briony treasure, or even care about? Avin Brone? He was too stern, too guarded. Who else?

For some reason, the guard captain Ferras Vansen came to her mind—but that was nonsense! What was he to her, with his ordinary face and his ordinary brown hair and his posture so carefully correct it almost seemed like a kind of swagger? If she recognized now that he had not been as guilty in the death of her older brother as she had once felt, he was still nothing to her—a common soldier, a functionary, a man who no doubt thought little beyond the barracks and the tavern, and likely spent what spare time he had putting his hands up the dresses of tavern wenches.

Still, it was odd that she should see his thoughtful face just now, that she should think of him so suddenly, and almost fondly . . .

Merolanna. Of course—dear old Auntie 'Lanna! Briony's great-aunt would be there for any triumphant return. But what must she be feeling now? Briony abruptly felt a kind of panic steal over her. Poor Auntie! She must be mad with grief and worry, both twins gone, the whole order of life overturned. But Merolanna would persevere, of course. She would hold together for the sake of others, for the sake of the family, even for the sake of Olin's newborn son, Anissa's child. Briony pushed away a pang of jealousy. What else should her great-aunt do? She would be protecting the Eddons as best she could.

Oh, Auntie, I will give you such a hug when I come back, it will almost crack your bones! And I'll kiss your old cheeks pink! You will be so astonished! The duchess would cry of course—she always did for happy things, scarcely ever for sad. *And you'll be so proud of me. "You wise girl," you'll say to me. "Just what your father would have done. And so brave . . . !"*

Briony nodded and drowsed, thinking about that day to come, so easy to imagine in every way except how it might actually come to pass.

★

They reached the hilly north Marrinswalk coast just as the rising sun warmed the storm clouds from black to bruised gray, rowing across the empty cove to within a few yards of the shore. Briony bunched the homespun skirt Ena had given her around her thighs and helped the Skimmer girl guide the hull up onto the wet sand. The wind was stingingly cold, the saltgrass and beach heather along the dunes rippling as if in imitation of the shallow wavelets frothing on the bay.

"Where are we?" she asked.

Shaso wrung water out of his saggy clothes. Just as Briony had been clothed in Ena's spares, he wore one of Turley's baggy, salt-bleached shirts and a pair of the Skimmer's plain, knee-length breeches. As he surveyed the surrounding hills, his leathery, wrinkled face gaunt from his long imprisonment, Shaso dan-Heza looked like some ancient spirit dressed in a child's castoff clothing. "Somewhere not far from Kinemarket, I'd say, about three or four days' walk from Oscastle."

"Kinemarket is that way." Ena pointed east. "On the far side of these hills, south of the coast road. You could be there before the sun lifts over the top."

"Only if we start walking," said Shaso.

"What on earth will we do in Kinemarket?" Briony had never been there, but knew it was a small town with a yearly fair that paid a decent amount of revenue to the throne. She also dimly remembered that some river passed through it or near it. In any case, it might as well have been named Tiny or Unimportant as far as she was concerned just now. "There's nothing there!"

"Except food—and we will need some of that, don't you think?" said Shaso. "We cannot travel without eating and I am not so well-honed in my skills that I can trap or kill dinner for us. Not until I mend a bit and find my legs, anyway."

"Where are we going after that?"

"Toward Oscastle."

"Why?"

"Enough questions." He gave her a look that would have made most people quail, but Briony was not so easily put off.

"You said you would make the choices, and I agreed. I never said that I wouldn't ask why, and you never said you wouldn't answer."

He growled under his breath. "Try your questions again when the road is under our feet." He turned to Ena. "Give your father my thanks, girl."

"Her father didn't row us." Briony was still shamed that she had argued with the young woman about landing at M'Helan's Rock. "I owe you a kindness," she told the girl with as much queenly graciousness as she could muster. "I won't forget."

"I'm sure you won't, Lady." Ena made a swift and not very reverent courtesy.

Well, she's seen me sleeping, drooling spittle down my chin. I suppose it would be a bit much to expect her to treat me like Zoria the Fair. Still, Briony wasn't entirely certain she was going to like being a princess without a throne or a castle or any of the privileges that, while she had been quick to scorn them, she had grown rather used to. "Thanks, in any case."

"Good luck to you both, Lady, Lord." Ena took a step, then stopped and turned around. "Holy Diver lift me, I almost forgot—Father would have had me skinned, stretched, and smoked!" She pulled a small sack out of a pocket in her voluminous skirt and handed it to Shaso. "There are some coins to help you get on with your journey, Lord." She looked at Briony with what almost seemed pity. "Buy the princess a proper meal, perhaps."

Before Briony or Shaso could say anything, the Skimmer girl scooted the wooden rowboat back down the wet sand and into the water, then waded with it out into the cove. She swung herself onto the bench as gracefully as a trick rider vaulting onto a horse; a heartbeat or two later the oars were in the water and the boat was moving outward against the wind, bobbing on each line of coursing waves.

Briony stood watching as the girl and her boat disappeared. She suddenly felt very lonely and very weary.

"A reliable thing about villages, or cities for that matter," said Shaso sourly, "is that *they* will not walk to *us*." He pointed across the dunes to the hills and their ragged covering of bushes and low trees. "Shall we begin, or do you have some pressing reason for us to keep standing here until someone notices us?"

She knew she should be grateful his old fire was coming back, but just now she wasn't.

His vinegary moment seemed to have tired Shaso, too. He kept his head down and didn't talk as they walked over the cold dunes toward a path that ran along the beginning of the hills.

Briony had at first wished to pursue the question of why they were going to Oscastle, Marrinswalk's leading city but still a bit of a backwater, and what his plans were when they reached the place, but she found herself just as happy to save her strength for walking. The wind, which had first had been steadily at their backs, now swung around and began to blow full into their faces with stinging force, making every step feel like a climb up steep stairs. The heavy gray clouds hung so low overhead it almost seemed to Briony she could reach up and sink her fingers into them. She was grateful for the thick wool cloaks the Skimmers had given them, but they were still damp with rainwater and Briony's felt heavy as lead. Her court dresses, for all their discomforts, suddenly did not seem so bad: at least they had been dry and warm.

After perhaps an hour Briony began to see signs of habitation— a few crofters' huts on hilltops, surrounded by trees. Some had smoke swirling from the holes in their roofs, or even from crooked chimneys, and Briony broke her long silence to ask Shaso if they could not stop at one of them for long enough to get warm again.

He shook his head. "The fewer the people, the greater the danger someone will remember us. Hendon Tolly and his men have no doubt begun to wonder whether we might have left the castle entirely, and soon they will be asking questions in every town along the coast of Brenn's Bay. We are an unusual pair, a black-skinned man and a white-skinned girl. It is only a matter of time until someone who's seen us meets one of Hendon's agents."

"But we'll be long gone!"

"We have to hide *somewhere*. Do you really want to tell the

Tollys they can stop searching the castle and all the rest of the surrounding lands and concentrate on just one place—like Marrinswalk?"

Thinking of a troop of armed men beating the countryside behind them made Briony shudder and walk faster. "But someone will have to see us eventually. If we go to Oscastle or some other city, I mean. Cities are full of people, after all."

"Which is our best hope. Perhaps our *only* hope. We are less likely to be noticed somewhere there are many people, Highness—especially where there are people of my race. And that is enough talk for now."

They followed the track down the edge of a wide valley. When they reached the broad river that meandered at its bottom, Shaso decided that they could at least take time to drink. They also encountered a few more houses, simple things of unmortared stone and loose thatching, but still so scattered that Briony doubted any man could see his neighbor's cottage even in full daylight with a cloudless sky. A goat bleated from the paddock behind one of them, probably protesting the cold day, and she realized that it was the first homely sound she had heard for hours.

They passed by several small villages as the hours passed but entered none of them, and reached Kinemarket by late morning, crossing over at a place where the river narrowed and some work by the locals had turned a lucky assembly of stones into a bridge. Kinemarket was a good-sized, prosperous town, with the turnip shape of a temple dome visible above its low walls. Shaso decided he should stay hidden in the trees outside town while Briony went to buy food with a coin from the purse Turley had provided—a silver piece with the head of King Enander of Syan, a coin so small that Briony felt sure almost half of its original metal had been shaved off. She was guiltily aware of having once declared that not only should coin-clippers be beaten in the public square, but that those who helped them pass their moneys should suffer the same punishment. It seemed a little different now, when someone else had already done the shaving and she needed the coin to buy food.

"Here—rub a little more dirt on yourself first." Shaso drew a line of grime on her face. She tried to back away. "Go, then, do it yourself. You've a head start on it, anyway, from the morning's walk."

She rubbed on a bit more, but as she made her way up the muddy track toward the town gate, hoping to lose herself in the crowd of people going to the market, she began to fear she and Shaso had given too little thought to disguising her identity. Surely even the oft-mended homespun dress and a few smears of dirt on her cheeks would not fool many people! Her face, she realized with a strange sort of pride, must be better known than any other woman's in the north. Now, though, being recognized could be deadly.

And although she tried not to meet their eyes, the first folk she passed on her way to the gate did look her over slowly and mistrustfully, but she realized after a moment that this man and woman were doing so only because most of the other travelers were dressed and clean for market: Briony was a dirty stranger, not a typical stranger.

"The Three grant you good day," said the woman. She held her gape-mouthed child tightly, as though Briony might steal it. "And a blessed Orphanstide to you, too."

"And you." The greeting startled her—Briony had almost forgotten the holidays, since it had been on Winter's Eve that her world had fallen completely into pieces. There certainly hadn't been any new year's feasting or gifts for her, and now it must be only a tennight or so until Kerneia. How strange, to have lost not just a home but an entire life!

She did not turn to watch the man and woman after they passed, but she knew that they had turned to look at her, doubtless wondering what kind of odd thing she was.

Go ahead and whisper about me, then. You cannot imagine anything near so strange as the truth.

Worried about attracting any kind of attention at all, she decided not to continue to the market, but passed through the gate and briefly into the bustle of the crowd on the main thoroughfare before turning down a narrow side street. She stopped at the first ramshackle house where she saw someone out in front—a woman wrapped in a heavy wool blanket scattering corn on the puddled ground, the chickens bustling about at her feet as though she were their mother hen.

The householder at first seemed suspicious, but when she saw the silver piece and heard Briony's invented story of a mother and younger brother out on the coast road, both ill, she bit her lip in thought, then nodded. She went into her tall house, which crowded against its neighbors on either side as if they were cho-risters sharing a small bench, but conspicuously did not ask Briony to follow her. After some time she reappeared with a hunk of hard cheese, a half a loaf of bread, and four eggs, not to men-tion several children trying to squeeze past her wide hips to get a look at Briony. It didn't seem a lot of food, even for a shaved fin-gerling, but she had to admit that what she knew about money had to do with much larger quantities, and the prices with which she was familiar were more likely to be the accounts for feeding an entire garrison of guards. She stared at the woman for a moment, wondering whether she was being dealt with honestly, and realized this was perhaps the first person she had ever met in her life who had no idea of who she was, the first person who (as far as this woman knew) owed her nothing in the way of respect or allegiance. Briony was further shocked to realize that this drab creature draggled with children, this brood-mother with red, wind-bitten face and mistrust still lurking in her eyes, was not many years older than Briony herself. Chastened, she thanked the young woman and wished her the blessing of the Three, then headed back toward the gate and the place outside the walls where Shaso waited.

And, it suddenly came to her, not only had no one recognized her, it was unlikely anyone would, unless they were Hendon's troops and they were already looking for her: in all of Marrinswalk only a few dozen people would know her face even were she wearing full court dress—a few nobles, a merchant or two who had come to Southmarch Castle to curry favor. Here in the countryside she was a ghost: since she could not be Briony, she was no one.

It was a feeling as humbling as it was reassuring.

Briony and Shaso ate enough cheese and bread to feel strengthened, then they began to walk again. As the day wore on they followed the line of the coast, which was sometimes only a stone's throw away, other times invisible and completely absent but for the rumble of the surf. The valley walls and trees protected them from the worst of the chilly wind. They slipped off the road when they heard large traveling parties coming and kept their heads down when they couldn't avoid passing others on the road.

"How far to Oscastle?" she asked Shaso as they sat resting. They had just finished scrambling up a wet, slippery hillside to go around a fallen tree that blocked the road and it had tired them both.

"Three days or more," Shaso said. "But we are not going there."

"But Lawren, the old Earl of Marrinscrest, lives there, and he would . . ."

"Would certainly find it hard to keep a secret of your presence, yes." The old man rubbed his weathered face. "I am glad to see you are beginning to think carefully." He scowled. "By the Great Mother, I cannot believe I am so tired. Some evil spirit is riding me like a donkey."

"The evil spirit is me," Briony said. "I was the one who kept you locked up for all that time—no wonder you are tired and ill."

He turned away and spat. "You did what you had to do, Briony Eddon. And, unlike your brother, you wished to believe I was innocent of Kendrick's murder."

"Barrick thought he was doing what had to be done, too." A flood of pain and loneliness swept through her, so powerful that for a moment it took her breath away. "Oh, I don't want to talk about him," she said at last. "If we're not going to Oscastle, where are we going?"

"Landers Port." He levered himself up to his feet, showing little of his old murderous grace or speed. "A grand name for a town that never saw King Lander at all, but only one of his ships, which foundered off the coast on the way back from Coldgray Moor." Shaso almost smiled. "A fishing town and not much more, but it will suit our needs nicely, as you will see."

"How do you know all this about Lander's ships and Coldgray Moor?"

His smile disappeared. "The greatest battle in the history of the north? And me master of arms for Southmarch? If I did not know any history, then you *would* have had a reason to hang me in irons in the stronghold, child."

Briony knew when it was a good time to hold her tongue, but she did not always do what was best. "I only asked. And merry Orphanstide to you, too. Did you enjoy your breakfast?"

Shaso shook his head. "I am old and my limbs are sore. Forgive me."

Now he had managed to make her feel bad again. In his own way, he was as difficult to argue with as her father could be. And that thought brought another pang of loneliness.

"Forgiven," was all she said.

By late afternoon, with Kinemarket far behind them and the smell of smoke rising from the cottages they passed, Briony was hungry again. They had sucked the meat from the eggs long before, but Shaso had kept back half the bread and cheese for later and she was finding it hard to think about anything except eating. The only rival to food was imagining what it would be like to crawl under the warm, heavy counterpane of her bed back home, and lie there listening to the very wind and rain that were now making her day so miserable. She wondered where they were going to sleep that night, and whether Shaso was saving the last rind of the cheese for their dinner. Cold cheer that would make.

Look at me! I am a pampered child, she scolded herself. *Think of Barrick, wherever he is, on a cold battlefield, or worse. Think of Father in a stone dungeon. And look at Shaso. Three days ago, he was in chains, starving, bleeding from his iron manacles. Now he is exiled because of me, walking by my side, and he is forty years or more my elder!*

All of which only made her more miserable.

The path they had been following for so long, which had never been anything more than a beaten track, now widened a bit and began to turn away from the coast. The cottages now were so thickly set that they were clearly approaching another large village or town—she could see the life of the place even at twilight, the men coming back from the rainy fields in their woolen jackets, each one carrying some wood for the fire, women calling the children in, older boys and girls herding sheep to their paddocks. Everyone seemed to have a place, all under the gods' careful order, homes and lives that, however humble, made sense. For a moment Briony thought she might burst into tears.

Shaso, however, did not stop to moon over rustic certainties, and had even picked up a little speed, like a horse on the way back to the barn for its evening fodder, so she had to hurry to keep up with him. They both kept their hoods close around their faces, but so did everyone else in this weather; people going in and out of the riverside settlements scarcely even looked up as they passed.

The path wound up the side of the valley, the river now only a murmur in the trees behind them, and Briony was just beginning to wonder how they would walk without a torch on this dark, rain-spattered night, when they reached the top of the valley and looked down on the marvelous lights of a city.

No, not a city, Briony realized after a dazzled moment, but at least a substantial, prosperous town. In the folds of the hills she could see half a dozen streets sparkling with torches, and more windows lit from within than she could easily count. Set against the great darkness behind it the bowl of lights seemed a precious thing, a treasure.

"That is the sea, out there," said Shaso, pointing to the darkness beyond Landers Port. "We have worked our way around to it again. The track is wide here, but be careful—it is marshland all about."

Still, despite the boggy emptiness on either side, they walked quickly to take advantage of the fast diminishing twilight. Briony was buoyed by a sudden optimism, the hope that at the very least they would soon be putting something in their stomachs and perhaps getting out of the rain as well. It was an altogether different matter, this unrelenting drizzle, when one had only to cross a courtyard or, at worst, Market Square—and she had been seldom allowed to do even that without a guardsman holding his cloak above her. But here in the wilderness, with drops battering the top of her head all day like a fall of pebbles and soaking her all the way to her bones, the rain was not an inconvenience but an enemy, patient and cruel.

"Will we stay at an inn, then?" she asked, still half-wishing they could stop in the comfortable house of some loyal noble, risks be damned. "That seems dangerous, too. Do you think no one will remark on a black-skinned man and a young girl?"

"People might remark less than you think," Shaso said with a snort. "Landers Port may never have seen the old king of Syan, but it is a busy fishing town and boats land every day from all parts of Eion and even beyond. But no, we will not be stopping in a tavern full of gossips and layabouts. We might as well announce our arrival from the steps of the town's temple."

"Oh, merciful Zoria," she said, knowing that going on about it only made her seem a pampered child, but at this moment not caring. "It's to be another shack, then. Some fisherman's hut stinking of mackerel, with a leaking roof."

"If you do not stop your complaining, I may arrange just such a lodging," he said, and pulled his cloak tighter against the rain.

Full night had fallen and the city gate was closing, the watchmen bawling curses at the stragglers. In the undifferentiated mass of wet wool hoods and cloaks, the jostling of people and animals, Briony and Shaso did not seem to attract much notice, but she still held her breath while the guards at the gate looked them over and did not let it out until they were past the walls and inside.

The old man took her by the arm, pulling her out of the crowd of latecomers and down a tiny side-alley, the houses so close that their upper levels seemed about to butt each other like rams in spring. Briony could smell fish, both fresh and smoked, and here and there even the aroma of fresh bread. Her stomach twisted with desire, but Shaso hurried her down dark streets lit only by guttering cookfires visible through the open doorways. Voices came to her, dreamlike in her hunger and cold, some speaking words she could understand but many that she could not, either because of thick accents or unfamiliar tongues.

They had obviously entered the town's poorest quarter, not a shred of horn or glass in any window, no light but meager fires in the crowded downstairs rooms, and Briony's heart sank. Reeking straw was going to be her bed tonight, and small, leggy things would be crawling on her in the cold dark. At least she and Shaso had a little money. She would settle for ᴅo leavings of cheese and bread from the morning. She would command, or at least demand, that he buy them something hot—a bowl of pottage, perhaps even some meat if there was such a thing as a clean butcher in this part of the town.

"Be very quiet now," said Shaso abruptly, putting out his arm to stop her. They were in the deepest shadow they had yet found, the only illumination the nearly invisible, cloud-dimmed moon, and it took her a moment to realize they were standing beside a high stone wall. When he had listened for a moment—Briony could hear nothing at all except her own breathing and the never-ending patter of rain—the old man stepped toward the wall and, to her astonishment, pounded his knuckles on what sounded like a wooden door. How he could have found such a thing in the near-perfect darkness, let alone known it was there in the first place, she had no idea.

There was a long silence. Shaso knocked again, this time in a discernible pattern. A moment later a man's low voice said something and Shaso answered, neither question nor reply in a language she recognized. The door creaked inward and light splashed out into the rain-rippled muck of the street.

A man in a strange, baggy robe stood in the entrance; as Shaso stepped back to let Briony step through the man bowed. For a moment she wondered if the robe marked him as a mantis, if this was indeed, despite Shaso's own denial, some back-alley temple, but when the gatekeeper finished his bow and looked up at her he proved to be a bearded youth as dark-skinned as Shaso.

"Welcome, guest," he said to her. "If you accompany Lord Shaso, you are a flower in the house of Effir dan-Mozan."

They entered the main part of the house by a covered passage beside a courtyard—Briony could dimly see what looked like a bare fruit tree at its center—which led into a low building that seemed to take up a great deal of space. A covey of women came to her and surrounded her, murmuring, only every fifth or sixth word in Briony's own tongue. They smelled charmingly of violets and rosewater and other, less familiar scents; for a moment she was happy just to breathe in as they took her hands and tugged her toward a passageway. She looked back at Shaso in bemusement and alarm, but he was already in urgent conversation with the bearded youth and only waved her on. That was the last she saw of him, or of any man, for the rest of the evening.

The women, a mixture of old and young, but all dark-skinned, black-haired Southerners like the man at the door, led her—herded her, in truth—into a sumptuous tiled chamber lit with dozens of candles, so warm that the air was steamy. Briony was so astounded to find this palatial luxury in the poorest quarter of a fishing town that she did not realize for a moment that some of the women were trying to pull her clothes off. Shocked, she fought back, and was about to give one of them a good blow of her fist (a skill learned in childhood to deal with a pair of brawling brothers) when one of the smaller women stepped toward her, both hands raised in supplication.

"Please," she said, "what is your name?"

Briony stared. The woman was fine-boned and handsome, but though her hair was shiny and black as tar, it was clear she was old enough to be Briony's mother, or even her grandmother. "Briony," she said, remembering only too late that she was a fugitive. Still, Shaso had passed her to the women as though she were a saddle-bag to be unpacked: she could not be expected to keep her caution while under attack by this murmuring pigeon flock.

"Please, Bri-oh-nee-*zisaya*," the small woman said, "you are cold and tired. You are a guest for us, yes? You cannot eat in the *hada* until you are bathing, yes?"

"Bathing?" Briony suddenly realized that the great dark rectangular emptiness in the middle of the room, which she had thought only a lower part of the floor, was a bath—a bath bigger than her own huge bed in the Southmarch royal residence! "There?" she added stupidly.

The women, sensing a lull in her resistance, swooped in and pulled off the rest of her sodden clothes, murmuring in pity and amusement as Briony's pale, goose-pimpled skin was exposed. She was helped to the edge of the bath—it had steps leading down!—and, to her further astonishment, several of the women disrobed and climbed in with her. Now at least she understood why the bath was so large.

The first shock of the hot water almost made her faint, then as she settled in and grew used to it a deep languor crept over her, so that she nearly fell asleep. The women giggled, soaping and scrubbing her in a way she would have found unduly intimate if it had been Rose and Moina, who had known her for years, but somehow she could not make herself care. It was warm in the bath—so blessedly warm!—and the scent of flowery oils in the steamy air made her feel as though she were floating in a summer cloud.

Out of the bath, wrapped in a thick white robe like those the women wore, she was led to a room full of cushions with a fire in a brazier at its center. Here too an inordinate number of candles burned, the flames wavering as the women walked in and out, talking quietly, laughing, some even singing.

Have I died? she wondered without truly believing it. *Is this what it will be like in Zoria's court in heaven?*

They seated her amid the cushions and the older woman brought her food; the others whispered in fascination at this, as though it were an unusual honor. The bowl was heaped with fruit and a cooked grain she did not recognize, with pieces of some roasted bird sitting on top, and Briony could not help remembering the woman back in Kinemarket with her broods of chickens and children. She wondered if that woman in her damp, smoky cottage could even imagine a place like this, less than a day's walk away.

The food was excellent, hot and flavored with spices Briony did not know, which at other moments might have put her off, but now only added to the waking dream. At last she lolled back on the cushions, full, warm, and gloriously dry. The younger women cleared away Briony's bowl and the empty goblet from which she had drunk some watered wine, and the older woman sat beside her.

"Thank you," Briony said, although that did not suffice.

"You are tired. Sleep." The woman waved and one of the others brought a blanket which they draped on Briony where she lay among the embroidered cushions.

"But . . . where am I? What is this place?"

"The *hada* of Effir dan-Mozan," the woman said. "My . . . married?"

"Your husband?"

"Yes. Just so." The woman smiled. One of her teeth was covered in gold. "And you are our honored guest. Sleep now."

"But why . . . ?" She wanted to ask why this house in such a strange place, why the bath, why all these beautiful dark-skinned women in the middle of Marrinswalk, but all that came out was that word again. "Why?"

"Because the Lord Shaso brought you here," the woman said. "He is a great man, cousin of our old king. He honors our house."

They didn't even know who she was. Shaso was the royalty here.

Briony slept then, floundering through confusing dreams of warm rivers and icy cold rain.

5
At Liberty

But the first son of Zo and Sva, who they named Rud, the golden arrow of the daytime sky, was killed in the fight against the demons of Old Night. Their younger son Sveros, lord of twilight, seized Rud's widow Madi Oneyna for his own, and swore that he would be a father to Rud's son Yirrud, but in truth he sent a cloud to breathe upon Yirrud where Onyena had hidden him in the mountain fastness and the child sickened and died.

Instead of giving Oneyna a new child to replace the one he had taken, Sveros also took her twin, Surazem, who we call Moist Mother Earth, and fathered three children upon her, who were the great brothers, Perin, Erivor, and Kernios.

—from *The Beginnings of Things*
The Book of the Trigon

FREEDOM WAS BOTH frightening and exhilarating. It was wonderful to be able to walk the streets on her own, with nothing between her and life but a hooded robe— she had not known such liberty since she was a young child, when she had known nothing else and had not appreciated what a sublime gift it truly was.

In fact, it was a bit confounding to have so many choices. Just now, Qinnitan couldn't decide whether to return to the main road winding through Onir Soteros, the neighborhood just behind the Harbor of Kalkas which she had called home for almost a month, or to continue following the winding streets farther into the great city, expanding her area of conquest as she had almost every day.

What a place in which to have gained her freedom! Hierosol was a huge city, perhaps not quite as large as Xis, the place she had escaped, but not a great deal smaller, either—a massive rumpled blanket of hills and valleys sitting athwart several bays, commanding both the Kulloan Strait and the Ostein Sea, nearly every inch covered with the constructions of several different centuries. Ancient Xis sat on a high plain as flat as a marble floor, and from any of its high places you could see all the way to both the northern sea and the southern desert. Here in Hierosol she had not yet managed to climb high enough to see anything but other hills, Citadel Hill the tallest of them all, looming above the others like a noble head gazing out across the straits, the rest of the city trailing down the slopes behind it like a cape.

Hierosol was so old and complex and ingrown that to Qinnitan every neighborhood seemed to be its own city, its own world—tree-covered Foxgate Hill sloping gently behind her, home of rich merchants, and just below the sailmakers' and shipwrights' quarter of Sandy Head, bustling with work from the adjacent Harbor of Kalkas. Not just a new city to explore but dozens of new *worlds,* all waiting for her and her newfound freedom. For a girl who had spent the last several years in the cloistered ways of the Hive and the Seclusion, it was dizzying to contemplate.

She had been brought here across the narrow sea from Xis by Axamis Dorza, the captain of the boat that had carried her away from her lifelong home when Dorza's master Jeddin fell suddenly and precipitously from the autarch's favor. When word of Jeddin's capture had caught up to them in Hierosol, most of the sailors on the *Morning Star of Kirous* had melted away into the shadowy alleys of the port. Those few that remained were even now scraping the ship's old name off the hull and repainting it. Qinnitan supposed Jeddin's slim, fast ship would belong to Dorza now, which must be at least some small compensation to him for being associated with the now infamous traitor.

It had been kind of Axamis Dorza, she knew, if also pragmatic, to take her into his home in the Onir Soteros district at the base of the rocky hills that leaned above Sandy Head. Although he could not know it, Dorza must suspect that Qinnitan was in even greater jeopardy than himself, and though hiding her from the autarch's spies might keep Dorza himself safe in the short run, it was bound to look bad if she was ever captured. In fact, the captain had made it clear that he was not happy with Qinnitan roaming the streets, even dressed in the fashion of a respectable Xandian girl (which left little of her visible) but she had made it equally clear to him that she would no longer be anyone's prisoner, especially in Dorza's small house. It was not his house at all, really, but the property of his Hierosoline wife, Tedora. Qinnitan suspected the captain had a larger, more respectable house and also a more respectable wife and family back home in Xis, but she was too polite to inquire. Qinnitan also suspected that she would not have been allowed such freedom in that other house, but Tedora was a woman of Eion, not Xand, and was more interested in drinking wine and gossiping with her neighbors than watching over the moral education of a fugitive Xixian girl. Because of that, and a certain confused subservience Qinnitan inspired in Dorza, most of the freedom which had been stolen from her since her girlhood in Cat's Alley had been returned.

In fact, other than her terror of the autarch and her fear of being recaptured, there was only one sizeable fly in the honey of her current Hierosoline harbor....

"Ho, there you are! Wait for me!"

Qinnitan flinched reflexively—in the back of her mind she was always waiting for the moment one of the autarch's minions would lay a hand on her—although within half a heartbeat she had known who it was.

"Nikos." She sighed and turned around. "Were you following me?"

"No." He was taller than his father Axamis, all the size of a man and none of the gravity or sense, the fuzz of his first black beard covering his chin, cheeks, and neck. He had trailed her like an oversized puppy since his father had first brought her home. "But he was, and I followed him." Nikos pointed at the small, silent boy who was standing so close to her he must have come within arm's reach without her even hearing.

"Pigeon!" she said, frowning at him. "You were to stay in bed until you're well."

The mute boy smiled and shook his head. His face was even paler than usual, and he had a fine sheen of sweat on his forehead. He held out his hands, palm up, to show that as far as he was concerned he was too healthy to be left at home.

"Where are you going, Qinnitan?" Nikos asked.

"Don't call me by that name! I wasn't going anywhere. I was thinking, enjoying the quiet. Now it's gone."

Nikos was immune to such remarks. "Some big ships just came in from Xis. Do you want to go down to the harbor to look at them? Maybe you know some of the people on board."

Qinnitan could not think of anything more foolish or dangerous. "No, I do not want to go look at them. I've told you—your *father* has told you—that I can have nothing to do with anyone from the south. *Nothing!* Do you never learn?"

Now he did look a little hurt, her tone finally piercing the armor of his nearly invincible disinterest in anything outside his tiny circle of familiarity. "I just thought you might like it," he said sullenly. "That you might be a little homesick."

She took a breath. She could not afford to anger Nikos as long as she lived in his house. The problem was, the boy fancied her. It was ludicrous that she was suffering from the unwanted attentions of a lumbering child her own age when only weeks before the greatest king in the world had kept her locked away in the Seclusion, threatening death to any whole man who so much as looked at her, but along with freedom, she was learning, came the costs of freedom.

She let Nikos trail after her as they climbed the winding streets of Foxgate Hill in the shadow of the old citadel walls, up into the crocus-starred heights where shops and taverns gave way to the houses of the wealthy, pretty white-plastered places with high walls that concealed gardens and shady courtyards, although all these secrets could be seen from the streets above, so that each level of society was exposed to the inspection of its wealthier neighbors. These houses, despite their size and beauty, still stood close together, side by side along the hilly roads like seashells left along the line of the retreating tide. She could only imagine what it would be like to live in such a place instead of Captain Dorza's noisy, rickety house that smelled of fish and spilled wine. She wondered even more acutely what it would be like to have a house of her own, a place where no one entered without her permission, where she did what she wanted, spoke as she wanted.

It was not to be, of course. She could hide here in Hierosol with people who spoke her language, or she could go back to Xis and die. What other choices were there?

Pigeon was tugging at her arm; she was suddenly reminded that her own life was not her only responsibility.

Freedom. Sometimes it seemed that the more of it she had, the more she lacked.

Nikos had pretended to bump against her for the fifth or sixth time, and this time had actually managed to put his hand on her rump and give it a squeeze before she could slap it away, when she decided to turn back to the captain's house. Her privacy stolen, her thoughts dragged down by Nikos' innocently stupid questions and less innocent attempts to paw her, she knew the best of the day was over. Qinnitan sighed. Time to go back to Tedora and that laugh of hers like the cry of an irritated goat, to the thick smoke in the air and the endless noise and the jumble of screeching children. She couldn't blame Nikos for wanting to spend time out of doors, she just wished he would spend it somewhere other than in her vicinity.

She put her arm around Pigeon, who pressed against her happily—he, at least, seemed quite content with their new life, and played with the younger children as comfortably as if they were his own brothers and sisters—then pulled her hood a little closer around her face, as she always did when she walked through the neighborhood around the captain's house, where nearly half the people seemed to come from Xis and many of them were sailors who shipped back and forth across the Ostean Sea several times a year. The house seemed oddly quiet as they walked down the long path: she could hear one of the younger children talking cheerful nonsense, but not much else.

The captain's wife Tedora looked up from her stool by the table. She had started her day of drinking wine early that morning—part of the reason Qinnitan had left the house—and judging by the jug and cup set beside her, not to mention the blurry, sly look on her seamed face, she had not slackened her pace in Qinnitan's absence.

She must have been pretty once, Qinnitan often thought. Pretty enough to catch a captain, no small trick in Onir Soteros. The bones were still good, but Tedora's skin was as cracked as old leather, her fingers knobby with age and hard work—not that Qinnitan had seen her do much of that.

"He's waiting for you." Tedora gestured to the bedroom, a sour smile flitting across her face. "Dorza. He wants to see you."

"What?" For a moment Qinnitan could make no sense of it. Was Tedora sending her in to become the master's concubine?

Then she realized that, of course, in a house so small, the single bedroom would be the only place to carry on a private conversation—she had seen Dorza take some of his crewmen back to talk about matters of the ship and of their involuntary exile from Xis.

A chilly heaviness lodged in her gut. A private conversation, was it? She felt certain she knew what he wanted, and had been fearing it for days. Axamis Dorza, saddled with the feeding of two people who should have not been his responsibility, was going to try to marry her off to young Nikos, to bind her properly to his household so that she could be set to work. Qinnitan had no doubt it was Tedora's idea. If, as she suspected, Dorza had another family back in Xis, he would be more than willing to do it, just to keep the peace here in his Hierosoline harbor. The thought made her heart as cold as her stomach.

"You asked to speak to me?" she said as the flimsy door fell shut behind her. It was dark in the room, only a single small oil lamp burning atop the large sea chest Dorza used as his captain's table. The shape there stirred, but so slowly and strangely that for a moment Qinnitan had to fight back an urge to scream, as though she had found herself locked in with a savage animal.

The captain looked up. His face, normally as clean-lined as a ship, seemed to have lost its bones, chin sunk against his chest, eyes almost invisible under his brows. "I have been . . . talking," Dorza said slowly. "With men newly come from Xis." She could smell the wine on his breath from halfway across the small room. "Why did you not tell me who you were?"

A different kind of chill descended on her now. "I have never lied to you," she said, although that was another lie. She wondered if sacred bees were dying in the Temple of the Hive, as a few were said to do whenever one of the acolytes abused the truth or thought an impure thought. *If that's so, I must have killed at least half of the poor bees by now. What a sinner I have become in this last year, in the simple matter of saving my own life!*

"You did not tell me all. I knew you were . . ." He lowered his voice. "I knew you were Jeddin's woman. But I did not understand . . ."

"I was *never* Jeddin's woman," she said, anger overcoming even her fear at Axamis Dorza's strange, grim mood. "He thrust himself upon me, put my life in danger. He did not lay with me, nor has any man!"

"Well, no matter that," said Dorza. He seemed a little surprised by her claim. "The knot at the center of the thing is this—you are fled from the autarch's own Seclusion."

She took a breath. "It is true. It was that or be handed over to Mokori the strangler, although I had done nothing wrong."

Dorza lurched to his feet, swaying. "But you have murdered *me!*" he roared.

"I've done nothing of the sort, Captain Dorza. You have done nothing wrong, and can say so. You gave a young woman passage on your master's order, without knowing your master had fallen out of favor—and certainly without knowing anything of the woman herself . . ."

He staggered a few steps toward her, looming over her like a tree that might topple. "Nothing wrong! By the fiery balls of Nushash, do you think the autarch will care? Do you think he will call off his torturers and say, 'You know, this fellow isn't so bad. Let him go back to his life again.' You liar. You heartless bitch! You slut . . . !" The captain's hand shot out and clutched her arm so hard she could not escape, although he could barely stand straight.

"I have done nothing wrong!" she shouted. "Nushash himself is my witness—I was taken as a virgin from the Temple of the Hive and Jeddin came to me in the Seclusion and told me he was in love with me. Is it my fault he was mad, the poor dead fool?"

Dorza's free hand rose up, trembling, to strike her, but then it fell again. He let go of her arm and stumbled back to his chair. "Then that son of a bitch Jeddin has destroyed me as surely as if he had shot me with a musket ball." He turned a red eye on Qinnitan again. "Go. Get out of this house and take that idiot child with you. I do not care where you go—I never want to hear your name again. When the autarch's men come to cut my head off and drag my wife and children into slavery, I will be certain to tell them what you said . . . that it was not your fault." He made a horrible barking sound, half laugh, half sob.

"You are casting me out? With nothing? Out of fear that some of the autarch's spies might find out . . ."

"The autarch's *spies?* Are you whores of the Seclusion really so ignorant? We always thought you knew more of events than we outside the palace ever could." He spat on the floor—shocking from such a tidy man. "It is only a matter of a few moons or so before the autarch's fleet sails. He is outfitting new warships and arming soldiers even now." Dorza took a key from his belt, then bent and clumsily unlocked the chest chained to the table leg. He took a few pieces of silver out and dropped them to the floor. One coin rolled right to Qinnitan's feet, but she did not stoop for it. "Take those. At least you may then get far enough from me before you're caught that I will gain a few more weeks of life."

"What do you mean, the autarch's fleet? Sails where?"

"*Here,* you foolish, foolish girl. He is coming here, to conquer Hierosol, then the rest of Eion after it. Now get out of my house."

6

Skurn

Here is truth! The light was Tso, and Zha was the wife he created out of the nothingness. She fled him but he followed. She hid, but he discovered. She protested, but he persuaded. At last she surrendered, and at their lovemaking the heavens roared with the first winds.

—from *The Revelations of Nushash,* Book One

GUARD CAPTAIN FERRAS VANSEN woke to the sickly glow of the shadowlands, unchanged since he had fallen asleep. His cloak was no longer covering his face and rain spattered him. He groaned and rolled over, scrabbling for the hem of the heavy woolen garment, but it was trapped between him and the dampening ground and he had to sit up, groaning even louder, to free it.

He was just about to roll back into sleep when he saw a hint of movement at the corner of his gaze. He held his breath and turned his head as slowly as he could, but saw nothing except the long, wet grass and the familiar lump of Barrick's sleeping form. Beyond lay the terrifying creature called Gyir, but the warrior-fairy also seemed to be asleep.

Vansen let out what he hoped sounded like the honest snort of someone whose slumber had been briefly but inconsequentially disturbed, then lay silently, praying that his heart was not really beating as loudly as it seemed to be. He knew he had seen something more than the simple bouncing of rain-bent grass.

Movement resumed beside the soggy remnants of last night's fire, a rounded shape bobbing along slowly only a few paces from the sleeping prince.

Vansen flung his cloak at it and dived after; the thing let out a muffled squawk and tried to escape, but it seemed to be tangled. Vansen scrambled across the wet ground on elbows and knees and managed to catch it before it disappeared into the darkness again. As he held it wrapped in the damp wool, he found it smaller than he had feared and surprisingly light, loose as a bundle of sticks and cloth in his hands: even with a poor grip on it, his strength seemed more than equal to the task of holding it. The captive creature let out a terrified, whistling shriek that sounded almost like a child's cry. He could feel by its struggles that it was a large bird of some kind, with wings that must stretch nearly as wide as a man's arms.

As he tried to protect his face from the darting beak something else rushed toward him, startling him so that he did not even fight when the bird was ripped out of his hands. By the time Vansen could turn his head, the shadow-man Gyir had a squat knife with scalloped edges pressed lengthwise against the creature's throat as the bird thrashed and made odd, almost human noises of fear. It was a raven, Ferras Vansen could see now, mostly black, with a few patches of white random as spatters of paint, but Vansen paid it little attention. He was terrified and astonished at the sudden appearance of Gyir's knife, and shamed by his own incompetence.

Great Perin, has he had that all along? He could have murdered us at any time! How did I miss it?

But he could not ignore the bird after all, because it had begun to talk.

"Don't kill us, Masters!" The voice rasped and whistled, but the words were clear. "Us'll never do wrong at you again! Us were only so hungry!"

"You can speak," said Vansen, reduced to the obvious.

The raven turned one bright yellow eye toward him, beak opening and shutting as it tried to get its breath. "Aye. And most sweetly, too, given chance, Masters!"

Prince Barrick sat up, tousle-haired and puffy-eyed, looking at least for this moment more like an ordinary sleepy young man and less like the maddening enigma he had been. "Why precisely are you two pummeling a bird?" He squinted. "It's rather spotty. Might it be good to eat?"

"No, Master!" the raven said, struggling uselessly. Patches of gray skin showed where it had lost feathers, making it seem even more pathetic. "Foul and tasteless, I am! Pizen!"

Gyir changed position to steady the squirming bird, poised to kill it.

"No!" Vansen said. "Let it be."

"But why?" asked the prince. "Gyir says it's old and going to die soon, anyway. And it was thieving from us."

"It speaks our tongue!"

"So do many other thieves." The prince seemed more amused than anything else.

"Aye," the bird panted, "speech it good and well, thy sunlander tongue. Learned it by Northmarch when I lived close by your folk there."

"Northmarch?" It was a name Vansen had barely heard in years, a haunted name. "How could that be? Men have not lived at Northmarch for two centuries, since the shadows rolled over it."

"Oh, aye, us were young then." The raven still struggled helplessly in Gyir's grasp. "Us had shiny pins and joints all supple, and us's knucklers were firm."

Vansen turned to Gyir, forgetting for a moment that it was harder to communicate with him than with the raven. "Two centuries old? Is that possible?"

The fairy came the closest to a human gesture Vansen had yet seen, a kind of slithery shrug. The meaning was clear: it was possible, but why should it matter?

"Yes, it matters." Vansen knew he was replying to words not spoken and perhaps not even intended, but at this moment he did not care: in the land of the mad, a land of talking animals and faceless fairies, madness was the only sane creed. "He talks like my mother's father, although that means nothing to you. I have not heard speech like that since I was a child." Vansen realized that he ached for conversation—ordinary talk, not the elliptical mysteries of spellbound Prince Barrick, each answer bringing only more questions. In fact, he realized, he was so lonely that he would accept comradeship even from a bird.

But it wouldn't do to make that clear just yet—even a bird could be suspect in these treacherous, magical lands. "So why shouldn't we kill you?" Vansen asked the struggling raven. "What were you doing in our camp, poking around? Tell, or I *will* let him slit your throat."

"Nay!" It was half shriek, half croak, a despairing sound that made Vansen almost feel ashamed of himself. "Mean no harm, us! Just hungry!"

"Gyir says he smells of those creatures," Barrick offered, "—the ones who attacked him and killed his horse. 'Followers,' they're called."

"Not us, Masters!" The raven struggled, but despite its size, it was helpless as a sparrow in the fairy-warrior's hands. "Was just following the Followers, like. Can't fly much now, us—pins be all a-draggled." It carefully eased one of its wings free, and this time Gyir allowed it. More than a few shiny black feathers were certainly missing. "Went to eat summat a few seasons gone by, but that summat be'nt quite dead yet," the raven explained, bobbing its head. "Tore us upwise and downwise."

"And the smell of those . . . Followers?"

"Us can't stay high or fly long like us did oncet. Have to follow close, go from branch to branch, like. Followers have a powerful stink." It ruffled its parti-colored feathers with its beak. "Can't smell it, usself. Poor Skurn is old now—so old!"

"Skurn? Is that what you're called?"

"Aye, or was. Us were handsome then, when that were our name." He poked his beak toward Gyir. "*His* folk drove all the sunlanders out from Northmarch. Life were good then, for a little while, in the fighting—dead 'uns every which side! But then sunlanders were gone and poor Skurn was leaved behind to shift as us could when twilight come down." The beak opened to let out a mournful sigh, but the shiny eyes looked to Vansen with calculating hope, like a child searching for the first light of forgiveness.

He had no stomach to kill the thing. "Let the bird go," he said. Nothing happened. Gyir was not looking at him but at Barrick. "Please, Highness. Let it go."

Barrick frowned, then sighed. "I suppose." He waved his hand at Gyir, still showing a remnant of the royal manner even here beneath the dripping trees. "Let it go free."

As soon as the blade was withdrawn the bird rolled to its feet and took a few hopping steps, quite nimble for all its professed age. It flapped its wings as though surprised and pleased to find it still had them. "Oh, thank you, Masters, thank you! Skurn will serve you, do everything you ask us, find all best hiding places, rotting dead 'uns, birds' nests, even where the fish go scumbling down in the muddy bottom! And eat so little, us? Never will you know us is even here."

"What is he talking about?" Vansen said crossly. He had expected it to bolt for the undergrowth or fly away, but the bird had distracted him and he had forgotten to watch where Gyir hid the knife; now the Twilight man's hand was empty again.

"You saved him, Captain." Amusement rippled coldly across Barrick's face. Suddenly he seemed a boy no longer, but more like an old man—ageless. "The raven's yours. It seems you'll finally taste the pleasures of being lord and master."

"Lord and master," said the raven, beginning to clean the mud from his matted feathers with his long black beak. He bobbed his head eagerly. "Yes, you folk are Masters of Skurn, now. Us will do you only good."

★

The forest track they followed seemed to have once been a road: only flimsy saplings and undergrowth grew on it, while the larger trees—most with sharp, silvery-black leaves that made Vansen think of them as "dagger trees"—formed a bower overhead, so that the horses paced almost as easily as they might have on the Settland Road or some other thoroughfare in mortal lands. If the going was easier, though, it was not a peaceful ride; Vansen had begun to wonder whether saving the wheezing raven might not have been his second-worst decision of recent days, exceeded only by the choice to follow Barrick across the Shadowline. Reprieved from death, Skurn could not stop talking, and although occasionally he said something interesting or even useful, Vansen was beginning to feel things would have been better if he had let Gyir the Storm Lantern spit the creature.

". . . The other ones, Followers and whatnot, are pure wild these days." Skurn bobbed his head, moving continuously from one side to the other off the base of the horse's neck like a cat trying to find the warmest place to sleep. It was a mark of how the last days had hardened Vansen's mount that it paid little attention to the creeping thing between its shoulders, only whinnying from time to time when the indignity became too much. "Scarce speak any language, and of course no sunlander tongue, unlikes usself. There, Master, don't ever eat that 'un, nor touch it. Will turn your insides to glass. And that other, yes, th'un with yellow berries. No, not pizen, but makes a fine stew with coney or water rat. Us'd have a lovely bit of that now, jump atter chance, us would. Knows you that soon you be crossing into Jack Chain's land? You'll turn, o'course. Foul, his lot. No love for the High Ones and wouldn't lift a hand but for their own stummicks or to shed some blood. They like blood, Jack's lot. Oh, there's a bit of the old wall. Look up high. A fine place for eggs . . ."

The nonstop chatter had begun to blend into one continuous rattle, like someone snoring across the room, but the bulwark of ruined stone caught Vansen's attention. It rose from a thicket of thorns, its top looming far above his head, and was sheathed in vines that flowered a dull blood red, the thick, heart-shaped leaves bouncing with the weight of raindrops.

"What did you say this was?"

"This old wall, Master? Us didn't, although us is pleased to name it if that be your wish. A place called Ealingsbarrow oncet in thy speech, if our remembering be not too full of holes—a town of your folk."

Vansen reined up. The crumbling golden stones looked as though they had been abandoned far more than two centuries ago: even the best-preserved sections were as pitted and porous as honeycomb. In many places trees had grown right through the substance of the wall and their roots were pulling out even more stones, like young cuckoos ousting other birdlings from a nest. The forest and the incessant damp were taking the wall apart as efficiently as a gang of workmen, tumbling the huge stones back to earth and wearing them away as though they were nothing more than wet sand, steadily removing this last trace that mortal men had once lived here.

"Why have we stopped?" asked Barrick. The prince had ridden beside Gyir all morning, and Vansen could not escape the idea that the two of them were conversing wordlessly, that the faceless man was instructing the prince just as Vansen had once been instructed by his old captain Donal Murroy.

"To look at this wall, Highness. The bird says it is part of a town named Ealingsbarrow. Northmarch must be only half a day's ride away or so." Vansen shook his head, still amazed. The old, cursed name of Northmarch reminded him that what had happened there and here in Ealingsbarrow might soon happen to all the mortal cities of the north—to Southmarch itself. "It is hard to believe, isn't it?"

Barrick only shrugged. "They did not belong here. No mortals did, building without permission. It is no wonder it came to this."

Vansen could only stare as the prince turned and rode forward again. Gyir, riding behind him, looked back a few moments longer, his featureless face as inscrutable as ever.

"Burned blue in the night for six nights when it fell, this place," said Skurn. "Like old star had fallen down into the forest. The keeper of the War-Stone gave it to the Whispering Mothers, you see."

Vansen was shivering as they left the last wall of Ealingsbarrow behind them. He did not know what the raven meant and he was fairly certain he was better off that way.

The rain began to abate in what Vansen estimated was the late afternoon, although as always he got no glimpse of sun or moon in the murky sky to confirm a guess about time. He had fed the hungry raven out of the last of his own stores, and had nibbled in a desultory way himself on some stale bread and a finger's width of dried meat, but he was feeling the grip of hunger in a way he hadn't before. Since the prince seemed to have become a little less strange and distracted, and since a full day had passed without any sign of the monstrous, faceless Twilight man Gyir trying to kill them all, Vansen's fearfulness had abated a little, but the respite only served to make him more aware of his other problems. The possibility of starving was one of them, although not the biggest.

I am completely ruled by something I cannot change or understand, he thought. *Worse even than if these fairy-folk had made me a prisoner. At least then I would expect to be helpless. But this—this is worse by far! Home is behind us, there is no reason to go on into this place of madness, and yet on we go, and it seems I can do nothing to stop it.*

"We cannot follow this road any farther, Master," said Skurn suddenly. His beak tugged at Vansen's sleeve. "Cannot, Master."

"What? Why?"

"The Northmarch Road, this is, and now I smell Northmarch too close. I told you we were coming near Jack Chain's land." The bird's eyes were blinking rapidly. He fidgeted on the horse's neck, almost comically frightened. "The bad is all on it, these days."

Northmarch Road! Of course, Vansen thought, no wonder they had found this so much easier a track than others they had followed. He could see nothing beneath his feet but undergrowth and grass and dead leaves, but still the hairs on the back of his neck stirred. Knowing the road was beneath him and had been for hours was like discovering he had been standing on a grave. Still, a part of him was loath to give up such ease of travel. "It has a fearful name, but surely it has been empty now for ages."

"You don't understand, good Master." Skurn flapped his wings in disquiet. "These lands be *not* empty. They be Jack Chain's and you will lose your life at least an' he catches you."

Vansen relayed the raven's words to Barrick. The prince paused for a moment, as though listening to something that silent Gyir might be telling him, then at last slowly nodded his head.

"We will make camp. There is much to decide."

Only days ago, in an ordinary world where the sun came up and the sun went down, Barrick Eddon knew he would have looked on the fairy Gyir as something hideously alien, but somehow he had come to know Gyir the Storm Lantern as well as he knew any other person, even those of his own family.

Except for Briony, of course—Briony, his other half . . . Barrick did his best to push the thought of her away. If he was to survive he must harden himself, he had decided, cast even the most precious of those beads of memory behind him. He couldn't let himself be weak as other men were weak—like Vansen the guard captain, still living in the old ways and as out of place here (or anywhere in the new world that was coming) as a bear sitting at a table with a bowl and spoon. Barrick knew that Vansen had saved the disgusting, corpse-eating raven mostly because it spoke his mortal speech, as if being able to mumble that outdated tongue was anything other than a mark of irrelevance.

The bird Skurn had many vile habits, and seemed to reveal a new one every few moments. Only an hour had passed since they had made camp and already the creature had defiled it, not even leaving the vicinity to defecate but instead simply pausing beside the campfire and discharging a spatter as wet and foul-smelling as the goose turds that had made it such a hazard to walk beside the pond in the royal residence back home. Now the disgusting old bird was crouched only a few steps from Barrick, noisily finishing off a baby rat he had found in a nest in the wet undergrowth, the tail danging from his mouth as he chewed the hindquarters. A moment later the whole of it, tail following to the very end, slid down his throat and disappeared.

Skurn belched. Barrick scowled.

Do not waste your fires on anger, Gyir told him. *Especially on one such as that. You will have need of every spark, cousin.* The words were simply there, as though whispered inside his skull. There was no sound, no quirks of speech as with regular talk, but the words had a shape and a feeling that Barrick could tell, even without comparison, made them Gyir's and no one else's.

Cousin? Why do you call me that?

Because we share something.

What? What could we share?

The love of our lady, and loyalty to her. She saved you as she saved me. Saved me from . . . And then the fairy's words trailed off, or changed, so that they felt like words no longer, but rather a sensation of cracking thunder and a rain as heavy and terrifying as a flight of arrows.

"Highness," said Vansen suddenly, his speaking voice as harsh as a frog's croak after the taut musicality of Gyir's soundless words. "I think we need to listen to what the bird says . . ."

"Listen!" snarled Barrick. "Listen! It is you who cannot listen!" How could the man continue to scrape and bray like that when he could have words *and* silence, music and stillness, both the plucked string and the expectant pause before the lute sounded? But perhaps the guardsman couldn't. Perhaps Barrick was being unfair. He himself had been touched by the Dark Lady—poor, earnest Ferras Vansen had not. "I apologize, Captain," he said, and was pleased by his own magnanimity. No wonder he had been chosen from the crowded, mad battlefield, singled out like the oracle Iaris, who of all men had been given the words of Perin to bear back to humanity. "What is it that . . . that squawking gore-crow has to say?"

"Cannot go this way," the raven said. "The High One with no food-hole, the caulbearer, *he* knows it. These be Jack Chain's lands

now, since the queen sleeps and the King has grown so old. Us that
care for our life don't go there."

"He's talking about Northmarch, Highness," Vansen said. "It
seems to belong to some enemy—some dangerous person."

"I am not stupid, Vansen. I understood that." Barrick scowled.
At this moment, the captain reminded him more than he would
wish of Shaso: the old man, too, had always been judging him,
always underestimating him, speaking words that sounded full of
reason to the ear but made him sting with shame. Well, half a year
in the stronghold had no doubt made Shaso dan-Heza a little less
proud and scornful.

A twinge of shame, a distant thing but still painful, made him
want to think about something else. Shaso had brought his doom
on himself, hadn't he? Nothing to do with Barrick.

"I am sorry, Highness," Vansen said, and bowed, the first time he
had done that since they had crossed over the Shadowline. "I have
overstepped."

"Oh, stop." Barrick's mood had gone sour. He turned to Gyir,
tried to form the words in his head so the other could understand
him. It was so easy when the faceless man spoke to him first—like
a flying dream, no labor, just the leap and then the freedom of the
air. *What is this creature talking about? Is it true?*

I do not know. I have not traveled here, in this part of . . . Here
another idea floated past that seemed to have no words, a jumble
of formless shapes that somehow spiraled inward like snailshells.
*Except when the army went to war, but none would have dared to attack
us in that force. Still, there are many here behind the Mantle that do not
love . . .* Again there was a picture rather than a word, this one a
paradoxical image of black towers and shining light. Only after it
had ceased to glow in his head did Barrick perceive the words that
went with it. *Qul-na-Qar.*

What is that? Is that you, your people?

That is the place we have made the heart of our . . . Here an idea that
seemed to mean not so much "rule" or "kingdom" as "story." *That
is where the Knowing make their home. Those Qar who know what was
lost, and what sleeps.*

Barrick shook his head—too many ideas he could not understand were floating through his mind, although he had finally come to understand one of Gyir's idea-sounds, *Qar*, meant "people like myself"—those Barrick still thought of in the back of his mind as "fairy folk." Still, even the clearest of Gyir's ideas were as slippery as live fish. *I need to know if what this unpleasant bird says is important*, Barrick said. *The . . . the Lady . . . has given you a charge, that you told me. You must do what she asked.* Although he had no idea of Gyir's task, he knew as well as he knew that his bones were inside his body that what the dark woman wanted must be done.

I am not allowed to delay, it is true. My errand is too vital. Still, it is hard to believe that one of our enemies has grown so strong here, an enemy that was thought dead. If it is true, I fear my luck—the luck of all the People, perhaps—has turned for ill. We are far from my home and in dangerous lands. I am wounded, perhaps crippled forever, your companion has my sword, and I have no horse.

Gyir's thoughts were heavy and fearful in a way that Barrick had not felt before. That alone was enough to make the prince really frightened for the first time since the giant's war club had swung up high above him and his old life had come to an end.

"I don't know what that fairy's done to you, Highness, what kind of spell he's put on you, but I'm not giving him back his sword. He may pretend friendship, but he'll likely kill us if we give him a chance. Don't you remember what he and his kind did to the men of Southmarch at Kolkan's Field? Don't you remember Tyne Aldritch, crushed into . . . into bloody suet?"

The prince stared at him. "We will talk more of this," Barrick said, and mounted his horse. The faceless man Gyir, with an agility that Vansen carefully noted—he was recovering very swiftly indeed from wounds that would have killed an ordinary man— swung himself up behind the prince.

Vansen pulled himself up into his own saddle. Unlike Barrick's strange black horse, Vansen's mount was beginning to look a little the worse for wear, despite the long pause for rest. It shuddered restively as Skurn climbed the saddle blanket with beak and talons and hopped forward to a perch on the beast's neck. Pleased with himself, the black bird looked around like a child about to be given a treat.

Mortal horses weren't meant for this place, Vansen thought. *No more than mortal men.*

Although a dragging succession of hours had passed, and Vansen himself had slept long enough to feel heavy in his wits, his head was foggy as the tangled forest into which Barrick and Gyir now rode.

"Where be they going, Master?" Skurn asked, agitated. "Us must turn back! Didn't uns listen? Don't uns see that this be all Jack Chain's land round about?"

"How should I know?" Vansen had no command of the situation, and the addition of the fairy-warrior to their party had made things worse, if anything. Gyir, the murderer of Prince Barrick's people, a proven enemy, now seemed to have become the prince's confidant, while Ferras Vansen, the captain of the royal guard, a man who had already risked his life for Barrick's sake, had become some kind of foe. "Why do you ask me, bird? Can't *you* understand that Gyir thing?"

The raven groomed himself nervously. Up close he was quite repulsive, scaly skin visible in many places, what feathers remained matted with the gods only knew what. "Not us, Master. That be a trick of the High Ones, to talk so, without voices, not such as old Skurn. Us knows nothing of what they are saying or where they think they go."

"Well, then, that makes two of us."

The remains of the ancient road stayed wide and relatively flat beneath them, but now the trees had grown thick again around them, shutting out anything but the briefest glimpses of the gray sky, as though they traveled down a long tunnel. Birds and other creatures Vansen could not identify hooted and whistled in the shadows; it was hard not to feel their approach was being heralded, as though he were back on one of the Eddons' royal progresses with the trumpeters and criers running ahead, calling the common folk to come out, come out, a king's son was passing. But Vansen could not help feeling that those who waited in this place did not wish them well.

His sense of danger, of being visible to some hostile, lurking force, grew stronger as the day of riding wore on. The unfamiliar bird and animal sounds died away, but Vansen found the silence even more foreboding. Barrick and the faceless man ignored him, no doubt deep in unspoken conversation, and even Skurn had fallen quiet, but Ferras Vansen's patience had become so thin that every time the little creature moved and he caught a whiff of its putrid scent, he had to steel himself not to simply sweep it off onto the ground.

"This was once a great road, Highness, just as the bird said," he called at last, and then wished he hadn't: the echoes died almost immediately in the thick growth on either side of the road, but even the absence of an echo made the noise seem more stark, more exceptional. He could imagine an entire gallery of shadowy watchers leaning forward to listen. He spurred his horse forward so that he could speak more quietly. "This is the old Northmarch Road, not simply a forest path. If we follow it long enough we will arrive at something—perhaps the raven's Jack Chain—but it will not be something we'll like. Can't you feel that?"

The prince turned his cool stare on him. Barrick's hair was stuck to his forehead in damp red ringlets. "We know, Captain. We are looking for another road, one that crosses this one. If we ride overland through this tangled forest, we will come to grief."

"But it is only a short way to Northmarch, and that is where Jack Chain has his hall!" squealed Skurn, hopping up and down, which made Vansen's horse snort and prance so that he had to tighten his grip on the reins. "Even if we are lucky and One-Eye bes far away, and there be no Night Men about, still Jack-Rovers and Longskulls there be all around here, as well as the Follower-folk who remember not sunlanders nor nothing even of the

High Ones! They will capture us, poor old Skurn. They will kill us!"

"They will certainly hear us if we stop to argue every few paces," Barrick said harshly. "I did not bring you here, Vansen, and I certainly did not bring that . . . bird. If you wish to find your own way, you may do so."

"I cannot leave you, Highness."

"Yes, you can. I have told you to do it but you do not listen. You say you are my liegeman, but you will not obey the simplest order. Go away, Captain Vansen."

He hung his head, hoping to hide both the shame and rage. "I cannot, Prince Barrick."

"Then do as you wish. But do it silently."

They had been riding for what seemed like most of a day when an astonishing thing happened, something that alarmed not only Vansen, but the raven, too, and even Gyir the Storm Lantern.

The sky began to grow dark.

It crept up on them slowly, and at first Ferras Vansen thought it no more than the ceaseless movement of gray cloud overhead, the blanket of mist which thickened and even sometimes thinned without ever diminishing much, and which gave the light of these lands its only real variety. But as he found himself squinting at trees beside the wide road, Vansen suddenly realized he could not doubt the truth any longer.

The twilight was dying. The sky was turning black.

"What's going on?" Vansen reined up. "Prince Barrick, ask your fairy what this means!"

Gyir was looking up between the trees, but not as though searching for something with his eyes—it was an odd, blind gaze, as though he were smelling rather than staring.

"He says it is smoke."

"What? What does that mean?"

Skurn was clinging to the horse's neck, beak tucked under a wing, mumbling to himself.

"What does he mean, smoke?" Vansen demanded of the raven.

"Smoke from what? Do you know what's happening here, bird? Why is it getting dark?"

"Crooked's curse has come at last, must be. Must be!" The black bird moaned and bobbed its head. "If the Night Men catch us or don't, it matters not. The queen will die and the Great Pig will swallow us all down to blackness!"

He could get nothing more out of him—the raven only croaked in terror. "I do not understand!" Vansen cried. "Where is the smoke coming from? Has the forest caught fire?"

"Gyir says no," Barrick said slowly, and now even he sounded uneasy. "It is from fire someone has made—he says it stinks of metal and flesh." The prince turned to look at silent Gyir, whose eyes were little more than red slits in his blank mask of a face. "He says it is the smoke of many small fires . . . or one very big one."

7

Chasing the Jackals

Twilight had been jealous from the first of his brother's gleaming songs, and when Daystar lost the depth of his music and flew away, Twilight climbed into his brother's place among the Firstborn. He made children with both Breeze and Moisture.

From the womb of Breeze came the brothers Whitefire and Silvergleam, and Judgment their sister. From the womb of Moisture came Thunder, Ocean, and Black Earth, and though their mothers were twinned, from the very first these six children could not find harmony among themselves.

—from *One Hundred Considerations*
out of the Qar's *Book of Regret*

EVEN THE WEAK MORNING LIGHT seeping in from the high, small windows was enough to tell Briony that she was not in her own paneled chamber in the royal residence. In fact, she was surrounded by white plastered walls and dark-skinned women in loose, soft dresses, all busy making beds or darning clothes, and talking in a quiet, musical language Briony could not understand. For a long moment she could only stare, dumbfounded, wondering what had happened.

The truth did not wait long, though: as she rolled over and sat up, clutching the blanket close around the flimsy nightclothes she had somehow acquired, memories began to leak back.

"Good morning, Bri-oh-nee-*zisaya*." Briony turned to find a slender middle-aged woman standing beside the bed. The woman smiled, showing a flash of unusual color. "Did you sleep well?"

Of course. Shaso had brought her to this place in the back alleys of whatever this Marrinswalk town was called . . . Lander's something . . . ? They had taken refuge in the house of one of Shaso's Tuani countrymen, and this was the gold-toothed mistress of the house.

"Yes. Yes, thank you, very well." Suddenly she felt shy, knowing she had been lying here sleeping, perhaps snoring, while these dark, delicate women worked quietly around her. "Is . . . I would like to speak to Shaso." She remembered the reverence with which the women had spoken of him, as though Princess Briony should be his servant instead of the other way around, something that irritated her more than she liked to admit. "Lord Shaso. Can you take me to him?"

"He will know you are waking and will be expecting you," the older woman said, smiling again. Briony could count half a dozen other women in the large room, and she seemed to recall there had been even more the previous night. "Let us help you dress."

It all went swiftly and even enjoyably, the women's talk mostly incomprehensible, a continuous dove-soft murmur that even in the waxing morning light made Briony feel sleepy again. It was so odd, these women and their foreign rooms and ways, their foreign tongue, as if the entire house had been lifted out of the sandy streets of some distant southern city by a mischievous god or goddess and spun through the air to land here in the middle of cold, muddy, winter's-end Eion. *Somebody* was definitely on the wrong continent.

The older woman, guessing correctly that Briony had forgotten her name, politely reintroduced herself as Idite. She didn't put Briony back into the Skimmer girl's tattered dress, but clothed her in a beautiful billowing robe of some pale pink fabric so thin she could easily see the light through it, so thin that she had to wear an underdress of a thicker, more clinging white cloth, with sleeves long enough to reach her fingertips. The Tuani women lifted her hair up and pinned it, cooing and giggling at its yellowness, then set a circlet of pearls on her head. Idite brought Briony a mirror, a small, precious thing in the shape of a lotus leaf, so she could see the result of all their work. She found it both charming and disturbing to discover herself so transfigured by a few articles of clothing and jewelry, turned so easily into a soft, pretty creature (yes, she actually looked pretty, even she had to admit it) of the kind she suspected all the men of Southmarch had always hoped she would become. It was hard not to bristle a bit. But the transformation was an act of kindness, not domination, so she smiled and thanked Idite and the others, then smiled some more as they complimented her at length, haltingly in her own tongue and fluently in their own.

"Come," the mistress of the house said at last. "Now you shall go to see the Dan-Heza and my good husband."

Idite and one of the younger women, a shy, slender creature not much older than Briony herself, with a nervous smile so fixed that it was painful to see, led her out of the women's quarters. The passageway turned so many times that it made the house seem even larger, but they emerged at last into what had to be the front room, although instead of looking out toward the front of the house all the furniture faced doors opening onto the rainy courtyard. Shaso stood there waiting beside three chairs, two empty, one occupied by a small, bald man in a simple white robe who looked to be a little more than Briony's father's age, with skin a half-shade lighter than Shaso's. The man's short fingers were covered with splendid, glittering rings.

"Thank you, Idite, my flower," he said; unlike his wife's, his words were scarcely accented. "You may go now."

Idite and the girl made courtesies and withdrew, even as the small man lifted himself from his chair and bowed in turn to Briony. "I am Effir dan-Mozan," he said. "Welcome to my house, Princess. You do us honor."

Briony nodded and seated herself in the chair he indicated. "Thank you. Everyone has been very kind to me."

Shaso cleared his throat. "I am sorry I left you so suddenly, Highness, but I had much to talk about with Effir."

"I had no idea there were such places in Marrinswalk!" Briony could not help laughing a little at her own surprise.

"If by 'such places' you mean Tuani *hadami*—houses of our people—you will find them in quite a few places, even here in the north. Even, I think, in your own city."

"In Southmarch? Truly?"

"Oh, yes—but this is rude, expecting a guest to make conversation when she has not even been fed. Forgive me." He raised a little bell from the arm of his chair and rang it. The bearded man who had opened the gate the night before suddenly appeared from behind a curtained doorway. He was even younger than she had thought then, perhaps only a year or two older than Briony herself. "Tal, would you please bring food and *gawa* for our guests—and for me, too. I was up early this morning and I am beginning to feel the need for a little something."

The young man bowed and went out, but not before giving Briony a long, unreadable look.

"My nephew Talibo," explained Dan-Mozan. "A good lad, although a little too enamored of these northern towns and northern ways. Still, he is a fast learner and perhaps these new ideas he so values will bring something useful to the House of Mozan. Now, let me ask, my child, was everything to your satisfaction? Did the women verily treat you well? Lord Shaso asked that you be given every kindness—not that you would have been less than an honored guest in any case."

"Yes, thank you, Lord Dan-Mozan. They all were very kind."

He chuckled with pleasure. "Oh, no, Princess, I am no lord. Only a merchant. Please call me Effir, and it will be to my ears as sweet honey on the tongue. I am glad you were treated well. A guest is a holy thing." He looked up as Talibo came back through the door leading an older man who seemed to be a servant, both of them bearing large trays. The food had obviously been prepared earlier and only waited her arrival. The youth and the older servant arranged the bowls and platters carefully on the wide, low table, putting out unleavened bread, fruit, bits of cold spicy fish, vinegar-soaked mushrooms, and other savories Briony did not recognize. Tal then poured a dark, steaming liquid from a pot into three cups. When Briony had finished filling a shallow bowl with things to eat, she followed the lead of Shaso and Effir dan-Mozan, curling her legs under her and placing the bowl on her lap. She took a careful sip of the hot liquid, expecting it to be tea, which she had learned to drink from her great-aunt Merolanna, but it was something much stranger, bitter as death, and it was all she could do not to spit it out.

"You do not like the *gawa*, eh?" Dan-Mozan smiled, not hiding his amusement very well. "Too hot?"

"Too . . . too bitter."

"Ah, then you must add cream and honey. I often do myself, especially in the evening, after a meal." He gestured to a smaller tray with two small pitchers on it. "May I do it for you?"

Briony wasn't sure she wanted it any way at all, but she nodded, just to be polite.

"Having you in my house is a privilege even greater than it is a surprise," Dan-Mozan said as he directed young Tal, with grimaces and flapping hands, through the delicate task of putting things in Briony's *gawa* cup. "Lord Shaso has told me something of what happened. Please be certain that you are welcome here as long as you need to stay, and that nothing of . . ." He paused, then looked at his nephew, who had finished with Briony's *gawa* and was waiting expectantly. "You may go now, Tal," he said, a little coolly. "We have things to talk about."

"*She* is staying?" Tal remembered himself and shut his mouth in a tight line, but the question clearly annoyed his uncle.

"Yes. She is a companion of Lord Shaso's, and more important, she is our guest—*my* guest. Now go. You and I will speak later."

"Yes, Uncle." Tal bowed, stole another quick look at Briony, then went out.

Dan-Mozan sighed, spread his hands in a gesture of resignation. "As I said, a good lad, but he has swallowed too many new ideas too quickly, like a naughty child given a whole bowl of sweetmeats. It has disturbed his constitution and he has forgotten how to behave."

"These northern lands can poison a young man," said Shaso, managing to look grim even as he piled mushrooms in his bowl.

"Of course, of course," Dan-Mozan said with a smile. "But young men are particularly susceptible wherever they find themselves. He will go back to Tuan after his year here, marry a good girl, and find himself again. Now, let us bless our food." He said a few words under his breath.

"Back to Tuan," Shaso said darkly. He looked drawn and tired despite the early hour. "There have been times when I wished I could do that, too, but it is not my Tuan, not anymore. How can it be, when it belongs to Xis?" He pursed his lips as though he might spit on the floor, but then seemed to think better of it. Effir dan-Mozan, who for a moment had looked concerned for his beautiful carpets, smiled again, but more sadly this time.

"You are right, my lord. Even though some of us unworthy ones must still keep ties there because of our trade, it is not the place we loved, not as long as those Xixian sons of whores—ah, your pardon, my lady, I forgot you were here—hold the keys to our gates. But that will change. All things change if the Great Mother wills it." He briefly assumed a pious face as he brought his hands together, then turned brightly to Briony. "Your food, Highness—is it to your liking?"

"Yes . . . yes, it's very nice." She had been eating slowly, wary of appearing too much of a pig in front of this small, neat man, but she was very hungry indeed and the food was excellent, full of tangy, unfamiliar flavors.

"Good. Well, my Lord Shaso, you wished to speak with me and here I sit, at your command. I am very pleased, of course, simply to see you free, and amazed by your story." The merchant turned to smile at Briony. "Your bravery was, it need not be said, a large and impressive part of Lord Shaso's tale."

Her mouth was full; she nodded her head carefully. She was also the person who had locked Shaso up in the first place and she was not entirely certain whether this small, amiable man might not be mocking her.

"I need information," Shaso said, "and I wished the princess to be here since it saves me the work of repeating it." He saw her irritated look. "And of course it is her right to be here, since she is heir to her father's throne."

"Ah, yes," said Dan-Mozan gravely. "We all pray for King Olin's safe and speedy return, may the gods give him health."

"Information," repeated Shaso, a bit of impatience coloring his voice. "Your ships go everywhere up and down the coasts, Dan-Mozan, and you have many eyes and ears on the inland waterways as well. What have you heard of the fairy-invasion, of the autarch, of anything I should know? Assume I know nothing."

"I would never be foolish enough to assume that, Lord Shaso," said Dan-Mozan. "But I take your meaning. Well, I will make as much sense of it as the Mother grants me to make. The north is all confusion, of course, because of the strange *d'shinna* army that has come from behind the Line of Shadows." He nodded, as though this was something he had long predicted. "The great army of Southmarch has been broken—I crave your pardon for saying it, estimable princess, but it is true. Those that have survived but could not reach the castle have scattered, some fleeing south toward Kertewall or into Silverside—they say that the streets of Onsilpia's Veil are crowded with weeping soldiers. Many others are heading on toward Settland or down into Brenland, convinced that the north will fall, hoping to find shelter in those places or take ship for the south. But the southern lands, they may find, will soon offer no safe harbor, either . . ."

Barrick, Barrick . . . ! She tried to imagine him free and alive, perhaps leading a group of survivors toward Settesyard. Her beloved other half—surely she would know if someone she had known and loved like a part of herself were dead! "What of the city and Southmarch Castle itself?" she asked. "Does it still stand? And how did you discover all this so quickly?"

"From the boats that fish in Brenn's Bay and supply the castle goods from the south, many of which belong to me," said Dan-Mozan, smiling. "And of course, my captains also hear much in port from the river-men coming down from the other parts of the March Kingdoms. Even in time of war, people must send their wool and beer to market. Yes, Southmarch Castle still stands, but the city on its shore has fallen. The countryside is emptied all around. The place is full of demons."

It all suddenly seemed so bleak, so hopeless. Briony clenched her jaw. She would not cry in front of these older men, would not be reassured or coddled. It was her kingdom—her father's, yes, but Olin was a prisoner in Hierosol. Southmarch needed her, and it especially needed her to be strong. "My father, the king—have you heard anything of him?"

The merchant nodded soberly. "Nothing that suggests he is not safe, Highness, or that anything has changed, but I hear rumors that Drakava's grip on Hierosol is not as strong as it might be. And there are other tales, mere whispers, that the autarch is readying a great fleet—that he might wish Hierosol for himself."

"What?" Shaso sat up, almost spilling his cup of *gawa*. Clearly this was new to him. "The autarch surely cannot be ready for that—he has only just pacified his own vassals in Xand—surely half his army must be garrisoned in Mihan, Marash, and our own miserable country. How could he move so soon against Hierosol and its mighty walls?"

Dan-Mozan shook his head. "I cannot answer you, my lord. All I can tell you is what I hear, and the whisper is that Sulepis has been assembling a fleet with great speed, as though something has happened which has pushed forward his plans." He turned to Briony, almost apologetically. "We all know that the Xixians have desired greater conquest on Eion, and that taking Hierosol would let them control all the Osteian Sea and the southern oceans on either side."

Briony waved away all this detail, angry and intent. "The autarch plans to attack Hierosol? Where my father is?"

"Rumors, only," said Dan-Mozan. "Do not let yourself be too alarmed, Princess. It is probably only these uncertain times, which tend to set tongues wagging even when there is nothing useful to say."

"We must go and get my father," she told Shaso. "If we take ship now we could be there before spring!"

He scowled and shook his head. "You will forgive me for being blunt, Highness, but that is foolishness. What could we do there? Join him in captivity, that is all. No, in fact you would be married by force to Drakava and I would go to the gibbet. There are many in Hierosol who wish me dead, not least of which is my onetime pupil, Dawet."

"But if the autarch is coming . . . !"

"If the autarch is coming to Eion, then we have many problems, and your father is only one of them."

"Please, please, honored guests!" Effir dan-Mozan lifted his hands and clapped. "Have more *gawa,* and we have some very nice almond pastries as well. Do not let yourself be frightened, Princess. These are the merest whispers, as I said, and likely not true."

"I'm *not* frightened. I'm angry." But she fell into an unhappy silence as Dan-Mozan's nephew Talibo returned and served more food and hot drinks. Briony looked at her hands, which she was having trouble keeping decorously still: if the youth was staring at her again, she was not going to give him the satisfaction of noticing.

Shaso, though, watched with a calculating eye as the young man went out again. "Do you think your nephew might have some spare garments he could lend us?" Shaso asked suddenly.

"Garments?" Dan-Mozan raised an eyebrow.

"Rough ones, not fine cloth. Suitable for some hard labor."

"I do not understand."

"He looks as though clothing of his might fit the princess. We can roll up the cuffs and sleeves." He turned to Briony. "We will put that anger of yours to some good work this afternoon."

"But surely you will come," Puzzle said. "I asked for you, Matty—I told them you were a poet, a very gifted poet."

Ordinarily, the chance to perform at table for the masters of Southmarch would have been the first and last thing solicited in Matt Tinwright's nightly prayers (if he had been the sort of person to pray) but for some reason, he was not so certain he wanted to be known by the Tollys and their friends at court, both old and new. The past tennight things had seemed to change, as though the dark clouds that these days always clung to the city across the bay had drifted over the castle as well.

Perhaps I am too sensitive, he told himself. *My poet's nature. The Tollys have done nothing but good in an ill time, surely.* Still, he had begun to hear tales from the kitchen workers and some of the other servitors with whom he shared quarters in the back of the residence that made him uneasy—tales of people disappearing and others being badly beaten or even executed for minor mistakes. One of the kitchen potboys had seen a young page's fingers cut off at the table by Tolly's lieutenant Berkan Hood for spilling a cup of wine, and Tinwright knew it was true because he had seen the poor lad being tended in a bed with a bandage over his bloody stumps.

"I . . . I am not certain I am ready to perform for them myself," he told Puzzle. "But I will help you. A new song, perhaps?"

"Aye, truly? Something I could dedicate to Lord Tolly . . . ?" As Puzzle paused to consider this and its possible results, Tinwright noticed movement on the wall of the Inner Keep where it passed around Wolfstooth Spire, a short arrow's flight from the residence garden where he and Puzzle had met to share some cooking wine that Puzzle had filched from the lesser buttery. For a moment he thought it was a phantom, a transparent thing of dark mists, but then he realized that the woman walking atop the wall was wearing veils and a net shawl over her black dress and he knew at once who it was.

"We will talk later, yes?" he said to Puzzle, giving the jester a clap on the back that almost knocked the old man over. "There is something I need to do."

Tinwright ran across the garden, dodging wandering sheep and goats as though in some village festival game. He knew Puzzle must be staring at his sudden retreat as though he were mad, but if this was madness it was the sweetest kind, the sort that a man could catch and never wish to lose.

He slowed near the armory and wiped the perspiration from his forehead with a sleeve, then straightened his breeches and hose. It was strange: he felt almost a little shamefaced, as though he were betraying his patroness Briony Eddon, but he shrugged the feeling away. Just because he did not wish to recite his poems before the whole of the Tolly contingent did not mean that he had no ambitions whatsoever.

He walked around the base of Wolfstooth Spire and made his way up its outer staircase, so that when he reached the wall he should seem to be encountering her by accident. He was gratified to see she had not continued on, which would have necessitated him trying to hide the fact of walking swiftly after her to catch up. She was leaning on the high top of the outer wall, peering out through a crenellation across the Outer Keep, her weeds fluttering about her.

When he thought he was close enough to be heard above the fluting of the wind, he cleared his throat. "Oh! Your pardon, Lady. I did not know anyone else was walking on the walls. It is something I like to do—to think, to feel the air." He hoped that sounded sufficiently poetic. The truth was, it was cold and damp here at the edge of the Inner Keep with the bay churning just below them. Were it not for her, he would much rather be under roof and by a fire, with a cup full of something to warm his guts.

She turned toward him and brushed back the veil to stare with cool, gray eyes. Her skin would be pale at the best of times, but here, on this dank, overcast day, with her black clothes and hat, her face almost disappeared except for her eyes and fever-red mouth. "Who are you?"

He suppressed an exultant shout. She had asked his name! "Matthias Tinwright, my lady." He made his best bow and prepared to kiss her hand, but it did not emerge from the dark folds of her cloak. "A humble poet. I was bard to Princess Briony." He realized phrasing things that way might seem disloyal, not to mention suggesting he was out of work. "I *am* bard to Princess Briony," he said, putting on his best, most pious aspect. "Because, with the mercy of Zoria and the Three, she will come back to us."

An expression he could not read passed across Elan M'Cory's face as she turned slowly back to the view. Why did she wear those widow's clothes, when he knew for a fact—he had pursued the question carefully—that she was not married? Was it truly in mourning for Gailon Tolly? They had not even been betrothed, or so at least the servants said. Many of them thought her a little mad, but Tinwright didn't care. One view of her with her hair hanging copper-brown against her white neck, her large, sad eyes watching nothing as the rest laughed and gibed at one of Puzzle's entertainments, and he had been smitten.

He hesitated, unsure of whether to go or not.

"A poet," she said suddenly. "Truly?"

He suppressed a boast and thus surprised himself. "I have long called myself so. Sometimes I doubt my skills."

She turned again and looked at him with a little more interest. "But surely this is a poet's world, Master . . ."

"Tinwright."

"Master Tinwright. Surely this your time of glory. Legends of the old days walk beneath the sun. Men are killed and no one can say why. Ghosts walk the battlements." She smiled, but it was not pleasant to see. Tinwright took a step back. "Do you know, I have even heard that mariners have lately returned with tales of a new continent in the west beyond the Smoking Islands, a great, unexplored land full of savages and gold. Think of it! Perhaps there are places where life still runs strong, where people are full of hope."

"Why should that not be true of this place, Lady Elan? Are we truly so weak and hopeless?"

She laughed, a small sound like scissors cutting string. "This place? Our world is old, Master Tinwright. Old and palsied—doddering, and even the young ones gasping in their cots. The end is coming soon, don't you think?"

While he was considering what to say to this strange assertion, he heard noises and looked up to see two young women hurrying along the battlements toward them, slipping a little on the wet stones in their haste. He recognized them as Princess Briony's ladies-in-waiting—the yellow-haired one was Rose or some other such flower name. They looked at Tinwright suspiciously as they approached, and for the first time he wished he was wearing better clothes. Oddly, it had not occurred to him during his conversation with Elan M'Cory.

"Lady Elan," the dark one cried, "you should not be walking here by yourself! Not after what happened to the princess!'

She laughed. "What, you think someone will climb the wall of the Inner Keep and steal me away? I can promise you, I have nothing to offer any kidnapper."

Ah, but you are wrong, thought Tinwright: if Briony Eddon was the bright morning sun, Elan M'Cory was the sullen, alluring moon. *In truth,* he thought, his mind as always leaping to the tropes of myth and story, *the goddess Mesiya must look much like this, so pale and mysterious, she who walks the night sky with her retinue of clouds.*

He remembered then that Mesiya was the wife of Erivor and mother of the Eddon family line, or so it was claimed, her wolf their battle-standard. How quickly these poetic thoughts grew muddled . . .

"Come with us," the two ladies-in-waiting were saying, tugging gently at the black-clad Elan's arms. "It is damp here—you will catch your death."

"Ho!" a voice cried from below, lazy and cheerful. "There you are."

"Never fear," Elan M'Cory said, but so quietly that only Tinwright heard her. "It has caught me instead."

Hendon Tolly stood at the base of the wall on the Inner Keep side, a small crowd of guardsmen in Tolly livery standing near him but at a respectful distance. "Come down, good lady. I have been looking for you."

"Surely you should go and lie down instead," said yellow-haired Rose, almost whispering. "Let us take care of you, Lady Elan."

"No, if my brother-in-law calls me, I must go." She turned to Tinwright. "It has been good speaking with you, Master Poet. If you think of any answer to my question, I shall be interested to know. It seems to me that things move more quickly toward an ending every day."

"I am waiting, my lady!" Hendon Tolly seemed full of rich humor, as though at a joke only he understood. "I have things I wish to show you."

She turned and walked behind the ladies, heading back toward the steps that Tinwright had climbed and the waiting master of Southmarch. Just before she reached them, when Tolly had looked away to talk to his guards, she turned back toward Tinwright for a brief moment. He thought she might nod or give some other sign of farewell, but she only looked at him with an expression as bizarrely full of mixed shame and excitement as a dog who has been caught gorging on the last of the family's dinner, who knows he will be fiercely beaten but cannot even run.

Matt Tinwright would see that face again and again in nightmares.

Briony wriggled, trying to ease herself. The scarf she had borrowed from one of Idite's daughters bound her breasts securely, but left an uncomfortable knot in the center of her back.

"Do the clothes fit?" Shaso had put on something similar to the loose homespun garments that one of the servants had brought to Briony. The pants were long; she had rolled them so they would not drag on the floor and trip her, but she was pleased to find that the rough shirt, though large, was not so big as to hinder her movements.

"Well enough, I suppose," she said. "Why am I wearing them?"

"Because you are going to learn something new." He was holding a bundle wrapped in oiled cloth, which he tucked under his arm, then led her down the hall and out to the courtyard. The rain had stopped but the sky was still heavy with dark clouds and the stones of the courtyard were wet. He gestured for her to sit down on the edge of the stone planter that housed the courtyard's lone quince tree, bare now except for the last few shriveled fruits the birds had not taken. "That should be dry."

"What am I going to learn?"

He scowled. "The first thing you must learn, like all Eddons, is to be patient. You are better at it than your brother—but not much." He raised his hand. "No, do not think of him. I shouldn't have spoken of him. We must pray that he is safe."

She nodded, willing her eyes to stay dry. *Poor Barrick! Zoria, watch over his every moment. Put your shield above him, wherever he is.*

"I would not have chosen to teach you swordplay, had you not wished it and your father not have given in to your whim." Shaso held up his hand again. "Remember—patience! But I have, and you have learned to fight well, for a woman. It is not the nature of women to fight, after all."

Again she started to speak, but she knew the look in the old man's eyes and did not have the strength for another argument. She closed her mouth.

"But whatever happens in the days to come, I think you will not be carrying a sword. You will not need one here, and if we leave this place we will go in secret." He placed his bundle down on the ground beside him, put his hand in and pulled out a wooden dowel that was only a little shorter than Briony's forearm. "I have taught you something of how to use a poniard, but primarily how to use it in combination with a sword. So now I am going to teach you how a Tuani fights *without* a sword. Stand up." He took the dowel in his fist. "Pretend this is a knife. Protect yourself."

He took a step toward her, swept the dowel down. She threw her hands up and shuffled backward.

"Wrong, child." He handed the bar of wood to her. "Do the same to me."

She looked at him, uncertain, then took a step forward, stabbing toward his chest, but unable to keep herself from holding back a little. Shaso put up a hand.

"No. Strike hard. I promise you will not hurt me."

She took a breath and then lunged. His hand flew out so quickly she almost could not see it move, knocking her hand aside even as Shaso himself stepped toward her, then put his leg behind her and pushed with his other hand against her neck. Just before she fell backward over his leg he caught at the sleeve of her shirt and kept her upright. He gently took the wooden rod out of her hand.

"Now you try what I have done."

It took her a dozen tries before she could get the trick of moving forward at the same time as she deflected his attack—it was different than swordfighting, far more intimate, the angles and speed affected by the small size of the weapon and the fact that she had no weapon of her own. When the old man was satisfied, he showed her several other blocks and leg-locks, and a few twisting moves meant not simply to deflect or stop an opponent's thrust but to loose the weapon from his hand.

The sun, climbing toward noon, finally made an appearance through the clouds. Briony was sweating now, and she had fallen down three or four times on the hard stones of the courtyard, bruising her knee and hip. By contrast, Shaso looked as calm and unruffled as when the lesson had first started.

"Take some moments to catch your breath," he said. "You are doing well."

"Why are you teaching me this?" she said. "Why now?"

"Because you are not royalty any longer," he said. "At least, you will have none of royalty's privileges. No men to guard you, no castle walls to keep your enemies away. Are you ready to begin again?"

She rubbed her aching hip, wondered if it was wrong to ask Zoria to grant Shaso a painful cramp—wondered if Zoria could even hear her, in this house of Tuan's Great Mother. "I'm ready," was all she said.

They stopped once for water and so that Briony could eat some dried fruit and bread that a wide-eyed servant brought out into the courtyard. Later, several of the house's women gathered under the covered walkway to watch, giggling inside their hooded robes, fascinated by the spectacle. Shaso showed her more unarmed blocks, grapple holds, kicks, and other methods of defending herself or even disarming an attacker, ways to break the arm of a man half again her size, or kick him in such a way that he would fight no more that day. When the old man was satisfied with her progress he brought out a second wooden dowel and gave it to her, then began to work with her on the skills of knife against knife.

"Do not let your enemy get his blade between you and him once you have closed," Shaso said. "Then even a backhand thrust can be fatal. Always turn it away, force the knife-hand out. There—see! If your enemy brings it too close, you can slash the tendons on the back of his hand or his wrist. But do not let him take your blade with his other hand."

By the time the sun had begun to slide behind the courtyard roof, and the women of the *hadar* had found even their deep curiosity satisfied and had gone back inside, Shaso let her stop and rest again. Her legs and arms were quivering with weariness and would not stop.

"We are finished for today," he said, wiping sweat from his forehead with his sleeve. "But we will do this again tomorrow and the days after, until I can sleep at night." He put the dowels back in the oilskin bundle. Something else inside it clinked, but he closed the wrapping and she did not see what it was. "This is not the world you knew, Briony Eddon. This is not a world that anyone knows, and what it will become is yet to be seen. Your part may be great or small, but I am sworn to your family and I want you alive to play that part."

She wasn't sure what he meant, but as she looked at the old man and saw that for all his seeming invincibility his hands were trembling as much as hers and his breathing was short and rapid, she was filled with misery and a kind of love. "I am sorry we had you imprisoned, Shaso. I am ashamed."

He gave her a strange look, not angry, but distant. "You did what you had to. As do we all, from the greatest to the smallest. Even the autarch in his palace is only a clay doll in the hands of the Great Mother." He tucked his bundle under his arm. "Go now. You did well—for a woman, very well."

The moment of affection disappeared in a burst of irritation. "You keep saying that. Why shouldn't a woman fight as well as a man?"

"Some women can fight as well as some men, child," he said with a sour smile. "But men are bigger, Briony, and stronger. Do you know what a lion is? It is a great cat that lives in the deserts near my country."

"I've seen one."

"Then you know its size and strength. The female lion is a great hunter, fierce and dangerous, a mighty killer. She brings down the gazelle and she slaughters the barking jackals that try to feed on her kill. But she gives way always before the male."

"But I don't want to be a male lion," Briony said. "I'd be happy just to chase away the jackals."

Shaso's smile lightened, became something almost peaceful. "That, anyway, I can try to give you. Go now, and I will see you in the morning."

"Won't I see you at supper?"

"In this house, the men and women do not eat together in the evening. It is the way of Tuan." He turned and walked, with just the hint of a limp, across the courtyard.

★

Dan-Mozan's nephew was waiting for her in the hallway. She groaned quietly as he stepped away from the wall where he had been leaning, eyes averted as though he had not yet noticed her, as though he had not been waiting here on purpose. All she wanted was to get into a hot bath, if such a thing could be found, and steam the aches from her muscles and the dirt from her scratched knees and feet.

"You are wearing my clothes," Talibo said.

"Yes, and thank you. Your uncle loaned them to me."

"Why?"

"Because Lord Shaso wished me to practice knife-fighting." She frowned at the expression of arrogant disbelief on his face, had to hold her tongue. How dare he look at her that way—Briony Eddon, a princess of all the March Kingdoms? He was no older than she was. It was true that he was not a bad-looking boy, she thought as she looked at his liquid brown eyes, the wispy mustache on his upper lip, but from the way his every feeling showed on his face he was still most definitely a boy. Seeing this one, she could imagine how Ludis' envoy Dawet dan-Faar must have looked in his youth, imagine the same look of youthful pride. Warrantless pride, she thought, annoyed: what had this brown-skinned boy ever done, living in a house, surrounded by women who deferred to him just because he was not a girl? "I have to go now," she said. "Thank you again for the use of these clothes."

She brushed past him, aware that the young man had more to say but unwilling to stand around while he worked up the nerve to say it. She thought she could feel his eyes on her as she walked wearily back to the women's quarters.

8

An Unremarkable Man

*When Onyena was ordered to serve her sister Surazem at
the birth she became angry, and cried out that she would
find some way to have vengeance on Sveros the Twilight, so
when the three brothers were being born from Surazem's
blessed womb Onyena stole some of the old god's essence.
She went away in secret and used the seed of Sveros
to make three children of her own, but she raised
them to hate their father and all he made.*

—from *The Beginnings of Things*
The Book of the Trigon

AT TIMES LIKE THIS, when Pinimmon Vash had to
look directly into his master's pale, awful eyes, it was hard
to remember that Autarch Sulepis had to be at least partly
human.

"All will be done, Golden One," Vash assured him, praying
silently to be dismissed and released. Sometimes just being near his

young ruler made him feel queasy. "All will be done just as you say."

"Swiftly, old man. She has tried to escape me." The autarch's gaze slid upward until he seemed to be staring intently at something invisible to anyone else. "Besides, the gods . . . the gods are restless to be born."

Confused by this strange remark, Vash hesitated. Was it something that needed to be understood and answered, or was he at last free to scurry away on his errand? He might be the paramount minister of mighty Xis, the old courtier reflected with some bitterness, and thus in theory more powerful than most kings, but he had no more real authority than a child. Still, being a minister who must jump to serve the autarch's every whim was much better than being a *former* minister: the vulture shrines atop the Orchard Palace's roofs were piled high with the bones of former ministers. "Yes, the gods, of course," Vash said at last, with no idea of what he was agreeing to. "The gods must be born, it goes without . . ."

"Then let it be done *now*. Or heaven itself will weep." Despite his harsh words, Sulepis began to laugh in a most inappropriate way.

Even as Vash hurried so swiftly from the bath chamber that he almost tripped over his own exquisite silk robes, he found himself hoping that one of the eunuchs shaving the autarch's long, oiled limbs had accidentally tickled him. It would be disturbing to think the man with life-and-death power over oneself and virtually every other human being on the continent had just giggled like a madman for no reason.

Partly human, Vash reminded himself. *He must be at least partly human.* Even if the autarch's father Parnad had also been a living god, the autarch's mother must surely have been a mortal woman, since she had come to the Seclusion as the gift of a foreign king. But whatever was mixed in with the heritage of godlike (although now fairly inarguably dead) Parnad, few mortal traits had made their way down to the son. The young autarch was as bright-eyed, remorseless, and inscrutable as his family's heraldic falcon. Sulepis was also full of inexplicable, seemingly mad ideas, as proved by this latest strange whim—the errand on which Vash now bustled toward the guard barracks.

As he left the guarded fastness of the Mandrake Court and hurried through the cavernous ministerial audience chamber at the heart of the Pomegranate Court, lesser folk scattered from his path like pigeons, as frightened of his anger as he was terrified of the autarch's. Pinimmon Vash reminded himself he should conduct a full sacrifice to Nushash and the other gods soon. After all, he was a very fortunate man—not just to have risen so high in the world, but also to have survived so many years of the father's autarchy and this first year of the son's: at least nine of Parnad's other high ministers had been put to death just in the short months of Sulepis' reign. In fact, should Vash need an example of how lucky he was compared to some, he only had to think about the man he was going to see, Hijam Marukh, the new captain of the Leopard guards—or more to the point, think about Marukh's predecessor, the peasant-soldier Jeddin.

Even Pinimmon Vash, no stranger to torture and execution, had been disturbed by the agonies visited upon the former Leopard captain. The autarch had ordered the entertainment conducted in the famous Lepthian library, so he could read while keeping an eye on the proceedings. Vash had watched with well-hidden terror as the living god danced his gold finger-stalls in the air in rhythm with Jeddin's shrieks, as though enjoying a charming performance. Many nights Vash still saw the terrible sights in his dreams, and the memory of the captain's agonized screaming haunted his waking mind as well. Near the end of the prisoner's suffering, Sulepis had even called for real musicians to play a careful, improvised accompaniment to his horrendous cries. At points, Sulepis had even sung along.

Vash had seen almost everything in his more than twenty years of service, but he had never seen anything like the young autarch.

But how could an ordinary man judge whether or not a god was mad?

★

"This makes no sense," said Hijam Marukh.

"You are foolish to say so," Vash hissed at him.

The officer known as Stoneheart allowed only a lifted eyebrow to animate his otherwise inexpressive face, but Vash could see that Marukh had realized his error—the kind that in Xis could swiftly prove fatal. Recently promoted to *kiliarch,* or captain, the Leopards' squat, muscular new master had survived countless major battles and deadly skirmishes, but he was not quite so used to the dangers of the Xixian court, where it was assumed that every public word and most private ones would be overheard by someone, and that one of those listeners likely either wanted or needed you dead. Marukh might have been cut, stabbed, and scorched so many times that his dark skin was covered in white stripes like a camp mongrel's, might have earned his famous nickname by passing unmoved through the worst carnage of war, but this was not the battlefield. In the Orchard Palace no man's death came at in him from the front or in plain sight.

"Of course," Hijam Stoneheart said now, slowly and clearly for the benefit of listening ears, "the Golden One must have his contest if he wills it so. But I am just a soldier and I don't understand such things. Explain to me, Vash. What good is there in having my men fight with each other? Already several are badly wounded and will need weeks of healing."

Vash took a breath. Nobody was obviously eavesdropping, but that meant nothing. "First of all, the Golden One is much wiser than we are, so perhaps we are not clever enough to understand his reasons—all we can know is that they must be good. Second, I must point out to you that it isn't your men, the Leopards, who are fighting for the honor of the autarch's special mission, Marukh. It is the White Hounds, and although they are valuable fighters they are only barbarians."

Vash had no more idea than the captain of why Sulepis had demanded a contest of strength among his famous troop of White Hounds, foreign mercenaries whose fathers and grandfathers had come to Xand from the northern continent, but as Vash knew better than almost anyone, sometimes gods-on-earth just did things like that. When the autarch had woken from a prophetic dream one morning in the first weeks of his rule and ordered the destruction of all the wild cranes in the land of Xis, it had been Paramount Minister Vash who had called the lower ministers to the Pomegranate Court to make the autarch's wishes known, and hundreds of thousands of the birds had been killed. When another day the autarch declared that every axhead shark in the city's salt-water canals should be caught and dispatched, the streets of the capital stank with rotting shark flesh for months afterward.

Vash forced his attention back to the combat. The abruptness of the autarch's demand had forced them to improvise this arena here in an unused audience chamber in the Tamarind Court, since the autarch's miners and cannoneers were all over the parade field and could not move their equipment on such sudden notice, even at threat of their lives—some of the artillery pieces weighed tons. Two sweaty men were struggling now in the makeshift ring. One was big by any ordinary standard and muscled like a bullock, but his yellow-bearded opponent was a true giant of a man, a head taller, with shoulders wide as the bed of an oxcart. This fair-haired monster clearly had the upper hand and even seemed to be toying with his adversary.

"Why is it taking so long?" Vash complained. "You said Yaridoras was by far the strongest of the White Hounds. Why does he not defeat his opponent? The autarch is waiting."

"Yaridoras will win." Hijam Stoneheart laughed sharply. "Trust me, he is a fearsome brute. Ah, look." The yellow-bearded one had just raised the other man over his head. The huge man held his opponent there just long enough for everyone to appreciate the glory of the moment, then flung him down onto the stony floor. The loser lay, senseless and bloody, as Yaridoras raised his arms above his head in triumph. The other White Hounds hooted in appreciation.

"Is that it?" Vash ached from standing and wanted only to lower himself into a hot bath, to be tended by his young boy and girl servants. He wished he had not been too proud to accept the *kiliarch's* offer of a chair. "Is it over? Can we finish with this?"

"There is one more challenger," said Marukh, "a fellow named Daikonas Vo. I am told he is the best swordsman of the White Hounds."

"But the autarch orderd them to prove themselves in bare-handed combat!" Vash shook his head in irritation, surveying the dozens of assembled Perikalese soldiers, perhaps four or five dozen in all. None of them looked big enough to give Yaridoras a contest. "Which one is he?"

For answer, Marukh stood and shouted, "Now the last fighter—step forth, Vo."

The man who rose was so unremarkable that, discounting his Perikalese heritage—the telltale fair hair and skin that marked him as a foreigner—any man of Xis might have passed him on the street without a second look. He was wiry but slightly built; his head barely reached Yaridoras' brawny chest.

"*That* one?" Vash snorted. "The big yellow-hair will snap his back like a twig."

"Likely." Marukh turned and bellowed, "You two may bring no weapons into the sacred space. So has our master Sulepis, the god-on-earth, the Great Tent, the Golden One, declared. You will fight until one of you can get up no longer. Are you ready?"

"Yes—and thirsty!" bellowed Yaridoras, making his fellow mercenaries laugh. "Let's get this over with so I can have my beer." The thin soldier, Daikonas Vo, only nodded.

"Very well," said the captain. "Begin."

At first, the smaller man put up a surprisingly good defense, moving with serpentine fluidity to stay out of Yaridoras' powerful grasp, once even hooking his foot behind the big man's heel and throwing him backward to the tile floor, which earned a percussive shout of surprised laughter from the other White Hounds, but the giant was up quickly, smiling in a way that suggested he himself was not very amused. After that Yaridoras was more careful, angling in to cut off his opponent's retreat, and Vo began to find it increasingly difficult to stay out of his hands. Vo did not give in easily, and several times he landed swift blows whose power was clearly greater than his size would have suggested, one of them opening a cut above Yaridoras' eye so that blood ran down one side of his face and into his beard. However inevitable the outcome seemed, the bigger man was clearly not enjoying the delay, and in the course of trying to get a finishing hold on his opponent left several long, bleeding weals across the small man's face and arms. The shouts and rowdy suggestions that had filled the room at the beginning of the bout began to die down, replaced by a murmuring of unease as the match slowly took on the look of something more desperate.

The big man lunged. Vo ducked under the groping arms and put a knee into his opponent's belly, so that Yaridoras' surprised gasp sent red froth flying, but the big man's knob-knuckled hand lashed out and caught Vo retreating, smashing him to the floor with an impact like a slaughterer's hammer. Yaridoras threw himself on top of his opponent before Vo had recovered his wits and for a moment it seemed as though the smaller soldier had been swallowed whole.

It's over now, thought Vash. *But he fought a surprisingly good fight.* The paramount minister was more than a little surprised: he had always thought of the Perikalese foreigners as benefiting mostly from their size and barbaric savagery. It was strange, even disturbing, to see one who could think and plan.

For a moment as they grappled on the floor, Yaridoras caught the smaller man's head between his legs. He began to squeeze, and Daikonas Vo's face darkened to a bruised red before he managed to elbow his opponent in the crotch and wriggle free. He was injured and tired, though, and he did not get far before Yaridoras caught him again, this time with a massive arm around his throat. The giant rolled his body over on top of his opponent, then began trying to sweep away the bracing arms and legs which were all that kept Vo from being pressed belly-first onto the floor. The big man grinned ferociously through the sweat and blood, while Vo showed his own teeth in a grimace as he struggled to get air.

"He'll kill him," Vash said, fascinated.

"No, he'll just choke him until he gives over," said Marukh.

"Yaridoras won't kill anyone needlessly, especially another White Hound. He is a veteran of such matches."

Daikonas Vo's purpling face was sinking closer and closer to the floor, his elbows bowing outward as the bigger man's weight overcame him. Then, to Pinimmon Vash's astonishment, Vo deliberately took one hand off the tiles and, just before he was driven to the ground, brought his elbow down so hard against the floor that a noise loud as a musket shot echoed through the room. A moment later the two of them collapsed in a writhing, grunting heap, and for a moment it was hard to make sense of the tangle of limbs. Then the two bodies lay still.

Face and upper body shiny with blood, Daikonas Vo at last pulled himself out from under Yaridoras, rolling the giant aside so that the long shard of stone floor tile sticking in the yellow-bearded man's eye rose into view like a sacred object being lifted above a parade of believers. The audience of White Hounds gasped and cursed in shock, then a roar of anger rose from them and several of them moved toward the exhausted, bloody Vo with murderous intent.

"*Stop!*" cried Pinimmon Vash. When they realized it was the autarch's chief minister who had commanded them, the White Hounds halted and fell into surly, murmuring attention. "Do not harm that man."

"But he killed Yaridoras!" growled Marukh. "The autarch's law was that no weapons could be used!"

"The autarch said that no weapons could be *brought into the arena,* Kiliarch. This man did not bring a weapon, he made one. Clean him up and bring him to the Mandrake Court."

"The Hounds will be angry. Yaridoras was popular . . ."

"Ask them to consider whether keeping their heads will be compensation enough. Otherwise, I'm sure their autarch will be happy to make other arrangements."

Vash shook his robe free of wrinkles and passed from the room.

The Golden One was reclining on the ceremonial stone bed in the Chamber of the New Sun, naked except for a short kilt decorated with jade tiles. On each side of him a kneeling priest bound the cuts in the autarch's arms, delicate wounds made only moments earlier by sacred golden shell-knives. The small quantity of royal blood, enough to fill two tiny golden bowls which at the moment were on a tray held by the high priest Panhyssir, would be poured into the Sublime Canal just after sunset to assure the sun's return from its long winter journey apart from its bride the earth.

Sulepis turned lazily as the soldier Daikonas Vo was led in, cradling his elbow as if it were a sleeping child. The man of Perikal had been wiped clean of blood, but his face and neck were still crisscrossed with raw, scraped flesh.

"I am told you killed a valuable member of my White Hounds," the autarch said, stretching his arms to test the fit of the bandages. Already tiny blooms of red could be seen through the linen.

"We fought, Master." Vo shrugged, his gray-green eyes as empty as two spheres of glass. There was nothing notable about him, Vash thought, except his accomplishment. He had forgotten the man's face in the short time since he had last seen him and would forget it again as soon as the man was gone. "At your request, as I understand it. I won."

"He cheated," said the captain of the Leopards angrily. "He broke a floor tile and used it to stab Yaridoras to death."

"Thank you, Kiliarch Marukh," said Vash. "You have delivered him and nothing more is required of you. The Golden One will decide what to do with him."

Suddenly conscious that he was drawing attention to himself in a place where attention was seldom beneficial, Hijam Stoneheart paled a little, then bowed and backed out of the chamber.

"Sit," said the autarch, surveying the pale-skinned soldier. "Panhyssir, bring us something to drink."

A strange honor for a mere brawler, to be served by the high priest of Nushash himself, thought Pinimmon Vash. Panhyssir was Vash's chief rival for the autarch's time and attention, but it was a contest Vash had lost long ago: the priest and the autarch were close as bats in a roost, always full of secrets, which made it seem all the more odd that the powerful Panhyssir should be carrying drinks like a mere slave.

As the high priest of Nushash moved with careful dignity toward a hidden alcove at the side of the great chamber, one of the autarch's eunuch servants scuttled up with a stool and placed it so that Daikonas Vo could seat himself within a few yards of the living god. The soldier did so, moving gingerly, as though his wounds from the combat with Yaridoras were inhibiting him. Vash guessed that they must be painful indeed: the man did not seem the type to show weakness easily.

Panhyssir returned with two goblets, and after bowing and presenting one to his monarch, gave the other to Vo, whose hesitation before drinking was so brief that Vash could have almost believed he had imagined it.

"Daikonas Vo, I am told your mother was a Perikalese whore," declared the autarch. "One of those bought and carried back from the northern continent to serve my troop of White Hounds. Your father was one of the original Hounds—dead, now. Killed at Dagardar, I'm told."

"Yes, Golden One."

"But not before he killed your mother. You have the look of your people, of course, but how well do you speak the language of your ancestors?"

"Perikalese?" Vo's nondescript face betrayed no surprise. "My mother taught it to me. Before she died it was all we spoke."

"Good." The autarch sat back, making a shape like a minaret with his fingers. "You are resourceful, I understand—and ruthless as well. Yaridoras is not the first man you have killed."

"I am a soldier, Golden One."

"I do not speak of killings on the battlefield. Vash, you may read."

Vash held up a leather-bound account book which had been brought to him by the library slave only a short while before, then traced down a page with his finger until he found what he sought. "Disciplinary records of the White Hounds for this year. *'By verified report extracted from two slaves, Daikonas Vo is known to have been responsible for the deaths of at least three men and one woman,'* " Vash read. " *'All were Xixians of low caste and the killings attracted little public attention so no punishment was required.'* That is just the report for this year, which is not yet over. Do you wish me to read from earlier years, Golden One?"

The autarch shook his head. A look of amusement crossed his long face as he turned back to the impassive soldier. "You are wondering why I should care about such things—whether you are to be punished at last. Is that not true?"

"In part, Master," said Vo. "It is certainly strange that the living god who rules us all should care about someone as unimportant as myself. But as to punishment, I do not fear it at the moment."

"You don't?" The autarch's smile tightened. "And why is that?"

"Because you are speaking to me. If you only wished to punish me, Golden One, I suspect you would have done so without wasting the fruits of your divine thought on someone so lowly. Everybody knows that the living god's judgments are swift and sure."

Some of the tension went out of the autarch's long neck, replaced by a certain stillness, like a snake sunning itself on a rock. "Yes, they are. Swift and sure. And your reasoning is flawed but adequate—I would not waste my time on you if I did not require something of you."

"Whatever you wish, Master." The soldier's voice remained flat and emotionless.

The autarch finished his wine and gestured that Daikonas Vo should do the same. "As you have no doubt heard, I am no longer content merely to receive tribute from the nations of the northern continent. The time is coming soon when I will take the ancient seaport of Hierosol and begin to expand our empire into Eion, bringing those savages into the bright, holy light of Nushash."

"So it has been rumored, Master," Vo said slowly. "We all pray for the day to come soon."

"It will. But first, I have lost something that I want back, and it is to be found somewhere in that northern wilderness—the lands of your forefathers."

"And you wish me to . . . retrieve this thing, Master?"

"I do. It will require cunning and discretion, you see, and it will be easier for a white-skinned man who can speak one of the languages of Eion to travel there, seeking this small thing which I desire."

"And may I ask what that thing is, Golden One?"

"A girl. The daughter of an unimportant priest. Still, I chose her for the Seclusion and she had the dreadful manners to run away." The autarch laughed, a quiet growl that might have come from a cat about to unsheathe its claws. "Her name is . . . what was it? Ah, yes—Qinnitan. You will bring her back to me."

"Of course, Master." The soldier's expression became even more still.

"You are thinking again, Vo. That is good. I chose you because I need a man who can use his head. This woman is somewhere in the lands of our enemies, and if someone learns I want her, she may become the object of a contest. I do not want that." The autarch sat back and waved his hand. This time it was only an ordinary servant who scurried forward to refill his goblet. "But what you are wondering is this: *Why should the autarch let me go free in the land of my ancestors? Even if I sincerely try to fulfill his quest, if I fail there is no punishment he can visit on me unless I return to Xis.* No, do not bother to deny it. It is what anyone would think." The young autarch turned to one of his child servants, a silent Favored. "Bring me my cousin Febis. He should be in his apartments."

As they waited, the autarch had the servant refill Vo's cup. Pinimmon Vash, who had some inkling of what was to come, was glad he was not drinking the strong, sour Mihanni wine, so unsettling to the stomach.

Febis, a chubby, balding man with the reddened cheeks of an inveterate drinker made even more obvious by the pallor of fear, hurried into the chamber and threw himself on his hands and knees in front of the autarch, bumping his forehead against the stone.

"Golden One, surely I have done nothing wrong! Surely I have not offended you! You are the light of all our lives!"

The autarch smiled. Vash never ceased to marvel at how the same expression that would bring joy if it were on the face of a young child or a pretty woman could, just by transferring it to the autarch's smoothly youthful features, suddenly become a thing to inspire terror. "No, Febis, you have done nothing wrong. I called you here only because I wish to demonstrate something." He turned to the soldier Vo. "You see, I had a similar problem with those of my relations, like Cousin Febis, who remained after my father and brothers had died—after I, by the grace of Nushash of the Gleaming Sword, had become autarch. How could I be certain that some of these family members might not ponder whether, as the succession had passed over several of my brothers upon their deaths and came to me, it might not continue on to Febis or one of the other cousins after *my* untimely death? Of course, I could have simply killed them all when I took the crown. It would only have been a few hundred. I could have done that, couldn't I, Febis?"

"Yes, yes, Golden One. But you were merciful, may heaven bless you."

"I was merciful, it's true. Instead, what I did was induce each of them to swallow a certain . . . creature. A tiny beast, at least in its infant form, which had long been thought lost to our modern knowledge. But I found it!" He smirked. "And you did swallow it, didn't you, Febis?"

"So I was told, Golden One." The autarch's cousin was sweating heavily, droplets dangling like glass beads from his chin and nose before splashing to the floor. "It was too small for me to see."

"Ah, yes, yes." The autarch laughed again, this time with all the pleasure of a young child. "You see, the creature is so small at first that the naked eye cannot see it. It can be swallowed in a glass of wine without the recipient even knowing." He turned to Daikonas Vo. "As you received it when you first drank."

Vo put down his goblet. "Ah," he said.

"As to what it does, it grows. Not hugely, mind you, but enough that when it lodges at last in the body of its host, it cannot be dislodged no matter what. But that does not matter, because the host will never be aware of it. Unless I wish it to be so." The autarch nodded. "Yes, let us say for the sake of argument that its host fails to carry out a task I have given him in the specified time, or in some other way incurs my anger . . ." He turned to burly, sweating Febis. "As, for instance, telling his wife that his master the autarch is mad and will not live long . . ."

"Did she say that?" shrieked Febis. "The whore! She lies!"

"Whatever the crime," the autarch went on evenly, "and no matter how far away its perpetrator, when I know of it, things will begin to happen." He gestured. "Panhyssir, call for the the *xol*-priest."

Febis shrieked again, a bleat of despair so shrill it made Pinimmon Vash's toes curl. "*No!* You must know I would never say such a thing, Golden One—never, please, no-o-o-o!" Weeping and burbling, Febis lurched toward the stone bed. Two burly Leopard guards stepped forward and restrained him, using no little force. His cries lost their words, became a sobbing moan.

The *xol*-priest came in a few moments later, a thin, dark, knife-nosed man with the look of the southern deserts about him. He bowed to the autarch and then sat cross-legged on the floor, opening a flat wooden box as though preparing to play a game of *shanat*. He spread a piece of fabric like a tiny blanket, then took several grayish shapes which might have been lumps of lead out of the box and arranged them with exacting care. When he had finished he looked up at the autarch, who nodded.

The man's spidery fingers picked up and moved two of the gray shapes and Febis, who had been twitching and sobbing obliviously in the grip of the guards, suddenly went rigid. When they let him go he tumbled to the floor like a stone. Another movement of the shapes on the little carpet and Febis began to writhe and gasp for breath, his arms and legs thrashing like a man about to sink beneath the water and drown. One more and he suddenly vomited up a terrible quantity of blood, then lay still in the spreading red puddle, unseeing eyes wide with horror. The *xol*-priest boxed up his gray shapes, bowed, and went out.

"Of course, the pain can be made to last much longer before

the end comes," the autarch said. "*Much* longer. Once the creature is awakened it can be restrained for days before it begins to feed in earnest, and each hour is an eternity. But I made Febis' end swift out of respect for his mother, who was my own father's sister. It is a shame he should have wasted that precious blood so." Sulepis looked a moment longer at the gleaming pool, then nodded, allowing the servants to rush forward and begin the removal of both the puddle and Febis' body. The autarch then turned to Daikonas Vo.

"Distance is no object, by the way. Should Febis have gone to Zan-Kartuum, or even the northernmost wastes of Eion where the imps live, still I could have struck him down. I trust the lesson is not lost on you, Vo. Go now. You will be a hound no longer, but my hunting falcon—the autarch's falcon. You could ask for no higher honor."

"No, Golden One."

"All else you need to know you will learn from Paramount Minister Vash." Sulepis started to turn away, but the soldier still had not moved. The autarch's eyes narrowed. "What is it? If you succeed you will be rewarded, of course. I am as good to my faithful servants as I am stern with those who are less so."

"I do not doubt it, Golden One. I only wondered if such a . . . creature . . . had been introduced to the girl, Qinnitan, and if so why you would not use so certain a method to bring her back to Great Xis."

"Whether such a thing has been done to her or not," the autarch said, "is beside the point. It is a clumsy and dangerous method if you wish your subject to survive. I wish the girl returned *alive and well*—do you understand? I still have plans for her. Now go. You sail for Hierosol tonight. I want her in my hands by the time Midsummer's Day arrives or you will be the most sorrowful of men. For a little while." The autarch stared. "Yet another question? I am minded to wake the *xol*-beast now and find someone less annoying."

"Please, I live to serve you, Golden One. I only wish to ask permission to wait until tomorrow to set out."

"Why? I have seen your records, man. You have no family, no friends. Surely you have no farewells to make."

"No, Golden One. It is only that I suspect I have broken my elbow fighting the bearded one." He held up the arm he had smashed against the tile floor, using his other arm to support it. The sleeve was a lumpy bag of blood. "That will give me time to have it set and bandaged, first, so I can better serve you."

The autarch threw back his head and laughed. "Ah, I like you, man. You are a cold-blooded fellow, indeed. Yes, go now and have it seen to. If you succeed in this task, who knows? Perhaps I will give you old Vash's job." Sulepis grinned, eyes as bright as if he were fevered. *That must be the explanation,* thought Pinimmon Vash: this man—or rather this god-on-earth—was in a perpetual fever, as though the sun's fiery blood really did run in his veins. It made him mad and it made him as dangerous as a wounded viper. "What do you think, old man?" the autarch prodded. "Would you like to train him as your replacement?"

Vash bowed, keeping his terrified, murderous thoughts off his face. "I will do whatever you wish, Golden One, of course. Whatever you wish."

9

In Lonely Deeps

Tso and Zha had many sons, of whom the greatest was
Zhafaris, the Prince of Evening. On his great black falcon
he would ride through the sky and when he saw beasts or
demons that might threaten the gods' tents he slew them
with his ax of volcano stone, which was called
Thunderclap—the mightiest weapon, O My Children,
that was ever seen.

—from *The Revelations of Nushash,* Book One

"I KNOW YOU THINK it is . . . because I am stout," said Chaven as he sagged against the corridor wall and fanned himself with his bandaged hand. "But it is *not.* That is to say, I am, but . . ."

"Nonsense," Chert told him. "You are not so fat, especially after the past tennight spent starving and hiding. If you need to rest, you need to rest. There is no shame in it."

"But that isn't it! I am . . . I am afraid of these tunnels." Even by the glow of the stonelights, which made everyone seem pale as mushroom flesh, his pallor was noticeable.

Chert wondered if it wasn't the dark itself that was unnerving the physician: even to Funderling eyes, the light was very dim here on the outer edge of the town, where Lower Ore Street began to touch the unnamed passages still being built or begun and then abandoned when Guild plans changed. "Is it the darkness you fear, or . . . something else?" Chert remembered the mysterious man Gil, who had taken him to the city to meet the Qar folk. Gil too had been wary, not of the tunnels themselves it had seemed, but of something that lurked in the depths below them. "Do I trespass by asking?"

"Trespass?" Chaven shook his head. "After saving my life and . . . taking me into your home, kind friend, you ask that? No, let me . . . catch my wind again . . . and I will tell you." After a few moments of labored breath he began. "You know I come from Ulos in the south. Did you know my family, the Makari, were rich?"

"I know only what you've told me." Chert tried to look patient, but he could not help thinking of Opal waiting at home, saddled with the painful burden of a child who had become a stranger. Already much of this morning had slipped away like sand running from a seam but Chert still did not know the purpose of their errand, let alone actually getting to it.

"They were—and may still be, for all I know. I broke with them years ago when they began to take gold from Parnad, the old autarch of Xis."

Chert knew little about any of the autarchs, living or dead, but he tried to look as though he routinely discussed such things with other worldly folk. "Ah," he said. "Yes, of course."

"I grew up in Falopetris, in a house overlooking the Hesperian Ocean, atop a great stone cliff riddled with tunnels just like these."

Chert, who knew that the honeycombed fastness of Midlan's Mount was not merely the chief dwelling, but the actual birthplace of his race, that the Salt Pool had seen the very creation of the Funderling people, felt a moment of irritation to have it compared to the paltry tunnels of Falopetris, but checked himself—the physician had not meant it that way. Chert was anxious to be moving on and he realized it was making him unkind. "I have heard of those cliffs," he said. "Very good limestone, some excellent tufa for bricks. In fact, good stone all around there . . ."

Now it was Chaven who looked a little impatient. "I'm certain. In any case, when I was small my brothers and I played in the caves—not deeply, because even my brothers knew that was too dangerous, but in the outer caverns on the cliff below our house that looked out over the sea. Pretended we were Vuttish sea-ravers and such, or that we manned a fortress against Xixian invaders." He scowled, gave a short unhappy bark of a laugh. "A good joke, that, I see now.

"It was on such a day that my older brothers grew angry with me for something I cannot even remember now and left me in the cave. We came down to it by a steep trail, you see, and at the end there was a rope ladder we had stolen from the keeper's shed that we had to clamber down to reach the entrance. My brothers and my sister Zamira went back up ahead of me, but took the ladder with them.

"At first I thought they would return any moment—I had scarcely five or six years, and could not imagine that anything else could happen. And in fact they probably would have come back once they had frightened me a little, but the younger of my brothers, Niram, fell from the trail higher up onto some rocks and broke his leg so badly that the bone jutted from the skin. He never walked again without a limp, even after it healed. In any case, they managed to lift him back to the trail and carry him home, but in their terror, and the subsequent hurry to bring a surgeon from the town, no one thought about me.

"I will not bore you with my every dreadful moment," Chaven said, as if fearing the other man's impatience, although that had faded now as Chert considered the horror of a child in such a situation, thought of Flint just days ago, alone in the depths, going through things he and Opal could never know. Chert shuddered.

"Enough to say that I heard screaming and shouting from the

hillside overhead," Chaven continued, "and thought they were trying to frighten me—and that it was succeeding. Then there was silence for so long that I at last stopped believing it was a trick. I became certain they had forgotten me in truth, or that they had fallen to their deaths, or been attacked by catamounts or bears. I cried and cried, as any child would, but at last the barrel was empty—I had no tears left.

"I do not remember much of what happened next. I must have found the hole at the back of the cave and wandered in, although I do not remember doing so. I dimly recall lights, or a dream of lights, and voices, but all that I can know for certain is that when my father and the servants came for me, bearing torches because it was hours after nightfall, they found me curled in a smaller, deeper cave whose entrance we had never found in all the times we had played there. My father subsequently had that inner cavern blocked and the ladder to the caves taken away. We never went there again—Niram could not have climbed down to them in any case." Chaven ran his hands over his balding scalp. "I have had a horror of dark, narrow places ever since. It took all I had those three days past simply to come down into Funderling Town seeking you, although I knew I would die if I did not find help."

It was hard to imagine feeling stone over your head as oppressive instead of sheltering—how much less secure to stand in some wide open space with no refuge, no place to hide from enemies or angry gods! But Chert did his best to understand. "Would you like to go back, then?"

"No." Chaven stood, still trembling, but with a resolution on his face that looked a little like anger. "No, I cannot leave my house to the plundering of the Tollys without even knowing what they do there. I cannot. My things . . . valuable . . ." The physician dropped into a mumble Chert could not understand as he pushed himself off from the wall and began walking again, heading bravely into the long stretches of shadow between stonelights, shadows which Chert knew must seem darkness complete and hopeless to a man from aboveground.

★

As he paused to drop a fresh piece of coral stone into the saltwater of the lantern Chert could not help thinking of his last two journeys through these tunnels, passing this way with Flint when they took the strange piece of stone to Chaven, then the other direction with Gil on their march to the fairy-held city on the other side of the bay. How could his life, such an ordinary thing only a year before, full of orderly days and restful nights, have been turned inside out so quickly, like Opal readying shirts to dry on a hot rock?

"And the stone, Flint's stone, was the thing that killed a prince . . ." Chert said half-aloud as he hurried to catch up to physician. Even after all the other things that had happened to him in the last days, he still found it hard to believe—found Chaven's entire story nearly impossible to grasp. He, Chert Blue Quartz, had carried that stone in his own hand!

Chaven, walking grimly ahead, did not seem to have heard him.

"If I had put that what-was-it-called stone in my own mouth," Chert said, louder this time, "would *I* have turned into a demon, too? Or did I have to say some magical words?"

"What?" Chaven seemed lost in a kind of dream, one that did not easily let go. "The *kulikos* stone? No, not unless you knew the spell that gave it life and power, and that would have needed more than words."

"More than words?"

"Such old wisdom, that men call magic, does not work like a door lock that any man can open if he has the key. Those among your people who work crystals and gems, do they simply grab a stone and strike it and it falls into shape, or is there more to the skill than that?"

"More, of course. Years of training, and still often a stone shatters."

"So it would be even if you held the *kulikos* in your hand right now and I told you the ancient words. You could say them a hundred times in a hundred ways and it would remain nothing but a lump of cold stone in your fingers. The old arts require training, learning, sacrifice—and even so, the cost is often greater than the reward . . ." He trailed off. When he spoke again his voice shook. "Sometimes the cost is terrible."

Chert put a hand on his shoulder. "We are coming near to the bottom of your house. We should go quietly now. If they have not found the lower door they might still hear us through the walls and come looking for what makes the noise."

Chaven nodded. He looked drawn and frightened, as though after telling the story of his childhood terror he had never managed to shake it off again.

Two more rough-hewn corridors and they stood in front of the door, which was as strange a sight as ever in this empty, untraveled place, its hardwoods and bronze fittings polished so that even the dim coral light raised a gleam. Chert suddenly wanted to ask whether Chaven had actually stepped out into the passage from time to time to clean the thing, since none of his servants had known of its existence, but he had to be quiet now until they learned who or what was on the other side.

Chert stared at the featureless door. It had no handle or latch or even keyhole on this side, nothing but the bellpull—and clearly they were not going to use that.

The physician tugged at his sleeve to get his attention, then made a strange gesture that the Funderling did not immediately understand. Chaven did it again, waving his bandaged fingers with increasing impatience until Chert realized that Chaven wanted him to turn around—that there was something the bigger man did not want him to see. It was impossible not to feel angered after all they had both been through, after he and Opal had given Chaven the sanctuary of their home and nursed him back to health, but now was not the time to argue. Chert turned his back on the door.

A quiet hiss as of something heavy sliding was followed by the chink of a lifting latch; a moment later he felt Chaven's touch on his shoulder. The door was open, spilling a widening sliver of light out into their passageway. Chaven leaned close, urgency on his face—he looked like a starving man who smelled food but did not yet know what he must do to get it. Chert held his breath, listening.

At last Chaven straightened up and nodded, then slipped through the open doorway. Chert hurried down the stone corridor after him holding the fading coral lantern. The physician paused in front of a hanging so bleached by age and dotted with mildew that the scene embroidered on it had become invisible, a thing weirdly out of place in such a damp, windowless, almost unvisited spot. For a moment Chaven hesitated, his burned fingers hovering in midair as though he would once again ask Chert to turn around, but then impatience got the best of him and he pulled back the hanging and ducked beneath it, making a lump under the ancient fabric. A moment later the lump disappeared as if the physician had simply vanished.

Despite a superstitious chill at the back of his neck, Chert was about to investigate, but something else caught his attention. He made his way as silently as he could down the corridor and past the hanging to the base of the stairs. He muffled his lantern, dropping the passageway into near-darkness as he stood, listening.

Voices, coming from somewhere upstairs—were Chaven's servants keeping the up house in his absence? Somehow Chaven did not think so.

A disembodied moan, quiet but still piercing, made Chert jump. He looked around wildly but the corridor was still empty. He hurried back to the hanging and pulled it aside to discover a hidden door, ajar. The noise came again, louder, the muffled wail of a lost soul, and Chert summoned up his courage and pushed the door open.

Chaven lay in the middle of the floor, writhing as though he had been stabbed, surrounded by rumpled lengths of cloth. Chert ran to him, turned him over, but could find no wound.

"Ruined . . . !" the physician groaned. Though his voice was quiet, it seemed loud as a shout to Chert. "*Ruined!* They have taken it . . . !"

"Quiet," the Funderling hissed at him. "There is someone upstairs!"

"They have it!" Chaven sat up, wild-eyed, and began to struggle in Chert's grasp like a man who had seen his only child stolen from his arms. "We must stop them!"

"Shut your mouth or you will get us killed," Chert whispered harshly clinging on to the much larger man as tightly as he could. "It might be the entire royal guard, looking for you."

"But they have stolen it . . . I am destroyed . . . !" Chaven was actually weeping. Chert could not believe what he saw, the change that had turned this man he had long known and respected into a mad child.

"Stole what? What are you saying?"

"We must listen. . . . We must hear them." Chaven managed to throw the Funderling off, but his look had changed from sheer madness to something more sly. He crawled across the room before Chert could get his legs under himself; a moment later he had snaked out under the faded hanging and into the corridor. Chert hurried after him.

The physician had stopped at the stairwell. He touched his lips to enjoin the Funderling to silence—an unnecessary gesture to someone as frightened as Chert was, both by the danger itself and Chaven's seeming madness. The physician was shaking, but it seemed a tremble of rage, not anything more sensible like a fear of being caught, imprisoned, and almost inevitably executed.

And me? Chert could not help thinking. *If they kill Chaven, the royal physician, what will they do with a mere Funderling who is his accomplice? The only question will be whether anyone ever learns of my death. Ah, my dear old Opal, you were right after all—I should have learned to stay at home and tend my own fungus.*

He took a deep breath to try to slow his beating heart. Perhaps it was only Chaven's own servants after all. Perhaps . . .

"I promise you, Lord Tolly, there is nothing else here of value at all." The reedy voice wafted down the stairwell, close enough to keep Chert stock-still, holding the last breath he took as if it must last him forever. To his horror, he saw Chaven's eyes go wide with that mindless, inexplicable rage he had shown earlier, even saw the physician make a twitching move toward the staircase itself. Chert shot out his hand and clung as if his fingers

were curled on scaffolding while he dangled over a deadly drop.

The other's voice was lazy, but with a suggestion somehow that it could turn cruel as quick as an adder's strike. *"Is that true, brother, or are there things here that you think might not be of value to me, but which you might quite like for yourself?"*

Confused, Chert guessed that Hendon Tolly and his brother, the new Duke of Summerfield, stood in the hallway above them. He could not understand the expression of heedless fury on Chaven's face. Earth Elders, didn't he realize that the Tollys owned not just the castle now but had become the unquestioned rulers of all Southmarch? That with a word these men could have Chaven and Chert skinned in Market Square in front of a whooping, applauding crowd?

"I tell you, Lord, you already have the one piece of true value. I promise that eventually I will winkle out its secrets, but at the moment there is something missing, some element I have not discovered, and it is not in this house . . ." The man's thin voice suddenly grew sharp, high-pitched. *"Ah, keep that away from me!"*

"It is only a cat," said the one he had called Lord Tolly.

"I hate the things. They are tools of Zmeos. There, it runs away. Good." When he spoke again his voice had regained its earlier calm. *"As I said, there is nothing in this house that will solve the puzzle—I swear that to you, my lord."*

"But you will solve it," the other said. *"You will."*

Fear was in the first one's voice again, not well hidden. *"Of course, Lord. Have I not served you well and faithfully for years?"*

"I suppose you have. Come, let us lock this place up and you can go back to your necromancy."

"I think it would be more accurate to call it captromancy, my lord." The speaker had recovered his nerve a bit. Chert was beginning to think he had guessed wrong—that one of these was a Tolly, but not both. *"Necromancers raise the dead. It is captromancers who use mirrors in their art."*

"Perhaps a little of both, then, eh?" said his master jauntily as their voices dwindled. *"Ah, what a fascinating world we are making . . . !"*

When the two were gone and the house was silent Chert could finally breathe freely, and found he was trembling all over, as if he had narrowly avoided a fatal tumble. "Who were those two men?"

"Hendon Tolly, to give one of the dogs a name," the physician snarled. "The other is the vilest traitor who ever lived—an even filthier cur than Hendon—a man who I thought was my friend, but who has been the Tollys' lapdog all along, it seems. If I had his throat in my hands . . ."

"What are you talking about?"

"Talking about? He has stolen my dearest possession!" Chaven's eyes were still wide, and it occurred to Chert it was not too late for the royal physician to go dashing out into Southmarch Keep and get them both killed. He grabbed Chaven's robe again.

"What? What did he steal? Who was that?"

Chaven shook his head, tears welling in his eyes again. "No. I cannot tell you. I am shamed by my weakness." He turned to stare at Chert, desperate, imploring. "Tolly called him brother because the man who helped him pillage my secrets is one of the brothers of the Eastmarch Academy. Okros, Brother Okros—a man who I have trusted as if he were my own family."

Chert had never seen the physician so helpless, so defeated, so . . . empty.

Chaven put his head on his arms, sagged as if he would never rise again. "Oh, by all the gods, I should have known! Growing to manhood in a family like mine, I should have known that trust is for fools and weaklings."

"Are you mad?" Teloni could not have been more astonished if her younger sister had suggested jumping off the harbor wall into the ocean. "He is a prisoner! And he is a man!"

"But look at him—he is always here and he seems so sad." Pelaya Akuanis had seen the prisoner a half-dozen times, and always the older man sat on the stone bench as quietly as if he listened to music, but of course there was no music, only the noises of birds and the distant boom and shush of the sea. "I am going to talk to him."

"The guards won't let you," one of the other girls warned, but Pelaya ignored her. She got up and smoothed her dress before walking across the garden toward the bench. Two of the guards stood, but after looking at her carefully one guard leaned back against the wall again; the other moved exactly one step closer to the bearded man they were guarding, which was apparently the solution to some odd little inner mechanics of responsibility. Then the two guards resumed their whispered conversation. Pelaya wished she looked more like the dangerous type who might free a prisoner, but the guards had judged her correctly—talking to him with her friends and the man's guards around her on all sides was quite enough of an adventure, however she might like to act otherwise.

As she reached him the man looked up at her, his face so empty of emotion that she was positive she could have been a beetle or a leaf for all he cared. She suddenly realized she had nothing to say. Pelaya would have turned and walked away again except that she could not bear to see Teloni give her one of those amused, superior looks.

She swayed a little, trying to think of how to begin, and he only watched her. For a moment the garden seemed very silent. He was at least her father's age, perhaps older, with long reddish-brown hair and beard, both shot with gray and a few curling wisps of pure white. Even as she examined him he was surveying her in turn, and his calm gaze unnerved her. "Who are you?" she said, blurting it out so that it sounded like a challenge. She could feel the blood rising in her cheeks and had to fight hard once more against the urge to flee.

"Ah, my good young mistress, but it is you who approached me," he said sternly. He sounded serious, and his face looked serious too, but something in the way he spoke made her think he might be mocking her. "You must name yourself. Have you never been told any stories, have you read no books on polite discourse? Names are important, you see. However, once given, they can never be taken back." He spoke the Hierosoline tongue with a strange accent, harsh but somehow musical.

"But I think I know yours," she said. "You are King Olin of Southmarch."

"Ah, you are only half right." He frowned, as though thinking hard about his words, then nodded slowly. "It seems that, in fairness, you must tell me half of your name."

"Pelaya!" her sister called, a strangled moan of embarrassment.

"Ah," said the prisoner. "And now I have received my due, will you, nill you."

"That wasn't fair. She told you."

"I was not aware we were involved in a contest. Hmmm—interesting." Something moved across his lips, fleeting as a shadow—a smile? "As I said, names are very important things. Very well, I will do my best to guess the other name without help from any of the bystanders. Pelaya, are you? A fair name. It means 'ocean.' "

"I know." She took a step back. "You are playing for time. You cannot guess."

"Ah, but I can. Let me consider what I know already." He stroked his beard, the very picture of a philosopher from the Sacred Trigon Academy. "You are here, that is the first thing to be pondered. Not everyone is allowed into this inner garden—I myself have only recently been granted the privilege. You are well dressed, in silk and a fine lace collar, so I feel rather certain you are not one of the pastry-makers gathering mint or a chambermaid on your way to air the linens. If you *are* either of those you are shirking your chores most unconscionably, but to me you do not have the face of a true idler."

She laughed despite herself. He was talking nonsense, she knew, amusing himself and her, but also there was more to it. He was showing her how he would think about things if he truly meant to solve a problem. "So, we must assume you are one of the ladies of the castle, and in fact I see that you have brought with you a formidable retinue." He gestured to Teloni and the others, who watched her with wide eyes, as though Pelaya had clambered down into a wolf's den. "One of them addressed you by first name, which suggests a familiarity a lady might show to one of her maids or other friends, but since there is a sameness to your features— yours are a bit finer, more delicate, but I hope you will keep that as our secret—I would guess that the two of you are related. Sisters?"

She looked at him sternly. She was not going to be so easily tricked into helping him.

"Well, then I will declare it so for the sake of my argument. Sisters. Now, I know well that my captor, the lord protector, has no declared offspring. Some might say he was the better for that— they can be difficult creatures, children—but I am not one of them. However much I pity his childlessness, though, I cannot make him your father, no matter how I puzzle the facts, so I must look elsewhere. Of his chief ministers, some are too dark or too pale of skin, some too old, and some too much inclined otherwise to be the fathers of handsome young women like your sister and yourself, so I must narrow my guesses to those whom I know to have children. I have been here more than half a year, so I have learned a little." He smiled. "In fact, I see now that your compan- ions are waving for you in earnest, and I must cut to the bone of the matter before they drag you away. My best guess is that your father is this castle's steward, Count Perivos Akuanis, and that you are his younger daughter, while the dark-haired girl there is his older daughter, Teloni."

She glared at him. "You knew it all along."

"No, I must sincerely protest that I did not, although it has become clear to me as we talked. I think I may have seen you once with your father, but I have only now remembered."

"I'm not certain I believe you."

"I would not lie to a young woman named after the sea. The sea god is my family's patron, and the sea itself has become very precious to me these days. From one corner of my room in the tower, if I bend down just so, I can see it at the edge of a window. Of such things are hearts made strong enough to last." He tipped his head, almost a bow. "And, the truth is, you remind me of my own daughter, who also has a weakness for old dogs and useless strays, although I think you are a few years younger." Now his face became a little strange, as though a sudden pain had bitten at him but he was determined not to show it. "But children change so quickly—here and then gone. Everything changes." For a moment whatever pained him seemed to take his breath away. It was a long time before he spoke again. "And how many years have you, Lady Pelaya?"

"I am twelve. I will be married next year or the year after, they say, after my sister Teloni is married."

"I wish you much happiness, now and later. Your friends look as though they are about to call for the lord protector to come rescue you. Perhaps you should go."

She began to turn, then stopped. "When I said you were King Olin of Southmarch, why did you say I was only half right? Isn't that who you are? Everyone knows about you."

"I am Olin of Southmarch, but no man is king when he is another man's prisoner." Even the sad, tired smile did not make an appearance this time. "Go on, young Pelaya of the Ocean. The others are waiting. The grace of Zoria on you—it has been a pleasure to speak with you."

Leaving the courtyard garden, the other girls surrounded Pelaya as though she were a deserter being dragged back to justice. She stole one look back but the man was staring at nothing again—watching clouds, perhaps, or the endless procession of waves in the strait: there was little else he could see from the high-walled garden.

"You should not have spoken to him," Teloni said. "He is a prisoner—a foreigner! Father will be furious."

"Yes." Pelaya felt sad, but also different—strange, as though she had learned something talking to the prisoner, something that had changed her, although she could not imagine what that might be. "Yes, I expect he will."

10

Crooked and his Great-Grandmother

The great family of Twilight was already mighty when the ancestors of our people first came to the land, and the newcomers were drawn to one or the other of the twin tribes, the children of Breeze or the children of Moisture, who were always contesting.

One day Lord Silvergleam of the Breeze clan was out riding, and caught sight of Pale Daughter, the child of Thunder, son of Moisture, as lovely as a white stone. She also saw him, so tall and hopeful, and their hearts found a shared melody that will never be lost until the world ends.

Thus began the Long Defeat.

—from *One Hundred Considerations*
out of the Qar's *Book of Regret*

BARRICK EDDON WOKE UP in the grip of utter terror, feeling as though his heart might crack like an egg. He could smell something burning, but the world was cold and astonishingly dark. For long moments he had no idea of where he was. Out of doors, yes—the rustle and creak of trees in the wind was unmistakable . . .

He was behind the Shadowline, of course.

Barrick felt as though he had just awakened from a long, bizarre dream—a feeling he knew all too well—but the waking was not much more reassuring than the dream. The endless twilight of these lands had actually ended, but only because the sky had turned black—and not just night-dark, but empty of stars, too, as though some angry god had thrown a cloak over all of creation. Had it not been for the last of the coals still glowing in the stone fire circle, the darkness would have been complete. And that terrible, acrid smell . . .

Smoke. Gyir said it was the smoke from some huge fire, filling the sky, killing the light. Barrick's eyes had stung for most of a day, he remembered now, and they had been forced to stop riding because he and Vansen the guard captain had trouble breathing.

Barrick crawled to the fire and poked the embers. Vansen was asleep with his mouth open, wearing his arming-cap against the chill. Why was the man still here? Why hadn't he turned and ridden back to Southmarch as any sane person would have done? Instead, here he lay beside his new friend, that ugly, splotch-feathered raven (which was sleeping too, apparently, its head under its wing). Barrick disliked the raven intensely, although he could not say why.

When he looked at Gyir Barrick's heart sped again, even as his stomach seemed to twist inside him. By all the gods, the fairy was a horror! He dimly remembered a feeling of friendship, of *kinship* even, between himself and this faceless abomination that had led an army of other monsters into the lands of real people, to burn and to kill. How could such madness be? And now he was virtually this creature's prisoner, being led toward the gods only knew what kind of horrible fate!

Barrick looked to the place the horses stood, mostly in shadow, Vansen's slumbering mount and the restless bulk of the Twilight horse which had somehow become Barrick's own, although he did not remember it happening. *I could be in the saddle and riding away in an instant,* he realized. Should he wake Vansen? Did he dare risk the time? Barrick's hand slid across the ground until it closed on the pommel of his falchion. Even better: he could have the long, sharp edge on the Gyir-creature's throat just as quickly.

But even as the fingers of Barrick's good hand closed around the corded hilt, Gyir's eyes flickered open and fixed on him just as if the fairy-man had smelled something of the prince's murderous thoughts. Gyir stared hard and knowingly at him for a moment, his pupils round and black in the dim light, but then he closed his eyes again as if to say, *Do what you will.*

Barrick hesitated. The loathing itself now seemed alien, just another unlikely feeling to grip him. *My blood, my thoughts—they turn and change like the wind!* He had always been moody and had often feared for his sanity, but now he felt a terror that he might lose his very self. *Father said own malady was better once he left the castle. For a while mine seemed the same, but now it is back and stronger than ever.*

Barrick tried to order his thoughts as his father had taught him, and could not help wishing he had spent more time listening and less sulking when the king spoke. He was trapped in a place where errors could kill him. How could he decide what was real and what was not? Only hours before he had thought of the faceless man as an ally, perhaps even a friend. Moments ago he had seemed an utter monster instead. Was Gyir really such a threat, or was he simply a warrior who served a foreign master?

Not master—mistress, Barrick reminded himself. And suddenly, as though everything had been tilting and threatening to tumble because of a single missing support, he saw the warrior-woman again in his mind's eye and his thoughts grew more stable. Gyir the Storm Lantern was not a monster, but not his friend, either. Barrick could not afford to trust so much. The Qar woman, the Lady Yasammez, had held him with her bottomless stare and had told him amazing things, although he could remember very few of them now. What had she said that had sent him so boldly across the Shadowline? Or had it been something else, not ideas but a spell to enslave him? *She told me of great lands I had never seen, the lands of the People, as she called them—of mountains taller than the clouds, and the black sea, and forests older than Time, and . . . and . . .*

But there had been more, and it was the *more* that he knew had been important. *She said she was sending me as a . . . a gift?* A gift? How could he be a gift, unless the Qar ate humans? *She sent me to . . . Saqri,* he remembered, *that was the name.* Someone of importance and power named Saqri, who had been sleeping but would awaken soon into a world that had moved farther into defeat. Whatever *that* might mean. Like any dream, it had begun to fade. Except for the fairy-woman's eyes, her predatory eyes, watchful and knowing, bright as a hunting hawk's, but with ageless depths— what he might have imagined the eyes of a goddess to look like, when he had still believed in such things.

But if I don't believe in the gods and their stories, he asked himself, *then what is all this around me? What has happened to me if I haven't been god-struck like the ones in the old stories, like Iaris and Zakkas and the rest of the oracles? Like Soteros who flew up to the palace of Perin on top of Mount Xandos and saw the gods in their home?*

Barrick realized that he had found, if not answers, a kind of peace with his predicament. Reasoning in the way his father would have had helped him. He looked at Gyir now and saw something fearful but not terrifying, a creature both like and unlike himself. They had spoken with their minds and hearts. He had felt the faceless Qar's angers and joys as he talked about his homeland and about the war with the humans, and had almost felt he understood him—surely that could not all have been lies. Could someone be both a bitter enemy and a friend?

Barrick felt sleep stealing over him again and let his eyes fall shut. Whether they were friends or enemies, as long as the Qar woman's enchantment drove Barrick on he and the Gyir the Storm Lantern must at least be allies. He had to trust in that much or he would go mad for certain.

With a last few flicks of his spur Ferras Vansen finished currying his horse, then bent to strap the spur back on. The one good thing about this cursed, soggy weather was that the beast seemed to pick up few brambles, although its tail was a knotted mess. He paused, eyeing the strange dark steed that had carried Prince Barrick away from the battle. The fairy-horse looked back at him, the eyes a single, milky gleam. The creature seemed unnaturally aware, its calm not that of indifference but of superiority. Vansen sniffed and turned away, shamed to be feeling such resentment toward a dumb brute.

"Gyir says the horse's name is Dragonfly."

Barrick's words made Vansen jump. He had not realized the prince was so close. "He told you that?"

"Of course. Just because you can't hear him doesn't mean he's not speaking."

Ferras Vansen did not doubt that the fairy-man spoke without words—he had felt a bit of it himself—but admitting it seemed the first step on a journey he did not wish to begin. "Dragonfly, then. As you wish."

"He belonged to someone named Four Sunsets—at least that's what Gyir says the name meant." Barrick frowned, trying to get things right. There were moments when, the subject of his conversation aside, he seemed like any ordinary lad of his age. "Four Sunsets was killed in the battle. The battle with . . . our folk." Barrick smiled tightly with relief: he had got it right.

Chilled, Vansen could not help wondering what it was he had been tempted to say instead. *Does he have to struggle to remember he's not one of them?* He shook his head. This was the puzzle the gods had set for him—he could only pray for strength and do his best. "Well, he is a fine enough horse, I suppose, for what he is—which is a fairy-bred monster."

"Faster than anything we'll ever ride again," said Barrick, still boyish. "Gyir says they are raised in great fields called the Meadows of the Moon."

"Don't know how they would know of the moon or anything else in the sky," said Vansen, looking up. "And it's got worse now, the sky's so dark with smoke." Their progress had been slowed to a walk—they led their horses now more often than they rode them. Vansen had hated the eternal twilight but he longed for it now. It seemed, however, that he was fated to realize such things only after it was too late.

Skurn hopped into the road to smash a snail against a stone embedded in the mud. The raven pulled out his meal and swallowed it down, then turned his dark, shiny eye on Vansen. "Shall us ride, then, Master?" Skurn shot an uneasy look at Barrick, who was staring at the raven with his usual disdain. "If us hasn't spoken out of turn, like."

"You seem in good cheer," Vansen said, still not quite accustomed to talking with a bird

"Broke us's fast most lovesomely this morning with a dead frog what had just begun to swell . . ."

Vansen waved his hand to forestall the description. "Yes, but I thought you were afraid of where we were going. Why have you changed?"

Skurn bobbed his head. "Because we go away, now, not toward, Master. This new road leads us away from Northmarch and Jack Chain's lands. 'Twas all us ever wanted."

Vansen felt a little better to hear that. If it had not been for the continual dreary, ashy rain, the lightless sky, and the fact that he knew he'd be spending another day's thankless journey surrounded by madmen and monsters out of dire legend, finishing with a bed on the cold, lumpy ground and a few bitter roots to gnaw, he might have been cheerful, too.

It was almost impossible to choose Skurn's single most annoying trait, but certainly high on the pile was the fact that unless something had terrified the bird into silence, he talked incessantly. Relieved by their new direction, the raven yammered on throughout the day, loudly at first, then more quietly after Vansen threatened to drag him on a rope behind the horse, naming trees and bushes and sharing other obscure bits of woodlore, and going on at great length about the wonderful things to eat that could be found on all sides—an urpsome subject that Vansen throttled shortly after being told how lovely it was to guzzle baby birds whole out of a nest.

"Can you not just stop?" he snarled at last. "Close your beak and just sit silently, for the Trigon's sake, and let me think."

"But us can't sit quiet, Master." Skurn squatted, holding his beak in the air in a way Vansen had learned was meant to suggest he was suffering—either that or he was fouling the saddle, one of his other charming traits. "You see, it is riding on this horse that has us so squirmsome, and when us talks not, us squirms more and the horse takes it ill. You have seen him startle up, have you not?"

Vansen had. Twice today already, Skurn had done something to make the horse balk and almost throw them. Vansen couldn't blame his mount: Skurn had trouble holding on, and when he lost his balance he sank in his talons, and if he happened to be off the saddle and on the horse's neck at the time, no matter.

Skyfather Perin, I beg you to save me, Vansen prayed. *Save me from everything you have given me. I doubt I am strong enough, great lord.* Aloud he said, "Then tell me something more useful than how to catch and eat yon hairy spiders, for I will not be doing that even if starvation has me in its grip."

"Shall us tell tha one story, then? To make time slip more easy, eh?"

"Tell me about the one you called Crooked, or this Jack Chain you are so frightened of. What is he? And the others, Night Men and suchlike."

"Ah, no, Master, no. No talk of Jack, not so close still to his lands, nor of Night Men—too shiversome. But us can tell you a little of the one us called Crooked. Those are mighty stories, and all know them—even my folk, from nestlings to high-bough weavers. Shall us speak on that?"

"I suppose so. But not too loudly, and try to sit still. I don't want to find myself in a ditch with my horse running away into the forest."

"Well, then." Skurn nodded his head, closed his tiny eyes, rocked slowly against the saddle horn.

"Here he came," the raven began in a cracked, crooning voice that seemed half song, *"tumble-dum, tumble-dum, crooked as lightning, but slow as the earth rolling over, all restless in her sleep. He limped, do you see? Though just a child then, he came through the great long war fighting at his father's side, and were struck a great blow near the end of it by the Sky Man, so that ever after, when it healed, one pin he had longer than the other. Was even captured, then, by Stone Man and his brothers, and they took away from him summat which they shouldn't have, but still he would not tell them where his father's secret house was hid.*

Later on, when his father and his mother was both taken away from him, and all his cousins and brothers and sisters were sent away to the sky lands, still he lived on in the world's lands because none of the three great brothers feared him. They mocked him, calling him Crooked, and that was his name always after.

Still, here he came through the world, tumble-dum, tumble-dum, one leg the shorter, and everywhere he went was mocked by those that had won, the brothers and their kin, although they were glad enough to have the things he made, the clever things he made.

So clever he was that when he lost his left hand in the forge fire he made another from ivory, more nimble even than the one he'd been born with, and when he touched pizen with his right hand and it withered away he made himself a new one from bronze, strong as any hand could ever be. Still they mocked him, called him not just Crooked but also No-Man because of what they themselves had taken from him, but, aye, they did covet the things he could make. For Sky Man he made a great iron hammer, heavier and grander than even his war hammer of old, and it could smash a mountain flat or knock a hole in the great gates of Stone Man's house, as it did once when the two brothers quarreled. He also made the great shield of the moon for her what had took his father's place, and for Night her necklace of stars, Water Man's spear what could split a mighty whalefish like a knife splits an apple, and a spear for

Stone Man, too, and many other wonderful things, swords and cups and mirrors what had the Old Strength in them, the might of the earliest days.

But he did not always know the very greatest secrets, and in fact when first he was become the servant of the brothers who had vanquished his people, though he was clever beyond saying, still he had much to learn. And this is how he learned some of it.

So here he came on this day, tumble-dum, tumble-dum, one leg shorter, walking like a ship in a rolling sea, wandering far from the city of the brothers because it plagued him and pained him to have to speak always respectfully to his family's conquerors. As he walked down the road through a narrow, shadowed valley, the which was fenced with high mountains on either side, he came upon a little old woman sitting in the middle of the path, an ancient widow woman such as could be seen in any village of the people, dry and gnarled as a stick. He paused, did Crooked, and then he says to her, "Move, please, old woman. I would pass." But the old woman did not move and did not reply, neither.

"Move," he says again, without so much courtesy this time. "I am strong and angry inside myself like a great storm, but I would rather not do you harm." Still she did not speak, nor even look at him.

"Old woman," he says, and his voice was now loud enough to make the valley rumble, so that stones broke loose from the walls and rolled down to the bottom, breaking trees as a person would break broomstraws, "I tell you for the last time. Move! I wish to pass."

At last she looked up at him and says, "I am old and weary and the day is hot. If you will bring me water to slake my thirst, I will move out of your way, great lord."

Crooked was not pleased, but he wasn't mannerless, and the woman was in truth very, very old, so he went to the stream beside the road and filled his hands and brought it back to her. When she had drunk it down, she shook her head.

"It does not touch my thirst. I must have more."

Crooked took a great boulder and with his hand of bronze he hollowed it into a mighty cup. When he had filled it in the stream he brought it back to her, and it was so heavy, when he set it down it made the ground jump. Still, the old woman lifted it with one hand and drained it, then shook her head. "More," she says. "My mouth is still as dry as the fields of dust before the Stone Man's palace."

Marveling, but angry, too, at how his journey had been halted and bollixed, Crooked went to the stream and tore up its bed, pointing it so that all the water flowed toward the old woman. But she only opened her mouth and swallowed it all down, so that within a short time the stream itself ran dry, and all the trees of the valley went dry and lifeless.

"More," she says. "Are you so useless that you cannot even help an old woman to slake her thirst?"

"I do not know how you do those tricks," he says, and he was so angry that his banished uncle's fire was a-dancing in his eyes, turning them bright as suns, pushing back the very shadows that covered the valley, "but I will not be courteous any more. Already I must carry the load of shame from my family's defeat, must I also be thwarted by an old peasant woman? Get out of my way or I will pick you up and hurl you out of the road."

"I go nowhere until I have finished what I am doing," the crone says.

Crooked sprang forward and grabbed the old woman with his hand of ivory, but as hard as he pulled he could not lift her. Then he grabbed her with his other hand as well, the mighty hand of bronze which its strength was beyond strength, but still he could not move her. He threw both his arms around her and heaved until he thought his heart would burst in his chest but he could not move her one inch.

Down he threw himself in the road beside her and said, "Old woman, you have defeated me where a hundred strong men could not. I give myself into your power, to be killed, enslaved, or ransomed as you see fit."

At this the old woman threw back her head and laughed. "Still you do not know me!" she says. "Still you do not recognize your own great-grandmother!"

He looked at her in amazement. "What does this mean?"

"Just as I said. I am Emptiness, and your father was one of my grandchildren. You could pour all the oceans of the world into me and still not fill me, because Emptiness cannot be filled. You could bring every creature of the world and still not lift me, because Emptiness cannot be moved. Why did you not go around me?"

Crooked got to his knees but bowed low, touching his forehead to the ground in the sign of the Dying Flower. "Honored Grandmother, you sit in the middle of a narrow road. There was no way to go around you and I did not wish to turn back."

"There is always a way to go around, if you only pass through my sovereign lands," she told him. "Come, child, and I will teach you how to travel in the lands of Emptiness, which stand beside everything and are in every place, as close as a thought, as invisible as a prayer."

And so she did. When Crooked was finished he again bowed his head low to his great-grandmother and promised her a mighty gift someday in return, then he went on his way, thinking of his new knowledge, and of revenge on those whom had wronged him."

It was strange, but Vansen was wondering if being lost again behind the Shadowline was not stealing his wits. Even after the raven's harsh voice had fallen silent Vansen could feel words in his head, as though someone was muttering just out of earshot.

"Foolishness," Barrick said after a long pause. "Gyir says the bird's tale is foolishness."

"All true it is, on our nest, us swears it." Skurn sounded more than a little irked.

"Gyir says that it is impossible that the one you call Crooked would not know his great-grandmother, who was the mother of all the Early Ones. It is a foolish raven story, he says, told from between two leaves."

"What does that mean?" asked Vansen.

"From where a raven sits, in a tree," Barrick explained. "We might say it is like groundlings discussing the deeds of princes."

Vansen stared for a moment, wondering if he were being

insulted, too, but Barrick Eddon's look was bland. "The fairy talks in your head, yes?" Vansen asks. "You can hear him as though he spoke to your ears?"

"Yes. Much of the time. When I can understand the ideas. Why?"

"Because a moment ago I thought I heard it. Felt it. I don't know the words, Highness. A tickling, almost, like a fly crawling in my head."

"Let us hope for your sake that you did indeed sense some of Gyir's thoughts, Captain Vansen. Because there are other things behind the Shadowline, as you doubtless already know, that you would not want crawling around in your head, or anywhere else on you."

Will you tell me now who this Jack Chain is that the raven has been prattling about? Barrick asked Gyir. *And the Longskulls? And the things he called Night Men?*

You are better not knowing most of that. The fairy-man's speech was growing more and more like ordinary talk in Barrick's head. It was hard to remember sometimes that they were not speaking aloud. *They are all grim creatures. The Night Men are those my folk call the Dreamless. They live far from here, in their city called Sleep. Be grateful for that.*

I am a prince, Barrick told him, stung. *I was not raised to let other people do my worrying for me.*

He could feel a small burst of resigned frustration from Gyir, something as wordless as a puff of air. *"Jack Chain" is a rendering of his name into the common tongue,* he explained. *Jikuyin he is called among our folk. He is one of the old, old ones—a lesser kin to the gods. The one in the bird's story, Emptiness, she was his mother, or so I was told. In the earliest days there were many like him, so many that for a long time the gods let them do what they would and take pieces of this earth for their own, to rule as they saw fit, as long as they gave the gods their honor and tribute.*

The gods? You mean the Trigon—Erivor and Perin and the rest? They're truly real? Not just stories?

Of course they are real, Gyir told him. *More real than you and I, and that is the problem. Now be quiet for a moment and let me listen to something.*

Barrick couldn't help wondering exactly what "be quiet" was supposed to mean to someone who wasn't talking out loud. Was he supposed to stop thinking, too?

There is nothing to fear, Gyir said at last. *Just the sounds that should be heard at this time, in this place.*

But you're worried, aren't you? It was painful to ask, painful even to consider. He was still uncertain how he felt about the fairy, but in these few short days he had grown used to the idea of Gyir as a reliable guide, someone who truly knew and belonged in this bizarre land.

Anyone who knew what I know and did not worry would be a fool. Gyir's thoughts were solemn. *Not all lands under the Mantle are ruled from Qul-na-Qar, and many who live in them hate the king and queen and the rest of the . . . People.* One word was a meaningless blur of idea-sounds.

What? What people? I don't understand.

Those like myself and like my mistress. Can you understand the idea of High Ones better? I mean the ruling tribes, those who are still close to the look of the earliest days, when your kind and the People were not so different. As if without witting thought, his hand crept up to the tight drumskin of his empty face. *Many of the more changed have grown to hate those who look similar to the mortals—as though we High Ones had not also changed, and far more than any of them could understand! But our changes are not on the outside.* He dropped his hand. *Not usually.*

Barrick shook his head, so beset by not-quite-understandable ideas that he almost felt the need to swat them away like gnats. *Were . . . were you mortals once? Your people?*

We Qar are mortal, unlike the gods, Gyir told him with a touch of dry amusement. *But if you mean were we like your folk, I think a better answer is that your folk—who long ago followed ours into these lands you think of as the whole world—your folk have stayed much as they were in their earliest days walking this world. But we have not. We have changed in many, many ways.*

Changed how? Why?

The why is easy enough, said Gyir. *The gods changed us. By the Tiles, child, do your people really know so little of us?*

Barrick shook his head. *We only know that your people hate us. Or so we were taught.*

You were not taught wrongly.

Gyir's thoughts had a grim, steely feel Barrick had not sensed before. For the first time since they had begun this conversation he was reminded of how different Gyir was—not just his viewpoint, but his entire way of *being*. Now Barrick could feel the fairy-warrior's tension and anger throbbing like muffled drums behind the unspoken but still recognizable words, and he realized that what the faceless creature was thinking of so fiercely was about slaughtering Barrick's own folk and how happily he, Gyir, had put his hand to it.

Very few of my people would not gladly die with their teeth locked in the throat of one of your kind, boy—sunlanders, as we call you since our retreat under the Mantle. Startled by the force of Gyir's thought, Barrick turned to look back at the fairy. He had the uncomfortable feeling that if the Storm Lantern had anything like a proper mouth, he would have grinned hugely. *But do not be frightened, little cousin. You have been singled out by the Lady Yasammez herself. No harm will come to you—at least not from me.*

In the days they had traveled together, Barrick had tried to winkle information about the one called Yasammez, with little success. Much of what Barrick did not know the faceless Qar thought too obvious for explanation, and the rest was full of Qar concepts that did not make words in Barrick's head but only smeary ideas. Yasammez was powerful and old, that was clear, but Barrick could have guessed that just from his own muddled memories, the bits of her that still seemed to drape his mind like spiderwebs. She also seemed to be in the middle of some kind of conflict between the fairy rulers Gyir thought of as king and queen, although even these concepts were far from straightforward—they all seemed to have many names and many titles, and some of them seemed to him oddly contradictory: Barrick had felt Gyir think of the king as recently crowned, but also as ageless, as blind but all-seeing.

It was hard enough just to understand the simple things. *You were going to tell me about Jack Chain. Jikuyin. Is he really a god?*

No, no. He is a child of the gods, though. Not like I am, or you are, or any thinking creature is—a child of great power. His kind were mostly spawned by the congress of the gods and other, older beings. The gods walk the earth no more—that is the first reason we are living the Long Defeat—but a few demigods such as Jikuyin apparently still remain.

Barrick took a deep breath, frustrated again. They had left the overgrown road hours ago because it had been blocked by a fallen tree, and had wandered far afield before they had spotted the road again, now on the far side of a rough, fast-moving stream. They were trying to make their way back to it on something that was closer to a deer track; the rains had stopped, but the trees were wet, and it had occurred to Barrick several times that every branch that smacked him in the face was one that did not hit Gyir, who rode behind him. *I don't understand any of that. I just want to know what this Jack Chain is and why he worries you. Why is the bird still so frightened? Aren't we going away from Northmarch where he lives?*

Yes, but Jikuyin is a Power, and like any of his kind, he rules a broad territory. I think among your people there are bandit lords like that, who respect no master but their own strength, yes?

There used to be. Barrick at first was thinking of the infamous Gray Companies, but then he remembered the adventurer who held their father even now—Ludis Drakava, the so-called Lord Protector of Hierosol. *Yes, we have people like that.*

So. That is Jikuyin. As the bird said, he has made the ruined sunlander city of Northmarch his own, although it was ours before it was yours—it is an old place.

The Qar lived in Northmarch?

So I am told. It was long before my time. There are certain places of power, and people are drawn to them, places like . . . Here another strange concept bounced uselessly in Barrick's head, a shadowy image of light the subtle gold of a falcon's eye gleaming from deep underwater, all muddled with something that was bright, piercing blue and as tangled and twined as a grapevine. *In the old days all the Children of Stone lived there in peace, and their roads ran beneath the ground in all directions—some say as far as the castle where you were born . . .* Gyir's words suddenly changed, insofar as Barrick was able to tell, the voice in his head growing suddenly cautious, withdrawn. *But all that does not matter. The simple tale is this—we are skirting Jikuyin's lair as widely as we can.*

But what about those . . . things that the bird said would be hunting us—Night Men and Longskulls . . . ?

Gyir was dismissive. *I do not fear the Longskulls, not if I am armed. And no Dreamless, I think, would be willing servants to Jikuyin—surely the world has not changed so much. They have their own lands and their own purposes . . .*

The Dreamless—Barrick shivered at the name. *Will we have to cross their lands, too?* he asked.

At some point, all who go to Qul-na-Qar, the great knife of the People, the city of black towers, must cross their lands. For a moment, there was something almost like kindness in Gyir's thoughts—almost, but not quite. *But don't fear, boy. Many survive the journey.* He considered for a moment; when he spoke again, his thoughts were somber. *Of course, none of your kind has yet tried it.*

11
A Little Hard Work

*The three children Oneyna birthed were Zmeos, the Horned
Serpent, his brother Khors Moonlord, and their sister
Zuriyal, who was called Merciless. And for long no one
knew these three existed. But Sveros was a tyrannical ruler,
and his true sons Perin, Erivor, and Kernios made compact
to dethrone him. They fought courageously against him
and threw him down, and then returned him to the
Void of Unbeing.*

—from *The Beginnings of Things*
The Book of the Trigon

THE SKIES OVER HIEROSOL were bright on this mild
winter day, clouds piled high and white as the snowfall
on the distant summit of Mount Sarissa and its neighbors. The thousand sails in the huge Harbor of Nektarios seemed
a reflection of those clouds, as if the bay were a great green
mirror.

The small inspector's boat that had tied up beside the much larger trading vessel now cast free, the rowers ferrying the petty official back to the the harbor master's office in the labyrinth of buildings behind the high eastern harbor wall where all legitimate business of the mighty port was transacted (and a great deal of its shadier workings, too). The trading ship, having duly submitted to the official's inspection—a rather cursory one, noted Daikonas Vo—was now free to move toward its designated harbor slip.

Vo did not think much of the harbor master's defenses against smuggling, and thought it likely that the lackey's visit had been more about the ceremonial exchange of bribes for permits than any actual search for contraband, but he could not help admiring the city's fortifications. Hierosol's eastern peninsula, which contained most of the anchorage, was as formidable as its reputation suggested, the seawalls ten times the height of a man, studded with gunports and bristling with cannon like the quills of a porcupine. On the far side of the Kulloan Strait stood the Finger, a narrow strip of land with its own heavy fortifications. Modern planners, reexamining the walls in this new age of cannonfire, had realized that if a determined attack should overthrow the much more thinly defended areas along the Finger, the heart of Hierosol would then be vulnerable to the citadel's own guns. Thus, they had mounted smaller guns in those forts on the western side of the isthmus facing the city—cannons which could reach the middle of the strait, well within the compass of the eastern guns, but could not themselves reach the eastern wall.

Vo respected that in his cold way, as he respected most types of careful planning. If, as rumors suggested, Autarch Sulepis truly intended a conquest of Hierosol, Xis' ancient rival, the Golden One would have hard work laid out before him.

Still, it would be interesting—a problem well worth the time and trouble, even without the rich reward of plunder, not to mention the choke hold a successful conqueror of Hierosol would gain on vast Lake Strivothos, the still mighty (and wealthy) kingdom of

Syan, and the rest of the interior of Eion. Perhaps, Vo mused, after his own project was successfully concluded he might find himself moving higher in the circles of the autarch's advisers. Yes, it would be a grand entertainment to devote adequate time and attention to cracking open Hierosol's mighty walls like a nut, exposing all the frail, human flesh within to the mercies of the autarch's armies, especially Vo's own comrades, the White Hounds. If such a day came the Hounds would bloody their muzzles well, there was no doubt about that. Vo did not think particularly highly of the cleverness of his fellow Perikalese mercenaries but he had a deep respect for their essential hunger for combat. They were well-named: you could kennel them for years, but when you let them out, they struck like red Nature.

As he thought about it he could almost smell blood in the salty air, and for a moment the seagulls' shrill cries seemed the lamentation of bereaved women. Daikonas Vo felt a thrill of anticipation, like a child being taken to the fair.

His belongings in a seabag slung across his shoulder, Vo gave the trading ship's captain a farewell nod as he stepped onto the gangplank. The captain, flush with the pride of a man about to unload a full cargo hold, returned the gesture with magisterial condescension.

The merchant captain had proved to be a garrulous fool, and for that Vo was grateful. During their conversations on the eight-day crossing from Xis to Hierosol he had told Vo so much about his fellow captain Axamis Dorza that he had saved Vo days of work, without ever once wondering why this low-level servant of the palace (for so Daikonas Vo had presented himself) should be asking all those questions. In ordinary circumstances Vo would have found it hard to resist killing the captain and throwing him overboard—the man talked with his mouth full as he ate, for one thing, and dribbled bits of food onto his beard and clothes, and he had an even more annoying habit of saying, "I swear it, by the red-hot doors of the house of Nushash!" a dozen times or so in every conversation—but Vo was not going to complicate his mission.

The memory of the autarch's cousin spewing blood and writhing helplessly on the floor was very much with him.

Daikonas Vo did not know whether he believed in the gods or not. He certainly did not much care whether they existed—if they did, their interest and involvement in human life was so capricious as to be, ultimately, no different in effect than pure chance. What he did believe in was Daikonas Vo: his own subtle pleasures and displeasures made up the whole of his cosmos. He did not want that cosmos to come to an early end. A world without Daikonas Vo at the center of it could not exist.

Very few people looked at him as he made his way along the busy harbor front, and those who did scarcely seemed able to see him, as though he were not fully visible. That was in part because of his outward appearance, which, because of his Perikalese ancestry, was similar to many of the folk he passed. He was also slight in build, or at least appeared that way, not short, but certainly not tall. Mostly, though, eyes slid off him because Daikonas Vo wanted it that way. He had discovered the trick of stillness when he was young, when first his father and then later his mother's other male friends had stormed through the house, drunk and angry, or his mother had played out her own shrieking madness; the trick had been to become so calm, so invisible, that all the rage blew past him like a thunderstorm while he lay sheltered in the secret cove of his own silence.

The passersby might not look at him, but Vo looked at them. He was a spy by nature, curious in a mildly contemptuous way as always about creatures that seemed to him like another species from himself, things that wore their emotions as openly as their clothes, faces that reflected fear and anger and something he had come to recognize as joy, although he could not connect it to his own more abstract pleasures. They were like apes, these ordinary folk, carrying on their private lives in the full sight of anyone with eyes to see, the adults as uncontrolled in their bleatings and grimaces as the children. In this regard the Hierosolines around him now were barely different from the people of Xis, who did at least have the sense to clothe the revealing nakedness of their wives and daughters from foot to crown, although not for the reason Vo would have done so. Here in Hierosol the women seemed to dress any way they chose, some decently modest in loose robes and veils or scarves that covered their heads and part of their faces, but some nearly as shameless as the men, with necks, shoulders, legs, and most especially their faces exposed for all to see. Vo had seen women naked, of course, and many times at that. Like his fellow Perikalese n rcenaries he had visited the brothels outside the palace's Lily Gate many times, although in his case it had been mostly because not to do so would have attracted attention, and Vo hated attention even more than he disliked pain. He had used some of the women as they chose to be used, but after the first time, when the oddness of the experience had some value in itself, it had meant little to him. He understood that copulation was a great motivator of mankind and perhaps even womankind as well, but to him it seemed only another ape trick, different from eating and defecating only because it could not be practiced solitarily, but required company.

Vo paused, his attention returned to the ships moving placidly in the gentle tides of the bay, tied up alongside the quay like so many great cows in a barn. That one, there, with the lean bow like the snout of a hunting animal: that must be the one he sought. The name painted in sweeping Xixian characters was unfamiliar, but anyone could change a name. It was less easy to hide the shape of a ship as swift as Jeddin's.

Daikonas Vo approached the gangway and looked up to the nearly empty deck. It could be that Dorza, her captain, was not here. If that was so, he would ask some questions and Dorza would be found. He felt confident that he could get everything else he needed from Axamis Dorza himself. It was an impossibly long coincidence that the captain should sail out from Xis in the disgraced Jeddin's own ship on the very night of both the Leopard captain's arrest and the disappearance of Vo's quarry. Captain Jeddin, despite torments that had impressed even Vo, had denied any involvement with the girl Qinnitan, but his denial seemed suspicious in itself: why would a man watching his own fingers and toes being torn loose from his body protect a girl he barely knew instead of assenting to anything the inquisitors seemed to want to hear? It certainly did not correspond with Vo's thorough experience of humanity in its final extremes.

He shouldered his bag and walked up the gangplank of the ship that had been the *Morning Star of Kirous,* whistling an old Perikalese work song his father used to sing while beating him.

Since Dorza had thrown her out, it had taken Qinnitan several days and many inquiries to find this woman, the laundry mistress. In the meantime, she had found herself in a situation she had never imagined in all her life, sleeping rough in the alleys of Hierosol, eating only what the mute boy Pigeon could steal. It could have been worse, but Pigeon had proved surprisingly adept at pilfering. From what Qinnitan could grasp of his story, he had not been fed well in the autarch's palace and he and the other young slaves had been forced to supplement their meager fare with thievery.

The citadel's laundry was huge, a vast space that had once perhaps been a trader's warehouse, but which now was filled not with cedar wood and spices but tubs of steaming water, dozens of them—the room, Qinnitan marveled, must exist in a permanent fog. Every tub had two or three women leaning over it, and scores more women and young boys were carrying buckets from the great cauldron set in the floor at the center of the room, which was kept continually bubbling by a fire in the basement. As Qinnitan watched, one of the girls slopped water over the edge of a bucket onto herself and then collapsed to the ground, shrieking. A woman of middle years, impressively thick-limbed but not fat, came over to examine the hurt girl, then gave her a cuff on the head and sent her off with two other washwomen before directing a third to take the bucket which the injured girl had somehow miraculously not dropped. The big woman stood with her hands on her hips and watched the wounded soldier being helped off the battlefield, her expression that of someone who knows that the gods have no other occupation but to fill her life with petty annoyances.

Qinnitan gestured for Pigeon to wait by the doorway. The laundry-mistress watched her approach, scowling at this clear sign that her day was about to be unfairly interrupted again.

"What do you want?" she said in flat, unfriendly Hierosoline.

Qinnitan made a little bow, not entirely for show: up close, the woman was quite amazingly large and her sun-darkened skin made her seem something carved out of wood, a statue or a ship of war or something else worthy of deferential approach. *"You . . . Soryaza are?"* she asked, aware that her Hierosoline was barbarous.

"Yes, I am, and I am a busy woman. What do you want?"

"You . . . from Xis? Speak Xis?"

"For the love of the gods," the woman grumbled, and then switched to Xixian. "Yes, I speak the tongue, although it's been years since I lived in the cursed place. What do you want?"

Qinnitan took a deep breath, one obstacle passed. "I am very sorry to bother you, Mistress Soryaza. I know you are an important person, with all this . . . " She spread her hands to indicate the sea of washing-tubs.

Soryaza wasn't so easily flattered. "Yes?"

"I . . . I have lost my father and my mother." Qinnitan had prepared the story carefully. "When my mother died of the coughing fever last summer, my father decided to bring me and my brother back here to Hierosol. But on the ship he too caught a fever and I nursed him for several months before he died." She cast her eyes down. "I have nowhere to go, and no relatives here or in Xis who will take me and my brother in."

Soryaza raised an eyebrow. "Brother? Are you sure you do not mean a lover? Tell the truth, girl."

Qinnitan pointed to Pigeon. The child stood by the door with his eyes wide, looking as though he might flee at a sudden loud noise. "There. He cannot speak but he is a good boy."

"All right, brother it is. But what in the gods' names could this possibly have to do with me?" Soryaza was already wiping her hands on her voluminous apron, like someone who is finished with something and about to move on to the next task.

This was the risky part. "I . . . I heard you were once a Hive Sister."

Both eyebrows rose. "Did you? And what do you know of such things?"

"I was one myself—an acolyte. But when my mother was dying I left the Hive to help her. They would have let me come back, I'm certain, but my father wanted me here in Hierosol, his home." She let a little of the very real tension and fear mount up from inside her, where she had kept it carefully bottled for so long. Her voice quivered and her eyes filled with tears. "And now my brother and I must sleep in the alleyways by the harbor, and men . . . men try . . ."

Soryaza's brown face softened a little, but only a little. "Who was the high priestess when you were there? Tell me, girl, and quickly."

"Rugan."

"Ah, yes. I remember when she was merely a priestess, but she had a head on her shoulders." She nodded. "Do the priests still come into the Hive every morning to collect the sacred honey?"

Qinnitan stared, surprised by such a strange, illogical question. Had things changed so much since this woman's days as a priestess? Then she realized she was still being tested. "No, Mistress Soryaza," she said carefully. "The priests never come in . . . except for a few Favored who tend the altar of Nushash, that is. No true men do. And the honey only goes to the priests twice a year." The amount sent in the winter ceremony was slight, only enough taken from the jars covered with holy seals to symbolize the light of the magnificent, holy sun that would survive the cold months and return again. Then, in summer, the high priestess herself and her four Carriers always took the wagon filled with jars of sacred honey to the high priest of Nushash during the important ceremony of Queening, when the new hives were begun and the weariest of the old hives were sacrificed to the flames. The high priest took that honey and presented it to the autarch, or so it was told: Qinnitan and the other acolytes never saw any of the ceremonies that took place outside the Hive, even one so important as the delivery of the god's honey.

"And the Oracle?"

"Mudri, Mistress. She spoke to me once." But that was telling more than she needed to. Fortunately, Soryaza didn't seem to notice.

"Ah, Mudri, was it? Hands of Surigali, she was there when I was a girl and she was old then."

"They say she has outlived four autarchs."

"The gods bless her and keep her, then. One autarch was enough for me, and now I hear there's a new one who means even less good than his father."

Qinnitan flinched at this casual blasphemy, so trained was she in the decorous and unthinking autarch-praise of the Seclusion. *Still,* she thought, *I could tell her things about this autarch that would freeze her blood.* She felt a small thrill of power even as the memories brought a rush of fear. She had survived—she, Qinnitan, had escaped. Had any other wife ever left the Seclusion except in a casket?

"Well, then, I believe your story, child," Soryaza said. "I will find work for you. You can sleep with the other girls, those who live here—some stay nights with their families. But you will work, I promise you! Harder than you've ever done. The Hive is a dream of paradise compared to the palace laundries."

"What about my . . . my brother?"

Soryaza regarded the boy sourly. He straightened up in an effort to look useful, even though from such a distance he could have no idea what was being discussed. "Is he clean? Does he have decent habits—or has he been allowed to run wild like most simpleminded children?"

"He's not simpleminded, Mistress, just mute. In truth, he's very clever, and he will work hard."

"Hmmmph. We'll see. I suppose I can find a few things for an able child to turn his hand to."

"You are very kind, Mistress Soryaza. Thank you so much. We won't give you any cause to regret . . ."

"I have regrets enough already," the laundry-mistress said. "More if you don't stop chattering. Go with Yazi—the one with the red arms, there. She's a southerner, too. She'll show you what to do." She turned to leave, then stopped and looked Qinnitan over, a disconcertingly shrewd appraisal. "There's more than you're telling me, of course. I can hear from your way of speaking, though, that the part about the Hive is true. No poor girl gets a place there, and no poor girl ever spoke like you. You'll have to learn to talk proper Hierosoline, though—you can't get away with Xixian here, someone will knock your head in. They don't care much for the autarch in this city."

"I will, Mistress!"

"What's your name?"

Qinnitan's mouth fell open. With all the talk about the Hive, she had forgotten the false name she had chosen, and now it had vanished as though it had never existed. In a stretching instant that seemed hours, her mind flitted wildly from one woman's name to another, her sisters Ashretan and Cheryazi, her friend Duny, even Arimone the autarch's paramount wife, but then lighted on that of a girl who actually had left the Hive, an older acolyte whom Qinnitan had envied and admired.

"Nira!" she said. "Nira. My name is Nira."

"Your name must be 'addled,' girl, if it takes you so long to remember. Go now, and I had better not catch you standing around with your mouth hanging open—everyone works here."

"Thank you again, Mistress. You have done . . ."

But Soryaza had already turned her back on Qinnitan and was on her way across the steaming laundry floor, off to deal with whatever practical joke rude Fate would next set in her path.

🌿

Axamis Dorza, sensing something wrong when no one responded to his greeting, came through the door with surprising delicacy for a big man. The captain seemed to have some idea of the pantomime Vo had prepared for him, but though he was obviously a clearheaded fellow and not to be underestimated, his eyes still grew wide when he saw the blood on the floor. When he in turn observed Dorza's heavily muscled arms, Vo took his blade back a few finger-widths from the boy's throat: he didn't want things happening too quickly. If he had to kill the boy he'd lose much of his leverage; if he had to kill Captain Dorza before he could be made to speak, the entire day's careful work would be wasted.

"What are you doing?" Axamis Dorza said hoarsely. "What do you want?"

"A few words. Some friendly conversation." Vo slowly moved the blade back until its needle-sharp tip touched the boy's convulsing throat. "So let us all move slowly. If you tell me what I need to know I will not harm the boy. Your son?"

"Nikos . . ." Dorza waved weakly. "Let him go. You cannot want anything from him. "

"Ah, but I can and do. I want him beside me while you answer my questions."

The captain's eyes darted away from his captive child, scanning the rooms for other bandits. Daikonas Vo could all but hear the man's thoughts: *Surely so confident a criminal as this one must have confederates.* There were no confederates, of course, which was how Vo liked it, but it also forced caution. Dorza was a head taller than him; if Vo hurt the boy the captain would be on him like a mad bear.

Vo wanted to head off the next problem too—anything to keep the man calm as long as possible. Any moment now he would notice the body crumpled on the floor just behind the door. Better simply to tell him.

"I have bad news for you, Captain Dorza. Your wife is dead. She caught me by surprise. I did not know she was in the house. She was a brave one, it must be said. She tried to kill me with that club—a belaying pin, I think you sailors call it? So I had to kill her. I am sorry. I did not wish to do it but it is done, and . . . ah, ah, careful . . . if you let anger get the best of you the boy will die, too."

"Tedora . . . !" Dorza looked around frantically, at last saw the blood-soaked shape behind the door. "You . . . you demon!" he shouted at Vo. "Nushash burn you, I'll send you to hell!" His eyes, red with tears, widened again. "The other children . . . !"

"Are under the bed. They are safe." Daikonas Vo prodded gently with his long blade at the boy's gorge, eliciting a squeal of fear. "Now speak to me or this one dies, too. You carried a young woman on your ship. Some say she was Guard Captain Jeddin's mistress. Where is she now?"

"I'll break you . . . !"

"Where is she?" He pulled the boy's chin back until it seemed the skin of his throat, downy with his first beard, might part without even the touch of the blade.

"I don't know, curse you! She stayed here with us but I threw her out when I found out what she was!"

"Liar." He pinked the boy just enough to make a drop of blood grow, wobble, then slide down into the neck of his shirt.

"It's true! She came to me with a note from Jeddin, saying to bring her here to Hierosol where he would meet us. I did not know she was the autarch's wife!"

"And you didn't know Jeddin was a traitor? You are surprisingly ignorant for a veteran captain."

"I didn't know anything until we arrived here. She hid it from me. She came with orders to leave that evening—the very evening when . . . when Jeddin was arrested."

"I do not think I like your answer. I think I will take one of the boy's eyes out and then we will try again."

"By the gods, I swear I have told you all I know! It was only a few days ago that I threw her out—she is doubtless still in the city! You can find her!"

"Did she know anyone here?"

"I don't think so. That was why she stayed with me—she and the child had nowhere else."

"A child? She had a child?"

"Not hers, he was too old. A little mute boy—her servant, I think." The captain ran his thick fingers through his beard. Though it was evening, and cool, his face was running with sweat. "And that is all I know. Here, even if you kill my son I can tell you nothing more, I swear on the blood of Nushash! On the autarch's head!"

"Swearing by the ruler you betrayed? Not a good choice of oaths, I think." Daikonas Vo experimentally lifted his blade until it hovered just a fingernail's breadth from the boy's eye, but the captain only wept. It seemed he truly had nothing more to say.

"Very well . . ." Vo began, then, with a fluidity learned only through long practice, snapped the knife across the room into Axamis Dorza's throat. *A good trick,* Vo thought, *but bad when you miss.* The man's hands flew to his neck, eyes wide with surprise. Gurgling, he sank to his knees.

"It had to be," Vo said. "Be glad I give you a quick death, Captain. You would not have liked to find yourself in the hands of the autarch's special craftsmen."

Shrieking like a much younger child, the boy suddenly began to thrash in Daikonas Vo's arms, trying to break away. Vo cursed his own inattentiveness—he had let his grip loosen when he threw the knife—but quickly managed to get the boy's arm twisted behind his back again. He turned him then, put a boot in his backside, and shoved the youth's head so hard into the table that the whole mass of oak tipped and turned. The boy was stunned but not dead. He lay bloody-headed in the broken crockery, weeping.

An instant later Vo was himself upended and knocked to the ground, a huge, red-smeared thing atop him like an angry mastiff. Dorza had not bled out as fast as Vo had thought he would, a misjudgment he was regretting already. Something smashed hard against his head, a blow he only partially managed to deflect with his forearm, and then the bloody face was right above his, eyes goggling with final rage and madness. Vo rolled so that he was on his side, then his hand went down his leg and another dagger came out of his boot. A moment later it was beneath the captain's ribs, and the man's bulk was jerking and stiffening even as Vo held him fast—as intimate as lovemaking, but somehow less distasteful. When the movement stopped, Vo rolled the corpse off and stood, wondering how he would get all the blood off his jerkin.

The boy was still on the floor, but he had drawn himself up onto his hands and knees, head wagging like an old dog's, blood drizzling down the side of his face.

"Someday . . ." he said, "someday I'll find you . . . and kill you."

"Ah . . . Nikos, was it?" Vo wiped his dagger on the captain's shirt before returning it to his boot, then tugged the other one loose from the gristle of the dead man's throat. "I doubt it. I don't leave enemies behind me, so there won't *be* a someday, you see." He took a few steps forward. Before the boy could pull away Daikonas Vo had his hair gripped tight, then slashed him beneath the throat like a pig held for slaughter.

Only now, as the boy wriggled in the spreading pool of red, did Vo hear the muffled sobbing of the children under the mattress, doing their best to be quiet but—understandably, given the circumstances—failing. He heaved up the heavy mass of the table and threw it on top of the pallet, then poured lantern oil on the floor and splashed it on the walls. He took a smoldering stick from the oven and tossed it over his shoulder as he went out the door. Flames had already begun to lick up the walls inside the house as he walked, swiftly but without obvious hurry, down the steep hill road.

So there's a child with her, he thought. One of the boy-eunuchs had disappeared from the Seclusion on the same night, but that escape had been linked only to the traitorous Favored Luian, not the girl he sought: Vo, like everyone else, assumed the boy had taken advantage of the confusion to run away, and now he was displeased with himself for making such an obvious but unwarranted assumption.

Well, if the child's with her, it will make them that much easier to find. He could see yellow light gleaming fitfully on the roofs of the houses he was passing, which meant that up the hill the captain's house must be burning well. Too bad about the children. He had nothing against children particularly, but he wanted no one knowing what he had questioned the captain about.

Yes, this might not be too difficult after all, he thought with satisfaction. Hiersol was full of girls and young women, but how many of them were traveling with a mute boy? Tracking down his quarry would be only a matter of time and effort, and Daikonas Vo had never been afraid of a little hard work.

12

Two Yisti Knives

When Zhafaris the Prince of Evening came to his manhood he became lord of all the gods. He took many wives, but highest among them were his nieces Ugeni and Shusayem, and I tell truth when I say they were as alike as two tamarind seeds. Soon both were heavy with the children of Zhafaris, but Ugeni was frightened and hid her children away, so that no one knew they had been born. However, Shusayem, her sister, brought forth her own children, Argal, Efiyal, and Xergal, and called them the heirs of Zhafaris.

—from *The Revelations of Nushash*, Book One

BRIONY SUPPOSED IT WAS POSSIBLE for a person to feel more exhausted than she did at this moment, dirtier, more sodden with sweat, and less ladylike, but she could not quite imagine it.

I wanted to be treated like a boy, didn't I? At the moment she was sitting on the ground sucking air, watching Shaso drink from a jar of watered wine. The old man had recovered some of his old bowstring-taut muscle during the days upon days they had been practicing; the sinews of his forearms writhed like snakes as he lifted the heavy jar. *I didn't want to be forced to wear confining dresses, or to be treated like a fragile blossom. Well, I've got my wish.*

Thank you, Zoria, she prayed with only the smallest tinge of irony. *Every day you teach me something new.*

"Are you ready?" Shaso demanded, wiping his bearded mouth with the back of his hand. After keeping himself shaved and carefully trimmed all Briony's life he had now let his whiskers and hair grow wild, and looked more than ever like some ancient oracle, the kind that had sailed across the sea on rafts to found the gods' temples when Hierosol was little more than a fishing village.

She groaned and sat up. No doubt the old oracles had been just as hard-minded as Shaso. It explained a lot. "Ready, I suppose."

"You have learned much," he said when she was standing again. "But wooden sticks are poor weapons in many ways, and there are tricks that can only be learned with a true blade." He squatted down and unfolded the leather bundle from which he had withdrawn the wooden dowels each day. Inside it lay four more objects, each wrapped in its own piece of oiled leather. "The first day we came here," Shaso said, "I asked the boon of Effir dan-Mozan that I could choose among some of his trade goods. These were the best pieces he had." He flipped open the wrappings, revealing four daggers, one pair larger than the other. The larger had curved crosspieces, the smaller barely any crosspieces at all. "They are Sanian steel, of excellent quality."

Her hand stole toward the knives, but stopped. "Sanian?"

"Sania is a country in the west of Xand. The Yisti metalworkers there are of Funderling stock, and make weapons that all Xandians covet. These four would cost you the price of a pair of warhorses."

"That much?"

"Yisti weapons are said to be charmed." He reached down and

took one of the larger daggers in his big hand, balancing it on his palm. He pointed at the simple, elegant hilt. "Polished tortoise-shell," he said. "Sacred to their god."

"Are they really magic?"

He looked up at her with amusement in his eyes. "No weapon can make a fighter out of a clumsy dolt, but a fine piece of steel will do what its wielder needs it to do. If it saves your life or takes the life from another, that is as powerful a magic as you could hope for, do you not think?"

Briony was a little breathless, and having taciturn Shaso turn poetic on her did not help. She reached out her finger and traced the length of one of the smaller, needle-sharp daggers. "Beautiful."

"And deadly." He picked up two of the knives, one large and one small, then took out their sheaths as well, hard, tanned leather with cords that could be tied around a waist or a leg. He scab-barded the two blades, then used the cords to secure the sheaths to the daggers' hilts. "Do that with yours, too," he said. "That way, we will not cut off any of each other's important parts as we work."

They worked for another hour at least as the sun slid down behind the walls and the courtyard filled with soothing shadows. Briony, who had thought she could not lift her arm one more time, instead found herself revived by the fascination of sparring with actual blades, of the weight and balance of them, the new shapes they made in her hand. She was delighted to find she could block Shaso's own blade with the crosshaft of her larger knife and then disarm him with no more than a flick of the wrist. When she had managed the trick a few times, he showed her how to move in below that sudden flick with the small knife, stabbing underneath her opponent's arm. It was strangely intimate, and as the point of the leather-clad blade bounced against his rib she pulled back, sud-denly queasy. For the first time she truly felt what she was doing, learning how to stab someone to death, to cut skin and pierce eyes, to let out a man's guts while she stared him in the face.

The old man looked at her for a long moment. "Yes, you must

get close to kill with a knife—close enough to kiss, almost. *Umeyana,* the blood-kiss, we call it. It takes courage. If you fail to land a deadly blow your enemy will be able to grab and hold. Most will be bigger than you." He frowned, then sank to his knees and began putting his blades back in their oilcloth wrapping. "That is enough for today. You have done well, Highness."

She tried to hand him the knives she had been using but he shook his head. "They are yours, Princess. From now on, I do not want you apart from them. Examine your clothes and find places you can keep them and then draw them without snagging. Many a soldier has died with his knife or sword-hilt caught in his belt, useless."

"They . . . they're mine?"

He nodded, eyes cold and bright. "The responsibility for one's own safety is no gift," he said. "It is much more pleasant to be a child and let someone else bear the burden. But you do not have that luxury anymore, Briony Eddon. You lost that with your castle."

That stung. For a moment she thought he was being intentionally cruel to her, humbling her further so she would be easier for him to mold. Then she realized that he meant every word he said: Briony, offspring of a royal family, was used to people who gave gifts with the idea of being remembered and needed—to make themselves indispensable. Shaso was giving her the only kind of gift he trusted, one that would make her better able to survive without Shaso's own help. He wanted to be unnecessary.

"Thank you," she said.

"Go now and get something to eat." Suddenly he would not meet her eye. "It has been a long day's exercise."

Strange, stubborn, sour old man! The only way he knows how to show love is by teaching me how to kill people.

The thought arrested her, and she stopped to watch the Tuani walk away. *It is love,* she thought. *It must be. And after all we did to him.*

She sat in the growing twilight for some time, thinking.

★

"How well do you know Lord Shaso?" she asked Idite. As much as she had been offended at first by not eating with the men of the house, she had come to enjoy these quiet evenings with the *hadar's* female inhabitants. She still could not speak the women's tongue and doubted she ever would, but some of the others beside Idite had proved able to speak Briony's once they had got over their initial shyness.

"Oh, not at all, Briony-*zisaya*." Idite always made the name sound like a child's counting game, one-two-three, one-two-three. "I have never met him before you came to our door twelve nights ago."

"But you speak of him as though you had known him all your life."

"It is true that I have, in some ways." Idite allowed a delicate frown to crease her lips as she considered. One of the young women whispered a translation to the others. "He is as famous as any man who ever lived, except for of course the Great Tuan, his cousin. I mean the old Great Tuan, of course. Where his eldest son is, the new Tuan, no one knows. He escaped before the autarch's armies reached Nyoru, and some say he is hiding in the desert, waiting to return and lift the autarch's cruel hand from our homeland. But he has waited a long time already." She forced a little laugh. "But listen to me, talking and talking and saying nothing, croaking like an ibis. Lord Shaso's name is known to every Tuani, his deeds spoken of around the cooking-fire. People still argue over Shaso's Choice, of course—so much so that the old Tuan made it a crime to discuss it, because people died from the arguments."

Briony shook her head. "Shaso's . . . choice?"

"Yes." Idite turned to the other women and said something in Tuani—Briony could make out Shaso's name. The women all nodded solemnly, some saying, *"sesa, sesa,"* which Briony had come to learn meant "yes, yes."

It was strange to think of Shaso as someone who had his own history—his own legends, even, although she had known that in his day he had been a much-respected warrior. "What choice,

Idite? I mean, surely you can talk of it now without breaking the law. He's only a few rooms away."

Idite laughed. "I was thinking of Tuan. There is no law here in Marrinswalk." In her accented speech it became *"Mah-reens-oo-woke,"* an exotic name that for a moment made it seem an exotic place to Briony, too. "But there is custom, and sometimes that is as strong as law. His choice was to honor the vow he made on the battlefield, to a foreign king, to leave his country and live in exile. Even when the Autarch of Xis attacked us, Shaso was not allowed to return and defend us. Some say that without his strong hand, without the fear he made when he led our armies, the Great Tuan had no chance against Xis."

It took Briony a moment to understand. "You're talking about how he came to serve my father? How he came to Southmarch?"

"Yes, of course—I almost forget." Idite lifted her hands in a gesture of embarrassment. "You are the daughter of Olin,"—*"Aw-leen"* was how she rendered it. "I meant no offense."

"I'm not offended, I'm just . . . tell me. Tell me about it."

"But . . . you must know all, yourself."

"Not what it meant to your people." It was Briony's turn to feel shamed. "I've never thought much about Shaso's life before now. Of course, that's in part because he's so closemouthed. Until a few months ago, I didn't even know he had a daughter."

"Ah, yes, Hanede." Idite shook her head. "Very sad."

"I was told she died because . . . because Dawet ruined her. Made love to her and then deserted her. Is that true?"

Idite looked a little alarmed. Some of the other women, bored or confused by the long stretch of conversation in Briony's tongue, seemed to beg for translation. Idite waved them to silence. "I do not know the facts—I am only a merchant's wife and it is not for me to speak of noble ones like the Dan-Heza and the Dan-Faar. They are above me like stars—like you are yourself, Lady."

"Huh. I'm not above you or anyone. I've been wearing borrowed clothes for nearly a month. At the moment I'm just grateful you've taken me into your house."

"No, it is our honor, Briony-*zisaya*."

"Do . . . do your people hate my father? For what he did to Shaso?"

Idite eyed her, the soft brown eyes full of shrewd intelligence. "I will speak honestly with you, Princess, because I believe you truly wish it. Yes, many of my people hated your father, but as with most things, it has more complicatedness—complication?—than that. Some respected him for forcing his own nobles to spare Shaso's life, but making a servant out of the Dan-Heza still was seen as dishonorable. Giving him land and honors, that was surprising, and many thought your father a very wise man, but then the people were furious that Shaso was not allowed to come back and fight against the old autarch (may he have to cross each of the seven hells twice!). These are things much discussed among our folk even now, and your father is seen as both hero and villain." Idite bowed her head. "I hope I have not offended."

"No. No, not at all." Briony was overwhelmed. She had been painfully reminded again how little she knew about Shaso despite his importance to both her father and herself, and she was just as ignorant about many others who had been her helpers and guardians and advisers. Avin Brone, Chaven, old Nynor the castellan—what did she know about any of them beyond the obvious? How had she dared to think of herself as a ruler for even one moment?

"You seem sad, my lady." Idite waved for one of the younger women to refill their guest's cup with flower-scented tea—Briony had not developed a taste for the Tuani's *gawa* as yet and she doubted she ever would. "I have said too much."

"You've made me think, that's all. Surely that's nothing to apologize for." Briony took a breath. "Sometimes we don't see the shape of things until we're a long way away, do we?"

"If I had learned that at your age," said Idite, "I would have been on the road to deep wisdom instead of becoming the foolish old woman that I am."

Briony ignored Idite's ritualized self-deprecation. "But all the wisdom of the world can't take you back to change a mistake you've already made, can it?"

"There." Idite smiled. "That is another step down the road. Now drink your tea and let us talk of happier things. Fanu and her sister have a song they will sing for you."

Briony woke on her thirteenth day in the house of the Dan-Mozan to find the women's quarters bustling. She had still not developed the habit of rising as early as the others—they seemed to get out of bed before the sun was above the horizon—but even so she was surprised by the degree of activity.

"Ah, she awake!" cried pretty young Fanu, and then added something in the Tuani tongue; Briony thought she recognized Idite's name in the fast slur of sounds.

Briony began sluggishly to pull off her nightdress so she could don her own garments, but the women gathered around her, waving their hands and laughing.

"Don't do!" said Fanu. "Later. For Idite wait."

Briony was grateful that she was at least allowed to wash her face and scrape her teeth clean before Idite arrived. The older woman was beautifully dressed in a robe of spotless white silk with a fringed girdle of deep red.

"They won't let me dress," Briony complained, shamed by Idite's splendid clothes and feeling more than ever that she was too large and too pale for this household.

"That is because we will dress you," Idite explained. "Today is a special day, and special care must be taken, especially for you, Briony-*zisaya*."

"Why? Is someone getting married?"

Idite laughed and repeated her remark. The other young women giggled. Idite had explained to Briony that most of them were the daughters of other well-to-do families, that they were not Effir's wives but closer to the ladies-in-waiting of Briony's own court. Only a few were true servants, and some, like Fanu, were relatives of Idite or her husband. Although Effir dan-Mozan was not a Tuani noble, not in the sense Briony understood it, it was clear that he was an important man and this was an important household, a fine place to send a daughter to learn from a respected woman like Idite.

"No, no one is to be married. Today is Godsday, and just as you go to your temple, so do we."

"But you didn't take me the last time." She remembered well the long morning she had spent on her own in the women's quarters, wishing she had something to read or even some sewing with which to occupy herself, much as she disliked it.

"Nor will we take you this time," Idite said kindly, patting Briony's hand. "You would be welcome, but you are a stranger to the Great Mother and Dan-Mozan my husband says it would be wrong to teach you the rituals, since you are a guest."

"So why do I have to dress in a special way?"

"Because afterward we are going out to the town," said Idite. The women behind her all murmured and smiled. "You have not been outside the walls of the *hadar* since you came. My husband thought you deserved to go outside today with the rest of us."

She was not certain she liked the word "deserved," which made her feel like a child or a prisoner, but she was excited at the thought of seeing something other than the inside of the merchant's house. A cautious thought occurred to her. "And Lord Shaso . . . ? He says it is allowed?"

"He is coming, too."

"But how can I go out? My face is well-known, at least to some . . ."

"Ah, that is why we must begin to work on you now, king's daughter." Idite smiled with mischievous pleasure. "You will see!"

By the time the sun had crept above the walls and morning had truly come, Briony sat alone in the women's quarters waiting for the others to return from their prayers, which were apparently led by a Tuani priest who came to the *hadar* and held forth in the courtyard. She lifted the beautiful little lotus mirror Idite had placed in her hands, wondering at the changes the women had made. Briony's skin, fair and freckled, at least in summertime, had been covered all over in powdery light brown paint from one of Idite's pots, so that she was now only a shade or two paler than Shaso himself. Her eyes had been heavily lined with kohl, her golden hair pulled back so that not a wisp of it showed beneath the tight-fitting white hood. Only her eyes had not changed, the green she had shared with her brother Kendrick as pale as Akaris jade. Idite and the other women had laughed at the contrast, saying that her eyes in that dark skin made her look like a Xixian witch, that she needed only flame-colored hair to complete the picture. This had made her think of redling Barrick, and to her horror she had suddenly found herself weeping, at which point everything had stopped while her eyes and cheeks were dabbed dry and repairs were made. The kohl had to be reapplied completely. As she looked in the mirror now, Briony saw a black spot of it that had dripped from her jaw to her wrist, and she dabbed it away.

Where was he? Where was her brother now?

For a moment a wave of such pure pain washed over her that she could barely breathe and she had to squeeze her eyes tightly shut. Every kindness that the people of this house did her only made her feel more lost, the life she knew farther away. She could live without the throne of Southmarch, even without Southmarch itself, strange and lonely as that was to contemplate, but if she could not ever see her father or her brother again she felt sure she would die.

Barrick, where are you? Where have you gone? Are you safe? Do you ever think of me?

Suddenly, prodded by something she could not understand, could barely feel, she opened her eyes. There, hovering in the mirror behind her own sorrowing features like the bottom of a pond seen through reflections on its surface, was her twin's death-pale face, eyes closed. His arms lay across his chest and his wrists were chained.

"Barrick!" she shrieked, but a moment later he was gone; only her own, now-alien face looked back. *I'm going mad,* she thought, staring at the horrified, dark-skinned stranger in the mirror, and again began to weep, this time with no thought for the painstaking work of Idite and the other women.

As they wound their way through the narrow streets of Landers Port, Briony, a little recovered but still shaken, was surprised by how nice it was merely to be in the chill open air. Still, despite her mummer's paint and head-to-toe garb, she felt almost naked being out among strangers, and every time she noticed someone looking at her she had to fight an urge to turn and hurry back to the shelter of the merchant's house. For the first time she really felt what Shaso had said so many times: if the wrong person saw her, it could mean her death. She kept her head down as much as she could, but after so long inside it was hard not to look around a little.

Many other people were out walking, most of them heading in the same direction as Briony's party, and the numbers grew as their small procession wound down toward the seafront. Most seemed to be Xandians, dressed in similar fashion to the merchant's family, the women in long robes, hoods, and veils, the men's pale garb made festive by long vests in bright colors, sparkling with gold thread. Effir dan-Mozan was at the front of their own little company, nodding gravely to other robed men, and even to a few workaday Marrinswalk folk who called greetings to him. His nephew Talibo walked behind him but in front of the women, head held high like a shepherd with a flock of prize sheep. Even Shaso had come, although he hid his features under high neck-scarf and a four-cornered Tuani hat pulled low over his eyes.

The women, with Briony at their center to keep her as far as possible from curious stares, her disguise notwithstanding, followed in a whispering, laughing crowd. This, as far as Briony could tell, was the one day they were always allowed out of the house, and despite the presence of the important men of the household, they seemed as confident and cheerful as they did in the privacy of the women's quarters.

Landers Port seemed bigger than Briony remembered—not that she had found much chance to examine it when she'd arrived after dark, exhausted and hungry and dripping wet. It was set on a hillside by a wide, shallow bay. A walled manor house and a gray stone temple watched over it all from the hill's crest. Shaso had told her that the manor belonged to a baron named Iomer, whom she had apparently met but did not remember, a stout landholder with more interest in his fruit trees and pigs than in life at Southmarch court, which perhaps explained his relative anonymity.

The poor part of town, of which the Dan-Mozan house was one of the few jewels, was located on the south side of the hill near the base, far from the ocean and far from the manor. Thus they did not climb now or descend on this journey so much as they made their way around the bulk of the hill. Since the rich lived high and the poor lived low, as in so many other towns in the March Kingdoms, they passed not from poor neighborhoods to wealthy ones, but from the part of town where the poor had mostly dark skin, or had the Skimmer cast, to places where poverty wore a skin as pale as Briony's own.

Or as pale as mine before they put all this paint on me, at least.

It was interesting and a little disturbing to be stared at for once, not for who she was—something she had grown used to over the years but was never fond of—but because she was traveling in a group of brown-skinned folk. Some people looked only with curiosity, but others, for no reason Briony could tell, stared with unhidden loathing. A few drunken men even leaned out of their doors to shout after them, but seemed to lose interest when they saw the knives on the Tuani men's belts.

Briony found it surprisingly hard to be glared at by people she did not know, although she was clever enough to understand it was the other side of the coin from all those folk who had cheered her and showered blessings on her only because she was part of King Olin's privileged family. But, other side of the coin or not, it was one thing to be loved by strangers, most definitely another to be hated by them.

So this is how it has been for Shaso as long as he's been here. She could make nothing of the thought just now, with so much happening around her, but she folded it like a letter and put it away to be examined later.

Soon, as the narrow road wound between the close-leaning houses, nearing the waterfront, Briony discovered that they were seeing more brown faces again and more wide-eyed, close-mouthed Skimmer folk. The smell of the bay also grew stronger, a slightly spoiled tang that seemed to flavor every breath, every thought. She wondered if she would ever again cross the wide waters of Brenn's Bay to return home openly and safely, whether her family would ever be together again. Seeing Barrick in the mirror that way had frightened her—was it an omen? Were the gods trying to tell her something? But she knew that people sometimes dreamed of things that worried them, and whether the gods had sent her this waking dream or not, it was certain that Barrick and his fate were the things that most worried her.

They reached a row of ramshackle warehouse buildings along a canal that emptied into Brenn's Bay, the bay itself visible only a stone's throw away between buildings, the masts of at least a dozen ships tilting gently just beyond the rooftops.

Effir dan-Mozan led them in through the doorway of one of the larger structures. Once through, Briony saw it was not a warehouse at all: the first room was long and low, but the walls were covered with beautiful tapestries in unfamiliar designs— birds and deer and trees of strange shape. A man even smaller and rounder than Effir stood in the center of the room, his arms spread wide, his bearded face stretched by a broad smile. "*Ziya* Dan-Mozan! You and your family grace my humble place of business!"

"You do me too much honor, Baddara," the merchant replied with a small bow.

"Come, come, I have saved the best room for you." Baddara took Dan-Mozan's hand and led him toward a door at the back of the room, gesticulating broadly and talking rapidly of ships and the price of *gawa*. The rest of the merchant's household followed.

Briony had edged up beside Shaso. "Why is he speaking our language?"

"Because he is not Tuani," the old man growled. "He is from Sania, and they speak a different language there. On the southern continent, Xixian and Mihanni are the tongues everyone shares. Here it is yours."

They were led through a large room filled with tables, many of them occupied by men in both southern and northern dress, several of whom greeted Effir dan-Mozan with obvious respect; just as obvious was his easy acceptance of their deference. Shaso, on the other hand, kept his head down, meeting no one's gaze, and Briony suddenly remembered that she, with her un-Tuani eyes, should most certainly be doing the same. Baddara led them to a private room whose walls were covered by more hangings, hunting scenes and boating scenes on shimmery fabrics done in a style Briony did not recognize. The little man shouted orders to several older bearded men who were clearly meant to serve the guests; then, after another elaborate bow, he hurried out.

Although the room was theirs alone, Briony noticed with some irritation that the Tuani notion of propriety was still present: she and the other women were seated at one end of the table, the men at the other, with an empty seat between the groups on each side. Still, it was a chance to see something other than the inside walls of the *hadar,* and she did her best to enjoy the change. The tapestries at least were beautiful to look at, many of them ornately decorated with thread of what looked like real gold, all of them woven with elaborate attention to color and detail—in fact, the tapestries were so compelling that she did not notice for some time that the room had no windows. The woven pictures themselves seemed to look out onto scenes far more soothing and uplifting than anything she could have seen in this small seaport.

Baddara's servers brought in several courses, pieces of fruit with a creamy sauce for dipping, and bread, cheese, and salted meats. The women and men both drank wine, although Briony suspected from the separate pitchers and the weak character of what was in her cup that the women's was more heavily watered. Watered or not, the combination of wine and unusual freedom cheered her companions immensely, and although they spoke in low voices there seemed to be a greater than usual amount of joking and giggling between the women, especially Fanu and the other young ones.

Meanwhile, as the courses came and went, men both of Xand and Eion wandered in from the rooms outside to engage in what looked like respectful audiences with Effir dan-Mozan, some clearly seafaring folk, others in the fine robes of merchants or bankers. Briony could see that although Shaso spoke to no one and did his best to be inconspicuous, he was listening carefully. She wondered how Dan-Mozan introduced him—as a relative? A stranger? Another merchant? And she wondered even more at what these men were saying. It was infuriating to have to sit here this way, amid this flock of ignored women, while important things about the state of the kingdom were doubtless being discussed.

If Shaso was paying close attention to the merchant's conversations, Dan-Mozan's nephew was not. In fact, Talibo appeared more interested in Briony, watching her with a fixation that unnerved her. At first she did her best to avoid his gaze, looking away whenever she caught him glancing her direction, but after a while the liberty he was taking began to annoy her. He was a child, practically—a handsome, stupid child! What right did he have to stare at her, and even more important, why should *she* feel compelled to look away? It touched her on the memory of Hendon Tolly humiliating her in front of her own court; it made the old injury sting all over again.

The next time she caught Tal looking at her she stared back coolly until at last it was the youth who looked away, his cheeks darkening with what she hoped was embarrassment or even shame.

Insolent boy. For a moment she found herself angry with everyone in the room, Shaso, Dan-Mozan, Idite, the other women, all of them. She was a princess, an Eddon! Why must she hide and skulk like a criminal? Why should she be grateful to people who were only doing their duty? If the Tollys were the active agents of her misfortune, all those who did not rise up against the usurpers and cast them out of Southmarch Castle, even these Tuani merchants, were their passive collaborators. They were all guilty!

Now she was the one feeling her face grow hot, and she stared down at her bowl, trying to compose herself. She should enjoy the meal—Baddara's kitchen was a good one, and many of the dishes were pleasurably unfamiliar—instead of brooding.

She took a deep breath and looked up again, composing herself, and found to her immense irritation that the merchant's nephew was looking at her again, his expression even more unreadable than before.

Gods curse him, anyway, she thought sourly, blocking him from view with her lifted cup. *And curse all men, young or old. And curse the Tollys, of course—curse them a thousand times!*

After the meal and their long walk back through town to the *hadar,* Briony was summoned to talk with Shaso and Effir dan-Mozan. She joined them in the courtyard garden where only a day before she had been trying to stick a real dagger—albeit with its blade wrapped in leather—into Shaso dan-Heza's ribs. She thought of the Yisti knives hidden beneath her bed and felt a moment of guilt: Shaso had told her she should keep them with her. She hoped he would not ask to see them.

But where are you supposed to carry knives while wearing such ridiculous clothes—no belts, billowing sleeves . . . ?

Shaso was standing, examining the quince tree as though he were an orchardman, but Effir dan-Mozan levered his small, round body out of his chair to greet her.

"Thank you for joining us, Princess Briony. We learned many things today and we knew you would want to hear as soon as possible what was said."

"Thank you, Effir." She looked at Shaso, wondering if he had been less eager to share the information than the merchant was suggesting: he had the look of a man who had eaten something sour.

"First off, a company of soldiers from Southmarch have been asking questions in Landers Port. They do not seem to have learned anything useful, however, and they moved on to other towns a day or two ago, so that will be some relief to you, I think."

"Yes. Yes, it is." The day's outing had made her realize how little she liked being out where people could see her, but she also knew she could not hide here in the merchant's house forever.

"Also," Dan-Mozan said, "everyone who has come from the south seems to agree that the autarch is pushing forward his ship-building at a great pace, which does make it seem as though he plans an attack on Hierosol. Most of the other nations in Xand are already pacified, and the strongest of those which resist him are in the mountainous regions to the south. There would be little use of a great navy there."

"But Hierosol . . . that is where my father is prisoner!"

"Of course, Highness." Dan-Mozan bowed as though acknowledging a sad but immutable fact, some ancient tragedy. "Still, I do not think you should be overly worried. Autarch Sulepis, even if he can put three hundred warships in the water, will not be able to overcome Hierosol."

"Why do you say that?" She wanted to believe it. It was horrid to think of being stuck here with Hierosol coming under attack. Foolish and probably fatal as it would be, it was all she could do these days not to steal a few days' worth of food and sneak out of the house, heading southward.

"Because the walls of Hierosol are the strongest defense on either of the two continents. No one has ever conquered them by force, not in almost two thousand years. And the Hierosolines have a mighty fleet of their own."

"But for all that, Hierosol has been conquered several times," growled Shaso, who had been silent until now, staring at the barren tree as though he had never seen anything so fascinating. "By treachery, usually. And Sulepis has made more than a few of his conquests that way—have you forgotten Talleno and Ulos?"

Effir dan-Mozan smiled and waved his hand as though swatting away the smallest of flying insects. "No, and Ludis Drakava has not forgotten either, I promise you. Remember, his followers can have no illusions about what comes in the wake of one of the autarch's triumphs. The Ulosians who turned to Xis did not have that knowledge and they paid dearly for it. Recall that Ludis and his men are interlopers, with no power except that which they hold in the great city itself. Not one of the lord protector's followers will believe he can make himself a better deal with Sulepis."

"Yes, but there are many that Ludis displaced, the old nobility of Hierosol, who might think precisely that."

Again the merchant waved a dismissive hand. "We will bore Princess Briony with this talk. She wants assurances and we give her debate." He turned his sharp gaze onto her. "You have my word, Highness. As the oracles teach us, only a fool says 'Forever,' but I promise you that the autarch will not take Hierosol this year or even next year. There is time enough to get your father back."

Shaso muttered something, but Briony could not make out the words.

"What else did you learn today?" she asked. "Anything about my brother or Southmarch?"

"Nothing we did not already know, at least in general terms. The only thing of interest I heard was that there is a new castellan at Southmarch—a man named Havemore."

Shaso cursed, but Briony did not recognize the name at first. "Hold—is that Brone's factor?" She felt sudden anger boil through her. "If he has appointed his own factor as castellan, then Avin Brone must be prospering under the Tollys." Could the lord constable, one of her father's oldest friends and closest advisers, have been with them all along? But if so, why had he told her and Barrick about the contact between the autarch and Summerfield Court? "It is all too confusing," she said at last.

"Not so confusing, at least in one respect." Shaso looked as though he wanted to swim back to Southmarch and get his large hands around someone's neck. "Tirnan Havemore is well-named. He has always been ambitious. If anyone would profit from the Tollys being in power, he would."

Shaso and Effir had gone in, and Briony had been left alone in the garden to mull over the latest tidings from Southmarch and elsewhere, large and small. She paced slowly, pulling her shawl close around her loose garment. Havemore being made castellan and the

Tollys' liegeman Berkan Hood being made lord constable, those changes were not all that surprising, just evidence of Hendon tightening his fist on power. No one knew much about Anissa, Briony's stepmother, and the new baby, but they had been seen, or at least Anissa and a baby had been seen.

It's not as if Hendon Tolly even needs a real heir, Briony thought bitterly. *The baby might have died that night, for all anyone will ever know. As long as Anissa swears it's true, any baby she claims is hers will be the heir, and the Tollys will protect the heir—which means the Tollys will rule.* It was especially bizarre to think that this child, if it *was* the real one, was her own half brother.

A sudden pang touched her. *Maybe he looks like Father, or like Kendrick or Barrick. For me, that would be reason enough to protect him.* For a moment she did not realize that she had made another promise to herself and the gods, but she had. *If that child is truly my father's, then Zoria, hear me—I will save him from the Tollys, too! He's an Eddon, after all. I won't let him be their mask.*

She was so deep in these thoughts that she had not noticed the man standing across the courtyard from her, watching her in the growing twilight gloom, until he began to move toward her.

"You are thinking," said Talibo, the merchant's nephew. His curly hair was wet, combed close against his head, and he wore a robe so clean and white it seemed to glow in the garden shadows. "What do you think about, lady?"

She tried to suppress her anger. How was he to know she wished to be alone with her thoughts? "Matters of my family."

"Ah, yes. Families are very important. All the wise men say this." He put his hand to his chin in a gesture so transparently meant to look like a wise man's pondering that Briony actually giggled. His eyes widened, then narrowed. "Why do you laugh?"

"Sorry. I thought of something funny, that's all. What brings you to the garden? I will be happy to let you walk in peace—I should go join the other women for the evening meal."

He looked at her for a moment with something like defiance. "You do not want to go. Not truly."

"What?"

"You do not want to go. I know this. I saw you look at me."

She shook her head. He was using words, simple words in her own language, but he was not making any sense to her at all. "What do you mean, Tal?"

"Do not call me that. That is a name for a child. I am Talibo dan-Mozan. You watch me. I see you watch me."

"Watch *you* . . . ?"

"A woman does not look at a man so unless she is interested in him. No woman makes such shameful eyes at a man if she does not want him."

Briony did not know whether to laugh again or to shout at him. He was mad! "You . . . you don't know what you're talking about. You were staring at me. You have been staring at me since I came here."

"You are a handsome woman, for an Eioni." He shrugged. "A girl, really. But still, not bad to the eye."

"How dare you? How dare you talk to me like . . . like I was a serving wench!"

"You are only a woman and you have no husband to protect you. You cannot make eyes at men, you know." He said this with the calm certainty of someone describing the weather. "Other men would take advantage of you." He stepped forward, trying to pull her toward him, first her hands, then—when she slapped his fingers away—moving even closer to put his arms around her.

Zoria, save me! She was so astonished she almost could not fight. He was going to try to kiss her! A small, sane part of her was glad she had left her knives behind, because at this moment she would happily have stabbed him through the heart.

She fought him off, but it was difficult: he was pushing blindly forward, as though determined on something he knew might be painful but needed to be done, and her own knees were weak with surprise and even fear. She was terrified and did not entirely know why. He was a boy, and Shaso and the others were only a few paces away—one shout and they would come to her aid.

She got her arm free and slapped at him, missing his face but striking him hard against the neck. He stopped in surprise, then began to step toward her again but she used one of Shaso's holds to grab his arm and shove him to one side, then she fled across the courtyard back toward the women's quarters, tears of rage and shame making it hard to see.

"You will come to me," he called after her, no more shaken than if someone at the market had rejected his first price. "You know that I am right." A moment later his last words came, now with a hot edge of anger. "You will not make a fool of me!"

13

Messages

Why was it ordered so? Why should the entwining of two hearts' melodies give birth to the destruction of the Firstborn and the People, too? The oldest voices cannot say. When Crooked spoke of it he called it "The Narrowing of the Way," and likened it to the point of a blade, which cuts where it is sharpest and which cannot shed blood without dividing Might Be from Is.

—from *One Hundred Considerations*
out of the Qar's *Book of Regret*

CHAVEN SEEMED A LITTLE BETTER with the cup of hot blueroot tea in his bandaged hands, but he was still shaking like a man with fever.

"What is all this about?" Chert demanded. "Your pardon, but you acted like a madman while we were in your house. What is happening?"

"No. No, I cannot tell you. I am ashamed."

"You owe us at least that much," Chert said. "We have taken you in—you, a wanted fugitive. If you are found here by the Tollys, we will all be thrown into the big folk's stronghold. How long do you think before one of our neighbors sees you? It has been nearly impossible, sneaking you in and out by night."

"Chert, leave the man alone," Opal growled at him, although she too looked frightened: the physician and Chert had come through the door with the harried look of two men chased by wolves. "It's not his fault he's fallen on the wrong side of those dreadful people."

"Ah, but it is my fault that I trusted one I should not." Chaven took a shaky sip of tea. "But how could Okros know of it? That was the one thing I never showed him—never showed anyone!"

"*What* is the one thing?" Chert had never seen the physician like this, trembling and weeping like a small child—not even after his escape from death and the horrors of Queen Anissa's chambers.

"Not so loud," Opal said, quietly but fiercely. "You'll wake the boy."

As if we did not have enough troubles already, Chert thought. *Two of the big folk in my house, one a grown man, both of them half mad. Just feeding them will kill us long before the castle guards come for us.* Not to mention the uncomfortable and unfamiliar brightness of having to burn lamps at all hours to make Chaven and his weak, uplander eyes more comfortable. "You owe us some explanation, sir," Chert said stubbornly. "We are your friends—and not the kind who have betrayed you."

"You are right, of course." Chaven took another sip of tea and stared at the floor. "You have risked your lives for me. Oh, I am wretched—wretched!"

Chert let out a hiss of air. He was losing his patience. Just before he got up in frustration and walked out of the main room, Chaven raised one of his wounded hands.

"Peace, friend," he said. "I will try to explain, although I think you will not care for me so much once you have heard my story. Still, it would only be what I deserved . . ."

Chert sat down, shared a glance with Opal. She leaned forward and filled the physician's cup with blueroot tea. "Speak, then." Despite his curiosity, Chert hoped it would not be a long story. He had already been up half the night and was so weary he could barely keep his eyes open.

"I have ... I had ... an ... object. A mirror. You heard Okros talk of captromancy—a clumsy word that means mirror-scrying. It is an art, an art with many depths and strange turnings, and a long, mysterious history."

"Mirror-scrying?" Opal asked. "Do you mean reading fortunes?" She refilled her own teacup and put her elbows on the table, listening carefully.

"More than that—far more." Chaven sighed. "There is a book. You likely have not heard of it, although in certain circles it is famous. *Ximander's Book,* it is called, but those who have seen it say it is merely part of a larger work, something called *The Book of Regret,* which was written by the fairy folk—the Qar, as they call themselves. Ximander was a mantis, a priest of Kupilas the Healer in the old days of the Hierosoline Empire, and he is said to have received the writings from a homeless wanderer who died in the temple."

Chert shifted impatiently. This might be the kind of thing that fascinated Chaven, but he was having trouble making sense of it. "Yes? And this book taught you mirror-scrying?"

"I have never seen it—it has been lost for years. But my master, Kaspar Dyelos, had either seen it or a copy of it when he was young—he would never tell me—and much of what he taught me came from those infamous pages. *Ximander's Book* tells us that the gods gave us three great gifts—fire, *shouma,* and mirror-wisdom ..."

"*Shouma?* What is that?"

"A drink—some call it the gods' nectar. It breeds visions, but sometimes madness or even death, too. For centuries it was used in special ceremonies in the temples and palaces of Eion, for those who wished to become closer to the gods. It is said that just as wine makes mortals drunk, *shouma* makes the gods themselves drunk. It is so powerful that it is not used anymore, or at least the

priests of our modern day mix only the tiniest bit into their ceremonial wine, and some say that it is not the true, potent *shouma*
anymore, that the knowledge of making that has been lost. In the
old days, many young priests used to die in *shouma* ecstasies at their
first investiture . . ." He trailed off. "Forgive me. I have spent my life
studying these things and I forget that not all are as interested as
me."

"You were going to speak of mirrors," Opal reminded him
firmly. "That was what you said. Mirrors."

"Yes, of course. And despite my seemingly wandering thoughts,
that is the subject closest to my heart just now. The last of the
gods' great gifts—mirror-wisdom. Captromancy.

"I will not task you with listening to much mirror-lore. Much
is what seems like mere folktales, fairy stories to help the initiated
remember complicated rituals—or at least so I believe. But what
cannot be argued is that with proper training and preparation mirrors can be used not for reflection of what is before them, but as
portals—windows, certainly, and some even claim as doors—to
other worlds."

Chert shook his head. "What does that mean—other worlds?
What other worlds?"

"In the old days," the physician said, "men thought that the gods
lived here beside them, on the earth. The peak of Mount Xandos
was said to hold Perin's great fortress, and Kernios was believed to
live in the caverns of the south, although I believe there are other
strains of wisdom that claim he dwelt somewhat closer, eh?" He
gave Chert a significant gaze.

What does he mean? Does he know something of the Mysteries?
Chert looked at Opal, but she was watching the physician with a
speculation Chert found unsettling, as if her mind was awhirl with
dangerous new thoughts. But why would Opal, Funderling
Town's least flighty person, the bedrock on which Chert had
based his whole life, be so interested in this obscure study of
Chaven's?

"In later years," Chaven went on, "when brave or sacreligious
men at last climbed cloud-wreathed Xandos and found no trace of

Perin's stronghold, new ideas arose. A wise man named Phelsas in Hierosol began to talk of the Many Worlds, saying that the worlds of the gods are both connected to and separate from our own."

"What does that mean?" Chert demanded. "Connected but separate? That makes no sense."

"Don't interrupt, old man," said Opal. "He's trying to explain if you'd just listen."

Chaven Makaros looked a little shamefaced at being the cause of such discord. Despite living in the house for several days he had not yet realized that this was Chert and Opal's way of speaking, especially Opal's, a kind of mock harshness that did not disguise her true and much warmer feelings—did not disguise them from Chert, at least, though outsiders might not recognize them.

"Have I spoken too much?" the physician asked. "It *is* late . . ."

"No, no." Chert waved for him to continue. "Opal is just reminding me that I'm a dunderhead. Continue—I am fascinated. It is certainly the first time any of these subjects have been discussed inside these walls."

"I know it is hard to understand," said Chaven. "I spent years with my master studying this and still do not altogether grasp it, and it is only one possible way of looking at the cosmos. The School of Phelsas says that the mistake is in thinking of our world or the world of the gods as solid things—as great masses of earth and stone. In truth, the Phelsaians suggest, the worlds—and there are more than two, they claim, far more—are closer to water."

"But that makes no sense . . . !" Chert began, then Opal caught his eye. "Apologies. Please continue."

"That does not mean the world is made of water," Chaven explained. "Let me explain. Just off the coast of my homeland Ulos in the south there is a cold current that moves through the water—cold enough to be felt with the hand, and even of a slightly different color than the rest of the Hesperian Ocean. This cold current sweeps down from the forbidden lands north of Settland, rushes south past Perikal and the Ulosian coast, then curves back out to sea again, finally disappearing in the waters off the western coast of distant Xand. Does that water travel through a clay pipe, like a Hierosoline water-channel bringing water hundreds of miles to the city? No. It passes through other water—it *is* water itself—but it retains its characteristic chill and color.

"This, says the School of Phelsas, is the nature of the worlds, our world, the world of the gods, and others. They touch, they flow through each other, but they retain that which makes them what they are. They inhabit almost the same place, but they are not the same thing, and most of the time there is no crossing over from one to another. Most of the time, one cannot even perceive the other."

Chert shook his head. "Strange. But where do mirrors fit into this?"

For once in the conversation, Opal did not seem to find him a waste of breath. "Yes, please, Doctor. What about the mirrors?"

Their guest shrugged in discomfort. Even after several days, it was still strange to see him here in their front room. Chert knew that Chaven was not particularly large for one of the big folk, but in this setting he loomed like a mountain. "You do not need to call me 'Doctor,' Mistress Blue Quartz."

"Opal! Call me Opal."

"Well. Chaven, then." He smiled a little. "Very well. *Ximander's Book* tells that mirror-lore is the third great gift because it allows men to glimpse these other worlds that travel as close to us as our own shadows. Just as an ordinary mirror bounces back the vision that is before it, so too can a special mirror be constructed and employed that will send back visions of . . . other places." He paused for a moment, as if considering what he was about to say very carefully. In the silence, Opal spoke up.

"It has to be a . . . special mirror?"

"In most cases and for most mirror-scrying, yes." Chaven looked at her in surprise. "You have heard something of this?"

"No, no." Opal shook her head. "Please go on. No, wait. Let me quickly look in on the boy." She got up and left the room, leaving Chert and Chaven to sip their tea. The blueroot had helped a little:

Chert no longer felt as though he might fall onto his face at any moment.

Opal returned and Chaven took a breath. "As I said, I will not bore you with too much mirror-lore, which is complicated and full of disputations—just learning and understanding some of the disagreements between the Phelsaians and the Captrosophist Order in Tessis could take years. And of course the Trigonate church has considered the whole science blasphemous for centuries. In bad times, men have burned for mirrors." As he said this, Chaven faltered a little. "Perhaps now I know why."

"What has your friend—your once-friend, I suppose—done to you, then?" Chert asked. "You said he stole something of yours. Was it a mirror?"

"Ah, you see where I am going," Chaven said almost gratefully. "Yes, it was a very powerful, very old mirror. One that I think was made carefully in ancient days to see, and even talk, between worlds."

"Where did you get it?"

Chaven's look became even stranger, a mixture of shame and a sort of furtive, almost criminal, hunger. "I . . . I don't know. There, I have said it. *I do not know.* I have traveled much, and I suppose I brought it back from one of my journeys, but with all the gods as my witnesses, I cannot say for sure."

"But if it is such a powerful thing . . ." Chert began.

"I know! Do not task me with it. I told you I was ashamed. I do not know how it came to me, but I had it, and I used it. And I . . . reached out and . . . and *touched* something on the other side."

It was the tortured expression on the physician's face as much as his words that made the hairs prickle on the back of Chert's neck. He almost thought he could sense movement in the room, as though the flames of the two lamps danced and flickered in an unfelt wind.

"Touched something . . . ?" asked Opal, and her earlier interest seemed to have vanished into fear and distaste.

"Yes, but what it was . . . what it is . . . I cannot say. It is . . ."

He shook his head and seemed almost ready to weep. "No. There are some things I cannot talk about. It is a thing beautiful and terrifying beyond all description, and it is mine alone—my discovery!" His voice grew harsh and he seemed to pull deeper into himself, as though prepared to strike or flee. "You cannot understand."

"But what use is such a thing to Okros—or to Hendon Tolly, for that matter?" Chert thought they seemed to have tunneled a bit far from the seam of the matter.

"I don't *know*," said Chaven wretchedly. "I don't even know what it is, myself! But I . . . woke it. And it has great power. Every time I touched it I felt things that no man can ever have felt before . . ." He let out a great, gasping sob. "I woke it! And now I have let Okros steal it! And I can never touch it again . . . !"

The sounds he was making began to alarm Chert, but to his relief Opal got up and went to the weeping physician, patting his hand and stroking his shoulder as though he were a child—as though he were not twice her size. "There, now. All will be well. You'll see."

"No, it won't. Not as long . . . not as long . . ." Another spell of sobbing took him and he did not speak for a long time. Chert found the man's weakness excruciatingly difficult to witness.

"Is there anything . . . would you . . . ? Perhaps some more tea?" Opal asked at last.

"No. No, thank you." Chaven tried to smile, but he sagged like a pennant on a windless day. "There is no cure for a shame like mine, not even your excellent tea."

"What shame?" Opal scowled. "You had something stolen from you. That isn't your fault!"

"Ah, but it meaning so much to me—that is my fault, without doubt. It has seized me—rooted itself in me like mistletoe on an oak. No, I could never be such a noble tree as Skyfather Perin's oak." He laughed brokenly. "It does not matter. I told no one. I made it my secret mistress, that mirror and what it contains, and I went to it afire with shame and joy. I spoke to no one because I was afraid I would have to give it up. Now it is too late. It's gone."

"Then it will be good for you," said Chert. "If it is an illness, as you say, then you can be cured now."

"You don't understand!" Chaven turned to him, eyes wide and face pale. "Even if I survive its loss, it is a terrible, powerful thing. You do not think Hendon Tolly and that bastard traitor Okros stole it for no reason, do you? They want its power! And what they will do with it, the gods only know. In fact, it could be only the gods can help us." He dropped his head, folded his bandaged hands on his chest—he was praying, Chert realized. "All-seeing Kupilas, lift me in your hands of bronze and ivory, preserve me from my folly. Holy Trigon, generous brothers, watch over us all . . . !" His voice dropped to a mumble.

"Doctor . . . Chaven," Opal said at last, "do you . . . can you do things . . . with any mirror?"

Chert gaped at her in astonishment—what *was* she talking about?—but Chaven stirred and looked up, hollow-eyed but a little more composed. "I'm sorry, Mistress. What do you mean?"

"Could you help our Flint? Help him to find his wits again?"

"Opal, what is this nonsense?" Chert stood, feeling bone-weary in every part of his body. "Can't you see that the man is ready to drop?"

"It's true I am too tired to be of any use just now," said Chaven, "but it is also true that after abusing your hospitality in many ways, there are things I could . . . explore. But we have no mirror."

"We have mine." Opal revealed the small face-glass she had been holding in her palm. She had received it as a wedding present from Chert's sisters, and now she held it out to Chaven, proud and anxious as a small child. "Could you use it to help our boy?"

He held it briefly, then passed it back. "Any mirror has uses to one who has been trained, Mistress. I will see what can be done in the morning." A strange light seemed to come into his eyes. "It is possible I could learn something of what Okros does as well." He passed a hand over his face. "But now I am so tired . . . !"

"Lie down then," said Opal. "Sleep. In the morning you can help him." She giggled, which alarmed Chert as much as Chaven's blubbering. "You can try, I mean."

The physician had already staggered to his pallet in the corner of the sitting room. He stretched out, face-first, and appeared to tumble into sleep like a man stepping off a cliff. Chert, overwhelmed, could only follow Opal into the darkness of their own bedchamber.

Sister Utta had just finished lighting the last candle, and was whispering the Hours of Refusal prayer when she noticed the girl.

She almost lost the flow of what she was saying, but she had been practicing the rituals of Zoria for most of her life; her tongue kept forming the near-silent words even as she observed the child who stood patiently in the alcove, hooded against the cold.

"Just as you would give your virtue to no man, so I shall hold mine sacred to you."

How long has the child been standing there?

"Just as you would not turn your tongue to false praise, I will speak only words acceptable to you.

"Just as you did walk naked into darkness to return to your father's house, so I will undertake my journey without fear, as long as I am true to you."

Ah. I know her now. It's young Eilis, the duchess Merolanna's maid. She is pale. It will be a long time until the spring sun, if the weather keeps up.

"And just as you returned at last to the bounty of your father's house, so will I, with your help and companionship, find my way to the blessed domain of the gods."

She kissed the palm of her hand and looked up briefly to the high window, its light dulled today by the cloudy weather. The face of her gloriously forgiving mistress looked down on her, reminding her that Zoria's mercy was without end, but Sister Utta still could not help feeling as though she had somehow failed the goddess.

Why has prayer brought me no peace? Is it my fault for bringing an unsettled heart to your shrine, sweet Zoria?

No answer came. Some days of deep sadness or confusion Utta could almost hear the voice of the goddess close as her own heartbeat, but today Perin's daughter seemed far away from her, even the stained glass window without its customary gleam, the birds that surrounded the virgin goddess not flying but only hovering, drab and distressed.

Utta took a breath, turned to the girl in the heavy woolen cloak. "Are you waiting for me?"

The child nodded helplessly, as if she had been caught doing something illicit. After a moment of wide-eyed confusion she reached into her cloak and produced an envelope with the seal of the dowager duchess on it. Utta took it, noting with surprise and sadness that the girl snatched her hand away as soon as the transfer had finished, as though she feared catching an illness.

What is that about? Utta wondered. *Am I the subject of evil rumors again?* She sighed, but kept it from making a sound. "Does she wish an answer now or shall I send one back later?"

"She . . . she wants you to read it, then come back with me."

Utta had to repress another sigh. She had much to do—the shrine needed sweeping, for one thing. The great bowl on the roof of the shrine needed filling so the birds could feed, a journey of many steps, and she also had letters to write. One of the other Zorians, the oldest of the castle's sisterhood, was ill and almost certainly dying and there were relatives who should be told, on the chance—however unlikely—that they would wish to come see her in the final days. Still, it was impossible to refuse the duchess, especially in a castle so unsettled by change, when the Zorian shrine had scarcely any protectors left. Hendon Tolly was openly contemptuous of Utta and the other Zorian sisters, calling them "white ants" and making it clear he thought the shrine took up room in the residence that could be better employed housing some of his kin and hangers-on. No, Utta needed Merolanna's continued goodwill: she was one of the few allies the sisterhood still retained.

Then again, perhaps the duchess was ill herself. Utta felt a clutch of worry. For all they were different, she liked the woman, and there were few enough among the castle folk these days with whom she felt anything in common.

"Of course I will come," Utta told the girl. She opened the letter and saw that it said nothing much more than the maid had suggested, except for a curious coda in the duchess' slightly shaky hand, *"if you have a pair of specktakle glasses, bring them."*

Utta did not, so she waved the girl toward the door of the shrine and followed her, but she could not help wondering what the duchess wanted of her that would require such a thing: Merolanna was an educated woman and could read and write perfectly well.

As she followed the girl Eilis through the nearly empty halls Utta could not help noticing how the interior of the residence seemed to mirror the weather outside. Half the torches were unlit and a dim gray murk seemed to have fallen over the corridors. Even the sounds of voices behind doors were muffled as though by a thick fog. The few people she passed, servants mostly, seemed pale and silent as ghosts.

Is it the fairy folk across the river? It has been a full month now and they have done nothing, but it is hard not to think of them every night. Is it the twins disappearing? Or is there something more—may the White Daughter protect us always—something deeper, that has made this place as cold and lonely as a deserted seashore?

When they reached the duchess' chambers, Eilis left Utta standing in the middle of the front room surrounded by a largely silent group of gentlewomen and servants, most of them sewing, while she went and knocked on the inner chamber door.

"*Sor* Utta is here, Your Grace."

"Ah." Merolanna's voice was faint but firm. Utta felt a little better: if the dowager duchess was ill, she did not sound it. "Send her in. You stay outside with the others, child."

Utta was surprised to find the duchess fully dressed, her hair done and her face powdered, looking in all ways prepared for any state occasion, but seated on the edge of her bed like a despondent child. Merolanna held a piece of paper in her hand, and she waved it distractedly, gesturing toward a chair high and wide enough to hold a woman wearing a voluminous court dress. Utta sat down. Because she wore only her simple robes, the seat stretched away on either side, so that she felt a bit like a single pea rolling in a wide bowl. "How may I help you, Your Grace?"

Merolanna waggled the piece of paper again, this time as if to drive away some annoying insect. "I think I am going mad, Sister. Well, perhaps not mad, but I do not know whether I am upside down or right side up."

"Your Grace?"

"Did you bring your reading spectacles?"

"I do not use such things, ma'am. I get along well enough, although my eyes are not what they were . . ."

"I can scarcely read without mine—Chaven made them for me, beautiful spectacle-lenses in a gold wire frame. But I lost them, curse it, and he's gone." She looked around the bedchamber in mingled outrage and misery, as though Chaven had disappeared on purpose, just to leave her half-blind.

"Do you want me to read something to you?"

"To yourself—but quietly! Come sit next to me. I already muddled it out, even without my spectacles, but I want to see if you read the same words." Merolanna patted the bed.

Utta herself did not wear scents, not because the Sisterhood didn't permit her to, but out of personal preference, and she found Merolanna's sweet, powdery smell a little disconcerting, not to mention almost strong enough to make her sneeze. She composed herself with her hands on her lap and tried not to breathe too deeply.

"This!" Merolanna said, waving the piece of paper again. "I don't know if I'm going mad, as I'm sure I already said. The whole world is topsy-turvy and has been for months! It almost feels like the end of the world."

"Surely the gods will bring us through safely, my lady."

"Perhaps, but they're not doing much to help so far. Asleep, perhaps, or simply gone away." Merolanna laughed, short and sharp. "Do I shock you?"

"No, Duchess. I cannot imagine a person who would never be angry at the gods or full of doubt in days like these. We have all—and especially you—lost too many that we love, and seen too many frightening things."

"Exactly." Merolanna hissed out a breath like someone who has waited a long time to hear such words. "Do I *seem* mad?"

"Not at all, my lady."

"Then perhaps there is some explanation for this." She handed Utta the piece of paper. It was a page of a letter, written in a careful and narrow hand, the letters set close as though the paper itself was precious and none of it was to be wasted.

Utta squinted. "It has no beginning or ending. Is there more?"

"There must be, but this is all I have. That is Olin's handwriting—the king. I believe it must be the letter that came to Kendrick just before the poor boy was murdered."

"And you wish me to read it?"

"In a moment. First you must understand why . . . why I doubt my senses. That page, that one page, simply . . . appeared in my room this morning."

"Do you mean someone left it for you? Put it under your door?"

"No, that is not what I mean. I mean it . . . *appeared*. While I sat in the other room with my ladies and Eilis, talking about the morning's service in the chapel."

"Appeared while you were at the service?"

"No, while I sat in the other room! Gods, woman, I do not think so little of my own wit that I would believe myself mad because someone left me a letter. We came back from the service. It was the new priest, that peevish-looking fellow. As you know, the Tollys drove my dear Timoid away." Her voice was as bitter as gall.

"I had heard he left the castle," Utta said carefully. "I was sorry to hear he was going."

"But all that doesn't matter this moment. As I said, we came back from the service. I came here to take off my chapel clothes. There was no letter. You will think I am a foolish woman who simply did not notice, but I swear on all the gods, there was no letter. I went out into the parlor room and sat with the others and we talked of the service and what we would do this day. The fire burned down and I went to get a shawl, and the letter was lying in the middle of this bed."

"And no one had come in?"

"None of us had even left the sitting room. Not once!"

Utta shook her head. "I do not know what to say. Shall I read it?"

"Please. It is eating away at me, wondering why such a thing was left here."

Utta spread the piece of parchment on her lap and began to read aloud.

" . . . *Men on Raven's Gate are slack. It seems our strong old walls work their spell not only on enemies, but on our own soldiers as well. I do not know if the young captain whose name escapes me inherited this problem from Murroy and has not been able or willing to fix it yet, or whether his governance of the guards has been slack, but this must change. I warn you that we must keep our eyes open for enemies within our city as well as outside, and that means greater vigilance.*

"I implore you also, tell Brone that I said the rocks beneath where the old and new walls meet outside the Tower of Summer must be examined and perhaps some other form of defense should be built there—an overhanging wall, perhaps, and another sentry post. That is the one place where someone might climb up from below and gain direct access to the Inner Keep. I know this must seem like untoward fretting to you, my son, but I fear the long peace is ending soon. I have heard whispers here in Hierosol that worry me, about the autarch and other things, and I was already fearful before I set off on this ill-starred quest.

"While I speak of the Tower of Summer, let me tell you one other thing, and this is meant for your eyes alone. If you read this letter to Briony and Barrick, DO NOT read this part to them.

"If a day should come when you know beyond doubt that I am

dead, there is something you must see. It is in the Summer Tower, in my library desk—a book, bound in plain dark cloth, with nothing written on its cover or binding. It is locked and the key may be found in a hidden cubby hole in the side of the desk, under the carved head of the Eddon wolf. But I beg of you, even order you so much as I am still your father and lord, do not touch it unless a time comes when you know as undeniable truth that I will not come back to you.

"That is all about that, or almost all. If you must share anything in that book with someone else, brave son, spare your brother and sister, and trust no one else but Shaso, who alone among my advisers has nothing to gain from treachery and everything to lose. For him, the fall of me or my heirs will mean exile, poverty, and perhaps even death, so I think he can be taken into your confidence, but only if you can see no way to shoulder the burden alone.

"Enough of this unhappy subject. I trust that I will still come back to you hale and well—Ludis wants bright gold in his hands, or at worst a living bride, but not a dead king. In the hours and days until then, please see that the castle is made safe. There are still too many places where we are vulnerable, and the slack methods of peacetime quickly become lasting regrets. Tell Brone also that the tunnels beneath the castle have not been surveyed in a hundred years, while the Funderlings have been burrowing like moles, and that there are so many holes in so many Southmarch basements that . . ."

"And there it ends," said Utta. "Except that there is a curious addendum written in the side margin, in quite a different fist."

"I could not make that out—read it to me," demanded Merolanna.

The Zorian sister squinted for a moment, trying to make sense of it. It was in an archaic-looking script, much smaller and more clumsily done than the king's writing, twisted so that it would fit into the letter's narrow margins, but the ink seemed quite fresh and new.

"If ye desire to knowe more, we wold speake with you. Say only, YES, and we will heare ye, howsoever."

Utta looked up at the duchess, perplexed. "I have no idea what that means."

"Nor do I. Any of it. But if someone is listening, I will say it. *Yes!*" She almost shouted the word. "There. How is that for madness? I am talking to ghosts. It will not be the first time this cursed year."

Utta ignored that, looking around the room, trying to spot anyplace that someone might hide and spy on them. The chamber had no windows, and since the duchess' part of the residence was on the topmost floor, nothing lay above them but the roof. Could someone be up there, crouching beside the bedchamber's small chimney, listening? But surely they would hear anyone moving about up there, or the guards would spot them.

The two women sat together in silence for long moments, waiting to see if anything would come of the strange request and Merolanna's accession, but at last the duchess raised herself shakily from the bed. "Whatever happens, I cannot in good faith keep you here all day, although it is a comfort to see you, Sister Utta. I do not trust many of those around me, and none of those who have sided with the Tollys, those damnable traitors."

"Please, my lady, not so loudly, even in your own chambers."

"Do you think they would have me tried and executed?" Merolanna laughed with something that sounded almost like pleasure. "Ah, but I'd scorch them first, wouldn't I? I'd speak my mind and burn the skin from their ears! Hiding behind a baby like that, claiming to protect Olin's throne when everyone knows they've been itching to get their hands on it since his poor brother died." She waved her hand in disgust. "Enough. I will walk you to the door. It is time I get out of this room, before I start seeing the phantoms I'm speaking to."

Merolanna bid her good-bye, offering her Eilis to walk back with her, but Utta politely refused. She wanted to walk by herself and think about what had happened.

Before she got two dozen steps down the hall, the door opened up again and Merolanna called after her in a cracked, frightened voice.

"Utta! Utta, come here!"

When she returned to the rooms, she let Merolanna lead her with trembling hand into the bedchamber. There, in the middle of the bed, lay another piece of paper—a torn scrap of parchment this time, but the writing was in the same crabbed, ancient style.

"Come to us to-morrow an howre after suns set, in the top of the Tower of Summer."

14
Hunted

Then Zmeos and his siblings reappeared, and disputed the right of Perin Skylord and his brothers to rule over heaven, but the three brothers met their scorn with peace. For a long time they all lived in uneasy alliance until the eye of Khors fell on Zoria, Perin's virgin daughter. Khors coveted her, and so he stole her from her father's house, taking her to his fortress.

—from *The Beginnings of Things*
The Book of the Trigon

SOMETHING WAS TUGGING at his hair.
Ferras Vansen had been lost in dreams of sunny meadows, but even in that fair place something dark had been lurking in the grass, and now it took him a few heartbeats to shake off the grip of the fearful dream.

"Master!" Skurn again took a clump of Vansen's hair in his beak and yanked. The bird's foul breath was right in his face. "Wake up! Something out there!"

Awake, dreaming, it made no difference—fear and misery were everywhere. Vansen rolled over. The bird hopped off him, flapping awkwardly back to the ground. "What?" he demanded. "What is it?"

"Us can't say," it whispered. "Smells like leather and metal. And noises there be, quiet ones."

A tall, menacing shadow fell over Vansen, blocking the faint glow of the guttering fire. Suddenly very much awake, he snatched at his blade, tangling it and himself in the cloak he used as a blanket, but the shadow did not move.

It was Gyir, his hand held out in a gesture of demand, the eyes in his featureless face staring at Ferras Vansen with an intensity that seemed to glow.

Give. Vansen could almost hear the word, although the faceless creature had not spoken aloud. *Give.*

"He wants his sword," Prince Barrick whispered, sitting up. "Give it to him . . ."

"Give him . . . ?"

"His sword! He knows this place. We do not."

Vansen did not move for a moment, his eyes swiveling between the prince and the looming, red-eyed fairy. At last he rolled over and pulled the scabbarded blade out from under his cloak. The fairy-man closed his fingers around the hilt and pulled it free, leaving Vansen holding the empty sheath as Gyir turned and vanished into the undergrowth around their small hillside encampment, swift and silent as a breeze.

"This is mad . . ." Vansen muttered. "He'll sneak back and kill us both."

"He will not." Barrick took off his boots and wiped his feet with the edge of his tattered, filthy cloak before pulling the boots back on. "He is angry, but not at us."

"What do you mean, angry?"

Skurn fluffed his feathers in worry. Small fragments of sticky eggshell flecked his beak and breast. Whatever had startled the raven seemed to have caught him midmeal. "Them all are mad, the High Ones," the bird said quietly. "Have lived too long in the Black Towers, them, staring into they mirrors and listening to voices of the dead."

"What does that mean? Have *all* of you lost your minds?"

"Gyir is angry because the raven heard the noises before he did," Barrick said calmly. "He blames himself."

"But why should . . . ?" Vansen never finished his question. From farther up the hillside echoed a noise unlike anything he had ever heard, a honking screech like a blast from a trumpet that had been bent into some impossible shape. "Perin's hammer," he gasped, "what is that?"

"Oh, Masters, them are Longskulls or worse!" squawked the raven.

"Whatever the bird scented, Gyir found." Barrick was still donning his boots, as calmly as if preparing for a walk across the Inner Keep back home.

Vansen struggled to his feet. "Shouldn't we . . . help him?" The thought was disturbing, but he had little doubt there were worse things afoot in these lands than Gyir. He had seen one of them take his comrade Collum Dyer, after all.

"Wait." Barrick held up his hand, listening. The youth still had that unthinking air of command—the inseparable heritage of a royal childhood—despite looking as disreputable as the poorest cotsman's urchin, even by the feeble glow of the fire. His hair, wet and festooned with bits of leaves, stuck out as eccentrically as Skurn's patchy feathers, and his clothes could only have looked more ragged and filthy if they had not originally been black. "It's Gyir. He wants us to come to him."

"Why? Is he . . . has he . . ."

"He is unharmed—but he is still angry." Barrick smiled a tight, secretive smile.

"Your Highness, what if he tricks us? I know you do not fear him, but think! He has his weapon back. Now would be the perfect time for him to murder us—it is dark, and he knows this forest much better than we do."

"If he wanted to kill us he could have done it any of the last few nights. He is not just angry—he is frightened, too. He needs us, although I am not quite sure why." Barrick frowned. "I cannot hear him anymore. We must go to him."

Without even a torch to light his way, Barrick started up the hillside in the direction of the scream. Vansen cursed and bent for a stick from the fire, then hurried after him.

The returning rains had washed the pall of smoke from the sky, but not the ever present Mantle, as Gyir called it: even in the middle-night a dull glow still bled through the close-knit branches above them, as though the murky skies had held onto a touch of the daylong twilight, soaking it up like oil so that it would sputter dimly through the night. But it was difficult to see even with the nightglow and the pathetic, makeshift torch: by the time he caught up to the prince, Vansen had scraped himself raw on several branches and had fallen down twice. Barrick turned to help him up the second time.

"Faster," said the prince.

But I was having such a good time dawdling and enjoying the sights, your Highness, Vansen thought sourly.

Skurn caught up with them in a moment—the raven could make faster time upslope than they could, hopping, sometimes flying awkwardly for a few yards at a time. The old bird seemed always to move in an odor of wet earth and a faint putridity: Vansen scented him a moment before he heard him flapping along behind them.

"Head down, Master," Skurn hissed. Vansen narrowly avoided running face-first into a low branch. Thereafter he found the bird's smell easier to bear.

Vansen gasped when Gyir abruptly stepped out of a copse of trees directly in front of them. The fairy-man's sword was dripping black, his jerkin and gloved hands also spattered.

Gyir gestured toward the copse behind him. Vansen went to look, still unable to shake off a fear that the faceless creature might turn on them at any moment. Because he was looking back over his shoulder, trying to locate Gyir in the nighttime dark, he almost stepped on the first body. Hand trembling, he held the brand down close, trying to understand what he was seeing.

The body seemed all *wrong,* somehow—folded into angles normal bones did not allow. It had a long, bony head which stuck out before and behind, and hard, leathery skin which only made the inhuman shape more obvious. The dead creature's arms were long and might have had an extra joint in them—it was hard to tell because of the darkness, but also because Gyir had made such a bloody mess of the thing. Still, it was the head that was most disturbing, especially the long, bony, beaklike snout, and although the dead creature's forehead was nearly human, the deep-set eyes might have belonged to a lizard.

The clothes that it wore were disturbing, too. The fact that this monster wore anything at all, much less a full battle-rig, an oily leather jerkin under chain mail, was enough to make Vansen's stomach squirm and a sour taste rise into the back of his mouth.

A second beak-faced corpse lay a few feet away, the bony head cut almost in half, the clawed, bloody hands still spread as if to ward off the deathblow.

"Perin's hammer, what are these . . . things?" Vansen asked. "Were they after us?"

"Don't know, but Gyir says they're Longskulls," Barrick said. "That's one of the reasons he's so angry. He's still suffering from the wounds the Followers gave him, he says, or he would have had all three of them."

"Longskulls," wheezed Skurn. "And not ordinary roving Longskulls either, this lot. They belong to someone, they do—can tell it by their wearings."

Gyir bent and turned the creature's ugly head with his sword blade so that they could see a mark scorched onto its bony face— a brand, several overlapping, wedge-shaped marks like a scatter of thorns.

"Jikuyin," Barrick said slowly. "I think that is how Gyir would say it."

The raven gave a croak of dismay. "Jack Chain? Them do belong to Jack Chain?" He fluttered awkwardly up onto Vansen's shoulder, almost overbalancing him. "We must run far and fast, Master. Far and fast!"

"The one you talked about?" Vansen looked from the silent Gyir to Barrick. "I thought we had left his territory behind!"

The prince did not answer for a moment. "Gyir says we will have to take turns sleeping and watching from now on," he said at last. "And that we must keep our weapons close."

The road was still overgrown, half-invisible most of the time beneath drifts of strange plants or the damage from roots and floods, but the trees were beginning to thin: ragged segments of gray sky appeared on the horizon, stretched between the trunks of trees like the world's oldest, filthiest linens hung out to dry. Even the rain was lightening to a floating drizzle, but Barrick did not feel a corresponding relief.

What are we running from? he asked Gyir. *Not those bony things?*

Take care. The fairy reached out a pale hand, pointing at a spot just ahead where the way forward dissolved into tumbled stones and shrubbery. Barrick reined up and the weirdling horse named Dragonfly walked around the ruined section before resuming its trot. Gyir leaned forward over the horse's long neck again, looking like the figurehead of a most peculiar ship.

What are we running from? Barrick asked again.

Death. Or worse. One of the Longskulls escaped. A wash of disgust moved underneath the fairy's thought, as obvious as a strong odor.

But you killed two by yourself. Vansen is a soldier, and I can fight, too. Surely we don't have anything to fear from the one that got away?

They do not hunt alone, or even in packs of three, sunlander. Gyir seemed to bite back a rage that, if freed, could not be captured again. *They are cowardly. They like company.*

Hunt?

In Jikuyin's service they are slavers or harvesters. Either way, those three were out hunting. They were scouts for a larger troop—I know it as I know that the White Root is in the sky overhead. This last came to Barrick as no more than the idea of a bright light shining through fog. The more disturbed Gyir became, the less work he put into choosing concepts Barrick could easily understand. *Would you rather be enslaved or eaten? It is not a good choice, is it?*

And who is Jikuyin? You keep talking about him, but I still don't know!

The one the bird calls Jack Chain. He is a power, an old power, and now that Qul-na-Qar has lost so much of its . . .—again an idea Barrick could not understand, something that came to him as "glow" but also "language" and perhaps even "music," an impossible amalgamation. *Clearly Jikuyin is confident of his strength, if he dares to spread his song so far into free territory.*

Barrick understood almost none of this. His arm was hurting him fiercely—the wet weather in these lands had done him no good at all—and the rib he had injured in a fall still pained him too. But it was rare to get Gyir to speak at any length. He was reluctant to give up the chance.

What kind of power is he? Is he another king, like the blind one you the talk about?

No. He is an old power. He is one of the gods' bastards, as I told you. We defeated most of them back in the Years of Blood, but some were too clever or too strong and hid away in deep places or high places. Jikuyin is one of those.

Some kind of god? And he's hunting . . . for us? Barrick suddenly felt as if he might fall out of his saddle—a swooning, light-headedness that for several heartbeats turned the forest around him into a meaningless rush of green. When the rushing ended, Gyir's arm was gripping his belt, holding him upright.

"I'm well, I'm well . . ." Barrick said out loud, then realized Vansen and the raven were staring at him. They were riding almost beside him when he had been certain they were a dozen or more lengths behind, as though he had lost a few moments of time during his spell of dizziness.

Shouldn't we turn back, if this . . . creature, this Jack Chain, is searching for us?

Not searching for us, I think. He would not send mere Longskulls to capture one like me. There was arrogance and pride in the thought, but also regret. *He could not know I have been . . . damaged.*

Damaged?

Now the regret felt more like shame. Barrick did not need to see Gyir's face (which obviously never revealed much anyway) to understand the fairy's grim mood. *The Followers, when they attacked me—I fell. They struck my head several times and then I hit it again on a stone. I am . . . blind.*

The word didn't seem right, somehow, but Barrick still reacted with astonishment. *What do you mean, blind? You can see!*

Only with my eyes.

While Barrick puzzled over this, Ferras Vansen rode up beside them again—as close as Vansen's mortal horse would come, anyway: even after a tennight traveling together, the animal always stayed at the stretched end of his tether when the company made camp, keeping as distant from the fairy-horse as he could. "Your Highness, are you ill?" the soldier asked. "You almost fell out of your saddle . . ."

"There is nothing wrong with me. Let me be." He wanted to talk to Gyir again, not swap braying mortal speech with this . . . peasant.

A peasant who came with you when he didn't have to, an inner voice reminded him, and for once he was hearing himself, not Gyir. *A peasant who came to this wretched place with full knowledge of what it was like.*

Barrick took a breath. "I do not mean to be . . . I am well enough, Captain Vansen." He could not bring himself to apologize. "You and I will talk later."

The soldier nodded and reined up a little, letting Barrick's horse take the lead again. As they fell back, the scruffy black bird crouching on Vansen's saddle watched the prince with disconcertingly shrewd eyes, like Chaven the physician seeing through one of Barrick's tantrums to the real matter beneath. For a moment the prince was painfully lonely again for Southmarch, for familiar faces and familiar things.

You said blind. Why? he asked. *Your eyes work, don't they?*

Gyir would not speak for long moments. *I am the Storm Lantern,* he said finally. *It is given to me to see in darkness, to see what is behind the light, to see things that are far away. I have an eye inside me, inside my head. Never before would three Longskulls have crept so close to me. Never before would I have to learn of it from a mere raven! But now I am blind.*

There was so much misery in this thought, so much fury, that for a moment, as the sensations buffeted him, Barrick felt as though he would vomit. He put one hand on the saddle to steady himself—he did not want Vansen riding up again, prying at him with questions.

Because of the wound to your head?

Yes. Yes, and now I am all but helpless—forced to hide and skulk in terror in my own country, like a forest elemental caught out by Whitefire in the naked sunlands!

Barrick didn't know what Gyir meant, but he knew that sort of rage and despair when he heard it—knew it all too well. *Will you get better?*

I do not know. The wound is healed, at least the flesh is. How can I say?

Barrick took a breath. *It does no good to fight against what the gods have done,* he told Gyir, repeating without realizing it something Briony had often said to him. *Perhaps we should find a place to hide, a place to wait and see if your wound finally heals? Wouldn't that be better than riding across this place you think is so dangerous, with those creatures out hunting?*

You do not understand, Gyir said. *We cannot afford so much time. As it is, we may be too late.*

Too late? For what?

I . . . I carry something. My mistress gave it to me, and I must take it to Qul-na-Qar, and soon. If I arrive too late—or do not arrive at all— many will die.

What are you talking about?

Many of your race and many of mine will die, little sunlander. There was no mistaking the grim certainty of the silent words. *At the very least, every human remaining in that castle of yours, and likely countless more—of both our kinds. I have been tasked to outrun doom.*

"I don't understand." Vansen's legs ached. They had been riding fast without a break for what must have been a few hours. "What are we running from?"

"Longskulls." Skurn was huddled so low against the horse's neck that he looked like little more than a particularly ugly growth. "Like the dead 'uns you saw."

"You said that already. Why are they after us?"

"Not after us'n, after whatever they can find—meat and slaves for Jack Chain."

"You keep talking about him? Who is he?"

"Not a him, not like you mean. An Old One. Does no good talking. Save your breath."

"But where are we? Where are we going?"

"Not our patch, this." The raven closed his eyes again and lowered his head near the horse's rolling shoulders and would not be roused to say any more.

Vansen knew that whatever small control he had maintained over this doomed expedition was long gone. Gyir was armed again, they were on the run from something Vansen could not understand, and now the fairy-warrior was actually leading them. All this in a place that Ferras Vansen had intended never even to approach again in his life—a place which had all but killed him once already. Yet here they were, careening along the ancient, over-grown road, heading . . . where? Deeper into the Twilight Lands, that was all he knew. So even if he could have forced himself to desert the prince, Vansen could no longer turn back—he would never find his way back to the sunlands on his own. *Doomed, doomed,* he mourned. *Why did I ever swear myself to these cursed, lost, mad Eddons?*

Half a day seemed to have gone by when they finally stopped to let the two horses drink. Vansen stood as his mount lapped water from a muddy streamlet that crossed the road. The trees were thinner here, the land ahead hilly but a bit more open, and even in unending twilight it was good at least to be able to see a little distance.

Skurn was drinking too, but farther downstream, since Vansen's horse had startled when he had fluttered down next to it. Some yards away from both of them, Barrick's gray steed drank with the same silent concentration it brought to everything else. Vansen's horse's ribs were still heaving as it caught its breath, but the fairy-horse seemed as fresh as when they had begun.

Is it truly stronger, Vansen wondered, *or is it merely that it is at home here and mine is not?* The same question, he reflected, could be asked about Gyir, who stood impatiently waiting while the horses drank their fill. Barrick had not even bothered to dismount, but sat and stared out at the road ahead, which was little more than a trail between rows of ghostly white trees of a sort Vansen had never seen, a tangle stretching away on either side like the traceries of frost on a window. The track itself looked considerably less magical, a lumpy swath of mud and pale grass, the stones of the old human road long since carried away by water or some more intentional pilferage.

"Highness," Vansen called—but not too loudly: it was easy to imagine those trees listening to the unfamiliar sound of human speech like coldly curious phantoms. "When will we stop and make camp? It must be day again, if we can call it such, and both you and I need food even if the fairy doesn't. In fact, we have used everything in my saddlebags, so before we can eat, we must also find something worth eating."

"Gyir says it is indeed day, but he does not want to stop until we have crossed the . . . the . . . Whisperfall."

"What is that?"

"A river. He says that Longskulls do not like the water. They can't swim."

Vansen laughed despite himself. "Perin's fiery bolts, what a world! Very well, then, we'll camp by the river. But we must eat before then, Highness."

"Us will catch summat for you," offered Skurn.

"No, we will find our own." He'd seen too much already of what Skurn thought edible. He and Barrick had struggled by so far on a few unfamiliar-looking birds and an injured black rabbit, all caught by Vansen with his bare hands—they could survive without the raven's help a little longer. "Unless you can find us something wholesome—eggs, maybe." He looked at the spotty old bird and decided he needed to be more specific. "Bird's eggs."

But can we afford to be particular? Vansen wondered. *I have no bow, so I can't even hope to bring down a squirrel, let alone a deer or something really toothsome.* In fact, now that he thought of it, other than the Followers and Longskulls Gyir had killed, they'd seen no creature bigger than Skurn during this whole venture into the shadowlands. He pointed this out to Barrick, who only shrugged.

"And what does that fairy eat?" Vansen asked suddenly. "We've been traveling together for over a tennight and I've never seen him eat. Even if he doesn't have a mouth, he must take food somehow!"

"When I was young," the prince said, "the nurse told me that fairies drank flower-nectar and ate stardust." His smile was mirthless. "Gyir tells me that what he eats is none of our affair, and that we must get riding again."

They found little more to fill their stomachs that day, only a few handfuls of pale, waxy berries Skurn and Gyir agreed the two sunlanders could probably eat without harm. They were sweeter than Vansen had feared, but still with a strange, smoky flavor unlike anything he had tasted. He also tried, at the raven's suggestion, a piece of fungus that grew on some of the trees they passed, which Skurn said would take the edge off his hunger. It was one of the most disgusting things Vansen had ever eaten in his life; for a veteran of several field campaigns (and a man who had dined more than once at the Badger's Boots Inn) that was saying something. The outside of the fungus was slimy with rain, so that putting it in his mouth was like biting into something plucked from a tidal pool, but the inside was dry, powdery, and as tasteless as dust. Still, he choked it down, and found that although it made him feel a little light-headed it did relieve the pain in his stomach. He pulled off a piece for the prince, who after a silent colloquy with Gyir, ate it with evident distaste.

They rode on with only a few short breaks for rest, cheered only by an occasional break in the cold drizzle. The forest continued to thin, and at times Vansen could see what looked like flatter, more open land in the distance. Once he even spotted the lead-colored gleam of what Gyir confirmed was the Whisperfall, although it was still far, far away.

"It looks like it will be easier going ahead," Vansen said to Skurn.

The bird stirred and flapped its wings. "Them be emptier lands, true, afar of the Whisperfall. Has to watch out, though. Be woodsworms there."

"Woodsworms? What are those?"

"Perilous big, Master. Dragons, some'd call they, but looks like trees—like fallen . . . what? Logs. Aye, lay up, they do, and wait for something to move too close. Then down them come, like a spider as has summat in's web." The raven peered at Vansen's expression. "Heard of they, have you? Heard them was fearful?"

"I've . . . oh, gods, I think I've seen one." Collum's dying scream was in his head, and always would be. *That thing . . . that horrible, sticklike thing . . .* "Is that the only way we can go?"

"Bad, they woodsworms, aye, but them are few. Jack Chain be worse, all say." And with these uncheering words Skurn fluffed his feathers and lowered himself against the saddle horn again.

Another hour or so went by and they did not see the Whisperfall again. Gyir at last and with evident reluctance allowed them to stop and make camp on a hillside overlooking a shallow canyon. Skurn found more berries the sunlanders could eat, and some dark blue flowers whose petals were sharply tangy but edible; when Vansen curled up under his cloak to sleep he had, if not a light heart, at least no heavier a mood than the night before.

He was shaken awake just as he had been the previous night, but this time by Barrick. "Get up!" the prince whispered. "They're on the ridge behind us!"

"Who?" But Vansen already knew. He grabbed his sword and rose to his feet. He patted his horse to keep it quiet while he stared up the wooded slope. He could see torches at the top, the flames strangely red against the half-light, and shadows moving down the hill toward them between the trees. "Where is *our* fairy?" Vansen hissed, half-certain they'd been betrayed, that all the pretense of companionship had been leading to this.

"Here, behind me," Barrick said. "He says ride straight down-hill, then turn downstream when you reach the bottom of the valley. When we come out of the trees we'll be on a slope heading toward the Whisperfall. If you can get to the river, he says ride out into the middle of it—we should be safe there."

Something in the heights above them loosed a honking bellow that sounded more like some giant, raw-throated goose than a dog, let alone a person. Vansen's skin, already prickling with fear, seemed to tighten and bunch all over his body.

"Go!" Barrick hurried toward his own horse. Gyir was already mounted; he helped the prince up. "They're coming—they know we're awake now!"

"Are those hounds they have? Wolves?"

Something thrashed down out of the tree and dropped onto him just as he climbed into the saddle. "Don't forget us, Master!" Skurn croaked, dodging Vansen's panicky swat. "Take us with!"

"Get behind me, then." He had to get low in the saddle and didn't want to be trying to see his way past the raven's south end.

The honking sounded again as Vansen spurred his mount downslope after the prince's horse, which he could already barely see through the trees and the shadowland's eternal evening. Branches slapped at him as though they were angry.

"Them be not hounds, Master," Skurn screeched, huddled close against Vansen's back, talons sunk through the fabric at his belt. "Them be those Sniffers. Need no hounds, them sniff so well." Another honking call split the night, closer now. "Loud, too," the little creature added needlessly.

The squawking and gabbling noises seemed to come from at least a half a dozen different places up the slope; when Vansen turned he could see the curious red torches in at least that many different spots, all moving steadily downward.

All we can do is pray that the horses do not stumble in the dark and break a leg, he thought. "Do they run well, these Longskulls?" he called back to Skurn. "Will they be able to catch us on flat ground?"

"Oh, Master, us thinks not, but them can track we forever. Smell a nest in the top of a tall tree, they can."

"Left!" Barrick shouted from somewhere below.

Vansen had just opened his mouth to ask him what he meant when the huge shadow heaved up directly in front of him—a rock the size of a cabin, a protruding bone of the hill's heavy stone skeleton. He yanked the reins and veered, almost falling headlong as the angle of the slope pitched more steeply downward.

Within moments they had swept out of the thickest woods and onto a patch of grassy slope. Vansen felt a flicker of hope, if only a tiny one: surely on horseback they could beat these honking monsters down to the river, and if Gyir was right about their dislike of water . . .

The beak-faced things were charging down through the trees on all sides, torches bobbing as the hooting clamor grew louder. He thought about drawing his sword, but instead bent even lower over the horse's neck and concentrated instead on staying in the saddle as branches whipped at his face. Barrick and Gyir were just a few yards ahead, but the dark fairy-horse was bigger than his and was beginning to pull away despite carrying two full-sized riders. Vansen dug his heels into his mount's ribs, afraid of falling too far behind in this dark, unfamiliar place.

He crashed out of a small spinney to see a scatter of torches had somehow appeared on the hillside just in front of him. Some of the pursuers had been farther down and had come out of the woods, missing Barrick's horse but cutting off Vansen's. He yanked at his sword hilt, praying for a clean pull. Skyfather Perin or someone heard him: the blade slid out in one swift glide and Vansen was swinging it at the nearest flame before he could even see the creature holding the brand.

His blade clacked against a stony skull. The thing fell away, its torch flying through the air. Another honking shape rose up in front of him but the gray horse, veteran of many battles, barely slowed as it trampled over the thing with a muffled crunch of bones, then Vansen's way was clear again. The line of torchbearers scrambled after him, but he was pulling away and had only lost a little ground to his companions.

He was almost down on flat ground now, following the course of what seemed to be a small stream toward the end of the valley, his mount stepping nimbly around thick, heathery bushes. He could actually see the opening of the valley now, a triangular piece of gray sky, and when he looked back the nearest torches were dozens of paces behind and falling back. He opened his mouth to shout something to Barrick, then suddenly the end of the valley ahead of them began to fill with more torches, as though dozens of flaming stars had fallen to earth.

"Trap!" he screamed. "They've trapped us!" But he knew that Barrick would not slow or turn back, that Gyir would not let him. Their only hope was that this new troop would not be strong enough to turn them back, that they could cut their way through and still escape into the valley and toward the distant river.

A hundred yards of open ground lay between them and the torches, a hundred yards that closed in what felt like a heartbeat. Only at the last moment did Vansen abruptly wonder how well-prepared this trap was—did the gabbling creatures have pikes? Would they have dug themselves in, then waited, as a human troop might have? The torches hurtled closer as if they had been thrown, and the eerie honking noises rose until he thought it would deafen him.

There were no pikes, but the line extended back beyond the torchbearers, three or four defenders deep at least. He saw Barrick's horse crash into the dark mass, heard shrieks and hooting screams and what sounded like a shout of anger from the prince, then Vansen was in the midst of the chaos himself, striking with his sword wherever he saw something move.

Some of the creatures had shields. Vansen could only hack his way a few yards into the crush of Longskulls before being driven back again, hammering away with his sword at the sharp points jabbing at him from all sides. The bony-headed creatures didn't have pikes or even swords as far he could tell in the confusion, but there were many axes and more than a few short stabbing-spears, as well as clubs. One shrieking creature swung something at him that looked like a pickax made of two heavy branches tied together, and although Vansen broke it with his blade, the force of the blow nearly knocked him from his saddle.

Unable to break through, Ferras Vansen yanked hard on the reins and his horse danced back out of the worst of the melee. He tried to spot another way through but it was like some children's game in a dark room, half-seen shapes everywhere. Where was the prince? Was he down, or had he and the fairy broken through?

A moment later Vansen saw Gyir on foot, dragging Barrick backward out of a clot of defenders, the fairy-horse lost or dead. Vansen spurred toward them and was suddenly aware of Skurn squawking in fear, squeezed underneath the arm he was using to hold the reins. The large, clumsy bird would only get in his way and there was no sense in the raven dying, too, if that was what was to happen. Vansen pulled Skurn loose, then threw him into the dark rushes waving near the stream.

The reverberating cry of the creatures grew suddenly louder as the rest of the force, the troop that had been pursuing Vansen and the others down the hill, came dashing out onto open ground, waving their torches, their oddly-jointed movements stranger than any nightmare.

Vansen reined up beside his companions. Barrick looked up with glassy, fatalistic eyes. Gyir, his sword already dripping black with blood, stared past him at the Longskulls on either side.

"We are surrounded!" Vansen pulled on the reins, trying to keep his restive, frightened horse from rearing. The pursuers on the hill-side had slowed from a full-tilt run to something more like a walk, but they still came on. Those at the head of the valley were moving closer now too, so that Vansen and his companions found themselves in the middle of a shrinking circle. Vansen looked for even a tiny opening—he would grab the prince and try to beat his way through—but their captors moved in without any jostling or confusion that might allow such an opening.

They were surrounded by many times their own numbers—perhaps a pentecount or more—but Vansen braced himself for a hopeless charge: better to die that way than be stuck as he stood like an exhausted boar at the end of a grueling hunt.

No. No, they've . . . stopped, he realized. Instead of finishing them off, the Longskulls watched the trio with calm interest, small eyes gleaming beneath heavy browridges, some of them opening and closing their bony, toothless mouths like fish. The two scouts Gyir had killed the night before had been better caparisoned than most of these club-wielding creatures, who wore little more than rags and shreds of chain mail and leather, but there were far more than enough of them to make up for any deficiency in their arms.

Gyir made the first speech-sound Vansen had ever heard from him, a hiss of air like a snake's warning, so loud it could be heard even above the gabble of the surrounding Longskulls. The fairy raised his sword, and Vansen knew beyond doubt that he was about to leap into the nearest mass of them and sell his life dearly, shedding blood and breaking bones, but Vansen knew just as clearly that even a fierce fighter like Gyir would fail and quickly be dragged down by sheer weight of numbers, and that he and Barrick would then follow him into death.

"Gyir, no! Barrick, stop him!" he shouted. "They're not going to kill us."

The fairy-man took a step forward. Vansen leaned down to grab at Gyir. He caught the collar of the fairy-man's cloak and hung on. The Storm Lantern's strength was surprising—Vansen was almost dragged out of the saddle, even with both legs gripping and his hand locked on the horn. "Curse you, give over!" he grunted at the fairy. "They mean to take us alive! *Look* at them!"

Barrick, after a moment of indecision, suddenly leaped forward and grabbed at Gyir's other arm. Trembling, the fairy-warrior turned on the young prince with a look of something like hatred, his eyes the only part of his face that lived, two burning slashes in the ivory mask. After a moment, though, he lowered his blood-stained blade. The Longskulls moved closer, hooting quietly, and began to disarm their new prisoners.

"We are a catch, it seems," Vansen said to the prince. "Better to surrender than die needlessly, Highness. For the living, there is always hope."

"Or torture." Barrick was shoved roughly to the ground even as he spoke. The prince's voice was flat and lifeless. "We will be slaves if we are lucky, or meat for their larders." A moment later Vansen had been shoved down to his knees beside him. The Longskulls fastened heavy chains around his arms and a hard, rough rope around his throat, then the same was done to Barrick and Gyir.

One of the Longskulls stepped forward and honked imperiously as he tugged on the rope around the prince's neck, forcing him to rise. For a moment it looked like Gyir might go mad when his own rope was pulled, but Vansen put out his hand and Gyir stilled, then allowed himself to be led. The Longskulls shared a gabbling hiss that might have been laughter. The creatures smelled of swamp mud and something else, an odor sharp and sour as vinegar.

As they trudged back up the dark hill they had ridden down such a short while before, Ferras Vansen could hear the heart-rending screams of his horse in the valley behind them as the Longskulls began to hack it into pieces.

Slaves or meat, he thought, feeling as hollow as a lightning-burned tree. *My horse is meat, but we are slaves—and still alive. At least for now.*

PART TWO

MUMMERS

15

The Boy in the Mirror

Zhafaris became a tyrant who did not observe the laws, and who cheated his relatives of their due, my children, and they began to whisper against him and his authority. Fiercest of all when it came to talking were the three sons of Shusayem, but in truth they were all afraid of their father.

Then Argal Thunderer said to his brothers, "I hear that in far off Xandos there is a mountain, and on that mountain lives a shepherd named Nushash, who is as strong as any man who ever lived." And it was true, because Nushash and his brother and sister were the true and first children of Zhafaris, although they had lived long in hiding.

—from *The Revelations of Nushash,* Book One

THE WIND HAD BLOWN THE CLOUDS into tatters, and although what remained was enough to keep the sun dodging in and out, for once the skies were dry. All over the castle people were emerging, eager to feel something other than rain on their faces.

A dozen young women came out into the garden of the royal residence. Matt Tinwright, who had been feeling sorry for himself and searching fruitlessly for something that rhymed with "misunderstood," stood and straightened his jerkin. His mood had suddenly improved, and not only because he could show his well-turned legs and new beard to some pretty girls: their arrival, bright and lively as a flock of migrating birds, felt like a harbinger of spring, although winter still had weeks to run. As he watched them scatter across the formal garden, some wiping the benches dry so they could sit, others forming a circle on the central lawn to toss a ball of feather-stuffed cloth, Tinwright could almost believe that things in Southmarch might again become ordinary, despite all evidence to the contrary.

He took off his soft hat and ran his fingers through his hair, wondering whether it would be more enjoyable to insert himself into the proceedings directly or wait a while, watching the play and smiling in a friendly but slightly superior manner. A moment later all thought of the ball game fled his mind.

She walked slowly, like a much older woman, and with the young maid beside her she might have been someone's dowager aunt—especially since on this day, when everyone else had chosen to wear something with a little color in it, she was still dressed head to foot in funeral black. But there was no mistaking that pale, resolute face, the fine, slightly sharp chin, the long fingers twined in prayer beads. At least she had left off her veil today.

What would have been quite sufficient for a casual game of ball and some seemingly accidental contact with the players was no longer enough to pass muster. Tinwright paused and pulled up his stockings, brushed a few crumbs from his chest—he had been eating bread and hard cheese while contemplating the unfairness of life—then made his way down the path looking only at plants, as if too taken by the harsh beauty of the winter garden to notice the arrival of several nubile young women showing more skin around the neck and bosom than they had in months. He wound in and out among the box hedges by a path so circuitous he might have been a foraging ant, crunching along gravel paths unraked since late autumn, until at last he approached the bench where the object of his garden quest sat with her maid.

Elan M'Cory was sewing something stretched on a wooden hoop; her eyes did not lift even when he stopped and stood for long moments, waiting. At last, his courage dying quickly, he coughed a little. "Lady Elan," he said. "I bid you good afternoon."

She finally looked up, but with such an unseeing, uncaring gaze that he found himself wondering against all sense whether he had approached the wrong woman, whether Elan M'Cory might have a blind or idiot sister. Then something like ordinary humanity came into her eyes. An expression that was not quite a smile, but almost, tugged at her lips.

"Ah, the poet. Master . . . Tinwright, was it?"

She remembered him! He could almost hear trumpets, as if the royal heralds had been called out to celebrate his now unmistakable and confirmed existence. "That is right, lady. You honor me."

Her gaze dropped to her sewing. "And are you enjoying the afternoon, Master Tinwright?"

"Much more for your presence, my lady."

Now she looked at him again, amused but still distant. "Ah. Because I am a vision of loveliness in my spring finery? Or perhaps because of the cloud of good cheer that surrounds me like a Xandian perfume?"

He laughed, but not confidently. She had wit. He wasn't certain how he felt about that. He didn't generally get on very well with women of that sort. On those occasions when he received compliments he wanted to be sure he understood them and that they were sincere. Still, there was something about her that pulled at him, just like the flame-loving moth he had so often cited in his poetry. So this was what it felt like! All poets should be forced to feel all the things they wrote about, Tinwright decided. It was a most novel way to understand the figures of poetry. It might change the craft entirely.

"Have I lost you, good sir? You were going to explain the subtle charm that draws you to me."

He started, ashamed at his own foolishness, standing slack-jawed when he had been asked a question, however sardonic. "Because you are beautiful and sad, Lady Elan," he said, uncertain whether he might not be overstepping the boundaries of propriety. He shrugged: too late—it had been said. "I wish there were something I could do to make you less so."

"Less beautiful?" she said, lifting an eyebrow, but there was something underneath the gibing that hurt him to hear—something naked and miserable.

"My lady points out rightly that I have made a fool of myself with my clumsy talk." He bowed. "I should go and leave you to your work."

"I hate my work. I sew like a farm laborer. I am more of an executioner than a chirurgeon when it comes to handcraft."

He didn't know what that meant, but she hadn't agreed he should go away. He felt a surge of joy but tried to hide it. "I am sure you underestimate yourself, lady."

She stared at him for a long moment. "I only like you when you tell the truth, Tinwright. Can you do that? If not, you may continue on your way."

What was she asking? He swallowed—discreetly, he hoped—and said, "Only the truth then, my lady."

"Promise?"

"On Zosim, my patron."

"Ah, the drunkard godling—and patron of criminals, too, I believe. A good enough choice, I suppose, and certainly appropriate for any conversation with me." She turned to the young maid beside her, who had been listening to them and watching open-mouthed. "Lida, you go," she said. "Play with the other girls."

"But, Mistress . . . !"

"I will be fine. I will sit right here. Master Tinwright will protect me from any danger. It is well known that poets fear nothing. Is that not right, Master Matthias?"

Tinwright smiled. "Known only to poets, perhaps, and not to

this one. But I do not think your mistress will be in any danger, child."

Lida, who was all of eight or nine years old, frowned at being called a child, but gathered her skirts and rose from the bench, a miniature of dignity. She spoiled the effect a little by sullenly scuffing her feet all the way down the path.

"She is a good girl," Elan said. "She came with me from home."

"Summerfield?"

"No. My own family lives miles from the city. Our estate is called Willowburn."

"Ah. So you are a country girl?"

She looked at him, her expression suddenly flat once more. "Do not flirt with me, Master Tinwright. I was about to ask you to sit down. Am I to regret my decision?"

He hung his head. "I meant no offense, Lady Elan. I only wondered. I was raised in the city and I've often wondered what it would mean to smell country air every day."

"Really? Well, sometimes it smells wonderful, and sometimes it is just as bad as anything to be found in the worst stews of a city. If you have not spent much time around pigs, Master Tinwright, you haven't missed a great deal."

He laughed. She might have more wit than was fitting in a woman, but she also spoke more engagingly than most of the women he knew—or the men either, for that matter. "Point taken, my lady. I will try not to overburnish the joys of country living."

"So you grew up in a city. Where?"

"Here. Well, across the bay, to be precise, in the outer city. A place called Wharfside. Not a very nice place."

"Ah. So your family was poor, then?"

He hesitated. He wanted to agree, to make himself seem as admirable as possible. Since he couldn't pass for nobility, he could at least be the opposite, someone who had lifted himself up from dire misery by bravery and brilliance.

"Truth," she reminded, seeing him hesitate.

"Most in Wharfside are poor, yes, but we were better off than the largest part of them. My father was a tutor to the children of some of the merchants. We could have lived better, but my father was ... he wasn't good with money." But good with spending it on drink, and a little too forthcoming in his opinions as far as some of his employers thought, Tinwright recalled, not without some bitterness even with the old man now years dead. "But we always had food on the table. My father studied at Eastmarch University. He taught me to love words."

Which was not exactly the strict truth, as promised—what Kearn Tinwright had actually taught him was to love words enough to be able to talk yourself out of bad situations and into good ones.

"Ah, yes, words," said Elan M'Cory, musingly. "I used to believe in them. Now I do not."

Tinwright wasn't sure he'd understood her. "What do you mean?"

"Nothing. I mean nothing." She shook her head; for a moment the brittle look of ordinary social cheerfulness crumbled. She looked down at her needlepoint work for the span of several breaths. "I have kept you too long," she said at last. "You must get on with your day and I must get on with ruining my sewing."

He recognized a dismissal, and for once was too gratified to try to tug loose a little more of something he coveted. "I enjoyed speaking with you, my lady," he said, and meant it. "May I hope to have the pleasure of doing it again sometime?"

The shrieks of the girls playing ball rose up and filled the long silence. She looked at him carefully, and this time it was as though she had retreated behind a high wall and peered down at him from the battlements. "Perhaps," she said at last. "If you do not hope too much. My company is nothing to hope for."

"Now it is you who does not tell the truth, my lady."

She frowned, but thinking, not disagreeing. "It is possible that some afternoons, when it does not rain, you may find me here, in this garden, at about this time of the day."

He stood, and bowed. "I will look forward to such days."

She smiled her sad smile. "Go on and join the living, Matt Tinwright. Perhaps we will meet, as you say. Perhaps we shall."

He bowed again and walked away. It took all his strength not to look back, or at least not to do so immediately. When he did, the bench where she had sat was empty.

Duchess Merolanna hesitated at the bottom of the tower steps as the door creaked shut behind them. "Oh, I'm a fool."

The creak ended in a low, shuddering thump as the door swung closed. The breeze set the torches fluttering in their brackets. "What do you mean, Your Grace?"

"I have brought us here without a single guard. What if these are murderers?"

"But you wished this kept a secret. Don't worry yourself too much, Duchess—I am reasonably fit, and I can use one of these torches to defend you, if necessary." Utta stretched up to lift one from its socket. "Even a murderer will not relish being struck in the face with this."

Merolanna laughed. "I was worrying about *you,* good Sister Utta, rather than myself. You do not deserve to be harmed because of these strange games I find myself playing. I care not what happens to me. I am old, and all my chicks are dead or fled or lost . . ." For a moment her face became painfully sober and her lip trembled. "Ah, well. Ah, well." The duchess took a breath and straightened, swelling her sizable bosom so that she seemed suddenly a small but daunting ship of war. "It does us no good to stand here whispering like frightened girls. Come, Utta. You have the torch. Lead the way."

They made their way up the winding staircase. The first floor was unoccupied. The single, undivided chamber contained several large tables bearing plaster models of the castle, some true to life and others showing possible improvements, the fruits of one of King Olin's enthusiasms now as forgotten as the dusty, mummified corpse of a mouse that lay in the middle of the doorway.

Merolanna eyed the tiny body with distaste. "Somebody should do something. What use is it having cats if they do not eat the mice instead of leaving them around to rot?"

"Cats don't always eat their prey, Your Grace," Utta said. "Sometimes they only play with them and then kill them for sport."

"Nasty creatures. I never did like cats. Give me a hound any day. Stupid but honest." Merolanna looked around for eavesdroppers—a reflex because they were quite alone. Still, when she spoke again it was in a low voice. "That's why I preferred Gailon Tolly, for all his faults, to his brothers. Hendon is a cat if ever there was one. You can see the cruelty—he wears it like a fancy outfit, with pride."

Utta nodded as they returned to the stairs, leaving the cobwebbed models behind. Even Zoria herself, she felt sure, would have found it hard to feel charitable toward Hendon Tolly.

The doors on the second and third floors were smaller, and locked. She guessed that at least the upper one contained part of King Olin's famous library. This tower had always been his private sanctuary, and even with him gone so long she felt disrespectful poking around without royal permission.

But I am with Merolanna—the king's own aunt, she reminded herself. *If that is not permission enough, what is?*

The door to the chamber which took up the entire top floor was open, although Utta felt oddly sure that in any ordinary circumstances it would be locked just like the floors below it. No light burned inside, and from where the two women stood on the landing at the top of the stairs, their torch barely threw light past the doorway. As Utta moved closer the shadows inside bent and stretched. Suddenly she felt short of breath. *Zoria, preserve me from dangers known and unknown,* she prayed, *from peril of the body and peril of the soul.* "Your Grace?"

Merolanna frowned as if irritated at herself. She had not left the top of the stairs. "Very well. I'm coming." She hesitated a moment longer, then walked forward to stand at Utta's side. Together they stepped into the doorway, both of them holding their breath. Utta lifted the torch.

If the room full of plaster models at the bottom of the tower had seemed cluttered, this was something else again. Books had been stacked everywhere across the floor in unsteady-looking towers, and across every surface, many of them open, covering the two long tables in heedless piles. More than a few of the volumes lay bent-backed, perched like clumsy nesting birds on tabletop or pile, in positions that likely had not changed since the king's disappearance. Many had lost pages: a mulch of creased parchments covered the floor like drifts of leaves. For Zoria, tutored in the thrifty ways of the Zorian sisterhood, where books were a precious, expensive resource and could be read only with the permission of the *adelfa,* the mistress of the shrine's sisterhood, this careless plenitude was both exhilarating and shocking.

"What a dreadful clutter!" said Merolanna. "And it's frightfully cold in here, too. I'm shivering, Utta. Would you see if there's any wood, and light a fire?"

"Light not any fires, great ladies!" a tiny voice piped. "I beg 'ee, or tha will scorch my own sweet mistress most cracklingly!"

Utta jumped and dropped the torch, which with great good fortune landed in one of the few places on the floor not covered with sheets of book paper. She snatched it up again, breathing thanks she had not set the entire tower aflame. "What was . . . ?"

Merolanna had given a little screech at the mysterious words, and now reached out and clutched Utta's shoulder so fiercely that the Zorian sister could barely restrain a cry of her own. "It was here! In this very room!" the duchess whispered. She made the sign of the Three. "Who speaks?" she demanded aloud, her voice cracked and quavering. "Are you a ghost? A demon spirit?"

"No, great ladies, no ghost. I will show myself presently." The faint, shrill voice might almost have come from the phantom of the dead mouse downstairs. A moment later, Utta saw something stirring on the tabletop. A minuscule, four-limbed shape crawled out from between two close-leaning piles of books. When it stood up, and was revealed to be a man no taller than Utta's finger, she nearly dropped the torch again.

"Oh, merciful daughter of Perin," Utta said. "It is a little man."

"No mere man," the stranger chirped, "but a Gutter-Scout of the Rooftoppers." He bowed. "Beetledown the Bowman, I hight. Beg pardon for affrighting thee."

"You see this too," Merolanna said, tightening her grip on Utta again until the other woman squirmed. "Sister Utta, you see it. I am not mad, am I?"

"I see it," was all she could say. At this moment Utta was not entirely certain of her own sanity. "Who are you?" she asked the tiny man. "I mean, what are you?"

"He said he was a Rooftopper," Merolanna said. "That's plain enough."

"A . . . Rooftopper?"

"Don't you know the stories? Ah, but you're from the Vuttish islands, aren't you?" Merolanna stared at Utta for a moment, then suddenly remembered what they were talking about and turned back to the astonishing little apparition on the table. "What do you want? Are you the one who . . . did you put that letter in my chamber?"

Beetledown bowed. It was hard to tell, he was so small, but he might have been a little shame-faced. "That were my folk, yes, and Beetledown played some part, 'tis also true. We took the letter and we brought it back. Any more, though, be not mine to tell. You must wait."

"Wait?" Merolanna's laugh was more than a little shaky. Utta half feared that the duchess would faint or run screaming, but Merolanna seemed determined to prove she was made of bolder stuff. "Wait for what? The goblins to come and play us a tune? The fairy-king to lead us to his hoard of gold? By the Holy Trigon, are all the stories coming to life?"

"Again, this one cannot say, great lady. But un comes who can." He cocked his head. "Ah. I hear her."

He pointed to the great, long-unused fireplace. A line of figures had begun to file out from behind a pile of books beside the hearth—tiny men like Beetledown, dressed in fantastical armor made of nut husks and rodent skeletons, carrying equally tiny swords and spears. The miniature troop marched silently across the floor (although not without a few nervous glances upward at Utta and Merolanna) and lined up before the fireplace. A platform descended slowly out of the flue and into the opening of the fireplace, winched down on threads with a feathery squeak like the cry of baby birds. When it was a half-foot above the ash-covered andiron, it stopped, swaying slightly. At the center of the platform, on a beautiful throne constructed in part from what appeared to be a gilded pinecone, sat a finger-sized woman with red hair and a little crown of gold wire. She regarded her two large guests with calm interest, then smiled.

"Her Sublime and Inextricable Majesty, Queen Upsteeplebat," announced Beetledown with considerable fervor.

"We owe you an explanation, Duchess Merolanna and Sister Utta," said the little queen. The stones of the fireplace, like the shape of a theater or temple, made her high voice easier to hear than the little man's had been. "We have information that we think you will find valuable, and in turn, we ask you to aid us in the great matters that are upon us all."

"Aid you?" Merolanna shook her head. The duchess was looking her age now, confused and even a little weary. "By the gods, I swear I understand none of this. Tiny people out of an old tale. What could we do to help you? And what information could you give us?"

"For one thing, Duchess," said the queen gently, as if to a restless child instead of to a woman many, many times her size, "we believe we can tell you what happened to your son."

"Are you sure?" Opal asked. "Perhaps you're still too tired."

His wife, Chert noted, seemed to be having second thoughts.

"No, Mistress," Chaven protested, "I am much recovered. In fact, I am ashamed at having let myself go so far last night." He did indeed look rather embarrassed. "I count you even better friends for your kindness, indulging me at a bad time."

"But, are you truly . . . ?" Opal looked at the physician, then at her husband, as though she wanted him to intervene. Chert was quite happy to sit with a sour smile on his face. This messing about with mirrors had been *her* idea, after all. "Will you really do it here? In our home?"

Chaven smiled. "Mistress Opal, this is not some great, dangerous experiment I will perform, only the mildest bit of captromancy. Nothing will damage your son or your house."

Son. Chert still wasn't sure how he felt about that, but kept his thoughts to himself. Just in the months since Flint had come to them, the boy had grown another handspan, and now he towered over Chert. How could you consider someone your son who first of all didn't belong to you, whose mother and father might be alive and living nearby, and who in a few years would be twice your own size?

Ah, I suppose it isn't the height but the heart, he thought. He looked at the boy, sitting sleepy-eyed and faintly distrustful, curled in his blanket in the corner he had made his own. *At least he's out of his bed.* These days Flint was like some ancient relative—asleep most of the day, barely speaking. The boy had never been talkative, of course, but until the moment he had woken up from his weird adventure in the Mysteries the vigor had practically sprayed off him like a dog shaking a wet coat.

"What do you need, Doctor?" Chert couldn't help being a little curious. "Special herbs? Opal could go to the market."

"*You* could go to the market, you old hedgehog," she said, but her heart wasn't in it.

"No, no." The physician waved his hand. He looked a bit better for a night's sleep, but Chert knew him well enough to see the hollowness behind the façade of the ordinary. Chaven Makaros was not a happy man, not remotely, which made Chert even more anxious. "No, I need only Mistress Opal's mirror and a candle, and . . ." Chaven frowned. "Can you make this place dark?"

Chert laughed. "Can we? You forget, you are a guest in Funderling Town now. Even what we usually walk about in would seem like deep dark to you, and what you think is ordinary light makes my head ache."

Chaven looked stricken. "Is that true? Have you been suffering because of me?"

He shook his head. "I exaggerate. But yes, of course, we can make it dark."

As Chert stood on a stool to douse the lantern burning high in the alcove above the fire, Opal left the room and returned with a single candle in a dish which she set on the table next to Chaven. Already the exchange of the lantern for this single small light had turned the morning into something else, into eerie, timeless twilight, and Chert could not help remembering the murk of Southmarch city across the bay, the ceaseless dripping of water, those armored . . . things stepping out of the shadows. He had dismissed Opal's worries about doing this in the house, thinking that she was concerned only about a mess on her immaculate floors, but realized now that something deeper troubled her: by this one act, the lighting of a candle, and the knowledge that more was to come, the day and their house itself had been transformed into something quite different, almost frightening.

"Now," said Chaven, "I will need something to prop this mirror—ah, the cup should do nicely. And I want to put the candle here, where it will reflect without being directly in front of him. Flint, that is the boy's name, yes? Flint, come and sit here at the table. On this bench, yes."

The straw-haired boy rose and came forward, looking not so much apprehensive now as confused—and why not, Chert thought: it was an odd thing for parents of any kind to do, fosterfolk or not, handing their child over to a strange, bespectacled fellow like this one, a man who might be small among his own kind but here was too big for any of the furniture, then letting him do the Elders knew what to the boy.

"It's all right, son," Chert said abruptly. Flint looked at him, then seated himself.

"Now, child, I want you to move a little so you can see nothing but the candle." The boy tilted a bit to the side, then moved the rest of his body at the physician's gentle direction. Chaven stood behind him.

"Perhaps you two should move to where he cannot see you," the physician said to Chert and Opal. "Just stand behind me."

"Will this hurt him?" Opal asked suddenly. The boy flinched.

"No, no, and again, no. No pain, nothing dangerous, only a few questions, a little . . . conversation."

When Opal had taken her place, gripping Chert's hand tighter than he could remember her doing for some time, Chaven began quietly to speak. "Now, look in the mirror, lad." It was strange to think this same fellow, so soothing now, had been shrieking like a man caught under a rockslide only a few hours earlier. "Do you see the candle flame? You do. It is there before you, the only bright thing. Look at it. Do not watch anything else, only the flame. See how it moves? See how it glows? The darkness on either side of it is spreading, but the light only grows brighter . . ."

Chert couldn't see Flint's face, of course—the angle of the mirror didn't permit it—but he could see the boy's posture beginning to ease. The bony shoulders, which had been hunched as though against a cold wind, now drooped, and the head tilted forward toward the mirror-candle that Flint could see but Chert could not.

Chaven continued to talk in this soft, serious way, speaking of the candle and the darkness around it until Chert felt that he was falling into some kind of spell himself, until the pool of light on the tabletop, the candle and Flint and the mirror, all seemed to float in a shadowy void. The physician let his voice trail off into silence.

"Now," Chaven said after a pause, "we are going to take a journey together, you and I. Fear nothing that you see because I will be with you. Nothing that you see can see *you,* or harm you in any way. *Do not be afraid.*"

Opal squeezed Chert's hand so hard he had to wriggle his fingers free. He put his own hand on her arm to let her know he was still there, and also to try to stave off any sudden urges on her part to crush his fingers again.

"You are a boy again, just a very small boy—a baby, perhaps still in swaddling, and you can barely walk," Chaven said. "Where are you? What do you see?"

A long pause was followed by a strange sound—Flint's voice, but a new one Chert hadn't yet heard, not the preternatural maturity of the nearly wild boy they had brought home, or the anxious sullenness that had come on him since his journey through the mysteries. This Flint sounded almost exactly like what Chaven had described—a very small child, only just up on his legs.

"See trees. See my mam."

Opal got hold of his hand despite Chert's best efforts and this time he didn't have the heart to pull away, despite her desperate grip.

"And your father? Is he there?"

"Han't got un."

"Ah. And what is your name?"

He waited another long moment before answering. "Boy. Mam calls me boy."

"And do you know her name?"

"Mam. Ma-ma."

There was another spell of silence while Chaven considered. "Very well. You are a little older now. Where do you live?"

"In my house. Near the wood."

"Do you know its name, this wood?"

"No. Only know I mustn't go there."

"And when other people speak to your mother, what do they call her?"

"Don't. Don't none come. Except the city-man. He comes with the money. Four silver seashells each time. She likes it when he comes."

Chaven turned and gave Chert and Opal a look that Chert could not identify. "And what does he call her?"

"Mistress, or goodwife. Once he called her Dame Nursewife."

Chaven sighed. "Enough, then. You are now . . ."

"She's not well," Flint said abruptly, his voice tremulous. "She said, don't go out, and I don't. But she's sleeping and the clouds are coming along the ground."

"He's frightened!" said Opal. Chert had to hold her back, wondering even as he did so whether it was the right thing to do. "Let go of me, old man—can't you hear him? Flint! Flint, I'm here!"

"I assure you, good Mistress Opal, he cannot hear you." Something odd and hard had entered Chaven's voice—a tone Chert hadn't heard from him before. "My master Kaspar Dyelos taught this working to me and I learned it well. I assure you, he hears no voice but mine."

"But he's frightened!"

"Then you must be quiet and let me speak to him," Chaven said. "Boy, listen to me."

"The trees!" Flint said, his voice rising. "The trees are . . . moving. They have fingers. They're all around the house, and the clouds are all around too!"

"You are safe," the physician said. "You are safe, boy. Nothing you can see can hurt you."

"I don't want to go out. Ma said not to! But the door's open and the clouds are in the house . . . !"

"Boy . . ."

Flint's desperate words came out in little bursts, as though he were running hard. "Not . . . the . . . don't want . . ." He was swaying on the bench now, boneless as a doll, his head rolling on his neck as though someone were shaking him by the shoulders. "The eyes are all staring! Where's my ma? Where's the sky?" He was weeping now. "Where's my house?"

"Stop this!" Opal shrieked. "You're hurting him with your horrible spell!"

"I assure you," Chaven said, a little breathless himself, "that while he may be remembering things that frightened him, he's in no danger . . ."

Flint suddenly went rigid on the bench. "He's not in the stone anymore," he said in a harsh whisper, throat as tight as if someone squeezed it in strong hands. "He's not just in the stone—*he's . . . in . . . me!*" The child fell silent, still stiff as a post.

"We are done now, boy," Chaven said after a long moment of

stunned silence. "Come back to your home. Come back here, to the candle, and the mirror, come back to Opal and Chert . . ."

Flint stood up so suddenly that he tipped the heavy bench over. It crashed onto Chaven's foot and the physician hopped back on one leg, cursing unintelligibly, then fell over.

"No!" Flint shouted, and his voice filled the small room, rattled from the stone walls. "The queen's heart! The queen's heart! It's a hole, and he's crawling through it . . . !"

And then he went limp and fell to the floor like a puppet with its strings cut.

"He only sleeps." Chaven spoke gently, an unspoken apology behind the words, but Opal was having nothing of it; the look on her face could have crumbled limestone. She angrily waved Chaven and her husband from the sleeping room so she could continue dabbing the boy's forehead with a wet cloth, as if the mere fact of their presence would compromise her healing abilities—or, as Chert thought more likely, as though the very sight of two such useless men made her feel ill.

"I do not know what happened," Chaven said to Chert as they turned the bench right-side-up and sat on it. Chert poured them both a mug of mossbrew out of a jug. "Never before . . ." He frowned. "Something has been done to that boy. Behind the Shadowline, perhaps."

Chert laughed, but it was not one of the pleasant kind. "We did not need any mirror-magic to know *that*."

"Yes, yes, but there is more here than I ever thought. You heard him. He did not merely wander across the Shadowline—he was taken. Something strange was done to him there, I have no doubt."

Chert thought of the boy as he had found him just days before, lying at the foot of the Shining Man at the very center of the Funderling Mysteries, with the little mirror clutched in his fingers. And then that terrifying fairy-woman had taken the mirror from Chert in turn. What was it all about? Was *she* the queen the boy was shouting about? He had said something about a hole, and Chert could see how a heart with a hole in it might describe her.

"I don't understand," Chaven said. "Not any of it. But I cannot help feeling that I need to."

"Well enough." Chert stood, wincing at the ache in his knees. "Me, I have more pressing things to worry about, like where we are going to go and how we are going to find something to eat without anyone noticing you."

"What are you talking about?" Chaven asked.

"Because not only isn't Opal going to feed us today," Chert told him, "I think it's pretty plain that you and I will be a lot healthier if we're not sitting here when she comes out."

"Ah," said the physician, and hastily drained his mug. "Yes, I see what you mean. Let us be going."

16
Night Fires

Pale Daughter told her father Thunder that she had seen a handsome lord dressed all in pearly armor, with hair like moonlight on snow, and that her heart now rode with him. Thunder knew that it was his half brother Silvergleam, one of the children of Breeze, and forbade her to go out of the house again. The music between father and daughter lost its purest note. The sky above the god's house filled with clouds.

—from *One Hundred Considerations*
out of the Qar's *Book of Regret*

AFTER SO MANY CENTURIES, it was hard for Yasammez to accustom herself to true daylight again. Even this shy, cloud-blanketed winter sun seemed to blaze into her eyes from the moment it rose until it slid down behind the hills. She disliked it, but also felt a sort of wonder: had it really been like this once, walking in these southern lands, moving beneath Whitefire's orb every day in light so bright that it turned shadows into stark black stripes? She could scarcely remember it.

She had taken the mortals' city, but it was meaningless without the castle—worse than meaningless, because time was against her. Yasammez had prepared herself for fire and blood, for her own long-forestalled death, for meaningless victory or the finality of defeat, but she could never have prepared herself for this . . . *waiting*. The dragging stalemate was beginning to feel as though it might last until the unfamiliar sun burned out and the world went dark. She cursed the Pact of the Glass and her own foolishness for agreeing—she should never have let her hands be tied. Even if it worked, it would buy the one she loved only a few more moons of life and make the eventual loss even more heartbreaking.

As usual, the traitor was waiting for her on the steps outside the great hall she had taken for her own, a market hall or court where the mortals had once performed the meaningless routines of their short, busy lives. The one the sunlanders had called *Gil-the-potboy* looked up as she approached and smiled his slow, sad smile. His face, so human now she could scarcely recognize what he had once been, seemed as unmoving and opaque as dough.

"Good morning, my lady," he said. "Will you kill me today?"

"Did you have other plans, Kayyin?"

Something that the King had done to him still prevented her speaking to him mind to mind, so they had fallen back on the court speech of Qul-na-Qar, the common tongue of a hundred different kinds of folk. Yasammez, never one to waste even silent words, could not help feeling that here was another way that blind Ynnir was thwarting her, robbing her mind of rest.

Kayyin rose to follow her inside, hands hidden in his robe. Two of the guards looked at her, waiting for her to order this strange creature kept out, but she made no gesture as he trailed her through the door.

"I do not wish to speak to you today," she warned him.

"Then I will not speak, my lady."

Their footsteps echoed through the hall. Other than two or three of her silent, dark-clad servants waiting in the gallery above, the tall, wood-timbered room was empty. Yasammez preferred it so. Her army had the whole of a city in which to nest. This place was hers, which made the presence of the traitor even more galling.

Yasammez the Porcupine curled herself into her hard, high-backed chair. Her unwelcome guest seated himself cross-legged at her feet. One of her servants from Shehen appeared as if stepping out of nowhere, and waited until Yasammez flicked her fingers in dismissal. She wanted nothing. Nothing was what she had. She had been outmaneuvered and now she was paying the price.

"I will not kill you today, Kayyin," she said at last. "No matter how you plague me. Go away."

"It is . . . interesting," he said, as if he had not heard the last part of what she said. "That name still does not seem entirely real to me, although it was how I thought of myself for centuries. But while living in the mortal lands I truly *became* Gil, and although in some ways I slept through those years, it is like trying to shake off a powerful dream."

"So first you betray me, now you would renounce your people entirely?"

He smiled, doubtless because he had lured her into conversation. Even when they had been close, when he had been allowed as near to her as Yasammez allowed anyone, he had always enjoyed the sport of making her talk. No one left alive cared about such things at all. It was one of the reasons the sight of his altered, now-alien face filled her with such disquiet. "I renounce nothing, my lady, and you know it. I have been a catspaw—first yours, then the King's—and cannot be faulted for insufficient loyalty. I did not even remember who I truly was until one moon ago. How does that make me a traitor?"

"You know. I trusted you."

"Trusted me, you say? You are still cruel, my lady, whatever else time has done." He smiled, but the mockery was mixed with true sorrow. "The King was wiser than you guessed. And stronger. He made me his. He sent me to live among the mortals. And it has borne fruit, has it not? For the moment, no one is dying."

"It would only have been sunlanders dying. We had won."

"Won what? A more glorious death for all the People? The King, apparently, has other ambitions."

"He is a fool."

Kayyin lifted his hand. "I do not seek to arbitrate the quarrels of the highest. Even when you lifted me up, you did not lift me far enough for that." He peered at her from the corner of his eye, perhaps wondering whether this little gibe had shamed her, but Yasammez showed him nothing but stone, cold stone. She had been old already when Kayyin's father had fought with her against Umadi Sva's bastard offspring, and she had held him as he died in the agony of his burns on the Shivering Plain. If it had been in her to weep at someone's death, she would have wept then. No, she had no shame in her—not about anything to do with Kayyin, at any rate.

After a long silence, the traitor laughed. "You know, it was strange, living among the sunlanders. They are not so different from us as you might think."

She did not honor such filth with a reply.

"I have considered it a great deal in the days since I returned to you, my lady, and I think I understand a part of the King's thinking. Perhaps he is less willing than you to destroy the mortals because he thinks that they are not entirely to blame."

She stared at him.

"It could even be that our king, in his labyrinthine wisdom, buttressed with the voices of his ancestors—your ancestors, too, of course—has come to believe that we may have helped to bring our woeful situation upon ourselves."

Yasammez rose from the chair in a blind rage, her aspect abruptly juddering about her, shadow-spikes flaring. Kayyin came closer to his promised death at that moment than ever before. Instead, she raised a trembling, ice-cold finger and pointed to the door.

He stood and bowed. "Yes, my lady. You need solitude, of

course, and with the burdens you bear, you deserve it. I await our next conversation."

As he walked out the room behind him came to life with flickering shadows.

The strange, glaring sun had long since set. Yasammez sat in darkness.

A soft voice bloomed inside her head. *"May I speak with you, Lady?"*

She gave permission.

The far door opened. The visitor glided in like a leaf carried on a stream. She was tall, almost as tall as Yasammez herself, and slender as a young willow. Her white, hooded robe seemed to move too slowly for her progress, billowing like something underwater.

"Have things changed, Aesi'uah?" Yasammez asked.

The woman stopped before the chair and made a ritual obeisance of spread hands as her strange, still face lifted to Yasammez. Her pale blue eyes gleamed like sunlight through stained glass, giving the face a little animation: but for that effulgent stare she might have been an ancient statue. *"Lady, things have, but only slightly. Still, I thought you should be told."*

Someone other than Yasammez, someone other than the famously imperturbable Lady Porcupine, might have sighed. Instead she only nodded.

Her chief eremite spread her arms again, this time in the posture of bringing-the-truth. Aesi'uah was of Dreamless blood, and although that blood had been diluted by her Qar heritage, she had inherited at least one trait beside her moonstone gaze from those ancient forebears: she had an extreme disinterest in lies or politic speech, which was why she had become Yasammez' favorite of all her eremite order. *"The touch of the King's glass has made him restless."*

"Is he awakening already?"

"No, Mistress." The face was placid but the words were not. *"But he is stirring, and something is different, although I cannot say what. He is like one fevered—restless, full of unsettling dreams."*

Yasammez would have scowled at that, but she had lost the habit of showing emotion in such a naked way. *"We know nothing of his dreams."*

"Just so." Aesi'uah bowed her head. *"But his sleep seems to be that sort of sleep, and what is just as important, his restlessness makes the other sleepers uneasy, too."*

She was just about to ask the chief eremite how much longer before everything ended for good and all when another voice spoke in her head, faint as a dying wind.

Where are you . . . do you hear me? Do you . . . know me?

Of course I know you, my heart. A claw of terror gripped Yasammez, but she tried to keep it from her thoughts. *How could you doubt it?*

Her beloved one was gone for a moment, then returned, sighing, tattered. *So . . . cold. So dark.*

Yasammez made the sign for "audience ended." Aesi'uah did not change expression. She spread her hands, then glided out of the chamber like a phantom ship sailing beneath the moon.

Speak to me, my heart, said Yasammez.

I fear . . . I am going soon into . . . that greater sleep . . .

No. Strength is coming to you. I have sent the glass.

Where is it? I fear it will never come. The thoughts were timid, simple as a child's. To Yasammez that was the worst torment of all.

Gyir brings it, she promised. *He is young and strong and his thoughts are clear. He will find his way to you in time.*

But what . . . what if he does not . . . ?

Do not even think it. Yasammez put every bit of strength she could behind the thought. *He will come and you will be strong again. I will bring the scorched stones of the sunlanders' cities to make you a necklace.*

But even so . . . even so . . . !

Quiet, my heart. Not even the gods themselves can unmake that which is. Rest. I will stay with you until you sleep—not the greater sleep, but only the lesser. Fear not. Gyir will come.

She held on, then, to that faint wisp of thought and gave it comfort, though it fluttered against the darkness like a dying bird, by turns terrified and exhausted. The shadows flickered again in the hall, moving and stretching all through the true night as she took her aspect upon her once more, but this time they were softer—not spikes but tendrils, not the black, reaching claws of death but the fingers of soft, nurturing hands, as Lady Porcupine struggled to soothe the only living being she had ever truly loved.

The day was cold and gray, seasoned with drifts of rain, and although the doors to Effir dan-Mozan's front room were open to the courtyard as usual, a large brazier had been lit to provide warmth. As Briony came in the merchant was bending forward—not an easy task over his rich-man's belly—and warming his small, beringed hands at the coals.

"Ah, Briony-*zisaya*," he said. "You have not left your meal too soon? I did not want to interrupt you."

"I was finished, Master dan . . . Effir. Thank you. The servant said you and Shaso wished to speak with me."

"Yes, but Lord dan-Heza is not here yet. Please, make yourself comfortable." He gestured to one of the chairs arranged in a semi-circle around the brazier. "It is a filthy day but I cannot bear to have the doors closed." He laughed. "I like to see the sky. When I look at it, I might be at home." The smile soured a little. "Well, not today. We do not have skies like this in Tuan. When the rains come, we go to our temples and give thanks. Here, I should suspect it is the reverse."

Briony smiled. "I have never seen a house like this one, so low, with the garden in the center. Do people live like this in Tuan?"

"More or less. The nicer houses, yes. Although I wish I could have shown you my family home in Dagardar. Much larger, much more finely furnished—until it was pillaged and then burned by the old autarch's soldiers. Still, I cannot complain. The March Kingdoms have been good to an exile."

"It is still a very nice house."

"You are kind. What you politely do not ask is why a rich man would dwell in such an unsalubrious part of Landers Port."

She colored a little. She had wondered just that many times. "They do seem to have better . . . views from higher up on the hill."

"Ah, yes, Princess. And they are jealous of them, too. A man like me can build himself a fine house here among the other dark-skinned folk and no one is too upset. But I promise you that were I to have built it somewhere that a lord like Iomer M'Sivon or the native merchant-folk had to look on me and my home every day, I would soon find that neighborhood even less pleasant than this one." His smile had a bit of a twist to it. "The important thing in this life is to know not just who you are but *where* you are."

Shaso came in, dressed as though he had been outside, his face hidden by scarf and drooping hat. He shook the rain off his cloak and draped it across a chair. Effir dan-Mozan did not look pleased to have water sprinkled across his carpeted floors.

Shaso took off his hat and sat down. "A ship came in from Hierosol," he said by way of explanation. "The sailors were drinking. And talking. I was listening."

"And what did you learn, Lord?" asked Effir, who had regained his equanimity.

"Hierosol is preparing. Several *dromons*—that is what they call their warships, Princess—that were awaiting repairs are being rushed through drydock. Drakava has also called back his captains, who were punishing reluctant taxpayers along the Kracian border. He seems to expect a siege."

"And my father?"

Shaso shook his head. "These tidings come from sailors, Highness. They know little and care less about politics or prisoners. No news, as they say, is doubtless good news. The only concern is what will happen when Drakava realizes he will get no ransom out of Southmarch now."

"What do you mean?" she said hotly, then realized a moment later that Shaso was right: the last thing Hendon Tolly wanted now was for King Olin to return. "Oh, those . . . swine! Will Ludis Drakava hurt him?"

"I cannot imagine he would." Shaso shook his head but wouldn't meet her eye. He was unpracticed at deception and did not do it well. "There is nothing to gain from it and much to lose—like any chance of help from the northern countries if he is attacked by Xis."

As if sensing Briony's doubt and fear, Effir suddenly clapped his hands. "Come, let us have something hot to drink! A chilly day like this gets into your bones if you are not careful. Tal! Ah, no, wait, he is not at home today—off on some errand of his own." He clapped again, and at last one of his older and more doddering servitors meandered in. When the ancient had been dispatched for mulled wine, Effir rubbed his hands and began talking, perhaps making sure the conversation did not wander back onto the uncertain ground of a few moments earlier. "We brought you here because the time has come to make plans, Princess."

"What plans?"

"Just so, just so." Effir turned to Shaso. "My lord?"

"You and I cannot stay here forever," the old Tuani said. "You have told me so yourself, Highness."

"Where will we go?" Her heart seemed to swell and grow lighter. "To my father?"

"No." The scowl turned his face into a mask. "No and no, Briony. I have told you, there is little we could do for him, and it would be even worse foolishness now that the autarch seems to be considering an attack on Hierosol. What we need are allies, but there are very few people we can trust."

"Surely there must be *someone* left who believes in honor." Briony balled her fists. "By the holy Trigon, will they all simply stand by and see our throne *stolen?* What about Brenland, or Settland—we've sent help to them more times than I can count!"

"Your fellow rulers will do what suits them—and their people. I would advise you no differently myself." He raised a hand to forestall her indignant objection. "That is not so bad as it sounds, Highness. Any alliances we can make will be more straightforward if we do not clutter them with ideas like 'honor.' As long as we can bring our new ally some benefit, he will remain our ally—a simple, clean arrangement. And things are not so helpless as I may have painted them earlier. We do not necessarily need an entire army to reclaim Southmarch. All we need is enough strength to prevent Tolly getting his hands on you and killing you outright or pronouncing you an impostor—we could get by with a fairly small force. Then, if we can avoid being overwhelmed immediately, we will be able to reveal you to the people of Southmarch and denounce the Tollys as murderers and usurpers. That is the first step."

Briony frowned. "Why is that only the first step? Surely if we could engineer such a thing that would solve the whole problem."

Shaso clicked his tongue at her. "Think, Highness! Do you believe that even if he is revealed as the worst sort of usurper, Hendon Tolly will simply surrender? No. He and his brother Caradon will know they must hold what they have stolen or die on a traitor's gibbet. Hendon will go to ground in Southmarch like a badger in a hole and Caradon will reinforce him. Anyone trying to force Hendon out will find himself trapped between the castle walls and the army of Summerfield."

"So we don't need an army, but we need an army? You're not making sense."

"Think on it carefully, Highness," Shaso told her.

She hated it when her elders talked that way. What it meant was, *I already know the answer because I'm grown and I know things, but you need to learn how to think, and then you can be wise and wonderful like me.* "I don't know."

"What is our true need—no more, no less?"

Effir dan-Mozan, meanwhile, was watching the exchange with bright-eyed interest, as though he were a spectator at some particularly fascinating contest. That reminded Briony of something. "What is it my father always says when he's playing King's Square?" she asked Shaso. "Something from one of those old philosophers, I think."

"Ah, yes. *'Errors of caution are more likely to be considered at leisure than errors of boldness—but less likely to be considered after a victory.'* In other words, if you are too careful, you are more likely to live, but less likely to win. It is one of his favorite epigrams—and one of the reasons I admire him."

"It is?" She was so pleased to hear someone, especially Shaso, talk about her father as a living person instead of as though he were already dead that she forgave the old man his lecturing ways.

"Yes. He is one of the most thoughtful men I have ever met, but he is not afraid to move swiftly and boldly when necessary—to take risks. It is how he beat me at Hierosol, you know."

"Tell me."

"Not now. We need to consider our present situation, not review ancient battles." Was that the hint of a smile? "Now think. What do we truly need?"

"To do something bold, I suppose. To get our castle back."

"Yes, and you will only get it with the Tollys out, or dead. But as I said, we do not necessarily need an army. We can raise that from the March Kingdoms and even within the walls of Southmarch itself, if we can keep you alive long enough."

"So we need an ally with at least a small force of soldiers." She thought. "But who? You've said we don't know who to trust."

"We must *make* trust—we must find an ally who wants to bargain with us. And we must do something bold to find that ally. Hendon has no doubt filled the roads to Brenland and Settland with spies and assassins. I do not doubt he has people in the courts of all the March Kingdoms as well, probably under the guise of being emissaries from the court of the infant prince."

"I'm going to kill him."

"Beware your own anger, Highness. But I think we must make a move Hendon does not suspect. As I said, I doubt any of your fellow rulers will do something for you out of the good of their hearts.

"Syan is our best hope, I think. To begin with, King Enander has no love for Summerfield Court, going back to the days when Lindon Tolly, the old duke, was trying to marry his sister to your father. When your father chose your mother instead, Lindon was so determined to build a link to the throne of the March Kingdoms that he snubbed one of King Enander's own nephews and married his sister Ethna to your father's younger brother, Hardis . . ."

Briony shook her head. "Gods give us strength, you remember more of this family lore than I do."

Shaso gave her a stern look. "This is not 'family lore,' as you know very well—this is the stuff of alliances . . . and betrayals." He frowned, thinking. "In any case, Enander of Syan might be sympathetic to your cause—he has never quite forgiven the Tollys—but he will exact a price."

"A price? What sort of price? By the gods, does the Treaty of Coldgray Moor mean nothing? Anglin *saved* them all, and Syan and the others promised they would always come to our aid." She bit back several unladylike words: Shaso had heard her worst while training her, but she felt shy about cursing in front of Effir dan-Mozan. "Besides, until we take Southmarch back we have nothing to give these greedy people . . ."

"Enander of Syan is not particularly greedy, but that treaty is centuries old, however much it is revered in the March Kingdoms. It could be he will settle for gold when we have your throne back, but I believe he also has a marriageable son, who is said to be a goodly man . . ."

"So I must sell myself to get my throne back?" She felt so hot in the face that she pushed herself back from the brazier. "I might as well marry Ludis Drakava!"

"I think you would find the Syannese prince a much more pleasant husband, but let us hope there is some other way." Shaso frowned, then nodded. "In fact, if you will excuse us, Highness, perhaps Effir and I can begin inquiries in Syan. Whatever we do, it should be soon."

Briony stood, angry and miserable but struggling not to show it. "I *will* marry to save my family's throne, of course . . . if it is the only way."

"I understand, Highness." Shaso looked at her with what could almost pass for fatherly fondness, if she had not known the old man to avoid it like an itching rash. "I will not sell your freedom if I can avoid it, having fought so hard in my life to keep my own."

Sad and confused, Briony had more than her usual small share of the sweet wine that Idite and the others liked so much. As a result, when she woke in the dark her head was heavy and it took long moments to make sense of where she was, much less what was going on.

One of the younger girls, wrapped head to toe in a blanket so that she looked like a desert nomad, was standing in the doorway.

"Mistress Idite, there are men at the gate, demanding to be let in!" she cried. "Your husband the Dan-Mozan, he is arguing with them, but they say they will break it down if he does not let them in!"

"By the Great Mother, who are they? Robbers?" Idite, although obviously frightened, was keeping her voice almost as level as she did during their evenings of storytelling.

The girl in the doorway swayed. "They say they are Baron Iomer's men. They say we are harboring a dangerous fugitive!"

Briony, who had just clambered out of bed, went wobbly in the knees and almost tumbled to the floor. A fugitive—who else could that be but herself? And Shaso, too, she remembered. He would still be called a murderer.

"Dress, girls—all of you." Idite raised her voice in an attempt to quiet the frightened murmuring. "We must be prepared for trouble, and at the very least we must be decently dressed if strangers burst in."

Briony was not so much concerned with being decent as being able to defend herself. She hesitated for only a moment before pulling on the loose tunic and breeches borrowed from Effir's nephew, then grabbed the one pair of practical shoes Idite had given her, leather slippers that would at least allow her to run or fight if she had to. She tucked her Yisti knives into the cloth belt of the tunic and then pulled her robe around herself to hide the male clothing and the knives, giving herself at least a chance to blend in with the other women.

As the sound of raised, angry voices came echoing through the house, Briony saw that Idite intended to keep the women hidden in the hopes that everything would be happily resolved without them ever having to come into contact with the baron's men. Briony was not willing to passively await her doom. The women's chambers had few exits, and if things turned bad she would be trapped like a rat in a barrel.

She pushed past young Fanu, who grabbed ineffectually at her arm as Briony stepped out into the corridor.

"Come back!" Idite shouted. "Br . . . Lady!"

As she ran toward the front of the *hadar,* Briony silently thanked Idite for having the good sense not to call out her name. The hallways were full of clamorous voices and flickering light, and for a dizzying moment it was as though she had stumbled into some eddy of time, as if she had circled back to the terrible night in the residence when Kendrick had been murdered.

She staggered a little as she reached the main chamber, stopping to steady herself on the doorframe. The smoke was thick here and the voices louder, men's harsh voices arguing. She peered into the weirdly crowded chamber and saw at least a dozen men in armor were shoving and shouting at perhaps half that number of Effir dan-Mozan's robed servants, bellowing at them as though they could force the men to understand an unfamiliar language by sheer force. Several robed bodies already lay on the floor at the soldiers' feet.

As Briony stared in horror, trying to see if one of them was Shaso, an armor-clad man kicked over a brazier, scattering burning coals everywhere. The barefooted servants shrieked and capered to avoid them even as they cringed from the soldiers' weapons.

"If you won't talk," shouted one bearded soldier, "we'll burn out this entire nest of traitors!" He stooped and lifted a torch that had been smoldering on an expensive carpet and held it to one of the wall-hangings. The servants moaned and wailed as the flames shimmered up the ancient hanging and began licking at the wooden rafters.

Briony was digging beneath her robe for her knife, although

she had no idea what she could do, when someone grabbed the belt of her robe and yanked her away from the door, back into the corridor.

Her heart plunged—trapped! Caught without even a weapon ready to fight back! But it was not another of the baron's soldiers.

"What are you doing?" hissed Effir's nephew Talibo. "I have looked everywhere for you! Why did you leave the women's quarters?" He grabbed at her arm before she could answer and began to drag her away down the hallway toward the back of the house.

"Let go of me! Didn't you see—they're killing the servants!"

"That is what servants are for, stupid woman!" The hall was rapidly filling with smoke; after only a few steps he doubled up coughing, but before she could pull away he recovered his breath and began tugging at her again.

"No!" She managed to wrench her arm free. "I have to find Shaso!"

"You fool, who do you think sent me?" Tal's face was so suffused with both rage and fear that it looked as though he might burst into tears or simply rip into pieces. "The house is full of soldiers. He wants me to hide you."

"Where is he?" She hesitated, but the shrieks of unarmed men being slaughtered like barnyard animals behind her were terrifying.

"He will come to you, I am sure—hurry! The soldiers must not find you!"

She allowed herself to be drawn away up the corridor. Almost as terrifying as the servants' screams was the low, hungry roar of the spreading fire.

She pulled away from him again as they reached the part of the residence across the garden from the main chamber. "What of your aunt and the other women?"

"The servants will lead them out! Curse you, girl, do you never do what you are told? Shaso is waiting for you!" He stepped behind her and grabbed both her elbows, shoving her forward at an awkward stumble, another dozen steps down the corridor and then out a door into the open yard at the back of the house, site of the donkey stables, the vegetable garden, and the kitchen midden. He pushed her toward the stable and had almost forced her through the doorway when she threw out her arms and caught herself. She stepped to the side so the front wall and not the open door was behind her, and put her hand into her robe.

"What are you doing?" Talibo was almost screaming, his handsome, slightly childish face as exaggerated as a festival mask. Briony could see flames now on top of the house, greedily at work in the roof. On the far side of Effir dan-Mozan's walls, torches and lanterns were being lit in the surrounding houses as the neighborhood woke up to the terror in their midst.

"You said Shaso was waiting for me. But first you said he would come to meet me. Where is he? I think you are lying."

He looked at her with a strange, wounded fury, as though she had gone out of her way to spoil some pleasant surprise he had planned for her. "Ah? Do you think so?"

"Yes, I do. I think . . ." But she did not finish because Talibo put both hands on her breasts and shoved her, bouncing her off the wall and into the doorway, then pushed her again, sending her stumbling backward to fall down in the mire of the stable.

"Close your mouth, whore!" he shouted. "Do what you are told! I will be back!"

But even as he scrambled for the door, Briony was sliding across the damp ground toward him. She grabbed at his leg and pulled herself upright, and when he turned, she shoved herself against him, forcing him back against the rough wattle of the stable wall, and pressed the curved blade of the Yisti knife against his throat. *Close enough to kiss,* Shaso had taught her, *close enough to kill.*

"You will never touch me again, do you hear?" she breathed into his face. "And you will tell me everything Shaso said to you, everything that has happened and that you saw. If you lie I will slash your throat and leave you to bleed to death right here in the shit and the mud."

Tal's long-lashed eyes widened. He had gone pale, she could see that even in the dim light of the single candle that someone had lit here in the stable—in preparation for her arrival?—and when he sagged Briony let her own muscles go a little slack. Where was Shaso? Was Effir's nephew really lying? How could they escape with soldiers everywhere—and how had the soldiers found out . . . ?

Talibo's hand was open, but his sudden blow to her face was still so hard and so unexpected that Briony flew backward, her knife spinning away into the darkness. For a moment she could do nothing but gasp in helpless anger and gurgle as blood filled her mouth. She spat, and spat again, but every drop in her body seemed to be streaming from her nose and lips. She scrabbled for the lost knife as the merchant's nephew approached but it was beyond her reach, beyond her sight—lost, just as she was . . .

"Bitch," he snarled. "She-demon. Put a knife to my throat. I should . . . I will . . ." He spat at her feet. "You will spend a month begging me to forgive you for that—a year!"

She tried to say something, but it felt as though her jaw had been broken and she could only murmur and spit blood again. She slid her hand down her leg and reached into her boot, but the sheath was empty—the other dagger had fallen out somewhere during the scuffle. Her gut went cold. She had no weapon.

"Shaso, your mighty Shaso, he is dead," said Talibo. "I saw the soldiers kill him—surrounded him like a wild pig, spearing, spearing. I told them where to find him, of course."

She coughed, rubbed at her broken mouth with the back of her hand. "Y–You . . . ?"

"And my uncle, too. Him I did myself. He will never again call me names—spoiled, lazy. Ha! He will rot in the shadows of the land of the dead and *I* will be the master here. My ships, my merchants, my house . . . !"

"You betrayed . . . ?" It hurt to speak, but the thought of Shaso murdered blazed in her like a fire, like one of the coals that had bounced across Effir dan-Mozan's chamber floor only moments ago, lifetimes ago. It couldn't be true—the gods could not be so cruel! "Betrayed us . . . all?"

"Not you, bitch, although now I wish I had. But I will keep you for my own and you will learn to treat me with respect." Panting, he took a few steps toward her and leaned over, keeping well out of reach, even though she had lost the curved blade. Briony took a certain grim pleasure in that, anyway: he craved respect, but it was he, Talibo the traitor, who had learned to respect her. His face was ridiculously young for the emotions that played across it in the candlelight, greed and lust and exultation in his own cruelty. "And if you had been a proper woman you would have been safe here until it was all over. Now, I will have to break you like a horse. I will teach you to behave . . . !"

Briony hooked his ankle with her foot, sending him crashing to the ground. Instead of running away, she threw herself onto him even as he thrashed on the slippery ground, struggling to get his feet under him. She knocked him back but he curled his hands around her throat. Something hard was pressing painfully into her back, but she scarcely noticed it. The merchant's nephew was slender but strong—stronger than she was—and within instants, as his fingers tightened, the light of the single candle began to waver, then to burst into flowers of radiance like the fireworks that had scorched the sky over Southmarch to celebrate her father's marriage to Anissa. Her hand found the thing that was digging into her back.

Talibo's grip was so powerful that it did not slacken immediately even after she had pulled the second, smaller Yisti dagger out from underneath her and rammed it up under his jaw with all her might. Talibo straightened, shuddering and wriggling like an eel in the bottom of a fisherman's boat, so that for a moment it seemed his death throes might break her in half, then at last his hands fell away.

She lay where she was for a long time, fighting for breath, coughing and sputtering. When at last her throat seemed to be open again she stood up. Swaying, legs trembling, she bent over the merchant's nephew cautiously, in case he might be shamming, but he was dead: he did not even twitch when she pulled the blade out of his throat, freeing a gush of dark blood. She spat on his handsome, youthful face—a gob that was red with her own blood—and then turned and went to look for her other knife.

When she emerged from the stable Effir dan-Mozan's entire house was in flames. Briony stared for long empty moments, as if she had turned to stone, then she limped across the open yard into the shadows by the wall. She found a place she could mount and climbed with quivering, exhausted muscles over the top, then she let herself drop into the cool, stinking darkness of a refuse heap.

When morning came, Briony found a bucket of icy water and did her best to wash the blood from her throbbing, aching face, then pulled her robe tight around her boy's clothes—the clothes of the boy whom she had killed, she reflected with little emotion. She dragged her hood down low and joined the crowd that had gathered outside the smoldering remains of Effir dan Mozan's house. Some of the baron's soldiers were still standing guard over the ruins, so she did not dare go too close, and many of the crowd spoke Xandian languages, since this was the poorest part of Landers Port, but she heard enough to learn that the women of the house, at least, had managed to escape, and were sheltering with one of the other well-known Tuani families. She thought briefly of going to Idite, but knew it was a foolish idea: they had lost everything because of her already—why put them in danger again? Nobody seemed to know for certain exactly what had happened, but many had heard that some important criminal had been captured or killed, that Dan-Mozan had been harboring him and had died trying to defend his secret.

Only one male member of the household had lived to escape. For a moment, hearing that, Briony felt a rush of hope, but then someone pointed out the survivor—a small, bowed old servant that she recognized but whose name she did not remember. He stood apart from the others, staring at the smoking, blackened timbers of what had been his home. Alone in the crowd, he looked the way Briony imagined she did beneath her hood, shocked, confused, empty.

There was nothing here for her anymore except danger and quite possibly death. The baron's men did not seem to have tried very hard to take Shaso alive, and he had been nowhere near as dangerous to the Tollys as she was. Briony felt certain that Hendon Tolly's hand was somewhere in all this—why else would Iomer, a man who cared little for politics, have struck in such a swift and deadly way?

She screwed up her courage and joined the crowd of people walking out the city gates for the day and stared at the ground as she walked, meeting no one's eye. It seemed to work: she was not challenged, and within an hour she was alone on the cliff road below Landers Port. Briony walked until she reached a place where the woods were thick beside the road, then staggered off into the trees. She found a hidden spot surrounded by under-growth and curled herself up in the wet leaves at the base of a mostly naked oak, well out of sight of the road, and then wept until she fell asleep.

17
Bastard Gods

Zmeos, brother of Khors, knew that Zoria's father and her uncles would come against their clan, so he raised an army and lay in wait for them. But Zosim the Clever flew to Perin in the form of a starling and told the great god that Zmeos and Khors and Zuriyal had laid a trap, so Perin and his brothers called out the loyal gods of heaven. Together they descended upon the Moonlord's castle in a mighty host.

—from *The Beginnings of Things*
The Book of the Trigon

FERRAS VANSEN AND HIS COMPANIONS were not the beak-faced Longskulls' only prisoners, as they discovered when they reached the creatures' camp after an exhausting trudge through the dark woods. The Longskulls seemed almost uninterested in them, despite the dozen or so of their number Vansen and the others had killed, most of them victims of the Storm Lantern's blade. If a prisoner strayed out of the line one of the snouted warders honked at him or even jabbed at exposed skin with a sharpened stick, but otherwise left them alone.

Despite being our ally, Gyir has shown more hatred toward me and the other mortals than these things do toward us, Vansen thought. *Why did they take us if they care so little about us?*

He quietly asked Barrick about it. The prince asked Gyir and passed on his words: "The Longskulls are more like animals than people, as we would see it. They are doing what they are trained to do, no more. If we hurt one it may well hurt us in return, but otherwise they are taught only to bring us back to their master." Their master was Jikuyin, the one the raven had called Jack Chain—a disturbing name then, even more ominous now.

"What does this Chain want with us?"

Barrick paused, listening again, then shrugged. Gyir's eyes were red slits. "He says we will not know until they bring us to him," Barrick said. "But we will not like it."

The Longskulls' hunting camp looked like something out of an ancient Hierosoline temple-carving—the antechamber of the underworld, perhaps, or the midden heap of the gods. Certainly there seemed to be at least one of every misshapen creature Ferras Vansen could have imagined in his wildest night-terrors—squint-eyed, sharp-toothed goblins; apish Followers; and even tiny, misshapen men called Drows that looked like ill-made Funderlings. There was also an entire menagerie of animal-headed creatures with disturbingly manlike bodies, things that crawled and things that stood upright, even some that crouched in the shadows singing sad songs and weeping what looked to be tears of blood. Vansen could not help shivering, as much to see the misery of his fellow prisoners as their strangeness. Many had their arms or legs shackled, some their wings cruelly tied, a few with no more restraint than a leather sack over their heads, as though nothing else was needed to keep them from escaping.

"Perin's great hammer!" he whispered hoarsely. "What are all these horrors?"

"Shadlowlanders," Barrick told him, then, after cocking his head toward Gyir for a moment, "Slaves."

"Slaves to what? Who *is* this Jack Chain?"

Gyir, who could understand Vansen even though he could not speak to him directly, bleakly spread his long-fingered hands as if trying to demonstrate something of improbable size and power, but then shook his head and let his hands drop.

"A god, he calls him," said the prince. "No, a god's bastard. A bastard god." Barrick let his head droop. "I do not know—I can't remember everything he said. I'm tired."

They were shoved off to a place in the center of the camp by themselves, for which Vansen was as grateful as he could be under the circumstances, and where they huddled under a sky the color of wet stone. Vansen and Barrick sat close to each other on the damp, leaf-carpeted ground, for the warmth and—at least in Vansen's case—the human companionship. The weird army of prisoners that surrounded them, dozens and dozens all told, seemed strangely quiet: only an occasional bleating noise or a spatter of unfamiliar, clicking speech broke the silence. Vansen could not help noticing that they behaved like animals who sensed that the hour for slaughter had come round.

He leaned close to the prince's ear. "We must escape, Highness. And when we do, we must try to make our way back to mortal men's country again. If we stay any longer in this never-ending evening, surrounded by godless things like these, we shall go mad."

Barrick sighed. "You shall, perhaps. I think I went mad a long time ago, Captain."

"Don't say such things, Highness . . ."

"Please!" The prince turned on him, his weariness forgotten for a moment. "Spare me these . . . pleasant little thoughts, Captain. *'Should not . . .'*—as though I might bring something bad down on myself. Look at me, Vansen! Why do you think I am here? Why do you think I came with the army in the first place? Because there is a canker in my brain and it is eating me alive!"

"What . . . what do you mean?"

"Never mind. It is not your fault. I could have wished you

would have made a busybody of yourself somewhere else, though." Barrick lifted his knees up to his chin and wrapped his arms around them.

"Do you know *why* I followed you, Highness?" The bleak surroundings seemed to be getting into Vansen's blood and his thoughts like a cold fog. *Soon I shall be as mournful and mad as this prince.* "Because your sister asked me—no, *begged* me to do so. She begged me to keep you safe."

Now Barrick showed fire again. "What, does she think I am helpless? A child?"

"No. She loves you, Prince Barrick, whether you love yourself or not." He swallowed. "And you are all she has left, I suppose."

"What do you know of it—a mere soldier?" Barrick looked as though he wanted to hit him, despite the shackles on his arms. Gyir, sitting a few paces away, turned to watch them.

"Nothing, Highness. I know nothing of what it is like to be a prince, or to suffer because of it. But I do know what it is like to lose a father and others of my blood. Of five other children in our family, I have only two sisters left now, and my mother and father both are years in the grave. I have lost friends among the guard as well, one of them swallowed by a demon-beast in these lands the first time I came here. I know enough about it to say that sometimes carelessness with your own life is selfishness."

Barrick seemed startled now, both angry and darkly amused. "Are you calling me selfish?"

"At your age, Highness, you would be odd if you were not. But I saw your sister before we rode out, saw her face as she begged me to keep you safe and told me what it would mean to her if she lost you too. You call me 'a mere soldier,' Prince Barrick, but I would be the lowest sort of villain indeed if I did not urge you to take care of yourself, if only for her sake. That is no burden, from where I see it—it is a mighty and honorable charge."

Barrick was silent for a long moment, anger and amusement both gone, absorbed into one of his inscrutable, cold-faced stares. "You care for her," he said suddenly. "Don't you, Vansen? Tell me the truth."

Ferras realized that even here in the dark heart of the Twilight Lands, on the way to what was almost certain death, he was blushing. "Of course I do, Highness. She is . . . you are both my sovereigns."

"Back home I could have you whipped for avoiding my question like that, Vansen. If I asked you whether we were being invaded, would you say, 'Well, we'll have more guests than we usually do at this time of the year'?"

Vansen gaped, then laughed despite himself, something he had not done for so long that it was almost painful. Gyir twisted his featureless face in a way that might almost have been a frown, then turned away from them. "But, Highness, even . . . even if it were so, how could I speak of such a thing? Your sister!" He felt his own face grow stern. "But I can tell you this—I would give my life for her without hesitation."

"Ah." Barrick looked up. "They are going to feed us, it seems."

"Pardon?"

The prince gestured with his good arm. "See, they are carrying around some kind of bucket. I'm sure it will be something rare and splendid." He scowled and suddenly seemed little more than a youth of fourteen or fifteen summers again. "You realize, of course, that there isn't a chance in the world it will ever come to anything?"

"What?"

"Stop pretending to be stupid, Captain. You know what I mean."

Vansen took a breath. "Of course I do."

"You like lost causes, don't you? And thankless favors? I saw you help that disgusting bird to escape, as well." Barrick smiled at him. It was quite nearly kind. "I see I'm not the only one who has learned to live with hopelessness. It makes an unsatisfying fare, doesn't it? But after a while, you begin to take a sort of pride in it." He looked up again. "And speaking of unsatisfying fare, here come our hosts."

Two Longskulls stood over them, appearing to Vansen like nothing so much as gigantic grasshoppers, although there was something weirdly doglike about them, too. Their legs were similar to men's, but the back of the foot and the heel were long and did not touch the ground, so that they perched on the front of their feet like upright rats. The eyes sunk deep in their loaf-shaped, bony heads did not exactly glisten with intelligence, but it was obvious they were not mere beasts, either. One made a little honking, gabbling noise and ladled something out of the bucket the other was holding. It pointed at Vansen's hands, then honked again.

I am living in a world of firelight tales, Vansen thought suddenly, remembering his father's old sea stories and his mother's accounts of the fairies that lived in the hills. *We are captives in some unhappy child's dream.*

He held out his arms, showing the guards his shackles. "I cannot hold anything," he said. The Longskull merely turned the ladle upside down and let the mass of cold pottage drop into his hands. It did the same for Barrick, then moved on to the next group.

In the end, he found he could eat only by bracing the heavy shackles on the ground, then crouching over his own outstretched hands, lapping up the tasteless vegetable pulp like a dog eating from a bowl.

When all the prisoners had been fed the watery pottage, the Longskull guards returned to the fire to eat their own food, which had been roasting on spits. Vansen could not see what they ate, but when the prisoners were hauled to their feet a short time later and set to marching again, he noticed the Longskulls hanging some empty shackles back on the massive wagon that held the slavers' simple belongings, and where they swung, clinking, as the wagon began to roll.

If Barrick had thought the Twilight Lands oppressive before, every miserable step of the forced march now seemed to take him into deeper and deeper gloom. It wasn't simply that the pall of smoke they thought they had escaped grew thicker above them with every step, turning the land dark as midnight and making breathing a misery, or even the dull horror of their predicament. No something even beyond these things was afflicting him, although Barrick could not say exactly what it was. Every step they took, even when they reached an old road and the going became easier, seemed to plunge them deeper into a queer malevolence he could feel in his very bones.

He asked Gyir about it. The fairy-warrior, who seemed almost as despondent as his companions, said, *Yes, I feel it, even despite the blindness my wounds have caused, but I do not know what causes it. Jikuyin is the source of some of it—but not all.*

Barrick was struck by a thought. *Will this blindness of yours get better? Will the illness or whatever it is leave you?*

I do not know. It has never before happened to me. Gyir made a sign with his long, graceful fingers that Barrick did not recognize. *In any case, I truthfully do not think we will live long enough to find out.*

Why are we prisoners? Is Jikuyin at war with your king?

Only in that he does not bow to him. Only in that Jikuyin is old and cruel and our king is less cruel. But we are prisoners, I think, only because we were captured. Look at those around us . . . He gestured to the slow-stepping band of prisoners on either side and stretching before and behind them farther than Barrick could throw a stone. *We may be rare things here,* Gyir told him in his wordless way, *but these others are as common as the trees and stones. No, we are all being taken to the same place, but the more I consider, the less I think it is because we were singled out.* He opened his eyes wide, something Barrick had come to recognize as a sign of determination. *But I think these creatures' master will take notice of us when he sees us. If nothing else, he will wonder what mortals are doing again in his lands.*

Again? I have never heard of him.

Jikuyin first made this place his own long, long before mortals roamed this country and built Northmarch, but he was injured in a great battle, and so after the Years of Blood he slept for a long time, healing his wounds. His name was lost to most memories, except for a few old stories. We drove the mortals out of Northmarch before he returned. That was only a very short time ago by our count. After they had fled we called down the Mantle to keep your kind away thereafter, banishing them from these lands for good and all.

Why did you do that?

Why? Because you would have come creeping back into our country from all sides as you did before, like maggots! Gyir narrowed his eyes, making crimson slits. *You had already killed most of us and stolen our ancient lands!*

Not me, Barrick told him. *My kind, yes. But not me.*

Gyir stared, then turned away. *Your pardon. I forgot to whom I spoke.*

The procession was just emerging from between two hills and into a shallow valley and a great stony shadow across the road—an immense, ruined gate.

"By *The Holy Book of the Trigon!*" Barrick breathed.

No oaths like that—not here, Gyir warned him sharply.

But . . . what is this?

The column of prisoners had shuffled to a weary halt. Those who still had the strength stared up at two massive pillars which flanked the road, lumps of vine-netted gray stone that despite being broken still loomed taller than the trees. Even the smaller lintel that stretched above their heads was as long as a tithing barn. Huge, overgrown walls, half standing, half tumbled, hemmed the crumbling gate like the wings of some god's headdress.

It is worse than I feared. The fairy's thoughts were suddenly faint as a superstitious whisper, hard for Barrick to grasp. *Jikuyin has left his lair in Northmarch and made himself a new home . . . in Greatdeeps itself. This is its outer gate.*

"What is this new misery?" Ferras Vansen was clearly feeling the strangeness of the place too, not just its size and immense age but even the hidden something that pressed ever more intrusively into Barrick's mind like cold, heavy fingers.

"Gyir says it was something called Greatdeeps, or at least the first gate."

"Greatdeeps?" Vansen frowned. "I think I know that name. From when I was a child . . ."

The Longskulls came hissing angrily down the line, poking and prodding, and at last even the most reluctant prisoners let themselves be driven under the massive lintel. It was carved with strange, inhuman faces that looked down on them as they passed— some with too few eyes, some with too many, none of them pleasant to see.

What lay beyond was equally disturbing. The wide, broken-cobbled road dipped down into a valley that lay almost hidden beneath a thick cloud of smoky fog as it wound between two rows of huge stone sculptures. Some of the stonework portrayed ordinary things cast in giant size, like anvils big as houses or hammers and other tools that a dozen mortals together could never have lifted. Other shapes were not quite so recognizable, queer representations of machinery Barrick had never seen and the uses of which he could not even guess. All the statues were old, cracked by wind and rain and the work of creepers and other plants. Many had fallen and been partially buried by dirt and leaves, so that the impression was that monstrous citizens who had once dwelled here had simply packed up one night and left, allowing the mighty road to fall to ruin after they were gone.

Despite the apparent emptiness, or perhaps because of it, Barrick's sense of oppression grew as they trudged forward. Even the Longskull guards grew quiet, their gabbling little more than a murmur as they moved up and down the line of prisoners, goading them forward.

What is this place? he asked Gyir. *What is Greatdeeps?*

The place where the gods first broke the earth, searching . . .

A tennight before this Barrick had not quite believed in the gods. Now, in a place like this, the mere word set his heart racing, brought clammy sweat to his skin. *Searching for what?*

Gyir shook his head. The weight that Barrick felt, the despairing thickness that seemed to lie on him like a net made of lead, seemed to weigh on the fairy even more heavily. Gyir's head was bowed, his back bent. He walked like a man approaching the gallows, struggling to get the smoky air in and out of his lungs. The fairy's thoughts were heavy, too, like stones—it made Barrick weary just to receive them. *I cannot . . . speak to you now,* Gyir told him. *I must understand what all this means, why . . . I must think . . .*

Barrick turned to Ferras Vansen. "You said you thought you remembered, Captain. Do you know anything of this Great-deeps?"

"A memory, and only a faint one. Something—a story we children told to frighten each other when I was young, I think . . ." He frowned miserably. "I cannot summon it. What does the fairy say?"

Barrick glanced quickly at the fairy, then back to Vansen. "Something about the gods breaking the earth here, but I can make little sense of it and he won't say more." The prince rubbed at his face as if he could scour away the discomfort. "But it is a bad place. Can you feel it?"

Vansen nodded. "A heaviness, as if the air was poisoned—and by more than smoke. No, not poisoned, but bad, somehow, as you say—thick and unpleasant. It makes my heart quail, Highness, to speak the truth."

"I'm glad it's not just me," Barrick said. "Or perhaps I'm not. What will happen to us? Where do you think we're being taken?"

"We shall find that out sooner than we want to, I think. What we should consider instead is how we might get away."

Barrick held up the shackles, which although not too large for an ordinary person his size, were cruelly heavy on his bad arm. "Do you have a chisel? If so, I think we'd have something to talk about."

"They haven't tied our feet, Highness," the soldier said. "We can run, and worry about freeing our arms later."

"Really? Just look at them." Barrick gestured to the nearest pair of Longskulls pacing the line with their strange, springy gait. "I don't think we'll outrun those, even without our legs shackled."

"Still, The Book of the Trigon bids us to live in hope, Prince Barrick." Vansen looked curiously solemn as he said it—or maybe it was not so curious, under the circumstances. "Pray to the blessed oniri to speak for us in heaven—the gods may yet find a way to save us."

"Speaking frankly," Barrick said, "just at the moment, it is the gods themselves I fear most."

The prince seemed a little more like his ordinary self again, which was the only hopeful thing Vansen had seen all day. Perhaps it was because Gyir the Storm Lantern had almost stopped talking to him.

Judging by the usual run of his luck and mine, he'll come back to himself just in time to be executed by our captors, Vansen thought with bleak amusement. *At least I'll probably be killed, too. Anything would be better than to face Barrick's sister with news of her brother's death.*

Where is she? he suddenly wondered. *In the castle, perhaps under siege? There's no chance that Gyir's people would have beaten us so badly and then just stopped in the fields outside the city . . .* He felt a moment of terror, worse than anything he had felt for himself, at the idea of Princess Briony being threatened by monstrous creatures like these, perhaps a prisoner herself. He could not let the thought run free in his head—it was too horrible. *Perhaps she fled, along with her advisers. Wherever she is, Perin grant she is safe.* And who was it the princess herself had sworn by so often? *Zoria—Perin's merciful daughter.* He had never thought to pray to the virgin deity before, but now he did his best to summon the memory of her kind, pale face. *Yes, blessed Zoria, put your hand on her and keep her from harm.*

Does Briony ever think of us? Of course, she must think of her brother all the time—but does she think of me at all? Does she even remember my name?

He forced such foolishness away. If there was anything more pitiable than mooning after an unobtainable princess, a young woman as high above him as the gods were above humanity, it was mooning while they were captives in the Twilight Lands, being marched toward the Three Brothers only knew what doom.

You think too much, Ferras Vansen. That's what old Murroy told you, and he was right.

The sprawling avenue of broken stones and gigantic leaning statues had become even more desolate as they marched on, most of the plinths empty, the stones themselves few and far between, as though scavengers had carried them away. Even the trees had been cleared here; the valley floor, sloping up on either side, seemed as stubbly as the face of an unshaved corpse.

Vansen was also becoming more and more aware of a smell beyond that of the smoke, a strong, sulphurous odor that seemed to lie over the valley like a fog. The worst of it came from holes in the ground on either side of the road, and Vansen could not help wondering what could be under the ground that stank so badly.

"Mines," said Barrick when Vansen voiced his question out loud. "Gyir said these are the first mines his people built, a long time ago, although the digging here began even earlier. They go down into the ground for miles."

"What did they mine here?"

"That's all I know." Barrick gestured with his good arm toward the faceless fairy. Gyir's eyes were almost closed, as though he slept on his feet. "He's still not talking."

The road, which Vansen thought must once have been the path of an ancient streambed, began to rise as the valley floor rose. Even as they climbed the smoke remained thick in the air, turning the cheerless vista of tree stumps and broken stones into something even more dispiriting, if such was possible. They were nearing the far end of the valley, and even though the road continued to mount upward, it became clear that unless it ended in a ladder half a mile tall it would never climb high enough to take them over the jagged face of rock that hemmed the valley.

Barrick looked up at the looming peak in dismay. "There's nowhere to go. Perhaps we're not to be slaves after all. Perhaps they're just going to kill us here."

"It seems a long way to march us simply to do that, Highness," Vansen reassured him. "Likely there is some secret pass ahead—a path through the heights." But he also wondered, and fear began to poison him again. Soon they would be pressed against the stony cliffs with nowhere to go, the Longskulls hemming them in with sharp spears . . .

If others had not been trudging through the growing dark ahead of him, Vansen would have tripped on the first impossibly

wide, high step. As the prisoners in front clambered up, Vansen followed, turning to help the prince climb despite Barrick's fiercely
resentful looks. One massive step ran into the next, one wearying
climb after another.

"It's . . . a . . . cursed . . . *staircase,*" Barrick said, fighting for breath.
They had been marching without a rest for hours, and each step
was a formidable obstacle. "Like the one in front of the great
temple back home—but monstrously big." He fell silent except for
his ragged breathing as he labored up two more steps behind
Vansen. All around him the other prisoners were struggling at least
as badly—some were simply too short to get up without help. The
Longskulls clambered in and out of the procession, jabbing with
their sticks and making irritated honking noises. "Gyir says that
this is it," Barrick reported at last.

"This is what, exactly?"

"Greatdeeps. The entrance to the ancient mine." Barrick closed
his eyes for a moment, listening to that silent voice. "He says we
must hold hands, because to get separated here might be worse
than death."

"A cheery thought," said Vansen as lightly as he could, but his
own heart was like a stone. They continued up the great staircase,
which seemed wider than the Lantern Broad in Tessis. At the top
yawned a great doorway, high as a many-storied house. Compared
to the twilight in the valley and on the stairs, its interior was dark
as night.

"There will be a fight here, mark my words," Vansen whispered
to Barrick. It felt strangely natural to hold the boy's hand, as
though this topsy-turvy land had given him back one of his
younger brothers. "No creature would let itself be driven into that
without a struggle."

But there was no struggle, or at least not much of one. As the
prisoners bunched in the doorway, some moaning and slumping to
the ground, some actively trying to turn back, the Longskulls
charged. They had been prepared, and now they leaped up the
stairs and onto the landing as a unified force, shoving, kicking,
poking, and even biting until all those who could do so clambered

to their feet and staggered through the door. Many were trampled, and as Vansen let himself and Barrick be drawn into the darkness, he wondered if in the long run those lying bloody and crushed on the top step might not be the lucky ones.

"Should we have tried to get away?" Barrick whispered. "Before they shoved us in here?"

"No, not unless your Gyir says we must. We do not know what is inside, but we might find a better chance for escape later on." Vansen wished he believed that himself.

They allowed themselves to be dragged along in the river of captive creatures, out of the initial darkness into sloping, timbered tunnels lit with torches, then down, down into the heart of the mountain.

He did not notice it at first, but after a short time of trudging through the dank, hot corridors Vansen began to realize that some of the other prisoners were disappearing. The group in which they traveled was perhaps half the size now that it had been when they had first been driven through the great doors, and as he watched he saw two of the Longskulls roughly separate a group of perhaps a dozen captives—it was hard to tell in the flickering shadows, because the prisoners were of so many odd sizes and shapes—and drive them away down a cross corridor. He whispered this to Barrick, and saw the prince's eyes widen in alarm.

"Is that because they mean something different for us? To kill us instead of making us slaves?"

"I think it's more likely that they haven't seen many of our kind before," Vansen reassured him. "These Longskull things don't seem the types to act without orders. They may want someone to tell them where we should be put." He didn't really want to talk—it was hard enough trying to keep some idea in his mind of what turns they'd taken, where they might be in relation to the original doorway. If there was a chance later for escape, he did not want to run blindly.

Soon there were only a few prisoners left beside themselves, a more or less manlike creature with wings like a dragonfly, taller than Vansen although much more slender, a pair of goblins with bright red skin, and one of the wizened mock-Funderlings—a Drow. This last walked just in front of Vansen, which gave him more chance to look at the little manlike creature than he might have wanted: it had a huge, lopsided head, a stumpy body, and hands that were almost twice as big as Vansen's, although the creature itself was far less than half his size.

The remaining Longskulls hurried the last prisoners along. Vansen had to trot, no easy feat with heavy shackles on his wrists, and also to help the prince when the boy stumbled, which was often. The pain in the prince's withered arm from the restraints must be great, Vansen knew, although Barrick refused to mention it: it took no physician's eye to see the boy's pale skin, his creased, wincing eyes, or to interpret the silence that had fallen over him in the last hour.

They reached a wide place in the corridor where several other passages branched out. The guards forced them down one of those branches, and within just a few more paces they emerged into a large open space where they stopped before another massive doorway, this one guarded by lowering apelike things that might have been Followers, but grown to the size of men and dressed in dusty, mismatched bits of armor. The Longskulls gabbled at these sentries, then stepped forward and used their spears to tap on the door, which despite their deferential touch made a hollow, brazen clang with each knock. The door slowly swung open and the quietly honking guards shoved the prisoners inside.

Behind the door lay the most demented place Vansen had ever seen, a cavern as large as the interior of the Trigon Temple in Southmarch, but furnished by a madman. Broken bits and pieces of the statues that had once lined the valley stood all around the immense space—here half a warrior crouching in the middle of the cracked floor, there a single granite hand the size of a donkey-cart. Moss and little threadlike vines grew patchily on the sculptures, and in many places on the rough-hewn walls and floor as well, and the air was damp with mist from an actual waterfall that poured from a hole high on one side of the cavern and followed a splashing course downward over stone blocks to fill a great pool that took up half of the vast room.

Across the pool from the doorway stood another huge statue of a headless, seated warrior, tall as a castle wall. Enthroned on this stone warrior's lap, with various creatures kneeling or lying at his feet like a living carpet, sat the biggest man—the biggest living thing—Vansen had ever seen. Two, no, three times the height of a normal man he loomed, massive and muscular as a blacksmith, and if it had not been so absolutely clear that this monstrosity was alive, Vansen would never for an instant have believed him anything but a statue. His hair was curly and hung to his shoulders, his beard to his waist, and he was as beautiful as any of the stone gods' statues, as if he too had been carved by some master sculptor, except that one side of his gigantic face was a crumpled ruin, one eye gone and the skin of cheek and forehead a puckered crater in which his disarranged teeth could be seen like loose pearls in a jewelry box.

Somewhere deep beneath them, something boomed like a monstrous drumbeat, a concussion that punched at Vansen's ears and made the entire rocky chamber shudder ever so briefly, but no one in the room even seemed to notice.

Chains of all sizes and thicknesses hung around the terrible god-thing's waist and dangled from his neck and shoulders, so that if he wore some other garment it could not be seen at all. Hundreds of strange, round objects hung from the chains. As his eyes became used to the light, Vansen realized that every one of the hanging things was a severed head, some only naked skulls or mummified leather, some fresh, with ragged necks still dripping— heads of men, of fairies, even animals, heads of all descriptions.

The full childhood memory came back to Vansen suddenly, the taunt of older boys to scare the younger ones— *"Jack-in-Irons! Jack-in-Irons be coming from the great deeps to catch you! He'll take your head!"*

Jack in Irons. Jack Chain. He was real.

The apparition raised an arm big as a tree trunk, chains swaying and clanking, the heads dangling like charms on a lady's bracelet. The bastard god grinned and his beautiful face seemed almost to split open as he displayed teeth as large as plates, as cracked and broken as the ruined stones.

"*I AM JIKUYIN!*" he roared, his voice so loud and so painful that Vansen fell to his knees and then slumped down to his belly with his hands over his ears in a fruitless attempt to protect himself from the deafening noise. It was not until the giant spoke again that Ferras Vansen realized he was hearing the words not with his ears, but echoing inside his mind.

All ordinary thought disappeared in the skull-thunder that followed.

"*WELCOME, MORTALS—AH, AND ONE OF THE HIGH ONES, TOO, I SEE. WELCOME TO THE UNDERWORLD. I PROMISE I WILL GIVE YOU A USEFUL DEATH, AND AFTERWARD I MAY EVEN SHOW YOU THE MATCHLESS HONOR OF WEARING YOUR SMALL BUT SHAPELY HEADS!*"

18

Questions with No Answers

*So then in that great battle matchless Nushash at last
pulled the sun itself down from the sky and hurled it full
into the face of Zhafaris, the old Emperor Twilight, whose
beard caught fire. He was burned into ashes, and that, my
children, was the end of his evil rule.*

*Nushash and his brother Xosh scattered the ashes in the
desert of Night. Then, in his generosity, Nushash invited his
three half brothers to join him in building a new city of the
gods on Mount Xandos. Argal the Thunderer and the others
thanked him and swore fealty, but already they were
planning to betray him and take the throne of the gods for
themselves.*

—from *The Revelations of Nushash,* Book One

ALTHOUGH SHE COULD NOT HAVE SAID exactly why, Pelaya found herself spending more time in the garden than had been her habit, even on days like today when the weather was less than ideal, with heavy gray skies and a biting wind from the sea. It was partly because her father Count Perivos had been so busy lately, busier than she'd ever seen him, with no time at all to give to his children. Sometimes he stayed so late examining the city's defenses that he even slept in the Documents Chamber and only came home to change his clothes. But much of her interest in the garden was simply her interest in the prisoner Olin—King Olin, however he might mockingly disclaim his title. On the occasions that he and Pelaya met each other she always enjoyed talking to him, although it was never quite as strange and exciting as it had been the first time, when he had been a complete stranger and her companions had watched with horror as she introduced herself to him, as though she had decided to leap off the city walls and swim to Xand.

Still, she enjoyed the grown-up way their conversations made her feel, and he seemed to enjoy them too, although he was always disappointed by how little news she could give him about his homeland. She knew that one of his sons had died, and his daughter and other son were missing, and that his country was in some kind of war. Sometimes when Olin spoke about his children he seemed to be hiding feelings so strong that it seemed he would burst into tears, but then only moments later he would be so coldly composed she wondered if she had imagined it. He was a strange man even for a king, very changeable, unfailingly polite but sometimes a little frightening to a girl like Pelaya, whose own father was, for all his intelligence, a simpler sort of man. She sometimes thought Olin Eddon's true feelings were as painfully imprisoned as he was himself.

He was not allowed into the garden very often, only a few days in every tennight. Pelaya thought that unkind of the Lord Protector. She wondered if she dared speak to her father about it—

he was steward of the entire stronghold, after all—but although there was nothing illicit in the friendship with the northern king, she didn't want to draw attention to it. Count Perivos was a serious man; he didn't think much of things that had no purpose and she doubted he'd ever understand the harmless attraction Olin's company held for her. Her father had doubtless heard something about the odd friendship, but so far he hadn't said anything to her about it, perhaps reassured by Teloni, who had decided the whole thing was a boring lark of Pelaya's and had stopped fussing at her about it. It was probably best to leave things that way, Pelaya decided, and not tempt the gods.

She was pleased to find that King Olin was out in the garden today, looking across the walls from atop a jutting ornamental stone not far from the bench, the one place a person could climb high enough see between the towers of the stronghold over all the Kulloan Strait. He sat cross-legged on the stone with his chin propped on his hands, more like a boy than a grown man, let alone a monarch. She stood by the base of the stone waiting for him to realize she was there.

"Ah, good Mistress Akuanis," he said with a smile. "You honor me with your company again. I was just sitting here wondering if a man could fashion wings like a gull's—out of wood and feathers, perhaps, although I suspect each feather would have to be tied in place separately, which would make for a great deal of work—and so fly like a bird."

She frowned. "Why would someone want to do that?"

"Why?" He smiled. "I suppose the freedom of a gull on the wind has more meaning to me just now than to you." He clambered down, landing lightly. "I muse, only—I see the birds fly and my mind begins to wander. I beg you not to tell your father of my interest in flight. I might lose the gift of this time in the garden."

"I wouldn't do that," she said earnestly.

"Ah. You are kind." He nodded, the subject concluded. "And how are you today, Mistress? Have the gods treated you well since I saw you last?"

"Well enough, I suppose. My tutor sets me the dreariest lessons you can imagine, and I will never, never be a seamstress, no matter how many years I try. Mother says my needlework looks like the web of a drunken spider."

He chuckled. "Your mother sounds like a clever woman. That is not the first thing she has said that made me laugh. Perhaps that is where you come by your own wit and curiosity."

"Me?" All she could think of were the lessons that Brother Lysas taught, reading at length from *The Book of the Trigon*, " . . . *Beloved of the gods are the daughters and wives who make themselves humble, who seek only to serve Heaven . . .*" "I'm not curious, am I?"

He smiled again. "Child, you are a fountain of questions. It is often all I can do not to unpack the entirety of my life and let you rifle through it like a trunk of clothes."

"You must think I'm annoying, then. A child who cannot be still." She hung her head.

"Not at all. Curiosity is a virtue. So is discretion, but that is usually learned at a later age. In fact, take your shawl—it is a bit cool—while I ask you something about that very subject." He handed her the delicate Syannese cloth, but did not immediately let go. She was surprised, and started to say something. "Take it but do not unfold it," he said quietly. "I have put a letter in it. Do not fear! It is nothing criminal. In fact, it is a letter for your own father. Give it to him, please?"

She took the shawl from him and felt the small, angular shape of the letter. "What . . . what is it?"

"As I said, nothing to fear. Some thoughts of mine about the danger of this threatened siege by the Autarch of Xis—yes, I have heard the rumors. I would have to be deaf not to. In any case, he may do as he wishes with my suggestions."

"But why?" She put the folded shawl in her lap. "Why would you help us when we're holding you prisoner?"

Olin smiled as if through something painful. "First, I am at risk also, of course. Second, we are all natural allies against the autarch, whatever Drakava may think, and I believe your father would recognize that. Last—well, it would not hurt to have a man like your father think well of me."

Pelaya felt quite out of breath. A secret letter! Like something from one of the old tales of Silas or Lander Elfbane. "I will do it, if you promise there is no dishonor."

He bowed his head. "I promise, good mistress."

They talked a little while longer about less consequential things like her younger brother's wretched temper or the dragging nego-tiations for Teloni's marriage to a young nobleman from the country north of the city. This pained Pelaya because her father had said he would not find a husband for his younger daughter until the oldest was married, and she was anxious to be a grown woman, with a household of her own.

"Do not be in too much of a hurry," Olin said kindly. "The married state is a holy one for a woman, but it can be full of woe and danger, too." He looked down. "I lost my first wife in child-birth."

"The gods must have needed her to be with them," Pelaya said, then was irritated with herself for parroting the pious phrase her mother always used. "I'm sorry."

"I sometimes think it has been harder on my children than on me," he said quietly, then did not speak for a long moment. His eyes were roving somewhere beyond Pelaya's shoulder, so that she thought he was watching the gulls again, dreaming of the walls of Hierosol dropping into the distance behind him.

"You were saying, King Olin?"

"What?" He forced himself to look at her. "Ah, I beg your pardon. I was . . . distracted. Look, please, and tell me—who is that girl?"

Feeling a prickle of something that she would only realize later was jealousy, Pelaya turned and looked across the garden but saw no one. "Who? My sister and the others have gone in."

"There. There are two of them, carrying linens." He pointed. "One slender, one less so. The thin one—there, see, the one whose hair has come loose from her scarf."

"Do you mean . . . those washing women?"

"Yes, that is who I mean." For a moment, and for the first time Pelaya could remember, he sounded angry with her. "Do they not exist because they are servants? They are the only girls in the yard beside yourself."

She was hurt, but tried not to show it. "Who is she? How should I know? A washing woman—a girl, as you said, a servant. Why? Do you think she is pretty?" She looked closely at the slender young woman for the first time, saw that the girl was only a little older than herself. Her arms where they emerged from her billowing sleeves were brown, and her hair, which had spilled free from beneath her scarf as Olin had pointed out, was black except for a small, strange streak the color of fire. The girl's features were attractive enough, but Pelaya could see little about the thin young girl that should have attracted the prisoner-king's attention. "She looks like a Xandian to me. From the north, I'd say—they are darker below the desert. Lots of Xandian girls work here in the kitchens and the laundry."

Olin watched the young woman and her stockier companion until they had vanished into the darkness of the covered passage. "She reminds me . . . she reminded me of someone."

Now Pelaya definitely felt a pang. "You said that *I* reminded you of your daughter."

He turned, as though seeing her for the first time since the servant girl had appeared. "You do, Mistress. As I said, there is a quality in you that truly reminds me of her, and your curiosity is part of it. No, that servant girl reminds me of someone else." He frowned and shook his head. "A member of my family, long dead."

"One of your relatives?" It seemed unlikely. Pelaya thought the captive king was ashamed to have been caught ogling a serving girl.

"Yes. My . . ." He trailed off, looking again at the place where the servant had disappeared. "That is very strange—and here, so far away . . ." He paused again, then said, "Could you bring her to me?"

"What?"

"Bring her to me. Here, in the garden." His laugh was short and harsh. "I certainly cannot go to her. But I need to see her up close." He looked at her and his eyes softened. "Please, good Mistress Akuanis. I swear I ask you a favor for no unworthy reason. Could you do that for me?"

"That makes two favors in one day." She tired to make her voice stern. "I . . . I suppose I could. Perhaps." She did not understand her own feelings and was not certain that she wanted to understand them. "I will try."

"Thank you." He stood up and bowed, his face suddenly distant. "Now I must go. I have much to think about and I have stolen enough of your time today." He walked toward the archway leading back to his tower rooms—comfortable enough, he had told her, if you did not mind a door that had a barred window in it and was locked from the outside—without looking back.

Pelaya sat, feeling oddly as though she wanted to cry. For the first time since they had met each other Olin had left the garden first. The prisoner had gone back to his cell to be alone rather than share her company any longer.

She remained on the bench, trying to understand what had happened to her, until the first drops of rain forced her inside.

"Who could ever live in such a place?" Yazi asked, wide-eyed. "You would tire yourself to fits just walking to the kitchen."

"People who live in such places don't walk to the kitchen," said Qinnitan. "They have people like you and me bring their food to them." She frowned, trying to remember which way they had turned on the inbound trip. Monarchs had been adding rooms and corridors and whole wings onto the citadel of Hierosol for so many centuries that the place was like the sea coral from one of her favorite poems by Baz'u Jev. Qinnitan entertained a brief fantasy that one day she would be able to take the boy Pigeon for a walk on the seashore without worrying she might be recognized, to see some of the mysteries that had so charmed the poet, the spiraling shells daintier than jewels, the stones polished smooth as statues. She had work to do, though, and even if she hadn't, she couldn't afford to loiter in the open that way.

"But look at us!" Yazi was from the Ellamish border country so she spoke fairly good Xixian, a good-hearted girl but a little slow and prone to mistakes. "We are lost already. Surely no one can find their way in such a big place. This must be the biggest house on earth!"

Qinnitan was tempted to say that she herself had once lived in the biggest house on earth, just to see Yazi's expression, but even though she had already told Soryaza the laundry-mistress she had been an acolyte of the Hive, there was no sense in telling everyone else, especially someone as innocently loose-lipped as Yazi. The fact that Qinnitan had once lived in the Royal Seclusion, where she had been one of the fortunate few who had their food brought to them by hurrying, silent servants, was certainly not going to be mentioned either, although the irony of the present conversation was not lost on her.

"I know it's back this way," she said instead. "Remember, we came down a long hall full of pictures just after we went through that garden?"

"What garden?"

"You didn't . . . ? Where you could see the ocean and everything?" She sighed. "Never mind." Yazi was like a dog that way—the girl had been talking about something, a dream she had, or a dream she wanted to have, and hadn't even noticed the garden, the one time today they had been out from under the castle roof. Qinnitan had noticed, of course. She had spent too much time kept like a nightingale in a wicker cage to ignore the glorious moments when she was free beneath the gods' great sky. "Never mind," she said again. "Just follow me."

"Breasts of Surigali, where have you two been?" Soryaza stood with her hands on her hips, looking as though she might pick up one of the massive washing tubs and dump its scalding contents all over the truants. "You were just supposed to take those up to the upstairs ewery and come straight back."

"We did come straight back," Qinnitan said in Xixian. She could understand Hierosoline well enough now—the tongues were similar in many ways—or at least make out the sense of most things said to her, but she still did not feel comfortable with her own clumsy speech. *"We got lost."*

"It's so big!" Yazi said. *"We didn't do anything wrong, Mistress. On the Mother, we didn't!"*

Soryaza snorted her disbelief, then spat on the wet floor. "Well, get back to work. And speak Hierosoline, both of you. You aren't in the south anymore!"

As the laundry-mistress stalked away several of the other women sidled over to find out what had happened. Qinnitan knew most of their names already, although two were new enough she had only seen them and not spoken to them.

"Is she always angry?" asked one of these new workers, an anxious, scrawny young thing with pink-tinged eyes and twitching nose—the others had already named her Rabbit.

"Always," Yazi said. "Her feet hurt. And her back hurts too."

"Pah!" said one of the other women. "She's been saying that for years. Didn't stop her from picking that boy Gregor up and throwing him out the door when she caught him sleeping in the drying room. Or from kicking over a tub or two when she's in the mood."

"Nira, someone said you were a priestess in Xis," the girl called Rabbit suddenly said to Qinnitan. "Is that true?"

She was always a little slow to recognize her own false name, although she was getting better at it, and speaking Hierosoline slowed her down even more, so it took a moment for the question to sink in. When it did, she felt a chill. *By the Dark Queen, does everyone know already? Curse this nest of busybodies, and curse Soryaza—she must have told someone.*

Out loud, she said, "I . . . was not priestess. Just . . ." She searched for a word, but her command of the language was still weak. "Just helper."

"In the Hive?" Rabbit asked. "Someone said it was in the Hive. I've heard of that place. Was it like they say—did the priests come in and . . . you know? With the priestesses?"

"Silence, girl," said one of the other new workers, an old woman with a burn-scarred face and a mouth where dark holes outnumbered ruined teeth. She glared at Rabbit. "Don't ask so many question. She does not want to talk, maybe." Her command of Hierosoline was better than Qinnitan's, but it was easy to hear that she too was a southerner.

"I only wanted to know . . . !" Rabbit squeaked.

"Tits of the Great Mother, what are you lazy bitches up to?" Soryaza's voice thundered through the dank room. Her bulky form loomed up out of the washtub fog and the women scattered. "The next one I catch standing and talking might as well go down to the harbor and find a place to stand on Daneya Street with the other whores, because you won't work for me another moment!"

"Yazi, why are there so many new people?" Qinnitan asked when they were standing over their washing tub again. New faces made her unhappy, and people asking about her history in Xis made her even more so.

"New?" The round-faced girl laughed. "You've only been here a tennight yourself."

"But so many! Rabbit, and that old toothless woman, and the one with the fat legs . . ."

"Oh, listen to you! Not everyone's a skinny little thing like you, Nira. As it happens, Soryaza told me she's hiring more because of the war."

"The war?"

"Don't you listen to anybody? There's a war coming, everyone says so. The autarch's going to send ships. They'll never break this place, of course—no one ever has. But the lord protector has called in troops from Krace and . . . and . . . and other places." She flushed, her tone of authority momentarily compromised. "And so we're going to be having more work."

Qinnitan felt a sudden chill—touched by a ghost, her family

had always called it. She had heard rumors but had not given them much credence—as the continent's greatest seaport, Hierosol seemed to breathe rumors like air, to serve them as meat and drink. A new continent discovered in the western oceans, one said. So much gold discovered on an island near Ulos that the overladen boat sank on the way back. Fairy armies marching in the north. The Autarch of Xis preparing to conquer all Eion. Who was to know what was truth and what was fancy?

"The ... autarch ... ?" she said now. Memories of his pale, mad eyes, never more than a moment away from her thoughts at the best of times, now pushed their way front and center. *Is it me?* she wondered. *Is it to find me, to torture me for running away?* It was silly, unbearably self-important, even to consider it, but she couldn't shake off the idea: she had seen enough of Sulepis to know he was a man of incomprehensible whims.

No, she told herself. *He and his father and his father's father have wanted to set their heel on Eion for years, especially Hierosol.* She had heard it talked of enough in the Seclusion. *This is only more of the same, if it's even true. And if he is coming, well, the walls will defeat him. And if they don't . . .*

Then I will be gone. I escaped him once, I will escape him again. Despite her terror, she felt a stubborn little glow inside her, a heat like a burning coal. *Or die. But one way or another, he won't have me . . .*

"Nira?" Yazi was pulling at her sleeve. "Pay attention, girl! If Soryaza sees you staring at nothing that way, she'll whip us both."

Qinnitan bent to the washing, but it was hard to keep her thoughts on the sheets and soapy water.

As Qinnitan walked with Yazi at sunset across the wide space of the Echoing Mall, she had a sudden feeling of being observed, troubling as an insect flying too near her head. She looked back and at first saw only the other washerwomen and ordinary working folk of the citadel dispersing to the outer gates or their cramped quarters within the great fortress itself; then a movement at the corner of her eye, where the newly-lit torches lined one of the colonnades, made her turn all the way around. A smear of sideways movement, at odds with the rest of the crowd, arrested her attention. She felt sure someone had stepped back into the colonnade just as she looked. Still, did it mean something, even so?

"Nira, stop that," said Yazi. "I'm so tired my feet are on fire. Keep walking, will you?"

Qinnitan walked forward, but after a dozen paces turned again. A man was walking along the edge of the colonnade, and although he was not looking at her she thought she saw him hesitate for an instant and almost break stride, as though he had just decided it was too late to step back out of sight again.

Qinnitan pointed up at the sky above the high walls of the Echoing Mall, shot red with the last light of the day, and said, "Isn't it pretty, with all those colors!" While performing this bit of show, she examined the man as best she could. He wore shabby, unobtrusive clothes—the kind any of the menial laborers might wear—and had somewhat the look of a northerner, with hair of the lackluster brown shade Qinnitan had learned was almost as common north of Hierosol as black hair was in Xand. He was studiously avoiding her eyes as he walked, and so Qinnitan swung around again.

"What are you talking about, the sunset?" asked Yazi. "If your thoughts wandered any farther, girl, you'd have to put bells on them, like goats."

When Qinnitan looked back the man was gone into the crowd. She didn't know what to think. Even Yazi suddenly seemed capable of having secret depths.

Pigeon came bounding out to greet her when they reached the dormitory hall, excited as a puppy. He threw his arms around her, then grabbed her hand to pull her back to the bed they shared, waving his free arm excitedly. He had taught her some of the hand-language he had spoken with the other mute servants back in the Orchard Palace, but at times like this he didn't bother trying to make his thoughts known in a more subtle way, nor did he need to. Some of the other women looked up as he dragged

Qinnitan down the open space between the tiny wooden beds, a few with indulgent smiles, remembering brothers or children of their own, many others with the generalized irritation of someone who had just finished a long, hard day's labor being forced to observe the endless energies of a child. It was strange, living with so many women again—almost a hundred in this dormitory alone, with several more buildings like it on this side of the citadel. The culture was oddly familiar, the same quick-blooming friendships and rivalries and even hatreds, as though someone had taken the wives of the autarch's Seclusion, dressed them in dirty smocks and sweat-stained dresses, then dumped them into this vast, depressing hall that had once been the royal stables for some long-dead king of Hierosol. These women were not so comely, and not so young—many of them were grand-mothers—but otherwise there seemed little difference between this and her former home, or even the Hive where she had lived before.

Cages, she thought. *Why do men fear us so that they must cage us all together and keep us apart from them?* Hierosol was better than Xis, but even here there were strict rules about keeping out men, even for those of the washerwomen who were married. Only Soryaza's intervention with the dormitory mistress had gained a place here for Pigeon, and he was one of but a dozen or so chil-dren, most babes in arms who stayed behind during the day to be cared for in an offhand way by a pair of washerwomen now too old to work, two crones who each morning found the sunniest place in the dormitory and sat there like lizards, muttering to each other while the children more or less looked after themselves.

"Soryaza says she has work for you again," Qinnitan told Pigeon, suddenly reminded. He had been banished to the dormi-tory for being underfoot—a crime worse than murder, to hear the laundry-mistress talk. "You'll come in with me tomorrow."

Pigeon seemed less interested in this news than in tugging her the last few steps toward their bed. In the middle of it, nested in a pile of wood chips and shavings like the legendary phoenix, sat a slightly irregular carving of a bird—a pigeon, she saw after a moment. Pigeon pointed to the sculpture, then dug the small knife he had stolen from Axamis Dorza's house out of the chips and proudly displayed it, too.

"Did you make this bird? It's very fine." But she could not help frowning a little. "I do wish you hadn't done it on the bed. I'll be sleeping in slivers tonight."

He looked at her with such hurt that she bent and picked up the carving to examine it. As she turned it over she saw that he had arduously carved her name (or at least his childish approximation of it) on the bottom of it in Xixian letters—"Qinatan." A rush of love for the boy collided with a burst of fear to see her real name written on something, even a child's rough carving. Yazi and Soryaza were not the only women here who could speak the language of Xis, and some of them might read it too. She already had enough problems with people asking questions.

"It's beautiful," she whispered. "But you must remember my name here is *Nira,* not . . . not the other. And you are Nonem, remember?"

This time he did not look hurt so much as anguished at his own mistake, and she had to pull him to her and hug him tight. "No, it's beautiful, it is. Let me just take it for a moment. And the knife, please." She kissed him on top of his head, smelling the strange boy-smell of his sweat, then looked around. Several women on either side were watching. She smiled and showed them the bird, then took it with her and headed for the privies on the far side of the dormitory hall. She sat down in one of the small cubicles there, so like an animal's stall that she felt sure they had once been just that, and, when she felt sure no one was looking, took the knife and quickly scraped the boy's childish letters off the bottom of the bird.

On the way back she stopped off to borrow a looking-glass from one of the other serving-women. In return for the loan she gave the woman the round ball of soap she had assembled from discarded slivers in the laundry. The mirror was the size of Qinnitan's hand, in a chipped frame of polished tortoiseshell.

"Mind you bring it back before bedtime," the woman warned.

Qinnitan nodded. "Just . . . for hair," she said in her fragmented Hierosoline. "Bring soon."

When she reached her bed again she saw that Pigeon had done his best to clear away the remnants of his day's carvings. She set the carved bird on the empty barrel she shared as a table with the next bed over, and borrowed a comb from the girl whose bed that was, and who luckily did not ask anything in trade.

Qinnitan set the mirror on her knee and stared at the reflection. To her despair, she saw that her unruly hair had escaped the scarf again right where the red streak emerged. As if she had not already left enough of a trail across the citadel! She no longer had access to the cosmetics and dyes the women had used in the Seclusion, so she had done her best to disguise the flame-colored patch with soot from the candles and the laundry fireplaces, but working in that damp, hot room ensured that the soot didn't work for long. She would have to get a bigger scarf, or cut her hair off entirely. Some of the older women here wore their hair very short, especially if they were past childbearing age. Maybe no one would think it too odd if she did the same . . .

"Nira, isn't it?" a scratchy voice asked.

Startled, Qinnitan looked up, hurriedly tucking her hair back under the scarf. It was the old woman from the laundry, the one with the burned face and missing teeth who had only been working there a few days. "Yes?"

"It's me, Losa. I thought that was you when I saw you across the room. And is this your little brother?"

Pigeon was looking at the old woman with mistrust, his usual expression with strangers. "Yes, his name is Nonem."

"Ah, lovely. I didn't mean to bother you, child, I was just . . ."

At that moment, just to add to the madcap air of sudden festivity, Yazi approached, followed by a young girl in a very fine dress—the kind of dress the laundrywomen only saw when they were called upon to clean things from the upper apartments of the citadel.

"Nira, I just . . ." Yazi saw the old woman. "Losa! What are you doing here?"

The woman smiled, then quickly pulled her lips together to hide her ruined teeth. "Oh, I couldn't get out the gate to get home. All kinds of soldiers coming in, and such a fuss! Wagons, oxen, people shouting. Someone said they were Sessians hired by the lord protector. I thought I'd ask if I could stay here."

"We'll talk to the dormitory mistress," said Yazi, "but I'm sure she wouldn't mind." At any ordinary time Yazi would have pressed the old woman for details and it would have been the subject of the evening's conversation all over the dormitory, but now something even more exciting was clearly pressing on her. "Nira, there's someone here to see you."

Qinnitan was beginning to feel quite overwhelmed. She turned to the very young girl in the beautiful blue dress and velvet petticoat. A crowd of women was beginning to gather as people came to see what had brought such an apparition into the dormitory.

"Yes?"

"I am to take you to my mistress," the girl said. "You are . . . Nira?"

Qinnitan's confusion quickly turned to panic, but she couldn't very well deny it. She struggled to frame the Hierosoline words. "Who . . . who is your mistress?"

"She will tell you herself. Come with me, please." Beneath the formal manners, the girl seemed a little anxious herself.

"Oh, that is too bad," old Losa said. "I was looking forward to a chat."

"You'd better go," Yazi told Qinnitan. "Maybe a handsome prince saw you when we were wandering around lost today. Should I come with you, in case he has trouble making himself understood when he proposes to you?"

"Stop, Yazi." Qinnitan just wanted everyone to go away and forget about this, but it was obviously going to be the talk of the dormitory, perhaps for days.

"She is to come alone," said the girl in the blue dress.

"But what about . . . my brother?" Qinnitan asked.

"I'll watch him," Yazi said. "We'll have fun, won't we, Nonem?"

Pigeon liked Yazi, but he clearly didn't like the idea of letting Qinnitan go away with some stranger. Still, after a warning look from her, he nodded. Qinnitan rose, leaving the comb and mirror for Yazi to return to their owners, and followed the girl out of the dormitory into the cold, torchlit night.

She felt in the pocket of her smock for Pigeon's carving knife and held it tightly as they walked back across the tiled immensity of the Echoing Mall.

"Who is your . . . mistress?" she asked the girl again.

"She will tell you what she wishes to tell you," the little girl in the blue dress said, and would say no more.

"I am not happy," said her father. Pelaya knew it was the truth. Count Perivos was not the sort of man who liked surprises, and all this had obviously come as just that. "Bad enough that a foreign prisoner should bribe my daughter to send messages to me when I already have so much else to worry on—using her as a . . . a go-between. But to find he also expects her to arrange some sort of *assignation* for him . . . !"

"It's not an assignation and he didn't bribe me." Pelaya stroked his sleeve. The cuff needed mending, which made her heart ache a little—he worked so hard! "Please, Babba, don't be difficult. Was there anything bad in his letter to you?"

Her father raised his eyebrow. "Babba? I haven't heard that since the last time you wanted something. No, his thoughts are at least interesting, perhaps useful, and all he asks in return is any news I can give him about his home or his family. There's nothing wrong with the letter, except that he knows too much. How could a foreign prisoner have so much to say about our castle defenses?"

"He told me he fought here twenty years ago against the Tuan pirates. That he was a guest of the Temple Council."

"I remember those days, but he remembers where every tower stairway is and how many steps it has, I swear! He must have a memory like a mantisery library." Count Perivos frowned. "Still, some of his warnings and suggestions show wisdom, and I am willing to believe he meant them in good faith. But what is this madness about a serving girl?"

"I don't know, Babba. He said she reminded him of someone." Pelaya spotted her servant coming across the garden with the dark-haired girl walking slowly behind her. "Look—here they come now."

"Madness," her father said, but sighed as if weak protest were all he was allowed.

Seeing the laundry maid up close, Pelaya was both relieved and confused. Relieved, without quite understanding why, to see that this girl was only a year or two older than she was, and that while she was by no means ugly, she was not astoundingly pretty, either. But something else about this laundry servant put her on edge, although Pelaya could not say what it was—something in the quality of the girl's watchfulness, in the cool and measured way she looked around the torchlit garden, was not what the steward's daughter expected from someone who spent every day up to her elbows in the citadel's washing tubs.

Now the girl turned that dark-eyed gaze onto Pelaya and her father, examining them as carefully as she had the surroundings, which was strange in itself: should she not have been looking first at the nobles who had summoned her? Pelaya found the inspection a little unnerving.

"Your name is Nira, is it not?" she asked the girl. "Someone wants to meet you. Do you understand me?"

The girl nodded. "Yes, Nira. Understand." Either she had not been in Hierosol long or she was far more stupid than she looked, because her accent was barbarous.

Not for the first time that day, Pelaya wondered what she had stumbled into. A simple friendship had become something larger and much less comfortable. She was reassured that her father and his bodyguard were here to ensure that nothing was passed between the prisoner and this servant girl and that no tricks were attempted.

Now Perivos stepped forward. He spent a moment examining the girl Nira as thoroughly as she herself had inspected everything and everyone else. "So this is her?"

"Yes, Father."

"I wish Olin Eddon would hasten himself. I have better things to do . . ."

"Yes, Father. I know." She took a breath. "Please, be kind to him."

He turned on her with a look of surprise and annoyance. "What does that mean, Pelaya?"

"He is a kind man, Father. *Babba*. He has always been polite to me, proper in his speech, and always insists that his guards stay— and my maid as well. He says I remind him of his daughter."

Her father gave a little snort of disbelief. "Many young women remind him of his daughter, it seems."

"Father! Be kind. You know his daughter has disappeared and both his sons are dead."

The count shook his head, but she could see him softening. More subtle than her sister, she had learned ways to bend him gently to her will, and sometimes he even seemed to collaborate in his own defeats. "Do not badger me," he said. "I will grant him the respect of some privacy—he is a king, after all—but I do not like it. And if anything untoward occurs . . ."

"It won't, Father. He's not like that." Pelaya Akuanis was far too ladylike to curse even to herself, and did not know any really useful curse words in any case, but Olin's favor was costing her more than the prisoner could know. She could not besiege her father for favors like this very often: it would be long months before she could expect to get her way in anything important again. *I hope it's worth it for him, talking to some laundry trollop.* But she knew even in her disgruntled state that wasn't quite fair: there was unquestionably something more to this girl, this Nira, although Pelaya still could not guess what it might be.

Olin and his guards arrived even as a quiet rumble of thunder growled through the northern sky. A storm was on the way. Pelaya's father stepped forward and bowed his head to the prisoner.

"King Olin, you are a persuasive man, or else we would not all be standing in this garden with the rains sweeping toward us and my supper waiting. My daughter has risked her father's love to bring you and this young woman here."

Olin smiled. "I think that might be an exaggeration, Count Perivos, from the things your daughter has said about you. I have a headstrong girl child myself, so I appreciate your position and I thank you for indulging me when you did not need to." He lowered his voice so the bodyguard standing a dozen steps away could not hear. "Did you receive the letter? And is it any help to you?"

Pelaya's father would not be so easily swayed. "Perhaps. We will talk about it at some other time. For now I will leave you to your conversation . . . *if* you will swear to me on your honor that it is nothing against the interests of Hierosol. It goes without saying that it is nothing lewd or immoral, either."

"Yes, it goes without saying," said Olin with a touch of asperity. "You have my word, Count Perivos."

Her father bowed and withdrew himself a little way.

"Do not be frightened, child," Olin said to the laundry girl. "Your name is Nira, I am told. Is that correct?"

She nodded, watching the bearded man with a different kind of attention than she had given to the garden or Pelaya or anything else, almost as if she recognized him—as if they had met before and the girl was trying to remember where and when. For a moment Pelaya felt a kind of chill. Had she done something truly wrong here after all? Was she unwittingly helping an escape plan, something that would cost her father his honor or maybe even his life?

"Yes," the girl said slowly. "Nira."

"All I want to know from you is a little about your family," Olin said gently. "That red in your hair—I think it is rare in this part of the world, is it not?"

The girl only shrugged. Pelaya felt a need to say something, if only to remind the man that she was still sitting here, part of the gathering. "Not so rare," she told him. "There have been northerners in Xand for years—mercenaries and folk of that sort. My father often talks about the autarch's White Hounds. They are famous traitors to Eion."

Olin nodded. "But still, I think such a shade is uncommon." He smiled and turned to the laundry girl. "Are there mercenaries from Eion in your family, young Nira? Northerners with fair hair?"

The girl hesitated for a moment as she made sense of his question. Her fingers moved up to the place where another little curl of hair escaped her scarf and pushed it back beneath the stained homespun cloth. "No. All . . . like me."

"I see something in you of a family that I know well, Nira. Be brave—you have done nothing wrong. Can you tell me if your family came from the north? Are there any family stories about such things?"

She looked at him a long time, as though trying to decide whether this entire conversation might be some kind of trick. "No. Always Xis." She shrugged. "Think always Xis. Until me."

"Until you, of course." He nodded. "Someone told me that your parents died. I am very sorry to hear it. If I can do anything— not that I have much favor here, but I have made a couple of kind friends—let me know."

She stared at him again, clearly puzzled by something. At last she nodded.

"Let her go now," Olin said, straightening. "I am sure she hasn't had her supper yet and I have no doubt she works hard all the day." He stood. "Thank you, Pelaya, and thank you, Count Perivos. My curiosity is satisfied. Doubtless it was just a fluke of light and shadow that tricked me into seeing a resemblance that was not there—that could not be there."

Pelaya's little maid took Nira back to the servants' dormitory, and Olin went with his guards back to his chambers. As she walked back across the garden toward their residence, a part of the citadel only a little less sumptuous than the lord protector's own quarters, Pelaya took her father's hand.

"Thank you, Babba," she said. "You are the best, kindest father. You truly are."

"But what in the name of the gods was that all about?" he said, scowling. "Has the man lost his wits? What connection could he be searching for with a laundry girl?"

"I don't know," Pelaya said. "But they both seem sad."

Her father shook his head. "That is what you said about that stray cat, and now I awake every morning to the sound of that creature yowling for fish. Both your King Olin and his laundry girl have places to live. Do not think to bring them home."

"No, Papa." But she too wondered what had brought two such strange, different people together in a Hierosol garden.

The sky thundered again and the first drops of rain began to spatter down. Pelaya, her father, and the bodyguard all hurried to get out of the open air.

19

Voices in the Forest

*But each night Pale Daughter heard Silvergleam singing
and her heart ached for him, until at last she fled her
father's house and ran to her beloved. So beautiful was she
that he could not bear to send her away, although his
brother and sister warned him that only evil would come of
it. But Silvergleam made Pale Daughter his wife, and
together they conceived a child who would make a new and
greater song of their two melodies, a strange song which
would thereafter sound through all the Tale of Years.*

—from *One Hundred Considerations*
out of the Qar's *Book of Regret*

EVEN WITH HER INJURIES, Briony knew she should
put as much distance as she could between herself and
Landers Port, but instead she stayed close to the walls of
the city in the two days after the attack, sheltering where she
could and eavesdropping on the conversations of other travelers,

trying to find out for certain what had happened to Shaso. The destructive fire that had taken the life of one of the city's wealthiest merchants was on everyone's lips, of course, and all seemed to agree that except for the one lone manservant she'd seen, only the women of Dan-Mozan's house had survived the night's terrible events.

Her last unlikely hopes finally dashed, Briony realized that if the baron's guards knew that more than one fugitive had taken refuge in the Dan-Mozan *hadar,* they would be looking for her. Young man's clothing was an indifferent disguise, especially when it was a young Tuani man's clothing and she no longer had the tools to make herself look like someone of that race. She daubed her face and hair with dirt, trying to make herself less noticeable, but she knew her disguise would not survive real scrutiny for more than a few moments. She had to leave Landers Port, that was all: if she was caught mooning around the town gates Shaso would have died for nothing—a bitter thought, but the only one that moved her when her own desires were muted by grief and rage. She missed the old man fiercely. Had Effir's nephew Talibo stood before her again, she would gladly have killed the little traitor a second time.

Foolishly thinking she had already lost everything, Briony was learning daily that the gods could always take more from you if they wished.

She quickly discovered that she was not suited for life as an outlaw—in fact, all the tales of romantic banditry she had ever heard now began to seem like the cruelest lies imaginable. It was impossible to live out of doors in even as mild a winter as this, even with the gods-sent gift of the woolen cloak she had taken from the *hadar* when she ran; Briony spent a large part of each day's travel just searching for unguarded barns or storehouses where she could sleep without freezing. Even so, after only a few nights she found herself with a wracking cough.

The cough and her sore mouth (still tender from where Talibo had struck her) made it difficult to eat, but she soaked bread in the little pot of wine so it would soften, then chewed very slowly and carefully so as not to pain her loosened teeth and split lips any more than necessary. Even so, her small cache of food was gone in a couple of days.

The only thing that saved her at first was the number of small towns and villages dotting the hillsides along the coast road west of Landers Port. She moved from one to the next, taking shelter where she could and finding an occasional scrap of untended food. She dared not attract attention when her enemies were doubtless searching for her, so she could not beg for help in public places. Despite her hunger, though, Briony did her best to avoid real theft—not for moral reasons so much as practical ones: what good to have escaped an attempt on her life only to be caught and imprisoned in some goatyard village in the middle of nowhere?

Still, within a few days the gnawing of her empty stomach began to overwhelm her. She had never been hungry for more than a short time in all her life and was painfully surprised to discover how it conquered everything else, drove out all other thoughts. Her cough was getting worse as well, wracking her body until she felt dizzy. Sometimes she stumbled and fell in the middle of the road for no reason other than weakness. She knew she could not go on much longer without becoming either a beggar or a thief. She decided she would rather risk the first—people didn't get hanged for begging.

The first place she approached in search of alms, a steading on the outskirts of a nameless village along the Karalsway, the market road that wound south from the Coast Road, proved unsympathetic to beggars: before she could speak to the wild-haired man standing in the doorway of the cottage he stepped aside and let out a huge brindle dog. The creature ran at her like the Raging Beast that had fought Hiliometes, and Briony only just barely got back over the steading's low wall before it caught her in its slavering jaws. As it was, she tore her lifesaving wool cloak on a stone, an injury which seemed as painful to her as if it had been her own flesh. She retreated into the woods, still sick and sore and hungry, and although she disliked herself for doing it, she wept.

She tried again with a little more success on the far side of the village—but not because of the qualities of godly mercy the mantis-priests liked to talk about so solemnly. The householder who owned this particular shambles of a cottage happened to be gone for the day, and although there was little of use inside the empty, smoke-darkened room but a bed made of leaves stuffed in a rough cloth sack, with a single threadbare blanket, she found an iron bowl half-full of cold pottage sitting underneath the table with a wooden plate set on top of it. She devoured it eagerly, and it was not until she had finished it—her stomach so full it seemed hung on her rather than connected to her—that she realized she had stolen, and stolen from one of her poorer subjects at that. For a moment, in an agony of guilt possible only because she had momentarily sated her hunger, she considered waiting until the cottage's owner returned and offering to make restitution, but quickly realized that other than her clothes, her Yisti knives, and her virginity—none of which she was willing to give up—she had nothing to offer. Still, she felt bad enough that she discarded her earlier plan of stealing the blanket as well, and stumbled dry-eyed but miserable out into the dying light of afternoon and a sparkle of lightly falling snow.

The days since Shaso's death turned into first one tennight, then another, and Briony crept west, stealing enough to stay alive when she could, almost always from those least able to protect what they had. Shame and hunger dogged her, whipsawing her back and forth, one growing less as the other grew greater. Her wounds and sore jaw had mostly healed, but her cough had become a constant thing, painful and frighteningly deep. And as things became harder for her, as hunger and illness made her thoughts difficult, the two other alternatives, surrender or death, began to seem more attractive.

Briony stared blearily at the bridge, at the dark, sluggish river and the empty lands on either side. The sky was like a bed of slates.

Orphanstide and the changing of the year have passed already. But they had been tolling the bells for Oni Zakkas' Day only a few sunrises ago in the last town she had passed that was big enough to have a temple (more of a shrine, really, this far out in the country) so that meant Dimene was just arriving—the Gestrimadi festival had not even begun yet. That was a terrible thought—at least another two months of winter still, with the worst of it yet to come!

In her breathless exhaustion she had wandered far south down the Karalsway, still uncertain whether she should go to Hierosol or Syan, but knowing in her heart that in her present condition she would reach neither. The villages became more scarce the farther south she went—she had been chased out of the last one two days ago by a group of drunken men who hadn't liked her look and had called her a plague-carrier—and there would be even fewer settlements in the empty lands between here and the Syannese border. She was beginning to feel truly desperate.

All through her childhood Briony had been prepared for a life of importance, but what had she truly learned? Nothing useful. She did not know how to start a fire on her own. She might have managed with a flint and iron, but she had spent the last coppers Shaso had given her on bread and cheese before realizing warmth would come to be even more important to her than filling her stomach. She did not know how to hunt or trap either, or which if any of the plants that grew wild might be eaten without poisoning her—things that even the most ignorant crofter's son could easily manage. Instead, her tutors had taught her how to sing, and sew, and read, but the books she had been given were filled with romantic poetry, or useless knowledge about the great gods and their adventures, with parables of gentle Zoria and her blameless suffering.

She stood now in a nearly empty land, staring miserably at the bridge over the muddy Elusine. Learning about suffering was useless—experience came easily enough. Learning how *not* to suffer would have proved much more practical.

Briony could recall just enough of her brother's lessons and things her father had told her to know that the territory on the other side of the Elusine was named the Weeping Moors. These marshy, treacherous lands stretched almost all the way south to the lakes of upper Syan, the mud cold and black, with no shelter from the vicious, freezing winds and gusting snows. She had wandered this far almost without thinking, and now she had nowhere to go but back to the towns she had already haunted with so little luck, or east to the Tollys' home in Summerfield, or southward along this dwindling road through the fens, then around the lakes and over the mountains to distant Syan and even more distant Hierosol, praying to strike lucky in whatever human habitations she might stumble across in the great, empty water-lands ahead.

Briony sank to a crouch. For the moment, she could see nothing but the reeds that surrounded her, the windblown stalks rubbing and whispering. She coughed and spat. The gobbet was tinged with red. It was pointless even to think about Syan—she would never survive a journey across the moors and mountains to reach it.

Unless I go west . . . she thought slowly, and squinted toward what looked an endless smear of dark forest on the muddy western horizon. That, she knew, must be the northernmost tip of the Whitewood. If she managed to cross through it alive, she would reach Firstford on the far side, the largest city in Silverside. There was a famous temple at Firstford that fed poor people from all over the March Kingdoms, and even provided beds for the sick.

"Silverside" began sounding over and over in her thoughts as soothing as the word "heaven."

But as the dull morning wore away and she still sat exhausted beside the bridge and the muddy, gurgling Elusine, she still could not make a decision. Singing about Silverside to herself was all well and good, but she was even more likely to die in the trees trying to get there than out on the open wrack of the Weeping Moors. The Whitewood was the second greatest forest in all of Eion, and in its depths lived wolves and bears and perhaps even some of the stranger creatures out of legend. After all, if the fairy folk could come down out of the misty north to invade the March Kingdoms, it stood to reason that goblins and ghouls could still be found in the depths of the Whitewood, just as the stories all told. No, it would be better to stay away from the almost certain death of either marsh or forest, to turn back instead and continue to haunt the fringes of Marrinswalk villages like a lost child. Better to stay where she was and pray for a miracle than to plunge into the forest and certain doom. Yes, she decided wearily, that made more sense. She would turn back.

It was very strange, then, that as the sun slipped down the sky toward evening Briony found herself wandering through the dense trees of the Whitewood, with the road and the bridge lost somewhere behind her and no real memory of how she had come there.

There's sky above me. There—a little. Between the branches. That is sky, isn't it? It's still day, I can see, so there must be sky somewhere.

She lurched a few more steps toward a place where the trees seemed farther apart, where the branches would not pull at her. Already her cloak was in tatters.

Food. So hungry. What will I . . . ?

Something had caught at the boyish trousers she wore. Brambles. She pulled herself free, only vaguely noticing new scratches on hands already crisscrossed with bloody little lines. Thank all the gods the cold was making her fingers numb! She wept to realize she had forgotten again which direction she had set herself to walk.

"Cloudy-eyed, line-handed," she named herself, mangling the famous story—and not entirely on purpose. She tried to laugh but could only make a ragged hooting noise. Barrick would think that was funny, she decided. He hated learning those stories.

But it was about *her,* that story. Well, no, not about her, but about Zoria, and hadn't that Matty Wringtight fellow, that poet, said that she *was* Zoria? A virgin princess? Wrongly stolen from her father's house?

But I ran away. It was the house that was stolen.

It didn't matter. She had always felt deeply about Zoria, the daughter of Perin. When she had been a little girl the tales of Perin and Siveda and Erivor and the others had interested her, but it was the tale of Zoria the merciful, Zoria the pure, brave shield-maiden, that had inspired her. Although she knew many of the old tales and romances, it was only the poems about Zoria she had learned by heart. She recited the line out loud—haltingly at first, then with more strength. It gave her a rhythm to push through the brambles, a marching cadence to keep putting one foot in front of the other.

" . . . *Clear-eyed, lion-hearted, her mind turned toward the day when her honor will again be proclaimed, the Lady of the Doves walks out into the night, toward the fires of her family.*"

Briony had little strength, and the words came out as scarcely more than a croaking murmur, but it was a pleasure to hear any voice, even if it was her own, so she said it again.

" . . . *Clear-eyed, lion-hearted, her mind turned toward the day when her honor will again be proclaimed, the Lady of the Doves walks out into the night, toward the fires of her family.*"

She had to stop for a moment while a coughing fit shook her. The next part of the tale was something about walking and singing. That seemed appropriate: she was walking right now, and she supposed she was singing, too, after a fashion. Branches slapped at her, wet leaves against her face like angry kisses, making it hard to think, but at last she came up with the next lines:

"*Walking, she sings, and singing, Perin's virgin daughter is truly free, despite her terrible wound and unstanched blood.*"

Briony felt better with something to think about, and it fit her mood of self-pity to think of how Zoria too had suffered. *Merciful goddess,* she prayed, *think of me and help me through these days of sorrow.* In Gregor of Syan's famous romance, the ice and snow had seemed to fill the world. Briony could still think clearly enough to be grateful that there was no snow here under the trees, but it was still cold enough to make her shiver. The pattering rain was coming down harder now, drizzling heavily through open spaces in the cover. These little waterfalls became another obstacle to be avoided as she trudged on, along with the worst of the brambles and the fallen trees.

Somebody came to help Zoria, she remembered—one of the other gods. Wouldn't that be fine, to be saved by a god! Except that god hadn't really saved her, had he . . . ?

> *"Zosim the Helper, grandson of old Kernios the Earth Master, hears Perin's daughter's tripping footfalls and offers to show her the way, but the night's shadows are long and confusing even for the grandchild of the Lord of Owls, and the dark magic of Everfrost delays them.*
>
> *"Thus the Moon King's fate is marked and sealed by the mysteries of his own great house . . ."*

Whatever that meant. Her voice trailed off.

A shadow seemed to jump from behind one tree to another at the top of the rise. Briony stopped, heart beating fast. She squinted but could make out nothing among the paper-white birches except the columns of weak sunlight between the trunks, each one shot through with falling rain so that they looked like pillars of smoky glass and diamonds.

Could it be a wolf? She touched the hilt of the long Yisti knife sheathed in her belt. She knew she might be able to fight one wolf, perhaps even kill it if she was lucky—but they hunted in packs, didn't they? For a moment she was overwhelmed by a dark vision of herself surrounded by wolves in a wet, lonely forest as darkness came on. She began to cry.

"Most beasts of forest and field are more afraid of you than you are of them," her father had once told her, and she tried hard to believe it now. *"They are right to fear us, of course—we men are more likely to be their death than the other way around."*

"That's me!" she said aloud, as harshly as she could. "Your death!" Nothing moved, no sound except the rain broke the silence after her words had echoed away. Briony coughed again and shook her head, leaned in toward the slope and started to clamber up again, scratching her hands as she grabbed for roots and vines when the way was steep.

"When morning's sun rises . . ."

she sang out, loud enough for the wolves to hear, trying to make her voice steady enough to scare them away,

" . . .All father Perin rides with the gods of his house behind him, the lightnings in his hands and his eye full of fury. The shining towers of Everfrost loom above the icy earth, burning with a pallid gleam like twilight, like bone, and a moat of killing ice surrounds it."

The story was making her feel cold again. She realized her hood had fallen back and her hair was getting soaked.

"Before his own door stood the Moonlord in shimmering armor of ivory and electrum, pale hair blowing, with his great sword Silverbeam in his hand."

Just before she reached the top of the rise she saw the shape once more, a movement of darkness a score of paces ahead. Afraid to see it too closely, fearful that it was some predatory beast moving just ahead of her and that the sight of it would freeze her throat, she raised her scratchy voice even louder.

" 'Go away from my door, Cousin,' " speaks Khors. *" 'You ride unasked in the Moon's Land, on the sovereign road of Everfrost. You have no rights here. This is not vasty Xandos, citadel of the gods.'*

" 'I have the right of a father,' " bellows Perin, *'and you have*

stolen that right from me when you stole my daughter! Set her here
before me, then never cross into my lands again, and I will let you
live.' "

At the top of the rise Briony could make out only a deer track
or old streambed at the base of the hill on the far side, a snaking
line of reddish mud. It was nothing like a road, but at least it was
a direction and she would not be pulling berry brambles from
her feet at each step. She made her way down toward it with cautious speed, aware for the first time in some hours that if she
stumbled or slipped and broke her leg she would certainly die
here. When she reached the stripe of rust-colored mud she raised
her voice again in a note of ragged triumph, a hymn to her newfound path.

When you are this badly beaten, she thought distractedly, climbing
over a huge, damp trunk, terrified that it might start rolling downward while she was on it—*when you are this badly beaten, you must*
take any victory you can find.

"'No one orders me on my own lands,'" Khors cries, "'and least of
all a braggart like you, Lord Storm-Cloud, heavy with thunder like
a tempest that blows and blows but does nothing more. She belongs
to me now. The dove is mine.'

"'Thief! Liar!'" shouts Perin. "'Now you shall learn for yourself
whether this storm is all wind, like the stables of Strivos, full of his
godlike stallions of the blowing gale, or whether it brings lightning,
too!'"

She reached the bottom of the hill at last, muddy and panting until
her lungs ached in her chest, but she had a clear track for walking
now and she wanted to go as far as she could before the light
failed.

And then what? a silent voice asked her—her own voice, the
sensible part she thought she had lost somewhere on the road outside the forest. *Then what? You cannot even make a fire, and in any case*
the wood is all wet. Will you sit on a damp rock all night and try to keep

the wolves at bay with your knife? And the next night? And the next . . . ?

No. Quiet! What else can I do? Go forward. Go forward. She raised her voice again, just as Allfather Perin raised high his weapon against his daughter's kidnapper. *Run, wolves! Run, all you enemies!*

"And with that he lifts his mighty hammer Oak Tree and rides at Khors and the world shakes at the sounds of his golden car, the very mountains swaying to the drumbeat of his horses' hooves.

"Khors is fearful, but rides out himself on his white horse, brandishing Silverbeam his potent blade, swinging the great net his father Sveros had given him, in which once the old god had captured the stars of the sky."

When the two meet it is as the shock of a thunderclap, so that all gods in both armies, who would have rushed at each other, must instead fight to keep their feet beneath them. Indeed, some like Yarnos of the Snows are thrown to the ground; Strivos is one, and as he lies there he is almost destroyed by Azinor of the Onyenai, always swift to strike and eager to slay his father's enemies.

"Back and forth across the great icy field upon which stands Everfrost the gods give battle, the light unto the dark, Perin and his brothers against Khors and the spawn of Old Mother Night, and ever hangs the balance on the cast of a spear, the flight of an arrow, the thrust of a sword, even the blink of a blood-spattered eye.

"White-Handed Uvis is wounded by a blow of Kernios' great spear, but Birin, Lord of the Evening Mist, meets his doom when the arrows of the Onyenai pierce his throat. The car of courageous Volios is thrown down by the bullish strength of Zmeos the horned one, and the war-god is trapped beneath it, his bones broken, his voice crying out to his uncles for vengeance. Even the great river Rimetrail is thrown from its banks by the force of their fighting, and flows brokenly in many directions."

She was following the deer track now. It was wider than it had looked, as though not deer but herds of cattle had made it, just as they had scraped the wide drover's roads across the valleys and hills of Southmarch from the farmlands into the city's markets. The relative ease of passage lifted her heart, although the rain was still falling and her face and hands were still numb. If there were wolves near her, then her proclaiming of the *Lay of Everfrost* was keeping them well at bay.

> *"In the forest, virgin Zoria is lost in the snow,"* Briony bellowed, but the wet trees swallowed most of the echoes, *"the Almond Princess pulled away from the aiding hand of Zosim by the wrath of Old Winter, so that she cannot see her fingers before her eyes, and can hear only the shriek of the snowy winds. Only a short distance away her family fights and dies for her honor, and everywhere else the screams of gods overtop even the storm.*
>
> *"Lost, her eyes shut against the wailing winds, her face bloodied by sleet, she stumbles. Lost, she wanders in howling darkness, and does not know that on the other side of the darkly sheltering, confounding wood, all is war, all is death, as her cousins murder her cousins and the endless snows cover all . . ."*

Briony fell silent, not because she had forgotten the words, the touching words that described how Zoria began her long wandering even as the Great War of the Gods blazed in earnest, but because something was definitely moving on the path ahead of her. The late afternoon light was beginning to weaken, but she could think of nothing but that shape just at the edge of sight, something dark that walked upright.

She smothered her first impulse to shout to the figure for help. After all, who would live in such a place? A kind woodsman, who would take her to his cottage and give her soup, like something in the stories of her childhood? More likely it was some half-savage madman who would ravage her or worse. She drew the longer of her knives and held it in her hand. The shape was moving away from her, so perhaps whoever or whatever it was hadn't heard her. But how could that be possible? She had been shouting loud enough to knock the leaves off the trees. Perhaps he was deaf.

A deaf madman. The prospects only get better and better, she thought sourly. Briony did not quite notice it, but something of her old self had come back to her as she stumbled through the trees crying old lines of poetry.

She walked a little faster, ignoring the ache in her legs, and she called out no more of Zoria's tale. Gregor's famous words may have kept her going but the time for them was over, at least for a while.

Another few hundred paces and she caught sight of the shape again, and this time could see it a little more clearly: it was man-like, walking on two legs, but seemed strangely bent, humped on its back beyond even the deformities of age, and she felt a thrill of superstitious fear run along her spine. What was it? Some half-human thing, part man, part animal? As the darkness came on would it tilt forward and run on all fours?

Despite her terror, she knew she must have food and shelter soon, even at risk that she was chasing some forest demon. She hurried on, moving as quickly and quietly as she could, trying to get a better look at whatever walked the path ahead of her.

At last, when she had closed the distance to only a hundred paces or so, she saw that the shape was not as unnatural as she'd feared: whatever walked before her in a dark cloak and hood carried a bundle of wood on its back. Her heart, which had been a stone in her chest, now lightened. *A person, at least—not something with teeth and claws.*

She thought it might be good to call now, with enough room between them to allow an escape if the other seemed dangerous. She stopped and shouted, "Halloo! Halloo, there! Can you help me? I'm lost!"

The dark figure slowed and stopped, then turned. For a moment she saw a hint of the face in the deep hood, of white hair and bright eyes as the wood carrier stared back at her, then the shape turned back to the path and hurried on.

"Gods' curses!" Briony screamed hoarsely. "I mean you no harm!" And she began to trot after the shape as fast as her tremblingly weary legs would carry her. But although the figure before her seemed to move no faster than she would expect of an aged woodcutter carrying a heavy burden, she could not seem to close the distance. She dug ahead as hard as she could, but still she could get no closer to the dark shape. "Wait! I don't want to hurt you! I'm hungry and I'm lost!"

The wide path looped between the trees, rising and falling, and the figure appeared and disappeared in the growing shadows. Briony's mind was full of old stories again, about malevolent fairies and will-o'-the-wisps who led travelers from their rightful path to their doom in the forest or marsh.

But I'm already lost! she thought miserably. *Where would the glory be in that?* She even shouted it, but the silent shape before her seemed to pay no attention.

At last, just before she was about to drop to her knees in surrender, give up on the mysterious figure and resign herself to another night alone in cold, rain-spattered despair, the dark-cloaked shape turned from the path—slowly, as if determined that Briony should take notice—and disappeared through the undergrowth into the thickest part of the wood. When she reached that spot on the path, Briony looked carefully but could see nothing unusual. If she had not seen the figure turn, she would have had no idea where it had gone.

Trap, a part of her warned, but that part was not strong enough to rule a mind so hungry and lonely and distraught. She turned off the track into the deep woods, her knife held out before her. Within a few steps she found herself on a steep slope, and after a few more paces stepped down out of the trees into a quiet, grassy dell. A campsite stood at the foot of the hollow—a rickety wagon, a sway-backed horse tied beside it cropping grass, and a fire. Standing beside the fire was the dark-cloaked shape she had trailed, the bundle of firewood lying on the ground at its feet.

The figure threw back the hood of the wet cloak, revealing a tangle of white hair and a face so old and so lined that at first Briony could not be sure if it was male or female.

"You took long enough, daughter," the ancient creature said. The voice marked her as a woman, although just barely, a throaty rasp halfway between a chuckle and a growl. "I thought I would have to lie down and have a nap to give you time to catch up."

Briony still had the knife out, but it seemed more important to bend double and keep her hands on her knees instead while she struggled to catch her breath. This was followed by a coughing fit that made her whimper at the pain in her chest. At last she straightened up. "I . . . couldn't . . . catch you . . ."

The old, old woman shook her head. "I fear for the breed," was all she said, then began laying new faggots on the fire. "Sit down, child. I can see you're ill—I'll have to do something about that. Are you hungry, too?"

"Who . . . who are you? I mean, yes—Oh, gods, yes, I'm starving."

"Good. We'll make you work for your supper, but I suppose you should rest and recover a bit first." The old woman gave her a sharp look. It was like being stared at by a wild beast. Briony's heart tripped again. The woman's eyes were not blue or green or even brown, but black and shiny as volcano glass. "One thing we *won't* ask you to do is sing. We've had quite enough of that tuneless caterwauling."

Even in the midst of all these unexpected happenings, Briony was stung. "I was just trying to keep myself going." She slumped to the ground and tucked the knife back into its sheath, still finding it hard to get her breath. The old woman was scarcely as high as Briony's own shoulder and looked to weigh no more than a roast Orphanstide duck.

"Maybe it was the song, then, daughter," said the old woman as she bent to rummage in a sack that hung from the front of the wagon. "I've never cared much for that Gregor. Too full of himself, and a dreadful man for a stretched rhyme. I told him so, too."

Briony, recovering her strength a little, shook her head. Perhaps this ancient was a little mad—surely she'd have to be, to live in the forest this way, by herself. "He's been dead for two centuries."

"Yes, he has, bless him, and not a moment too soon." She straightened up. "Hmmm. If I'd known yesterday I would have company, I would have gathered more marsh marigold, and maybe some chestnuts. But I didn't know until this morning."

"This morning what?"

"That you'd be coming. It took you long enough." She shrugged her thin shoulders, two bony points beneath the cloak. "It's not just Gregor, though, it's that song of his—more of it wrong than right, you know. Zosim the Helper—there's a laugh. That snake-eyed trickster helped himself to a few things, but that's all the helping he ever did. And the snow. Pure nonsense. Khors' castle wasn't made of ice or anything like that, it shone that way because of the elfglass it was covered with—fairy-shimmer, they used to call the stuff. And 'Everfrost!' " She smacked her lips in disgust, as if she'd eaten something that tasted foul. "He just took the real story and mixed it up with that Caylor story about the Prince of Birds—and *that* was a mumbled-up porridge of the story of the Godswar in the first place!"

Briony blinked. She wished that the woman would stop talking and get cooking. Only the griping pain in her stomach was allowing her to remain upright. "You . . . sound like you know . . . a great deal about . . . about the War of the Gods."

The old woman snickered, then the snicker became a full throated laugh. She laughed until she was wheezing and had to sit down beside Briony. "Yes, daughter, I do know a great deal about it." She chuckled again and wiped her eyes. "I ought to, child. I was there."

20

A Piece of the Moon's House

As the battle began, innocent Zoria escaped the fortress and on her pale, bare feet went in search of her family, but although Zosim found her and tried to help her, they were separated by a great storm, and so Perin's virgin daughter wandered far from the battlefield.

Before the walls of Khors' mighty fortress, Kernios the Earthlord was killed by the treachery of Zmeos, but the tears of his brother Erivor raised him again and he was thereafter undefeatable by any man or god.

—from *The Beginnings of Things*
The Book of the Trigon

IT TOOK SISTER UTTA LONGER than she would have liked to clear away the books and rolls of parchment on the least cluttered chair, but when she had finished Merolanna sank into it gladly. Once she saw that the duchess was only light-headed—and no surprise; Utta was feeling a bit dizzy herself—she cleared herself a place to sit, too. This task was not made any easier by the fact that a pentecount of miniature soldiers standing at attention on the floor had been joined by at least that number of tiny courtiers, so that there was almost nowhere Sister Utta could put her foot or anything else down without first having to wait for finger-high people to clear the way. King Olin's study now looked like the grandest and most elaborate game of dolls a little girl could ever imagine. At the center of it all, as poised and graceful as if she were the ordinary-sized one and Utta and the duchess were the inexplicable atomies, sat Queen Upsteeplebat on her hanging platform in the fireplace.

Merolanna fanned herself with a sheaf of parchments. "What did you mean, you can tell me about my son? What do you know about my son?"

Utta could make no sense of this: she had lived more than twenty years in the castle, and to the best of her knowledge Merolanna was childless. "Are you all right, Your Grace?"

Merolanna waved a hand at her. "Losing my mind, there is no doubt about that, but otherwise I am well enough. I am more grateful than I can say that you are here with me. You *are* seeing and hearing the same things I am, aren't you?"

"Tiny people? Yes, I'm afraid I am."

Upsteeplebat raised her arms in a gesture of support, or perhaps apology. "I am sorry if I shocked you, Duchess Merolanna. I cannot explain how we know about your son, but I can promise you it was not by deliberately intruding on your privacy." The queen showed them a smile tinier than a baby's fingernail. "Although I must confess we have been guilty of that in other circumstances with other folk. But I can tell you no more about any of it, because we are offering you a bargain."

"What sort?" asked Utta.

"Don't be ridiculous," said Merolanna. "You don't have to bargain with me. Tell me what you want and I'll get it for you—food? You must live a dreadful, poor life hiding in the shadows if all the old stories now turn out to be true. Surely you can't want money . . ."

The Rooftopper queen smiled again. "We eat better than you would suppose, Duchess. In fact, we could triple our numbers and still barely dent what is thrown away or ignored in this great household. But what we want is something a bit less obvious. And we do not want it for ourselves."

"Please," said Merolanna with an edge of anger in her voice, "do not play at games with me, madam. You tease me with the prospect of learning something about my son, which if you know of his existence at all, you must know I would do anything to achieve. Just tell me what you want."

"I cannot. We do not know."

"What?" Merolanna began to stand and then fell back in the chair, fanning vigorously. "What madness—what cruel prank . . . ?"

"Please, Your Grace, hear us out." Upsteeplebat spoke kindly, but there was a note of authority in her own voice that Utta could not help remarking. "We do not play at games. Our Lord of the Peak, to whom we owe our very existence, has spoken, and told us what to do, and what to say to you."

"Is that your Rooftopper king?" Utta rose from her own chair and went to stand by Merolanna's. She set her hand on the duchess' shoulder and could not help noticing how the woman was trembling.

Upsteeplebat shook her head. "Not in the sense you mean. No, I rule the Rooftoppers here among the living. But the Master of the Heights rules all living things and we are his servants."

"Your god?"

She nodded her head. "You may call him thus. To us, he is simply the Lord."

Merolanna took a long breath; Utta could feel her shudder. "What do you want? Just tell me, please."

"You must come with us. You must hear what the Lord of the Peak has to say."

"You would take us . . . to your god?" Utta wondered that a few moments ago she had thought things as strange as they could get.

"In a way. No harm will come to you."

Merolanna looked at Utta, her expression a grimace somewhere between despair and hilarity. Her voice, when she finally spoke, shared the same air of resigned confusion. "Take us, then. To Rooftopper's Heaven or wherever else. Why not?"

The tiny queen gestured toward a door in the wall at the back of the library, half-obscured by bookshelves and piles of loose books. "Please know that this is a rare honor. It has been centuries since we invited any of your kind into our sacred place."

"Through that door? But it's locked," said Merolanna. "Olin always talked about how the storeroom here at the top of the tower hadn't been opened since his grandfather's day—that the key was lost and that nothing short of breaking it down would ever get it open."

"Nor would it," said Upsteeplebat with a tone of satisfaction. "It has been wedged on the far side in a thousand places and the key is indeed lost—at least to your folk. But now the Lord of the Peak has called for you, so my people have labored for two days to remove the wedges and other impediments." She waved her hands and three of her tiny soldiers stepped out from their line along the base of the fireplace bricks. They lifted trumpets made of what looked like seashells and blew a long, shrill, tootling call. As if in reply, Utta heard a thin scraping noise, and then a metallic *plink,* as of a small hammer striking an equally small anvil.

"All praise to the Lord of Heights," Upsteeplebat said, "the oil was sufficient to loosen the lock's workings. It was the matter about which my council argued and argued. Now pull the door, please—but gently. My subjects will take some while to climb out of the way."

"You do it," Merolanna whispered to Utta. "Small things, oh, they make me jump so."

Utta cleared the books piled on the floor, then did her best to move the book cabinets without tipping them—no easy task. The door resisted her pull for a moment—she wondered if the Rooftoppers had remembered to oil the hinges as well at the latch—but then, with a shriek that made her wince, it swung toward her.

"Carefully!" came Upsteeplebat's piping cry, but there was no need. Utta had already taken a step back in dismay from what she took to be half a dozen huge spiders dangling in the doorway before she realized they were Rooftoppers hanging from ropes like steeplejacks, slowly climbing back up to the top of the doorframe.

Most of them looked at her with anxiety or even fear—and small wonder, since she was dozens of times their size, as tall in their eyes as the spire of a great temple—but one tiny climber who seemed barely more than a boy kicked his legs and gave her a sort of salute before he disappeared into the darkness above the door.

"Fare you well," Utta whispered as the rest of the climbers also reached the safety of the doorframe. She turned to the queen, who still stood on her platform in the fireplace like an image of Zoria in a shrine. Utta could not help wondering if that was coincidence or more of the Rooftopper's planning. "Your people are brave."

"We fight the cat, the rat, the jay, the gull," said the Rooftopper queen. "Our walls are full of spiders and centipedes. We must be brave to survive. You may enter now."

Utta leaned forward into the doorway.

"What . . . what do you see?" Merolanna's voice quivered a little, but she had been at court for most of a century and was good at masking her feelings even in the most extreme of situations. "Can we get on with this?"

"It's dark—I'll need the torch."

"A candle only, if you please, Sister Utta," said the queen. "And if you'll be kind enough to take my good Beetledown on your shoulder, he will help you to walk carefully in our sacred place."

The little man, who had been standing silently on the hearth, now bowed. Utta got a candle on a dish—they had been left everywhere around the room, as if Olin had liked to use dozens at a time—then lowered her hand and let the Rooftopper climb on.

Merolanna stood, not without a little huffing and wheezing. "I'm coming with you. Whatever it is, I want to see it."

"I will join you inside." The Rooftopper queen lifted her hand. The royal platform slowly began to rise upward, back into the fireplace flue.

"Do thee step careful, like un told thee," said Beetledown. The voice so close to her ear made Utta itchy. She lifted the candle and led Merolanna through the open door.

The floor of the room beyond was scarcely half the size of the one in the king's library, but the room itself extended farther upward: with candle lifted, Utta could see the rafters of the tower top itself, latticed with what she first took for spiderwebs, then realized were dozens, perhaps hundreds, of rope bridges, none any wider than her hand. Some were only a foot or so long, but a few stretched for a dozen feet or more in sagging parabolas braced with slender crosswires.

"Watch tha foot!" cried Beetledown. Utta looked down to see that she had nearly stepped on a ramp that led from the floor to an old rosewood chest no higher than the middle of her thigh. The lid was flung back and the hinges, badly rusted, had given way, so that the lid hung unevenly, half resting on the ground, but it was the inside of the chest that caught her eye. A row of tiny houses had been built inside it, along the back—half a dozen simple but beautifully constructed three-story houses.

"Merciful Zoria," said Utta. "Is this where your people live?"

"Nay," said Beetledown, "only those as tend the Ears."

"Tend the ears?"

"Step careful, please. And watch tha head, too."

Utta looked up just before walking into one of the hanging bridges. Up close, she could see it was much less simple than she had thought: the knotwork was regular and decorative, the wooden planks clearly finished by hand with love and care. She resolved to move even more slowly. Just the loss of one of these bridges to her clumsiness would be a shame.

"Did you ever imagine such a thing was here, under our noses?" she asked Merolanna.

"This castle has always been full of secrets," the other woman said, sounding oddly mournful.

They moved deeper into what might have once been a simple storeroom but had long since become a weird, magical place of miniature bridges and ladders, of furniture turned into houses, with small wonders of fittings and drapery inside them that Utta could only glimpse, and tiny lanterns glowing in the windows like fireflies.

"Where are all your people?" she asked.

"There be only few of we folk who live in this place—only those who serve the Lord of the Peak direct and personal," the little man explained. "Those stay inside, so as not to be trod on by giants." He coughed, a sound like a bird sniffing. "Beggin' tha pardon, ma'am."

Utta smiled. "No, that sounds very sensible. How long have your people been here, hiding from us blundering giants?"

"Forever, ma'am. Long as remembered. The Lord of the Peak, he made us and gave us this place for our own. Well, not *this* place, 'haps—this room we took for ours in my great-grands' day. But our lands, our walls, our roofs, we have had forever."

"But then why is your god named the Lord of the Peak?" Utta asked. "If you have always been here, what mountain can you know?"

"Why, the great peak your folk do call Wolfstooth," Beetledown said, as if it was the most obvious thing in the world—which, to him, it doubtless was. "That is where the Lord lives."

Utta shook her head, but gently, so as not to dislodge the little man. Wolfstooth Spire, the castle's central tower, was the Rooftopper's Xandos—the home of their god! What a world this was, both his and hers. What a strange, wonderful world.

The queen now appeared from a hidden door somewhere on the far side of the room, riding in a chariot drawn by a herd of white mice, with a small phalanx of soldiers behind her. She waved in an imperial sort of way, then led Utta and Merolanna a little farther down what was clearly the attic room's main thoroughfare, between rows of chests and other furniture—each, Utta had no doubt, converted into temples or mantiseries or congregations of sisters, all in service to the god who they believed lived at the top of a nearby tower.

Upsteeplebat's chariot drew to a halt at the end of the aisle; her mice settled on their haunches and began most unceremoniously to groom themselves. Against the wall, at the end of a sort of plaza a couple of yards across made when the furniture had been pushed back was a high dresser of the kind used by wealthy women. Its drawers had been pulled out, the bottommost the farthest, the topmost the least, and a fretwork of ladders and ramps connected the drawers together. More of the spidery steeplejacks were at work here, but it took a moment for her to make out what they were doing. A long bundle, almost like an insect wrapped in webbing by a spider, was being carefully lowered down from the topmost drawer to the floor.

"Could you kneel, please," Upsteeplebat said in her high, calm voice. "We have delicate work to do, and all of us will be safer if you are sitting or kneeling."

"Can we get on with things?" Merolanna grumbled. "This dress isn't meant for such games. If you'd told me I'd be down on the floor like a child playing tops I'd have worn my nightclothes instead."

Utta could not blame the dowager duchess for complaining. Though she herself was in good, healthy fettle, and much more conveniently garbed in a simple robe, her old bones did not particularly enjoy the exercise, either.

When they were seated, a small troop of soldiers and a trio of shaven-headed creatures (whose delicate features Utta guessed must be female) brought out a cushioned bed made from what had obviously once been a jewel case. The bundle from the uppermost drawer was lowered into it, then unwrapped to reveal a Rooftopper woman with dark hair and pale skin, dead or sleeping.

"I present to you the Glorious and Accurate Ears," the queen said, "whose family has for centuries been our link to the Lord of the Peak, and who will today, for the first time, share the Lord's words straightly with your folk."

The trio of priestesses, if that was what they were, stepped forward to stand at the head and either arm of the Ears. They lit bowls of some stuff that smoked and waved them over her and then began to chant words too quiet to be heard. This went on for long moments; Utta could feel Merolanna shifting impatiently beside her. In the quiet room, the rucking and crinkling of the duchess' dress sounded like distant thunder.

At last the priestesses stepped back and bowed their heads. The silence continued. Utta began to wonder if she or Merolanna were expected to ask a question, but then the woman in the bed began to move, first to twitch as in a fever-dream, then to thrash weakly. Suddenly she sat up. Her eyes opened wide, but she did not seem to be looking at anything in the room, not even the two giant women. She spoke in a surprisingly low voice, a slurry string of quiet sounds like bees buzzing. The priestesses swayed.

"What does she say?" demanded Merolanna.

"She says nothing," the queen of the Rooftoppers corrected her. "It is the Lord of the Peak himself who speaks, and *he* says, *'The end of these days comes on white wings, but it bears darkness like an egg. Old Night waits to be born, and unless the sea swallows all untimely, the stars themselves will rain down like flaming arrows.'* Those are the words of the Lord of High Places."

Vague, apocalyptic prophecy was not what the dowager duchess had come to hear. "Ask about my son," she said in a sharp whisper. But Utta could tell that a bargain was being struck, even if she did not yet know with whom they were bargaining—the Rooftoppers and their queen? Their god? Or simply this one Rooftopper oracle?

"We have been told that you know something of this woman's son, O Lord of the Peak," Utta said slowly and clearly, hoping that if the Rooftoppers spoke her language, so did their god. "Will you tell us of him?"

The woman thrashed again and almost fell from her bed. Two tiny, shaven-headed priestesses stepped forward to hold her as she mumbled and rasped again.

" *'The High Ones took him, fifty winters past,'* " the queen said, translating or simply amplifying the Ears' quiet mumble. " *'He was carried behind the cloud of unknowing mortals call the Shadowline. But he yet lives.'* "

Merolanna let out a little shriek, swayed, and collapsed against Utta, who did her best to hold her upright: the duchess was of a size that she would destroy much of the Rooftoppers' religious quarter if allowed to fall. "She will thank you for this news—but I think not today," Utta said, a little out of breath. She bent closer to Queen Upsteeplebat. "Can your god not tell us more?" she whispered. "Is there a way to find her child?"

For long moments the Ears lay like a dead woman—much like Merolanna, who seemed to have fainted. Then the tiny shape stirred and spoke again, but so quietly that Utta could only see her lips move. Even the little queen had to lean against the rail of her chariot to hear.

"The Lord of High Places says, '*The world's need is great. Old Night pecks at its shell, yearning to breathe the air of Time. This castle's priest of light and stars once owned a piece of the House of the Moon, ancient and powerful, but now it has been taken. Find where that stolen piece has gone and in return Heaven will speak more of this mortal woman's son.*'"

With that the Ears fell into a deep, deathlike sleep. When it was clear she would speak the god's words no longer, the priestesses wrapped her up again. This time the tiny soldiers moved in and carried the entire bed away into the shadows like a funeral bier.

Utta held Merolanna, who groaned like a woman in a bad dream, and wondered and wondered at the surpassing strangeness this day had brought.

The duchess stirred in her bed and sat up, hands clawing out as though something had been pulled away from her.

"Where are they? Did I dream?"

"You did not dream," Utta told her. "Unless I dreamed the same dream."

"But what else did that little creature say? I cannot remember!" Merolanna fumbled for the cup of watered wine on the chest by her bed, drank it so fast that a pinkish rivulet spilled and ran down her chin.

Utta told her the rest of the Ears' pronouncement. "But I can make no sense of it."

"My child!" Merolanna fell back against the pillows, her chest heaving. "I gave him away," she moaned, "and now the fairies have him. Poor, poor boy!" In halting words, she told Utta of the child's secret birth and disappearance. Utta was surprised, but not astonished—the Zorians did not believe humans could be perfected, only forgiven.

"If the little people's oracle spoke correctly, that was almost fifty years gone, Your Grace," she told Merolanna. "Still, we must try to understand the god's words—if it really was a god who spoke. A piece of the Moon's House, the little woman said. And that it belonged to the castle's priest of light and stars."

"Priest? Do they mean Father Timoid? But he is gone!" Merolanna tossed her head as if in a fever. "Why should some god send this message to torture me?"

"Perhaps they mean Hierarch Sisel." Utta reached out to take the duchess' hand, hoping to calm her. "He is the highest priest of all, so . . ."

"But he is gone too, to his house in the country. He told me he could not bear to see what the Tollys were doing." Merolanna tried to calm herself. "Would he be the priest of light and stars, though? He is the great priest of the Trigon, and they are air, water, and earth . . ." She moaned again. "Ah, if only Chaven were here. He knows of such things—he studies the stars, and knows almost as much about the old tales of the gods as Sisel . . ."

"Wait," said Utta. "Perhaps that is who it means. Chaven is a priest of sorts—a priest of logic and science. And his is the particular study of light and the stars, with those lenses of his. Perhaps Chaven had some powerful object that is now lost."

"But *Chaven* is the one who's lost!" said Merolanna. "He's vanished! And that means my son is lost forever . . . !"

"No one simply disappears," said Utta. "Unless the gods themselves take them. And the Rooftoppers' god, at least, does not seem to know what's happened to Chaven, so perhaps he is still alive." She stood. "I will see what I can discover, Your Grace."

"Be careful!" Merolanna cried as Utta moved to the door. She extended her arms again as though to draw the Zorian sister back. "You are all I have left!"

"We have the gods, Duchess. I will pray for my gracious lady Zoria's help. You should do the same."

Merolanna slumped back. "Gods, fairies . . . the world has run utterly mad."

Utta called in the little maid Eilis. "See to your mistress," she told the girl. "Take good care of her. She has had a shock."

But who will see to me? she wondered as she left Merolanna's chambers. *Who will take care of me in this mad time when legends spring to life at our feet? Zoria, merciful goddess, I need your help now more than ever.*

Even to Matty Tinwright, who had never found it easy to say no to a celebration or a feast, especially if someone else was paying the tally, it seemed a bit much. Surely with an invading force just across the river—an invading force of monsters and demons at that—all these fetes and fairs were a waste, if not worse?

Perhaps Lord Hendon is only trying to divert us from our troubles. If so, he had set himself a hard task, because troubles were plentiful. The creatures across the bay had not attacked the keep, but they had certainly cut off all supplies coming to the overfilled castle from the west, and the short, terrifying war had emptied the valleys to the west and south as well, so there were no cattle or sheep being driven in from Marrinswalk and Silverside and no wool or cheese from Settland, only such supplies as could be brought in by ships, which lay crammed in Southmarch harbor like driftwood against a seawall.

Despite all this, the merriment went on. Tonight, to celebrate the first evening of Gestrimadi, the festival in honor of the Mother of the Gods, there would be a public fair in Market Square and here in the castle a great supper and masked fete, with music and dancing.

And yet surely there has not been a darker Dimene-month since the Twilight folk last marched on us, two hundred years gone?

It was strange, Tinwright thought, that a place as solemn and silent during the day as this should spring to life so feverishly at night, as though the chambers were tombs which discharged their occupants only after sunset, so that they could dance and flirt in imitation of the living.

It was a powerful image, and he thought suddenly that he should write it down. Surely there was a poem in it, the courtiers emerging from their stony dens at nightfall, wearing masks that hid everything but their too-bright eyes ...

But Hendon Tolly and his circle will not like it, and these days that is a very dangerous thing. Didn't Lord Nynor disappear after being heard criticizing the Tollys' rule? Still, the lure of the idea was strong. He decided that he could write it and keep it hidden until better times, when his foresight would be recognized, and his brilliance (if not his courage) honored.

Poets are not made to be hanged, he reminded himself. *They are made to admired. And even if I could only be admired for being hanged, I would choose obscurity, I think.* No, he would stay alive. In any case, he had other things to live for, these days ...

"Oh, most effective, Master Tinwright!" said Puzzle approvingly. Now that he had been picked up by Hendon Tolly's set, however mockingly, the old jester had developed a loud heartiness to his tone that Tinwright found irritating. Strangely, though, his wrinkled face suddenly crumpled into sadness. "You will captivate many a young heart tonight, that is certain."

Tinwright looked down at the forest-green hose, which had a disturbing tendency to twist between ankle and crotch so that each leg's seam looked more like a winding country road than a straight royal thoroughfare. The colors were pleasing, though no real traveling minstrel ever wore such peacockery as this. It was a party costume that had belonged to Puzzle's dead friend Robben Hulligan, and the old man was actually weeping now to see him in it.

"He was fair of face and shapely of leg, my good old Robben." Puzzle rubbed his eyes. He had dressed for the masked fete himself in a black mantis' robe, and it suited him strangely, making his long, dour face seem for the first time to have found its proper set-ting. "He too loved the ladies, and the ladies loved him."

Tinwright didn't say anything. He had heard this Robben-talk before and knew the old man would have his say no matter what Tinwright did.

"He was murdered by bandits, poor fellow," said Puzzle, shaking his head. Tinwright could have recited the rest of his speech with him, so many times had he heard it. "Taken by Kernios long before his time. Have I told you of him? Sweet singing Robben."

Tinwright was even thinking of going to the temple for the services, just to avoid the rest of the old man's maundering, but was saved that ignominious fate by the arrival of a small boy, a page, bearing a message to Puzzle from Hendon Tolly's squire.

"Ah, it seems I am wanted!" the old man said with a pleasure he could barely contain. "The guardian wishes me to sit with him during the feast, so that I may entertain him."

The guardian must be trying to keep himself from eating too much, Tinwright thought but of course did not say: he was fond of Puzzle, if a bit tired of spending so much time with him. The old fellow's recent rise in favor had made him cheerful, but had made him a bit boastful as well, and Matt Tinwright's more dubi-ous fortunes made it hard sometimes to enjoy his friend's triumphs. "Does it say anything about me?"

"I fear not," said Puzzle. "Perhaps you could come with me, though. I could sing my lord one of your songs, and surely . . ."

Tinwright thought back on the disastrous and humiliating reception he had received the last time he had tagged after Puzzle. That made it much easier to remember something that was true, if not useful to a man in search of advancement: he had decided he truly disliked Hendon Tolly. No, more than that—Tinwright was terrified of him. "Fear not, good friend Puzzle," he said aloud. "As you pointed out, there are doubtless many fair young faces and firm young bosoms that await my attention tonight. I hope you will have good fortune at the guardian's table." He could not help dispensing a little advice, though, since Puzzle these days seemed as innocently smitten of attention as a child. "Be careful of that man Havemore, though. He does not love anyone, and will go to subtle lengths to be cruel."

"He is a good enough fellow in his way," said Puzzle, quick to defend any of the wealthy, powerful men who had so unexpectedly taken him up. "When next you come with me, you will see and know him better."

"Let's hope not," said Matt Tinwright under his breath. If Tolly was a predator, Tirnan Havemore was a scavenger, a graveyard dog that would snatch up whatever it could find and hold onto it with stinking jaws. "Be well and be merry, Uncle."

He waved as Puzzle went out, and then realized he had forgotten to ask him whether Hulligan's borrowed costume was buttoned correctly in the back. He wished he had a dressing-mirror, but only a rich man—or at least a man who made poems for rich men—could afford such a thing.

Ah, Princess Briony, where did you go? Your poet needs you. At least you appreciated my true quality, if scarcely anyone else did . . . or does . . .

The castle was strung with parchment lanterns, and in every corner stood little altars to Madi Surazem covered with greenery, with pale hellebore blooms, firethorn, and holly surrounding white candles, each arrangement a silent prayer that the swelling within the belly of Moist Mother Earth would bear forth in another spring of healthy crops.

But what crops? Tinwright thought *And who to harvest them? The fairies have laid waste to all the western and northern lands.* It was strange that he should be the one fretting about such things. His father had once called him (exaggerating only slightly, Tinwright had to confess) the laziest and most self-centered youth on either side of Brenn's Bay. Now he watched the courtiers in their masks and finery trip out into the garden and come back in, soaked from the rain and laughing, only to rush out again, and felt like a despairing parent himself. He wondered if his earlier idea, how-ever poetic, might not be wrong: the dead could afford to make merry, having nothing to lose. The people around him seemed more like children, playing games beneath a teetering boulder.

Something bumped him and almost knocked him to the floor. "Sing us a song, minstrel!" shouted a drunken voice. Swaying in front of him, wearing a mask with an obscenely long nose, was Durstin Crowel, one of Tolly's closest followers, a red-faced young lord who would have looked more natural, Tinwright thought, on a platter at the center of a banquet with a quince stuffed in his mouth. Crowel stood in the middle of the corridor with four or five of his friends, none of whom looked any better for drink than the Baron of Graylock. He was soaking wet and wearing a dress. "Go on," Crowel said, pointing an unsteady finger at Tinwright. "Sing something with some swiving in it!" His companions laughed but they did not move on. They had sensed an edge in Crowel's tone that meant more interesting things might be coming.

"Go to, then!" one of them shouted. "You heard! Entertain us, minstrel!"

"It is a costume, only," Tinwright said, backing away. At least they did not seem to have recognized him behind his bird mask. Sometimes it was good to be beneath the notice of the great.

"Ah, but my dagger is real." Crowel pulled something with a long, slender blade from his bodice—the noble seemed to be dressed as a tavern maid. "To protect my dear virtue, you see . . ." He paused for the laugh, which his friends dutifully provided, "so I'm afraid you will sing—or I will make you sing." He belched and his friends laughed again. "Minstrel."

For a moment it seemed as if it would be easier simply to do it—to mop and mow a little for the benefit of these drunken arsewipes, to play the part and sing a sad song of love and let them mock him. He knew enough of Crowel to know the man had beaten at least one servant to death and crippled another, just in the time he had been living in the Tollys' wing of the residence— surely it was better simply to give the man what he wanted.

But why should I think they will stop at mockery?

"My lord's command," he said aloud, and bent his knee in a bow. "I will be pleased to sing for you . . . another day."

Tinwright turned and ran for the residence garden. He was out into the cold rain before Crowel and the others realized what had happened.

This was the part of the plan I didn't think about as carefully as I might, Tinwright admitted to himself as he huddled soaking wet in the lee of a tall hedge. The wind was chill and sharp as a razor—he thought he could feel his skin beginning to turn to ice. Still, he was not ready to go back inside. He was fairly certain that Graylock hadn't recognized him, so all he had to do was stay away from them just for tonight. He considered sneaking back to the room he shared with Puzzle, but if he didn't go back through main halls of the residence he would have a long walk back in the biting, bitter wind.

Better just to wait until they drink themselves to sleep.

In any case, he was feeling more than a little sorry for himself when he realized he had not heard voices or seen movement in the garden for some time.

If they're not looking for me out here, at least I could find somewhere a little more warm and dry to hide, he thought. He pulled the minstrel's floppy cap down over his ears again—he had already nearly lost it to the wind several times—and wrapped the thin cape tight around his shoulders, wishing he had picked a more sensible disguise.

I could have been a monk with a hood—or a Vuttish reaver with a fur-lined helmet! But no, I wished to show my legs to the ladies in a minstrel's hose. Fool.

He found one of the covered arbors at last; it was only when he had thrown himself down on the bench with a loud grunt of despair that he realized someone else was already sitting there.

"Oh! Your pardon, Lady . . ."

The woman in the dark dress looked up. Her eyes were red—she had been crying. An ivory-colored mask sat on her lap like a temple offering bowl. Tinwright's heart jumped, and for a moment he could not speak. He leaped to his feet, bowed, then remembered to take off his mask.

"Master Tinwright." She turned away and lifted her kerchief, drying her tears in a slow, deliberate fashion. Her voice was hard. "You find me at a disadvantage. Have you followed me, sir?"

"No, Lady Elan, I swear. I was only . . ."

"Wandering in the garden? Enjoying the weather?"

He laughed ruefully. "Yes, as you can see I have quite immersed myself in it. No, I was . . . well, I must be frank. The Baron of Graylock and some of his friends had taken it into their heads that I should entertain them, and it wasn't clear how much I should have to suffer for my art." He shrugged. "I decided that I would entertain them with a game of hide and seek instead."

"Durstin Crowel?" Her voice grew harder still. "Ah, yes, dear Lord Crowel. Do you know, when I first came here, he asked Hendon if he could have me. 'I'll break her for you, Tolly,' he said—as if I were a horse."

"You mean he wanted to marry you?"

For the first time she turned to look at him, her face a mask of bitter amusement. "Marry me? Black heart of Kernios, no, he wanted to bed me only." Her face twisted into something else, something truly disturbing. "He did not know that Hendon had other plans for me. But yes, I know Baron Durstin." She composed herself, even tried to smile. "Very well, Master Tinwright, you are forgiven for your intrusion. And in fact, you may keep the arbor for yourself and I'll tell no one where you are. I must go back inside now. Doubtless my lord and master is looking for me."

She had risen, the mask halfway to her face, when Tinwright at last found the words.

"What is he to you?"

"Who?" She sounded startled. "Do you mean Hendon Tolly? I should think that was obvious, Master Tinwright. He owns me."

"You are not his wife but his sister-in-law. Will he marry you?"

"Why should he? Why should he pay for a cow whose milk is already his?"

It sickened him to hear her speak so. He took a breath, tried to find calm words. "Does he at least treat you well, my lady?" .

She laughed, a cracked, unpleasant sound, and put the white

mask to her face so that she seemed a corpse or a ghost. "Oh, he is most attentive." Her shoulders slumped and she turned away again. "Truly, I must go."

Tinwright grabbed at the sleeve of her velvet gown. She tried to pull away and something tore. For a moment they both stood, half in, half out of the rain.

"I would kill him for causing you unhappiness," he said, and realized in that moment it was true. "I would."

She lowered the mask in surprise. "Gods help us, do not say such things! Do not even go near him. He . . . you do not know. You cannot guess what evil is in him."

Tinwright still held her sleeve. "I . . . would not treat you so, Lady Elan. If you were mine, that is. I would love you. As it is, I think of you day and night."

She stared at him. Tears welled in her eyes again. "Ah, but you are a boy, Master Tinwright."

"I am grown!"

"In years. But your heart is still innocent. I am filthy and I would begrime you, too. I would stain you as I myself am stained, corrupted . . ."

"No. Please, do not say such things!"

"I must go." She gently pulled free of his grip. "You are kind— you cannot know how kind—to say such things to me. But you must not think of me. I could not bear to have another's soul on my conscience."

Before she could turn away again he stepped forward and took her shoulders, felt her trembling. Could it be she had some feelings for him? She looked so startled at his touch, so frightened, as if she expected to be hit, that he did not kiss her mouth, although he wished to at this moment beyond any dream of riches or fame he had ever coveted. Instead he let his hands slide down her arms. As if his fingers stole her vitality where they passed, she let the mask drop clattering to the walkway. He took both her hands in his, lifted them to his lips, and kissed her cold fingers.

"I love you, Lady Elan. I cannot bear to see you, and to know you are in pain."

Her cheeks were wet, her eyes bright and frightened. "Oh, Master Tinwright, it cannot be."

"Matthias. My name is Matthias."

She looked at him for a long moment, then pulled his hands up to her mouth and kissed them in turn. "Would you really help me? Truly?"

He was soaking with rain, but he could feel her tears on his hands like streaks of hot lead. "I would do anything—I swear by all the gods. Ask me."

She turned to look out into the darkness. When she turned back her face was strange. "Then bring me poison. Something that will cause a quick death."

For a moment Matt Tinwright could not breathe. "You . . . you would kill Tolly?"

She let go of his hands and wiped at her eyes with her sleeve. "Are you mad? With my sister married to his brother Caradon? The Tollys would destroy her. They would burn my parents' house to the ground and murder them both. Not to mention that Southmarch Castle would be left in the hands of Crowel and Havemore and others almost as blackhearted as Hendon, but not as clever. The March Kingdoms would be drowned in blood in half a year." She took a breath. "No. I want the poison for myself."

She pulled away from him again, bent and picked up her mask. When she stood, she was again a phantom. "If you love me, you will bring me that release. It is the only gift I can ever take from you, sweet Matthias."

And then she was gone into the rain.

21

The Deathwatch Chamber

Brave Nushash was out riding and saw Suya the Dawnflower, the beautiful daughter of Argal, and instantly knew she must be his. He stopped beside her and held out his hand, and at once she too fell in love with him. Thus it is when the heart speaks louder than the head—even gods must listen. She reached up to him and let the fire god draw her up into the saddle. Together they rode away.

—from *The Revelations of Nushash,* Book One

VANSEN LAY ON HIS FACE, still trembling, unable to find the strings to make his limbs lift him again and un-certain that he wanted to. The terrible voice that had blasted through his head like a crack of thunder was still echoing, although whether that was inside or outside his skull, or both, he could not have said.

"DO MY WORDS PAIN YOU? OR IS IT THE WAY I SPEAK THEM?"

Vansen whimpered despite himself. He felt as though an ocean wave had picked him up and dashed him onto the rocks. He clung to the floor and wondered if he could hit his head hard enough on the stone flags to kill himself and end this throbbing, agonizing clamor.

When the voice rolled over and through him again, the words and the mocking laugh were quieter—painful but not crippling. *"Well, then, I will speak more softly, for the comfort of my guests. Sometimes I forget what the voice of a god can do . . ."*

"Half a god," said a voice Vansen had never heard before, but which seemed somehow weirdly familiar. It was vastly less intrusive than the one-eyed monster's, but it sounded inside Ferras Vansen's head in the same way. *"Half a god, half a monster."*

"Is there a difference?"

"Why do you take us from our lawful business, Old One?"

"To help me in **my** *lawful business,"* the rumbling voice said. *"But what brings one of the Encauled so close to my adopted kingdom? What is this lawful business of which you speak?"*

"We are riding home to the House of the People, but were driven out of our way. Why should you interfere?"

Now that Jack Chain's voice no longer rattled his bones with each utterance, Vansen slowly began to lift himself from the ground. He ached as if he had been beaten, but if he was going to die he would do his best to meet that death standing, as a soldier of Southmarch. The dusty stone beneath him was splotched with red; he lifted his hands to his face and realized his nose was streaming blood.

"Interfere? You trespass on my land, little hobgoblin, and then claim I have interfered with you?" The monstrous, one-eyed creature lolled on his statue-throne, his splayed legs longer than Vansen was tall, the handsome, ruined head as big as a temple bell. Jikuyin was smiling down at a small figure standing before him—Gyir the Storm Lantern.

"I am on the king's business," said Gyir's voice.

By the Three, Vansen thought, *I can understand him!* He was as astonished by this as everything else that had happened to them. *I can hear him in my head now, just as the prince can!*

He turned to tell Barrick, but was horrified to see the boy lying on his side with blood running from his nose and ears. Vansen threw himself down beside him and was only slightly relieved to feel the rise and fall of Barrick's chest.

"He is hurt!" Vansen shouted. "Help him, you god or whatever you are—it was your great barking voice that did this to him!"

Jikuyin laughed long and hard; the sound rolled and crashed in Vansen's skull like untethered barrels slamming in the hold of a storm-tossed ship. *"Help him! I like you, little mortal—you are very amusing! But like the fly on the horse's back who tells his host which way to go, you have a flawed notion of your own importance."* He turned his single eye on Gyir. *"As for you, slave of the Fireflower, I do not know how one of the Encauled could let himself be taken unawares—and by Longskulls, no less . . .!"* The god-thing chortled, and several of the other prisoners in the great room laughed, too, if not with the same heartiness as their master. *"But it signifies nothing, in any case. You will be part of my great work."* Jikuyin grinned, showing the true horror of his ruined mouth and shattered teeth. He stroked the chains across his chest, making the severed heads sway. *"And even if you cannot help me in any profound way, you will at least, as I promised, prove ornamental."*

The giant stood then for the first time, and even though Ferras Vansen had thought himself full to sickening with strange miracles, it was a horrible, astonishing sight: Jikuyin was so tall that his great head seemed to rise into the heights of the chamber like the pock-faced mooon, beyond the reach of the torches and lanterns, until much of it had passed into shadow and only the lower, broken half could be seen.

"Take them away," he rumbled. A host of shapes scurried forward from the dark edges of the massive room—the guard-Followers, man-sized and heavier than the Longskulls, with stubs of sharp bone poking through their matted pelts and small piggy eyes glinting like coals. *"Give them to the gray one and tell him to keep them safe until I need them."*

Gyir stood firm as the red-eyed things began to surround him, and clearly would have fought, but one of the apelike creatures had already stolen up behind him unseen. It hit Gyir in the back of the head with its massive fist and the Storm Lantern was pulled down and dragged away.

Vansen was too weak to resist. All he could do was try to keep a hand on Barrick's unmoving form as they were carried out of Jikuyin's throne room by the bristly, foul-smelling creatures. As they were roughly hurried down what seemed an endless succession of lightless tunnels he struggled against his heavy shackles, doing his best to cling to the prince so that they would not be separated, as a mother who has fallen into a river with her child will still keep a hand clenched on the infant's garment even after death has stolen away her breath.

Even in the center of his own great house, the fortress that had been given to his family from the gods' own hands, the blind king Ynnir dina'at sen-Qin, Guardian of the Fireflower, Lord of Winds and Thought, could not simply walk to the Deathwatch Chamber. First the Guard of Elementals must be supplicated, allowed to perform their warlike rites in his honor, and in honor of the one they were protecting—the Salute of the Bone Knife, the Song of the Owl's Eye (blessedly shorter in these latter days, thanks to an edict by Ynnir's own grandfather: once the chant would have lasted an entire day), and the Arrow Count. When all these duties were finished and the Guard-Commander of the Elementals had removed his helmet in salute—even without sight, Ynnir always found that part difficult—the king moved on.

The Celebrants of Mother Night did not perform official duties, but they had been allowed to make their camp of suffering outside the Deathwatch Chamber. Merely to move among them, to hear their moaning and weeping and feel the naked misery of their grief, was like walking through biting winds and needle-sharp sleet. Pale Daughter herself, fleeing her lover's house with an infant godling in her belly, could have felt nothing more chillingly painful.

It was a relief, after a time that felt like days, to pass out of the chambers where the Celebrants shrieked and tore at themselves and into the silence of the final antechamber, to face Zsan-san-sis, the ancient chieftain of the Children of the Emerald Fire. Zsan-san-sis had returned from the underground pools in which he had spent more and more time as he aged; it was a measure of the crisis that he should appoint himself the final guardian of the Deathwatch Chamber when it was only one of his young grand-nephews who stood watch outside the Hall of Mirrors itself.

"Moonlight and Sunlight," said the king.

"And thus roll the days of the Great Defeat unto Time's sleep," said the other, completing the ceremonial greeting. "I bid Your Majesty welcome." His tone seemed even more curt than usual, the glow from inside his ceremonial robe dim and noncommittal, so that his mask was almost invisible in the shadowed hood. The king had always had trouble reading the moods of Zsan-san-sis, as if his own sightlessness and the Emerald Fire chieftain's silver mask were impediments as real to him as they would be to a mortal. The Children had long favored the queen's cause, although the old chieftain had been the most conciliatory of his clan. In days past Ynnir had often wondered what would happen when Zsan-san-sis eventually sank to the bottom of his pool and did not surface again, a day when someone less willing to compromise might rise to lead the Emerald Fire Children. Now it no longer seemed to matter.

"How is she today?"

"I have not gone in to her, Majesty. I feel her, but barely—a breath faint as a whisper from Silent Hill." His thoughts and words both—for they came to the king as a single thing—were clouded with regret and resignation. "Even were we to triumph, Majesty, she could never travel now. She would die before we left our own lands."

Ynnir brought his open hand to his chest, then spread his fingers, a gesture called *Significance Incomplete*. "We can only wait and be patient, old one, hard as that is. Many threads still remain unbroken."

"I would not have spent my last seasons this way," said Zsan-san-sis. "Holding together what is broken, knowing that my daughter's daughter's daughters will bear their young in pools without light."

Ynnir shook his head. "We all do what we can. You have done more than most. This defeat was authored when Time began—all we do not know is the hour of its coming."

"Who could not say with certainty that it is upon us?"

"I could not." Ynnir said it gently, letting it pass to the ancient guardian with an undertone of spring, of hope, of renewal even after death. "Neither should you. Do as you have always done—do as your broodsire raised you. We will face it bravely, and who knows? We may yet be surprised."

Zsan-san-sis' glow guttered for a moment, then burned more strongly. "You are more king than your father was, or his father before him," he said.

"I *am* my father, and his father before him," said the blind king. "But I thank you."

He did not clasp the old chieftain's hand—it would be unwise even for the king to touch one of the Children of the Emerald Fire—but he nodded his head so slowly it might almost have been a bow. He left the robed guardian in a posture of surprise as he walked into the Deathwatch Chamber.

The beetles on the walls shifted minutely as he entered and the movement of their iridescent wingcases sent a ripple of changing colors across the entire chamber. They settled again; the flickers of blue and pale green were replaced by an earthier tone that better reflected the gray and peach of the cloud-wreathed sunset outside the open window. Blind for centuries, Ynnir could smell the sea as powerfully as a drowning man could taste it, and he hoped that his sister-wife could smell it too, that it gave her a little relief in the growing dark.

He stood over the bed and looked at her, so wan, so still. It had been a full turning of the seasons since she could even bear to be sat up in Hall of Mirrors like some obscene, floppy icon. He was almost grateful that those humiliating days had passed, that she had slipped down into herself so far that she could not even be moved.

Even as he stared in silent contemplation he realized he saw no traces of life at all. Alarmed, he looked to her lips, the pink now paler than ever, almost white, and felt a moment of real fear. Always before, even on the worst days, she had greeted him before he spoke. So still . . . !

My queen, he called to her, shaping each word so clearly that he could imagine it as a stone dropped into a still pond, the ripples sending everything that swam beneath them scattering, until the stone itself struck into the softness at the bottom. *Can you hear me? My twin?*

Despite all that had gone between them, the fair and the foul, his heart leaped in his breast when he at last heard her words, as quiet as if they did indeed issue from beneath the mud at the bottom of a deep, deep pond.

Husband?

I am here, at your bedside. How are you today?

Weaker. I . . . I can barely hear you. I sent my words to Yasammez. She did not think the name, but rather a flutter of ideas— Grandmother's Fierce Beautiful Sister of the Bloodletting Thorns and the Smoking Eye. *I should not have done it,* she told him, almost an apology. *I did not have the . . . strength . . . but I was . . .*

Afraid she would use up what little of her music remained, he hastened to finish her thought. *You were wondering if she had succeeded. And she told you she had.*

Succeeded at your plan. Fulfilled the Pact. Not at what I wished . . .

Which would have availed you nothing. Trust me, my sister, my wife. Many things have passed between us over all these years, but never lies. And it could yet be my own compromised plan, like the despised, bent tree in the corner of the orchard, that will bear fruit.

What would it matter? There is nothing that can be done now. All that we love will perish. Her thoughts were so full of blackness he could almost feel himself pulled down by them, like a man so fixed on the swirling clouds below his mountain path that he leans toward them and falls free . . .

No. He pulled himself back, disentangling himself from her. *Hope is the only strength left to us and I will not give it up.*

What hope? For me? I . . . doubt it. And even if so, then what of you . . . ? He sensed her amusement, that old, bitter mirth that sometimes over the long centuries had felt to him like a slow poison. *What of you, Ynnirit-so?*

I ask for nothing I cannot bear. And Yasammez has given the glass to her dearest, closest servitor, Gyir.

The Encauled One? But he is so young in years . . . !

He will bring it to us. He will stop for nothing—he knows its importance. Do not despair, my queen. Do not go down into the darkness yet. Things may change.

Things always change, she told him, *that is the nature of things . . .* but she was fading now, weary and in need of that deeper blackness that was her sleep, and which might last days. A last bubble of dark amusement drifted up to him. *Things always change, but never for the better. Are we not the People, and is that not the substance of all our story?*

Then her thoughts were gone and he stood alone with her silent, coolly slumbering shell. The beetles shifted on the walls again, a quiet unfurling and resettling of wings that rippled sunset-colored lightning all around the chamber until they too settled down to sleep once more.

They were back.

The dark men, the faceless men, once more pursued him through burning halls, sliding in and out of the rippling shadows as though they were nothing but shadows themselves. Was it a nightmare? Another fever dream? Why couldn't he wake up?

Where am I? The tapestries curled and smoked. *Southmarch.* He knew the look of its corridors as completely as he knew the sound and feel of his own blood rushing through his veins. So had all the rest been a dream? Those endless hours in the dripping forest behind the Shadowline? Gyir and Vansen, and that bellowing, one-eyed giant—had they all been fever-fancy?

He ran, gasping and clumsy, and the faceless men in black oozed behind him like something that had been melted and poured, losing bodily form as they flowed around corners and snaked along the walls in sideways drips and smears only to regain shape once more, a dozen shapes, and spring out after him, heads following his every movement, fingers spreading and reaching. But even as he ran for his life, even as the tapestries flamed and now even the roofbeams began to smolder, he felt his thoughts float free, light and insubstantial as the flakes of ash swirling around him on hot winds.

Who am I? What am I?

He was coming apart, fragmenting like a kori-doll on an Eril's Night bonfire, his limbs flailing but useless, his head a thing of straw, dry tinder, full of sparks.

Who am I? What am I?

Something to hold—he needed something cool as a stone, thick and hard as bone, something real to keep himself from falling into flaming pieces. He ran and it was as though he grew smaller with every step. He was losing himself, all that made him up char-ring, disappearing. The rush and thump of the faceless men's pursuit echoed in his head as if he were listening to his own blood coursing through the gutters of his body, his own filthy, corrupted blood.

I'm like Father—worse. It burns in me—it burns me up!

And it hurt like the most dreadful thing he could imagine, like needles under his skin, like white-hot metal in his marrow, and it shifted with every movement, driving bolts of pain from joint to joint, rushing up into his head like fire exploding from a cannon's barrel. He wanted only to get away from it, but how? How could you run away from your own blood?

Briony. If Southmarch itself was no longer his home, if its pas-sageways were full of fire and angry shadows and the galleries hung with leering, alien faces, his sister was something different. She would help him. She would hold him, remember him, know him. She would tell him his name—he missed it so much!—and put her cool hand on his head, and then he would sleep. If only he could find Briony the faceless men would not find him—they would give up and scuttle, slide, ooze back into the shadows, at least for a while. Briony. His twin. Where was she?

"Briony!" he shouted, then he screamed it: "*Briony!* Help me!"

Stumbling then, and falling; a bolt of pain shooting through him as he struck his injured arm—how could this be a dream when it felt so real? He scrabbled to lift himself from the hot stone, arm aching worse than even the burning of the skin on his hands. He could not stop, could not rest, not until he found his sister. If he stopped he would die, he knew that beyond doubt. The shadow-men would eat him from within.

He stood, even in this dream world forced to cradle his throbbing, aching arm, that thing he carried through his life like a sickly child, loving it and hating it. He looked around. A vast, empty room stretched away on all sides, dark but for a few slanting columns of light falling down from the high windows—the Portrait Hall, and it was empty but for him, he could feel it. The faceless men had not caught him yet, but he could smell smoke and sense the growing murmur of their pursuit. He could not stop here.

A picture hung before him, one he had seen before but seldom paid much attention to—some ancient queen whose name he could not remember. Briony would know. She always knew things like that, his beloved show-off sister. But there was something about the woman's eyes, her cloud of hair, that caught his attention . . .

The sound of his pursuers rose until it seemed they were just beyond the Portrait Hall door, but he stood transfixed, because it was not the face of some ancient Eddon pictured there, some long-dead queen of Southmarch, but his own, his features haggard with fear and terror.

A mirror, he thought. *It's been a mirror all this time.* How often had he passed through this place and its ranks of frowning dead without realizing that here, in the center of the hall, hung a mirror?

Or is it a portrait . . . of me . . . ? He stared into the hunted, haunted eyes of the sweating red-haired boy. The boy gazed back. Then the mirror began to dim as if clouds were forming on its surface, as if even from this distance he fogged it with his own hot, fretful breath.

The clouds dimmed and then dissolved. Now it was Briony who looked back at him. She wore a strange hooded white dress he had never seen before, something a Zorian sister would likelier wear than would a princess, but he knew her face better than his own—much better. She was unhappy, quietly but deeply, a look he had never seen so much as he had since first they had word their father had been betrayed and made a prisoner.

"Briony!" he shouted now, "I'm here!"

He could not reach her, and he knew that she was not hearing his words, but he thought she could at least feel him. It was glory to see her, cruelty to have so little of her. Even so, just the sight of her utterly familiar and perfect Briony-face reminded him of who he was: *Barrick.* He was Barrick Eddon, whatever might have happened to him, wherever he might be. Even if he had been dreaming this—even if he was dying and it had all been some strange illusion the gods had set for him on the doorstep of the next world—he had remembered who he was.

"Briony," he said, but more quietly now as the clouds covered the face in the mirror. For a moment, just before it disappeared, he thought he saw a different face, a stranger's face, astoundingly, a girl whose black hair was streaked with a red like his own. He could not understand what was happening—to go from that most familiar of all faces to one he had never seen before . . . !

"Why are you in my dreams?" she said in surprise, and her words pattered in his head like cooling rain. Then the black-haired girl was gone too, and so was almost everything else—the faceless men gone, the Portrait Hall gone, the flames of the terrible conflagration grown as transparent as wet parchment and the castle itself going, going . . .

As the terror lost its grip a little he was startled, frightened, confused, and even excited by the memory of that new face—seeing it had felt like cold water in a parched mouth—but he let it go for the moment so he could cling instead to what was more important: Briony had touched him, somehow, across all the cold world and more, and that great goodness had kept him in the world during a moment when he would otherwise have chosen to leave. He was still footless and confused by the dream he was in, but he understood that he had chosen to remain for now on the near side of Immon's fateful gate, however wretched and painful living might be.

Like a man fighting upward from the bottom of deep water, Barrick Eddon began to thrash his despairing way back toward the light.

Vansen had just finished making a space for the prince and wrapping him in his own tattered, stained wool guardsman's cloak when Barrick's feverish murmuring quieted and the boy's body, which had been as tight as a bowstring, suddenly went limp. Even as horror flooded through Vansen . . .

I lost the prince! I let him die!

. . . The boy's eyes snapped open. For a moment they rolled wildly, fixing on nothing, as if he tried to stare right through the stone of the long, low cavern cell in search of freedom. Then the young prince narrowed his gaze on Ferras Vansen. The soldier thought that the boy was going to say something to him—thank him, perhaps, for carrying him all this way, or curse him for the same reason, or perhaps just ask what day it was. Instead, the prince's eyes abruptly welled with tears.

Sobbing, snuffling, Barrick thrashed his way out of both the cloak and Vansen's restraining grasp, then crawled across the floor to an empty spot near the adjoining wall where he huddled with his face in his hands, weeping unrestrainedly. Several of the other prisoners turned to watch him, the expressions on their inhuman faces varying from mild interest to uncomprehending blankness. Vansen clambered to his feet to follow the prince.

I suspect he will not thank you. Gyir's voice in his head was still a novelty, and not an entirely pleasant one—like a stranger making himself at home in your house without permission. *Let the boy grieve.*

"Grieve for what? We're alive. There's still hope." Vansen spoke aloud—he didn't know the trick of talking without words and did not care to learn. Already this place, this shadowland, was doing its best to take away all that made him who he was. He was *not* going to help speed the process.

Grieve for all he has realized he is losing. The same thing to which you also cling so tightly—his old idea of who he was.

"What do you . . . ? Get out of my head, fairy!"

I do not dig into your thoughts, sunlander. Vansen could feel the irritation—no, it was something deeper—in Gyir's words. The featureless face showed no more emotion at this moment than the prow of a boat, but the words came with pulses of anger, as though each thought hummed like an apple wasp. *Even as diminished as I am, I cannot help knowing a little of your strongest feelings,* Gyir said, speaking ideas that Vansen somehow understood as words. *Any more than if you were sick or frightened someone could avoid smelling the stink in your sweat.* Another wave of contempt came from him. *And in truth I can do that as well, much to my sorrow. You sunlanders all smell like corruption and death.*

Struck by curiosity, Vansen ignored the insult. "How is it I can understand you at all? I couldn't before."

I did not know you could until just now. In other, less dangerous circumstances, it would be quite an interesting puzzle to consider.

Vansen watched Prince Barrick as the boy's sobbing grew weaker. A few of the smaller prisoners that had been driven off by Barrick's sudden move had edged back into the area surrounding him, but they seemed to be regarding him with more fear than interest. "Will any harm come to him there?"

Gyir briefly turned his yellow eyes toward Barrick. *I think not.*

Most of those in this room are afraid of me. They are right to be, even crippled as I am.

Vansen saw that the fairy spoke the truth: even in this large underground prison chamber, stuffed to overcrowding with scores of creatures of at least a dozen different types and sizes, some of which appeared quite fierce, the three of them were being given a great deal of room to themselves. "But they're not afraid of you enough to let you go."

The nearly faceless creature watched Vansen for a long moment, as though considering his existence for the first time. *You too can speak to me without speaking aloud, Ferras Vansen.* It was not his own name Vansen sensed in Gyir's wordless speech so much as his face. It was unutterably strange to see himself both so clearly and so strangely, even to see his face suddenly pull into a scowl of frightened disgust—as if someone had put a looking glass inside his thoughts.

"Stop! I want nothing to do with such . . . black magic."

You would refuse to stop talking aloud, even if it means that you are endangering the boy—your prince? We will never find a way to escape if half our conversation is spoken out loud. There are still folk in this land who understand the sunlander tongue, as the raven did. I do not doubt Jikuyin has a few among his slaves.

Ferras Vansen thought for a long time, then nodded, although the very idea of sharing the substance of himself with the faceless, inhuman creature made him feel queasy and terrified. "Well, then. Show me."

It is simple, man of the hills. All you need to do is think that you are speaking the words—hear yourself speaking but keep the sounds locked inside you. I will guide you.

Strangely, the fairy was right—it *was* simple. Once he found the proper trick of imagining himself talking in just the right way, he discovered that Gyir could hear what he said as clearly as if he had formed it with air and tongue and lips. Had it been the power of the godling Jikuyin's voice that had unlocked this skill? But then why had Barrick Eddon been able to do it from the first?

Why can I suddenly understand you? he asked the fairy. *And what can we do to escape this place?*

If I knew already how we might free ourselves, Gyir said with an undercurrent of something that felt a little like scorn, or perhaps was the bitter tang of self-dislike, *I would not be conversing about the boy's mood and how you gained the gift of true speech, but beginning to make a plan.* Now Vansen could feel the fairy's anger clearly, as a man in water would feel another man thrashing helplessly close by. *I dislike being a prisoner, too—perhaps more than you do. We will talk later about escape.*

Then, with a considered effort that Vansen could feel like a gust of cooling air, Gyir swept away his own fury. *For now, we must try to understand better why we are being held,* he said, and it was as if the moment of rage had never happened. *That is our first step— it will set the direction for all others.* The fairy paused for a long time then, and Vansen felt the silence in a way he never had before. *As for what has made you able to understand me,* Gyir said at last, *I said it was interesting because it seems to hint at an answer to a question my people have long debated—at least those in the Deep Libraries to whom such tasks are given.* This came as a blur of ideas Vansen could only barely riddle out, and he was certain he was missing most of what the fairy intended. *There is little we can do at this moment except . . .*

Interesting? I don't understand you? He looked to Barrick again, who had recovered himself a little. The boy's eyes were red and his cheeks still wet, but he seemed to be listening to Vansen's conversation with Gyir. *I don't understand,* he repeated.

Ah, but you do, and that is the crux. Gyir, who had been crouching, finally sat down and pushed his back against the sooty, rough-carved stone wall. *Look around you. Do you see these creatures? Drows and bokkles and all manner of things even less savory? These are the Common Ones—all creatures of our lands, some even related to my folk, but they are not the trueblood People.* Vansen could feel the emphasis with which Gyir spoke the word, as if it were a thing of power, something to conjure with. *Most especially, they are not High Ones. Among the Twilight folk, only those called the High Ones have the gift of speaking with their hearts, as we say it—the True Speech, which cannot lie, the speech we are using now.*

So why should I be able to do it? Vansen asked. He was fearful of what the answer might be—some taint in his family, some witchy blood, another mark of shame laid on his quiet, hard-working, abashed people.

Some say that all the sunlanders once could speak with us this way— that they, or at least some of them, were of the same great branch as the People, that they came of the People and not just after them. Perhaps Jikuyin merely thrust the gift of True Speech upon you, somehow—his kind, the Old Ones, are grandchildren of the Formless and have many powers that are unknown. But also it may simply be that when he spoke to you the power of his voice cleared the channels of your heart as a great flood may scour clean riverbeds long filled with silt. It is possible he only gave back to you that which is the birthright of your kind.

But . . . but Prince Barrick . . . Vansen turned and saw the boy staring back at him with something in his eyes that looked almost like hatred. Shaken, it took him a moment to remember what he had been saying and to form the words in his mind. *Prince Barrick could speak to you already, and understand you, long before we met this thing you call Jikuyin.* Vansen could not approach the complexity of images which Gyir used when he "spoke" their captor's name, but he felt certain just his horrified memory of the ogre's massive, ravaged face would be enough.

Prince Barrick is different, Gyir said abruptly, *otherwise he would have been dead long ago and you would not have followed him here. That is all I may say.*

"Don't talk about me." The boy wiped angrily at his eyes. "Don't."

Why can't I hear him—Barrick—in my head? asked Vansen.

It could be in time you will, Gyir replied. *Or it could be that both of you can only speak with me.*

Vansen wanted to go to the prince, to bring him back to sit with them, but something in the boy's expression kept him seated where he was. *Why are we here in this mine or prison or whatever it is? Why aren't we dead? And what is the monster who's captured us? Does he have any weaknesses? You said he was one of the Old Ones, a god or a god's bastard.*

Gyir looked at him for a few moments before answering. *As to why we are not dead, I cannot say, Ferras Vansen, but it is clear that Jikuyin wants slaves more than he wants corpses.* The fairy looked as though he was almost asleep, red eyes only half open. *What he wants them for, I do not know, but this place has an old, grim reputation. As to what he is, I told you—a grandchild of the Formless.*

This means nothing to me. I have never heard of such a god.

You have, but among your people the true lore is almost lost. Even here, in our own land, the stories have become children's tales. You remember the raven's little tale of Crooked and his great-grandmother, Emptiness? There were bones of truth buried in it, but the flesh was corrupt. The truth at its core is that the Formless begat both Emptiness and Light, and those two in turn begat gods and monsters. The One in Chains is such a one—a small monster, not a god but a demigod. Still, he is a great power.

And that's whose prisoner we are? asked Vansen. His head was beginning to hurt from all this think-talking. *Why have I never heard of them—of any of them?*

"You have," said Barrick. He sounded as though he had a mouthful of something bitter. "You know them all, Captain—Sva, the Void, and Zo, her mate, the First Light. All the rattling nonsense the priests talked . . . and it's all real." He seemed on the verge of tears again. "All of it! The gods are real and they will destroy us all, for not believing. We can no longer pretend it isn't true."

They will not destroy us, said Gyir, *and although your kind and mine may well destroy each other, it will not be the gods' doing.* But he did not sound as certain as he had before, and Vansen wondered suddenly if it was really true that the True Speech could not lie. *They are all gone from the earth now, long gone. Only a few of their lesser children like this crippled demigod remain.*

Vansen had to take a breath, pained by such sacrilege from an inhuman creature—the gods gone? *I still do not understand you. Sva and Zo? I have heard of them, but what of Perin and the Trigon? What of the gods we know, at whose temples we worship?*

They are all one family, said Gyir. *One family and one blood. And long before your folk or mine had even thought to clothe ourselves, they were spilling that blood.*

"It's pointless," protested Barrick, putting his hands over his ears as though he could block out the soundless words that way. "This talking—any of this! It changes nothing." His face reddened and seemed to crumple. The boy was crying again, rocking in place. "I thought it was all priest's lies. Instead, I am being p–p–punished . . . punished for my miserable, flyblown, shit-stained pride!"

Vansen clambered to his feet and hurried to the prince's side. "Your Highness, it is not your fault . . ."

"Leave me alone!" the boy shrieked. "Do not speak to me of things you know nothing about! What could you know of a curse like mine?" He threw himself down on his stomach and banged his forehead against the stone, like a man in a terrible hurry to pray.

"Prince Barrick . . . ! Barrick, get up . . ." Vansen put his arms around the boy's chest and tried to lift him, but the prince fought his way loose, and as he did so struck Vansen hard in the face.

Barrick did not even seem to notice. "No! Don't you touch me!" he groaned. " I am filthy! On fire!" A froth of spittle hung at the corners of the boy's mouth and on his lower lip. "The gods have chosen me for this suffering, this curse . . . !"

Vansen hesitated only a moment, then drew back and slapped the prince full in the face. Barrick stumbled and fell to his knees, shocked into silence. His hand slowly came up to his cheek. He drew it away and stared at it as though expecting to see blood, although Vansen had hit him only with his open hand. "You . . . you *struck* me!"

"I apologize, Your Highness," Vansen said, "but you must calm yourself, for your own sake if nothing else. We cannot afford to bring down the guards, or start a fight with other prisoners. You may punish me for my crime as you wish if we make it home to Southmarch again. You may even have me put to death for it, if it pleases you . . ."

"Death?" said Barrick, and in an instant the flailing child was gone, his place taken by someone who looked like him but was eerily self-possessed. Barrick's anger, hot a moment before, had suddenly turned icy. "You're a fool if you think you're going to get off that easily. If the impossible occurs and we return to Southmarch alive, I'm going to tell my sister how you feel about her and then order you to join her bodyguard, so you have to look at her every day and know that she is looking back at you with disgust, that she and all the other ladies of the court are marveling together at the sight of the most arrogantly foolish and pitiful idiot who ever lived."

The prince turned away from him. Gyir seemed lost in his own secret thoughts. Ferras Vansen had no choice but to sit silently, holding his stomach as though he had been kicked.

22

A Meeting of the Guild

As a marriage gift, Silvergleam gave to Pale Daughter a box of wood, carved with the shapes of birds, and in it she put all that she could remember of her family and old home. When she opened the box, its music soothed her heart. But her father Thunder could not make music to cool the burning of his own anger. He called out to his brothers that he was afflicted, dying, that his heart was a smoldering stone in his chest. They came to him and he told them of the theft of his daughter, his dove.

—from *One Hundred Considerations*
out of the Qar's *Book of Regret*

"I DON'T LIKE IT," OPAL SAID. "No good can come of telling everyone."

"I'm afraid this once I can't agree with you." Chert looked around the front room. Evidence of the distractions of the last days were everywhere—tools uncleaned, dust on the tabletop, unwashed bowls and cups. "I am no hero, old girl. I've come to the limit of what I can do."

"No hero—is that what you say? You certainly have been acting like you thought you were one."

"Not by choice. In all seriousness, my love, you must know that."

She sniffed. "I'll put the kettle on. Did you know the flue is blocked? We'll be lucky if the smoke doesn't kill us."

Chert sighed and sank deeper in his chair. "I'll see to the flue later. One thing at a time."

He had been so tired that when the ringing began he did not at first realize what it was. Half in dream, he imagined it as the bells of the guildhall, that the great building was floating away on some underground river, being sucked down into the darkness below Funderling Town . . .

"Is that our bell?" Opal shouted. "I'm making tea!"

"Sorry, sorry!" Chert climbed onto his feet, trying to ignore the protesting twinges from his knees and ankles. No, he was definitely *not* a hero.

I should be settled back to carve soapstone and watch grandchildren play. But we never had children. He thought of Flint, strange Flint. *Until now, I suppose.*

Cinnabar's bulky form filled the doorway. "Ho, Master Blue Quartz. I've come on my way back from quarry, as I promised."

"Come in, Magister. It is kind of you."

Opal was already waiting by the best chair with a cup of blue-root tea. "I am mortified to have visitors with the house in this state—especially you, Magister. You do us an honor."

Cinnabar waved his hand. "Vistiting the most famous citizen of Funderling Town? Seems to me I'm the one being honored with an audience." He took a small sip of the tea to test it, then blew on it.

"Famous . . . ?" Chert frowned. Cinnabar had a rough and ready sense of humor, but the way he'd said it didn't sound like a joke.

"First you find the boy himself, then when he runs away you bring him back with one of the Metamorphic Brothers holding the litter? Big folk visitors in and out? And I hear rumors even of the Rooftoppers, the little folk out of the old tales. Chert, if anyone in the town is *not* talking about you and Opal, they would have to be as ignorant as a blindshrew."

"Oh. Oh, dear," Opal said, although there was a strange under-tone of something almost like pride in it. "Would you like some more tea, Magister?"

"No, I've still got supper waiting at home for me, Mistress Opal. It's one thing to work late, but to come home to Quicksilver House without an appetite after my woman's been in the kitchen all afternoon is just asking for trouble. Perhaps you could tell me what's on your minds, if I'm not rushing you?"

Chert smiled. How different this fellow was from Chert's own brother, who was also a Magister: Nodule Blue Quartz was not nearly so important as Cinnabar in Funderling Town, but you would never know it from the airs Nodule put on. But Cinnabar—you couldn't fail to like a man who was so easy in himself, so uninterested in position or rank. Chert felt a little bad for what he was about to do.

"I'll get to the point, then, Magister," he said. "It's about our vis-itor. I need your help."

"Problems with the boy?" Cinnabar actually looked mildly concerned.

"Not the boy—or at least that's not the visitor we mean." He raised his voice. "You can come out now, Chaven!"

The physician had to bend at the waist to make his way through the doorway of the bedchamber, where he had been sitting with Flint. Even with his head bowed so as not to touch the ceiling, he loomed almost twice Cinnabar's height.

"Good evening, Magister," he said. "I think we have met."

"By the oldest Deeps." Cinnabar was clearly amazed. "Chaven Makaros, isn't it? You're the physician—the one who's supposed to be dead."

"There are many who would like that to be true," said Chaven with a rueful smile, "but so far they have not had their wish granted."

Cinnabar turned to his hosts. "You surprise me again. But what is this to me?"

"To all of us, I'm beginning to think," said Chert. "My bracing can't take the weight of all these secrets any longer, Magister. I need your help."

The head of the Quicksilver clan looked up at the physician, then back at Chert. "I've always thought you a good and honest man, Blue Quartz. Talk to me. I will listen. That much at least I can promise."

When Ludis saw that his visitor had arrived, the Lord Protector of Hierosol gestured for his military commanders to leave. The black-cloaked officers rolled up their charts of the citadel's defenses, bowed, and departed, but not without a few odd glances at the prisoner.

Ludis Drakava and his guest were not left entirely alone, of course: besides the Golden Enomote, half a pentecount of soldiers who never left the lord protector's presence even when he slept, and who stood now at attention along the throne room walls, the lord protector also had his personal bodyguards, a pair of huge Kracian wrestlers who stood cross-armed and impassive on either side of the Green Chair. (The massive jade throne of Hierosol was reputed to have belonged to the great Hiliometes, the Worm-Slayer himself, and certainly was big enough to have seated a demigod. In recent centuries, more human-sized emperors had removed much of the throne's lower foundation so they could sit with their feet close enough to the ground to spare their pride.)

Ludis, a former mercenary himself, was broad enough in chest and shoulders to mount the Green Chair without looking like a child. He had once been lean and muscled as a heroic statue, but now even the light armor that he wore instead of the robes of nobility—perhaps to remind his subjects he had won the throne by force and would not give it up any other way—could not hide the thickness around his middle, nor could his spadelike beard completely obscure his softening jaw.

Ludis beckoned the prisoner forward as he seated himself on the uncushioned jade. "Ah, King Olin." He had the rasping voice of a man who had been shouting orders in the chaos of battle all his grown life. "It is good to see you. We should not be strangers."

"What should we be?" asked the prisoner, but without obvious rancor.

"Equals. Rulers thrown together by circumstance, but with an understanding of what ruling means."

"You mean I should not despise you for holding me prisoner."

"Holding you for ransom. A common enough practice." Ludis clapped his hands and a servant appeared, dressed in the livery of House Drakava, a tunic decorated with a stylized picture of a red-eyed ram, a coat of arms that had not been hanging in the Herald's Hall quite as many years as the other great family crests. *You can make yourself emperor in one day,* warned an old Hierosoline saying, *but it takes five centuries to make yourself respectable.* "Wine," commanded Ludis. "And for you, Olin?"

He shrugged. "Wine. One thing at least; I know you will not poison me."

Ludis laughed and pawed at his beard. "No, no indeed! A waste of a valuable prize, that would be!" He flicked his hand at the servant. "You heard him. Go." He settled himself, pulling the furry mantle close around his shoulders. "It is cold, this sea wind. We plainsmen never get used to it. Are your rooms warm enough?"

"I am as comfortable as I could be any place with iron bars on the doors and windows."

"You are always welcome at my table. There are no bars on the dining hall."

"Just armed guards." Olin smiled a little. "You will forgive me. I cannot seem to lose my reluctance to break bread with the man who is holding me prisoner while my kingdom is in peril."

The servant returned. Ludis Drakava reached up and took a goblet from the tray. "Or would you like to choose first?"

"As I said." Olin took the other goblet and sipped. "Xandian?"

"From Mihan. The last of the stock. I suppose they will make that foul, sweet Xixian stuff now." Ludis drank his off in one swallow and wiped his mouth. "Perhaps you scorn my invitations because you are a king and I am only a usurper—a peasant with an army." His voice remained pleasant, but something had changed. "Kings, if they must be ransomed, like to be ransomed by other kings."

Olin stared at him for a long moment before replying. "Beggaring my people for ransom is bad enough, Drakava. But you want my daughter."

"There are worse matches she could make. But I am told her whereabouts are . . . unknown at the present. You are running out of heirs, King Olin, although I also hear your newest wife has whelped successfully. Still, an infant prince, helpless in the hands of . . . what is their name . . . the Tolly family . . . ?"

"If I did not have reasons already to wish to put my sword through you," said Olin evenly, "you would have just given me several. And you will never have my daughter. May the gods forgive me, but it would be better if she truly is dead instead of your slave. If I had known then what I know about you now I would have hanged myself before allowing you even to suggest such a match."

The lord protector's eyebrow rose. "Ah? Really?"

"I have heard of what happens to the women brought to your chambers—no, the girls. Young girls."

Ludis Drakava laughed. "Have you? Perhaps as you curse me for a monster you will tell me what your own interest is in girl-children, Olin of Southmarch. I hear you have developed a . . . friendship with the daughter of Count Perivos."

Olin, still standing, bent and put down his goblet on the floor, sloshing a little wine onto the marble tiles. "I think I would like to go back to my rooms now. To my prison."

"My question strikes too close to home?"

"All the gods curse you, Drakava, Pelaya Akuanis is a child. She reminds me of my own daughter—not that you would understand such a thing. She has been kind to me. We talk occasionally in the garden, with guards and her maids present. Even your foul imagination cannot make that into anything unseemly."

"Ah, perhaps, perhaps. But that does not explain the little Xixian girl."

"What?" Olin looked startled, even took a step back. His foot tipped over the goblet and the dregs pooled on the floor.

"Surely you don't think you can meet with a chambermaid, or laundry-maid, or whatever that little creature is, let alone my castle steward, without my knowing it. If such a thing happened I would have to poison all my spies like rats and start over." He brayed a laugh. "I am not such a fool as you think me, Southmarch!"

"It was curiosity only." Olin took a deep breath; when he spoke again his voice was even. "She resembled someone, or so I thought, and I asked to meet her. I was wrong. She is nothing."

"Perhaps." Ludis clapped for the servant again, who came in with an ewer of wine and refilled the lord protector's cup. He saw the goblet on the floor and looked accusingly at Olin, but did not move to clean it up. "Tell the guards to bring in the envoy," Ludis ordered the man, then turned back to his captive. "Perhaps all is as you say. Perhaps. In any case, I think you will find this interesting."

The man who came in, accompanied by another half-pentecount of the lord protector's Rams, was hugely fat, his thighs rubbing against each other beneath his sumptuous silk robes so that he swayed when he walked like an overpacked donkey. His head and eyebrows were shaved and he wore on his chest a gold medallion in the shape of a flaming eye. He paused when he reached the foot of the throne and looked at Olin with casual suspicion, like someone who had spent most of his life making quick decisions on court precedent and disliked seeing anyone he could not quickly put into an appropriate list in his head.

"Pay no attention to my . . . counselor," Ludis Drakava told the fat man. "Read me your letter again."

The envoy bowed his huge, shiny head, and held up a beribboned scroll of vellum, then began to recite its contents in the high tones of a child.

"*From Sulepis Bishakh am-Xis III, Elect of Nushash, the Golden One, Master of the Great Tent and the Falcon Throne, Lord of All Places and Happenings, may He live forever, to Ludis Drakava, Lord Protector of Hierosol and the Kracian Territories.*

"*It has come to Our attention that you hold prisoner one Olin Eddon, king of the northern country called Southmarch. We, in our divine wisdom, would like to speak with this man and have him as Our guest. Should you send him to Us, or arrange for him to return with Favored Bazilis, Our messenger, We will reward you handsomely and also look kindly on you in the future. It could even be that, should Hierosol someday find itself part of Our living kingdom (as is the manifest wish of the great god Nushash) that you, Ludis Drakava, will receive a guarantee of safety and high position for yourself in Our glorious empire.*

"*Should you refuse to give him to Us, though, you will incur Our gravest displeasure.*"

"And it is signed by His sacred hand, and stamped with the great Seal of the Son of the Sun," the eunuch finished, letting the vellum roll close with a flourish. "Do you have an answer for my immortal master, Lord Protector?"

"I will give you one by morning, never fear," said Ludis. "You may go now."

The huge man looked at him sternly, as at a child who seeks to shirk responsibility, but allowed himself to be led out again by the soldiers.

Soon the throne room was empty again of all save Olin and Ludis and the bodyguards. "So, will you give him what he wants?" Olin asked.

Ludis Drakava laughed hard again. His cheeks were red, his eyes only a little less so. He had been drinking for much of the afternoon, it seemed. "He is readying his fleet, the Autarch—that poisonous, eunuch-loving child. He will be coming soon. The only question is, why does he want you?"

The northern king shrugged. "How could I know? They say this Sulepis is even more of a madman than his father Parnad was."

"Yes, but why you? In fact, how did it come to his attention that you are my . . . guest?"

"It's hardly a secret." Olin smiled in an ugly way. "You have made sure that all of Eion knows I am your prisoner."

"Yes. But it is also interesting this should come so soon after you spoke with that Xixian girl. Could your innocent meeting have been an opportunity for you to . . . send a message?"

"Are you mad?" Olin took a step toward the Green Chair. The two huge guards unfolded their arms and stared at him. He stopped, fists clenched. "Why would I want to put myself into such a madman's hands? I have fought him and his father for years—I would be fighting them now, if you and cursed Hesper had not conspired to take me prisoner in Jellon." He slapped his hands together in frustration. "Besides, I spoke to that girl only a few days ago—how could any message go back and forth to Xis so swiftly?"

The lord protector inclined his head. "All that you say seems reasonable." He seemed satisfied merely to have angered Olin. "But that does not mean it is true. These are unreasonable times, as you should well know, with your own castle attacked by changelings and goblins." He looked up, fixing Olin with his reddened eyes. "Let me tell you this—you belong to Ludis. I bought you, and I will keep you. If I sell you, I alone will profit. And if the Autarch of Xix somehow manages to knock down the citadel walls, I will make sure with my last breath that he does not get you. Not alive, anyway." The master of Hierosol waved his hand. "You may go back to your chambers now to read your books and flirt with the chambermaids, Eddon." He clapped his hands and the prisoner's guards appeared from outside the throne room door. "Take him out."

The minutely carved roof of the cavern that shielded Funderling Town was renowned throughout Eion. In better times people actually traveled up from distant countries like Perikal and the Devonisian islands just to see the fantastical forest of stone, the loving work of at least a dozen generations of Funderlings.

The ceiling of the House of the Stonecutters' Guild was not so famous, and certainly nowhere near so large, but was in its own way just as stupefying a piece of art. In a natural concavity on the underside of Southmarch Castle's foundation slab a combination of limestone, cloudy quartz, beams of ancient black ironwood and the Funderlings' own matchless skills had been crafted into something the gods themselves might envy.

Chert had seen it many times, of course—his grandfather had been part of the team which had performed its last major repairs—but even so it never failed to impress him. Staring up at it from his lonely position at the ceremonial Outcrop, the ceiling seemed a window through quartz crystal and limestone clouds to some distant part of heaven, but those clouds were braced with great spars of ironwood far too thick and workmanlike to be merely ornamental. It was only when the viewer's eyes adjusted to the darkness (which grew paradoxically greater as the empty space ascended) that he saw the robed and masked figure surrounded by smaller robed and veiled figures, all seated upside down at the apex, glaring down from the vault, and he realized that the view was not that of someone looking up, but looking *down* into the depths of the earth—a great tunnel leading downward into the J'ezh'kral Pit, domain of the Lord of the Hot, Wet Stone—Kernios, as the big folk called him.

But of course, the true cleverness of the room was beneath the viewer's feet—something Chert had time to appreciate now as he waited for the noisy reaction to his last words to die down. The Magisters' semicircle of benches and the four stone chairs they faced sat around the edge of a huge mirror of silvered mica, so that everything above was reflected below. Chert and the others seemed to be sitting around the rim of the great Pit itself, looking down into the very eyes of their god. To approach the Highwardens was to seem to walk on nothing above the living depths of Creation.

It was disconcerting at the best of times. Tonight, with the whole Guild joined together to judge Chert's actions, it was downright frightening.

"You did *what?*" His own brother, Nodule, was predictably leading the charge against him. "You cannot imagine the shame I feel, that one of our family . . ."

"Please, Magister," said Cinnabar. "No one here has even determined that anything wrong's been done, let alone that Chert has brought shame to the Blue Quartz family."

"To the entire Quartz clan!" cried Bloodstone, Magister of the Smoke Quartz branch. Fat and bulging-eyed, he was an ally of Nodule's and quick to join Chert's brother in most things—including, it seemed, in being horrified by what Chert had done. He was not alone: the Magisters of the Black, Milk, and Rose Quartz families had also been grumbling all through Chert's appearance at the Outcrop.

Nice to see my family hurrying to my aid. Chert could only hope that the silence of the other members of the large Quartz clan augured more open minds.

"Strangers in the Mysteries?" Bloodstone shook his head in apparent amazement. "Big folk hiding from their rightful lords here in Funderling Town? What madness have you brought to us, Chert?"

"Your concern has been noted," said Cinnabar, sounding as though he meant the opposite. As Magister of his own Quicksilver family and one of the most important leaders of all Metal House—most thought he would someday replace old Quicklime Pewter as one of the four Great Highwardens, the most exalted of Funderling honors—he was a good ally to have. On top of everything else, he was also fair and sensible. "Perhaps," he said now, "we should see if any of the other Magisters or our noble Highwardens have questions before we start shouting about shame and tradition."

Scoria, Magister of the Gneiss family since his father was lifted to the rank of Highwarden, stood up, his thin face full of fretful anger. "I wish to know why you took in this newest upsider, Chert Blue Quartz. The rest is beyond my understanding, but this seems simple enough. He is a criminal and the king's regent searches for him. If he is found here we will all suffer."

"With respect, Magister," Chert said, "the physician Chaven is a good man, as I said. He was also one of King Olin's most respected advisers. If he swears that the Tollys have murdered people to seize the throne, and will murder him as well to silence him—well, I'm only a foreman, a working man, but it seems more complicated to me than merely saying he's a criminal."

"But that doesn't change the risk we're in," pointed out Jacinth Malachite, one of the few female Magisters. "Chert, many of us know you, and know you as a good man, but there's a difference between doing a deed of good conscience on your own and dragging all Funderling Town into a quarrel with the castle's rulers . . ."

A noise like wet sand rubbing on stone interrupted her: Highwarden Sard Smaragdine of Crystal House was clearing his throat. Unlike the Magisters, the Highwardens did not rise to speak; ancient Sard remained shrunken in his chair like a sack of old chips and samples. High on the wall above his head the Great Astion, seal of Funderling Town, gleamed like a star buried in the stone. "Too many questions here to go about it in such a backward way," rasped Sard. "Which questions are the most important? That must be answered first. Then we will move our way down, layer after layer, until we have reached the bedrock of the whole matter." He waved a spindly arm. "What do the Metamorphic Brothers think? Has this . . . incursion . . . into the sacred Mysteries angered the Earth Elders?"

Chert looked around, but it seemed nobody at this hastily assembled meeting of the Guild had thought to bring along any of the order. "They knew I went down into the Mysteries in search of my . . . in search of the boy, and they knew I brought him back up." The Metamorphic Brothers did *not* know everything that had happened down there, of course, and Chert didn't intend to tell the entire story to the Guild, either; as Opal liked to remind him, there was such a thing as having too much trust in your fellows. "They knew the little Rooftopper went down part of the way with me. The only thing that they seemed worried about was that somehow this all seemed to match some of old Brother Sulfur's dreams."

"When it comes to the Earth Elders," said Travertine, another of the Highwardens and almost as old as Sard, "Sulphur has forgotten more than the rest of you ever knew ..."

"Yes, thank you, Brother Highwarden," Sard rasped. "Let us continue. Chert Blue Quartz, why did you first bring this upgrounder boy among us? It is ... not our custom."

"It was something about the strangeness of where we found him, I suppose. But if truth be told, much of it was because my wife Opal wanted to take him home and I could not argue her out of it." A ripple of laughter passed through the room, but only a small one: the matters at hand were far too daunting. "We have no children, as most of you know."

Sard cleared his throat again. "Is there anything other than the timing that makes you think there is any connection between what this physician claims is happening in the castle above us and the strange child you brought home?"

Chert had to think for a moment. "Well, Flint found the stone that Chaven says was used to murder Prince Kendrick. That may be happenstance, but for a child who found his way to the Rooftoppers when no one else has seen them, let alone spoken to them, for generations ..."

"I take your meaning," the oldest Highwarden said, nodding. He waved his hand, looking like an upended tortoise struggling to rise. "Do any of my fellows have anything more to ask or to offer?" He squinted his old, near-blind eyes as he looked to the masters of Fire Stone and Water Stone houses, but they shook their heads. Only Quicklime Pewter, the Highwarden of Metal House, had anything to say.

"Is the physician here, brothers?" he asked. "We cannot make up our minds on hearsay alone."

One of the younger Magisters opened the chamber door and beckoned. Chaven came through with his bandaged hands clasped before him, head lowered and shoulders hunched, although the door to the Magisterial Chamber was one of the few in Funderling Town he could walk through upright. He saw the size of the room and stopped, then looked down at the mica floor, startled by what appeared to be an abyss beneath his feet.

"It's a mirror," Chert said from where he stood at the Outcrop. "Don't be afraid."

"I've never seen one even near such a size," said Chaven, half to himself. "Wonderful. *Wonderful!*"

"You may step down, Chert Blue Quartz," wheezed Sard. "Chaven of Ulos, you may take his place at the Outcrop. We have some questions we wish to ask you."

The physician was so fascinated by the mica mirror beneath his feet that he almost bumped into the Magister nearest the end, but at last made his way to the Outcrop and stood at the edge of the circular floor, the tall stone chairs of the Highwardens on his left, the stone benches of the Magisters at his right.

As Chaven repeated the story that others had already related, Chert felt a flush of guilty gratitude that the physician did not know all of the tale. Because of Chaven's seeming madness on the subject of mirrors, Chert had chosen to keep back the full story of Flint's glass, and likewise had not told the officers of the Guild about his own journey under Brenn's Bay to meet the victorious Twilight People in mainland Southmarch. Chert still had no idea what any of that meant, but feared that if he told Cinnabar and the others that he had actually handed something over to the Quiet Folk, as they were sometimes euphemistically called, something that the boy had brought from behind the Shadowline in the first place, the Guild might decide keeping the boy was a risk that Funderling Town could not afford.

And that would be the end of me, he thought. *My wife would never speak to me again. And,* he realized, *I'd miss the boy something fierce.*

"You realize, Chaven Makaros," said the Water Stone Highwarden, Travertine, "that by coming here, you may have embroiled our entire settlement in a struggle with the current lords of Southmarch." He gave the physician a stern look. "We have a saying, *'Few are the good things that come from above,'* and nothing you have done makes me inclined to think we should change it."

Even with his head bowed Chaven still towered above the Highwardens. "I was wounded, feverish, and desperate, my lords. I did not think of greater matters, but only hoped to find help from my friend, Chert of the Blue Quartz. For that, I apologize."

"Foolishness is no excuse!" called out Chert's brother Nodule. Several of the other Magisters rumbled their approval of the sentiment.

"But desperation may bring true allies together," said Cinnabar, and many other Magisters nodded. During his brief time in power, Hendon Tolly had taken all building around the castle out of the hands of Funderlings, keeping his plans secret and using hand-picked men of his own brought in from Summerfield. Many of the Funderling leaders already feared for their livelihood—work on sprawling Southmarch Castle had provided much of their income in recent years. Chert suspected that as much as anything else might make them more willing to take risks than usual.

"Does anybody else wish to speak?" asked Highwarden Sard after a long pointless speech advocating caution by Magister Puddingstone of the Marl family had dragged to an end. "Or may we get on with our decision?"

"Which decision, Highwarden?" asked Cinnabar. "It seems to me we have three things to ponder. What, if anything, should be done about Chert Blue Quartz taking outsiders into the Mysteries? What, if anything, should be done to punish the boy Flint for visiting the Mysteries without permission (although he seems to have suffered more than a little for his mischief already, and was sick for many days thereafter)? And what should we do about this gentleman, the physician Chaven, and what he says about the Tollys and the attack on the royal family?"

"Thank you, Magister Quicksilver," said Highwarden Caprock Gneiss. "You have summed things up admirably. And as the best informed of the Magisters, you may stay and help the four of us with our deliberations."

Chert's spirits rose a little. One of the Magisters was always picked to help prevent a deadlock among the four Houses, and he could not have hoped for anyone better than Cinnabar.

The five got up—Sard leaning heavily on Cinnabar's arm—and retreated to the Highwardens' Cabinet, a room off the Council

Chamber that Chert had heard was very sumptuously appointed, with its own waterfall and several comfortable couches. The informant had been his brother Nodule, who as always was eager to emphasize the difference in his and Chert's status. Nodule had once been the Magister picked to provide the fifth vote and still talked about it several years later as if it were an everyday occurrence.

While the Highwardens were absent the others milled about the Council Chamber and talked. Some, anticipating a long deliberation, even stepped out to the tavern around the corner for a cup or two. Chert, who had the distinct feeling he was the subject of almost every conversation, and not in a way he'd like, went and joined Chaven, who was sitting on a bench along the outer wall with a morose expression on his round face.

"I fear I've brought you nothing but trouble, Chert."

"Nonsense." He did his best to smile. "You've brought a bit, there's no question, but if I'd come to you the same way, you'd have done the same for me."

"Would I?" Chaven shook his head, then lowered his chin to his hands. "I don't know, sometimes. Everything seems to be different since that mirror came to me. I don't even feel like precisely the same person. It's hard to explain." He sighed. "But I pray that you're right. I hope that no matter how it's got its claws into me, I'm still the same man underneath."

"Of course you are," said Chert heartily, patting the physician's arm, but in truth such talk made him a bit nervous. What could a mere looking glass do to unsettle a learned man like Chaven so thoroughly? "Perhaps you are worrying too much. Perhaps we should not even mention your own mirror, the one Brother Okros has stolen."

"Not mention it?" For a moment Chaven looked like someone quite different, someone colder and angrier than Chert would ever have expected. "It may be a weapon—a terrible weapon—and it is in the hands of Hendon Tolly, a man without kindness or mercy. He must not have it! Your people . . . we must . . ." He looked around as though surprised to find that the person speaking so loudly was himself. "I'm sorry, Chert. Perhaps you are right. This has all been . . . difficult."

Chert patted his arm again. The other Funderlings in the wide chamber were all watching him and the physician now, although some had the courtesy to pretend they weren't.

"We have decided," said Highwarden Sard, "not to decide. At least not about the most dangerous issue, that of the legitimacy of the castle's regent, Lord Tolly, and what if anything we should do about it."

"We know we must come to a decision," amplified Highwarden Travertine. "But it cannot be rushed."

"However, in the meantime, we have decided about the other matters," continued Sard, then paused to catch his breath. "Chert Blue Quartz, stand and hear our words."

Chert stood up, his heart pounding. He tried to catch Cinnabar's eye, to glean something of what was to come, but his view of the Quicksilver Magister was blocked by the dark, robed bulk of Highwarden Caprock.

"We rule that the boy Flint shall be punished for his mischief, as Cinnabar so quaintly put it, by being confined to his house unless he is accompanied by Chert or Opal Blue Quartz."

Chert let out his breath. They were not going to exile the boy from Funderling Town. He was so relieved he could barely pay attention to what else the Highwardens were saying.

"Chert Blue Quartz himself has done no wrong," proclaimed Sard.

"Although his judgment could have been better," suggested Highwarden Quicklime Pewter.

"Yes, it could have been," said old Sard with a sour look at his colleague, "but he did his best to remedy a bad situation, and then realized that he could not go on without the advice of the Guild. To him, no penalty, but he must no longer act without the Guild's approval in any of these matters. Do you understand, Chert Blue Quartz?"

"I do."

"And do you so swear on the Mysteries that bind us all?"

"I do." But though he was reassured by what had been said so far, Chert found he was not as confident about what would be done in the long run. Also, he had grown used to doing things that others—especially the Magisters and Highwardens—might think were beyond his rights or responsibilities. He and his family were dug very deep into a strange, strange vein.

"Last we come to the matter of the physician Chaven," said Sard. "We have much still to discuss about his claims and will not make a decision recklessly, but some choices must be made now." He stopped to cough, and for a moment as his chest heaved it seemed he might not go on. At last he caught his breath. "He will remain with us until we have determined what to do."

"But he cannot remain in your house, Chert," said Cinnabar. "It is already nearly impossible to keep our people from whispering, and it's likely that only the fact these Tollys have banned us from working in the castle has kept his presence secret from them this long."

"Where will he go . . . ?"

"We will find a place for him here at the guild hall." Cinnabar turned to the Highwardens. Sard and Quicklime nodded, but Travertine and Gneiss looked more than a little disgruntled. Chert guessed that Cinnabar had cast the deciding vote.

"I am sure Opal will want to keep feeding him," Chert said. "Now that she's learned what he eats." He smiled at Chaven, who seemed not entirely to understand what was happening. "Upgrounders don't like mole very much, and you can't get them to eat cave crickets at knifepoint."

A few of the other Magisters laughed. For the moment, things in the Council Chamber were as friendly as they were likely to be—still tense, but no one in open rebellion.

"So, then." Sard raised his hand and all the Magisters stood. "We will meet again in one tennight to make final decisions. Until then, may the Earth Elders see you through all darknesses and in any depths."

"In the name of He who listens in the Great Dark," the others said in ragged chorus.

Chert watched the Magisters file out before turning to Chaven, who was still staring down at the floor of the Council Chamber like a schoolboy caught with his exercises unlearned. "Come, friend. Cinnabar will show us where you'll stay, then I'll go back to my house and pack up some things for you. We've been very lucky—I'm surprised, to tell you the truth. I suspect that having Cinnabar on our side is what saved us, because old Quicklime trusts him. Cinnabar will probably replace him one day."

"And I hope that day is far away," said the Quicksilver Magister, striding up. "Quicklime Pewter has forgotten more about this town and the stone it's built with than I'll ever know."

As they began to walk toward the chamber door, Chaven at last looked up, as if wakening from a dream. "I'm sorry, I . . ." He blinked. "That veiled figure," he said, pointing at the fabled ceiling. "Who is that? Is it . . . ?"

"That is the Lord of . . . that is Kernios, of course, god of the earth," Chert told him. "He is our special patron, as you must know."

"And on his shoulder, an owl." The physician was staring down again.

"It is his sacred bird, after all."

"Kernios . . ." Chaven shook his head. "Of course."

He said no more, but seemed far more troubled than a man should who had just been granted his life and safety by the venerable Stone-Cutter's Guild.

23

The Dreams of Gods

The war raged for years before the walls of the Moonlord's keep. Countless gods died, Onyenai and Surazemai alike.

Urekh the Wolf King perished howling in a storm of arrows. Azinor of the Oneyenai defeated the Windlord Strivos in combat, but before he could slay him, Azinor was himself butchered by Immon, the squire of great Kernios. Birin of the Evening Mists was shot by the hundred arrows of the brothers Kulin and Hiliolin, though brave Birin destroyed those murderous twins before he died.

—from *The Beginnings of Things*
The Book of the Trigon

"I T . . . IT SOUNDED LIKE you said . . . that you were *there*." Briony didn't want to offend her hostess (especially not before she'd shared whatever food the crone had to spare) but even in the throes of fever and starvation, the habits of a princess died hard: she didn't like being teased, especially by grimy old women. "When the gods went to war."

"I was. Here, I'll put a few more marigold roots in the pot for you—you'd be surprised how nicely they cook up once you boil the poison out. I've been in flesh so long I can scarcely remember anything else, but one thing I don't miss about the old days—all that bloody, smoking meat! I don't know what they thought they were doing."

"Who? Wait, poison? What?" Briony was trying to keep still and avoid sudden movements. It had only just occurred to her that an old woman who lived by herself in the middle of the Whitewood was likely to be quite mad. She felt sure that even as weak and sick as she was, she could defend herself against this tiny creature, bony as a starveling cat—but how could she protect herself when she slept? She didn't think she could survive another night on her own in the rainy wood.

"I'm talking about those bloody men and their bloody sacrifices!" the old woman said, which explained very little. "They used to be everywhere in this part of the forest, chopping wood, hunting my deer, generally making a nuisance of themselves. Some of them were handsome, though." She smiled, a contraction of wrinkles that made her face look even more like a knot in the grain of a very old tree. "I let some of them stay with me, bloody-handed or not. I was not so particular then, when my youth was on me."

It was no use trying to make sense of what the woman was saying. Briony shivered and wished the fire were big enough to keep her warm. Her hostess stared at her as she dropped more roots into a clay pot sitting on the stones beside the fire, then began to wrap two wild apples in leaves. When she had finished, the old woman reached out toward her. Briony shied away.

"Don't be stupid, child," she said. "I can see you're ill. Here, let me feel your brow." The old woman put a hand as rough as a chicken's foot against Briony's forehead. "That's a bad fever. And you've other wounds as well." She shook her head. "Let me see what I can do. Sit still." She brought up her other hand and flattened both palms on Briony's temples. Startled, Briony reached for the knife in her boot, but the woman only moved her hands in slow circles.

"Come out, fever," the old woman said, then began to sing in a quiet, cracked voice. Briony could not understand the words, but her head had begun to feel increasingly hot and vibrantly alive, as though it were a beehive in high summer. It was such an odd sensation that she tried to pull away, but her limbs would not obey her. Even her heart, which should have sped up when she found herself helpless, did not comply. It bumped along, beating calmly and happily, as though having an ancient stranger set your head on fire with her bare hands were the most ordinary thing in the world.

The heat traveled down from her skull into her spine and spread throughout her body. She felt boneless, woozy: when the woman at last released her it was all Briony could do not to tumble onto her face.

"The rest of the healing you must do yourself," the old woman said. "Pfoo! I have not expended so much energy in a while." She clapped her hands together. "So, do you feel well enough to eat now?" When Briony did not immediately answer, because she was more than a little stunned by what had just happened, the old woman spoke again, more sharply. "Briony Eddon, daughter of Meriel, granddaughter of Krisanthe, where are your manners? I asked you a question."

Briony stared at her for a long moment as her thoughts caught up with her ears. Her fingers went numb and hair rose on her neck and scalp. She snatched out her small knife and held it out before her in a trembling hand. "Who *are* you? How do you know my name? What did you just do to me?"

The old woman shook her head. "Every time. By the sacred, ever-renewing heartwood, it happens every time. What did I do? Made you better, you ungrateful little kit. How do I know your name? The same way as I know everything I know. I am Lisiya Melana of the Silver Glade, one of the nine daughters of Birgya, and I am the patroness of this forest, as my sisters were the protectors of Eion's other forests. My father was Volios of the Measureless Grip, you see—a god. You may call me Lisiya. I am a goddess."

"You're . . . you're . . ."

"Do I mumble? Very well, a demigoddess. When my father was young, he fathered a brood on my mother, who was a tree-spirit. It was all very romantic, in a brutal sort of way—but it's not as if my father stayed around to help raise us. I didn't call him 'Papa,' as you did with yours, and sit on his knee while he chucked me under the chin. The gods aren't like that—weren't then, and certainly aren't now." She chuckled at some private joke. "Like tomcats, really, and the goddesses weren't much better."

Briony lowered her knife to her lap but did not put it away. Even if the woman was completely mad, she had skills. Briony felt much better. She was still cold and tired, and still definitely hungry, but the weakness and misery of her illness and her many wounds seemed to have vanished. "I . . . I don't know . . ."

"You don't know what to say. Of course you don't, daughter. You think I might be mad but you don't want to offend me. In your case, you're being careful because you're cold and lonely and hungry, but you have the right idea. It's never a good idea to annoy a god. If a mortal offended us in the old days, even in the smallest of ways, well, we were likely to turn him into a shrub or a sand-crab." The old woman sighed and looked at her wrinkled hands. "I don't know that I could manage anything that impressive anymore, but I'm fairly certain that at the very least, I could give you back your fever and add a very bad stomachache."

"You say you're a goddess?" It wasn't possible. A forest-witch, perhaps, but surely goddesses never looked like this.

"Only a demigoddess, as I already admitted, and please don't rub my face in it. There aren't any true goddesses left. Now don't be dull." Lisiya frowned. "I can hear some of your thoughts and they're not pretty. Very well. I hate doing this, especially after I already spent so much vigor healing you—ai, my head is going to hurt tomorrow!—but I suppose we won't be able to get on with whatever the music has in mind unless I do." The old woman stood, not without difficulty, and spread her thin arms like an underfed raptor trying to take flight. "You might want to squint your eyes a bit, daughter."

Before Briony could do more than suck in a breath the fire billowed up in new colors and the darkening sky seemed to bend in toward them, as though it were the roof of a tent and something heavy had just landed on it. The old woman's figure grew and stretched and her rags became diaphanous as smoke, but at the center of it all Lisiya's staring eyes smoldered even brighter, as though fires bloomed behind volcanic glass.

Briony fell forward onto her elbows, terrified. The maid Selia had changed like this, taking on a form of terrible darkness, a thing of claws and soot-black spikes; for a moment Briony was certain she had fallen into some terrible trap. Then, drawn by a glow gilding the ground around her, she looked up into a face of such startling, serene beauty that all her fear drained away.

She was tall, the goddess, a full head taller than even a tall man, and her face and hands, the only parts of her flesh visible in the misty fullness of her dark robes, were golden. Vines and branches curled around her; a corona of silvery leaves about her head moved gently in an unfelt wind. The black eyes were the only things that had remained anything near the same, although they glowed now with a shimmering witchlight. How terrifying anger would be on such a face! Briony didn't think her heart could stand the shock of seeing it.

The seemingly immobile mask of perfection moved: the lips curled in a gentle but somewhat self-satisfied smile. "Have you seen enough, daughter?"

"Please . . ." Briony moaned. It was like trying to stare at the sun. "Yes—enough!"

The figure shrank then, like parchment curling in a fire, until the old woman stood before her once more, wrinkled and stooped. Lisiya lifted a knobbed knuckle to her eye and flicked something away. "Ah," she said. "It hurts to be beautiful again. No, it hurts to let it go."

"You . . . you really are a goddess."

"I told you. By my sacred spring, you children of men these

days, you're practically unbelievers, aren't you? Just trot out the statues on holy days and mumble some words. Well, I hope you're happy, because now I am quite exhausted. You will have to tend the roots." The old woman gingerly settled herself beside the fire. "Every season it is harder to summon my old aspect, and every time it takes more out of me. The hour is coming when I will be no more than what you see before you, and then I will sing my last song and sleep until the world ends."

"Thank you for helping me." Briony felt much better—that was undeniable. The mist of fever had cleared and her breath no longer rattled in her lungs. "But I don't understand. Any of this."

"Nor do I. The music has decreed that I should find you, and that I should feed you, and perhaps give you what advice I may—not that I have much to offer. This is no longer my world and it hasn't been for a long time."

Briony could not help staring at the old woman, trying to see the terrible, glorious shape of the goddess, once more so well hidden beneath wrinkled, leathery flesh. "Your name is . . . Lisiya?"

"That is the name I am called, yes. But my true name is known only to my mother, and written only in the great Book itself, child, so do not think to command me."

"The great book? Do you mean *The Book of the Trigon*?"

She was startled by how hard the goddess laughed. "Oh, good! A very fine jest! That compendium of self-serving lies? Even the arrogant brothers themselves would not try to pass off such nonsense as truth. No, the tale of all that is and shall be—the *Book of the Fire in the Void*. It is the source of the music that governs even the gods."

Briony felt as though she had been slapped. "You call *The Book of the Trigon* lies?"

Lisiya flapped her hand dismissively. "Not purposeful lies, at least not most of them. And there is much truth in it, too, I suppose, but melted out of recognizable shape like something buried too long in the ground." She squinted at the pot. "Spoon those hot stones out, child, before the water all boils away, and I will try to explain."

The night had come down in earnest and Briony, despite the

strangeness of her situation, was feeling the tug of sleep. She had been frightened by the woman's display, by seeing what Lisiya had called her true aspect, but now she also found herself strangely reassured. No harm could come to her in the camp of a forest goddess, could it? Not unless it came from the goddess herself, and Lisiya did not seem to bear her any ill will.

"Good," she said, spooning up the marigold root soup.

"It's the rosemary. Gives it some savor. Now, that song you were singing, there's an example of ripe modern nonsense, some of it stolen from other poems, some of it straight out of the Trigonate canon, especially that foolishness about Zoria being helped by Zosim. Zosim the Trickster never did anyone a good turn in his life. I should know—we were cousins."

Briony could only nod her head and keep eating. It was glorious to feel well again, however preposterous the circumstances. She would think about it all tomorrow.

"And Zoria. She was not stolen, not in the way that the Surazemai always claimed. She went with Khors of her own free will. She loved him, foolish girl that she was."

"Loved . . . ?"

"They teach you nothing but self-serving nonsense, do they? The heroism of the Surazemai, the evil of the Onyenai, that sort of rubbish. I blame Perin Thunderer. Full of bluster, and wished no one had ever been ruler of the gods but himself. He was named Thunderer as much because of his shouting as the crashing of his hammer. Oh, where to begin?"

Briony could only stare at her, dazed. She took a bite of the marigold root and wondered how long she could keep her eyes open while Lisiya talked about things she didn't understand. "At the beginning . . . ?" Maybe she could just close her eyes for a bit, just to rest them.

"Oh, upon my beloved grove, no. By the way, that's not just a bit of idle oathmaking—this place where you sit used to *be* my sacred grove." Lisiya waved her gnarled fingers around the clearing. "Can you tell? The stones of this fire pit were once my altar, when all men still paid me homage. All gone to wrack and ruin hundreds of years ago, of course, as you see—a lightning fire took the most glorious of my trees. More of the Thunderer's splendid work, and I've not always believed it was an accident. A sleeping dog can still growl. Ah, but they were so beautiful, the ring of birches that grew here. Bark white as snow, but they gleamed in moonlight just like quicksilver . . ." Lisiya coughed. "Mercy on me, I am so old . . ."

Briony belched. She had eaten too fast.

The goddess frowned. "Charming. Now, where was I? Ah, the beginning. No, I could not hope to correct all you do not know, child, and to be honest, I do not remember all the nonsense that Perin and his brothers declared their priests must teach. Here is all you need to know about the oldest days. Zo, the Sun, took as his wife Sva, the Void. They had four children, and the eldest, Rud the Day Sky, was killed in the battle against the demons of the Old Darkness. Everyone knows these things—even mortals. Sveros, who we called Twilight, took to wife his niece Madi Onyena, Rud's widow, and she bore him Zmeos Whitefire and Khors Moonlord. Then Sveros Twilight was lured away from her by Madi Onyena's twin sister Surazem, who had been born from the same golden egg. Surazem bore him Perin, Erivor, and Kernios, the three brothers, and from these five sons of Twilight—and some sisters and half sisters, of course, but who talks of them?—sprang the great gods and their eternal rivalries. All this you must know already, yes?"

Briony did her best to sit up straight and look as though she were not falling asleep. "More or less . . ."

"And you have to know that Perin and his brothers turned against their father Sveros and cast him out of the world into the between-spaces. But the three brothers did not then become the rulers of the gods, as your people teach. Whitefire, the one you call Zmeos, was the oldest of Sveros' chilren, and felt he should have pride of place."

"Zmeos the Horned One?" Briony shuddered, and not just from her still-damp clothing. All her childhood she had been told of the Old Serpent, who waited to steal away children who were wicked or told lies, to drag them off to his fiery cave.

"So Perin's priests call him, yes." Lisiya pursed her lips. "I never had priests myself. I do not like them, to be honest. In the days when people still sacrificed to me I was happy enough with a honeycomb or an armful of flowers. All that bleeding red meat . . . ! Animal flesh to feed priests, not a goddess. And I would not have been caught dead in their stone temples, in any case. Well, except for once, but that is not a story for tonight . . ." The old woman's eyes narrowed. "You are falling asleep, child," she said sternly. "I begin to tell you the true tale of the gods and you cannot even keep your eyes open."

"I'm sorry," Briony murmured. "It's just been . . . so long since . . ."

"Sleep, then," said Lisiya. "I waited a day for you—and years since my last supplicant. I can wait a few more hours."

"Thank you." Briony stretched out, her arm beneath her head. "Thank you . . . my lady . . ."

She did not even hear if the goddess said anything, because within moments sleep reached up and seized her as the ocean takes a shipwrecked sailor grown too weary to swim.

For a moment after waking she lay motionless with the thin sunlight on her closed eyelids, trying to remember where she was and what had happened. She felt surprisingly well—had her fever broken? But her stomach felt full, too, almost as if the dreams had been . . . real.

Briony sat up. If the last night's events had been dreams, then the dreams still lingered: only a few yards away from her sleeping spot the fire was burning in its pit of stones, and something was cooking, a sweet smell that made her mouth water. Other than Briony, though, the little clearing was empty. She didn't know what to think. She might have imagined the old woman who claimed to be a goddess, but the rest of this—the fire, the careful stack of kindling beside it, the smell of . . . roasting apples? In late winter?

"Ho there, child, so you've finally dragged yourself upright." The voice behind her made Briony jump. "You didn't get your sweet last night, so I put some more in the coals."

She turned to see the tiny, black-robed figure of Lisiya limping slowly down into the dell, a pair of deer walking behind her like pet dogs. The two animals, a buck and a doe, paused when they saw Briony but did not run. After a moment's careful consideration of her with their liquid brown eyes, they stooped and began to crop at the grass which peeked up here and there through the fallen leaves and branches.

"You're real," Briony said. "I mean, I didn't dream you. Was . . . was *everything* real, then?"

"Now how would I know?" Lisiya dropped the bag she was carrying, then lifted her arms over her head and stretched. "I stay out of mortal minds as a rule—in any case, I spent the night walking. What do you recall that might or might not be a dream?"

"That you fed me and gave me a place to sleep." Briony smiled shyly. "That you healed me. And that you are a goddess."

"Yes, that all accords with my memory." Lisiya finished her stretch and grunted. "Ai, such old bones! To think once I could have run from one side of my Whitewood to another and back in a single night, then still had the strength to take a handsome young woodsman or two to my bed." She looked at Briony and frowned. "What are you waiting for, child? Aren't you hungry? We have a long way to go today."

"What? Go where?"

"Just eat and I will explain. Watch your fingers when you take out those apples. Ah, I almost forgot." She reached into her sack and pulled out a small jug stoppered with wax. "Cream. A certain farmer leaves it out for me when his cow is milking well. Not everyone has forgotten me, you see." She looked as pleased as a spinster with a suitor.

The meal was messy but glorious. Briony licked every last bit of cream and soft, sweet apple pulp off her fingers.

"If we were staying, I'd make bread," Lisiya said.

"But where are we going?"

"You are going where you need to go. As to what will happen there, I can't say. The music says you have wandered off your course."

"You said that before and I didn't understand. *What* music?"

"Child! You demand answers the way a baby sparrow shrieks to have worms spat in its mouth! The music is . . . *the music*. The thing that makes fire in the heart of the Void itself. That which gives order to the cosmos—or such order as is necessary, and chaos when that is called for instead. It is the one thing that the gods feel and must heed. It speaks to us—sings to us—and beats in us instead of heart's blood. Well, unless we are wearing flesh, then we must listen hard to hear the music over the plodding drumbeat of these foolish organs. How uncomfortable to wear a body!" She shook her head and sighed. "Still, the music tells me that you have lost your way, Briony Eddon. It is my task to put you back on the path again."

"Does that mean . . . that everything will be all right? The gods will help us drive out all our enemies and we'll get Southmarch back?"

Lisiya threw her a look of dark amusement. "Not expecting much, are you? No, it doesn't mean anything of the sort. The last time I helped someone to get back onto his path, a pack of wolves ate him a day after I said farewell. *That* was his rightful path, you see." She paused to scratch her arm. "If I hadn't stepped in, who knows how long he would have wandered around—he and the wolves both, I suppose."

Briony stared openmouthed. "So I'm going to die?"

"Eventually, child, yes. That's what's given to mortals—it's what 'mortal' means, after all. And believe me, it's probably a good deal more pleasant than a thousand years of ever-increasing decrepitude."

"But . . . but how can the gods do this to me? I've lost everything—everybody I love!"

Lisiya turned to her with something like fury. "You've lost everything? Child, when you've seen not just everybody you love but everybody you *know* disappear, when you've surrendered all that I have—beauty, power, youth—and the last of them slipped away centuries in the past, *then* you may complain."

"I thought . . . I thought you might . . ."

"Help you? By my grove, I *am* helping you. You're not starving anymore, are you? In fact, it seems like that's my sacred offering of cream on your chin right now, and Heaven knows I don't get many of those these days. You had a dry night's sleep, too, and you're no longer coughing your liver and lights out. Some might count those as mighty gifts indeed."

"But I don't want to get eaten by wolves—my family *needs* me."

Lisiya sighed in exasperation. "I only said the last person I guided was eaten by wolves—the remark was meant as a bit of a joke (although I suppose the fellow with the wolves wouldn't have seen it that way). *I don't know* what's going to happen to you. Perhaps the music is sending some handsome prince your way, who will sweep you up onto his white horse and carry you away into the sunset." She scowled and spat. "Just like one of that Gregor fellow's unskilled rhymes."

Briony scowled right back. "I don't want any prince. I want my brother back. I want my father back, and our home back. I want everything like it was before!"

"I'm glad to hear you're keeping your demands to a minimum." Lisiya shook her head. "In any case, stop thinking about wolves— they're not relevant. There's a stream over that rise and down the hill. Go wash yourself off, then drink water, or make water, or whatever it is you mortals do in the morning. I'll pack up, then if you need more explanations, I'll provide them while we walk. And don't dawdle."

Briony followed the goddess' instructions, walking so close past the grazing deer on her way to the stream that one of them turned and touched her with its nose as she went past. It was an unexpected thing, small but strangely reassuring, and by the time she'd washed her face and run her fingers through her hair a few times she felt almost like a person again.

With her worse fears placated, a little food in her belly, and the company of a real person—if a goddess as old as time could be said to be real—Briony found that there was much to admire about the Whitewood. Many of its trees were so old and so vast that younger trees, giants themselves, grew between their roots. The hush of the place, a larger, more important quiet than in any human building no matter how vast, coupled with the soft light filtering down through the leaves and tangled branches, made her feel as though she swam through Erivor's underwater realm, as in one of the beautiful blue-green frescoes that lined the chapel back home at Southmarch. If she narrowed her eyes in just the right way Briony could almost see the dangling vines as floating seaweed, imagine the flicker of birds in the upper branches to be the darting of fish.

"Ah, there's another one," said Lisiya when Briony shyly mentioned the chapel paintings. "Don't your folk hold him as an ancestor, old Fish-Spear?"

"Erivor? Why, is that a lie, too?"

"Don't be so touchy, child. Who knows if it's true or not? Perin and his brothers certainly put themselves about over the years, and there were more than a few mortal women willing to find out what it felt like to bed a god. And those were only the ones who participated by choice!"

"This is all . . . so hard to believe." Briony flinched at Lisiya's expression. "No, not hard to believe that you're a goddess, but hard to . . . understand. That you know the rest of the gods, know them the way I know my own family!"

"It isn't quite the same," said Lisiya, softening a bit. "There were hundreds of us, and we seldom were together. Most of us kept to ourselves, especially my folk. The forests were our homes, not lofty Xandos. But I did know them, yes, and while we met each other infrequently, we did gather on certain occasions. And many of the gods were travelers—Zosim, and Kupilas in his later years, and Devona of the Shining Legs, so the news of what the others did came to us in time. Not that you could trust a word that Zosim said, that little turd."

"But . . . but he is the god of poets!"

"And that fits, too." She looked up, swiveling her head from side to side like an ancient bird. "We have made a wrong turn. Curse these fading eyes!"

"Wrong turn?" Briony looked around at the endless trees, the unbroken canopy of dripping green above their heads and the labyrinth of damp earth and leaves between the trunks. "How can you tell?"

"Because it should be later in the day by now." Lisiya blew out a hiss of air. "We should have lost time, then gained a little of it back, but we have gained all of it back. It is scarcely a creeping hour since we set out."

Briony shook her head. "I don't understand."

"Nor should you, a mortal child who never traveled the gods' paths. Trust me—we have made a wrong turn. I must stop and think." Lisiya suited word to deed, lowering herself onto a rounded stone and putting her fingers to her temples. Briony, who was not lucky enough to have a rock of her own, had to squat beside her.

"We must wait until the clouds pass," Lisiya announced at last, just as the ache in Briony's legs was becoming fierce.

"Shall we make a fire?"

"Might as well. It could be that we cannot travel again until tomorrow. Find some dry wood—it makes things easier."

When Briony had returned to the spot with half a dozen pieces of reasonably dry deadfall, Lisiya piled them into a tiny hill, then took the last piece in her bony grip and said something Briony could not understand, a slur of rasping consonants and fluting vowels. Smoke leaked between Lisiya's fingers. By the time she put the stick down among the others, fire was already smoldering from a black spot where she had held it.

"That's a good trick," Briony said approvingly.

Lisiya snorted. "It is not a trick, child, it is the pitiable remains of a power that once could have felled half this forest and turned the rest into smoking ruin. Mastery over branch and root, pith and grain and knot—all those were mine. I could make a great tree burst into flower in a moment, make a river change course. Now I can scarcely start a fire without burning my hand." She held up her sooty palm. "See? Blisters. I shall have to put some lavender oil on it."

As the goddess rummaged through her bag Briony watched the

fire begin to catch, the flames barely visible in the still-strong afternoon light. It was strange to be in this between-place, this timeless junction between her life before and whatever would come next, let alone to be the guest of a goddess. What was left to her? What would become of her?

"Barrick!" she said suddenly.

"What?" Lisiya looked up in irritation.

"Barrick—my brother."

"I know who your brother is, child. I am old, not an idiot. Why did you shout his name?"

"I just remembered that when I was in . . . before I found you . . ."

"You found *me?"*

"Before you found me, then. Merciful . . . ! For a goddess, you certainly are thin-skinned."

"Look at me, child. Thin? It barely keeps my bones from poking out—although there does seem to be more of the wrinkly old stuff than there once was. Go on, speak."

"I was looking in a mirror and I saw him. He was in chains. Was that a true vision?"

Lisiya raised a disturbingly scraggly eyebrow. "A mirror? What sort? A scrying glass?"

"A mirror. I'm not certain—just a hand mirror. It belonged to one of the women I was staying with in Landers Port."

"Hmmmm." The goddess dropped her pot of salve back into her rumpled, cavernous bag. "Either someone was using a mighty artifact as a bauble or there are stranger things afoot with you and your brother than even I can guess."

"Artifact . . . do you mean a magic mirror, like in a poem? It wasn't anything like that." She held up her fingers in a small circle. "It was only that big."

"And you, of course, are a scholar of such things?" The goddess' expression was enough to make Briony lower her gaze. "Still, it seems unlikely that a Tile so small, yet clearly also one of the most powerful, should be in mortal hands and no one aware of it, passed around as if it were an ordinary part of a lady's toiletry."

Briony dared to look up again. Lisiya was apparently thinking, her gaze focused on nothing. Briony did her best to be patient. She did not want the goddess angry with her again. She did not—O merciful Zoria!—want to be left in the forest by herself. But after the sticks in the fire had burned halfway down, she could not keep her questions to herself any longer.

"You said 'tile'—what are those? Do you mean the sort of thing that we have on the floor of the chapel? And what is Zoria like? Is she like the pictures to look at? Is she kind?" Once, she recalled, her own lady-in-waiting, Rose Trelling, had gone back to Landsend for Orphanstide and had been asked an extraordinary number of questions by her other relatives—about Briony and her family, about life in Southmarch Castle, a thousand things. *So we wonder about those who are above us—those who are well-known, or rich, or powerful. Are they like us?* It was funny to think that ordinary folk thought of her as she thought of the gods. Who did the gods envy? Whose doings made *them* sit up and take notice? There were so many things Briony wanted to know, and here she sat with a living, breathing demigoddess!

Lisiya let out a hissing sigh. "So you have determined on saving me from this painful immortality, have you? And your killing weapon is to be an unending stream of questions?"

"Sorry. I'm sorry, but . . . how can I not ask?"

"It's not that you ask, it's *what* you ask, kit. But it is always that way with mortals, it seems. When they have their chances, they seldom seek important answers."

"All right, what's important, then? Please tell me, Lisiya."

"I will answer a few of your questions—but quickly, because I have concerns of my own and I must listen carefully to the music. First, the Tiles used in the most potent scrying glasses are pieces of Khors' tower, the things that the foolish poem you were bellowing through the forest called 'ice crystals' or some such nonsense. They were made for him by Kupilas the Artificer—'Crooked,' as the Onyenai call him . . ."

"Onyenai?"

"Curse your rabbiting thoughts, child, pay attention! Onyenai, like Zmeos and Khors and their sister Zuriyal—the gods born to Madi Onyena. You know the Surazemai—Perin and his brothers, the gods born to Madi Surazem. The Onyenai and Surazemai were the two great clans of gods that went to war with each other. But old Sveros fathered them all."

Chastened, Briony nodded but did not say anything.

"Yes. Well, then. Crooked helped Khors strengthen his great house, and the things that he used to do it ensured that Khors' house was not found just in Heaven any longer, nor was it on the earth, but opened into many places. Kupilas used the Tiles to make this happen, although some said the Tiles only masked its true nature and location with a false seeming. In any case, after the destruction of the Godswar, after Perin angrily tore down Khors' towers, some of the remnants were saved. Those are the Tiles we speak of now. They appear to be simple mirrors but they are far more—scrying glasses of great power."

"But you don't think that's how I saw Barrick . . . ?"

"I am old, child, and I am no longer so foolish as to think I know anything for certain. But I doubt it. In all the world only a score or fewer of the Tiles survive. I find it hard to believe that after all these ages another would wind up in a lady's cosmetics chest in . . . where did you say? Landers Port?"

Briony nodded.

"More likely something else is afoot with you and your brother. I sense nothing out of the ordinary from your side, nothing magical—other than your virginity, which always counts for *something*, for some reason." She let out a harsh, dry chuckle. "Sacred stones, look at Zoria. Millennia have passed, and they *still* call her a virgin!"

"What do you mean?"

"A rare possession among both the Surazemai and Onyenai, I can promise you. In fact, other than perhaps the Artificer himself——there's irony there, isn't there?—only our Devona remained unsullied, and I think that may have been as much from inclination as anything else. Just as among mortals, the gods were made in all sorts of shapes and desires. But Zoria . . . certainly not, poor thing."

"Are you saying that the blessed Zoria isn't . . . wasn't . . . she's not . . . a . . ."

Lisiya rolled her eyes. "Girl, I told you, Khors was her lover and she loved him back. Why do you think she ran away from the meadows and the Xandian hills? To be with him! And had her father not come with all his army of relatives to defend his own honor—foolish men and their honor!—she would have happily married the Moonlord and borne him many more children. But that was not fated to be, and the world changed." For a moment the brittleness seemed to soften; Briony watched a sadness so deep it looked like agony creep over the goddess' gaunt face. "The world changed."

Her expression was too naked—too private. Briony looked down at the fire.

"To answer your earlier, unfinished question . . ." Lisiya said suddenly, then cleared her throat. "No, Zoria was not a virgin. And now she simply is not—nor are any but we pathetic few, stepchildren and monsters, castoffs of Heaven. Like insects crawling out of the scorched ground when a forest fire has passed, only we survived the last War of the Gods."

"You mean . . . the other gods are dead?"

"Not dead, but sleeping, child. But the sleep of the gods has already been ages long, and it will continue until the world ends."

"Sleeping? Then the gods are . . . gone?"

"Not entirely, but that is another story. And I do not doubt that a few more aging demigods and demigoddesses like me are still caring for their forests, or landlocked lakes that once were small seas. But I have not talked to one of my kin in the waking world for so long I can scarcely remember."

"No gods? They left us?"

Lisiya's smile was grim. "Not by choice, mortal kit. But they have slept since your ancestors first set stone on stone to build the earliest cities, so it is not as though anything has changed."

"But we pray to them! I have always prayed, especially to Zoria . . . !"

"And you may continue to pray to her if you wish, and the others as well. They may even answer you—when they sleep, they dream, and their dreams are not like those of your kind. It is a restless sleep, for one thing . . . but *that* is most definitely a tale for another time. As it is, we have dallied too long. Come, rise."

"What? Are we going to walk again?"

"Yes. Follow." And without looking back to see if Briony had obeyed her, Lisiya went limping away through the forest.

The late afternoon sun was burrowing into the distant hills when they reached the edge of the Whitewood. As they stood with the great fence of trees behind them, Briony looked out over the meadowlands of what she could only guess was Silverside. The grassy plains stretched away as far to the north and west as she could see, beautiful, peaceful, and empty. "Why have we come here?" she asked.

"Because the music calls you here." Lisiya fumbled in her shapeless robes and drew out something on a string, lifting it over her head with surprising nimbleness. "Ah, a little sun on my bones is a kindly thing. Here, daughter. I am sorry we have not had more time. I miss the chance to speak to something less settled and slow than the trees, and for a mortal child you are not too stoneheaded." She held out her claw of a hand. "Take this."

Briony lifted it from her hand. It was a crude little charm made from a bird skull and a sprig of some dried white flowers, wrapped around with white thread. "I am too old to come when summoned," Lisiya said, "and too weak to send you much in the way of help, but it could be that this might smooth your way in some difficult situation. I have one or two worshipers left."

As she drew the leather cord around her neck, Briony asked, "Have we reached the place you were talking about? You're not going yet, are you?"

Lisiya smiled. "You are a good child—I'm glad it was given to me to help you. And I hope this path will lead you to at least a little happiness."

"Path, what path?" Briony looked around but saw nothing, only damp grass waving in the freshening evening wind. It was the middle of nowhere—no road, no track, let alone a town. "Where am I supposed to go . . . ?"

But when she turned back the old woman had vanished. Briony ran back into the forest, calling and calling, looking for some sign of the black-robed form, but the Mistress of the Silver Glade was gone.

24

Three Brothers

Listen, my children! Argal and his brothers now had the excuse they needed and their wickedness flowered. They went among the gods claiming that Nushash had stolen Suya against her will, and many of the gods became angry and said they would throw down Nushash, their rightful ruler.

—from *The Revelations of Nushash,* Book One

"T HIS DOES NOT SEEM A GOOD IDEA to me," Utta whispered. "What does he want from us? He is dangerous!"

Merolanna shook her head. "You must trust me. I may not know much, but I know my way around these things."

"But . . . !"

She fell silent as the new castellan, Tirnan Havemore, walked into the chamber. He held a book in his hands and was followed by a page carrying more books with—rather dangerously—a writing-tray balanced atop them. Havemore wore his hair in the Syannese style that had swept the castle, cut high above the ears, and because he was balding he looked more like a priest than anything else—a resemblance, Utta thought, that Havemore was only too eager to encourage. Even when he had been merely Avin Brone's factor he had seen himself as a philosopher, a wise man amid lesser minds. She had never liked him, and knew no one outside of the Tollys' circle who did.

Havemore stopped as though he had only just realized the women were in the room. "Why, Duchess," he said, peering at them over the spectacles perched on his narrow nose, "you honor me. And Sister Utta, a pleasure to see you, too. I am afraid my new duties as castellan have kept me fearfully busy of late—too busy to visit with old friends. Perhaps we can remedy that now. Would you like some wine? Tea?"

Utta could feel Merolanna bristling at the mere suggestion that she and this upstart were old friends. She laid her hand on the older woman's arm. "Not for me, thank you, Lord Havemore."

"I will not take anything, either, sir," the duchess said with better grace than Utta would have expected. "And although we would love to have a proper conversation with you, we know you are a busy man. I'm certain we won't take much of your time."

"Oh, but it would be a true joy to have a visit." Havemore snapped his fingers and waved. "Wine." The page put down the books and the teetering tray on the castellan's tall, narrow desk, a desk which had been Nynor Steffen's for years and which had seemed as much a part of him as his skin and his knobby hands. Unburdened, the page left the room. "A true joy," Havemore repeated as though he liked the sound of it. "In any case, I will have a cup of something myself, since I have been working very hard this morning, preparing for Duke Caradon's visit. I'm sure you must have heard about it—very exciting, eh?"

It was news to Utta. *Hendon's older brother, the new Duke of Summerfield, coming here?* Doubtless he would bring his entire retinue—hundreds more Tolly supporters in the household, and during the ominous days of the Kerneia festival as well. Her heart sank to think of what the place would be like, full of drunken soldiers.

"So, my gracious ladies," said Havemore, "what can I do for you today?"

Utta could not imagine anything that Tirnan Havemore could do for them that would not immediately be reported to Hendon Tolly, so she kept her mouth closed. This was Merolanna's idea; Utta would let the dowager duchess take the lead. *Zoria, watch over us, here in the stronghold of our enemies,* she prayed. Even if they knew nothing of the astonishing business she and Merolanna had embarked upon, the ruling faction held little but contempt for either of them, for one key reason: neither one of them had anything to bargain with, no strength, no land, no money. *Well, except Merolanna is part of the royal family and a link to Olin. I suppose the Tollys want to keep her sweet at least until they've got their claws well into Southmarch.*

"But Lord Havemore, you must know what you can do for us," Merolanna said. "Since you called us here. As I said, I don't want to intrude on your time, which is valuable to all of Southmarch, and especially to Earl Hendon, our selfless guardian."

Careful, Utta could not help thinking. Merolanna had moved and was out of range of an admonitory squeeze of the arm. *Don't be too obvious. He doesn't expect you to like him, but don't let your dislike show too openly.*

"Hendon Tolly is a great man." Havemore's grin looked even more wolfish than before—he was enjoying this. "And we are all grateful that he is helping to guard King Olin's throne for its legitimate heir."

The page returned with wine and several cups. Utta and Merolanna shook their heads. The page poured only one and handed it to the castellan, then stepped back to the wall and did his best to look like a piece of furniture. Havemore seated himself in his narrow chair, pointedly leaving the dowager duchess standing.

"You mean for King Olin, of course," Merolanna said cheerfully, ignoring the calculated slight. "Guarding the throne for *King*

Olin. The heir is all well and good, but my brother-in-law Olin is still king, even in his absence."

"Of course, Your Grace, of course. I misspoke. However, the king is a prisoner and his heirs are gone—perhaps dead. We would be foolish to pretend that the infant heir is not of the greatest importance."

"Yes, of course." Merolanna nodded. "In any case, leaving aside all this quibbling about succession, which I'm sure is of scarcely any real interest to a scholar like yourself, you did call us here. What have we done to deserve your kind invitation?"

"Ah, now it is you who feigns innocence, Your Grace. You asked to speak to Avin Brone, but you must know that he has . . . retired. That his duties have all been taken up by me and Lord Hood, the new lord constable. Our dear Brone has worked so hard for Southmarch—he deserves his rest. Thus, I thought I might save him the unnecessary work of trying to solve whatever problem you ladies might have by volunteering my own attention to it, instead." His smile looked like it had been drawn with a single stroke of a very sharp pen.

"That is truly kind, Lord Havemore," said Merolanna, "but in truth we wanted—*I* wanted—to see Lord Brone only out of friendship. For the sake of old times. Why, I daresay Avin Brone and I have known each other longer than you've been alive!"

"Ah." Havemore, like many ambitious young men, did not like being reminded of allegiances that predated his own arrival. "I see. So there is nothing I can do for you?"

"You can remember your kind offer to share yourself more with the rest of us castle folk, Lord Havemore." The duchess smiled winningly. "A man of your learning, a well-spoken man like you, should put himself about a bit more."

He narrowed his eyes, not entirely sure how to take her remark. "Very kind. But there is still a question, Your Grace. I can understand your desire to reminisce with your old friend Lord Brone, but what brings Sister Utta along on such a mission? Surely she and Brone are not also old friends? I had never heard that old Count Avin was much on religion, beyond what is necessary for appearances." Havemore smiled at this little joke shared among friends and for the first time Sister Utta felt herself chilled. This man was more than ambitious, he was dangerous.

"I do consider Brone a friend," Utta said suddenly, ignoring Merolanna's flinch. "He has been kind to me in the past. And he is a man of good heart, whether he spends much time in the temple or not."

"I am glad to hear you say that." Tirnan Havemore now looked at Utta closely. "I worked for him for many years and always felt his best qualities were ignored, or at least underappreciated."

Merolanna actually took a step forward, as if to stop the conversation from straying into dangerous areas. "I asked her to come with me, Lord Havemore. I am . . . I am not so well these days. It makes me easier to have a sensible woman like Utta with me instead of one of my scatterbrained young maids."

"Of course." His smile widened. "Of course, Your Grace. So great is your spirit, so charming your manners, that I fear I'd forgotten your age. Of course, you must have your companion." It was almost a leer now.

What is he thinking? Utta did not want to contemplate it for long.

"By all means, go and see your old friend, Count Avin. I'm afraid he has changed his chambers—I needed more space, of course, so I took these old ones of his over. When Brone is not at home in Landsend you will find him in the old countinghouse next to the Chamber of the Royal Guard. He still comes in, although he has little to do these days." The smile had changed into something else now as Havemore rose, something that celebrated an enemy well and truly dispatched. "You will come see me again? This has been such a delight."

"For us all," Merolanna assured him. "We are honored by your interest in two old women like ourselves, Lord Havemore, now that you've become such an important man in Southmarch."

"Were you not perhaps spreading the fat a little thick?" Utta asked as they made their way across the residence garden, hoods pulled low against the chilly rain. "You do not need to make an enemy of him."

Merolanna snorted. "He is already an enemy, Utta, never doubt that for a moment. If I weren't one of the only people left related to Olin, I'd be gone already. The Tollys and their toadies have no love for me, but they can't afford to see me off—not yet. Perhaps if they get through the winter they'll start thinking about how I might be encouraged to die. I'm very old, after all."

Startled, Sister Utta made the sign of the Three. "Gods protect us, then why did you suggest to him that you were in ill health? Give them no excuse!"

"They will kill me when they want to. I'm convinced now that they had something to do with Kendrick's murder, too. By reminding Havemore, I was just reassuring him that whatever I got up to, I wouldn't be around to make trouble much longer." She stumbled and caught at Utta's arm. "And I'm *not* all that well these days, in truth. I find myself feeble, and sometimes my mind wanders . . ."

"Hush. Enough of that." Utta took the older woman's elbow and held it tightly. "You have frightened me with all this . . . intrigue, Your Grace, all this talk of threats and plots and counter-plots. I am only a Zorian sister and I'm out of my depth. Besides, *I* need you, so you may be neither ill nor feeble, and you certainly may not die!"

Merolanna laughed. "Talk to your immortal mistress, not to me. If the gods choose to take me, or simply to make me a doddering old witling, that's their affair." She slowed as they entered the narrow passage between Wolfstooth Spire and the armory. The paint had faded, and tufts of greenery grew in the cracks in the walls. "By the grace of the Brothers, I have not been to this part of the castle in years. It's falling apart!"

"A suitable place, then, for those who are no longer necessary—Brone, and you, and me too."

"Well said, my dear." Merolanna squeezed her arm approvingly. "The more worthless we are, the less anyone will suspect what devilry we're up to."

★

"Your Grace, this is . . . this is quite a surprise." Brone's voice was a bit thick. Other than a pair of young, wary-looking guardsmen who acted more like they were watching a prisoner than protecting an important lord, the countinghouse was empty. "And Sister Utta. Bless me, Sister, I haven't seen you for a long time. How are you?"

"Fine, Lord Brone."

"You'll forgive me if I don't get up." He gestured at his bare left leg, propped on a hassock, the ankle swollen like a ham. "This cursed gout."

"It's not the gout, it's the drinking that's keeping you in that chair," Merolanna said. "It is scarcely noon. How much wine have you had today, Brone?"

"What?" He goggled at her. "Scarcely any. A glass or two, to ease the pain."

"A glass or two, is it?" Merolanna made a face.

In truth, he looked much the worse for wear. Utta had not seen him for some time, so it was possible the new lines on his face were nothing odd, but his eyes seemed sunken and dark and the color of his skin was bad, like a man who has been weeks in a sickbed. It was hard to reconcile this bloated, pasty creature slumped like a sack of laundry with the big man who only a short time ago had moved through the castle like a war galleon under full sail.

Merolanna rapped on the table and pointed at one of the guards. "Lord Brone needs some bread and cheese for the sake of his stomach. Go fetch some."

The guard gaped at her. "Y—Your Grace . . . ?"

"And you," she said to the other. "I am old and I chill easily. Go and bring a brazier of coals. Go on, both of you!"

"But . . . but we are not supposed to leave Lord Brone!" said the second guard.

"Are you afraid the Zorian sister and I will assassinate him while you're gone?" Utta stared at him, then turned to the count. "Do you think we're likely to attack you, Brone?" She didn't give him time to reply, but took a step toward the guards, waggling her fingers like she was shooing chickens out of a garden. "Go on, then. Hurry up, both of you."

When the baffled guards were gone, the count cleared his throat. "What was *that* about, may I ask?"

"I need your help, Brone," she said. "Something is gravely amiss, and we will not solve it without you—nor in front of Havemore's spies, which is why I sent those two apes away."

He stared at her for a moment, but his eyes failed to catch light. "I can be no help to you, Duchess. You know that. I have lost my place. I have been . . . retired." His laugh was a rheumy bark. "I have retreated."

"And so you sit and drink and feel sorry for yourself." Utta cringed at Merolanna's words, wondering how even a woman like the duchess could talk to Avin Brone that way, with such contemptuous familiarity. "I did not come here to help you with that, Brone, and I will thank you to sit up and pay attention. You know me. You know I would not come to you for help if I did not need it—I am not one of those women who runs weeping to a man at the first sign of trouble."

The specter of a smile flitted across Brone's face. "True enough."

"Things may have seemed bad enough already," Merolanna said, "with Briony and Barrick gone and the Tollys riding herd over us all—but I have news that is stranger than any of that. What do you know about the Rooftoppers?"

For a moment Brone only stared at her as though she had suddenly started to sing and dance and strew flowers around the room. "Rooftoppers? The little people in the old stories?"

"Yes, *those* Rooftoppers." Merolanna watched him keenly. "You really do not know?"

"On my honor, Merolanna, I have no idea what you're talking about."

"Look at this, then, and tell me what you think." She pulled a sheet of parchment from out of the bodice of her dress and handed it to him. He stared at it blankly for a moment, then reached up— not without some discomfort—to take down a candle from the shelf on the wall behind him so he could read.

"It's . . . a letter from Olin," he said at last.

"It was the *last* letter from Olin, as you should know—the one that Kendrick received just before he was murdered. This is a page from it."

"The missing page? Truly? Where did you find it?"

"So you know about it. Tell us." Merolanna seemed a different woman now, more like the spymaster Brone used to be than the doddering old woman she called herself.

"The entire letter was missing after Kendrick's murder," he said. "Someone put it among my papers some days later, but a page was missing." He scanned the parchment with growing excitement. "I think this *is* the page. Where did you find it?"

"Ah, now that is a story indeed. Perhaps you had better have another drink, Brone," Merolanna said. "Or maybe some water to clear your head would be better. Understanding this is not going to be easy, and this is only the beginning."

"So the Rooftoppers . . . are real?"

"We saw them with our own eyes. If it had been only me you might be able to blame it on my age, but Utta was there."

"Everything she says is true, Lord Brone."

"But this is fantastic. How could they be here in the castle all these years and we never knew . . . ?"

"Because they didn't want us to know. And it is a big castle, after all, Brone. But here is the question. How am I going to find that piece of the moon, or whatever it is? Sister Utta thinks it is Chaven the little woman was talking about, but where is he? Do you know?"

Brone looked around the small, cluttered room. There was no sign of the guards returning, but he lowered his voice anyway. "I do not. But I suspect he is alive. It would be easy enough for the Tollys to trump up some charge against him if all they wanted was an execution. I still have a few . . . sources around the castle, and I hear Hendon's men are still searching for him."

"Well, tell your sources to find him. As swiftly as possible. And it would not hurt to inquire into this moon-stone or whatever it is, either."

"But I don't understand—why did these little people ask *you*?

And you said they wanted to bargain with you. How? What did they offer?"

"Ah." Merolanna smiled, and it was almost fond this time. "Once a courtier, always a courtier, I see. Do you not believe they might have come to me because they recognized me as a person of kindness and good will?"

Brone raised an eyebrow.

"You're right. They told me they would give me news of my child."

Avin Brone's eyes went wide as cartwheels. "Your . . . your . . . ?"

"Child. Yes, that's right. Don't worry about Utta—she's been told the whole dreadful story."

He looked at her with a face gone pale. "You told her . . . ?"

"You're not speaking very well, today, Brone. I fear the drink is doing you damage. Yes, I told her of my adultery with my long-dead lover." She turned to Utta. "Brone already knows, you see. I have few confidantes in the castle, but he has long been one of them. He was the one who arranged for the child to be fostered." She turned back to Brone. "I told Barrick and Briony, also."

"You *what?*"

"Told them, the poor dears. They had a right to know. You see, on the day of Kendrick's funeral, I saw the child. My child."

Brone could only shake his head again. "Surely, Merolanna, one of us is going mad."

"It isn't me. I thought for a time it must be, but I think I know better now. Tell me, then—what are you going to do?"

"Do? About what?"

"All of this. About finding Chaven and discovering why the fairies took my little boy." She saw the look on Avin Brone's face. "Oh, I didn't tell you about that, did I?" She quickly related the words of Queen Upsteeplebat and the oracular Ears. "Now, what are you going to do?"

Brone seemed dazed. "I . . . I can inquire quietly again after Chaven's whereabouts, I suppose, but the trail has probably long gone cold."

"You can do more than that. You can help Utta and myself make our way to the camp of those fairy-people, those . . . what are they called? Qar? We've always called them the Twilight Folk, I don't know why everyone has to change. In any case, I want to go to them. After all, they are only on the other side of the bay."

Now it was Utta's turn to be astonished. "Your Grace, what are you saying? Go out to the Qar? They are murderous creatures—they have killed hundreds of your people."

The duchess flapped her hands in dismissal of Utta's concern. "Yes, I'm sure they are terrible, but if they won't tell me where my son is then I don't much care what they do with me. I want answers. Why steal my child? Why put me through year upon year of torture, only to send him back as young as the day he was taken? I saw him, you know, at Kendrick's funeral. I thought I'd truly gone mad. And why should this happen *now*? It has something to do with all this other nonsense, mark my words."

"You're . . . you're really certain you saw him?" Utta asked.

"He was my child." Merolanna's face had gone chilly, hard. "Would·you fail to recognize your revered Zoria if she appeared in your chapel? I saw him—my poor, dear little boy." She turned back to Brone. "Well?"

He took a deep, ragged breath, then let it out. "Merolanna . . . Duchess . . . you mistake me for someone who still wields some power, instead of a broken old warhorse who has been beaten out to pasture."

"Ah. So that is how it is?" She turned to Sister Utta. "You may go, dear. If you will do me the kindness of coming to my chambers this afternoon perhaps we may talk more then. We have much to decide. In the meantime, I have a little persuasion to do here." She turned a sharp eye toward Brone. "And tell that page waiting in the hall outside that when I'm done, his master will need a bath and something to eat. The count has work to do."

Utta went out, awed and a little frightened by Merolanna's strength and determination. She was going to bend Brone to her will somehow, there seemed little doubt, but would that force of character be enough when it came time to deal with all their enemies—with cruel Hendon Tolly, or the immortal and alien Twilight People?

Suddenly the castle seemed no longer any kind of refuge to Utta, but only a cold box of stone sitting in the middle of a cold, cold world.

"Don't I know you?" the guard asked Tinwright. He took a step closer and pushed his round, stubbled face close to the poet's own. "Wasn't I going to smash your skull in?"

Matt Tinwright's knees were feeling a bit wobbly. As if things weren't bad enough already, this was indeed the same guard who had objected to Tinwright having a little adventure with his lady friend some months back in an alley behind *The Badger's Boots*. "No, no, you must be thinking of someone else," he said, trying to smile reassuringly. "But if there's anything else I can do for you, other than having my skull smashed . . ."

"Leave him be," said the other guard with more amusement than sympathy. "If Lord Tolly's got it in for him, they'll do worse to him soon than you could ever imagine. Besides, he might want this fellow unmarked."

The fat-faced guard peered at the trembling poet like a short-sighted bull trying to decide whether to charge toward something. "Right. Well, if His Lordship doesn't flog you raw or something like, then you and I still have a treat to look forward to."

"By the gods, how sensible!" Tinwright stepped away, putting his back against the wall. "Wouldn't want to interfere with His Lordship's plans, of course. Well considered."

And it would have been a narrow escape, except that Tinwright did not for a moment believe he would be alive to avoid future meetings with the vengeful guard. Surely it could not be a coincidence that Hendon Tolly had summoned him so soon after his moment of madness in the garden with Elan M'Cory, kissing her hands, protesting his love. Before this, Tolly had paid Matt Tinwright no more attention than one of the dogs under the table.

He's going to kill me. The thought of it made his knees go wobbly again and he had to dig his fingers into the cracks of the wall behind him to remain upright. He barely resisted the impulse to run. *But, oh, gods, maybe it is something harmless. To run would be to declare guilt . . . !*

Matty Tinwright had received the summons in the morning from one of the castellan Havemore's pages. Tinwright had thought the boy was looking at him strangely as he handed over the message; when he read it, he knew why.

Matthias Tinwright will come to the throne room today after morning prayers.

It was signed with a "T" for "Tolly" and sealed with the Summerfield boar-and-spears crest. The moment the page had left the room Tinwright had been helplessly, noisily sick into the chamber pot.

Now he clung to the wall and watched the fat guard and his friend talk aimlessly of this and that. Would they or anyone else remember him when he was dead? The fat one would celebrate! And no one else in the castle would care, either, except poor, haunted Elan and perhaps old Puzzle. Such a fate for someone who hoped to do great things . . . !

But I have done no great things. Nor, to be honest (and I might as well try to get in practice if I'm going to be standing before the gods soon) have I really tried. I thought becoming a court poet would bring greatness with it, but I have done no work of note. A few lines about Zoria for the princess, but nothing since Dekamene—a poem I thought might be my making, but with Briony gone it has ground to a halt. Not my best work, anyway, if I'm telling the truth. And what else? A few scribbles for Puzzle, songs, amusements. A commission or two for young nobles wanting some words to put their sweethearts in a bedable mood. In all—nothing. I've wasted my life and talent, if I ever truly had any.

He was still cold as ice behind his ribs, but the numbness above the waist was coupled with a sudden, fierce need to piss.

That's a man in his last hour, Tinwright thought miserably. *Thinking about poetry, looking for the privy.*

The door to the throne room crashed open. "Where's the poet?" said a brawny guardsman. "There you are. Come on, don't pull away—it'll all be over soon enough."

The throne room was crowded, as usual. A pentecount of royal guards dressed in full armor and the wolf-and-stars livery of the Eddons stood by the walls, along with nearly that many of Hendon Tolly's own armed bravos, distinguishable from the nobles and rich merchants by the coldness of their stares and the way that even as they talked, they never looked at the person with whom they were speaking, but let their eyes rove around the room. The other courtiers were more conventionally occupied, quietly arguing or gossiping. Almost none of them looked up as Tinwright was led through the room, too deeply occupied in the business of the moment. In the current court of Southmarch, with much property newly masterless and hundreds of nobles vanished in the war against the fairies, the pickings were rich. A man of dubious breeding could quickly become a man of fortune.

Still, the court had always been a bustling place, a hive of ambition and vanity, but one thing was certainly different from the way things had been here only a few months ago: during the short regency of Barrick and Briony the throne room had been raucous, less quiet and orderly than in Olin's day (or so Tinwright had been told, since he had never been *in* the throne room, or even the Inner Keep, in Olin's day) but even at its most respectful and ritualistic, the missing king's throne room had been a place of clamorous conversation. Now it was nearly silent. As Tinwright was led across the room by the guard, the knots of people unraveling before them so they could pass, the noise never rose above a loud whisper. It was like being in a dovecote at night—nothing but quiet rustling.

Like a cold wind through dry leaves, he thought, and felt his stomach lurch again. *Gods of hill and valley, they're going to kill me!* The oath, one of his mother's that he hadn't thought of, much less used, for years, brought him no solace. *Zosim, cleverest of gods, are you listening? Save me from this monstrous fate and I . . . I'll build you a temple.*

When I have the money. Even to himself, this sounded like a hollow promise. What else would the patron of poets and drunkards desire? *I'll put a bottle of the finest Xandian red wine on your altar. Don't let Hendon Tolly kill me!* But Zosim was famous for his fickleness. The sickening weight pressed down on Tinwright and he struggled not to weep. *Zoria, blessed virgin, if you ever loved mankind, if you ever pitied fools who meant no harm, help me now! I will be a better man. I promise I will be a better man.*

Hendon Tolly was not in the chair where he ordinarily held court. Tirnan Havemore stood beside the empty seat instead, peering at a sheaf of papers in his hand, his spectacles halfway down his nose.

"Who is this wretch?" Havemore asked, looking at the poet over the rim of his lenses. "Tinwright, isn't that it?" He turned and held out his hand. The page standing behind him put a piece of thick, official-looking parchment in his hand. Havemore squinted at it. "Ah, yes. He's to be executed, it says here."

Matty Tinwright screeched. The world spun wildly, it seemed, then he realized it was himself—or rather it wasn't him, it *was* the world: he was flat on his back and the world wasn't simply spinning, it was whirling like a child's top, and he was about to be sick. He only just swallowed the bile back down.

As he lay with his cheek against the stones and the sour taste of vomit in his mouth, he heard Havemore speak again, in irritation. "Look at what you've done, lackwit! It's not Tinwright at all to be executed, this says someone named *Wainwright*—fellow who strangled a reeve." The poet heard a grunt and a squeak of pain as the castellan struck his page. "Can't you read, idiot child? I wanted the order for 'Tinwright,' not 'Wainwright'!" Matt Tinwright could hear more rustling of parchment and the whispering of the surrounding courtiers rose again like a flock of bats taking flight. "Here it is. He's to wait for His Lordship."

"No need—I am here," said a new voice. A pair of black boots trimmed with silver chains stopped beside Tinwright's face where it rested against the floor. "And here is the poet. Still, it seems a strange place to wait."

Tinwright had just enough sense to scramble to his feet. Hendon Tolly watched him rise, the corner of his mouth cocked in a charmless grin, then turned away and moved to his regent's chair, which he dropped himself into with the practiced ease of a cat jumping down off a low wall. "Tinwright, isn't it?"

"Yes, Lord. I was . . . I was told you wanted to see me."

"I did, yes, but not necessarily in that strange position. What were you doing on the floor?"

"I . . . I was told I was to be executed."

Hendon Tolly laughed. "Really? And so you fainted, did you? I suppose it would be the kind thing, then, for me to tell you that nothing like that is planned." He was grinning, but his eyes were absolutely cold. "Unless I decide to execute you anyway. The day has been short on amusements."

Oh, merciful gods, Tinwright thought. *He plays with me as if I were a mouse.* He swallowed, tried to take a breath without bursting into helpless sobs. "Do . . . do you plan to kill me, then, Lord Guardian?"

Tolly cocked his head. He was dressed in the finery of a Syannese court dandy, with pleated scarlet tunic and black sleeves immensely puffed above the elbow, and his hair was dressed in foppish strands that hung down into his eyes, but Tinwright knew beyond doubt that if the mood took him this overdressed dandy could murder the poet or anyone else as quickly and easily as an ordinary man could kick over a chair.

The guardian of Southmarch narrowed his eyes until they were almost closed, but his stare still glinted. "I am told you are . . . ambitious."

Elan. He does know. "I—I'm not sure . . . what you mean, Lord."

Tolly flicked his fingers as if they were wet. "Don't parse words with me. You know what the word 'ambitious' means. Are you? Do you have eyes above your station, poet?"

"I . . . I wish to better myself, sir. As do most men."

Tolly leaned forward, smiling as though he had finally found something worth hunting, or trapping, or killing. "Ah, but is that so? *I* think most men are cattle, poet. I think they hope to be ignored by the wolves, and when one of their fellows is taken they all move closer together and start hoping again. Men of ambition are the wolves—we must feed on the cattle in order to survive, and it makes us cleverer than they. What do you think, Tinwright? Is that a, what do you call it, a metaphor? Is it a good metaphor?"

Puzzled, Tinwright almost shook his head in confusion, but realized it might be mistaken as a denial of Hendon Tolly's words. Did the guardian fancy *himself* a poet? What would that mean for Tinwright? "Yes, Lord, of course, it is a metaphor. A very good one, I daresay."

"Hah." Tolly toyed with the grip of his sword. Other than the royal guardsmen, he was the only one in the room with a visible weapon. Tinwright had heard enough stories about his facility with it that he had to struggle not to stare as Tolly caressed the hilt. "I have a commission for you," the guardian of Southmarch said at last. "I heard your song about Caylor and thought it quite good work, so I have decided to put you to honest labor."

"I beg your pardon?" Matt Tinwright could not have listed a group of words he had less expected to hear.

"A commission, fool—unless you think you are too good to take such work. But I hear otherwise." Tolly gave him that blank, contemplative stare again. "In fact, I hear much of your time is spent making up to your betters."

This made Tinwright think uncomfortably about Elan M'Cory again. Was the talk of commission just a ruse? Was Tolly just playing some abstract, cruel game with him before having him killed? Still, he did not dare to behave as anything other than an innocent man. "I would be delighted, Lord. I have never received a greater honor."

His new patron smiled. "Not true. In fact, I hear you were given an important task by a highborn lady. Isn't that true?"

Tinwright knew he must look like a rabbit staring at a swaying serpent. "I don't catch your meaning, my lord."

Tolly settled back in the chair, grinning. "Surely you have not forgotten your poem in praise of our beloved Princess Briony?"

"Oh! Oh, no, sir. No, but . . . but I confess my heart has not been in it of late . . ."

"Since her disappearance. Yes, a feeling we all share. Poor Briony. Brave girl!" Tolly did not even bother to feign sorrow. "We all wait for news of her." He leaned forward. Havemore had reappeared beside his chair and was rattling his papers officiously. "Now, listen closely, Tinwright. I find it a good idea to keep a man of your talents occupied, so I wish you to prepare an epic for me, for a special occasion. My brother Caradon is coming and will be here the first day of the Kerneia—Caradon, Duke of Summerfield? You do know the name?"

Tinwright realized he had been staring openmouthed, still not certain he would survive this interview. "Yes, of course, sir. Your older brother. A splendid man . . . !"

Hendon cut off the paean with a wave of his hand. "I want something special in honor of his visit, and the Tolly family's . . . stewardship of Southmarch. You will provide a poem, something in a fitting style. You are to make your verses on the fall of Sveros."

"Sveros, the god of the evening sky?" said Tinwright, amazed. He could not imagine either of the Tolly brothers as lovers of religious poetry.

"What other? I would like the story of his tyrannical rule—and of how he was deposed by three brothers."

It was the myth of the Trigon, of course, Perin and his brothers Erivor and Kernios destroying their cruel father. "If that is what you want, Lord . . . of course!"

"I find it highly appropriate, you see." Tolly grinned again, showing his teeth and reminding the poet that this man was a wolf even among other wolves. "Three brothers, one of them dead—because Kernios was killed, of course, before he came back to life—who must overthrow an old, useless king." He flicked a finger. "Get to work, then. Keep yourself busy. We would not want such a gifted fellow as you to fall into idleness. That breeds danger for young men."

Three brothers, one dead, overthrow the king, Tinwright thought as he bowed to his new patron. *Surely that's the Tollys taking Olin's*

*throne. He wants me to write a celebration of himself stealing the throne of
Southmarch!*

But even as this idea roiled in his guts, another one crept in. *He's
as much as said he'll kill me if I cause him any trouble—if I go near Elan.
Clever Zosim, protector of fools like me, what can I do?*

"You will perform it at the feast on the first night of Kerneia,"
Tolly said. "Now you may go."

Before going back to his rooms Tinwright stumbled into the
garden so he could be alone as he threw up into a box hedge.

"What are you doing, woman?" Brone tried to get up, grimaced in
pain, and slumped back down into his chair.

"Don't speak to me that way. You will refer to me as 'Your
Grace.' "

"We're alone now. Isn't that why you sent the priestess away?"

"Not so you could insult me or treat me like a chambermaid.
We have a problem, Brone, and by that I mean you and I."

"But what were you thinking? You have kept the secret for
years, and now it seems that everyone in the castle must know."

"Don't exaggerate." Merolanna looked around the small room.
"It's bad enough you stay seated when a lady is in the room, but
have you not even a chair to offer me? You are nearly as rude as
Havemore."

"That miserable, treacherous whoreson . . ." He growled in frustration. "There is a stool on the other side of the desk. Forgive me,
Merolanna. It really is agony to stand. My gout . . ."

"Yes, your gout. Always it has been something—your age, your
duties. Always something." She found the stool and pulled it out,
settling herself gingerly on its small seat, her dress spreading around
her like the tail of a bedraggled pheasant. "Well. Now is the time
when you can make no more excuses, Brone. The fairies are across
the bay. Olin and the twins are gone and their throne is in terrible
danger—the Eddons are your own kin, remember, however
distant."

"You don't need to tell me that I have failed my family and my king, woman," Brone growled. "That is the song I sing myself to sleep with every night." He didn't seem anywhere near as bleary as he had only a short time ago.

"Then listen now. The Tollys have their hands around the throat of the kingdom. And somehow—somehow, though I don't pretend to understand it—my child is involved. Our child."

"I cannot believe you told Barrick and Briony."

She scowled. "I am not a fool. I said the father was dead."

He looked at her and his face softened. "Merolanna, I did my best. I never turned my back on you."

"Too little and too late, always."

"I offered to marry you. I begged you . . . !"

"After your own wife was dead. By then I had grown quite used to widowhood, thank you. Twenty years after I was foolish enough to fall in love with you. Too late, Avin, too late."

"You were the wife of the king's brother. What was I to do, demand he give you a bill of divorce?"

"And I was older than you, too. But I recall that neither of those things stopped you when you wanted my favors." She paused, took a ragged breath. "Enough of this. It is also too late for fighting this way. We are old, Brone, and we have made terrible mistakes. Let us do what we can now to repair some of them, because the stakes are bigger than our own happiness."

"What do you want me to do, Merolanna? You see me—old, sick, cut off from power. What do you want me to do?"

"Find Chaven. Find this moon-stone. And help me to cross the bay so I can meet these fairy folk and ask them what they did with my son."

"Do you mean it? You *are* mad. But mad or not, I can't help you."

She dragged herself to her feet. "You coward! Everything you worked for your entire life is being stolen by the Tollys, and you sit there, doing *nothing* . . . !" She leaned across the table and raised her hand as though she would strike him. Brone reached up and caught at it, folding his immense paw around hers.

"Calm yourself, Merolanna," he said. "You do not know as much as you think you do. Do you know what happened to Nynor?"

"Yes, of course! They pushed him out so they could give his honors and duties to your lickspittle factor, Havemore! Nynor's gone back to his house in the country."

"No, curse it, he's *dead*. Hendon's men killed him and threw his body in the ocean."

For a moment the duchess faltered and if Brone had not been holding her hand, she might have fallen. She pulled away and sat down. "Nynor is dead?" she said at last. "Steffens Nynor?"

"Murdered, yes. He was talking against the Tollys and he spoke to someone he shouldn't have. Word got back to Hendon. Berkan Hood dragged Nynor out of his bed in the middle of the night and murdered him." Brone clenched his fists until his knuckles went white. "I heard it myself from someone who was there. They cut that good old man into pieces and smuggled his body out of the castle in a grain barrel. They can't quite get away yet with slaughtering their enemies without even a mock trial. Not quite."

"Oh, by all the gods, is that true? Killed him?" Merolanna abruptly began to cry. "Poor Steffens! The Tollys are demons—we are surrounded by demons!" She made the sign of the Three, then wiped at her face with her sleeve and tried to compose herself. "But that is all the more reason you must help me, Avin! There are things going on that . . ."

"No." He shook his head again. "There are certainly things going on, and you don't know all of them, Merolanna." He looked around again. The guards were still not back, but he dropped his voice even lower. "Please, understand me, Your Grace—I have worked hard to convince Hendon and his party that I am no threat so I could put plans of my own into motion. I cannot afford for them to suspect otherwise. I will do what I can to find Chaven, because that would not seem unusual—the physician and I knew each other well. But I can do nothing else. I will not risk the small chance we have of saving Olin's throne. Everything is balanced on a knife-edge."

The duchess stared at him for a long time. "So that is your defense, is it?" She smiled a little, but her words had a bitter edge. "That you are already hard at work on other, more important things? Well and good. But I will discover this moon-piece myself if I must, and find out what happened to my child—*our* child— even if I have to pull this castle down stone by stone to do it."

"You are no spy, Merolanna," Brone told her gently.

"No. But I am a mother." She reached a trembling hand up to touch her face. "Sweet Zoria, I must be a terrible mess. You've made me cry, Brone. I'll have to repair myself before I go talk to Utta." She gazed around the cluttered room, slowly and wearily now, energy mostly spent. "Look at this. We sit at the center of the capital of all the March Kingdoms but you do not even have a glass for an old woman to fix her face. How can it be so hard to find a simple mirror?"

PART THREE

MACHINES

25

The Gray Man

The Firstborn were as large as mountains and as small as gems in the private earth. They came from all parts, choosing to side with either the children of Moisture or the children of Breeze, because the wounds would not close themselves and in the rising storm the only songs that could be heard were of blood and answers. Thus came the War in Heaven.

The children of Moisture first drew a ring around the house of Silvergleam, which had as many rooms as the number of times the People have drawn breath.

—from *One Hundred Considerations*
out of the Qar's *Book of Regret*

H E HIT ME.

Barrick's anger had shrunk to a cold, hard thing inside his chest but it was not going away. He was glad: it gave him life, of a sort—better angry than empty. He stared at

Ferras Vansen, who was chewing a piece of stale bread. The rest
of the prisoners, quickly sorted into winners and losers after the
goblin guards had thrown the bowl of slops into the middle of
the cell, were nursing either their meals or their wounds. Some
of the smaller ones were so thin and undernourished that it was
clear they had given up competing for food and were just
waiting to die. But Barrick did not care about such hapless
creatures.

He had no right!

Stop. Gyir pushed Barrick's hand with the heel of bread in it.
Eat. He brought you food.

But he hit me!

*I would have hit you myself if I had been closer. You were acting like a
nestling—no, not even that. No child of the People would be so foolish.
This is a dangerous place—how dangerous we do not even know yet. There
is no time to waste on such tricks.* A percussive thump jarred the floor
of the cell like a giant hammer falling in the depths of the earth
below them. Barrick had heard the thunderous noise, like a
cannon firing, many times since being captured; the other prisoners did not even look up.

Gyir pulled a chunk from his own loaf, one of the largest pieces
any of the prisoners had secured, and slipped the rest into his
cloak. *What you don't eat, save. We may need it later.*

Why? Barrick asked, making the thought as bitter as he could.
*You don't even eat, do you? Besides, this is a god who has captured us.
What can we do?*

*No, I said Jikuyin was a demigod, not a god. Trust me, there is a world
of difference. What can we do? Wait and watch—and, especially, think.
They have taken our weapons but not our wits.* The fairy hesitated for
a moment, as if he had something more to say. Then, to Barrick's
astonishment, Gyir's face peeled away from the bone, rolling up
from his chin to just below his eyes.

No, that wasn't it, the prince realized after a boggled moment.
The featureless skin between what would have been the chin and
nose on an ordinary man had folded back, flexible as a horse's
upper lip, exposing even paler flesh beneath, shiny with damp, and

a small, almost circular mouth. Vansen was staring now, too. Ignoring them both, Gyir pushed a piece of bread into the toothy hole. Bones and muscles worked beneath the second layer of skin—his jaw was clearly hinged in a different way than theirs—as he chewed, then swallowed. The fairy stared back at his two companions as if daring them to speak.

Yes, your question is answered now, Gyir said at last. He seemed almost angry. *This is how one of the Encauled eats. It is not pretty,*

But how do you breathe? Barrick asked. *You keep it . . . your mouth . . . covered all the time.*

Gyir brushed his lank, dark hair back from the side of his head. *There are slits here behind my ears, like a fish's gills. When necessary, I can close them.* The next thought was a curious, wordless burst of something Barrick could not at first grasp. *That way, I do not drown when it rains hard,* he finished. The wordless sensation had been a laugh, Barrick realized, although not a happy one.

Gyir ate the rest of his piece of bread, then the flap of skin folded back down again, curling just beneath his chin like the skin of a drum, leaving him smooth as ivory once more beneath the red eyes. *So,* he said. *Your curiosity has been satisfied. That is what it means to be born with the Caul. Now perhaps we can go back to thinking about what is truly important.* Gyir rose and stretched. Several of the other prisoners scuttled away, but he ignored them. *I feel stronger than I did—I think the power of our enemy's voice has affected me, somehow—but I could not directly challenge a force like Jikuyin on my best day. Still, if he is as careless as he has been in the past, we have a chance.*

"What do you mean?" Vansen said aloud.

Do not use your voices, Gyir ordered. *I will interpret between the two of you when necessary.*

Barrick scowled. Only a day before it had been him alone to whom Gyir would speak, but now the soldier was included in everything. What good was suffering as Barrick had suffered if it did not make him special?

The immortals, for all their power, always had one weakness, Gyir said. *They do not change and they do not learn. Jikuyin is fearsome but he was always a fool—one who thought himself greater than he was.* Gyir spread his fingers in an unfamiliar gesture, something that smacked of ritual. *He took the side of the Onyenai—our side, I can call it, because my folk also fought with the Onyenai—in one of the last great battles of gods, monsters, and men. But Jikuyin did not attack when he should have, thinking perhaps to let both sides damage themselves to his own betterment. Even then, he was ambitious.*

When he did come to the field with his legion of Widowmakers, it was too late. The Onyenai had been defeated, but the Surazemai—Perin and his brothers and their allies—were still strong. Jikuyin was trapped and could not retreat. In his foolish pride, he attacked great Kernios himself, killing one of the Earthfather's sons, the demigod Annon. But Kernios in his rage was far beyond Jikuyin. One cast of his great spear Earthstar shattered Jikuyin's shield, broke his helmet, and destroyed his face. He would have died then but his Widowmakers, seeing that there would be no spoils for them, managed to drag their wounded lord from the field. Many thought him dead afterward, but the People have always said that no one knew Jikuyin's true fate. We were right to be cautious.

So what does he want? Barrick could make little sense of the story itself, which seemed like a confused shadow-version of what Father Timoid had taught them about the gods. *Why take us prisoner? What does he mean to do with us?*

Gyir lifted his hand, his eyes suddenly grown tensely alert in his featureless face. *Say no more. Someone is coming.*

Creatures of various sorts had been passing in and out of the huge prison cavern for hours—guards leading individual captives and groups away or bringing them back, the limping, overburdened goblins with their buckets of food. A few times the Longskulls had even showed up with ragged bands of new prisoners, but this was the first time Gyir had appeared to take any notice. Barrick felt his heart speed.

The heavy bronze door of the cell swung open and a squadron of the bristling, apelike guards came in, their menacing appearance and heavy clubs quickly clearing a space as prisoners hurried to get out of their way—even those still bickering over food went still and shrank back against the walls. Silence fell over the chamber. Was the giant demigod himself coming? Barrick suddenly found it hard to breathe. Would the monster even fit through the massive cell doors without getting down on his hands and knees?

Instead, the individual who entered the prison chamber was of ordinary man-size, wearing a hooded robe so black that the light of the torches seemed to fall into it and die, as if someone had taken a knife to the fabric of what was visible and simply cut out a piece. Hands so fleshless they seemed nothing but bone, sinew, and skin pulled back his hood, revealing a shaved head and a face as gaunt as a Xandian mummy, nearly every line of his skull visible beneath pearly gray skin that was thin as a lady's fine silk stocking. He might have been a corpse just beginning to putrefy but for his eyes, which glistened silvery blue-green like twin moons in the depths of his dark sockets.

"My master told me to make sure you were comfortable." The terrifying stranger's voice was as expressionless as his face. He did not blink. As far as Barrick could tell, he did not even have eyelids, his gaze as fixed and unchanging as that of a fish. "Comfortable . . . and secure. But I think with such a one as the Storm Lantern in your company, you should have more private accommodations." He raised his bony hand and beckoned them. "Follow."

The brutish guards stepped forward, tiny eyes almost invisible beneath their thick brows, stone clubs lifted menacingly. Barrick tried to rise, but he was trembling uncontrollably and managed it only with Vansen's help. He shook the soldier off and fell in behind Gyir, who was following the black-robed figure toward the back of the long, high-ceilinged chamber. The stranger moved in a disturbingly graceful glide, as though his feet did not quite touch the floor.

Who is this gray man? Barrick asked, fighting down terror. *What is he going to do with us?*

Gyir did not turn his head. *Do not speak—aloud or otherwise—and do not resist. This is Ueni'ssoh of the Dreamless. He is not a god but he is very old and very powerful. Silence!*

Barrick stumbled after Gyir, hemmed in by the shaggy giant Followers. Even with his stomach all but empty the sour stink of their fur made him feel ill. The three prisoners were forced into a narrow stone room that had been carved into the naked rock at the back of the vast prison chamber, closed off from the rest of the cavern by another heavy door with a barred window. This smaller cell was empty except for a single stinking hole in the floor for waste, dark except for the torchlight leaking in through the window in the door. Barrick had to breathe deeply simply to keep down the scream that was building in him.

The gray man appeared in the doorway. For long moments he stared at them in silence.

You have come down in the world, Ueni'ssoh, said Gyir. *Once you were mighty among your own people. Now it seems you have become court conjurer for a bandit-lord.*

If this was meant to goad or distract the gray man somehow, it failed. His voice remained as bloodless as before. "The master said you were a strange little company, and he spoke truly. Your presence here makes no sense to me. That is something I do not like. You—the young one. Come here. Storm Lantern, if you try to interfere these brutes will kill you."

Tell him nothing! Gyir's words flew into Barrick's head like arrows. *Think of other things. Tell nothing!*

Ueni'ssoh's unblinking stare was fixed on Barrick; there seemed nothing else in the narrow cell but those eyes shining like two blue flames. Before he knew it, Barrick had stumbled forward and stood helplessly in front of the gray creature, swaying in the icy heat of that mortal glare. He could feel the Dreamless plucking and prying at his deepest thoughts as if those long, cadaverous fingers had opened his skull like a jewel box.

No! He shut his eyes tight. *Think of something else,* he told himself desperately. *Anything!* He tried to imagine nothingness, true nothingness, but the featureless white that he summoned gradually took on shape, until it became snow in the garden outside his chamber in the residence at Southmarch—a view he had seen countless times. Barrick Eddon could feel the gray man's interest like a moving ache. He tried desperately to turn his mind somewhere else, struggling to protect himself from this terrible, fearful prying, but the snow in his mind's eye was all but real now—deep, new snow, mounded against the chimneys and on the skeletal branches of the trees. His own sitting room, chill on an Ondekamene morning despite the fire burning in the hearth behind him. Leaning on his good arm, staring out his window . . . alone? No, not alone . . .

"What are you looking at, redling?"

"Ravens. They're comical. That one's stolen something from the kitchen, see? And the other's trying to get it from him."

"They're hungry. That's not comical." She stepped up beside him, then, her golden hair like a sudden appearance of the sun. "We should feed them."

"Feed the ravens?" He laughed harshly. "You're mad, strawhead. What should we do after that, go out into the hills and feed the wolves? Even if we took them the whole of Bronze's litter, the wolves would be hungry again tomorrow." He pretended to consider. "But perhaps there might be enough of those whelps to feed the ravens . . ."

Briony hit him—not hard—and scooped the puppy up off the bed. "Did you hear that, Nelli? Did you hear what he said about you and your brothers and sisters? Isn't he a cruel monster?"

He turned and looked at her then, really looked at her. The light in her eyes was magical. Sometimes he felt as though she were the only person beside himself in the great castle that was truly alive. "Mad," he said, and let himself smile. "See? Talking to dogs. Mad as can be."

"It's not me who's mad, Barrick Eddon. It's you. Now stop this nonsense about snow and ravens. Tell me what I want to know."

"What are you talking about?"

"Look at me," she said, but she didn't sound quite like herself any more. "Tell me why you are here."

"Why . . . ? I don't understand you."

"You understand—you do. Don't waste my time. Why are you here?"

He felt his breath catch in his chest. That's not . . . Briony wouldn't . . . !

A cold wave of surprise and fear suddenly washed over him and he found himself staring into the coldly gleaming eyes of Ueni'ssoh once more.

A tiny smile curled the slate-colored lips. "So. Stronger than I would have guessed, and with some . . . interesting flavors. What about the other sunlander? Might he prove a little less stubborn?"

The gray man abruptly swiveled to look at Gyir, as if he felt some movement from his direction. "No, I will not strive with you, Storm Lantern—not yet. I will enjoy that too much, and I like to anticipate my pleasures." The cadaverous face turned to Ferras Vansen and Barrick felt himself abruptly released, as if a powerful hand had let go of the nape of his neck. He slumped helplessly to his knees as Vansen trudged past him and then stopped before the black-robed man like an obedient servant.

After staring at the guardsman for several heartbeats, Ueni'ssoh raised his hand. Vansen swayed and crumpled to the floor.

"Interesting," Ueni'ssoh said, showing long, narrow teeth as gray as his skin. "You both shield yourself with the thought of the same female. I shall ponder on this." He turned and glided out of the low-ceilinged chamber, followed by the bestial guards. The door slammed, plunging the room into almost complete darkness as the bolt rattled home.

What will they do with us? Barrick asked Gyir, but the faceless warrior did not answer him. "What's going to happen?" Barrick finally said aloud. "Are . . . are they going to kill us?"

"Even if they keep us alive," Vansen said grimly, "I doubt we'll like it much."

I said you two should be silent and I meant it. Gyir's anger blew into Barrick's head like a winter wind. *We are in terrible danger and every word you speak aloud is a risk.*

But you won't talk to me! Barrick knew it sounded petty, but he didn't care. What had happened to the Barrick Eddon of a few days ago, when he had not cared whether he was alive or dead? *You just sit there.*

I am not being silent out of some ill humor, Gyir told him. *I am . . . testing myself. And thinking.*

What does that mean?

Stop. Gyir closed his eyes. *Let me be alone with my thoughts, boy. Otherwise, the lives of far more than we three may be forfeit.*

Miserable and terrified, with no room to pace, Barrick could only sit and breathe in the dreadful, stretching silence.

Prince Barrick had fallen asleep at last, for which Vansen was grateful. Gyir stirred and then, in one smoothly nimble motion, rose to his feet—impressive, considering he had been sitting on the hard stone for hours.

Are they just older than us, these fairies, and schooled in different ways? Vansen wondered. *Is it all tricks of magic they've learned? Or are they truly stronger and better than we are in everything?* He would never be able to forget the way the Twilight People had slashed through his men at Kolkan's Field like wolves through pampered house dogs.

Gyir moved to the door of the cell and stood close to the grille, looking out into the larger prison room beyond.

Is someone coming? Vansen was beginning to feel disturbingly comfortable with this unspeaking speech.

The fairy lifted his pale hand. *Quiet.*

Rebuked, Vansen clambered to his feet to see for himself, but Gyir waved him back. The fairy was doing more than observing, Vansen realized: Gyir had an expression of fierce concentration in his narrowed eyes, and, as the torchlight from the door grille moved across the fairy's face Vansen could even see veins bulging at the sides of the Storm Lantern's ivory brow.

Ferras Vansen watched as the fairy looked from one side of the chamber to the other. Gyir's gaze lit on one of the larger, more human-looking prisoners, manlike but shaggy and yellow as a buttercup, with long, splay-toed feet and a starry snout like a burrowing mole. The creature raised its head and looked around with nothing more than slow curiosity at first, but then began to twitch as though beset by flying insects. It grabbed at its ears as if to shut out some loud noise, then staggered upright and lurched toward Gyir and the bronze door.

The yellow fairy stopped, its flowerlike muzzle only inches from the grille, its eyes wide. Gyir lifted a hand and its eyes fell shut, then he extended his long fingers through the bars until he could touch the creature lightly on the forehead, then he closed his own eyes.

For long moments they stood that way, unmoving, as if sharing some ancient ritual. At last the yellow fairy took an awkward step backward, shook its head, then turned and walked away without a backward glance. Gyir stood watching it for a moment before he swayed and collapsed.

Ferras Vansen caught the fairy as he fell, grunting at the weight, although Gyir was lighter than his size would have suggested. As he lowered the Storm Lantern to the cell floor Vansen could not help noticing the fairy's smell, an odd mixture of ocean tang, leather, and cloying, flowery scents.

Fear not—I will survive. There was a dry edge to Gyir's thoughts which Vansen recognized as amusement. *Just let me rest.*

What did you do?

Must rest. The fairy did not even lay his head on his arm—the red eyes simply shut.

Prince Barrick had awakened by the time Gyir sat up again, rubbing his head as though it ached. "What have you two done?" the boy demanded of Vansen. "*He* won't tell me." Vansen had no doubt the prince was speaking aloud to irritate Gyir, and couldn't help wondering if the boy's father had ever simply taken Barrick over his knee and given him a good thrashing.

"I couldn't tell you, Highness, because I didn't understand it myself."

I have asked several times for silence. I will not ask again. Gyir's brow wrinkled, which was his way of frowning. *Listen.* Outside their tiny cell Vansen could hear the growling of the guards and the moans and shrills of protesting prisoners. *They are harrying the next gang out to work and I must . . . narrow my thoughts. Deepen them. I am going to look through the eyes of one of them—the yellow one that*

Captain Vansen saw. I will see what he does, where he goes, and discover something of this place.

Vansen was puzzled. *But I thought you were . . . crippled, you said. By what those Followers did to you.*

I have recovered, somewhat. In fact, I think my recovery was caused, or at least hastened, by being in the presence of Jikuyin, battered by his voice. It would be nice to think that in capturing and imprisoning us, he has unwittingly given me back something of myself. He paused, clearly listening to something Barrick was saying.

I do not know if I have the strength, Gyir said at last. Then: *Very well, you may be right. I will try. But if I grow too weak, I will cut the rope, as it were, and let the two of you fall away rather than give up my own connection.*

What does that mean? Try what? Vansen asked, careful not to speak aloud again.

The young prince wants me to let you both see what I see through the eyes of the prisoner.

Can you really do that?

The fairy sat down with his back against the door, then beckoned Vansen and the prince toward him. *Take my hands and close your eyes, shut out all distraction.* He extended one long hand toward Vansen and the other toward Barrick, palms up, white fingers curled like the petals of water flowers. *Go—take it.*

Vansen did and was bemused to find nothing different, other than the obviously strange situation of holding the fairy's chill, smooth hand.

No, you must shut out distraction. If you look around, if you squirm, if you even think too much, you make it more difficult for me to hold everything in my thoughts.

Vansen did his best to comply. At first he saw nothing except the floating sparks that usually populated the darkness behind closed lids. Then one of the sparks began to grow, its glow swelling, until it pushed out the blackness and filled his mind's eye.

It was more than just sight, though, he realized as the great door swung open before him and he followed the small, hairy back of another prisoner out into the passageway. He thought he could even feel something of the yellow creature's thoughts, although they were as strange to him as trying to hear meaning in birdsong. The thing he was inhabiting longed helplessly for home, an ache Vansen understood, but "home" to this creature seemed to mean deep woods and tangling leaves and the silver of snail-tracks undisturbed on a damp forest floor. The thing had a name, too—something like "Praise-Sweet-Lisiya's-Grace," as far as Vansen could tell. It was terribly frightened, but had dissolved its fear in a passivity he could not understand, a certainty that nothing would change or even could change, that it could only follow what was before it, from meal to miserable meal and from one command to the next, unless something came at last to change this nightmare, even if that something was death itself.

It was a chilling way to feel, worse still to experience such hopelessness as if it were his own. Vansen did not try to sample any of the river of memories that ran just beneath the slow, awkward thoughts. He wanted only to get out of the creature's thoughts entirely, as quickly as he could—he hated being in this trapped, pathetic, doomed thing . . . !

Something wrapped around him, soothing him as a parent would a child. It was Gyir, acting not out of pity, but because Vansen's discomfort was affecting the fairy's own composure. Vansen felt a wash of shame and did his best to choke down his discomfort and fear. *Just watch,* he told himself. *Be strong. It's not me. This thing is not me.* But it was more frightening than he would ever have guessed to be trapped in someone else's body.

The line of prisoners trudged downward through several sloping corridors and once down a flight of spiral steps so long that Vansen feared he would soon be seeing the face of Immon the immortal gatekeeper. In these depths they could better hear the thunderous sounds that had rumbled up to the prisoner chamber. They were not constant, or even regular, but every hundred dragging steps or so a loud thump seemed to rattle the very stone around them.

They passed dozens of the hairy guards and hundreds of other prisoners returning from the depths, most of the groups as queerly mixed as their own, but some more obviously collected for a certain limited task, like the group of short, heavy-muscled creatures with heads sunk deep between their huge shoulders, each one carrying a bronze pick like a spearman marching to war. The most chilling thing about these squat diggers was not their silence or their faintly luminous, mushroom-colored skin, but the absence of eyes in the crude faces nestling just above their breast-bones.

When they reached the bottom of the stairs at last, the guards marched the yellow fairy and his companions through a few more corridors and down one last slope, then through a heavy wooden door. A wheeled cart the size of a large hay wain stood untended in a chamber slightly bigger than the one in which the prisoners were housed, its wheels sunk deep into tracks through what looked like centuries worth of dust. At the far end of the chamber was an open door large enough for the cart to pass through, with only darkness visible behind. At the near end of the room a shaft led straight down, with a system of large pulleys strung above it and ropes cobwebbing down into the measureless depths.

Vansen did his best to understand what he was seeing through the forest-fairy's eyes, but could make little sense of it. Were they supposed to take something from the door at one end and then lower it down the shaft? Gold? Jewels? Or did the exchange more likely go the other way around, the dirt and rubble from the mine's digging, source of all this dust, sent aboveground for disposal?

The brutish guards finished herding the rest of the prisoners into the room but did not stop to give directions, if they were even capable of such a thing. Instead, a few of the shaggy, club-wielding creatures stayed behind to guard the prisoners—it was hard to tell exactly how many, since the star-nosed yellow fairy was doing his best to avoid eye contact with any of them—while the rest trooped out of the chamber. Whatever their work might be, the prisoners did not immediately spring to it, and the remaining guards did not seem to expect them to do so. The yellow fairy and his companions waited in attitudes of dull patience, but they did not have to wait long.

Vansen felt rather than heard a ragged sound—a shout from below—and most of the prisoners hurried to the pulleys above the deep, square pit, while others went to bring the wagon nearer. The slaves hauling on the ropes grunted and moaned until they had hauled a huge wooden basket up from the unseen depths, then they swung the basket out on a hinged arm until it dangled over the bed of the huge wagon. When they tipped it down several dozen corpses fell out in a limply flopping heap.

Vansen almost lost his grip on Gyir, or the fairy nearly lost his hold on Vansen.

One of bodies slid off the top of the pile and tumbled onto the stone floor beside the cart wheel, limp as a grain sack. The yellow fairy bent with another prisoner to lift the body—in life it had been a goblin, Vansen guessed, although the small creature's hairy pelt was so caked with dust it was hard to be certain. There were no obvious marks of violence, at least not anything fatal: long weals ran across the dead goblin's back, crisscrossed through the fur like roads being swallowed by undergrowth, but the skin had scarred long ago: it had not been the whipping that had killed this creature.

The yellow forest-fairy went about its grisly chores as though sleepwalking, which was just as well, since Ferras Vansen found it hard to watch what the creature was doing. It wrestled another fallen body back onto the cart, a bumpy-skinned corpse of the star-nosed thing's own type, with blood on its face but no other sign of violence. Vansen caught only the briefest moment of hesitation as the creature saw one of its own kind, then it turned away without looking at the face, pulling an emptiness over its thoughts that Vansen could feel. Nevertheless, it did not linger beside the corpse of its star-nosed kin, but walked around the back of the cart just as the creaking vehicle began to roll away from the pit. The yellow fairy bent one last time to pick up the corpse of a hard-shelled creature whose half-closed eyes and sagging mouth were the only parts of its face not covered by leathery plates of skin. The buglike thing was clearly heavier than the yellow fairy had expected; after a moment's struggle, he decided to drag it instead of trying to lift it. As he pulled it scraping across the floor one of the other prisoners came to help—something that Vansen found oddly touching—and together they heaved the shelled thing back onto the cart.

Beyond the doorway at the chamber's far end, a more or less level track led away into darkness. Within a few hundred paces the track grew deep with dust and the wagon slowed, then stopped. The yellow fairy and several other prisoners stepped up and pushed until it the wheels came free and began to roll again. Another thumping crash shook the cavern—Vansen could not hear it so much as he could see the way it knocked the yellow fairy and everything around him off-kilter—and for a moment the eyes through which he was looking stared straight down into nothingness: on the left side the path dropped away and the shadows stretched so deep the torchlight could not find their ending.

The prisoners steered the heavy cart very slowly around a bend in the track, trying not to let themselves or the wagon get too near the edge. Even so, one small captive was caught between the front wheel and the edge of the track; with a scream Vansen could barely hear, although he knew it must be hideously shrill in the yellow fairy's ears, the little creature was swept off into darkness. The rest of the prisoners stopped, frightened and miserable, but blows from the guards' clubs quickly set them moving again.

After they had finally coaxed the wagon around the difficult bend, they found themselves face-to-face with more of the hairy beast-guards coming along the track toward them. This group had scarves wrapped around their faces so that only their tiny eyes could be seen, which made them even more ominously strange. These new ape-things did not like to see their way blocked by the cart, and pointed forked spears at the prisoners, gesturing and grunting angrily until the yellow fairy and his comrades shrank back against the cliff face and let the masked creatures shove by. When they were gone, the woodsprite and his fellow prisoners laboriously heaved the corpse-wagon into motion again.

The part of Vansen that still thought as Vansen had wondered why they should be traveling so far, and where the bodies were being taken. Now he learned. As the wagon creaked onward the light grew stronger: there was clearly some other source besides the torches high on the walls above the narrow path. Only another hundred yards or farther the path turned and then turned again. The light and the sickening smell bloomed, and those prisoners who still wore rags of clothing tried to cover noses and mouths. The yellow fairy could do nothing except spread his hand over his muzzle, squeezing the star-shaped protuberance closed like a parent wrapping his fist around a child's hand. Even through the curious dislocation of Gyir's spell, Vansen could smell rotting flesh—the true stench must have been almost beyond belief.

For a moment Vansen could feel not just the woodsprite's dull horror, and his own, but a flare of despair and dread from Prince Barrick as well, as though the boy were standing just beside him, or even just *inside* him. Barrick was fighting to get away, somehow, pushing back from the scene that stretched before them in the billowing firelight. Vansen felt Gyir's connection to them all grow thin.

No! Gyir's thoughts came like hammer blows. *Do not turn away! Wait!*

Dozens of guards, many in sacklike hooded robes that covered them almost entirely, swarmed along the floor of the vast cavern, which was little more than a shelf around a huge, open pit full of corpses, thousands of dead creatures of all kinds and sizes. Dirt brought in on ore carts by other guards was being shoveled in on top of the uppermost bodies. Fires burned everywhere, great bonfires at each corner of the huge hole and smaller fires tended by the guards in several of the wider places on the shelf around the pit, meant to disperse or consume the stench. The smoke and sparks swirled upward, and the heat of the fires and the air drawn in from the corridors that emptied into the pit chamber on all sides made the stinking winds rush in circles around the cavern before at last rising upward into the darkness of the cavern's roof.

No. So many . . . ! It is . . .

Vansen did not know if the thoughts were his own now or Barrick's, or perhaps even Gyir's. All he knew was that the terrible sight blurred before him as if his eyes were filling with tears, then it all flew away into darkness and he was back in his own frail body once more, sprawled on the floor of the cell beside Gyir and Barrick, weak, ill, and horror-stricken.

26
Rising Wind

*Uvis White-Hand, favorite of dark Zmeos, was wounded
by Kernios and was taken from the field to die. In his
rage, the Horned One beat down brave Volios of the
Measureless Grip, stabbing him with his terrible sword
Whitefire until the war god's blood turned the river
Rimetrail red, and at last the giant son of Perin
staggered, fell, and died.*

—from *The Beginnings of Things*
The Book of the Trigon

PINIMMON VASH, THE PARAMOUNT MINISTER
of Xis and its possessions all across Xand, looked at his
closet with disaffection. Three boys, naked except for artful decorations of gold around their necks and ankles, cringed on
the carpet. The slaves knew what it meant when their master was
in an unhappy mood.

"I do not see my silk robe with my family nightingale crest. It should be in the closet. That robe is worth more than your entire families to the seventh generation. Where is it?"

"You sent it to be cleaned, Master," one of the slaves ventured after a long silence.

"I sent it to be cleaned and brought back. It has not been brought back. I am going on a voyage. I must have my nightingale robe."

Vash was just debating which one of them to beat, and if he had time to beat two, when the messenger came. It was one of the Leopards, dressed in the full panoply of warfare and very conscious of the days of fire and blood just ahead. The soldier stood straight as a broomstraw in the doorway, touched his palm to his forehead in salute, and announced, "Our lord Sulepis, the Master of the Great Tent, requires your immediate attendance."

Pinimmon Vash carefully hid his irritation: it was not wise in these days of universal upheaval to give anyone even the slightest thing to mention to an ambitious courtier or (might all gods forbid it!) the autarch himself. Still, it *was* annoying. He could not imagine when he would find the time before leaving to give these boys the discipline they deserved, and even his large shipboard cabin was a place of little privacy. Nothing to be done, though. The autarch had called.

"I come," he said simply. The Leopard guard turned smartly on his heel and strode out of the room. Vash paused in the doorway.

"I will be back very soon," he told his servants. "If the nightingale robe is not in the closet, all of you will go up the gangplank limping and weeping. If the robe is not in excellently clean condition, I will be taking other servants on my voyage. You three will be floating down the canal past your parents' houses, but they will not recognize you to weep over you."

The look on their faces was almost worth the tedium of having to go and listen to the ravings of his mad and extremely demanding monarch. Vash was an old man and he enjoyed the few simple pleasures left to him.

★

The autarch was being bathed in a room filled with hundreds of candles. Vash was all too used to seeing his master naked, but he had never quite grown unused to it. It was not because the autarch's nakedness was an ugly thing, not at all: Sulepis was a young man, tall and fit, if a trifle too slender for Vash's taste (which tended toward round cheeks and small, childlike bellies). No, it was that his nakedness, which should have provoked thoughts of vulnerability or intimacy, seemed . . . unimportant. As though Sulepis wore a body only because it was convenient, or demanded by his station, but really would have been just as comfortable with nothing more than a skeleton or skinless meat or the stone limbs of a statue. The autarch's nakedness, Vash had decided, had nothing much of the human about it. He never felt even a twinge of desire, shame, or disgust looking at the autarch, when any other unclothed man or woman would summon one of those feelings, if not all.

"You called for me, Golden One?"

The autarch stared at him for a long moment, as though he had never seen his paramount minister before—as if Pinimmon Vash were some stranger who had wandered into the monarch's bath chamber. The candlelight rippled across the monarch as though his long body was something drifting at the bottom of the Eminent Canal. "Ah," he said at last. "Vash. Yes." He gestured limply toward a figure on his other side, half obscured by the steam of the huge bath. "Vash, you must greet Prusus, your scotarch."

Vash turned to the crippled creature, who swayed in his litter as though caught in a high wind. Many thought he was simple-minded, but Pinimmon Vash doubted it. "A pleasure, Scotarch, as always. I hope I find you well?"

Prusus tried to say something, grimaced, then tried again. His round face contorted as though he were in agony—speaking was hard for him at the best of times, and even more difficult in front of the autarch—but he only got out a few grunting syllables before Sulepis laughed and waved his hand.

"Enough, enough—we cannot wait all day. Tell me, Prusus, how do you pray? Even Nushash must lose patience with your jerking and mumbling. Ah, and our other guest, Polemarch Johar. Vash, you and Johar already know each other, yes?"

Vash bowed slightly to the spare, cold-eyed man, as almost to an equal. Ikelis Johar, high polemarch of the autarch's troops, was a power unto himself and although he and Vash had not yet clashed over policy, it was inevitable that one day they would. It was equally inevitable that one of them would not survive the clash. Looking at Ikelis Johar's cruel, humorless mouth, Vash found himself looking forward to that day. One could have too much leisure, after all. "Of course, Golden One. The Overseer of the Armies and I are old friends."

Johar's grin was as humorless as that of a lion sniffing the breeze. "Yes—old friends."

"Johar is in a cheerful mood—aren't you, Overseer?" said the autarch, stretching his arms so a slave could oil them. "Because soon he will have a chance to give his men some exercise. Life has been dull the last few moons, since Mihan capitulated."

"With all respect, Golden One," Johar said, "I'm not certain I'd call besieging Hierosol merely exercise. It has never fallen by force in all its long history."

"Then your name will live in glory beside mine, Overseer."

"As you say, of course, and I am grateful to hear it. The Master of the Great Tent is never wrong."

"That's true, you know." The autarch sat up as if struck with a sudden and pleasing thought; one of his slaves, trying desperately to avoid an incorrect contact with his master, almost slipped and fell on the wet floor. "It is the god in me, of course—the blood of Nushash himself running through me. I cannot be wrong and I cannot fail." He sat back just as suddenly as he had risen, making the water rush back and forth in waves from one end of the large tub to the other. "A very comforting thing."

But if that is so, my very great lord, Pinimmon Vash could not help thinking, *it did not save your brothers, who also had the blood of the god in them, from losing a great deal of that holy blood when you took the throne.* This thought naturally stayed private, but he could not avoid a pang of fright when the autarch looked at him and smiled with wicked amusement, as if he knew just what heretical ideas his paramount minister was harboring.

"Come, there is much to do—even for one like me who cannot make mistakes, eh, Vash? Someone take the scotarch to his chambers. Yes, farewell, Prusus. No, save your breath. We all must prepare for the ceremonies of departure, the consecration of the army, and everything else." The autarch's smile twisted. "I need my most loyal servant at my side. Will you stay with me while the slaves dress me?"

The old minister bowed. "Of course, Golden One."

"Good. And you, Johar, doubtless have many details to see to. We depart at dawn."

"Of course, Golden One."

The autarch smiled. "Two strong men but the same obedient words. The harmony of infallibility. What a beautiful, melodious world this is, my dearly beloved servants. How could it be better?" The autarch laughed, but with an odd harshness, as though he fought some kind of doubt. But the autarch never doubted, Vash knew, and the autarch feared nothing. In all the years he had known Sulepis, from his silent, studious childhood to his sudden and violent ascension to the throne, Pinimmon Vash had never seen the autarch anything other than confident almost to the point of madness.

"It is a beautiful world indeed, Golden One," Vash said in the silence after the laughter, and despite the sudden chill that squeezed his heart he did his very, very best to sound as though he meant it.

She walked right out the door and no one stopped her. One moment all was light and warmth and the reassuring sound of her brothers and sisters breathing in their sleep, the next moment Qinnitan had stepped into the sudden, surprising cold of a night with no moon.

The houses and shops of Cat's Eye Street were only shadow-shapes, but it didn't matter. She knew the place as well as she knew the geography of her own body, knew that Arjamele's doorway would be just *here,* and the loose stone of the next doorway along would catch her toe if she didn't step over it. She knew the shape of everything, but she also knew that something was different— something in the dark, cold street had changed.

The well. The lid was off the well.

But that was impossible: the well was always covered at night. Still, even though she could not see it—could see almost nothing but the indistinct shapes of the buildings looming around her, black against the deep velvety purple of the sky—she knew it was uncovered. She could feel it like a hole in the night, a deeper black than anything she could see with her eyes. And worse, she could feel something in it—something *waiting*.

Still moving helplessly as though led by some god, she walked forward, feeling her bare soles against the gritty sand. The stones of her street, a street almost as old as Xis itself, had long since surrendered to the flowing sands which got into everything. No matter how hard the women of Cat's Eye Street swept, the stones would never be seen again. But it was said that some of the oldest houses had cellar rooms with doors that had once let out onto this very street when the stones had still been visible, although now those doors could no longer be opened, and would admit only centuried dust if they were.

Qinnitan felt the well before she saw it, the waist-high ring of stone with emptiness at its center like an untended wound. She thought she could hear a faint noise as of something in the depths gently pushing the water to and fro.

She leaned forward, although she did not want to, although every sense she had screamed out for her to turn back toward the house and the safety of her sleeping family. Still she leaned farther, until her face was over the invisible hole, until the faint noises were rising straight up to her ears—*slish, splush, slish,* something gently stirring down in the darkness.

Was it a monstrous eight-legger such as she had seen in the market, a sort of wet sea spider with limbs as slippery and loose as noodles? But how could such a thing get into the well? Still, whatever it was, she could feel it as well as hear it, sense its inhuman presence somewhere below her.

Now she could feel it moving. Coming upward. Climbing, with inhuman strength and patience, up the smooth, clammy stones, climbing right up toward her where she leaned helplessly over the well mouth, her limbs stiff as stone. She could feel it in her head as well—cold thoughts, alien wishes unclear but unmistakable as fingers around her throat. It was climbing toward her as intently as if she had called it . . .

"Briony! Help me!"

At first she thought the startling voice came from the thing in the well, but it sounded like a real person—a young man, frightened as she was frightened. Was someone calling her? But why call her by that unfamiliar name?

The thing in the well did not stop or even slow the sticky slap of its climb. Qinnitan tried to scream, but could not. She tried again, but the scream could only build and build inside her until it seemed she would burst like a flooded dam.

"Briony! I'm here!"

She could feel him, as if he stood just on the other side of the well—could almost see him, a pale, pale boy with hair as flame-red as the streak in her own dark locks, a boy staring at her without seeing, his eyes haunted . . .

"Briony!"

She was terrified. The thing's wet fingers were curling on the lip of the well and the boy couldn't even see it? She wanted to know why he called her by that strange name, but instead when she found her voice at last she heard herself ask him, *"Why are you in my dreams?"*

And then the blackness burst up from below and the boy blew away like smoke and the shriek at last came rushing out of her, rising, ragged. . . .

Qinnitan sat up, gasping. Something had a grip on her and for a moment she struggled fruitlessly against it until she realized it was not huge and chilly but small and warm and . . . and frightened. It was Pigeon. Pigeon was hanging onto her, grunting with fear. He was terrified, but he was trying to comfort *her*.

"Don't worry," she said quietly. She found his head in the darkness, stroked his hair. He clung to her like a street musician's monkey. "It was just a bad dream. Were you frightened? Did you call me?"

But of course he couldn't have called her—not in words. The voice had been a dream, too. *Briony.* What a strange name. And what a terrible dream! It had been like the nights when she had lived in the Seclusion, when the priest Panhyssir had given her that dreadful elixir called the Sun's Blood, that poison which had left her feverish and terrified that it was stealing her mind.

Remembering, Qinnitan shivered helplessly. Pigeon was already asleep again, his bony little body pressed against her so that she couldn't lower her arm, which was already beginning to ache a little. How could she have believed that the autarch would simply let her go? She was a fool to linger here in Hierosol, only a short distance across the sea from Xis itself. She should pack up in the morning, leave the citadel and its laundry behind.

As she lay cradling the boy in the darkness, she heard something moaning: outside the dormitory, the winds were rising.

A storm, she thought. *Wind from the south. What do they call it here? "Red wind"—the wind from Xand. From Xis . . .*

She rolled over, gently dislodging Pigeon. His breathing changed, then settled into a low buzz again, soothing as the drone of the sacred bees, but Qinnitan could not be so easily calmed. *Winds push ships,* she thought. Suddenly, sleep seemed farther away than the southern continent.

She got up and made her way across the cold stone floors to the main room, reassuring herself by the sound of the sleeping women she passed that all was ordinary, that only night's darkness was making it seem strange. She stepped to one of the windows and lifted the heavy shutter, wanting a glimpse of moonlight or the sight of trees bending in the wind's grasp, anything ordinary. Despite evidence of the ordinary all around her, she half-expected to find Cat's Eye Street and the uncovered well outside, but instead she was soothed to see the high facades of Echoing Mall. Something was moving on the otherwise empty street, though— a manlike figure in a long robe walking away down the colonnade with casual haste. It might simply have been one of the citadel's countless other servants returning home late, or it might have been someone who had been watching the front of the dormitory.

Holding her breath as if the retreating shape might hear her from a hundred paces away, Qinnitan let the shutter down quietly and hurried back across the dark house.

There were times that the great throne room of Xis seemed as familiar to Pinimmon Vash as the house in the temple district where he had spent his childhood (a large dwelling, but not too large, a dream of wealth to the servants but only one residence out of many that belonged to the eminent Vash clan). This throne room was the Paramount Minister's place of work, after all: it was understandable that he might sometimes fail to notice its size and splendor. But sometimes he saw it for what it truly was, a vast hall the size of a small village, whose black and white tiles stretched away for hundreds of meters in geometric perfection until the eye blurred trying to look at them, and whose tiled ceiling covered in pictures of the gods of Xis seemed as huge as heaven itself. This was one of those times.

The hall was full. It seemed as if almost every single person in the court had come to see the Ceremony of Leavetaking—even twitching Prusus was here, who generally only left his chambers when Sulepis demanded his attendance, and who Pinimmon Vash was seeing for an almost unprecedented second time in one day. Vash was glad to see that the scotarch, nominal successor to the monarchy, had been dressed as was fitting in a sumptuous robe too dark to show the spittle that dripped occasionally from his chin.

The monstrous chamber was so crowded that for the first time since the autarch's crowning, Vash could not see the pattern on the floor. Everyone was dressed as if for a festival, but instead they had been standing in silence for most of the morning as the parade of priests and officials filed past to take their places in front of the Falcon Throne, dozens upon dozens of functionaries who only appeared on these state occasions:

The Prophets of the Moon Shrine of Kerah
The Keepers of the Autarch's Raptors
The Master of the Sarcophagus of Vushum
The Chiefs of the Brewers of Ash-hanan at Khexi
The Eyes of the Blessed Autarch of Upper Xand
The Eyes of the Blessed Autarch of Lower Xand
The Oracle of the Whispers of Surigali
The Master of the Sacred Bees of Nushash
The Scribe of the Tablet of Destinies
The Wardens of the Gates of the Ocean
The Supplicators of the Waves of Apisur
The Wardens of the Royal Canals
The Keeper of the Sacred Monkeys of Nobu
The Sacred Slave of the Great Tent
The Master of the Seclusion of Nissara
The Chief of Royal Herds and Flocks
The Master of the Granaries of Zishinah
The Priests of the Coming-Forth of Zoaz
The Guardians of the Whip that Scourges Pah-Inu
The Wardens of the Digging-Stick of Ukamon
The Priests of the Great Staff of Hernigal

There were other priests, too, many more: Panhyssir, high priest of Nushash and the most powerful religious figure in the land next to the autarch himself, along with priests of Habbili and priests of Sawamat (the great goddess who, truth be told, had far more priestesses than priests, but whose female servants, like the priestesses of the Hive, were subordinated to their male masters and had only a token presence)—priests of every god and goddess who ever lived, it seemed, and of a few that may have existed only in the tales of other deities.

And as many court functionaries crowded the chamber as

priests, the Favored of the palace and the whole men of the autarch's army and navy, stable masters and kitchen masters, the clerks of records and the scribes of all the granaries and butteries and storehouses of the gigantic Orchard Palace, not to mention the ambassadors of every tame country that now danced to the autarch's tune: Tuan, Mihan, Zan-Kartuum, Zan-Ahmia, Marash, Sania, and Iyar, even a few abashed envoys from the northern continent, representing captive Ulos, Akaris, and Torvio. There were islanders from distant Hakka wearing their skirts of palm fronds, and chieftains of the desert herders, camel masters and sneeringly proud horsemen of the red desert, from whom the autarch's own family had sprung, but who had the sense now to bend their knees beside everyone else. (To be master of the desert and kin to the autarch himself might be a matter of pride, but too much pride in the presence of the Golden One was foolishness; the few fools bred by the sands did not usually live to adulthood.)

Sulepis himself, the Master of the Great Tent, the Golden One, the God-on-Earth, stood before this assembly like the sun in the sky, clad only in a spotless white loin cloth, his arms raised as though he were about to speak. He said nothing, however, but only stood as the Slaves of the Royal Armor, under the direction of the high official known as the Master of the Armor—a position reserved for the closest thing to a friend the autarch had, a plump young man named Muziren Chah, eldest son of a middling noble family; Muziren had shared a wet nurse with the infant Sulepis but had no royal blood himself. Under Muziren's silent (but still obviously anxious) direction, the Slaves of the Royal Armor clothed the autarch first in billowing pants and blouse of red silk embroidered with the Bishakh falcon, then pulled on the monarch's boots and belt and emblems of office, the amulet and the great necklace, both made of gold and fire opal. Then they began to draw on his golden armor, first the breastplate and kilt of delicate, tough chain, then the rest, finishing with his gauntlets. They draped his great black cape on which the spread wings of the falcon had been stitched in golden wire, and then lowered the flame-pointed Battle Crown onto his head.

When the priests had perfumed the autarch with incense it was Vash's turn. He carried up the cushion bearing the Mace of Nushash, gold-plated and shaped like a blazing sun. Sulepis looked at it for a long instant, a half-smile on his face, then winked at Pinimmon Vash and lifted the mace high in the air. For a moment the paramount minister felt certain the autarch was about to dash out his brains right here in front of all these gathered notables—not that any one of them would have dared even to murmur in surprise, let alone protest—but instead he turned to face the sea of people and bellowed in his high, strong voice.

"We will not rest until the enemies of Great Xis have been subdued!"

The crowd roared its approval, a noise that started low like a moan of pain, then rose until it seemed as if it would rattle the tiled images of the gods overhead right out of their heaven and bringing them crashing down to earth.

"We will not rest until our empire spreads over the world!"

The roar grew louder, although why any of them should have cared whether Xis stretched its sway one inch, Vash couldn't imagine.

"We will not rest until Nushash is lord over all—the living God on Earth!"

And now the noise really did threaten to dislodge the tiles from the ceiling and even shake the pillars that kept heaven and earth separated.

The autarch turned and said something to Vash, but it was lost in the storm of approval. He turned back and waved his hands for quiet, which came quickly.

"In our absence, the Master of the Armor, Muziren Chah, will care for you as I care for you, like a herdsman his goats, like a father his children. Obey him in all things or I will return and destroy you all."

Wide-eyed, the assembled courtiers nodded their heads and mumbled praise and in general did their best to look as if they could not even imagine what disobedience meant; Vash, though, had to struggle to keep his face expressionless. Muziren? The autarch was leaving the simpleton Master of the Armor on the throne? Surely that was the role of Prusus, the crippled scotarch, or even of Vash himself as paramount minister—what could be the reason for such a bizarre choice? Was it merely that Muziren was no threat to take the throne? It was hard to believe Sulepis could feel that he would become so vulnerable simply by leaving the city, not with a quarter of a million men at his command and the blood of a hundred kings in his veins?

Muziren Chah took the circlet of regency from the autarch and then dropped to his knees to kiss Sulepis' feet. The autarch dismissed the crowd. (None of them were so foolish as to move from the spots where they stood until Sulepis himself had departed.) The autarch turned to Pinimmon Vash.

"To the ships," he said, grinning. "Blood is in the air. And other things, too."

Vash had no idea what he meant. "But . . . but what of Prusus, Golden One?"

"He is going with me. Surely our beloved scotarch deserves to see a little of the world, old friend?"

"Of course, Golden One. It is just that he has never traveled before . . ."

"Then enough talk. I will need my most trusted minister, too. Are you ready?"

"Of course, Master of the Great Tent. Packed and ready to travel, ready to do your bidding, as always."

"Good. We shall have a most interesting adventure."

The autarch stepped back into his litter—now that he was dressed in the royal armor, he could not set foot outside the throne room in the normal way, and in fact could not touch ground in Xis until he reached his ship. His brawny slaves lifted him and carried him out of the room, leaving Vash to wonder why it seemed to him as though the world had suddenly spun a little way out of its accustomed orbit.

27

The Players

*Fearing for the safety of his new bride Suya, Nushash took
her to Moontusk, the house of his brother Xosh, a great
fortress built from the ivory of the moon (which becomes a
tusk each month and then falls from the sky.) But hear me!
Argal, Xergal, and Efiyal learned from Shoshem the
Trickster where she was, and raised a great army
to come against it.*

—from *The Revelations of Nushash,* Book One

ALONE AGAIN. *Lost again. Cursed and lost and alone . . .*
Briony wiped hard at her cheeks with the back of her
hand, scrubbing away the tears. *No. Get up, you stupid girl!*
What was she doing, weeping like a child? How long had she
been sitting here alone at the edge of the forest as the sun began
to set? What kind of fool would sit blubbering while the moon
rose and the wolves came out?

She staggered to her feet, weak-kneed and exhausted although she hadn't moved for a long, long time. Had it all been a dream, then—the demigoddess Lisiya, the food, the stories of the gods and their battles? Only the dream of someone lost and wandering?

But wait—Lisiya had given her something, some amulet to carry. Where was it? Briony patted at the pockets in the sleeves of her ragged clothing, the long blouse of the boy she had killed, spattered with the dried brown of his blood . . .

Defending myself, she thought, feeling a warming glow of anger. *Defending myself from kidnap and rape!*

She could find no trace of any goddess-given trinket. Her heart seemed heavy and cold as a stone at the bottom of a well. She must have imagined it all.

She still had something left in her of the Briony Eddon who had been a queen in all but name, however, the young woman who had woken up every morning for months with the weight of her people's well-being pressing down on her, the Briony who had learned to trust herself in the midst of flattering counselors and scheming enemies. That Briony possessed more than a little of her family's famously stubborn strength and was not going to give in so easily, even now. She began to retrace her own steps—although noting with another pang that hers seemed to be the only footprints—searching along the forest fringe for any trace of her hours with Lisiya, for any real evidence of what had happened.

She found the amulet at last, almost by pure chance: the white threads had caught on a hanging branch several hundred steps into the forest, where it dangled like a tiny oblong moon. Briony gently teased the bird skull free, sending a prayer of gratitude to Zoria, and then belatedly to Lisiya herself, for this proof she had not imagined it all. She held it to her nose and smelled the dried flowers whose strange, musty tang reminded her of the spice jars in the castle kitchens, then slipped it into her pocket. She would have to find a cord for it, to keep it safe.

Could it all have been *true,* then—all Lisiya's words, her strange tales?

Briony had a sudden, horrifying thought: if the charm was real, then Lisiya had brought her to the edge of the forest for a reason—but Briony was no longer there.

Slipping, stumbling in the growing dark, she hurried back over the wet and uneven, leaf-slicked ground, through the skeletal trees.

She burst out of the forest into the misty emptiness of early evening on the featureless meadows, and for a moment saw nothing. Then, just before she was about to throw herself down to the damp, grassy ground to gasp some breath back into her chest, she saw a single bobbing light moving away from her into the murk to her left, a lantern on a wagon going south toward Syan and faraway Hierosol. The witch, the goddess, whatever or whoever she was, had brought Briony here for a reason after all. She hobbled after the receding light, praying that these strangers were not bandits and wondering how she would explain why she was walking alone on the empty grasslands beside the Whitewood.

The two wagons on either side of the large fire made a sort of counterfeit town: for a few moments Briony could almost feel herself back in the midst of civilization. The man talking to her was certainly civilized enough, his speech as round and precise as his appearance. She knew him slightly, although she had not realized it until he gave his name, Finn Teodoros, and she was desperately grateful that they had never met in person. He was a poet and playwright who in years past had done some work for Brone and others at court, and had once or twice written pretty speeches for Orphanstide or Perinsday ceremonies. The rest of his traveling companions were players (as far as she could tell from the things they said to each other) taking their wagons on a winter tour of the provinces and beyond. As Teodoros questioned her, some of the others at the fire listened with interest, but most seemed far more involved with eating, or drinking as much wine as possible. Among the latter was another Briony thought she had heard of, Nevin or Hewney by name, another poet and—as her ladies Rose and Moina had informed her in tones mixing horror with a possibly indecent fascination—a very bad man indeed.

"So you say your name is Timoid, young man?" Finn Teodoros nodded at her sagely. "It smacks somewhat of a straw-covered bumpkin just off the channel boat from Connord. Perhaps we should call you Tim."

Briony, who had picked the name of the Eddon family priest, could only nod.

"Strange, though, since the channel boat does not, as far as I know, make landfall in the midst of the Whitewood. Nor do you sound Connord-fresh. You say you have been wandering here how long?"

"Days, maybe weeks, my lord." She tried to keep her voice boyishly gruff and her words what she imagined would be peasant-simple. "I do not know for certain." This at least was true, but she was glad her dirty face would hide the flush of her fear. "And I am not from Connord but Southmarch." She had hoped to pass herself off as a wandering prentice, but she had expected to encounter some tradesman or merchant, not this shrewd-faced familiar of her own court.

"Do not task him so," said the tall one named Dowan—a giant of a fellow, so big that Briony did not reach near to his shoulder, and Olin Eddon's daughter was not a small girl. "The lad is weary and hungry, and cold."

"And looking to ease those deficits at our expense," said a woman the others had called Estir. Her dark hair was shot with gray and although her face might be called pretty, she had the soured look of someone who remembered every slight ever done to her.

"We could use another hand on the ropes," offered a handsome, brown-skinned youth, one of the few who seemed near Briony's own age. He spoke lazily, as one accustomed to getting his way, and she wondered if he was related to the owner of the troop. Finn Teodoros had introduced the company as Makewell's Men, which was the usual sort of name for a troop of traveling players—

perhaps the young man was Makewell's son, or even Makewell himself.

"Well, that is at first easy enough to accomplish without loss, Estir," said Teodoros. "He shall have my share tonight, since my stomach pains me a bit. And he shall sleep with me in the wagon—unless that is not mine to grant?"

The woman named Estir scowled, but waved her hand as though it was of little import to her.

"Come, then, wandering Tim," said Teodoros, rising heavily from his seat on the wagon's narrow steps. He was no older than her father and what hair he had showed little gray, but he moved like an aged man. "You can have my meal and we can speak more, and perhaps I shall sniff out what use you might be, since no one travels with us who cannot earn his way."

"That's not all you'll sniff out, I'll wager," said one of the drinkers. His words were mumbled in a way that suggested he had started his drinking long before sunset. He was handsome in a thick-jawed way, with a shock of dark hair.

"Thank you, Pedder," said Teodoros with a hint of irritation. "Estir, perhaps you could see that your brother puts a little food in his stomach to offset the drink. If he is ill again this tennight I fear we will have another disaster with *Xarpedon,* because Hewney does not know it."

"I *wrote* it, curse you!" bellowed Hewney, a bearded, balding man with the look of an aging courtier who still clung to the memory of his handsome youth.

"Writing it and remembering it are two different things, Nevin," said Teodoros reasonably. "Come along, young Tim—we will talk while you eat."

Once inside the tiny wagon the scrivener lowered himself onto the small plank bed and gestured at a covered bowl sitting on the folding shelf that seemed, judging by the quills, pens, and ink bottles hanging in a pocketed leather pouch, to double as a writing table. "I did not bring a spoon. There is a basin of water you can use to wash your hands."

While Briony began to consume the lukewarm stew, Teodoros

watched her with a small, pleasant smile on his face. "You might do for some of the girl's roles, you know. We lost our second boy in Silverside—he fell in love with a local, which is the curse of traveling companies. Feival cannot play all the women, Pilney is too ugly to play any but the nurses and dowagers, and we will not have money to hire another actor until we are installed in our next theater."

Briony swallowed. "A player—me? No. No, my lord, I cannot. I have no training."

Teodoros raised an eyebrow. "No training in imposture? That is a strange argument coming from a girl pretending to be a boy, don't you think? What matter it if we add one more twist to the deception and have you pretend to be a boy pretending to be a girl?"

Briony almost choked. "A girl . . ."

Teodoros laughed. "Oh, come, child. Surely you did not think to pass yourself off as a true manchild? Not among players—or at least not around me. I have been brushing rouge on principal boys and tightening their corsets since before you were born. But it is up to you—I cannot imagine forcing someone onto the stage against her will. You will sleep in the wagon with me and we will find you other employ."

Suddenly the stew seemed to become something like paste in her mouth, sticky and tasteless. She had never spent much time around writers, but she had heard stories of their vicious habits. "Sleep with you . . . ?"

Teodoros reached out and patted her knee. She flinched and almost dropped the bowl into her lap. "Foolish child," he said. "If you were a real boy, handsome as you are, you might have some cause to fear me. But I want nothing from you, and if Pedder Makewell thinks you are mine, then he will leave you alone, too. He likes a charming lad, but dares not offend me because even with his name on the company, it is my contacts in Tessis that will keep us alive and plying our craft."

"Tessis? You're going all the way to Syan?" Briony swayed a little on her tiny stool, dizzy with relief. *Bless you, Lisiya—and you, dear, kind Zoria.*

"Eventually we shall wind our way thither, yes. Perhaps a few testings of our new material in the outlying towns—*The Ravishment of Zoria* has never seen a true audience and I would like to let it breathe a few free breaths before it is stifled by the jades in Tessis."

"*The Ravishment* . . . I don't understand."

"*The Ravishment of Zoria.* It is a play of mine, newish, concerning the abduction of Zoria by Khors and his imprisonment of her, and the fateful beginning of the war between the gods. With real thunderstorms, lightning, magical sleights, and the fearful rumble of the gods on their immortal steeds, all for two coppers!" He smiled again. "I am rather proud of it, truth to tell. Whether it is my best work, though, only time and the *hoi polloi* of Syan will say."

"But you . . . you're all from the March Kingdoms, aren't you? Why are you going to Syan? Why can't you do your plays in Southmarch?"

"Spoken as someone who understands little of the doings of artists and nobles," said Teodoros, his smile gone now. "We were Earl Rorick's Players, inherited by the earl from his father of the same name. We were also the best and most respected of the Southmarch players—whatever you have heard about the Lord Castellan's Men is rubbish. The Firmament itself was ours until it burned (that is a theater, child) and then afterward the Odeion Playhouse inside the castle walls and the great Treasury Theater in the mainland city both fought for our works. But young Rorick is dead, you see."

"Dead? Rorick Longarren?" She only realized after she said it that perhaps it would seem strange she should know his full name.

Teodoros nodded. "Killed by fairies, they say. In any case, he did not come back from the battle at Kolkan's Field and he has no heir, so we are left without a patron. The country's guardian, kindly Lord Tolly, does not like players, or at least he does not like players with connections to the monarchy that was. He has given his own support to a group of players—players, hah! They are bandits, so criminal is their writing and their declaiming—under the patronage of a young idiot baron named Crowel. And so there is nothing for us to do but starve or travel." He gave a rueful chuckle. "We decided travel would be more graceful and less painful."

After Teodoros went back out to join his fellow players by the fire, Briony curled up on the floor of the wagon—choosing not to put Finn Teodoros' professed disinterest in women to too harsh a test—and pulled the playwright's traveling cloak over her. The news that her cousin Rorick was dead had disturbed her, even though she had never liked him. He had been in the same battle as Barrick and had not survived it. She did her best to let the sounds of talking and singing from outside the wagon soothe her. She was among people, even if they were only rough sorts, and not alone anymore. Briony fell asleep quickly. If she dreamed, she did not remember it in the morning.

The physician had made himself fairly comfortable. Besides a bed and a chair, the Guild-masters had given Chaven a table and what looked like every book in the guildhall library. It pained Chert's head to think of reading so many of the things. Except for consultation here in the hall over a few particular and difficult problems over the years, he had not opened a book himself since soon after he had been introduced to the Mysteries. Chert of the Blue Quartz had a deep respect for learning, but he was not much of a reader.

"I should have come down here years ago," said Chaven, hardly even looking up at Chert's entrance. "How could I have been such a fool! If I had even guessed at the treasures down here . . ."

"Treasures?"

Chaven lifted the book in his hands reverently. "Bistrodos on the husbandry of crystals! My colleagues all over Eion believe this book lost when Hierosol first fell. And if I can find someone to help me translate from the Funderling, I tremble to think what knowledge your own ancestors have preserved here in these other volumes."

"Chaven, I . . ."

"I know you do not feel up to such a challenge yourself, Chert, but perhaps one of the Metamorphic Brothers? I am sure they have scholars among their number who could help me . . ."

The idea of the conservative Metamorphic Brothers agreeing to allow ancient Funderling wisdom to be translated into one of the big-folk tongues was preposterous enough; Chert didn't even want to imagine asking them to help with the project. In any case, he had more important matters at hand. "Chaven, I . . ."

"I know, I'm supposed to be solving my own problems—those I have brought with me which have become your people's problems now, too. I know." He shook his head. "But it is so hard to ignore all this . . ."

"Chaven, will you listen to me?"

The physician looked up, surprised. "What is it, friend?"

"I have been trying to speak to you, but you will go on and on about these books. Something has happened, something . . . disturbing."

"What? Nothing wrong with the boy Flint, I hope?"

"No," said Chert. There at least was one thing in the world to be grateful for: Flint still had not recovered his memories, but he seemed more ordinary after his session with Chaven's mirrors. He paid attention now, and though he still spoke little, he at least took part in the life of the household. Opal was the happiest she had been in a month. "No, nothing like that. We've had a message from the castle."

"So?"

"From Brother Okros. He asks the Funderlings' help."

Chaven's eyes narrowed. "That traitor! What does he want?"

Chert handed the letter to the physician, who fumbled for his spectacles and found them at last in his pockets. He had to set down his copy of Bistrodos so he could put them on and read the letter.

"To the esteemed Elders of the Guild of Stone-Cutters, greetings!
From his honor Okros Dioketian, royal physician to Olin
Alessandros, Prince Regent of Southmarch and the March
Kingdoms, and to his mother Queen Anissa."

Chaven almost dropped the letter in his fury. "The villain! And look, he puts his own name before the royal child and mother. Does he know nothing of humility?" It took him a moment until he was calm enough to read again.

"I request the help of your august Guild with a small matter of
scholarship, but one which will nevertheless carry with it my gratitude
and that of the Queen, guardian of the Prince Regent. Send to me
in the castle any among you who is particularly learned in the craft
of Mirrors, their making, their mending, and the study of their sub-
stance and properties.

"I thank you in advance for this aid. Please do not speak of it
outside your Guild, for it is the Queen's express wish it be kept
secret, so as not to excite rumor among the ignorant, who have many
superstitions about Mirrors and suchlike."

"And here he's signed it—oh, and a seal, too!" Chaven's voice was icy with disgust. "He's come high in the world."

"But what do you think about it? What should we do?"

"Do? What we must, of course—send him someone. And it must be you, Chert."

"But I know nothing about mirrors . . . !"

"You will know more when you read Bistrodos." Chaven picked the book up again, then let it fall back on the tabletop—the heavy volume made a noise like a badly-shored corridor collapsing. "And I will help you learn to speak like a master of captromancy."

This was so preposterous he did not even argue. "But why?"

"Because Okros Dioketian is trying to learn the secrets of *my mirror*—and you must find out what he plans." Chaven had become unnaturally pale and intent. "You *must* do it, Chert. You alone I trust. In the hands of someone like Okros there is no telling what mischief that mirror could perform!"

Chert shook his head in dismay, although he did not doubt the task would indeed fall to him. He was already imagining Opal's opinion of this latest outrage.

Despite Lisiya's healing hands, Briony was still sore in many places, but she was much happier than she had been on her own. It was better by far to walk in company, and the miles of empty grassland, broken only by the occasional settlement, village, or even more infrequent market town, went much more easily than they would have otherwise. She spoke little, not wanting to risk her disguise, although on the second night Estir Makewell had sidled up to her at the campfire and quietly said, "I don't blame you for traveling as a boy in these dire territories. But if you make any trouble for me or the troop, girl, I will snatch the hair out of your head—and I'll beat you stupid, too."

It was a strange sort of welcome from the only other female, but Briony hadn't planned on the two of them being friends in any case.

So if she could stay with them until Syan, what then? She was grateful for their fellowship, but she couldn't imagine any of the players could help her in Tessis. Besides Teodoros, the soft-spoken but sharp-eyed eminence of the group, the troop was named for Pedder Makewell, Estir's brother, the actor who liked his wine (and, according to Teodoros, also handsome young men). Makewell's Men had chosen him as their figurehead because he had a reputation for playing the great parts and playing them loudly and well. The groundlings loved Makewell, Teodoros had told her, for his bombast but also for his tragic deaths. *"His Xarpedon gasps out his life with an arrow in his heart,"* Teodoros had said approvingly, *"and although this mighty autarch has put half of Xand to the sword, the people weep to hear him whisper his last words."*

The playwright Nevin Hewney was at least as well known as Makewell, although not for his acting—Teodoros said Hewney was a middling player at best, indifferent to that craft except as a way of attracting the fairer sex. He was, however, infamous for his plays, especially those like *The Terrible Conflagration* that some called blasphemous. But no one called him an indifferent poet: even Briony had heard something of Hewney's *The Death of Karal,* which the royal physician Chaven had often claimed almost redeemed playwrighting from its sordid and sensational crimes against language.

"When he found his poetic voice, Hewney burst upon the world like fireworks," Finn Teodoros told her as they walked one morning while the man in question limped along ahead of them, cursing the effects of the previous night's drinking. "I remember when first I saw *The Eidolon of Devonis* and realized that words spoken on a stage could open up a world never seen before. But he was young then. Strong spirits and his own foul temper have blunted his genius, and I must do most of the writing." Teodoros shook his head. "A shame against the gods themselves, who seldom give such gifts, to see those gifts squandered."

Makewell's sister Estir was the group's only female member, and although she did not play upon the stage she performed many other useful services as seamstress and costumer, and also collected the money at performances and serviced the accounting books. The giant Dowan Birch had the beetling brow and frown of some forest wild man, but was surprisingly kind and intelligent in his speech—Teodoros called him "a quaffing of gentlemanry decanted into a barrel rather than a bottle." But for his size and looks, he seemed distinctly unfit to play the demons and monsters that were his lot. The other leading actor was the handsome young man Feival, who although he had ended his dalliances with Teodoros and Makewell years earlier was still youthful and pretty enough to treat them both like lovesick old men. He seemed not to take advantage of this except in small ways, and Briony decided she rather liked him: his edge of carelessness and his occasional snappishness reminded her a little of Barrick.

"Your other name is Ulian," she said to him as they walked beside the horses one day. "Does that mean you are from Ulos?"

"Only for as long as it took me to realize what a midden heap it was," he said, laughing. "I notice you did not spend long sniffing the air of Southmarch, either."

Briony was almost shocked. "I love Southmarch. I did not leave because I disliked it."

"Why, then?"

She realized she was already wandering into territory she wished to avoid. "I was treated badly by someone. But you, how old were you? When you left Ulos, I mean."

"Not more than ten, I suppose." He frowned, thinking. "I have numbers, but not well. I think I have eighteen or nineteen years now, so that seems about right."

"And you came to Southmarch and became an actor?"

"Nothing so straightforward." He grinned. "If you have heard players and playhouses are the dregs of civilization, then know that anyone who says so has not seen the true cesspits of a place like Southmarch—let alone Tessis, which has Southmarch beat hollow for vice and depravity!" Feival chuckled. "I am rather looking forward to seeing it again."

"There was a . . . physician in Southmarch," Briony said, wondering if she might be going too far. "I think he lived in the castle. Chaven, his name was. Some said he was from Ulos. Do you know anything of him?"

He gave her a quizzical look. "Chaven Makaros? Of course. He is from one of the ruling families of Ulos. The Makari would be kings, if Ulos had such creatures."

"So he is well known?"

"As well known where I grew up as the Eddons are in Southmarch." Feival paused to make the sign of the Three. "Ah, the poor Eddons," he sighed. "May the gods watch over them. Except for our dear prisoned king, I hear they are all dead, now." He looked at her intently. "If you were perhaps one of the castle servants, I do not blame you for running away. They are in hard times there. Frightening times. It is no place for a young girl."

"Girl . . . ?"

"Yes, *girl,* sweetling. You may fool the others, but not me. I have spent my life playing one, and recognize both good and bad imitations. You are neither, but the true coin. Also, you make a fairly wretched, unmanly boy." He patted her on the shoulder. "Stay away from Hewney, whatever guise you wear. He is hungry for youth, and will take it anywhere he can find it."

Briony shivered and only barely resisted making the sign of the Three herself. She was less disturbed to find another player had penetrated her disguise than by what Feival had said about the Eddons all being dead now . . .

Not all, she told herself, and found a little courage in that bleak denial.

They walked for several days and made rough camp each night until they reached the estate of a rural lord, a knight, where they had apparently received hospitality in past years and were again welcomed. The company did not have to perform a play for their rent, but Pedder Makewell—after being forced to bathe in a cold stream, much against his will, for both his cleanliness and sobriety—went up to the house to declaim for the knight and his lady and household. Peder's sister Estir went along to watch over him (but also, Briony thought, to have the chance at a better meal than the rest of the players enjoyed down by the knight's stables). She couldn't really blame the woman. Had she not feared being recognized, she would have gladly taken an evening by an indoor fire herself, eating something other than boiled onions and carrots. Still, carrots and onions and two loaves to split between them were better than most of what she had enjoyed for the last month, so she tried not to feel too sorry for herself. As she was learning, most of her subjects would be delighted with such fare.

Teodoros left the gathering early, returning with his soup bowl to the wagon because he said he had thought of some excellent revisions for his new play—something he promised he would show Briony later. "It may amuse you," he said, "and certainly will at least instruct you, and in either case make you a more fit travel-ing companion." She wasn't certain what that meant, but although she was left alone with the other players, she had spent much of the afternoon helping to haul the wagons out of a muddy rut, rub-bing her hands bloody on the rope in the process, and so they were willing, at least for tonight, to treat her as one of their own.

"But in truth we are a desperate fraternity, young Tim," Nevin Hewney said to her, pouring freely from the cask of ale the knight had sent down as payment, along with lodging in the stables, for Makewell's evening of recitation. "You should never take mem-bership, even in the most temporary way, if you are not willing to incur the opprobrium of all gods-fearing folk."

Briony, who in the recent weeks had survived fire, starvation, and more deliberate attempts to kill her—not least of which had been demonic magic—was not impressed by the playwright's drunken conceit, but she nodded anyway.

"Gods-fearing folk fear *you,* Hewney," said young Feival, and winked at Briony. "But that is not because you are a player—or not simply because you are a player. It is because you stink."

The giant Dowan Birch laughed at that, as did the three other men whose names Briony had not learned by heart yet—quiet, bearded fellows who did their work uncomplainingly, and seemed to her too ordinary to be players. Nevin Hewney stared at the Ulosian youth for a moment, then leaped to his feet, eyes goggling, his mouth twisted in a grimace of rage. He snatched something out of his dirty doublet and leaped forward, thrusting it toward Feival's throat. Briony let out a muffled shriek.

"That belongs in the pot, not at my gullet," said Feival, pushing the carrot away. Hewney continued to stare ferociously for a moment, then lifted the vegetable to his mouth and took a bite.

"The new boy was frightened, though," he said cheerfully. "A most unmanly squeal, that was." Sweat gleamed on his high fore-head. He was already drunk, Briony thought, her heart still beating too fast. "Which makes my point—and underscores it, too, thin-keth I." He turned to her. "You thought I would murder our sweet Feival, did you not?"

Briony started to shrug, then nodded slowly.

"And if I had instead played the gentleman . . . like this . . . and begged this tender maiden for a kiss . . . ?" He suited action to words, pursing his lips like the most lovesick swain. Feival, the principal boy, lifted his hand and pretended to flutter a fan, keeping the importunate suitor at bay. "Or perhaps if I turned seductively to you, handsome youth," Hewney said, leaning toward Briony, "with your face like Zosim's smoothest catamite . . . ?"

"Leave the lad alone, Nev," rumbled Dowan Birch before Briony's alarm became something she had to act on. She did not want anyone coming close enough to see that she was a girl, but most especially not an unpredictable drunk like Hewney. "You are in a bad temper because Makewell was invited to the house but not you."

"Not true!" Hewney made a careless gesture, then found himself off balance and did his best to turn his stumble into something like a deliberate attempt to sit down on the ground by the small fire. The frozen earth around it had thawed into muck, and he had to perform an almost acrobatic twist to land on the log the others were sharing. "No, as I was saying when I was interrupted by the princess of Ulos, I merely demonstrated why we are such a fearful federation, we players. We display what all other people hide—what even the priests hide. We show what the priests speak—but we also show it as nonsense. The entrance to a theater is the door to the underworld, like the gate Immon himself keeps, but beyond ours terrifying truth and the most outrageous sham lurk side by side, and who is to say which is which? Only the players, who stand behind the curtain and dress themselves in such clothes and masks as will tell the tale." Hewney lifted his cup of ale and took a long swig, as though satisfied that he had made his point.

"Oh, but Master Nevin is talkative tonight," said Feival, laughing, "I predict that before the cask is empty he will have explained to us all yet again that he is the round world's greatest living playwright."

"Or fall asleep in his own spew," called one of the other players.

"Be kind," said the giant Birch. "We have a visitor, and perhaps Tim was raised more gently than you fleering lot."

"I suspect so," said Hewney, giving Briony an odd look that made her stomach sink. The playwright struggled back onto his feet. "But, pish, friend Cloudscraper, I speak nothing but truth. The gods themselves, Zosim and Zoria and artificing Kupilas, who were the first players and playmakers, know the wisdom of my words." He took another long draught of ale, then wiped his mouth with his sleeve. His beard gleamed wetly in the firelight and his sharp eyes glittered. "When the peasant falls down on his knees, quaking in fear that he will be delivered after death to the halls of Kernios, what does he see? Is it the crude paintings on the temple walls, with the god as stiff as a scarecrow? Or is it our bosom companion High-Pockets Birch that he remembers, awesome in robes of billowing black, masked and ghostly, as he came to take Dandelon's soul in *The Life and Death of King Nikolos*?"

"Would that be a play by Nevin Hewney?" gibed Feival.

"Of course, and none of the other historicals as good," Hewney said, "but my point has flown past you, it seems, leaving you as sunken in ignorance as previously." He turned to Briony. "Do *you* take my meaning, child? What do people see when they think of the great and frightening things in life—love, murder, the wrath of the gods? They think of the poets' words, the players' carefully practiced gestures, the costumes, the roar of thunder we make with our booming drums. When Waterman remembers to beat his in the proper time, that is."

The company laughed heartily at this, and one of the bearded men shook his head in shamed acknowledgment—obviously a mistake he had not been allowed to forget, nor probably ever would be.

"So," Hewney went on, draining his cup and refilling it, "when they see gods, they see us. When they think of demons and even fairies, it is our masks and impostures they recall—although that may change, now that those Qarish knaves have come down from the north to interfere with honest players' livings." Hewney paused to clear his throat, as though acknowledging the shadow suddenly cast on their amusement. "But, hist, that is not the only way in which we players and poets are the most dangerous guild of all. Think! When we write of things that cannot be, or speak them, do we not put ideas in people's mind—ideas which sometimes frighten even kings and queens? It is always the powerful who are most fearful (now that I think on it) precisely because they have the most to lose!" He wiped his mouth again, almost roughly, as though he did not feel much from his own lips. "In fact, in all other occurrences, is counterfeiting not a crime punishable by the highest courts? To make a false seeming of gold enough to gain the artisan the stockade at best, or the white-hot rod, or even the hangman's rope? No wonder they fear us, who can counterfeit not just kings and princes, but the gods themselves! And there is more. We counterfeit *feeling* . . . and even *being*. There is no liar like a player!"

"Or a drunken scrivener," said Feival, amused but also a little irritated now. "Who loves to see what shiny things come from his mouth like a child making bubbles of spit."

"Very good, young Ulian, very good," said Hewney, and took another drink. "You yet might make a poet yourself."

"Why bother, when I can get poetry from most of 'em any time I want just by showing my bum?"

"Because someday that alabaster fundament will be old and rad-dled, wrinkled as a turkey's neck," said Hewney. "And I, once the prettiest boy in Helmingsea, should know."

"And now you are a buyer, not a seller, and any fair young tavern maid can have your poetry for a copper's worth of pre-tending, Master Hewney." Feival was amused. "So lying, too, is for sale—that is the whole of what you're saying. It seems to me that what you describe is the marketplace, and any peasant knows how a market works."

"But none know so well as players," Hewney repeated stub-bornly. Briony could detect just the smallest slur in his words now.

The others gathered by the fire seemed to recognize this as a familiar game. They urged him on, pouring more ale for him and asking him mocking questions.

"What are players afraid of?" shouted one.

"And what exactly is it that players know?" said the fellow named Waterman.

"Players are afraid of being interrupted," snapped Hewney. "And what they know is . . . everything that is of worth. Why do you think that the common people say, 'Go and ask in the innyard,' when they deem something a mystery? Because that is where the players are to be found. Why say, 'As well ask the mask whose face it covers?' Because they know that the matter of life is secrets, and that we players know them all and act them all, if the price is right. Think of old Lord Brone—or our new Lord Havemore! They know who it is who hears all. Who knows all the filthiest secrets . . . ." Hewney's head swayed. He seemed suddenly to have lost his thread of discourse. "They know what . . . they know who . . . will sniff out the truth in the back alleys. And for a little silver, who will tell that truth in the halls of the great and powerful . . ."

"Perhaps it's time for you to take a walk, Nevin," said a voice from just behind Briony, startling her so that she almost squeaked again. Finn Teodoros was standing on the steps of the wagon, his round form almost completely hiding the painted door. "Or simply to go to your bed. We have a long day tomorrow, far to walk."

"And I am talking too much," said Hewney. "Yes, Brother Finn, I hear you. All the gods know I would not want to offend anyone with my o'er-busy tongue." He smiled at Briony as sweetly as a squinting, sweaty man could manage. "Perhaps our newest player would like to come for a walk with me. I will speak of safer subjects—the early days of the theater, when players were criminals and could never set up in the same pasture two nights running . . ."

"No, I think Master Tim will come with me." Teodoros gave him a stern look. "You are a fool, Nevin."

"But undisguised," said Hewney, still smiling. "An honest fool."

"If snakes are honest," said Feival.

"They are honestly snakes," Hewney replied, and everyone laughed.

★

"What was he talking about?" Briony said. "I hardly understood any of it."

"Just as well," said Teodoros, and then spoke quickly, as if he did not wish to dwell on the subject. "So tell me, Tim . . . my girl," he grinned. "How long has it been since you left South-march?"

"I do not know, exactly." She didn't want to set things exactly the same as in truth—no sense making anyone think too much about Princess Briony's disappearance. "Sometime before Orphanstide. I ran away. My master beat me," she said, hoping to make it all sound more reasonable.

"Had the fairies come?"

She nodded. "No one knew much, though. The army was going out to fight them, but I have heard . . . heard that the fairies won." She caught her breath. Barrick . . . "Has anyone . . . learned more about what happened?"

Teodoros shook his head. "There is not much to report. There was a great battle west of Greater Southmarch, in the farmlands outside the city, and fewer than a third of the soldiers made it away again, bringing reports of great slaughter and terrible deeds. Then the fairies took the mainland city, and as far as I know they are still there. Our patron Rorick Longarren was killed, as were many other noble knights—Mayne Calough, Lord Aldritch, more than anyone can count, the greatest slaughter of chivalry since Kellick Eddon's day."

"And the prince—Prince Barrick? Has anyone heard anything of him?"

Teodoros looked at her for a long moment, then sighed. "No word. He is presumed dead. None can go close enough to the battlefield—all are terrified of the fairies, although they have done no violence since then, and seem content to sit in the dark city, waiting for something." He shrugged. "But no one travels west any more. The Settland Road is empty. No one passes through the mainland city at all. We had to take ship to Oscastle to begin our own journey."

Briony felt as though someone pressed her heart between two

strong hands—it was hard to breathe, hard even to think. "Who . . . who would believe such times would come?"

"Indeed." Teodoros suddenly sat forward. "Now, though, you must brighten a little, young Tim. Life goes on, and you have given me a most splendid idea."

"What do you mean?"

"Simply this. Here, these are the foul papers of *The Ravishment of Zoria*. I thought it was finished, but you have provided me with such a daring inspiration that I am adding page upon page. For just the jests alone I would owe you much praise—you can never have too many good jokes in a work where many bloody battles are fought, after all. The one sends the audience back for the other, like sweet and savory."

"What idea are you talking about?" Did all playwrights babble like this? Could none of them speak in plain, sensible words?

"It is simply this. Your . . . plight put me in mind of it. Often in plays we have seen a girl passing for a boy. It is an old trick—some daughter of the minor nobility playing at being a rustic, calling herself a shepherd or some such. But never has it been a goddess!"

"A . . . what?"

"A goddess! I had my Zoria steal out of the clutches of Khors the Moonlord disguised as a serving wench, and thus did she pass herself among the mortals. But with you as my worldly inspiration, I have changed her disguise to that of a boy. A goddess, not merely passing as a mortal, but as a human boy—do you not see how rich that is, how much it adds to the business of her escape and her time among the mortal herd?"

"I suppose." Briony was feeling tired now, sleepy and without much strength for being talked at anymore. She remembered all Lisiya had said, and could not resist tweaking Teodoros a little. "Here's another thought for you to consider. What if Zoria wasn't ravished by Khors? What if she truly loved him—ran away with him?"

Teodoros stared at her for a long moment, more shocked than she thought a man of ideas should have been. "What do you mean? Would you speak against all the authority of *The Book of the Trigon?*"

"I'm not speaking against anything." It was hard to keep her eyes open any longer. "I'm just saying that if you want to look at things differently, why settle for the easy way?"

She slid off the edge of Teodoros' bed to the floor and curled up under the blanket he had loaned her, leaving the playwright staring into the shadows the single candle could not reach, his expression a mixture of startlement and surmise.

28

Secrets of the Black Earth

*When Pale Daughter's child was born he reached his full
growth in only a few seasons. He was called Crooked, not
because of his heart, which was straight as an arrow's flight,
but because his song was not one thing or the other and flowed
in unexpected directions. He was mighty in gifts, and by the
time he was one year old he had become so great in wisdom
that he created and gave to Silvergleam his father the Tiles that
would make their house mighty beyond all others.*

*But then the war came and many died. The oldest voices
remember how the People took the side of the children of
Breeze, even though they died like ants before the anger of
Thunder and his brothers. And ever after the firstborn
children of Moisture hated the People for opposing them,
and persecuted them. But in later days those who took
Thunder's side would prosper because of their fealty to
Moisture's brood.*

—from *One Hundred Considerations*
out of the Qar's *Book of Regret*

AT FIRST VANSEN COULD NOT even muster the will to sit up. The memory of the corpse-pit was like a weight on his chest.

I will say it again. Rise, Ferras Vansen.

It was not his own name that resounded in his head so much as an image of himself, although it seemed a distorted view, the skin too dark, the features coarse as those of the inbred families of the upper dales he used to see in the market at Greater Stell when he was a child. It was the Storm Lantern's view of him, perhaps.

What do you want? Let me sleep.

We must try to make sense of what we have seen, sunlander—and there is something else, too.

Vansen groaned and opened his eyes, then forced himself into a sitting position, scraping his back and elbows on the cell's rough wall. Barrick was still asleep, but he twitched and moaned quietly, as if trapped in a nightmare.

Let him be for the moment. I have words to share with you.

The memory of the pit would not go away. *Gods protect us, what are they doing down there to work all those creatures to death?*

Gyir nodded. *So you too noticed that most of them showed no sign of what killed them. Yes, perhaps they were worked to death.* The fairy touched the palm of one hand to the back of the other. *Whatever the tale behind it, it is certainly a new page for the Book of Regret.* The thought that accompanied the words was not so much of a real book as of a sort of frozen storm of ideas and pictures and feelings too complex, too alien for Vansen to grasp.

What else could it be? They looked like they'd just fallen down dead. No marks on most of them. Vansen was more familiar with corpses than he wished to be, especially those found on a battlefield, each one its own little Book of Regret, the ending written in cruel wounds for all to read.

We must not make the mistake of supposing that which we do not know for certain, Gyir said. *The waters in these deep places are sometimes poisonous. Or it could be that they were felled by a plague. Or it might be something else . . .*

Even while his skin crawled at the thought of being locked in a massive prison with plague raging through it, Vansen could not help being struck by the quality of the Storm Lantern's thinking. The creature he had considered little more than a beast, a blood-lusting wolf, was proving instead as careful as an Eastmarch scholar. *Something else? What?*

I do not know. But I fear the answer more than I fear poison or plague. Gyir looked to Barrick, still murmuring in fitful sleep. *I wished to spare the boy talk of the dead we have seen. His thoughts are already fevered with terror and other things I do not entirely understand. But now we must wake him. I have something to say to both of you—something important.*

More important than plague?

Gyir crouched beside the prince and touched his shoulder. Barrick, still twitching, immediately calmed; a moment later the boy's eyes opened. The fairy reached into his jerkin and pulled out a handful of bread he had hoarded from the earlier meal, went to the barred window in their cell door and, as Vansen watched in astonishment, threw it into the center of the outer chamber.

After a moment of surprised hesitation the other prisoners rushed to the scattered bread like pigeons, the bigger taking from the smaller, those of similar size or health fighting viciously among themselves to keep what they had grabbed or to steal what they had failed to get by quickness. In a few heartbeats the chamber outside went from a place of quiet misery to a nest of yowling, screeching mad things.

Now we may talk—at least for a moment, Gyir said. *I feel someone is listening close by—Ueni'ssoh or one of his lieutenants, perhaps—but just as noise will cover the sound of spoken voices, enough anger and fear will muffle our conversation from anyone near who can hear unspoken words.*

Vansen did not like the sound of that. *People can hear us talking in our heads?*

Speaking this way is not a secret, sunlander, only a matter of skill or birth—or perhaps in your case, strange fortune. The Dreamless,

Uein'ssoh, can certainly do it when he is close. Now give me your attention. He turned to look at Barrick, who still looked bleary. *Both of you.*

Gyir took something else out of his jerkin, but this time kept his hand closed. *I will not show this thing I hold to you,* he said. *I dare not expose it, even in this chaos—but this will show you its size in case you must take it later.*

Vansen stared. Whatever lay in the fairy's long-fingered hand was completely hidden, small as an egg. *What . . . ?*

Gyir shook his head. *It is a precious thing, that is all you need to know—unspeakably precious. My mistress gave me the duty of carrying it to the House of the People. If it does not reach them, war and worse will break out again between our two folk, and the suffering will not stop there. If this is not delivered to the House of the People, the Pact of the Glass will be defeated and my mistress Yasammez will destroy your castle and everyone in it. Ultimately, she will wake the gods themselves. The world will change. My people will die and yours will be slaves.*

Vansen glanced at Barrick, who did not look as dumbfounded as Vansen felt. The boy was staring at Gyir's fist with what seemed only passing interest. *Why . . . why are you telling us this?*

I am telling you, Ferras Vansen, because the prince has other burdens to carry—struggles you cannot know. Yasammez has laid a task on Barrick as well. I do not know it or understand its purpose, but she has sent him to the same place as I go—the House of the People. The Pact of the Glass must be completed, and so I tell you now because I know that even if you do not believe all I say, you will follow the prince wherever he goes. Listen!

He fixed Vansen with his weird red eyes, demanding, pleading: his words swam in fearful thoughts like fish in a swift cold, current. *Understand this—if I die here, you two must take this thing from me and carry it to the House of the People. You must. If you do not, all will be lost—your people, mine, all drowning in blood and darkness. The Great Defeat will have a swifter, uglier end than anyone could have believed.*

Vansen stared at the strange, almost entirely expressionless face.

You are asking me to perform some task . . . for you? Or for your mistress, as you call her—the one who has put a spell on the prince? For your people, who slaughtered hundreds of my guardsmen, burned towns, killed innocents? He turned without thinking to Barrick, but the prince only stared at him as though trying to remember where they had met before. *Surely this is madness.*

I cannot compel you to do anything, Ferras Vansen, said the fairy. *I can only beg this boon. I understand your hatred of my kind very well—believe me, I have all those feelings for your folk, and more.* Gyir lifted his head, listening. *We can speak of this no longer. But I beg you, if the time should come—remember!*

How could I forget? Vansen wondered, but this time his thoughts were only for himself. *I have been asked to help the murderers of my people. And, may the gods help me, I think I will have to do it.*

After the confusing conversation between Gyir and Vansen, only a little of which he remembered, let alone understood, Barrick fell back into sleep again. The nightmares that plagued him in the next hours were much like others he had suffered in his old life—dreams of rage and pursuit, dreams of a world that he did not recognize but which recognized him and feared him—but they seemed fuller now, deeper and richer. One thing *had* changed, however: the girl with dark hair and dark eyes now appeared in every dream, as though she were as much his twin as Briony, his own flesh and blood. Barrick did not know her, not even in the suspended logic of a dream, and she took no active part in any of his dire fancies, but she was there through it all like a shepherd on a distant hilltop, remote, uninvolved, but an indisputable and welcome presence.

Barrick woke up blinking. His companions had moved him into the single shaft of light (if something so weak could be graced with the name) that fell through the grille and into their cell, illuminating the crudely mortared stones.

He sat up, but the cell spun around him and for a moment he felt as if the corpse-pit itself they had seen had somehow reached up to clutch him, to pull him down into the stink and the jellying flesh. He managed to crawl to the privy-hole at the far end of the narrow cell before vomiting, but his aim was hampered by his convulsive movement. Even though his stomach had been almost empty, the sour tang quickly filled the small space, adding shame to his misery. Ferras Vansen turned away as Barrick retched again, bringing up only bile this time—an act of courtesy by the guard captain that only made Barrick feel worse. He still had not forgotten that Vansen had struck him—must the man condescend to him as well? Treat him like a child?

He tried to speak but could not summon the strength. He was hot where he shouldn't be, cold where he shouldn't be, and his bad arm ached so that he could barely stand it. Vansen and Gyir were watching him, but Barrick waved away the guard captain's helping hand and ignored the throbbing of his arm long enough to crawl back to the cell wall. He wanted to tell them he was only tired, but weakness overcame him. He let them feed him a morsel of bread moistened with water, then he fell yet again into miserable, feverish sleep.

What day was this? It was a discordant thought: the names of days had become as much of a vanishing memory as the look of the sky and the smell of pleasant things like pine needles and cooked food. The silence suddenly caught his attention. Barrick rolled over and sat up, certain in his panic that the Qar and the guardsman had been taken away and he had been left alone. He gritted his teeth through a moment of dizziness and fluttering sparks before his eyes, but when the sparks cleared he saw that Vansen and Gyir were only a short distance away, slouched against the wall, heads sagging in sleep.

"Praise all the gods," he whispered. At the sound of the prince's voice Gyir opened his red eyes. Vansen was stirring, too. The soldier's face was gaunt and shadowed with unkempt beard. When had the man become so thin?

"How are you feeling, Highness?" Vansen asked him.

It took Barrick a moment to clear his throat. "Does it matter? We will die here. Everything I ever thought . . . said . . . it doesn't matter now. This is where we'll die."

Do not give in to despair yet. Gyir's words were surprisingly strong. *All is not lost. Something in this place seems to have strengthened my . . .* Barrick could not understand the word—the feeling was of something like a small, fierce flame. *My abilities, you would say—that which makes me a Storm Lantern.*

Funny. I feel worse than I have since I left the castle. It was true: Barrick had actually experienced some easing of the nightmares and strange thoughts after leaving home, especially during the days he had ridden with Tyne Aldritch and the other soldiers, but since he and his companions had entered this hellish hole in the ground the old miseries had come back more powerfully than ever. He could almost feel doom following just behind him like a shadow. *Do you think it is that horrible Jikuyin who has done it to me, that giant? I felt as though his voice . . . it hurt me . . .*

Gyir shook his head. *I do not know. But there is something strange about this place—stranger even than the presence of the demigod himself, I think. I have spent much of the last days casting out my net, gleaning what thoughts I can from the other prisoners, and even some of the guards, although most of them are little more than beasts.*

You can do that?

I can now. It is strange, but this place has not only given my strength back to me, I think it has even made me a little stronger than I was before.

Barrick shrugged. *Strong enough to get us out of here?*

He felt sure that Gyir would have smiled regretfully if he had a mouth like an ordinary man. *I think not—not by pitting strength alone against the powers of both Ueni'ssoh and great Jikuyin. But do not despair. Give me a while longer to think of something. I need to learn more of the great secret of this place.*

Secret? Barrick saw that Vansen was listening raptly, too—might even be carrying on his own conversation with Gyir. Instead of the burst of jealously such a realization usually caused, this time he felt oddly connected to the man. There were moments he hated the guard captain, but others when he felt as though he were closer to Ferras Vansen than to any other living mortal—except Briony, of course. *Gods protect you,* he thought, his heart suddenly, achingly full. *Oh, strawhead, what I would give just to see your face, your real face, in front of me . . . !*

I have not wasted the time while you were lost in fever dreams, Gyir told him. *I have found a guard who works sometimes in the pit—one who watches over the prisoners who put the bodies on the platform and send them up to the wagon-slaves.*

Can you . . . see his thoughts? Can you see what's down below us?

No. The guard has a curious emptiness where those memories should be.

Then what good is he to us? Barrick was weary again. How absurd, when he had been awake such a short time!

I can follow him—stand inside him as I stood inside the thoughts and feelings of the woodsprite. I can see what he sees down in the depths.

Then I will go with you again, like last time, Barrick said. *I want to see.* Gyir and Vansen actually exchanged a look, which infuriated him. *I know you two think me weak, but I will not be left behind in this cell.*

I do not think you are weak, Barrick Eddon, but I do think you are in danger. Whatever about this place troubles you grew worse when I carried your thoughts with me last time. And Ferras Vansen and I will not leave— only our thoughts will. You will not be alone.

Barrick should have been too weak for fury, but he wasn't. *Don't speak in my head and tell me lies. Alone? How could I be more alone than stuck here with your empty bodies? What if something happens to you and your thoughts are . . . lost, or something like that? I would rather it happens to me, too, than to be left here with your corpses.*

Gyir stared at him a long time. *I will consider it.*

"I don't think it's a good idea, either," Vansen said out loud.

Barrick did his best to regain his mask of cold control. "I know you don't follow orders you don't like, Captain Vansen, but unless you have given up your allegiance to me entirely, you are still sworn to my family as your liegelords. I am the prince of Southmarch. Do you think to order me as to what I may and may not do?"

Vansen stared at him, a dozen different expressions moving across his face like oil spreading on a pool of water. "No, Highness," he said at last. "You will do what you think best. As always."

The guardsman was right, of course, and Barrick hated that. He was a fool to take such a risk, but he had told the truth—he was far more terrified of being left alone.

"Doirrean, what are you doing? He is too far from the fire—he will be cold and then ill." Queen Anissa leaned forward in her bed to glare at the nurse, a sturdy, sullen girl with pale, Connordic features.

"Yes, Highness." The young woman picked up both the baby and the cushion underneath him, taking care to show just how much trouble she was being put to, and then used her foot to move the chair closer to the large fireplace. Sister Utta could not help wondering whether a healthy baby was not at more risk from flying sparks than from a few moments naked in an otherwise warm room. *Of course, I've never had a child, though I've been present for my share of births. Perhaps it feels different when it's your own.*

"I just cannot understand why I am saying things over and over," Anissa declared. Her thin frame had rounded a little during her pregnancy, but now the skin seemed to hang loosely on her bones. "Does no one listen? Have I not had enough pain and suffer . . . sufferance?"

"Don't fret yourself too much, dear," Merolanna told her. "You have had a terrible time, yes, but you have a fine, fine son. His father will be very proud."

"Yes, he is fine, is he not?" Anissa smiled at the infant, who was staring raptly up at his nurse in that guileless, heart-tugging way that babies had—the only thing about them that ever made Utta regret her own choices in life. It *would* be appealing, she thought, perhaps even deeply satisfying, to have an innocent young soul in your care, to fill it like a jewel case with only good things, with kindness and reverent thoughts and love and friendship. "Oh, I pray that his father comes back soon to see him," the queen said, "to see what I have done, what a handsome boy I have made for him."

"What will you name him?" Utta asked. "If you do not mind saying before the ceremony."

"Olin, of course. Like his father. Well, Olin Alessandros— Alessandros was my grandfather's name, the grand viscount of Devonis." Anissa sounded a bit nettled. "Olin. What else would I name him?"

Utta did not point out that the king had already had two other sons, neither of whom had been given his name. Anissa was an insecure creature, but she had reason to be: her husband was imprisoned, her stepchildren all gone, and her only claim to authority was this tiny child. Small surprise she would want to remind everyone constantly of who the father was and what the child represented.

Somebody knocked at the chamber door. One of the queen's other maids left the group of whispering women and opened it, then exchanged a few words with one of the wolf-liveried guards who stood outside. "It is the physician, Highness," she called.

Merolanna and Utta exchanged a startled look as the door swung open, but it was Brother Okros, not Chaven, who stepped into the room. The scholar, dressed in the wine-colored robes of Eastmarch Academy, bowed deeply and stayed down on one knee. "Your Highness," he said. "Ah, and Your Grace." He rose, then added a bow for Utta and the others. "Ladies."

"You may come to me, Okros," called Anissa. "I am all in a trouble. My milk, it hardly ever flows. If I did not have Doirrean, I do not know what I would do."

Utta, who was impressed that Anissa was nursing at all—it was not terribly common among the upper classes, and she would have guessed the queen would be only too glad to hand the child over to a wet nurse—turned away to let the physician talk to his patient. The other ladies-in-waiting came forward and surrounded the queen's bed, listening.

"We haven't spoken to Okros yet," said Merolanna quietly, "and this would be a good time."

"Speak to him about what?"

"We can ask him about those strange things the little person said. That House of the Moon jabber. If it's to do with Chaven, then perhaps Okros will recognize what it means. Perhaps it's something that any of those doctoring fellows would know."

Utta felt a sudden pang of fear, although she could not say exactly why. "You want to . . . tell him? About what the Queen's Ears said?"

Merolanna waved her beringed hand. "Not all of it—I'm no fool. I'm certainly not going to tell anyone that we heard all this from a Rooftopper—a little person the size of my finger."

"But . . . but these matters are secret!"

"It's been a tennight or more and I'm no closer to finding out what happened to my son. Okros is a good man—a smart one, too. He'll tell us if he recognizes any of this. You let me take charge, Utta. You worry too much."

Brother Okros had finished with the queen and was writing down a list of instructions for her ladies. "Just remember, he is too young for sops."

"But he loves to suck the sugar and milk from my finger," said Anissa, pouting.

"You may give him milk on your finger, but not sugar. He does not need it. And tell your nurses not to swaddle him so tightly."

"But it will give him such a fine neck, my handsome Sandro."

"And bent shoulders, and perhaps even a pigeon chest. No, tell them to swaddle him loosely enough that the act would not wake him if he was sleeping."

"Nonsense. But, of course, if you are saying it must be so . . ."

Anissa looked as though she would probably deliberately forget this advice as soon as the physician had left the room.

Okros bowed, a smile wrinkling his thin, leathery face. "Thank you, Your Highness. Blessings of the Trigon—and Kupilas and our good Madi Surazem—upon you." He made the sign of the Three, then turned to Merolanna and Utta, bowing again. "Ladies."

Merolanna laid a hand on his arm as he passed. "Oh, would you wait for a moment outside, Brother Okros? I have something I would ask you. Will you excuse us, Anissa, dear? I mean, Your Highness? I must go and have a little rest—my age, you know."

Anissa was gazing raptly at her infant son again, watching Doirrean swathe him in linen. "Of course, dear Merolanna. You are so kind to visit me. You will come to the Carrying, of course—Sandro's naming ceremony? It is only little while from now, on the day before the Kerneia—what do you call that day here?"

"Prophets' Day," said Merolanna.

"Yes, Prophet's Day. And *Sor* Utta, you are most certainly welcomed for coming, too."

Utta nodded. "Thank you, Highness."

"Oh, I would not miss it for a bag of golden dolphins, Anissa," Merolanna assured her. "Miss my newest nephew being welcomed into the family? Of course I will be there."

Okros was waiting for them in the antechamber. He smiled and bowed again, then turned to walk beside them down the tower steps. Utta saw that the duchess really was tired—Merolanna was walking slowly, and with a bit of a limp because of the pains in her hip.

"What can I offer you, Your Grace?" Okros asked.

"Some information, to be honest. May I assume you still have not heard anything from Chaven?"

He shook his head. "To my deep regret, no. There are so many things I would like to ask him. Taking on his duties has left me with many questions, many confusions. I miss his counsel—and his presence, too, of course. Our friendship goes back many years."

"Do you know anything about the moon?"

Okros looked a little startled by the apparent change of subject, but shrugged his slender shoulders. "It depends, I suppose. Do you mean the object that rides the skies above us at night and sometimes in the day—yes, see, there it is now, pale as a seashell! Or the goddess Mesiya of the silver limbs? Or the moon's effect on women's courses and the ocean's tides?"

"Not any of those things," said Merolanna. "At least I don't think so. Have you ever heard of anything called the House of the Moon?"

He was silent for so long that Utta thought they had upset him somehow, but when he spoke he sounded just as before. "Do you mean the palace of Khors? The old moon demon conquered by the Trigon? His palace is spoken of in some of the poems and stories of ancient days, called by that name, House of the Moon."

"It could be. Did Chaven ever own something that could be called a piece of the moon's house?"

Now he looked at her carefully, as though he hadn't really noticed the duchess until just this moment—which was nonsense, of course. Utta knew it was her own nerves making her see phantoms.

"What makes you ask such a question?" he said at last. "I never thought to hear such dusty words of scholarship from you, Your Grace."

"Why shouldn't I?" Merolanna was annoyed. "I'm not a fool, am I?"

"Oh, no, Your Grace, no!" Okros laughed—a little anxiously, it seemed to Utta. "I meant no such thing. It's just that such old legends, such . . . trivial old stories . . . it surprises me to hear such things from you when I would more expect them from one of my brother scholars in the Eastmarch library." He bowed his head, thinking. "I remember nothing about Chaven and anything to do with the House of the Moon, but I will give it some thought, and perhaps even have a look at the letters Chaven sent to me over the years—it could be some investigation he had undertaken that I have forgotten." He paused, rubbing his chin. "May I ask what makes you inquire about this?"

"Just . . . something that I heard," Merolanna said. "Doubtless a mistake. Something I thought I remembered him saying once, that's all."

"And is it of importance to you, Your Grace? Is it something that I, with my humble scholarship and my friends at the academy, could help you to discover?"

"No, it's really nothing important," said Merolanna. "If you find anything about Chaven and this House of the Moon thing, perhaps we'll talk more. But don't worry yourself too much."

After Okros had taken his leave the women made their way across the Inner Keep toward the residence. Flurries of snow were in the air, but only a few powdery scatterings had collected on the cobbled paths. Still, the sky was dark as burned pudding and Utta suspected there would be a lot more white on the ground by morning.

"I think that went rather well," said Merolanna, frowning. Her limp had become more distinct. "He seemed willing to be helpful."

"He knows something. Couldn't you see?"

"Yes, of course I could see." Merolanna's frown deepened in annoyance. "All these men, especially the scholars, think that such knowledge belongs to them alone. But he also knows now that he'll have to give something to get something."

"Did it ever occur to you such a game might be dangerous?"

Merolanna looked at Utta with surprise. "Do you mean Brother Okros? The castle is full of dangers, dear—just the Tollys alone are enough to give someone nightmares—but Brother Okros is as harmless as milk. Trust me."

"I'll have to, won't I?" said Utta, but she could not stay angry with her friend for more than a few moments. She took Merolanna's elbow, letting the older woman lean on her as they walked back through powdery snow in swiftly darkening afternoon.

Even with a dumb brute like this it will not be as easy as prying at unprotected thoughts, Gyir said. *I must have silence just to bring him to the door of our cell.*

Barrick was only too happy to comply. He was already regretting his insistence. The memory of being trapped in the woodsprite's dull, hopeless thoughts, of handling corpses like they were discarded bits of clothing dropped on the floor, still roiled his stomach and made him light-headed.

A bestial, leathery face appeared in the grille, the brow so bony and low that Barrick could not even see the creature's eyes. It grunted and then snarled, angered by something, but was clearly compelled to remain where it was.

Gyir stood eye-to-eye with it for what seemed to Barrick like a terribly long time, in a silence broken only by the occasional pained cry of a prisoner in the other chamber. The guard-beast swayed but could not free itself from Gyir. The fairy stood almost motionless, but Barrick could sense a little of the tides of compulsion and resistance flowing back and forth between the two of them. At last the creature made a strange, rough-throated noise that could have been a gasp of pain. Gyir wiped sweat from his pale brow with his sleeve, then turned toward them.

I have him, now.

Barrick stared at the guard, whose tiny eyes, rolled up behind half-open lids, had finally become visible as slivers of white. *But if you've mastered him, couldn't he free us? Help us to escape?*

He is only a minion—one who brings food. He has no keys for this inner cell. Only Ueni'ssoh has those. But this dull savage may yet give us better aid than any key. Sit down. I will show you something of his thoughts, his sight, as I send him on his way.

Even as Barrick settled himself on the hard stone floor, the guard turned and staggered away across the outer cell. Prisoners scurried to avoid him, but he walked past them as though they were invisible.

Gyir's presence pressed on Barrick's thoughts. He closed his eyes. At first he could see nothing but red darkness, then it slowly began to resolve into shapes he could recognize—a door swinging open, a corridor stretching out beyond.

Barrick could feel very little of the creature's own thoughts beyond the muted jumble of perceptions, of sight and sound, and he wondered whether that was because the guards were not much more than mindless beasts.

No. The fairy's voice came swiftly and clearly: Gyir truly had gained strength. Barrick could even feel Vansen's presence beside him in the beast's thoughts, like someone breathing at his own shoulder. *He is not just an animal,* Gyir said. *Even the animals are not just animals in the way you are thinking. But I have quashed his mind with my own as best I can, so that he will do what we like and not remember it afterward.*

The guard-beast trudged down into the depths, a long journey that took him far beneath even the level of the corpse-room. Despite the odd gait forced on him by Gyir's awkward control of his movements, he was avoided by prisoners and the other guards barely seemed to acknowledge his existence. They might not be mere beasts, Barrick decided, but even among their own kind they showed little life. For the first time it occurred to him that maybe these large, apelike guards were, in their own way, prisoners just as he and his companions were.

Every few hundred paces something boomed and rumbled in the depths, a noise Barrick could feel more than hear through the creature's muffled perceptions.

What is that noise? It sounds like thunder—or cannons!

You are closer with the second. Gyir was silent for a moment as the creature stumbled, then righted itself. *It is Crooked's Fire, or at least so we call it. Your people call it gun-flour.*

Then they truly are shooting off cannons down there?

No. I suspect they are using it to dig. Now let me concentrate.

Down and down and down they went, until the guard-beast reached a room where corpses were being loaded into the huge corpse basket to be winched to the top by more of the neckless, mushroom-colored men. The dead were being unloaded from ore wagons pushed by more servitors, and the guard-beast followed the dirt track of the wagons down into darkness.

They were still descending, but this slope was more gradual so that the haulers could push their carts up it. The wagons were not just bearing bodies, either: at least ten times as many were coming up from the depths full of dirt and chunks of raw stone, but these were being rolled away down another branch of the tunnel.

Barrick could almost *feel* Vansen and Gyir trying to make sense of the arrangement, but he was already feeling queasy from the depth, the heat, and the frequent rumble of the concussive, hammering sounds farther down in the deeps. *If they put me to work here,* he thought, *I wouldn't last long.* Barrick Eddon had fought all his life against being called frail or sickly, but living with a crippled arm had made him hate lying to himself as much as he hated it when others did it to soothe him. *I could not do what these creatures are doing, working with hardly any water in this dreadful, dust-ridden place. I would die in a matter of hours.*

The guard-beast trudged downward into an ever increasing throb of activity. The inconstant thundering of what Gyir called Crooked's Fire was much stronger now, so loud that the staggering guard-beast almost fell over several times. Hundreds of prisoners pushed carts past him up the long, wide, sloped passage, but no matter how monstrous their burden, they always moved out of the guard-beast's way.

At last Barrick saw the end of the passage, a huge, low arch at least twice as wide across as the Basilisk Gate back home. When the guard stepped through it into the cavern beyond, a monstrous chamber which dwarfed even the cave that housed the corpse-pit, Barrick could feel hot air rush up at his host, tugging the matted fur, bringing tears to the creature's already blurry vision. A line of torches marked the broad track down through the swirling dust and marked off the cross-paths where other guards and prisoners labored with the weight of ore carts. To Barrick each step seemed to take a terrible effort—the powerful discharge of hot air he had felt at the doorway continued to buffet the guard-beast at every step, as though he walked down the throat of a panting dragon. It pressed at Barrick's thoughts like crushing hands and Barrick thought he might faint away at any moment, simply swoon into insensibility like the frailest girl-child.

Can't you feel it? he cried to the others, his thoughts screaming. *Can't you? This is a bad place—bad! I can't hold on anymore!*

Courage. Gyir's thought came with the weight of all his power and knowledge, so that for a moment Barrick remembered what it was to trust him completely.

I'll try. Oh, gods, don't you and Vansen feel it?

Not as powerfully as you do, I think.

Barrick hated being weak, hated it worse than anything. All through his childhood nothing could more easily prompt him to act foolishly than the suggestion, however kindly meant, that his crippled arm or his young age might give him an excuse to avoid doing something. Now, though, he had to admit he could not hold out much longer. No amount of steadying words could obliterate the cramping pain from his stomach, the queasiness that did not grow any less wretched by having been nearly constant since they had reached this place.

Why do I feel this way? I'm not even really here! What is doing this to me? This was more than just pain and weariness—waves of fear rolled through him. He had spoken a truth to Gyir that he could feel in his bones, in his soul: this was a bad place, a wrong place.

We don't belong here. He might have said it so the others could hear. He didn't know and he didn't care. He wasn't even ashamed anymore.

The air grew hotter and the sounds grew louder. The guard-beast was clearly familiar with it all, but still seemed to feel almost as frightened as Barrick did himself. The rising stench was not that of spoiling bodies and unwashed slaves, although there was a hint of each—Barrick could clearly recognize them even through the alien thoughts of the guard. Instead something altogether stranger billowed over him, a scent he could not identify, something that had metal in it, and fire, and the tang of ocean air, and something even of flowers, if flowers ever grew in blood.

The edge of the pit was just before him now, glaring with the light of hundreds of torches, swimming in the haze of the burning, dust-laden air. If he could have hung back while the other two went forward, he would have—would have happily acknowledged himself a coward, a cripple, anything to avoid seeing what was in that chasm before him. But he could not leave them. He no longer knew how. He could only cling to the idea of Gyir and the idea of Vansen, cling to the creature that carried them as if it were a runaway horse and wait for it all to end. The chaos in his head was constant now and seemed to have little to do with what was actually around him—mad sounds, unrecognizable voices, moving shadows, flashes of ideas that made no sense, all hissing in his skull like angry wasps.

The light was bright. Something sang triumphantly in his head now above all the other noise, sang without words, without a voice, but *sang*. He stumbled forward, or the thing that carried him stumbled forward, like a blind man into a cave full of shrieking bats. He stood at the edge and looked down.

The great hole in the stone had been dug almost straight downward. Far below, the bottom of the pit was alive with the beetling bodies of slaves like a carcass full of maggots, hundreds of them with sweating, naked bodies and rags around their heads and faces. In the center, its peak half a hundred feet below him, sunk into the very stone of the wall and only half-uncovered by digging, was a strange shape that Barrick could not at first understand, something upright and unbelievably huge. It gleamed strangely in its exposed matrix of rock, a monstrous rectangle of black stone trimmed with dull gold and fishscale green beneath the shroud of dust and stone that clung to its exposed surface. It was astonishingly tall—almost as high as Wolfstooth Spire and far, far wider. Somebody had carved a rune deep into the black stone, a pine tree that covered most of the black rock face. Another carved shape, a crude bird with two huge eyes, had been superimposed over the tree. The far-distant shape looked immensely old, like something that had fallen down to the earth from the high stars. In the chaos of his thoughts, Barrick struggled to make sense of it, then abruptly saw it for what it was.

A gate—a gigantic stone portal scribed with the ancient signs of the pine tree and the owl. The symbols of Kernios, god of death and the black earth.

Dizziness at its sheer size overcame Barrick then. He let go of Gyir, let go of the guard-beast's dull, terrified thoughts, and fell away into emptiness, unable to look at the blasphemous thing a moment longer.

29
Bells

*At last, after battling each other for a year without
stopping, Perin Skylord defeated Khors the ravisher and
slew him. He cut the Moonlord's head from his body and
held it up for all to see. At this Khors' allies fled or
surrendered. In the confusion, many of those evil ones called
the Twilight People hid themselves in forests and other dark
places, but some fled to the chill and deadly northern wilds
and raised themselves there a black fortress which they
called Qul-na-Qar—home of the demons.*

—from *The Beginnings of Things*
The Book of the Trigon

HER DREAMS WERE BECOMING STRANGER
every night, full of shadows and fire and the movements
of barely seen pursuers, but all distant, as though she
watched events through a thick fog or from behind a streaked and
dirty window. She knew she should be frightened, and she was—

but not for herself. *They will catch him,* was all she could think, although she did not know who *he* was, or who *they* were, for that matter. The boy she had dreamed about, the pale one with red hair in sweaty ringlets—was he the quarry of the shadowy creatures? But why should she dream repeatedly of a face she did not recognize?

Qinnitan woke to find Pigeon half underneath her. Although the mute boy himself remained happily asleep, his bony elbows and chin and knees were poking her in so many places she might as well have been trying to get comfortable on a pile of cypress branches. Despite the aches, though, it was hard to look at his face and be angry. His innocently gaping mouth with that pitiful stub of tongue behind his teeth made her ache with a love for him unlike anything she'd felt even for her own younger brothers and sisters, perhaps because she was responsible for Pigeon in a way she hadn't been for them.

It was odd to lie here in this cramped, uncomfortable bed in a foreign land thinking about two people, one the child lying next to her (shivering slightly now that she had made some space for herself), the other entirely a creature of dream. How had her life come to this? Once she had been an ordinary girl in an ordinary street, playing with the other children; now she had traveled on her own to a far country, fleeing from the autarch himself.

Qinnitan still didn't understand it all. Why had Sulepis, the ruler of all the southern world, chosen her in the first place? It was not as though she were a rare beauty like Arimone, his paramount wife, or even much of a beauty at all: Qinnitan had seen her own long features enough times, her thin lips pursed, her watchful, slightly suspicious eyes peering back at her from the polished mirrors of the Seclusion, to know that beyond question.

Enough worrying, she decided, and yawned. It must be almost dawn, although she hoped the wheels of Nushash's great cart were at least an hour from the daylight track: she wanted a little more sleep. She arranged Pigeon so that she could stretch out; he made a scraping sound of annoyance through his nose but allowed himself to be prodded into a less painful configuration.

As she was drifting back down into the warmth of slumber she heard a dull tone so low that she could feel it rumbling in the floor. It was followed a moment later by another, pitched higher. The two notes sounded again, then a third tone joined them—bells, she finally realized, ringing in the distance. At first, in her sleepy confusion, Qinnitan thought it must be the summons to morning service in the Hive, then she remembered where she was and sat up, freeing herself from the complaining boy. Around her others were beginning to stir. The ringing went on.

Qinnitan climbed out of bed and hurried across the dormitory room and out into the dark hallway. A few other women stumbled out with her, clumsy phantoms in their shapeless nightdresses. The bells were so loud and constant now that she could not remember what it had been like only moments before, in the silence of the night.

She clambered up to the passage window, the one that looked east toward mighty Three Brothers temple. The sun hadn't risen, but she could see lights in the tower windows where the bells were ringing. It was so strange—what did it mean? She looked down to see if anyone was in the streets yet, and by the light of the lantern burning at the corner of the courtyard she saw a smear of pale-haired head as a man—the man she had seen the previous night, she felt certain—moved with a certain casual hurry from below the residence window into the shadows. Her heart felt squeezed in a cold hand. Him again. Watching her, or at least watching Kossope House, the dormitory in which she lived. Who was he? What did he want?

She stood as the first sheen of dawn turned the sky purple, cold air on her face, her skin pebbled with goosebumps. Bells were ringing all over the city. Something terrible was happening.

The bells in Three Brothers began to peal while Pelaya was saying the Daybreak Prayer in the family chapel, ringing so loud that it seemed the walls might tumble down. She and her sisters, brother, and mother were all crowded into the chapel, and when Pelaya turned she almost knocked her brother Kiril off the bench.

"Zoria's mercy!" Her mother hurried to the chapel door and handed Pelaya's infant sister to the nurse as the bells continued to crash and clang. "It is a fire! Get the children to safety."

"That's not the fire bell," Pelaya said loudly.

Despite her fear, Teloni was irritated. "How do you know?"

"Because the fire bell is only one bell, rung over and over. *All* the bells are ringing."

Her mother turned to Kiril, Pelaya's younger brother. "Go and find your father. Find out what is happening."

"He's not old enough." Pelaya was too excited and frightened to stay with her mother and sisters. "I'll go!"

She was up before her mother could stop her, heading for the chapel door. "You headstrong little beast!" her mother called. "Teloni, go with your sister, keep her out of trouble. No, Kiril, you'll stay, now—I'll not have all my children scattered."

Pelaya was out the door just as Kiril's bellow of dismay erupted, but it was still loud enough to hear even above the clangor of the bells.

"You're wicked!" gasped Teloni, catching up to her on the first landing. "Mama said Kiril was to go."

"Why? Because he's a boy?" She pulled up her skirts so she wouldn't trip over them as she hurried up the stairs. Already the stairwell and the landings were filling with people, some still half-dressed in their nightclothes, wandering out like sleepwalkers to see what the clamor was about.

"Slow down!"

"Just because you climb like a cow trying to go over a gate doesn't mean I have to wait for you, Teli."

"What if it *is* a fire?"

Pelaya rolled her eyes and began leaping the stairs two at a time. Didn't anyone else take note of things but her? That was why she enjoyed talking to the foreign king, Olin Eddon: *he* paid attention to what was around him, and he complimented her cleverness when she did so too. "It's not a fire, I told you. It's probably the autarch attacking the city."

Teloni slid to a stop and grabbed at the wall to keep herself from falling. "It's *what?*"

"The Autarch of Xis, stupid. Don't you ever listen to what Babba says?"

"Don't you dare call me that—I'm your elder sister. What do you mean, the autarch . . . *attacking?*"

"Babba's been preparing for it for months, Teli. Surely you must have noticed something."

"Yes, but . . . but I didn't think it was really going to *happen*. I mean, why? What does the autarch want with Hierosol?"

"I don't know, what do men ever want with the things they fight wars about? Come on—I want to find Babba."

"But he can't get in, can he? The autarch? Our walls are too strong."

"Yes, the walls are too strong, but he might besiege us. Then we'd all have to go hungry." She poked her sister's waist. "You won't last long without sweetmeats and honey-bread."

"Stop! You are a beast!"

"But you'll get better at climbing stairs. Come *on!*" The jokes rang a little hollow even to Pelaya herself. It was hard to tease her sister, who was good and kind most of the time, with those terrible bells sounding all across the citadel hill, echoing and echoing.

They found their father in an antechamber to the throne room, surrounded by frightened nobles and patient guardsmen. "What are you girls doing here?" he asked when he saw them.

"Mama wanted to send Kiril to ask you what is happening," Teloni said quickly. "But Pelaya ran quick like a rabbit and I had to run after her."

"Neither of you should be here—you should be with your mother, helping with the little ones."

"What is it, Babba?" Pelaya asked. "Is it the autarch . . . ?"

Count Perivos frowned at her, not as if he were angry, but as if he wished she hadn't asked him the question at all. "Probably. We've had a signal from the western forts that they are under attack, and also reports of a great army marching down the coast from the north toward the Nektarian Walls—the land walls." He shook his head. "But it may be exaggerated. The autarch knows he can never break down our fortifications, so it may be he simply wishes to frighten us into giving him the right to navigate our waters on his way to attack someone else."

Pelaya didn't believe it, and she felt fairly certain her father didn't either. "Well, then. We'll tell Mama."

"Tell her we should move the family down to the house near the market. Here on top of the citadel it may be dangerous, although even if the autarch manages somehow to take the western forts, the guns cannot reach us here. Still, better to spend your last dolphin on your roof, as my father used to say, just in case it rains. Go tell her to pack up. I'll be back before the noon prayers."

Pelaya stood on her tiptoes to kiss his cheek. Only a few years earlier she could only reach his face if he bent almost double. Now she could put her arms around his broad chest and smell the pomander scent in his robes. "Go," he said softly. "Both of you. Your mother will need your help."

"We'll be all right down in the city," Teloni said as they trotted back down the citadel's main staircase, weaving through distracted and fearful folk, all scurrying as if the bells were summoning them to the gods' judgment. "Even if the Autarch does fire his cannons, they can't reach *that* far."

Pelaya wondered what Teloni thought armies carried heavy cannons around for if not to fire them. "Unless he brings that army up to the Salamander Gate and fires into the city from that side." She felt almost cruel saying it.

Teloni's eyes went wild and she stumbled as they reached the landing at the base of the stairs; Pelaya had to grab her sister's sleeve. "He wouldn't!"

Pelaya realized there was nothing she could do by talking, even about truthful things, except make life worse for her sister, and soon thereafter, for her mother and the little ones as well. She gave Teloni's arm a quick squeeze.

"I'm sure you're right. Go tell Mama. I'll be there in a short while—I need to go do something."

Her older sister watched in openmouthed astonishment as Pelaya abruptly turned and darted across the hall toward the gardens. "What . . . where are you going?"

"Go to Mama, Teli! I'll be there soon!"

She cut through the Four Sisters Courtyard and very nearly ran headlong into a colum of citadel guards wearing the Dragonfly on their sky-blue surcoats, the symbol of the old Devonai kings, still the touchstone for legitimacy in Hierosol centuries after the last of them had reigned. The guards, who in ordinary circumstances would have at least paused to let her by, hardly even broke stride, booted feet slapping on the floor as they hurried on, their faces set in looks so firm-jawed and unrevealing it made her chest hurt.

Surely Babba's right—the autarch must know better than to try to conquer Hierosol. No one has ever managed in a thousand years! But she couldn't believe things would be quite so easy. She felt a disturbing thrill in the air, like a wind carrying scents from savage foreign lands. Even the bells finally falling silent did not make the world seem any less strange; if anything, the silence that followed seemed to quiver just as dangerously as it had while the bells clamored.

Olin Eddon was just being led back inside by his guards when she reached the garden. After a few moments' discussion, he managed to convince them to let him linger for a moment at the wall on the side of the garden that looked out across the low western roofs of the palace and the seawall, out across the strait and, beside it, the wide, green ocean. The water, despite the chill wind that circled through the garden, looked smooth as the marble of a painted statue. She remembered what her father had said about the western forts and looked out toward the peninsula, but she could see nothing there except a bank of mist; the water of the strait and the gray morning sky seemed to blur together into a single vagueness.

"I did not expect to see you today, and certainly not so early."

His smile was a little sad. He looked thinner than the last time she'd seen him. "Don't you have your lessons in the morning? *Sor* Lyris will be angry."

"Don't tease. You heard the bells—how could you not hear them?"

"Ah, yes. I did notice something ringing . . ."

She scowled. She didn't like him saying foolish things and pretending he was serious about them, treating her like a child who needed to be amused. She wondered if he had done that with his own daughter, the one he spoke of so sadly, the one he so clearly missed. (He didn't speak about his son very much, though, she couldn't help noticing.) "Enough. I have to hurry back to my family. What of you, Your Majesty?"

"A formal title. Now I *am* worried." He nodded his head, almost a bow. "I will be well, my lady, but I thank you for your concern. Go with your family. I have a nice, safe room with bars on the window and a warm coverlet." He stopped. "Oh, but you are truly frightened. I'm sorry—it was cruel of me to make sport."

She was about to deny it, but suddenly felt warmth in her face. She was terrified she might cry in front of this man who, for all their friendly conversations, was a stranger, a foreigner. "A little," she admitted. "Aren't you?"

For a moment something showed through his mask of charming manners—a deep, bleak wretchedness. "My fate is entirely in the hands of the gods." A moment later he had regained his composure and it was as if the mask had never slipped.

Of course it is, she thought. *And my fate is, too. Why should that be so frightening, if we do as they want us to do?* Aloud, she said, "But what do you think the autarch wants with us?"

"Who can say?" Olin shrugged. "But Hierosol has stood for a long time. Many kings have tried to pull it down and failed— many autarchs, for that matter. A hundred years ago Lepthis . . ." He paused, then frowned. "Forgive me, but I cannot remember which Lepthis, the third or fourth. They called this one 'the Cruel,' as if that was enough to mark one Lepthis from another, let alone one autarch from the rest of the bloody-handed crew. In any case, this autarch swore he would shatter this city's walls with his cannon, which were the mightiest guns in the world. Do you know about that?"

"A little." She took a shaky breath. Olin had seemed genuinely upset to have frightened her, and now she could not help wondering who was making whom feel better. "He failed, didn't he?"

Olin laughed. "Evidently, for we are speaking Hierosoline and you see no temple of fiery Nushash or black Surigali here on Citadel Hill, do you? Lepthis the Cruel swore to destroy the temples of all the false gods, as he called them, and put all Hierosol's inhabitants to the sword. He pounded the walls with cannonfire for a year but could not even nick them. The flies and mosquitoes bit and bit down in the valley below the northern walls, and the Xixians died there in droves of fevers and plagues. Thousands more died of fiery missiles from inside the citadel. At last his men demanded he let them go back to Xis, but Lepthis would not hear of such a compromise to his honor. So his men killed him and made his heir the autarch instead, then they all sailed back to the shores of Xand."

"His own men killed him?"

"His own men. Ultimately, even the most bloody-minded troops will not fight when they are hungry and exhausted, or when they understand their deaths will be for nothing except to glorify their commander."

She stared out at the expanse of blue-green water in the strait, then looked south toward the place where she knew the great city of Xis must lie somewhere beyond the mists, its long walls hot and dry and white as bones bleaching in the desert sun. "Do you think that will happen this time? That we will have to live through a siege of a year—or even more?"

"I do not think it will be so bad," Olin said. "I suspect that the present autarch mainly wants to keep Hierosol's fleet occupied and her defenders busy so that he can turn his attentions on other, less well-defended targets—perhaps the Sessian Islands, which still hold out against him."

For the first time since the bells had begun to ring Pelaya felt a little looseness in her chest, which had felt so tight she feared breathing too deeply. Both her father and Olin said that all would be well. They were grown men, noble and educated men: they knew about such things. "I hope . . ." she began, then stopped. Without thinking, she raised her hand to shade her eyes then realized that the sun was behind her. It was only the low-lying mist causing that glare on the water, making it so hard to see out into the southern strait.

"Pelaya? What is it?"

She realized after a moment that she was praying to the Three, mumbling words she had known since childhood but which had never seemed as desperately important as they did now. "Look," she said.

King Olin moved up to the wall and stood beside her, staring out across the strait toward the Finger. "I see nothing. Your eyes are young and strong . . ."

"No, not there. Toward the ocean."

He turned, following her finger, and even as he did the bells began to ring again, all across Citadel Hill, loud as the gods clanging spears against their battle-shields.

As it rolled toward them out of the southeast, the great, low-lying blanket of spiky shadow seemed to Pelaya an immense thicket of trees and clouds—as though somehow an entire forest had torn free of the shore and floated out into the middle of Kulloan Strait and was now drifting toward the walls of Hierosol. It was only when she could see the shapes more clearly that she realized they were ships. It took several moments more before she understood that this was the autarch's fleet, hundreds upon hundreds of warships—thousands, perhaps, a snowstorm of white sailcloth bearing down upon Hierosol out of the fog.

"Siveda of the White Star preserve us," said Pelaya quietly. Her own name had become a horrid jest—the ocean was now the city's worst enemy. "Three Brothers preserve us. Zoria and all Heaven preserve us." So many ships filled the strait that surely the gods themselves, looking down, would not be able to see water between them. "May Heaven save us."

"Amen, child," said Olin Eddon in a stunned whisper. "If Heaven is still watching."

The streets were full of murmuring crowds as Daikonas Vo reached his rooming house, a dilapidated place near the Theogonian Gate, just inside the city's ancient walls and just beneath the ramshackle hillside cemetery which had once been the estate of a wealthy family. The narrow street was not in the least fashionable now, but that didn't bother Vo, and in all other ways a house full of transients suited him excellently.

Most of the people seemed to be heading for the nearest Trigonate temple or across the city toward Three Brothers and the citadel. When he had passed through Fountain Square on his way back from the stronghold, hundreds of citizens had already gathered outside the citadel gates, staring anxiously at the lightening sky as though the clamor of bells would be explained by heaven itself.

Many of them had guessed the cause of the alarm, and shouts and curses directed toward the Autarch of Xis were mixed with some harsh words about their own so-called protector, Ludis Drakava.

Vo, of course, was pleased. He had thought the invasion still months away, and had been creating and examining plan after plan for smuggling the girl out of the city. He had experienced a few bad moments when she seemed to attract the attention of one of the noble prisoners in the citadel, Olin Eddon, the king of Southmarch, but to Vo's relief whatever flash of interest had provoked the northerner seemed to have died away. He had been aghast at the idea that the Marchlander might plan to make the girl his mistress: nothing would make his task harder than having to smuggle her out of Drakava's own palace under the noses of Drakava's own guards. But instead, she was still in Kossope House and still unprotected as far as he could tell.

He would be able to sneak her out of Hierosol now in the confusion of the autarch's attack. Easier still, if the triumph of the invaders was quick, he would be able to walk out of the city with Autarch Sulepis' safe-conduct in his hand and approach the Living God-on-Earth in high honor, to hand over the prisoner and receive his reward—and, he hoped, to have the noxious thing inside him removed. Daikonas Vo was not so naïve as to feel certain that would happen—after all, why should the autarch take him off the leash precisely when he had proved helpful? But the Golden One was notoriously whimsical, so perhaps if Vo pleased him he would do just as he had promised.

Just now, Daikonas Vo couldn't imagine needing more from life than to serve a powerful patron like autarch Sulepis, but he was no fool: he could imagine a time might come when he might wish to be free from this living god. Vo decided that if the autarch didn't immediately remove the invader from inside his body, he should find his own way to loose himself from his master's fatal control, just to be on the safe side.

He reached the inn by the Theogonian Gate. Most of the patrons seemed to be out, summoned from their flea-infested beds even earlier than usual by the clamoring bells. He made his way up the rickety stairway and into his room, which was empty now. He climbed under the reeking blanket and listened to the sound of a city woken to war. Everything would change. Death would lay a skeletal hand on thousands of lives. Destruction would reshape everything around him. And Vo would move through it as he always did, stronger, faster, smarter than the others, a creature that lived comfortably in disaster and thrived on chaos.

It was exciting, really, to think about what was to come. He closed his eyes and listened to his blood rushing and buzzing in sympathy with the vibration of the bells.

30

The Tanglewife

Soshem the Trickster, her cousin, came to Suya and gave her a philter to make her sleep so he could steal her away for himself in the confusion of the gods' contending. But when he carried her away, the stinging grit of the sandstorm woke her and she fled from him, becoming lost in the storm, and his dishonest plan was defeated.

—from *The Revelations of Nushash,* Book One

MATT TINWRIGHT STOOD FOR A LONG TIME in the muddy, rain-spattered street, surprised at his own timidity. It wasn't going back to the Quiller's Mint that made him fret so, or even having to deal with Brigid, although he certainly hadn't forgot her cuffing him silly the last time he'd seen her. No, it was the line he was about to cross that frightened him. Elan M'Cory, sister of the wife of the Duke of Summerfield— who was he to have anything to do with her at all, let alone to meddle in this most profound and dreadful of decisions?

Courage, man, he thought. *Think of Zosim, stepping forth to save Zoria herself, the daughter of the king of heaven!* Tinwright had been considering the god of poets and drunkards quite a bit—he was thinking of making him the narrator of the poem Hendon Tolly had demanded. Zosim had acted bravely, and he was but a small god.

God? He had to laugh, standing in the street with cold rain dribbling from his hat brim and running down his neck. *And what of me?* He wasn't even much of a man, according to most. He was just a poet.

Still, he thought to himself, *if we do not reach, as my father used to say, our hands will always be empty.* Of course, Kearn Tinwright had likely been talking about reaching for his next drink.

"Look what the wind has blown in." A sour smile twisted Brigid's mouth. "Did they run out of room up at the castle? Or did you leave something behind the last time you were here?"

"Where's Conary?"

"Down in the cellar trying to kill rats with a toasting-fork the last I heard, but that was hours ago. He never bothers to tell me anything—just like you." Even the false smile disappeared. "Oh, but of course, you don't remember me, do you? You were telling your wrinkled old friend just that while he stared at my tits as if he'd never seen anything like them."

At this time of the morning there were only two or three other patrons nodding in the dim lamplight—all flouting the royal licensing laws, which said that no one might visit a tavern until an hour before noon. Tinwright suspected it was because they had all slept on the straw floor and only recently woken up. Conary, the proprietor, must be getting slack not to have noticed them, but it was fearfully dark in the place with the window shuttered against the winter chill and the fire not yet built up again.

Tinwright stared at Brigid, who had gone back to gathering tankards from beneath the stained benches. He was about to make an excuse for his last visit—for a moment a multitude of explanations swarmed in his head, although none of them seemed entirely convincing—but then, and somewhat to his own surprise, he shrugged his shoulders. "I'm sorry, Brigid. That was a shabby thing to say, about not remembering your name. But don't blame Puzzle for staring—you are something fine to look at, after all."

She looked hard at him, but her hand stole up and brushed a curl of her dark hair away from her face, as if she remembered all the sweet words he had whispered to her only the previous spring. "Don't try to honey-talk me, Matty Tinwright. What do you want? You *do* want something, don't you?" Still, she seemed less angry. Perhaps there was something to be said for a simple, truthful apology. Tinwright wasn't certain he wanted to make a regular practice of it, though. It would take up a lot of his time.

"Yes, there is something I'd like to ask, but it's not just as a favor. I'd pay you for your trouble."

Now suspicion returned. "The Three know that enough men come in here asking if I'll do the honors for their sons, but I can't say anyone's ever come in asking on behalf of his great-grandfather. I'm not going to let your ancient friend poke me, Tinwright."

"No, no, nothing like that!" It was too disturbing to think about, in fact. People Puzzle's age were done with the sweaty business of love, surely. It would be indecent otherwise. "I need to find someone. A . . . a tanglewife."

"A tanglewife? Why, have you got some castle serving-maid up the country way, then?" Brigid laughed, but she seemed angry again. "I should have known what kind of business would bring you back begging to me."

"No. It's not . . . it's not about a baby."

She raised her eyebrow. "A love potion, then? Something to moisten up one of those wooden-shod harlots you're following around these days?"

He let out a long breath in frustration. Why must she make everything so difficult? Of course, she always had been a woman with her own mind. "I . . . I can't tell you, not yet. But it isn't the kind of thing you think. I need help to . . . to save someone a great deal of pain." His heart stuttered for a moment at the enormity of what he was thinking. "And I have another favor to ask, too." He reached into the sleeve-pocket of his shirt and produced a silver gull. He had needed to borrow money from Puzzle, money he had no way of paying back, but for once something greater than even his own self-interest drove him. "I'll give you this now and another just like it afterward if you'll help me, Brigid—but not a word to Conary. Bargain?"

She stared at the coin in real surprise. "I'll not help you murder someone," she breathed, but she looked as though she wasn't even certain about that.

"It's . . . it's complicated," he said. "Oh, gods, it is horribly complicated. Bring me a beer and I'll try to explain."

"You'll need another starfish to pay for the two beers, then," she said, "—one of them for me, of course!—if I'm to be getting that whole gull."

He couldn't remember the last time he had visited the neighborhood around Skimmer's Lagoon in daylight—not that he had come here so many times. It was surprising, really, since the Mint, the tavern in which he had lived and spent most of his time, was only a few hundred steps away on the outer edge of the lagoon district. Still, there was a distinct borderline at Barge Street, which took its name from an inn called the Red Barge at one end of it: except for the poorest of the Southmarch poor, who shared the lagoon district's damp and fishy smells, only Skimmers spent much time in the area. The exception was after nightfall, when groups of young men came down to patronize the various taverns around the lagoon.

Tinwright turned now onto Barge Street and made his way along it toward Sealer's Walk, the district's main thoroughfare, which ran along the edge of the lagoon until it ended in Market Square in the shadow of the new walls. There was no sun to speak of, but Tinwright was grateful for such light as the gray, late-morning sky offered: Barge Street was so narrow that he could imagine Skimmer arms reaching out to grab him from doorways on either side. In reality, he saw almost no one, only a few women emptying slops into the gutters or children who halted their games to watch with wide, unblinking eyes as he passed. There was something so unnerving about these staring children that he found himself hurrying toward Sealer's Walk, a street he knew fairly well, and where he might find a few of his own kind.

Sealer's Walk was perhaps the only part of Skimmer's Lagoon that most castle folk ever visited, fishermen and their women to purchase charms—the Skimmers were said to be great charmwrights, especially when it came to safety on the water—and others to visit the lagoon-side taverns and eat fish soup or drink the oddly salty spirit called wickeril. Many though, especially from outside Southmarch, came for no purpose more lofty than to see something different, because Sealer's Walk, the lagoon, and the Skimmers themselves were about the strangest things that anyone in the March Kingdoms could see this side of the Shadowline. Even visitors from Brenland and Jael and other nations came to the lagoon, because outside of the lake-folk of Syan and a few settlements in the far southern islands, the Skimmers of Southmarch were unique.

Their food came almost entirely from the bay and the ocean beyond—they ate seaweed!—and even wickeril tasted like something scooped from the bottom of a leaky boat. The long-armed Skimmer men wore few clothes above the waist even in cold weather, and although the women generally wore floor-length dresses and scarves wrapped around their heads, Tinwright had heard it was only for modesty—that they were no more susceptible to the cold than were their menfolk. In other circumstances, as with some female travelers he'd seen, even an occasional woman from Xand, bundled in secrecy to the eyeballs, he'd found the mystery quite appealing, but something about Skimmer women was different. He'd heard men boast of their exploits among the lagoon women—tellingly, though, never in front of Skimmer men—but he himself had never been particularly tempted. Even in the bawdy house behind the Firmament Playhouse, the knocking-shop Hewney and Teodoros had liked so much, Matt Tinwright had never found the Skimmer girls particularly interesting. They had cold skin, for one thing, and even bathed and perfumed they had an odor he found disturbing—not fishy, but with a certain undeniable whiff of brine. And even the naked faces of Skimmer girls were disconcerting to him, although he could not actually say why. The shape of their cheekbones, the size and slant of their eyes, the almost complete lack of eyebrows—Tinwright had always found them obscurely shuddersome.

Still, there were worse places to visit than Sealer's Walk; Tinwright had even been looking forward to seeing it again. It had a vigor unlike any other part of Southmarch, even the exciting bustle of Market Square. When the catch came in each morning just before dawn, or the fishermen who went far out to sea returned at evening, the place was alive with strange songs and exotic sights.

Today, though, the district seemed much more subdued, even for the doldrums of late morning. The people were quiet and fewer were on the street than he would have expected. Most of the men he saw seemed to be gathered at the site of a recent fire, where a row of three or four houses and shops had burned. Half a dozen adults and twice that many children were picking through the blackened rubble; a few turned to look at him as he passed, and for a moment he felt certain that they were staring angrily at him, as though he had done something wrong to them and then returned to gloat.

As he passed a fishmonger's warehouse, two other Skimmer men gutting fish with long, scallop-backed knives also stopped to stare at him, their heads swiveling slowly as he walked past. It was hard not to imagine something murderous in their cold-eyed, gape-mouthed gazes.

He came at last to narrow Silverhook Row and turned right as Brigid had told him, following its wandering length for a few hundred paces until he found the tiny alley that seemed to match her description. On either side loomed the windowless backs of tall houses, blocking out all but a sliver of the gray sky, but at the end of the short, dark passage stood the narrow front façade of another house, with a few steps leading down to the door.

Tinwright was about to knock, but stopped when he saw the long, knurled horn, as long as a man's arms outstretched, hanging over the door. A superstitious prickle ran up his back. Was it a unicorn horn? Or did it come from some even stranger, more deadly creature?

"Planning to steal it?"

He jumped at the unexpected voice and turned to see a short, lumpy shape blocking the entrance to the alley. Thinking of the Skimmer men with their scalloped blades he took a step back and almost fell down the stairs. "No!" he said, waving his arms for balance. "No, I was just . . . looking. I've come to see Aislin the tanglewife."

"Ah." The figure took a few steps forward; Tinwright balled his fingers into fists but kept them behind him. "Well, that would be me."

"You?" He couldn't help sounding surprised—the voice was so low and scratchy he'd thought it a man's.

"I do surely hope so, drylander, otherwise I've been living someone else's life this last hundred years." He still couldn't see much of her face, which peered out of a deep hood. He could see the eyes, though, wide and watery, yet somehow quite daunting even in the darkened alley. "Move out the way, you young clot, so I can open the door."

"Sorry." He sprang to one side as she shuffled past him. He felt uncomfortable watching her mottled hand reach out with the key, so he turned his eyes up to the great horn above the door. "Is that from a unicorn?"

"What? Oh, that? No, that's the tusk from an alicorn whale taken up in the Vuttish Seas. Unless you're in the market for a unicorn's horn, that is, in which case I could be persuaded to change my story." Her laugh was halfway between a gurgle and a hacking cough, and she emphasized it by leaning into him and jabbing him with her elbow. If this really was Aislin, she smelled to the high heavens, but he found himself almost liking her.

The door open, she went gingerly down the steps. Tinwright followed her inside and found himself beneath a ceiling so low he could not stand straight and so crowded with objects hanging from the rafters that he might have been in a hole beneath the roots of a huge tree. Dozens of bundles of dried seaweed and other more aromatic plants, sheaves of leathery kelp stems and bunches of flowers brushed his face everywhere he turned. Countless charms of wood and baked clay dangled between the drying plants, spinning and swinging as he or the tanglewife brushed them, so that even just standing in one place made him dizzy. Many of the charms were in the shape of living things, mostly aquatic beasts and birds, seals and gulls and fish and ribbony eels. Those not hanging from the ceiling had been set out on every available surface, including most of the floor.

Tinwright had to walk carefully, but he was fascinated by the profusion of animal shapes. Some even had little glass eyeballs pressed into the clay or glued to the wood, making them seem almost alive . . .

"Ah, there you are, small bastard," said Aislin suddenly, to no one he could see. "There you are, my love."

The black and white gull, which had been staring back at Tinwright so raptly he had thought it only another particularly well-made object, yawped and shrugged its wings. Tinwright flinched back and almost fell over. "It's alive!"

"More or less," she cackled. "He's missing a leg, my Soso, and he can't fly, but the wing should heal. Still, I don't think he'll go any-where—will you, my love?" She leaned down and offered her pursed mouth to the gull, which pecked at it in an irritated fashion. "You have it too good here, don't you, small bastard?"

Aislin had taken her hood off and unwrapped her head scarf, freeing a bristling tangle of white hair. Her face showed the usual Skimmer features, eyes far apart, lips wide and mobile. Like other old Skimmer-folk he'd seen she also had a curious hard look to her skin, as though instead of sagging and growing loose as ordinary folk's flesh did when they aged, hers had begun to turn into something thick and rigid. Even the curl of inky tattoos on each cheek and at the bridge of her nose seemed to be disappearing into the horny flesh like unused roads disappearing under grass and weeds.

"Will you have something to drink, then?" she asked. "Warm yourself up?"

"Wickeril?"

"That muck?" She shook her head. "Wouldn't drink it. That's for Perikali sailors and other barbarians. Black Wrack wine, that's your drink." She slid between dangling charms toward the corner of the little house where pots and pans hung from wooden pegs—the kitchen, you'd have to call it, Tinwright supposed. She was shaped like a brewer's barrel, but without the heavy cloak she moved with surprising nimbleness through the confines of her crowded nest.

"What's it made with?" he asked—"Black Wrack" didn't sound all that promising.

"What do you think? Don't you know what wrack is? Seaweed! Grandsire Egye-Var protect you, boy, what do you expect? You wanted a tanglewife—what do you think 'tangle' means? Seaweed, of course."

Tinwright didn't say anything. He hadn't known—he'd thought it was just the word for an old woman who made healing simples and . . . and other things.

"What do they call someone like you in a place where they don't have seaweed—or Skimmers?"

She chortled with pleasure, a sound like a joiner's rasp. "A witch, of course. Now drink this. It will take the hair right off your chest."

Aislin was frowning as she emptied her cup. She clearly contemplated pouring herself yet another, but instead sat back in the room's only chair with a sigh. Tinwright was balanced much more precariously on his stool, especially after finishing his own cup. He couldn't remember how much of the smoky wine he'd drunk while trying to explain the difficult, frightening business that had brought him, but he had downed more than a few. The wine was almost as salty as blood but still quite refreshing, and his fear had receded into a general smear of unconcern. He stared at the old woman, trying to remember how exactly he had come to this strange place.

"It's not that I have any scruples, boy," she said. "And I'm not frightened of much of anything, which you can see by me letting you in here in the first place."

Tinwright shook his head. Soso the gull gave him a baleful look and feinted toward his ear. The bird didn't seem as fond of the poet as he was of Aislin, and he especially didn't like it when Tinwright moved—he'd given him a few painful pecks on the ankles and hands already. "What do you mean, letting me in? I wouldn't hurt you."

"Hurt me? Should say not—I'd pop you like a bulb of rock-weed, boy," she said with an evil, self-satisfied chuckle. "No, because you're a drylander ... what was your name?" She stared at him, blinking slowly. "Ah, never mind. Because you're a drylander, and your kind isn't much liked around here just now."

"Why?" There was no resisting the notion, once it had crept into his head, that Aislin the tanglewife looked and sounded like nothing so much as a huge, gray-haired frog in a shapeless dress. It made conversation tricky. That last cup of wine wasn't helping, either.

"Why? By the Grandsire's soggy cod, boy, didn't you see? Big piece of Sealer's Walk burned down? Who do you think did that?"

Tinwright stared aghast at the goggle-eyed Skimmer woman. "It wasn't me!"

"No, you fool, and be glad it wasn't, but it was drylanders from up in the town, a gang of them, young and stupid and hateful. Three of our people were killed, one of them a child. Folk around here aren't very happy."

"Why did they do it?" Suddenly he understood the way some of the Skimmers had watched him and a chill swept over him. "I hadn't heard anything about a fire."

"You wouldn't. We take care of our own, and what happens here doesn't interest the ordinary run of castle folk—not unless the whole place went up in flames and threatened the rest of the town." The tanglewife settled back again, waving her broad hands as though to waft away a foul smell. "It's been bad ever since those Qar creatures crossed the Shadowline. We folk are different—they used to call us kilpies and sea-fairies, did you know?—so things go bad for us. It happened when they came the last time, too, in my great-grandmother's day. Everyone was driven out of Southmarch by them, eventually, but *our* folk were driven out first—and by our own neighbors."

"Sorry." The cursed wine had fogged his brain—how had they started talking about this? "What's . . . what's a Kwar?"

"You're not quite saying it right, but close enough for a dry-lander. Qar is another name for the Old Ones living beyond the Shadowline—the Twilight People." She stared at him for a moment. "You've been sitting here much of the afternoon, boy. Better get up and going before it turns dark. I don't think it's going to be a good night for someone like you to be wandering around land-legged on Sealer's Walk."

"Right, then." Tinwright stood up, sketched a somewhat uneven bow, and began to bob through the dangling charms in search of the door, doing his best to ignore the black and white gull pecking aggressively at his feet.

"What are you doing?" Aislin called. "Didn't you come here to buy something from me?"

He stopped, a thought suddenly gnawing at his mind. "Ah. Yes."

"You have no head for Black Wrack, boy, that's certain." She grunted as she lifted herself to her feet. "Let me get to my powders and potions. Don't sit down again, you'll fall asleep."

After she had been gone for no little time (a span during which Tinwright and the gull eyed each other with feigned disinterest) she came back carrying a small stoppered glass bottle no bigger than a child's thumb.

"This venom comes from an octopus out of the southern seas—a small thing you would never think to be so deadly. Dip a needle in it and use that *one drop only*. Just that, and her journey will be painless. But be careful with it or you will murder yourself. This poison knows no master."

Tinwright took it and stared at the thing in his hand. It was hard to know for certain through the blue glass vial, but the fluid inside looked clear and harmless as water. "Careful . . ." he breathed. "I'll be careful."

"You had better." Her laugh was sharp and raw. "There's enough in there to kill a dozen strong men. I don't like handling it, myself. I had an accident once." She sat down heavily. "And it goes without saying that from here out, you don't know me and I don't know you. I've no qualms about much of anything but I don't want trouble with the Tollys. So remember, if someone comes down here asking about me and blue glass bottles, someone will come looking for you in turn. Understand?"

"Yes." Those Skimmer men testing the blades of their fish-gutting knives as they watched him pass was a picture he wouldn't soon forget. The Black Wrack in his stomach seemed to sour and bubble. He hesitated for a moment before carefully putting the little flask into his sleeve pocket.

"Grandsire's sake, boy, wrap it in something," she said, disgusted. "Here, take this bit of kelp leaf, that's thick enough. If you fall down and break the jar while it's sitting in your shirt like that, you'll never get up again."

When he was finished Tinwright was feeling ill indeed. He stared at Aislin for a moment, swaying, then swiveled toward the door.

"Didn't you forget something?"

"Pardon?" He turned back. "Oh, yes. Thank you. Thank you very much."

"No, you daft herring, my money. That's a gull and two coppers you owe me." She smirked. "And I'm giving you the lovesick poet's rate."

"Of course." He fumbled out the money, handed it to her. After a moment's assessment, which seemed mostly to consist of running her thumb around the circumference of each coin, she whisked them down the gap in her shiny, wrinkled bosom, an expanse which looked like nothing so much as a well-worn saddle. "Now be on your way. And remember what I said. Better you drink that whole jar right now than breathe a word to anyone of where you got it."

Feeling as though some poison had already taken away his powers of thought and speech, Tinwright nodded and staggered toward the door, then out into the cold gray day, or what was left of it.

When he reached Silverhook Row he turned to look back down the alley. Aislin the tanglewife stood in her doorway beneath the great length of pale horn, staring at him. She lifted a hand as if to wave him farewell, but her strange, pop-eyed face had gone cold and remote. She turned and went back inside.

Matt Tinwright hurried out of the lagoon district as fast as he could, acutely conscious of both the fast fading afternoon light and the tiny jar full of treason and murder concealed in his shirt.

Opal came back from market with her sack mostly empty and her face full of worry.

"You look terrible, my old darling," Chert told her. "I'll only be gone up to the castle for the day. I'm sure there's nothing to fear."

"I'm not worrying about you," she growled, then shook her head angrily. "No, of course I'm worried about you, all caught up in this big-folk madness again. But that's not what's bothering me. There's nothing to eat in this house and scarcely anything to be had even at the market."

"Why is that?"

She snorted. "You *are* a dunderhead, Chert! Why do you think? The castle is surrounded by fairy folk, half the merchants won't send their ships here to Southmarch, and there's no work for the Funderlings. Surely in your time loitering around the guildhall you must have heard something of that?"

"Of course." He scratched his head. She was right: it wasn't as though there were no ordinary problems. "But Berkan Hood, the new lord constable, promised that he'd put two hundred of ours to work repairing the castle walls, so Cinnabar and the rest are saying not to worry."

"And what are they going to pay them with?" She had her shawl off now and was washing her hands vigorously in a bowl of water. "The Tollys are already spending money hand over fist trying to lure merchants to bring in food and drink for Southmarch, not to mention the ships they've had to buy and mercenary seamen they've had to hire, all to protect the harbor."

"You heard all this at the market?"

"Do you think we spend all day talking about vegetables and sewing?" She dried her hands off on her shapeless, oft-mended old dress and Chert felt a pang that his wife had nothing nicer to wear. "Honestly, you menfolk. You think you do it all yourselves, don't you?"

"Not for years, my good old woman." He laughed ruefully. "Not since I've had you around to keep me straightened out."

"Well, just go and talk to the boy before you disappear for the day. He's had a bad night and I have a hundred things to do if I'm going to make a meal out of these sad leavings."

Flint was sitting on the bed, his white-gold hair disarranged, his face distant and mournful.

"How are you, lad?"

"Well." But he didn't meet Chert's eye.

"I wonder if that's really true. Your mo . . . Opal says you had a bad night." He sat down beside the boy and patted his knee. "Did you not sleep well?"

"Didn't sleep."

"Why not?" He peered at the pale, almost translucent face. Flint looked as though he needed sun. It was a strange thought—he certainly couldn't remember ever thinking it about anyone else. Of course, most of the people he knew never even saw the sun if they could help it.

"Too noisy," the boy said. "Too many voices."

"Last night?" It was true that in the early part of the evening Cinnabar and some of the other Guildsmen had stopped by to talk about where Chert was going today, but they had been gone by the time the darklights came on. "Really? Well, we'll try to keep it more quiet."

"It's too crowded," Flint said. Before Chert could ask him to explain, he added: "I have bad dreams. Very bad."

"Like what?"

Flint shook his head slowly. "I don't know. Eyes, bright eyes, and someone holding me down." His chest heaved with a sob. "It hurts!"

"Come on, lad. Don't be feared. Things will get better, you've just had a rough time." Helplessly, Chert put his arm around him and felt the child's entire body shudder.

"But I want to go back to sleep! Nobody understands. They won't let me sleep! They keep calling me!"

"Lie down, then." He did his best, half helping, half forcing the child back into the bed. He pulled the blanket up to his chin. "Ssshhh. Go to sleep, now. Opal's just in the other room. I have to go out to work, but I'll be back later."

Flint miserably allowed himself to be stroked and soothed into a thin, restless slumber. Chert got up as quietly as he could, desperate not to wake him.

What have we done to that boy? he wondered. *What's wrong with him? Odd as he was before, he was always alert, lively. He seems only half alive since I found him down in the Mysteries.*

He didn't even have the heart to talk about it to Opal, who felt the boy's distraction and strangeness even more than he did: he only waved to her as he passed, tying on his tool belt.

"Vermilion Cinnabar had a message for you from her husband," Opal called.

Chert stopped in the doorway. "What's that?"

"She said to tell you that Chaven wants to see you again before you go upground."

He sighed. "Why not?"

The physician was waiting in the middle of the mirrored floor of the Guild's great hall. Several Funderlings were preparing the hall for the next meeting, politely avoiding him as he stood staring down, like children circling an absentminded father. For the first time Chert's own people looked small to him in their own great hall.

The physician didn't look up even after Chert coughed politely. "Chaven?" he said at last. "You wanted to speak to me?"

Startled, Chaven turned. "Oh, it's you! Sorry, so sorry, it's just . . . this place. I find it strangely . . . restful is not the right word, not quite. But it is one of the few places where my cares, they just . . . slip away . . ."

Chert had never felt the presence of the Lord of the Hot Wet Stone to be particularly restful, even in statue form. He looked up to the image of Kernios sunk deep in the ceiling, then down to the mirror-version below their feet. Being suspended, as it were, between *two* versions of the black-eyed, somber-faced earth god seemed even less soothing, especially when the mirroring rendered Chaven and himself as blobs with feet in the middle and heads at each end, suspended halfway between Heaven and the Pit. "I heard you wanted me."

Chaven dragged his attention away from the representation of the god. "Oh, yes. I just felt I should talk to you again about what you should say."

"Fracture and fissure, man," Chert cursed, "we've been over this a dozen times already! What more can there be to say?"

"I am sorry, but this is very important."

Chert sighed. "It would be different if I were actually going to pretend to know something I don't, but if he asks me something I don't know an answer for I'll just make important-sounding humming noises, then tell him I need to confer with my Funderling colleagues." He gave Chaven an annoyed look. "And then, yes, I'll come right to you and tell you, and find out what to say."

"Good, good. And what will you look for to know if it's my mirror?"

"A dark frame of cypress wood, with wings that open out. It is carved with pictures of eyes and hands."

"Yes, but if there's no frame, or if he's put a new one on it?"

Chert took a deep breath. *Patience,* he told himself. *He's been through a great deal.* But it was more than a little like dealing with a drunkard, someone forever trying to shake the last dribbles of mossbrew out of an empty jar. "The glass itself has a slight outward curve to it."

"Yes. Good!"

"May I go now? Before Okros decides to ask someone else to do it instead?"

"Will you write down anything you are unsure about? It will help me understand what Okros is trying to do. Do you promise?"

Chert said nothing, but tapped the slate hanging on a string around his neck. "Really, I must go now."

Worriedly repeating all that they had just discussed, Chaven followed him to the door but, to Chert's relief, went no farther, as if he did not want to travel far from the reassuring presence of the earth lord and the haven of the guildhall's great room.

Chert hadn't been out of Funderling Town for many, many days—was it almost a month?—and he was surprised by the obvious differences since the last time he'd been upground. The spirit of ragged camaraderie he'd seen everywhere in the castle had now just as obviously expired, overcome by weariness and fear of the unchanging siege conditions, the strange, suspended watchfulness that in some ways was worse than even a real and imminent danger of attack.

The faces bundled up in scarves and hoods were red with cold and very grim, even as he reached the Raven Gate and the vicinity of the royal residence itself, where at least the people did not yet have to worry about starving. Still, these comparatively well-fed courtiers had a wolfish look about them, too, as though even the most kindly and cheerful of them were spending a large part of their thoughts considering what they were going to do and to whom they were going to do it when things became really bad, when they would have to struggle to survive.

The castle itself looked different, too. The walls around the Inner Keep were built over with wooden hoardings and crawling with guards, the greens were full of animals (mostly pigs and sheep) the wells were guarded by soldiers, and there seemed to be twice as many folk as usual milling in the narrow roads and public squares. Still, when he showed the letter from Okros he received only cursory attention before being allowed through Raven's Gate, although he thought he heard a few of the guards mutter uncomplimentary things about Funderlings. That was certainly not the first time in Chert's life such a thing had ever happened, but he was a little surprised by the vehemence in their voices.

Well, bad times make bad neighbors, he reminded himself. *And there were always rumors that the king fed us—as though we were animals in a menagerie, instead of us earning our own way, which we always have. Just the kind of thing to make the big folk resentful when times are hard.*

It was disturbing to find that Okros had openly usurped Chaven's residence in the Observatory, but Chert supposed it made sense. In any case, he was not even supposed to know Chaven, so he certainly wasn't going to say anything about it.

A young, jug-eared acolyte in an Eastmarch robe opened the door and silently led him to the observatory itself, a high-ceilinged room with a sliding panel in the roof, permeated with the smell of damp. Okros rose from a table piled with books, brushing off his dark red smock. He was a slender man with a fringe of white hair and a pleasant, intelligent expression. It was hard to believe he was the villain Chaven believed him, even though Chert himself had heard Brother Okros talking to Hendon Tolly about Chaven's glass.

In any case, he would let discretion rule. He bowed. "I am Chert of the Blue Quartz. The Guild of Stone-Cutters sent me."

"Yes, you are expected. And you know much of mirrors?"

Chert spoke carefully. "I am of the Blue Quartz. We are part of the Crystal clan and a mirror is merely an object made from crystal or glass, so all Funderling mirror-work is overseen by us. And yes, I do know some few things. Whether that will be enough for your needs, my lord, we shall see."

Okros gave him an appraising look. "Very well. I will take you to it."

The scholar took a lantern from the tabletop and led Chert out of the high-ceilinged observatory and down a succession of corridors and stairways. Chert had been in Chaven's house before, of course, but not often, and he had little idea where they were now except that they were traveling downward. For a moment he became fearfully certain that the man was taking him to the secret door Chert himself had employed when Chaven lived here, that he knew exactly who Chert was and what had brought him here, but instead, when they had gone down several floors, the little physician opened a door off the hallway with a key and beckoned him inside. An object covered with a cloth stood in the middle of an otherwise empty table, like an oddly shaped corpse waiting burial—or resurrection.

Okros removed the cloth with careful fingers. The mirror was just as Chaven had described it, but Chert did his best to look at it as though he had never seen it or heard of it before. Carved hands, the fingers spread in different arrangements, alternated with crude but compelling eyes around the dark wood of the frame. The curve was there, too, just enough of a convexity to make the reflection slightly unstable to a moving observer: in fact, it was disturbing to look at it for more than a few moments.

"And what exactly did you wish to know, my lord?" Chert asked carefully. "It looks like an ordinary . . . that is, it looks as though it is . . . unbroken."

"Yes, I know!" For the first time, Chert could detect a hint of something strange under the physician's words. "It is . . . it does nothing."

"Nothing? I'm sorry, what . . . ?"

"Don't pretend you are ignorant, Funderling." Okros shook his head angrily, then calmed himself. "This is a scrying glass. Surely you and your people did not think I would send for help to deal with an ordinary mirror? It is an authentic scrying glass—a 'Tile,' as they are sometimes called—but it remains dead to me. Do you still pretend ignorance?"

Chert kept his eyes on the glass. The man was not just angry, he was frightened somehow. What could that mean? "I pretend nothing, Lord, and I am not ignorant. I just wished to hear what it was you wanted. Now, what more can you tell me?" He tried to remember Chaven's words. "Is it a problem of reflection or refraction?"

"Both." The physician seemed mollified. "The substance seems intact, as you see, but as an object it is inert. As a scrying glass, it is useless. I can make nothing of it."

"Can you tell me anything of where it comes from?"

Okros looked at him sharply. "No, I cannot. Why do you ask?"

"Because the literature of scrying glasses, and the unwritten lore as well, must be applied to that which is known, to help discover that which is unknown." He hoped he didn't sound too much like he was making things up (which he was): Chaven had told him a few facts and a name or two to drop when the occasion seemed to warrant, but there was no way of knowing ahead of time precisely what Okros would want to know. "Perhaps I could take it back to the Funderling Guild . . ."

"Are you mad?" Okros actually put his arms around the thing as if guarding a small, helpless child from a ravening wolf. "You will take nothing! This object is worth more than Funderling Town itself!" He stared at Chert, eyes narrowed to slits.

"Sorry, my lord. I only thought . . ."

"You will remember that it is an honor even being called to consult. I am the prince-regent's physician—the royal physician!—and I will not be trifled with."

Chert suddenly and for the first time felt frightened, not just of Okros himself—although the man could call the guards and have Chert locked in a dungeon in moments if he wished—but of his strange feverishness. It reminded him more than a little of the odd behavior he had seen from Chaven. What was it about this mirror that turned men into beasts?

"If anything," Okros said, "I should come and examine the library in Funderling Town. The Guild would make it available to me, of course."

Chert knew this would be a bad idea in many ways. "Of course, my lord. They would be honored. But most of the knowledge about subjects like these glasses cannot be found in books. Most of it is in the minds of our oldest men and women. Do you speak Funderling?"

Okros stared at him as though he were joking. "What do you mean, speak Funderling? Surely no one down there speaks anything but the common tongue of the March Kingdoms?"

"Oh, no, Brother Okros, sir. Many of our older folk have not left Funderling Town in years and years and they speak only the old tongue of our forefathers." Which was not entirely a lie, although the numbers who could only speak Old Funderling were tiny. "Why don't you let me go back to the Guild with your questions—and my observations too, of course—and see what answers I can bring back in a day or two. Surely for someone as busy as yourself, with all your responsibilities, that would be the best solution."

"Well, perhaps . . ."

"Let me just make a few notes." He rapidly sketched the mirror and its frame and made notations in the margin just as he would have while planning a particularly intricate scaffolding installation. When he had stalled as long as he could, he remembered something else Chaven had told him, which had made no sense but which he wanted Chert to discover. There had been some artful way he had wanted Chert to pose the question, but he couldn't remember, so he just asked bluntly. "Have you seen anything unusual in the mirror? Birds or animals?"

Okros looked at Chert as though he had suddenly sprouted wings or a tail himself. "No," he said at last, still staring. "No, I told you it was lifeless."

"Ah. Of course." Chert bowed, hung his slate around his neck, and backed toward the door. He no longer thought Okros quite as friendly and harmless as he first had. "Thank you for the honor of asking for us, my lord. I shall consult with my fellows in the Guild and return soon."

"Yes. Well, just do not wait too long."

Chert had his hood up against the cold, so even though she was twice his height he nearly walked into her when she stepped out of the shadows near the Raven's Gate. Startled, he stopped and looked up, but it took him a moment to recognize her—he had only seen her once, of course, and that had been well over a month ago.

"You're the one who came to my house," he said. She still had the same distracted look, like a sleepwalker. "You never told me your name."

"Willow," said the young woman. "But it does not matter. That was someone's name who is gone now, or has changed." She did not move on. Clearly, she wanted something, but Chert began to feel if he did not ask her she might never disclose it, that they would both remain standing here until night fell and then dawn came again.

"Do you need something?"

She shook her head. "Nothing you can give me."

Chert's patience, never his best feature, had been tested beyond belief this year, and it seemed the tests were far from over. "Then perhaps you will excuse me—my wife will be holding supper."

"I wish to speak to you about the one called Gil," she said.

Chert suddenly remembered. "Ah, of course. You were very attached to him, weren't you?" She didn't speak, but only watched him attentively. "I'm very sorry, but we were both captured by the fairy-soldiers. They let me go, but their queen, or their general, or whatever she was, sentenced Gil to death. He's dead. I'm sorry I could not do more for him."

She shook her head. "No. He is not dead."

He saw the look in her eyes. "Of course. His spirit lives on, no doubt. Now I must go. Again, I'm sorry for how things happened."

The young woman smiled, an almost ordinary thing, but it still had a quality of ineffable strangeness. "No, he is not dead. I hear his voice. He speaks to Lady Porcupine every day. She hates what he has to say, because he speaks with the king's voice."

"What are you talking about?"

"It does not matter. I only wished to tell you that I heard Gil speak of you just yesterday, or perhaps it was today." She shook her head, as though Chert must know how hard it was to remember when one last heard from dead people. "He said he wished he could tell you and your people that they are not safe beneath the castle. That soon the world will change, and that the door will open under Funderling Town and dead time will escape." She nodded as though she had performed some small trick with an acceptable level of skill. "I am going now."

She turned and walked away.

Chert stood in the lengthening shadows, feeling a chill crawl across his body that was out of all proportions even to the cold day.

31
The Dark-Eyed Girl

When the gods had fought for one hundred years, Pale Daughter was so dismayed that she resolved to go out and surrender to her father to end the war, but her husband Silvergleam, his brother, and sister would not let her go, fearing her death. But her cousin Trickster came to her in secret and piped her a sweet tune, telling he would help her to slip away from her husband's house. Trickster intended to keep her for himself, and would have, but a great storm came and he lost her in its howling discord. She lost herself as well, wandering a long time without knowing who she was.

In the battle Whitefire killed Thunder's son, Bull, and Thunder in his rage beat down and killed Silvergleam, husband of Pale Daughter, father of Crooked. Many died that day, and the music of all things was thereafter more somber, even unto this hour.

—from *One Hundred Considerations*
out of the Qar's *Book of Regret*

H E HAD BEEN FALLING for so long he could not remember what it was like *not* to fall, could not remember which direction was up, or even what having an up and down meant. The last thing he remembered was seeing the gates, the sign of the owl and pine tree, and then—as if those monstrous gates had swung open and a black wind had lifted him and carried him through—he had been tumbling in darkness like this, helpless as a sparrow in a thunderstorm.

Sister, he called, or tried to, *I'm falling. I'm lost . . .!* But she did not come, not even as a ghost of memory; they were separated by some gulf that even their blood tie could not bridge.

Sister. I'm dying . . . He could never have guessed that it would happen this way—that they would have no last farewell. But she must know how he loved her. She was the only thing in this corrupted world that mattered to him. He could take solace in that, anyway . . .

Who . . . are . . . you . . . ?

It came to him as a whisper—no, less than a whisper, it came like the sound of a flower unfolding on the far side of a meadow. Still, in the midst of such utter emptiness, it was a glorious sound, glad as trumpets.

Who's there? Is that you, Storm Lantern? But he knew that the fairy's words could never feel like that in his mind, each one as cool, gentle and precise as water dripping from a leaf after the rains had stopped. It was a woman speaking, he could feel it, but that still didn't seem quite right: the touch seemed even too light for that. And then he knew. It was the dark-haired girl, the one who had watched over his other dreams.

Who are you? he asked the emptiness. He was still falling, but the movement seemed different now, no longer plunging toward something but sailing outward. *Do I know you?*

Who am I? She was silent for a time, as if the question surprised her. *I . . . I don't know. Who are you?*

A silly question, he thought at first, but found he had no easy answer. *I have a name,* he insisted, *I just can't think of it right now.*

So do I, she told him, still no more than a ghostly voice. *And I can't think of mine, either. How strange . . . !*

Do you know where we are?

He could feel the negation even before he caught the word-thoughts. *No. Lost, I think. We're lost.* For the first time he recognized the sadness in her voice and knew he was not the only one who was afraid. He wanted to help her, although he could not help himself or even say what it was that troubled him. All he knew was that he was falling endlessly outward through nothing, and that it was a blessing beyond price to have someone to share it with.

I want to see you, he said suddenly. *Like before.*

Before?

You were watching me. That was you, wasn't it? Those things were chasing me, and the halls were on fire . . .

That was you. It was not a question, but almost a sweet note of satisfaction. *I was afraid for you.*

I want to see you.

But who are you? she demanded.

I don't know! When he grew angry her presence became fainter and that frightened him. Still, it was interesting to know he could still feel anger. When he had been falling alone, he had felt almost nothing. *I just know that I was by myself, and then you were here. I haven't felt . . .* It would have been almost impossible to explain in his waking life—in this wordless, directionless place it was far beyond impossible. *I haven't felt anyone in my heart since I lost her.* He could not summon the name, but he knew her, his sister, his twin soul, his other half.

The other was silent for a long moment. *You love her.*

I do. But there was a misunderstanding between them, a sort of cloud of confusion, and again the girl's presence became remote. *Don't go! I need to see you. I want to . . .* There was no word for what he wanted—there weren't even thoughts that could be strung together—but he wanted a reason to exist. He wanted a place to be, and to feel someone waiting for the thoughts in his head, so that he knew there was more to the universe the gods had made than simply a few whispers in endless darkness. *I want to . . .*

There is a place around us, she said suddenly. *I can almost see it.*

What do you mean?

Look! It's big, but it has walls. And there's . . . a road?

He could see it now, at least its faint lineaments. It was a space only slightly smaller than the endless dark through which they had been falling, and only a little more bright, but it had shape, it had boundaries. At the center of it he saw what she had called a road, an arching span of safety over an astonishing, terrifying dark nothing—a nothing even more profound than the void through which he had been falling. But this pit of blackness beneath the span was not simply *nothing,* it was a darkness that wanted to make everything else into a nothing, too. It existed, but its existence was a threat to all else. It was the raw stuff of *unbeing.*

No, that's not a road, he said as the one stripe of *something* slowly hardened into visibility. *It's a bridge.*

And then they were facing each other on the curving span, the boy and the girl, shifting and vague as objects seen through murky water. Neither of them were really children, but neither were they grown or anywhere close to it. They were raw, frightened, excited, and still new enough to the world that a thing like this made as much sense as anything else.

Her eyes were what held him, although he could not keep his stare fixed on them for more than a moment—everything here was inconstant, shifting and blurring as though he had exhausted his sight with hours of reading instead of just regaining it.

It wasn't the eyes themselves that fascinated him, although they were large and kind, brown like the eyes of some creature watching with caution from the forest depths. Rather it was the way her eyes looked at him and *saw* him. Even in this fit of madness (or whatever had swallowed him) the brown-eyed girl saw *him,* not what he said or what he seemed or what others imagined him to be. Perhaps it was only because they were in this place without names—perhaps she could have seen him here in no other way—but the way she looked at him felt like a welcoming campfire summoning a freezing, exhausted traveler. It felt like something that could save him.

Who are you? he asked again.

I told you, I don't know. Then she smiled, a surprising flash of amusement that transformed her solemn little face into something astounding. *I'm a dreamer, I suppose, or maybe I'm a dream. One of us is dreaming this, aren't we?* But that was a jest, he knew. She was no idle wisp of either his fancy or her own—she was strong and practical. He could feel it. *And who are you?*

A prisoner, he told her, and knew it was true. *An exile. A victim.*

Now for the first time he felt something other than kindness from her, a sour taste in her reply. *A victim? Who isn't? That isn't who you are, that's just what's happening to you.*

He was torn between his desire to feel her sweetness again and the need to explain just how badly life and the gods had treated him. The gods? They were trying to kill him!

You don't understand, he said. *It's different with me.* But he found that here on this bridge over Unbeing, this span that led away in either direction to unseen and unknowable ends, he couldn't explain why that was. *I'm . . . wrong. Crippled. Mad in the head.*

If you expect me to feel sorry for you because you dream of impossible places and people without names, she said, some of her sly humor creeping back, *then you'll have to try something else instead.*

He wanted to let himself enjoy her, but he could not. If he did—if he belittled his own miseries—how could he even exist? The only thing that made his suffering bearable was the knowledge that it also made him different—that he had been elected somehow for this pain. *But I didn't ask to be like this!* His despair rose up in a howl of fury. *I didn't want things to be this way! I don't have the strength for any more!*

What do you mean? Her amusement was gone—she was looking at him again, really looking. He would not recognize this blurry, occulted phantom even if he stood face-to-face with her, at least not by her features, but he would know the quality of attention she gave him anywhere, in any disguise.

I mean it's too much. One horror after another. The gods themselves . . .

The monstrousness of it all could not be explained. *I'm cursed, that's all. I'm not strong enough to live with it any longer. I thought I could— I've tried—but I can't.*

You don't mean that. It's a kind of . . . showing off.

I do mean it! I'd rather be dead. Dead, he might not see his beloved twin soul ever again—or this one either, this new friend in darkness—but at this moment he didn't care. He was tired of the burden.

You can't ever say that. Her thoughts were not plaintive but angry again. *We all die. What if we only get one chance to be alive?*

What if it's all pain?

Push against it. Escape it. Change it.

Easy to say. He was disgusted and furious, but suddenly terrified she would leave him alone on this bone-white span over nothing—no, worse than nothing.

No, it's not. And it's even harder to do, I know. But it's all you have.

What is?

This is. All of it. You have to fight.

Will you . . . will you come back to me if I do?

I don't know. A flash of sweetness in the nothing, a smile like a fluting of birdsong in the dark before sunrise. *I don't know how I found you, so I can't say if I'll ever find you again, dear friend. Who are you?*

I can't say—I'm not sure. But come back to me—please!

I'll try . . . but live!

And then the bridge, the pit, the girl, everything was gone, and Barrick Eddon was swimming slowly back up through the ordinary soundings of dream and sleep.

Ferras Vansen was relieved to see that the prince's miseries seemed to have eased a bit. Barrick was no longer making that terrible wheezing noise, and although he still lay stretched on the stone floor of their cell he seemed to be resting now instead of suffering. Vansen, who had tried to comfort the prince once and had been hit in the face by a flailing hand for his trouble, let out a breath.

Apparently he would live, although Vansen was still not entirely certain what had sickened him so badly. It seemed to be something to do with . . .

So what was that thing? he demanded of Gyir. *That . . . door. You haven't told me anything since we came back into our own heads except "Grab the boy's legs" when he was thrashing on the floor. Why do you keep silent?*

Because I am trying to understand. Gyir's thoughts traveled slowly as summer clouds. *What we saw seemed to have only one explanation and I do not trust such seemings. But the more I think, the more I come back again and again to the same conclusion.*

What conclusion? Vansen looked to the prince, who had sat up, but was hunched over like a small child with a bellyache. *I am only a soldier—I know nothing of gods, fairies, magic. What is happening here?*

You saw the pine tree and the owl, Gyir said. *They are Black Earth's symbols. What else could we have seen except the fearful gate of Immon, as you would name him—the way into the palace of Immon's master, bleak Kernios himself?*

It was not the familiar Trigonate god Vansen saw in his mind's eye now, not a statue or a painting on a church wall, but a memory from his early life in the dales—whispers of the dark man with his mask and his heavy gloves, who would grab wicked children (or maybe even good ones if he caught them alone) and drag them down beneath the ground.

Kernios . . . the god of the dead? Are you telling me that we are standing on top of the entrance to his palace? It was one thing to meet even a terrifying giant like Jikuyin and be told he was a demigod, another thing to be told that one of the all-powerful Trigon made his home just beneath their feet in this very spot, the dark brother whose frowning eyes had been on Ferras Vansen since he had drawn breath, the shadow that had haunted his dreams as long as he could remember. *But how could that be? Why would it be here?*

It could be anywhere. It simply happens to be here. Or a doorway does, at least. Where other doorways are, who can say . . . ?

But what does that mean? If the gate's here, the whole palace has to be here, too, doesn't it? Buried down there in the stone?

Gyir shook his head. There was a small furrow between his eyes that showed his worry, the only sign of recognizable feelings on that bleak expanse. *The ways of the gods, their dwellings and habits, are not like ours. They walk different roads. They live in different fields, some of which we cannot even tread. One side of a doorway is not always in the same place or even time as what is on the other side.* The fairy lifted both hands, made a sign with them that spoke first of connection, then separation. *It is confusing,* he admitted.

Vansen thought about his own experiences trying to find his way around behind the Shadowline, then tried to imagine something that would confuse even creatures like Gyir who had been born and raised in these shifting, unfixed lands. *But why are they digging it out?* he asked. *The giant and that gray man—why would they want to go near it?* Ferras Vansen had a sudden, terrifying thought. *Is . . . Kernios on the other side of that? Waiting?*

No, he is gone, Gyir said. *All the gods are gone, Perin Shatterhand and Kernios and Immon the Black Pig—at least all those gods whose names I know. Banished to the lands of sleep.*

"Then why are they digging?" In his agitation Vansen spoke aloud. After so much time, the croaking sound of his own voice irritated him. "For treasure?"

"Because they are mad," grunted Barrick, rolling over. "The Qar are mad, but the gods and demigods are even more so. This whole land is cracked and deathly." The prince couldn't yet sit up straight, but he was doing his best to hide his discomfort, and Vansen couldn't help admiring him for it.

Gyir must have said something to him then, because there was a pause before the prince said aloud, "Because I can't. It hurts my head too much. I'll just have to be careful what I say. Can you talk to both of us at the same time?"

I will try, Gyir said. *You think us all mad, man-child? I wish it were only so, then our problems might not be so great. You speak from pain, because the essence of the gods hurts you, even when they are absent. In a way, you seem much like me. We have both felt the power of this place, only in different ways.*

"What are you talking about?" Barrick asked.

You are sensitive, it seems, as I was and as all the Encauled would be—sensitive to the voice of Jikuyin, sensitive to the Pig's gate and to the throne room of Black Earth beyond. But it is a little strange, almost as if . . . as if . . . Gyir closed his eyes for a moment, thinking. *No,* he told them, opening his eyes again. *It matters not. Listen, though, and I will tell you some things that do matter.* The fairy settled himself on the stone floor of the cell and briefly closed his red eyes in thought.

When Kernios was driven out, he told them at last, *he left behind everything that was material, all that was of flesh or the world . . .*

Vansen was puzzled, uncertain if he had understood Gyir correctly. *Driven out?*

"Explain," Barrick said. "I'm tired of guessing."

Yes, driven out. He and the other gods were banished from these lands and cast into the realm of sleep and forgetting.

"Banished by who?"

I will try to explain all, but you two must not interrupt me with questions—especially you, Prince Impatience, since you are speaking aloud so anyone can hear. Gyir's anger flashed like lightning through his thoughts. *We are fortunate—I sense there is no one near who can hear what I say in your heads or who speaks your mortal tongue—but do not stretch your luck. We are in terrible, terrible danger—worse even than I had feared.* The fairy raised his fingers to his temples as though his head pained him. *Please, let me begin where I need to begin.* Even to Vansen, still not entirely familiar with this way of conversing, it was impossible to mistake the desperation in Gyir's every thought.

Prince Barrick raised his hand in surrender or permission.

First you must understand something of my own history. I am not merely a warrior. In fact, it is the most unlikely thing I could have become. Those of my folk who are most like your people in shape—for it was a shape we all shared, once—are called "the High Folk," not because looking like a sunlander is comely, but because it is the old way of seeming. But even some of the High Ones are so different from your kind as to be almost unrecognizable, either born dissimilar or because they can change their outward appearance. Some of them have been figures of terror to your kind for thousands of years. Others, like the Guild of Elementals, take earthly shapes only when it suits them, like the gods themselves.

And then there are folk like me, who although we come from the great families of power that have kept the most of the old seeming, yet we ourselves are born different—freakish even among our varied folk. I am one such—one of the Encauled, as those of my malady are named. We are born with this tissue of flesh over our faces that we must wear all our lives, but we are granted other gifts—senses that are stronger than most, an understanding that allows us to find our way when even the powerful might become lost. Among the People, we Encauled often become the guides, the searchers, those who explore different ways. Some of us take service in the Deep Library in the House of the People, which is our great city and capital. The Library is where we speak with the spirits of those who have left their flesh, as well as with some who have never worn flesh. Serving the Library is an exacting and noble pursuit.

That would likely have been my calling, but my parents fell afoul of one of the court rivalries and my father was killed. My mother was driven out of the House of the People by a faction who held strong allegiance to King Ynnir—although, to be fair, they did not always act as the king would have wished, nor could he always control them. My mother and I wandered for years, taking service at last with Yasammez—Lady Porcupine, the great iconoclast, the woman who belongs to no one but herself. In her house in the Wanderwind Mountains I grew, and when my mother at last became weary of the many defeats and disappointments of her life and surrendered to death, I was raised in Yasammez's martial service, my gifts used not for contemplation but for warfare on behalf of the woman who had taken me in and raised me almost as her own.

Because of her, Jikuyin is not the first of the demigods I have met. When I was barely old enough to carry a sword I fought with my mistress at Dawnwood against Barumbanogatir, a fearsome bastard of old Twilight— the one you sunlanders call Sveros the Evening Sky. Giant Barumbanogatir killed three hundred of my lady's finest warriors before she brought him down at last with a spear through his great shield and into his throat. After that we fought other wars for the People, against the Dreamless and the treacherous mountain Drows, struggling and dying to keep our people safe even as the people themselves shunned us—even as all but Queen Saqri treated us like vicious animals to be tied at the edge of camp but never to be allowed any closer.

You see, only Saqri of the Ancient Song recognized us for what we were—the sharp sword in the People's sheath, which even when it is not drawn gives others pause, makes them think and weigh their lusts against their fears. Yasammez is of the queen's own family, and Saqri honored her as one of the oldest and purest of the High Ones still living. Queen Saqri knew that my mistress had been given in long life and in courage what the king and queen and their ancestors had surrendered in return for the gift of the Fireflower, the boon of the last god to our ruling family.

A boon that has now become a curse . . .

Ferras Vansen could feel thousands of years of confusing, dangerous history swirling like deep black waters just behind the fairy's words. He wanted to ask what the Fireflower was, but Gyir for once was speaking so openly that Vansen feared to distract him.

My lady Yasammez had been fighting for the People long centuries before ever I was born. At the dreadful, infamous battle of Shivering Plain, during one of the last of the wars of the gods, she destroyed the earthly form of Urekh, no god's bastard but a true god himself, who wore the pelt of a magical wolf as his invulnerable armor. For that alone she would be remembered and celebrated until time's candle gutters out, but it is not why I speak of that battle. That was the same day of which I told you before, where Jikuyin delayed his coming, hoping to manipulate the results to his own advantage, and instead was struck down by Kernios himself, blinded and nearly killed.

Vansen remembered the story of Jukuyin riding late onto the field with his Widowmakers, then realizing he had bought more trouble than he could afford, since Perin, Kernios, and the gods called the Surazemai were winning and the rest of the gods and Qar were already in flight. *Kernios hurt him, you said.*

Indeed. Black Earth wounded Jikuyin so gravely that he would never heal. But now, for some reason, the demigod is digging his way into the very throne room of Black Earth—the one your kind call Kernios.

So what is Jikuyin going to do?

Make right what was done to him, somehow. Perhaps the god's mighty spear Earthstar lies behind that gate, or perhaps Jikuyin seeks a more subtle prize. But if he does manage to open that doorway into Kernios' earthly realm, I can feel that Jikuyin will gain in power—gain immeasurably. His long-ago defeat cast him down into weakness—what you see before you is scarcely a shadow of what he was on the day he rode out onto Shivering Plain—but he is one of the last living bastards of the true gods. If he gains that strength back he will be the most powerful thing that walks on the green world.

But we can't do anything to stop him, Vansen said. *Can we?*

I fear we must, said Gyir.

Are you telling me it is up to us to defend all the world? Vansen turned to Barrick to see if the boy understood Gyir's riddling words, but the prince only stared back at him balefully, still struggling for breath.

Of course—but also to save our own lives. Great magicks—the oldest, most powerful magicks—need blood and essences—what your kind call the souls of people or animals—to succeed. They need sacrifices. The word came like the tip of a dagger, cold and sharp, almost painless at first. *Especially the sacrifice of those who are themselves powerful in some way.*

What are you talking about? But Vansen had already guessed.

I suspect now that we have not been worked to death like the other poor creatures poisoned by the gateway to the gods' realm because Jikuyin needs one of us—most likely me, since I am of the Encauled—or perhaps even all of us to unlock the way into Kernios' throne room. He needs our blood. He needs our souls.

One thing you had to say for Ferras Vansen, Barrick decided. The guard captain never stopped . . . trying. If his stolid normality and his rude health had not already been sufficient reasons to hate him, then his relentless willingness to keep pushing and fighting—as if life were a game and there would be some ultimate tally, some adding-up of accounts—would have more than sufficed. Barrick had always thought optimism was another name for stupidity.

But the dark-eyed girl would admire him, he realized with a pang.

"So what do we do?" Vansen asked Gyir quietly, speaking aloud so the prince could hear. The man was also thoughtful. Barrick wanted to hit him with something. "Surely we cannot simply wait for them to . . . to burn us on some barbarous altar."

"You might want to consider the small matter of a mad demigod and all the demons and beasts who serve him and who would happily tear us to shreds," Barrick pointed out with more pleasure than one would normally expect to accompany such a sentence. He was tempted to help Gyir and the soldier anyway, just so they could discover the futility of all such scheming. He supposed it wasn't entirely their fault. They had not felt, as he had, the true strength of this place, the horrific, overwhelming power that remained in Greatdeeps even if the god himself was gone—if he *was* truly gone. Whatever made Barrick sensitive also clearly made him wise: he alone seemed to understand the pointlessness of all this discussion.

But would *she* think it was pointless? Barrick knew she wouldn't, and that made him feel ashamed again. *Shame or certain death,* he thought —*what splendid choices I am always given.*

Of course, said Gyir. *We would be fools if we thought our chances anything but bad. However, we have no choice. As I told you, I have something here which must be carried to the House of the People at any cost, so we must resist Jikuyin and his plans.*

"It's all very well to talk," Barrick said. "But what can actually be done? What hope do we have?"

There must be no more talking in spoken words, Gyir told him, *even if it causes you pain. I will speak to both of you, and I will translate what each of you say to me, back and forth. It will be slow, but even though I do not feel anyone spying on us, if we are going to talk about what we might do, I can no longer risk being wrong.*

Very well, Barrick said. *But what point is there in talking about fighting Jikuyin, anyway? He's a giant—a kind of god!*

Gyir slowly nodded. *Pointless? Likely. It will take preparation and luck, and even so we will probably gain nothing but a violent death—but at least the death will be of our own choosing, and that is worth more than a little. However, first I must find the serpentine, and think of a way to lay my hands on it.*

The what? Barrick did not recognize the idea that went with the snaky word–picture—a trail of fire, a sudden expansion like a pig's bladder too full of air. *What do you mean?*

Gyir paused for a moment as if listening. *I spoke of it before. The burning black sand, the Fire of Kupilas. Ah, Ferras Vansen reminds me that your people call it "gun-flour."*

Gun-flour? How would we get our hands on such stuff, locked in this cell? demanded Barrick. *Might as well ask for a bombard or a troop of musketeers while we're at it—we won't get any of them.*

They are using the swift-burning serpentine in the earth below us every day, Gyir told him. *They pack it into the cracks and speed their digging that way, by smashing apart the stones. It is here in Greatdeeps, somewhere. We have only to find it, and steal some.*

And then fly away like birds, said Barrick. *How will we do any of those things? We are prisoners, don't you realize? Prisoners!*

Gyir shook his head. *No, child. You are only a prisoner when you surrender.*

32

Remembering Simmikin

The renegade gods Zmeos the Horned One and Zuriyal the Merciless (who was his sister and wife) were banished to the same Unbeing which had swallowed Sveros, father of all, and for a while peace reigned on heavenly Xandos. Mesiya, the wife of Kernios, left him to shepherd the moon in the place of dead Khors, and Kernios generously took Zoria to be his wife, caring little what dishonor she had suffered.

—from *The Beginnings of Things*
The Book of the Trigon

I T WAS ODD, BRIONY REFLECTED, how much traveling with a troop of players was like going on a royal progress. In each town you stopped for a night and entertained the locals to keep them sweet, pretending as though you had never been in a more delightful place until they were safely behind you, then complaining about the take and the poor quality of local food and lodgings.

The main difference between this journey and her father's occasional jaunts through the March Kingdoms was that as part of the king's progress you stood a smaller chance of having stale vegetables thrown at you if the local citizens didn't like the way you spoke your piece. That, and the royal faction brought along enough armed guards that no one cheated anyone too obviously.

Tonight, this thought occurred to her with some force. Although the hour was long past midnight, instead of sharing a comfortable hayloft or even a spare tavern room, they were making their way along a rutted roadway through southernmost Kertewall in a drenching rain. It had turned out that the keeper of Hallia Fair's biggest tavern, which they had just left, was also the brother of the local reeve, and when he had claimed that the Makewell troop had cheated him on the takings from the night's performance—although Pedder Makewell's sister Estir swore it was the other way around—they got no support from the reeve and his men, and in fact were stripped of an even larger pile of coin than the innkeeper had claimed in the first place. Thus, here they were, poor and hungry again despite an evening's hard work, soaking wet in the middle of the night as they trudged off in search of a town more congenial to the playmaking arts.

Briony was walking in the cold rain because the giant Dowan Birch was unwell and she had given him her place in the wagon. She did not mind doing so—he was a kind person, and even when he wasn't ill walking made his oversized feet ache—but she wished this adventure could have begun in a friendlier month of the year, like Heptamene or Oktamene, with their bonny, balmy nights.

"Zoria, give me strength," she murmured under her breath.

Finn Teodoros lifted the shutter and leaned his head out the tiny window of the wagon. "How are you faring, young Tim?" It amused the poet to call her by her boy's name, and he did so as often as possible.

"Miserable. Miserable and wet."

"Ah, well. The price we must pay for the gifts the gods grant us."

"What gifts are those?"

"Art. Freedom. Masculine virtue. Those sorts of things."

Pleased with himself beyond any reason, the fat playwright pulled the shutter down just before she could hit him with a gob of mud.

In this most extraordinary of times, traveling with the players had begun to seem almost ordinary. It had been almost half a month since Briony had come upon them, and possibly longer—it was hard to keep track without the machineries of court etiquette to remind her of things like what day it was. Eimene, the year's first month, had become Dimene, although it was hard to tell the difference: there had been little snow in this dark, muddy year, which was a small blessing, but the rains continued to fall and the wind continued to blow, frigid and unkind. Despite all that had happened since Orphanstide, Briony was not used to living out of doors and doubted she ever would be.

They had made their way roughly south, following the Great Kertish Road along the Silverside border, back and forth across the edge of Kertewall, stopping in every town big enough to have a place to perform and enough money in the citizen's pockets to make it worthwhile. That said, on every stop some people paid with vegetables or other foodstuffs, and in many of the smaller villages there were no coins at all in the box at the end of the night, but a few small loaves set on Estir Makewell's wooden trunk (which served as the company's turnstile gate) along with enough dried peas and parsnips to provide the players with a meal of soup and bread after they had finished performing. Although the spiritual instruction of *The Orphan Boy in Heaven* was popular, and scenes from the *Theomachy* (the war of Perin and his brothers against the bad, old gods) were always a favorite, what the villagers liked best were the violent history plays, especially *The Bandit-King of Torvio* and Hewney's infamous *Xarpedon,* where Pedder Makewell always provided such a monstrous, entertaining death for the title character. Briony, who had seen too much of the true heart's essence of late, was still not entirely comfortable with watching Makewell or Nevin Hewney staggering about spouting pig's blood from a hidden bladder, but the spectators could not seem to get enough of it. Although they reacted with anger and outrage over the death of a hero or an innocent, especially if it was well-staged, they yelped with glee when the wicked, horned god Zmeos was pierced with Kernios' spear, and they laughed uproariously as Milios the Bandit-King coughed out his life after having been mauled by a bear, moaning, "What claws! What foul, treacherous claws!"

The rainswept roads of Kertewall and southern Silverside were surprisingly busy, with peddlers' carts bumping in the rutted tracks and unbound peasants, whole families or even small companies, heading south to seek work for the coming spring. Briony, who had long since recovered from wounds and burns got in Dan-Mozan's house, and from her worst starving days lost in the forest, was feeling stronger and healthier than she had in a long time. For one thing, the pleasure of getting up each day and putting on boy's clothes did not dim, although she could have wished them a deal cleaner and less lousy. It was not that she loved the clothes themselves or wished to be a boy, although she had always envied her brothers their ease of movement and expression, but she mightily loved the freedom of wearing nothing more confining than a loose tunic and rough hose. She could stand, sit, bend over, and on those few occasions where she was allowed to, even ride the company's hard-working horse without having to give thought to propriety or practicality. Why had no one back in Southmarch been able to understand that?

Thinking of the old days at Southmarch and the almost daily battle with Rose and Moina over what she should wear made her feel homesick, but although she missed the two girls very much, not to mention Merolanna, Chaven, and many others, it was as nothing compared to how she ached every time she thought of Barrick.

Had she really seen him in Idite's looking glass, or had it just been her pained heart creating a phantom of what it wished to see? What had the demigoddess Lisiya meant when she had said, "There are stranger things afoot with you and your brother than even I can guess"? That it hadn't just been a dream or Briony's feverish imagination, but somehow the truth? But Briony knew she was no Onirai—the gods chose their oracles early in life. In any case, the Barrick she saw had been a prisoner—shackled and miserable. It was almost better to think she had not truly seen him, even though that vision proved him alive, than to think of him so wretched, so . . . alone.

That was the nub of it, of course: she and her brother were both alone, and in a way that only twins could be, who had scarcely been separated their entire lives before this, and certainly never in such fearful conditions. If it was a true vision, had he seen her too? Did he mourn for her as she did for him, or was he still such a prisoner of anger and discomfort that he spared hardly a thought for his loving sister?

And what, she suddenly thought, *has happened to Ferras Vansen, charged with my brother's safety?* She had to fight through a flare of anger at the thought he had let her poor, crippled brother be captured. After all, who was to say that the guard captain had not saved Barrick from something worse? Or that he hadn't given up his own life trying to protect the prince?

That last thought brought a shockingly powerful pang of remorse—even of fear: Vansen dead and her brother alone? She could not in that moment say which would be the worse result.

I must pray for them, she told herself. She saw Vansen in her mind's eye, tall but not overbearing, his hair the color of a walnut husk, his face either carefully expressionless or open and wounded like that of a puzzled child's. Who was he to stay in her thoughts so? Others far more important were also lost, like her brother and father, and Shaso and Kendrick were dead. Why should she think of Vansen? He was a guardsman, a nobody—a failure, to be absolutely fair, since he had lost half his troop or more the first time he had been given a responsibility. What female weakness or pity or even—the Three defend her from her own foolishness!—desire had made her give him a second chance, she wondered, and especially with the care of the most precious thing she could have given him to protect?

She pushed all thoughts of Vansen out of her mind, tried to concentrate on her brother, to make sense out of the mysterious mirror-vision. How had it come to her? If Lisiya was alive, was some other god watching over them too? Had Erivor, their house's patron, granted her the vision for some reason she was too blind to understand?

Great lord of the sea, help your foolish daughter! Zoria, lend me your wisdom for a little while!

Her heart sank again to think of her brother lost in some foreign place. He had always been like a hermit crab, the claws of his anger no real threat to others at all. Only his shell protected him, because without it he was too soft to live, too frightened to keep the world at bay.

One year—they had both been, what, nine or ten?—their father had allowed the Master of Hounds to give them a puppy to be their own, a beautiful black hound. Barrick had wanted to name him Immon, but Briony had refused. She had been very religious then and had not used even the mildest curses, not even silently to herself. Barrick had always laughed at her, calling her "the Blessed Briony," but she had been firm. They were certainly not going to name him after the powerful god of burial, the Earthfather's gate-keeper—that would be blasphemy. She named the puppy Simargil instead, after the faithful dog of Volios (although she toyed with sacrilege herself by generally referring to him as "Simmikin") and except for the ordinary high spirits and growling, nipping play of a young male dog he had been an exceptionally sweet animal. Briony had been as attached to him as if he had been a baby brother. She had been shocked, then, when Barrick refused to play with him, saying that he was vicious and evil.

Being who she was, Briony would not let her brother rest until she had forced him to join her in playing with the dog—or at least being in the same room with the animal, since at first Barrick hung back in the doorway while Briony scratched Simargil's stomach and engaged him in playful, mock-fights, the dog growling in delight and throwing himself from side to side as he struggled to catch up with Briony's moving hand.

When she at last convinced Barrick to come forward, she quickly saw the problem. He approached the dog like someone entering a wolf's den. Simargil was already on his guard, watching Barrick not as he had watched Briony, with the bright gaze of a friend waiting to see what new fun would come, but with the narrowed eyes of someone who expected to be cheated or worse.

"Just stroke him gently," she said. "Reach out and scratch his head—he likes that. Don't you, Simmikin? Don't you, my Simmikin?"

The dog looked to Briony, white showing at the corners of his eyes as he struggled to keep watch on Barrick, too. If he had spoken to her, told her out loud that he was confused by this sudden change of mood, the animal could not have more clearly let her know what he felt.

Barrick's hand moved toward the dog's face as though toward a hornet's nest. When Simargil let out a low growl, Barrick snatched it back, making the dog lunge. Briony caught his collar.

"Do you see?" Barrick said.

It was her brother, not the dog. Something about him, perhaps only his mistrust, but maybe some scent of fear, had the dog's hackles up. Still, Briony could not believe that her beloved Simmikin could ever do anything really bad—not with her right here on the floor beside him. "Stroke him again. I'll hold his head. He just needs to get to know you."

"He has known me since he was born, and each day he hates me worse."

"Hush! That's not true, redling. Just let him smell your hand and don't yank it away just because he growls."

"Oh, should I let him bite it off?" He scowled. "It's not as though I have one to spare like most folk."

Briony rolled her eyes. She felt sorry about her brother's terrible injury, of course, and would have done anything to spare him the pain it brought him every day, but she was not going to let it be an excuse to treat him like a child half his age. "Stop sniveling. Put your hand out."

His scowl deepened but he did as he was told. Simargil

growled, but only for a moment, and Barrick actually managed to touch his head. Briony should have known that the dog's sudden silence was a bad sign rather than good, but she was too pleased with her own peacemaking activities between her favorite animal and her beloved twin to pay the sort of attention she should have. As Barrick gave the animal a tentative touch on the head, letting his fingers slip down near Simargil's throat, Briony let go of the collar to stroke the dog's chest. The dog's ears went back and he snarled, a high sound almost like a yelp of fear, and snapped at Barrick's right hand, getting his sharp teeth into the meat behind the knuckles. Barrick shrieked and leaped back. For a moment, the dog hung on, but Barrick hit him on the snout hard enough to make him whimper and let go.

An instant passed, the dog's ears still back, Barrick staring at the beast as though he had never seen anything worse in his life. Her brother's face was bone-white, his eyes wide in horror. Then blood came flooding back into his features like waves rushing onto a muddy strand, a demon-mask of red that almost blurred into the roots of his hair, as though his entire head had caught fire. He snatched up one of Briony's bows from where it leaned against the wall and brought it whistling down so fast she could not even move as the end of the staff hissed past her face. He beat at the dog until the bow cracked and the animal scrambled snarling and whining onto the floor, then tried to retreat under Briony's bed, snapping at the bloody weals on its own back as Barrick continued to belabor its hindquarters. Shrieking, she grabbed her brother's arm, and was splattered by blood that might have been from his hand or the dog's tattered back, or both.

At last, with the dog wedged so far under the edge of the bed that only its feet could be seen, Barrick had thrown down the splintered bow and run out, sobbing and cursing the gods.

If it had been anyone else but her brother, Briony would not have understood now why she missed him with such a painful yearning. Simargil would not have understood: the dog had limped thereafter, and used to lay himself down on the floor at the first sound of a raised voice. Although her brother never touched him again, he would also dart out of any room some time before Barrick arrived, which often made it easy to track the prince: wherever black Simargil was moving hurriedly, she had only to retrace the dog's steps to find Barrick.

If it had been anyone else, Briony would have cursed them as a bully and a coward and that would have been the end of it—an enemy forever. No one else convicted of such crimes in her private court could expect to have the sentence of her disgust commuted. But she knew her twin too well, had known even at that tender age that all his worst angers were the spawn of his fears, those night terrors that followed him around in the way that Simargil, before he limped, had followed Briony herself.

Barrick *was* monstrous sometimes, but she ached for him. No one but Briony knew the sweetness that lay behind that sour, even cruel mask he showed the world. Since their mother had died, only she had held him in the night, when he woke crying and uncertain where he was or even who he was. Only she had heard him say she was his very heart, that without her he would die. And how he feared that when he did die his soul would wander homeless forever, because of his blasphemous thoughts and his stiff neck which would not bend even to Heaven, as Father Timoid always said of him.

"My black thorn bush," their father had often called Barrick, alluding to the colors the boy had worn ever since he was old enough to choose his own clothing. "Fit to lash the fiercest penitent's back," Olin had gently mocked.

Had her father always known the curse he had passed on to his younger son? It was painful to think about it—not the thing itself, their shared ailment, although that was terrible enough, but the fact that her twin and her beloved father had conspired to keep this thing secret from her. It made all Briony's other memories seem suspect or outright false. At best they felt shallow now, as though her entire childhood, her life, had been nothing more than something devised by her family to keep her busy while the real matters of importance were being settled.

Each thought of her lost brother and father carried enough pain that the gods would have forgiven her for trying never to think of either of them again. And yet, of course, she did think of them, and suffered anew when she did so, which was at least once in almost every hour of every single day.

As they reached the lake lands near the Syannese border the road wound between the fens and across the ridges of the tiny principality of Tyrosbridge, and Makewell's Men went several days without encountering a town or even a village large enough to be worth mounting a performance. They were short of food and drink, so, on a large farmstead just inside the border of Syan they earned themselves a few meals and a few nights' dry lodging by helping the landowner to repair his old lambing pen and sheepfold and to build a new lambing house and several new walls around his pasture land as well. The work of carrying and stacking stones was hard, the day cold and wet, but the company was good, and to Briony's surprise she found herself feeling almost happy.

But what kind of life is this when our family's throne has been stolen? Up to my knees in mud like a peasant, hands red and sore, struggling in the rain to prop up a stone wall, doing nothing to save my family or get revenge on the Tollys. Still, they had reached Syan, the first of her destinations, and she had to admit it was a relief to deal with only what stood just in front of her, to think about nothing but the action of the moment. Most of the people of her kingdom worked this hard every day, she realized. No wonder they flocked to see the players. And no wonder they grew restive in hard times, when their lives were already so hard! If she ever regained her throne she would have all her courtiers join her in building sheepfolds in the dampest, most chill pasture she could find.

She laughed out loud, startling huge, kind Dowan Birch.

"Blood of the Three, boy!" he swore. "I thought I dropped a stone on you and crushed you, a noise like that."

"I'll try to find a different way to laugh when I've been crushed, so you'll know," she said.

"Hark to him," Birch called to Feival, the principal boy. "Our Tim has a tongue as sharp as Hewney's."

"Let us hope for the child's sake his tongue has not been in as many foul spots as Master Nevin's has," said Feival tartly. "Nor uttered half so many blasphemies."

"Did the child live six lifetimes," Hewney shouted, "he could not curse as much in all of them together as I do each morning when I wake up with my head and bladder both swollen misery-full of last night's ale and realize I am still a part of this wretched troop of thieves, blockheads, and he-whores."

"He-whore? He-whore? Do I hear an ass braying?" Finn Teodoros, who with the excuse of his age and portly figure, seemed to spend more time resting than working, pushed himself away from the wall. "Ah, no, it is only our beloved Nevin kicking at the door of his stall again. But were we to throw the door open, would he run away or fling himself at our feet and beg to be put back in harness?"

"It is an inexact metaphor," Hewney grumped. "No one keeps an ass in a stall. Unless he is so rich that he is able to act the ass himself."

"Besides," said Feival, "no one will ever get a harness on Hewney until he's dead, which will be too late to get any good out of him."

"Unless someday a man is needed who can drink a river of ale dry and save a city, as Hiliometes drained the flood," said Pedder Makewell.

"Too much talking, not enough working," his sister complained. "The sooner we finish, the sooner we can go claim our meal and some dry lodgings."

"Which will be a stable," Feival said. "Leaving none happy but our lead donkey, Master Hee-haw Hewney."

"Quiet, you, or you will find out what a kick truly is," Hewney said, glowering.

Briony worked on, amused and, for the moment, cold but content.

★

"Here," she said to the red-faced young player Pilney. "Try again. Remember, this stick is a sword now, not a stick. You don't beat someone with it, you use it as an extension of your arm." She scraped an empty place in the straw to make better footing, then lifted her own stick. "And if you're going to hack at someone like that, they're going to do *this*." She flicked his weapon aside, sidestepped his crude charge, and poked him in the ribs.

"Where did you learn that?" he asked, breathless.

"My . . . my old master. He was gifted at swordplay."

"Gather around me, children," Finn Teodoros called. "You may beat each other to death later."

Most of the company was already seated in the comfortable straw of the large stable, quite willing to ignore the smell of the horses and cows, since the presence of so many animals kept the place as warm as a fire would have.

"I have been thinking," said Teodoros, "that we will be in Tessis in less than a tennight, and if we are to impress the Syannese in that venerable capitol, we will have to show them something new. They have enough players of their own, after all, and the audiences are a hardened lot. Tessis has more theaters east of the river than exist in all the north of Eion put together. So we must bring them a spectacle."

"My *Karal* is spectacle enough," growled Hewney. "Even Makewell cannot help but make a royal impression in it."

"Never have a drunkard's words had such fair speaking before," Makewell said. "I refer to my playing of Hewney's work, of course. But he is right—the Tessians love *The Death of Karal,* since it is their own beloved king whose life we play. And we have other historicals and a comedy that we can give them."

"Yes, they loved *Karal* when we brought it to them four years ago," Teodoros agreed. "And it has remained in good enough favor that several Tessian companies have mounted it, too. But that does not mean the groundlings will come to see it again."

"Even with the playwright himself upon the stage?" Hewney was so outraged that he spilled some of his ale on his sleeve, which he then lifted to his mouth and sucked dry.

"What are you saying, Finn?" Estir Makewell demanded. "That we must buy some Tessian court play, some bit of froth done up for the Revels? We cannot afford it. We shall barely be able to feed ourselves until we get to Tessis, even with the money we had from . . ." She trailed off as Teodoros gave her a harsh look.

"Less speaking, more listening," he growled. Something had just happened, although Briony could not recognize what it was. "A loose tongue is an unbecoming ornament to anyone, but especially to a woman. I do not speak of buying anything. I have written a play—you have all heard it. *Zoria, Tragedy of a Virgin Goddess* is its name."

"Heard it?" Makewell put his hand on Feival Ulosian's knee, but the boy removed it. "We have rehearsed it for most of a year, and even performed it a few times in Silverside. What is new about that?"

"If nothing else, it would be new to the Tessians," Teodoros said with an air of great patience. "But I have changed it—rewritten much of the play. Also, I have made a larger part for you, Pedder, as great Perin, and for you, Hewney, as the fearsome dark god Zmeos, despoiler of a thousand maidenheads." He smiled. "I know it will test you to play so against your own character, but I feel certain you will give it your best."

"Sounds like rubbish," said Hewney. "But if it's good rubbish, it won't chap me to mount it in Tessis."

"And I suppose you feel certain that I will let you clap a hundredweight of new speeches on me as the beleaguered virgin?" said young Feival. "I won't have it, Finn. Already I have twice the lines of anyone."

"Ah, but now we come to my idea," said Teodoros. "I sympathize with your plight, Feival, and so I have written you a new part instead—shorter, but with a great deal of verve and bite, so that the eyes of the audience will be rapt upon you whenever you enter."

"What does *that* mean? What part?"

"I have made the goddess Zuriyal an important part of this new play—the wife of Zmeos and Khors' sister-in-law. Although darkly beautiful, my Zuriyal is jealous and fierce and murderous, and it is she whose cruelties most threaten pure Zoria."

"Darkly beautiful is not beyond my skills," Feival said lazily, "but surely in a play called after Zoria the virgin goddess, somebody must play the virgin herself? I would be happy to carry a lesser load, but is not Waterman here a jot too thickset and whiskery to play the divine mistress of all the pure virtues?"

"Doubtless—so why not let Tim play the part?" Teodoros spread his hands and gestured toward Briony like an envoy delivering a gift to a jaded monarch. "He is younger than you, even, and fair enough in his way to pass for a girl, if not viewed from too closely?" He turned and gave Briony a pleased smile that made her want to take a stick to him.

"Are you mad?" sputtered Makewell. "The child has no training, no skill. Does he know the Seven Postures of Femininity? Just because he held a spear for us when we played *Xarpedon* in some cow-byre does not mean he can stand up before the Tessians and pass as a woman—let alone a goddess! Are you really so desperate to claim another share, Teodoros, that you would put this boy up as a cheap front for your ambition?"

"In other times I would have you for that, Makewell," said the playwright coldly. "But I realize I have brought this to you as a surprise."

"I think he could do it," said Birch. "He is clever, young Tim."

"Thank you, Dowan," Briony said. "But I do not *want* to be a player at all, still less to go on the stage and mime my dear, holy Zoria, who would never forgive me."

"What, is our craft too low for you, then?" said Hewney. "Were we mistaken? Do we have a duchess in our midst after all, traveling in secret?"

Briony could only stare at him. He must be making fun of her, but he was uncomfortably close to the mark.

"Do not look so frightened," Feival said, laughing. "Everyone here knows you are a girl by now."

"What?" Dowan Birch shook his head. "Who is a girl?"

Feival Ulian whispered in his ear. The giant's eyes grew round.

"I knew he could not be a boy when he chose to stay with you, Teodoros," said Pedder Makewell haughtily. "No handsome young man would subject himself to your pawings."

"And I haven't seen anything but halfwit farm boys succumb to your charms, dear Pedder," said Teodoros. "But this is beside the point."

"You *all* know?" Briony could not shake off her astonishment. And she had thought herself so clever!

"You have traveled with us two tennights or more, after all," Teodoros said kindly.

"*I* didn't know," said Birch, wide-eyed. "Are you sure?"

"Enough of this yammering," said Feival. "If anyone should be unhappy at the thought of our Tim—shall we still call you that?— playing at the goddess Zoria, it should be me, since it is my contracted due to play the leading woman's role. But if I like this Zuriyal-bitch that Finn has jotted out for me, I will raise no objection." He smiled. "I am with Dowan on this. I think you have many hidden depths."

"Think on it, Tim," said Teodoros. "And yes, we shall still call her . . . him that, because you may remember it is not lawful to have a woman on stage. If you will consent, we would have a new play for the Tessians, one that I can humbly say is my best. Much of my inspiration came from the talks you and I have had."

"Talks, is it?" Makewell shook his head and made a razzing noise with his lips. "Does that mean there are many scenes in this new work of a fat old playwright futtering a disguised child? I thought your winds only blew one direction, Finn."

"Don't be jealous, Pedder," said Teodoros serenely. "I promise you my relationship with young Tim has been as chaste as it would have been with Zoria herself. But Tim, the crudeness of Master Makewell left to one side, what do you say? You could be a great help to us and earn yourself a player's share, which can be rich indeed in Tessis, since the Syannese love plays the way the Hierosolines love religious processions."

"I am flattered, I suppose," Briony said carefully—she would be traveling with these people for days more, perhaps months, and didn't want to offend them. "But the answer is no. Under no circumstances. It will not happen in this world or any other. You must think of something else."

She only had a tennight to learn the lines. There were dozens upon dozens of them, in teetering rhyme-that-was-not-rhyme. Rehearsals came at night after whatever performance they made for their supper, so most of the work was done by candlelight in tavern courtyards and barns, while chill winds blew outside and snow and rain fell, but they could also speak lines and discuss blocking—a word she had learned meant where the actors went in and out or stood—as they made their way down the Great Kertish Road toward Syan.

I have fallen so far, she thought. *From a princess in a castle to a false goddess with no home, with straws in my hair and fleas in my woolen hose.*

Still, there was an unfamiliar freedom in such a collapse from grace. Briony was not happy, but she was not sad, either, and she had to admit that however lonely and uncomfortable it might be, and however much she missed her home and family, she was having something that could only be described as an adventure.

33

The Crocodile's Roar

Argal and his brothers launched their attack upon the fortress Moontusk, and many gods were slain, o my children, a thousand times a thousand.

In the end, betrayed by one of his own family, Nushash was prevented from destroying his half brothers, so he withdrew to the sun with his sister-wife, Surigali, Mistress of Justice. His true brother remained in the moon, taking as a spoil of war Nenizu, the wife of Xergal, to be his own wife.

—from *The Revelations of Nushash*, Book One

ALREADY SMOKE LAY OVER the Kulloan Straits like thick fog, great curtains of gray and black torn ragged by the wind. The Xixian ships churned up and down before the walls of Hierosol, their long banks of oars stabbing at the water like the legs of insects, fire spouting from their cannons. The defenders fired back: white spouts leaped up to show where the

Hierosoline cannons were finding their range, and many of the Xixian sails were tattered, the flaming eye insignia in flames, but none of the besiegers had been sunk yet. Still, it was a little solace to Pelaya to see that the cannonfire that reached Hierosol's walls did almost no damage.

"Look, Babba," she said, tugging on her father's arm. "They bounce off like pebbles!"

He smiled, barely. "Our walls are strong and thick. But that does not mean I want you here watching. You have given me your mother's message, and my midday meal." He turned to the armed servant, a tall man with the long-suffering look of someone in minor but almost constant pain. "See her back, now, Eril. And tell my wife that she and the children are no longer to come to the palace, not unless I say they may."

The servant bowed. "Yes, *Kurs* Perivos. And I will inform the *kura,* as you say."

Pelaya rose onto the tips of her toes to throw her arms around her father's neck, not caring one little bit about either Eril's frown of disapproval or her father's distracted, half-attentive squeeze in return.

"You should not act so, *Kuraion,*" the servant reproached her as they made their way out of the antechamber and onto the landing. He had called her "Little Mistress" since she was small enough to enjoy it—a time long past. "Not before strangers."

"What strangers, Eril?" She was particularly nettled because she always did her best to uphold the honor of her house—and it was high honor, too: the Akuanai were of the blood of the Devonai, the dynasty that had ruled all Hierosol only a few short centuries before, and whose funeral masks lined the entrance hall of the family estate in Siris like an assembly of patient, placid ghosts. She might not be as timid as Teloni of speaking out in public, but neither did she run or giggle like a child: those who saw her, she had always felt sure, saw a young woman as grave and serious-minded as befitted her upbringing and her noble house.

"There were soldiers there," he said. "Your father's men."

"Theo and Damian? And Spiridon? They have all been in our

house," she told him. "They are not strangers, they are like uncles." She thought of Damian, who was really quite handsome. "Young uncles, perhaps. But they are not strange to me, and it is no shame to embrace my father in front . . ."

She did not finish her statement because something outside the antechamber boomed like thunder, making the statue of Perin sway in the wall shrine above the landing. Pelaya squeaked with fear despite herself, then ran to the window.

"What are you doing, child?" The servant almost grabbed her arm to pull her away, but then thought better of taking such a liberty. "Come away. A cannonball will kill you!"

"Don't be foolish, Eril." Whatever else she might be, Pelaya was her father's daughter. "They cannot shoot their cannon this far, all the way to the citadel, not unless they are inside our walls already. But, oh, sweet mother Siveda, look!"

A thick plume of gray black smoke was rising beside the ancient walls—one of the buildings along the quay of the Harbor of Nektarios.

"It must be the powder magazine, hit by some stray shot. Oh, look at it burn!" Had her forward-thinking father not moved much of the powder stored for convenience in the immense harbor magazine, parceling it out to at least a dozen different storage places all over the city, half of the city's black powder would be gone now, not to mention the harbor itself, which would have almost certainly been destroyed. Instead, it looked as though only one building, the magazine itself, had been ruined, and if the fire could be put out quickly the loss would be bearable.

"I must tell my father," she said, leaving Eril to catch up as best he could as she scuttled back up the stairs.

"What are you *doing?*" her father shouted as she came in. He looked angry, truly angry, and for the first time she realized that the city might fall—that they all might die. She was so overwhelmed by this sudden, terrifying understanding that for a moment she could not speak.

"The magazine . . ." she said at last. "The one in the Harbor of Nektarios. It was hit by . . . it's exploded."

His expression softened a little. "I know. There is a window in the next room, do not forget. Go, and hurry to your mother as I told you. She will be frightened—I'm sure she could hear that crash in Landsman's Market."

He is defending the whole city, she thought, staring at him. Her father had already turned back to the table and was examining his charts again, his big hands splayed across the curling parchments like the roots of tall trees. For a moment she found it hard to breathe.

Pinimmon Vash, Paramount Minister to the Golden One Sulepis, Autarch of Xis, did not like traveling on ships. The sea air that had so delighted his ancestors when they came out of the deserts of Xand and settled on the northern shore of the continent smelled to him of putrefaction. The rolling motion of the waves made him feel again as he had in his childhood, when he had caught the bilious fever and lain for days near death, unable to keep anything in his stomach, shivering and sweating. In fact, his survival of that fever had been so unexpected that his father had dedicated the sacrifice of an entire ram to the goddess Sawamat (something that Vash would never have mentioned to the autarch, who barely acknowledged that any other gods beside Nushash existed).

Now, as he teetered down the ramp, he was so grateful to be on dry land again that he offered a silent prayer of thanks to her and to Efiyal, lord of the sea.

The long bight of land known as the Finger, which jutted out into the Kulloan Strait parallel to the western shore of Hierosol, was almost invisible from where he stood at its southernmost tip. Billows of gray and stinking yellow smoke hung close to the ground, so that in the few places where the walled fortifications could be seen at all they seemed to float atop clouds like the palaces of the gods. The fighting, which had begun at midnight with an invasion of the autarch's marines from both the landward edge of the Finger and the place where Vash's ship had just landed, was almost over. The Hierosoline garrisons, undermanned because Drakava had (against the recommendations of his leading advisers) withdrawn so many soldiers in preparation for the siege, had put up a brave resistance, but the small fortresses had proved vulnerable to the missiles of burning sulfur and straw the autarch's catapults had flung over the walls by the hundreds before the morning sun had climbed above the horizon. The defenders, choking, blinded, many of them dying from the poisonous smoke, had been unable to repel the autarch's marines, who, protected by masks of wet Sanian cotton, were able to hoist their siege ladders and clamber over the walls almost unopposed once the worst of the smoke had blown away. The defenders had offered resistance, but weakened, breathless, and blinded, they had fallen before the marines like brave children fighting grown men.

If we could use that tactic on Hierosol itself, Vash thought, *the war would be over in a few days.* But there was not enough sulfur for that in all of Xand, nor enough catapults to throw it, even in the autarch's huge army. Still, he could not help admiring how well Ikelis Johar and the other polemarchs had planned for the siege. The cannons jutting from the walls of the fortresses along the Finger might not be able to reach the walls of Hierosol, but they were an invaluable aid to its defense, able to rake the near side of any ships in the strait, or drive them in under the bigger guns of the city walls.

The autarch's pavilion had already been mounted on the slope beside the gangplank of his flagship, the *Flame of Nushash,* a towering four-masted warship painted (in defiance of any secrecy about its semi-divine passenger) in blindingly bright shades of red and gold and purple, with the great, flaming god's eye on either side of the bow and the autarch's royal falcon spread-winged in gold across the red sails. The recently erected pavilion was no more restrained, a striped cone almost fifty paces across flying two dozen falcon banners. Vash limped toward it, angrily waving away the offers of help from his guards. Sulepis, the Golden One, had already made it clear he suspected his paramount minister's loyalty: the last thing Vash needed was for the youthful autarch to see him staggering in on the arms of soldiers. He might as well announce himself old and useless and be done with it.

The autarch, dressed in his fanciful battle-array of golden armor and the flame-scalloped Battle Crown, was sitting on his war throne atop a raised platform at the center of the tent, talking to the Overseer of the Armies. Dozens of slaves and priests surrounded him, of course, along with a full troop of his Leopard guards in armor, muskets in hand, their eyes as brightly remorseless as those of their namesakes.

"Vash, welcome!" The autarch spread his fingers like claws, then scratched himself under the chin with the figured tip of his golden gauntlet. "You should have stayed on the ship a little longer, resting yourself, since we are going back to the landing spot soon anyway."

"I'm sorry, Golden One, I don't understand."

The autarch smiled and looked to Ikelis Johar, who nodded but maintained his customary stony expression. "The Royal Crocodiles are coming ashore."

For a moment Vash was completely confused, wondering what bizarre new plan his impulsive master had conceived. Was he going to put some of the massive reptiles from Xis' canals into the strait, or even introduce them somehow to the waterways behind the Hierosoline walls? The great beasts were certainly fearsome enough, even the younger adults longer than a fishing boat and armored like a siege engine, but who could make them do anything useful?

It was a mark of how strange and impulsive the autarch was, and how unpredictable life was in his service, that Vash was still trying to understand how crocodiles could be used in warfare even as he and Ikelis Johar and a crowd of servants and soldiers followed the autarch's litter back toward the ships. Only as he saw the monstrous thing being swung up from the hold of one of the six biggest cargo ships did Pinimmon Vash remember.

"Ah, Golden One, of course! The guns!"

"The largest, most beautiful in the history of mankind," said the autarch happily. "Each crafted like exquisite jewelry. What a roar they will make, my crocodiles! What a fiendish, terrifying roar!"

The immense bronze tube was six or seven times the length of a man, and even without its undercarriage, its weight was clearly staggering—several pentecounts of seamen were pulling on the ropes, trying to steady it as they swung the cannon barrel out over the side of the boat, the massive winding-wheels and pulleys creaking with the strain. The weapon had indeed been cast to resemble some monstrous river reptile, with inset topaz eyes and fanged jaws stretched wide to make the cannon's mouth, and the creature's rounded back ridged with scaly plates. This one and its brothers would fire huge stone balls, each missile ten times the weight of a man, and if the autarch's engineers were correct (they had been informed they would die painfully if they were wrong) they would easily be able to reach the far side of the strait from the forts along the Finger.

"Come," said the autarch after they had watched the sweating sailors lower the gun onto a giant wheeled wagon. "How fortunate for us that the old emperors of Hierosol made this fine, paved road for their supply wagons, otherwise we would have to drag the guns through the sand and the waiting would be even more tedious. I will have my morning meal, and then perhaps about midday we will be able to hear our first lovely crocodile speak. Come, Vash. We will attend to all other business as I eat."

The autarch had rather conspicuously not said anything about his paramount minister being fed. An hour on dry land had settled Vash's stomach and he was feeling extremely hungry, but he effortlessly stifled a sigh: all of the autarch's servitors either mastered the art of hiding their feelings and stifling their needs, or else their cooling bodies were picked clean on the vulture shrines.

Vash bowed. "Of course, Golden One. As you say."

"I ask your pardon for disturbing you, King Olin," said Count Perivos.

The bearded man smiled. "I am afraid I cannot entertain you in the way I could have in my old home, but you are welcome, sir. Please, come in." He waved to the page, who was watching with trepidation: Olin was only a foreign king, but everyone knew his visitor was of an important and ancient Hierosoline family. "Be so good as to pour us some wine, boy," Olin said. "Perhaps some of the Torvian."

Perivos Akuanis looked around the king's cell, which was furnished in moderate comfort, though not exactly overlarge. "I am sorry you must live this way, Your Highness. It would not have been my choice."

"But Ludis wished it so. He must have some hidden qualities, the lord protector, that he has a man as famous as you in his employ."

Perivos began to say something, then looked over to the guards standing on either side of the door. "You may wait outside, you two. I am in no danger."

They eyed him for a moment before going out. Count Perivos cleared his throat.

"I will be honest with you, Olin Eddon, because I believe you are an honorable man. It is not so much loyalty to Ludis that keeps me here, although the man did pull the country back into stability after a long civil war, but loyalty to my city and nation. I am a Hierosol man, through and through."

"But you are of high blood yourself. Why is it that you yourself did not try to take the throne, or support someone more to your liking?"

"Because I knew with things being as they are I could do more good this way. I am not a king or even a king's counselor. I am a soldier, and of a particular kind at that. My science is siege war, which I learned from Petris Kopayis, the best of this age. I knew I had no choice but to use that knowledge to try to save my city and its people from the bloody-handed autarchs of Xis. Thus, I could not afford to take sides in the last throes of the civil war."

"I remember Kopayis—I met him when we fought the Xandian Federation here twenty years ago. Gods, he was a clever man!" Olin smiled a little. "And everything I have heard suggests you are his true successor. So you do not bear a grudge against Ludis, you say—and he bears none against you?"

Perivos frowned. "Never underestimate him, King Olin. He is a rough man, and his personal habits are . . . are disturbing. But he is no fool. He will employ any man who can help him, whether that man admires him or not, whether that man fought for him or not. He has servants of all shapes and religions and histories. Two of his advisers fought against him in the civil war, and came to their new positions straight from the gallows-cells, and one of his chiefest envoys is a black man out of Xand—from Tuan, to be precise."

Olin raised his eyebrow in amusement. "An unusual choice, but not unheard of."

"Ah, that is right—you had a Tuani lord as your retainer too, did you not? But things have not gone so well with him, I hear."

The March King's face twitched with pain—it was almost shocking to see in a man so controlled. "Do not remind me, I pray you. I have been told he murdered my son, although I can scarcely believe it, and now there is talk he has taken my daughter as well. It is . . . agony to hear such things and be able to do nothing—you are a father, Akuanis, you can imagine! Agony beyond words." Olin rose and paced for a moment, then returned to take a long swallow of his wine. When he lowered the cup his face was precisely expressionless again. "Well," he said at last, "we obviously have some measure of each other, Count Perivos. If for no other reason, I would give you whatever assistance I honorably can because of the kindness your daughter has shown me. So what do you wish?"

Akuanis nodded. "It is about Sulepis of Xis. You have fought against one of the autarchs before, and you have warned about the Xixian menace for a long time. Your suggestions were canny and I am skilled enough at what I do that I have no shame in asking others for help. What else can you suggest that will help me save this city? You must know that the strait is full of his warships, and that already he has made two different landings on Hierosoline soil."

"Two?" Olin looked puzzled. "I had heard about his assault on the Finger forts—the guards were full of talk about it this morning. But what else?"

Count Perivos looked to the door, then back to Olin, his thin face with its two-day growth of beard pale and troubled. "You must speak of this to no one, King Olin. The autarch, although only the gods of war know how, has managed to land a sizable force at the northern mouth of the strait, near Lake Strivothos. King Enander of Syan sent a force of twenty pentecounts led by his son Eneas to reinforce the garrison on the fort at Temple Island north of the city, and on their way they met a Xixian army on the Kracian side of the strait. The Xixians fired on them, but luckily for the Syannese the autarch's men had not set their cannon yet and were able to use only muskets. Some of the Syannese escaped and were able to send us the news."

"And grim news it is," said Olin. "How could the Xixians have got there? Did they slip unnoticed up the strait?"

"I am cursed if I can tell you." Akuanis scowled. "But you can see my desperation. If they conquer our forts on the Finger we cannot keep more of their ships from sailing up the western side and reaching the great lake. They will be able to seal in our allies there, especially the Syannese. We will face this siege entirely alone."

Olin shook his head. "I would not dare to tell you your craft, Count Perivos. Your reputation has traveled where you have not, and I knew your name before I began my . . . visit here in Hierosol. I have studied this autarch a little but not fought him, of course—the southerners I fought here twenty years ago were a loose collection of Tuani and others, and although Parnad's troops fought with them, it was a very different sort of battle." He raised his hands. "So you see . . ."

"But you have been studying him a long time—is there anything you can tell me about this Sulepis, any weakness my spies have missed I might exploit? It goes without saying I will honor my end of the bargain with any news of your family and home I can discover."

"To be honest, I bargained only when I did not know you and

feared you would not trust me otherwise—I would not knowingly aid the autarch and will do anything I can do to help." He frowned. "But I am certain a man like yourself has explored every angle." Nevertheless, Olin spent much of the next hour describing what he remembered of the Xixian military at war and everything he had heard about this young autarch, Sulepis.

When he had finished the count sat silent for a while, then put down his wine cup and smacked his hands on his thighs in frustration. "It is this news about Xixian marines in Krace that frights me most. He has ten or twenty times our numbers, and if we cannot be reinforced except over land, up the steep, steep valley roads, I fear that Hierosol will fall at last, if only from starvation."

"That will take months," Olin said. "Many things may change in that time, Count Perivos. Other ideas will come, or even new allies." He looked at him keenly. "If I were free, it is possible I could bring a northern army to help break the siege."

Perivos Akuanis laughed without anger. "And if I could persuade Ludis Drakava to do something he so profoundly does not wish to do, *I* would be a god and could save the city by myself." He reached down for his cup and finished it with a swallow. "I am sorry, King Olin. Even with our enemies all around us, the lord protector still has hopes for using you to make some useful bargain—if not for your daughter, the gods protect her, then for something else. I cannot imagine any trade the autarch would make that Drakava would agree to, despite his strange offer for you. Whatever the case, our lord protector is not done with you yet. Apologies, your Highness, and thank you for your time. Now I have work to do."

Before he could reach the door, Olin had sprung from his bench and grabbed the count's arm. "Hold! Hold, damn you!"

Akuanis had his knife out in a moment and pressed it against Olin's throat. "I will not call the guards because I still believe you a gentleman, but you abuse our hospitality, King Olin."

"I . . . I am sorry . . ." Olin let go and took a clumsy step backward. "Truly. It is just . . . you said something about the autarch trying to bargain . . . for *me* . . . ?"

"Hah!" Count Perivos stared at him carefully. "I assumed your sources had told you already. Sulepis offered the lord protector some piddling promises in exchange for you. Drakava was not interested."

"But that makes no sense!" Olin held up his fists before him, not as someone who planned to use them, but as a man searching for something to grasp to keep himself from falling. "Why would the autarch be interested in the king of a small northern federation who has never even met him? I am no threat to him."

The count stared at him for a long moment, then sheathed his knife. "Perhaps he thinks you are. Can you guess at why? Perhaps there is something you have forgotten—something I can *use*." The weariness and desperation of Count Perivos became evident for the first time. "Otherwise we will have the siege, and fire, and starvation, and perhaps worse."

Olin sagged back onto his bench. "Forgive my behavior, but it seems I am to suffer one shock after another. It makes no sense. I am nothing to him."

"Think on it. I will send you what I can find of your family. As for your kingdom, I hear it is safe despite all these mad rumors of fairies. Your relatives the Tollys hold a regency as defenders of your infant child, or so I am told." He looked suddenly stricken. "You did know you had a new son, King Olin, didn't you?"

"Yes." He nodded heavily, like a man who can barely keep awake after a day's exhausting labor. "Yes, I had a letter from my wife. Olin Alessandros, he will be named. Healthy, they say."

"Well, that is one small blessing, anyway." Perivos Akuanis bowed his head. "Farewell, Olin. The gods grant we can talk again in days ahead."

Olin laughed sourly. "The gods? So you fear that Drakava will sell me to the autarch after all?"

"No, I fear that the autarch will find a way over the walls and kill us all." He made the sign of the Three, then sketched a mocking salute. "At which point, I will be home in Siris, waiting to die with my family, and you will be meeting your own fate. If it comes to that, the gods grant us good deaths."

"I would prefer that the gods help protect you and your family instead, Count Perivos. And mine."

The two men clasped hands before the Hierosoline nobleman went out.

It was actually the middle of the afternoon before the first of the great guns had been assembled and mounted on its mighty carriage behind the walls of the captive fortress. The air was still putrid with the eggy stench of the sulfur, and Vash was just as glad he had only managed to nibble a bit of food here and there—some flat bread, a few olives, a single tangerine.

"It is impressive, Ikelis, is it not?" The autarch smiled at the giant gun with the doting pride of a father.

"Gunnery has never had a better tool," said the Overseer of the Armies, looking sternly at Vash as though the paramount minister might dare to argue. "We will reach the citadel itself with that. We will send the dog Drakava scuttling."

"Oh, I will not waste this beautiful machine lobbing stones at Drakava," Sulepis said. "May my sacred father himself protect Ludis Drakava—I do not want him dead! That might slow this entire venture down to a fatal degree."

"I'm afraid I do not understand, Golden One." Johar's latest look at Vash was a great deal more humble. He clearly did not have as much experience as the paramount minister at dealing with the autarch's strange, sudden, and sometimes apparently mad changes of plan. "Surely you wish Hierosol to fall."

"Oh, yes, we are going to knock the walls down," said the autarch. "We are going to knock them down so that we do not have to waste time on a siege."

"But, Golden One, I do not think even such missiles as those," —Johar pointed to the huge, spherical stone being rolled up a ramp toward the cannon's mouth by a dozen sweating slaves— "can punch through the walls of Hiersol. Those walls are two dozen yards thick, and the stonework is immaculate!"

For the first time, the autarch's smile vanished. "Do you think I am unaware of that, High Polemarch?"

Like a man who has stepped one foot over the edge of a bottomless chasm, Ikelis Johar abruptly backtracked. "Of course, Golden One. You are the Living God on Earth. I am only a mortal and a fool. Instruct me."

"Someone ought to, clearly. We will fire the cannons at a single place on the wall until it collapses. Then we will land our troops and send them in."

"But . . . but trying to force through a single breach in those wide, wide walls? They will rain fire and arrows and burning oil on our soldiers. We will lose thousands of men in such an assault!" Johar was surprised enough to momentarily forget his own danger. "Tens and tens of thousands!"

"My destiny—the world's destiny—rides on my shoulder." Sulepis' pale eyes glinted, impossibly alert, impossibly lively. "These men are happy to live for their autarch, why should they not die for him happily, too? Either way, they will spend eternity in the golden glow of my father Nushash." The autarch laughed, the musical trill of someone contemplating with absolute, amused indifference the murder of thousands. "Now, let us see our first Royal Crocodile sing for his supper, eh?"

Johar, his brown face looking a touch more wan than usual, bowed several times as he backed away from the autarch's chair and descended from the golden litter, then waved his arms and bellowed an order to his generals. The command was passed rapidly down the chain of command until the gunnery master bowed and ordered a last few creaks of the wheel, lifting the elevation of the snarling, reptilian muzzle. When he was satisfied, the gunnery master stood up straight, wiping at the sweat that covered his face on this chill day.

"On the Master of the Great Tent's word!" he bawled. "For the glory of Heaven and of eternal Xis!"

The god-on-earth waved a languid hand. "You may set it off."

"Give it fire!" shouted the gunnery master. A shirtless man dropped the head of a flaming torch on the cannon's touchhole.

For a moment the gun was so silent that it seemed to have sucked all the noise out of the world. It was only as Vash realized that the waves were still murmuring in the strait and the gulls still keening overhead that the cannon went off.

Some moments later the paramount minister of Xis scrambled up onto his knees, certain that he would never hear anything again: his head was buzzing like the hive of the fire god's sacred bees. A pall of smoke hung in the air around them, slowly being fanned away by the wind. The cannon had rolled back several yards, crushing two unfortunate soldiers beneath it. The gunnery master was frowning at the bloody ruin beneath the wheels. "We'll have to put sand underneath them, or chain them," he said. "Otherwise we'll have to roll it back each time and firing will take even longer." It sounded to Vash's throbbing ears as though he whispered the words from miles away.

"It does not matter," said the autarch, his voice almost as muffled. "Ah, it was beautiful to see. And look!" He pointed with his gauntleted hand.

On the far side of the strait a chunk of pale rock the size of a palace door had been knocked out of Hierosol's great seawall, leaving a darker spot like a wound. Atop the walls tiny soldiers scurried like startled ants, unable to believe in anything so powerful, unwilling to think anything could throw a stone so far, let alone actually chip the mighty, ancient defenses.

"Ah, they hear us knocking on their door," said the autarch, clapping his hands together in delight; Vash could barely hear the sound they made. "Soon we will come in and make ourselves at home!"

A few moments later, and for the first time since the previous day, the bells of Hierosol began to ring again.

34

Through Immon's Gate

With his death, Silvergleam's house fell. Whitefire and Judgment were banished into the same Unbeing to which old Twilight had been dispatched, and most of their servants slaughtered. Crooked only was kept alive because the children of Moisture coveted his arts. They tormented him first, cutting away his manhood so that he would never spread the seed of Breeze's children, then they made him their slave.

Even the victors did not sing of these deeds, but made false tales to hide their shame and grief. The truth could not be encompassed. The true story is called Kingdom of Tears.

—from *One Hundred Considerations*
out of the Qar's *Book of Regret*

THE MYSTERIOUS DARK-HAIRED GIRL had not appeared to him in days. His hours in the cell were long and empty, he was still angry with Vansen, Gyir had shown no evidence of having come up with the promised plan of escape (nor done much at all except sit in oblique silence), and Barrick was desperate for something to distract him from his own discomfort and dread, so he brooded about her.

He had even begun to wonder if she might have been a herald of his own death—whether, despite all her words about courage and resistance, her presence actually meant he was nearing the end of his life. Perhaps she was some daughter of Kernios, awakened or summoned by the nearness of the monstrous gate. Barrick didn't know whether Kernios *had* a daughter—he had never been able to keep up with Father Timoid's endless recitations of the lineages of gods, even if his family claimed relationship to one—but it seemed possible.

Still, if the dark-haired girl was an emissary of the ultimate, he was not as afraid of dying as he had thought he would be. This Death had a kind, clever face. But so young! Younger than he was, certainly. Then again, if she was a goddess, how she appeared meant little—after all, the gods could become whatever they wanted, trees or stars or beasts of the field.

But what was the use of wondering, in any case? Day after day of throbbing pain in his head and blurred thoughts, night after night of frightening visions—Barrick was not even quite certain of what was real anymore. Why had he been chosen for this particular torment? Not fair. *Not fair.*

Push against it. He heard her voice again, but only in memory. *Escape it. Change it.*

What had Gyir told him? *You are only a prisoner when you surrender.* Even steadfast, stolid Vansen seemed to reproach Barrick for his weakness—everyone else was so cursedly certain about things *they* didn't have to suffer.

Barrick opened his eyes a little. Vansen was sleeping next to him, the soldier's thin face now softened by a beard which obscured but could not completely hide the hollowness of his cheeks. Though they drained every drop of the swill Jikuyin's guards gave them, they were all slowly wasting away. Barrick had been slender to begin with, but now he could watch each bone sliding and moving beneath his skin, see the deformity of his shattered arm in more detail than he had ever wanted.

For a moment, then, his eyes half shut, he could almost see King Olin's features hovering before him instead of Vansen's.

I hope you're happy, Father. You were so ashamed of what you did to me that you couldn't even speak of it. Soon I'll be dead and you'll never have to see me again.

But was it really all his father's fault? It was the curse, after all, a poison in the Eddon blood they shared, and even his father's blood was not as corrupted as Barrick's. For proof, he need look no farther than the days and nights just passed: when Olin had escaped the castle his own curse had become less—his letters had all but said so. Barrick, though, was in the grip of even worse fevers of madness than he had experienced at home.

He shut his eyes tight but sleep would not come. A quiet shuffling noise made him open them again. The latest shift of prisoners had just come back from their labors and one of the apish guards was coming right toward their cell. Gyir, who had been propped in a corner of the stony cell with his chin against his chest, slowly looked up. Barrick's heart raced—what could the guard want? Had the time come for the blood sacrifice Gyir had feared?

The creature stopped in front of the grille, cutting off most of the outside light. Gyir moved toward the door, but with a swift, easy grace that took a little of the edge off Barrick's fear: he had learned to read the fairy's movements a bit, and what they said now was not *danger* but only *caution*.

The beastlike guard stood in silence, its face pressed against the bars. Nothing visible passed between the guard and Gyir, but after a dozen or so heartbeats the shaggy creature shook itself and then turned away, a puzzled, perhaps even frightened expression on its inhuman face.

★

During the course of the following hours and days, many more guards and more than a few returning prisoners enacted a similar ritual as Barrick watched with fascination. He couldn't help wondering what this had to do with the Storm Lantern's talk of gun-flour, since there was none of the black powder to be seen. Instead, it was like watching the Bronzes ceremony at the Southmarch court, when the leading nobles of the March Kingdoms came and laid their weapons at the feet of the king sitting in the Wolf's Chair and each of their names was marked on a bronze tablet which was then blessed and then laid into the vault at the great Trigonate temple. But the beasts of Greatdeeps were bringing the fairy nothing that Barrick could see, nor were they taking anything away.

He realized that almost a year had come and gone since King Olin had performed the Bronzes ceremony before leaving on his ill-fated voyage. He wondered if Briony would take the fealty of the Marchwardens this year, and was suddenly filled with a homesickness so powerful it almost made him burst out sobbing. It was followed by a wave of loathing at his own helplessness, his own uselessness.

Look at me! I lie here like a child, doing nothing, waiting for death. And what is my death? A warrior's death? A king's death, or even a prince's death? No, it takes the form of a girl, a doe-eyed girl full of sympathy, and I wait for her like some smitten bard, some . . . poet. Then, the thought burning like fire in his guts: *And even she thinks that I have given up—that I am a coward.*

Barrick dragged himself upright, ignoring the sharp pain in his arm, which was always worst the first time he bent it after having been asleep. He made his way over to Gyir and sat down beside him. The fairy, whose eyes had been closed as if in sleep since the last visitor or tributary had shuffled away, opened them to fix Barrick with the banked fire of his gaze.

You do not need to sit near me to talk. I could speak to you from the House of the People, almost. You grow stronger every day.

Why are those guards and other creatures coming to you? he asked.

I am schooling them in what I need, Gyir told him. *I do not want to say more, since we will risk all on this throw.*

Barrick sat quiet for a while, thinking. *Why is all of this happening now?* he finally asked. *Not what I was just asking about, but . . . everything.*

Narrow your question, please.

Everything that hasn't happened before, or at least not for hundreds of years—the Shadowline moving, your people attacking Southmarch and warring against my people. And this demigod Jack Chain, or whatever he is, digging up the palace of Kernios. You can't pretend those sorts of things happen all the time.

Gyir let out the gust of bitter amusement that Barrick had come to recognize as a laugh. *Your people and my people at each other's throats is not so unusual. You slaughtered us for years. And, to be fair, we have attacked you twice since then.*

You know what I mean.

Gyir stared at him, then nodded. *Yes, I do. There are things I cannot tell you even though circumstances make us allies—promises I have made to others and oaths I have sworn. But here are some things I can tell, and should. Your companion must hear this, too.* The fairy paused. Barrick turned and watched Ferras Vansen slowly push himself into an upright position, woken by the Storm Lantern's silent call.

Our time is short, Gyir said. *You both must listen well.* He spread his pale fingers. *There are two ways other than experience that wisdom comes to the People. One is the gift of the Fireflower*—this made an idea in Barrick's mind he could barely contain, something that was as large and complicated as anything Gyir had ever said—*and the other is the Deep Library.*

In the most hidden places within the House of the People, the wisdom of our oldest days remains mostly in the form of the Preserved and their Voices—that is the Deep Library. These Voices speak the wisdom of the Preserved and thus are the People taught and reminded. Gyir's thoughts were rhythmic, almost singsong, as though he passed on a story that he had learned in childhood. *These Voices, along with the wisdom of the Fireflower, which is sometimes called the Gift, are what lifts the High*

*Ones above the rest of the People and what has brought us dominion over
our lands and songs.*

*You have heard that the gods have been banished from this world into
the realms of sleep. That was the work of the god we call Crooked, and
about that mystery I can say little, but it is the foundation of all that comes
afterward. The place where those events burned brightest, and where they
still smolder thousands of years later, is at the place we name Godsfall—
the place your people call Southmarch. Yes, Prince Barrick, your home.*

Barrick stared at him, confused. Was the fairy trying to say that
the gods had lived in Southmarch? Or died there? It was so bizarre
a thought that for a moment he feared he was dreaming again.

Only a few years ago, Gyir continued, *the Voices began to warn us
that the slumber of the gods in their exile had grown very shallow, very
fragile. Just as the moon may pull on the earthly tides when he swings
close, creating perturbations in the blood of those most sensitive, so the gods,
even in sleep, are closer to us now than they have been since they were
driven from the waking lands.* Gyir paused to listen to something
Vansen asked. *No, I cannot say more about it now. It is enough to know
the gods were driven out of the waking lands, that for a long time they have
been gone, almost as though they were dead.*

*But now the gods loom close, pushing into the minds and dreams of
both your people and mine, and in countless other ways as well. That would
be grim enough—dangerous too, because even in their eternal sleep the gods
can still make mischief both small and great, and they ache to have back
what was theirs. But by a grave chance, this ominous hour has arrived when
another terrible thing was already happening to the High Ones of my folk,
a thing that has plunged all of the House of the People into terror and
mourning. Our Queen Saqri, the Mistress of the Ancient Song, is dying.*

Barrick had never seen the fairy show much in the way of
emotion, but it was obvious from the pain in his thoughts that
what he was saying struck him to his core.

The High Ones, Gyir went on at last, *at least those in the Line of
the Fireflower, do not die as mortals die. We can all of us meet a violent
end, and we are prey to illnesses and accidents just as you sunlanders are,
but those of our highest house like Saqri and Ynnir are not like the rest of
living things, either in their mortality or their immortality. That is all I can*

tell you. No, I hear your questions but it is not my secret to share with your kind. I have not the right.

But I can tell you this. Queen Saqri is dying, and that which she needs most was to be found only in the old sacred place of our people—your people's home, the castle called Southmarch. Desperation had driven us to recapture it two hundred years before, but we were driven out again. Now desperation has driven us back there once more.

But this time, there was the matter of the gods' restless sleep to consider. Your Southmarch is a place that touches closely on the realms of the gods. Even the Voices of the Deep Library agreed that there was a terrible chance that an attempt to recapture the sacred place and use its virtues to save Queen Saqri would wake the gods from their slumber and bring an era of blood and darkness over the earth.

But why? Barrick could not help asking. *Why would waking the gods do such a thing?* He looked to Vansen, but even in the dim light he could see that the soldier had gone quite pale, as though he had just been told the incipient hour of his own death.

"Blood and darkness . . . ?" Vansen whispered. He looked as though he had been stabbed in the heart.

The gods would not be able to avoid it, Gyir declared, *any more than a wolf could let itself starve to death while a piece of bloody meat lay before it. Such is the nature of their godhood—they have been trapped in sleep for century upon century, powerless as great beasts caught in hunters' nets. One of the gods' most fearsome attributes is the mightiness of their angers. But even faced with such terror, humans would not easily give up dominion. When the gods lived on the earth in the distant past, mortals were their servants, small in numbers and weaker in self-regard, but they have grown in both wisdom and numbers. If the gods wake, there will be a war to end all wars. In the end, though, the gods will triumph and the pitiful survivors will begin sifting the ruins of their cities to build new temples to their greedy, victorious, immortal masters.*

Barrick wasn't certain he understood everything, but it was impossible to ignore the dreadful certainty in Gyir's thoughts.

So in our fear of waking the gods, the House of the People became divided between those who wished to see the queen saved at any cost, led in spirit by my lady Yasammez, and those who sought some other path.

That was King Ynnir's way, and although I fear it will only delay the inevitable, or perhaps make it worse when it comes, his wishes had enough support that a compromise was made.

We call that compromise the Pact of the Glass, and at this moment it is all that stands between your people and annihilation, because we of Yasammez's party believe that what we serve is more important than any mercy and is worth any risk.

Barrick felt light-headed again. *And . . . and you still feel that way, Gyir? That killing every man, woman, and child in Southmarch would be an acceptable cost to reach your goal?*

You will never understand without knowing the true stakes. The fairy's thoughts came to him like drips of icy water on stone. *And I cannot tell you all—I have not the stature to open such secrets to mortals.*

So what are you saying? That your king and queen are at war with each other? But they've made some kind of truce?

War is too simple a word, Gyir told him. *When you understand that they are not only our lord and lady, husband and wife, but also brother and sister, you of all people may understand something of the complexities involved.*

They're brother and sister . . . ?

Yes. Enough. I do not have time to explain the full history of my people to you, or any great urge to defend the Line of the Fireflower against the ignorance of sunlanders. Be silent and listen! Gyir's frustration was so palpable that his words came almost like blows. *The Pact of the Glass is the most fragile of wisps, but at the moment it holds. We defeated your army but we have not attacked your stronghold. But if we must, we will, and I promise you with no joy that if we do the blood will run like rivers.*

Barrick was angry now, too. *Say your piece, Storm Lantern.*

I do not wish your love, man-child, only your understanding. I am sorry if you thought that friendship between us might change the facts, but the gods themselves could not undo what is coming, even if they wished to do so.

So why do you tell us all this, curse you? If we're all doomed, what difference does it make?

Because as I once told you, things are still balanced on a knife's edge. We must do what we can to keep that balance from tilting. Here. He reached into his tattered shirt and pulled out a tiny bundle wrapped in dirty rags, held it out in his open hand. *This is the thing I told you about but would not show you. Now I must abandon caution, hoping you will understand the terrible danger we face and how important this is. This is the prize my lady Yasammez ordered me to carry to King Ynnir. On this small thing may rest the fate of all.*

What is it? It was smaller than the palm of Barrick's hand, vaguely round in shape. He stared at it, bemused.

It is the very scrying glass around which the Pact of the Glass is built. If it does not reach the king soon, Lady Yasammez will renew her attack upon Southmarch, this time without mercy.

He handed it to Barrick, who was so surprised he almost dropped it. *Why are you giving this to me?*

Because I fear that Jikuyin intends to use me in some way to open Immon's Gate into the palace of the Earthfather. If that happens, if I am lost while I still carry the Glass, then all is lost with me.

But why me? Barrick shook his head. *I can barely stand up! I'm full of mad thoughts—I'm sick! Give it to Vansen. He'll get it where you need it to go. He's a soldier. He's . . . honorable.* He looked over to the guard captain and realized that he meant it—despite everything he had said about the guard captain, every petty dislike he had expressed, Barrick admired the man and envied his strength and determination. In another world, another Barrick would have given much to have such a person as a friend.

I intended to, said Gyir, *but I have been thinking.* There was a brief silence in Barrick's head as the fairy spoke only to Vansen, then he turned his scarlet stare back onto Barrick. *Ferras Vansen is brave, but he does not carry Lady Porcupine's touch. My lady singled you out, Barrick Eddon and gave you an errand of your own to the House of the People—one that even I do not know. Her command will carry you on when all else would fail. But it will not keep you alive if Fate intends otherwise,* the fairy could not help adding, *so do not be foolhardy! Ferras Vansen can go with you, but you must be the one to carry it.*

So you want me to do a kindness for the woman who wants to kill all my people?

Must I have this argument with every sunlander who can draw breath?

Gyir shook his head. *Have you not listened? If this does not reach King Ynnir, then Yasammez will destroy all in her way to recapture Godsfall— your home—for our folk. If the Pact of the Glass is fulfilled there is at least a faint hope she will hold back, but only if the glass reaches the king's hand.*

Barrick swallowed. He had spent most of his young life trying to avoid just such situations—a chance to fail, to prove that he was less than those around him, those with healthy limbs and unshadowed hearts—but what else could he do?

Very well, if we must. He thought of the brown-eyed girl, of what she would think of him. *Yes, then! Give it to me.*

Do not look into it, Gyir warned. *You are not strong enough. It is a powerful, perilous thing.*

I don't want to look into it. Barrick tucked the ragged bundle into his shirt, trying to make sure it went into the one pocket that did not have a hole.

Ah, blessings. May Red Stag keep you ever safe on your path. The relief in the Storm Lantern's thoughts was clear, and for the first time Barrick realized that Gyir, too, might have been carrying a painful, unwanted burden. Then Gyir abruptly stiffened, becoming as still as a small animal under the shadow of a hawk. *Quickly,* he said, *what day is this?* He turned his burning red eyes from Barrick to Ferras Vansen, who both stared back helplessly. *Of course, how would you know? Let me think.* Gyir laid one hand over the other and then brought them both up to cover his eyes, and for the space of perhaps two dozen heartbeats he sat that way, silent and blind to the world. *We have a day, perhaps two,* he said abruptly, dropping his hands away from the smooth mask of flesh.

A day until what? Barrick asked. *Why?*

Until the ceremony of the Earthfather begins, Gyir said. *The sacrifice days of the one you call Kernios. Surely you still mark them.*

It took Barrick a moment, but then as it dawned on him he turned to Vansen, who had also understood. "The Kerneia," he said aloud. "Of course. By all the gods, is it Dimene already? How long have we been locked in this stinking place?"

Long enough to see your world and mine end if I have the day wrong, said Gyir. *They will come for us when the sacrifice days begin, and I am not yet ready.*

He would not say any more, but fell back into silence, shutting his two fellow prisoners out as thoroughly as if he had slammed a heavy door.

It was bad enough to suppose that the Kerneia marked the day of your doom, Ferras Vansen kept thinking, but it was made far worse by being trapped deep beneath the earth with no certain way of knowing what day it was in the world outside. This must be what it had been like to be tied to a tree and left for the wolves, as he had heard some of the old tribes of the March Kingdoms had done to prisoners, stopping the condemned's ears with mud and blindfolding their eyes so that they could only suffer in darkness, never knowing when the end would come.

Vansen slept only fitfully following Gyir's announcement, star-tled out of his thin slumbers every time Prince Barrick twitched in his sleep or some other prisoner growled or whimpered in the crowded cell outside.

Kerneia. Even during his childhood in Daler's Troth it had been a grim holiday. A small skull had to be carved for each family grave, where it would be set, nestled in flowers, on the first light of dawn as homage to the Earthfather who would take them all someday. Vansen's own father had never stopped complaining about the laziness of his adopted folk in Daler's Troth, who made their skull carvings out of soft wood. Back home in the Vuttish Isles, he would declare at least once each year, only stone was acceptable to the Lord of the Black Earth. Still, Ferras Vansen didn't doubt that with three of his own children gone to their graves and also the resting places of his wife's parents and grand-parents to be adorned, Pedar Vansen must have secretly been grateful he could make his death-tokens in yielding pine instead of the hard granite of the dales.

Skulls, skulls. Vansen could not get them out of his thoughts. As he had discovered when he came to the city, people in Southmarch purchased their festival skulls in the Street of Carvers, replicated in either stone or wood, depending on how much they wanted to spend. In the weeks before Kerneia you could even buy skulls baked of special pale bread in Market Square, the eye-sockets glazed dark brown. Vansen had never known what to think of that: eating the offerings that should go to Kernios himself seemed to trifle with that which should be respected—no, feared.

But then, they always said I was a bumpkin. Collum used to make up stories to amuse the other men about me thinking thunder meant the world was ending. As if a country boy wouldn't know about thunder!

Thinking about poor, dead Collum Dyer, remembering Kerneia and the black candles in the temple, the mantises in their owl masks and the crowds singing the story of the god of death and deep places, Vansen wandered in and out of something that was not quite sleep and that was certainly not restful, until at last he woke up to the tramp of many feet in the corridor outside.

The gray man Ueni'ssoh drifted across the floor as though he rode on a carpet of mist. His eyes smoldered in the dull, stony stillness of his face and even the prisoners in the large outer cell shrank back against the walls. Vansen could barely stand to look at him— he was a corpse-faced nightmare come to life.

"It is *time,*" he said, his words angular as a pile of sharp sticks. The brutish guards in their ill-fitting armor spread out on either side of Vansen and his two companions.

"For what, curse you?" Vansen raised himself to a crouch, although he knew that any move toward the gray man would earn him nothing except death at the ends of the guard's sharp pikes.

"Your final hour belongs to Jikuyin—it is not for me to instruct you." Ueni'ssoh nodded. Half a dozen guards sprang forward to shackle Gyir and loop a cord around his neck like a leash on a boarhound. When Barrick and Vansen had also been shackled the gray man looked at them all for a moment, then silently turned and walked out of the cell. As the guards prodded Vansen and the others after him, the prisoners in the outer cell turned their faces away, as if the three were already dead.

Do not despair—some hope still exists. Gyir's thoughts seemed as faint to Ferras Vansen as a voice heard from the top of a windy hillside. *Watch me. Do not let anything steal your wits or your heart. And if Ueni'ssoh speaks to you, do not listen!*

Hope? Vansen knew where they were going and hope was not a very likely guest.

The brute guards drove them deep into the earth, through tunnels and down stairs. For much of the journey the slap of the guards' leathery bare feet was the only sound, stark as drums beating a condemned man's march to the gallows. Since Vansen had only seen these passages through the eyes of the creatures Gyir had bespelled, it was strangely dreamlike now to travel them in his own body. They were not the featureless stone burrows he had thought them, but carved with intricate patterns, swirls and concentric circles and shapes that might have represented people or animals. He *could* recognize some of the shapes on the tunnel walls, and some of them were hard to look at—great, lowering owls with eyes like stars, and manlike creatures with heads and limbs divided from their torsos and the body parts piled before the birds as though in tribute. Other ominous shapes and symbols lined the passages as well, skulls and eyeless tortoises, both symbols of the Earthfather that Vansen knew well, along with some he did not recognize, knotted ropes and a squat cup shape with stubby legs that he thought might be a bowl or cauldron. And of course there were images of pigs, the animal most sacred to Immon, Kernios' grim servant.

"*The Black Pig has taken him!*" A despairing cry rang in his head, a childhood memory—an old woman of the Dales, cursing her son's untimely death. "*Curse the pig and curse his coldhearted master!*" she had screeched. "*Never will I light a candle for the Kerneia again!*"

Kerneia. In a faraway land where the sun still rose and set, the crowds were likely gathering on the streets of Southmarch to watch the statue of the masked god go by, carried high on a litter.

They would be drunk, even early in the morning—the litter-bearers, the crowds, even the Earthfather's priests, a deep, laughing-sad drunkenness that Vansen remembered well, the entire city like a funeral feast that had gone on too long. But here he was instead in the heart of the Earthfather's domain, being dragged to the god's very door!

A fever-chill swept over him and Vansen had to fight to keep from stumbling. He wished he could reach out to the prince, remind Barrick Eddon that he was not alone in this terrible place, but his shackles prevented it.

The way into the cavern that held the god's gate suddenly opened wide before them. The enormous chamber was lit by a mere dozen torches, its obsidian walls only delicately streaked with light and the ceiling altogether lost in darkness, but after the long trip through pitch-black tunnels Ferras Vansen found it as overwhelming as the great Trigon Temple in Southmarch on a bright afternoon, with color streaming down from its high windows. The gate itself was even more massive than it had seemed through the eyes of Gyir's spies, a rectangular slab of darkness as tall as a cliff, resembling an ordinary portal only in the way that the famous bronze colossus of Perin was like a living mortal man.

The guards prodded Vansen and the others toward the open area near the base of the exposed rock face. The slaves already assembled there, a pathetic, hollow-eyed and listless crowd watched over by what seemed almost as many guards as prisoners, shuffled meekly out of the captives' way, clearing an even larger space in front of the monstrous doorway.

The guards shoved the prisoners to their knees. Vansen wallowed in drifts of stone dust, sneezing as it billowed up around him like smoke and Barrick collapsed beside him as though arrow-shot, scarcely stirring. Vansen nudged the youth, trying to see if he had been injured somehow, but with the heavy wooden shackles around his wrists he could not move much without falling over.

Remember what I said . . .

Even as Gyir's words sounded in Ferras Vansen's skull, guards and workers began to stir all over the room—for a moment he thought that they had also heard the fairy's thoughts. Then he heard a thunderous, uneven rhythm like the pounding of a mighty drum. When he realized he was hearing footfalls, he knew why the guards, even those whom nature had made helplessly crooked, suddenly tried to straighten, and why all the kneeling slaves began to moan and shove their faces against the rough floor of the great cavern.

The demigod came through the door slowly, the chained heads that ornamented him swaying like seaweed in a tidal pool. As terrifying as Jikuyin was, for the first time Vansen could see something of his great age: the monster limped, leaning on a staff that was little more than a good-sized young tree stripped of its branches, and his great head lolled on his neck as though too heavy for him to hold completely upright. Still, as the ancient ogre looked around the chamber and bared his vast, broken teeth in a grin of ferocious satisfaction, Vansen felt his bladder loosen and his muscles go limp. The end had come, whatever Gyir might pretend. No one could fall into the hands of such a monstrous thing and live.

The other prisoners, many of them smeared with blood from their labors, struck their heads on the floor and wailed as the demigod approached. The awful, gigantic chamber, the hordes of shrieking creatures with bloody hands and filthy, despairing faces prostrating themselves before their giant lord—for a moment Vansen simply could not believe his eyes any longer: he had lost his wits, that was all it could be. His mind was regurgitating the worst tales the deacon in Little Stell had told to terrify Ferras Vansen and the other village children into serving the gods properly.

"Perin Skylord, clothed in light,"

Vansen murmured to himself,

"Guard us through the awesome night
Erivor, in silver mail
Smooth the seas on which we sail
Kernios, of death's dark lands
Take us in your careful hands . . ."

But it was pointless trying to remember childhood prayers—what help could such things be now? What good would anything do? The huge shape that was Jikuyin, so massive that he crushed stones that a strong man couldn't lift into powder beneath his feet, was limping toward them, each grating step like something as big as the world chewing, chewing, chewing . . .

Do not despair! The words came sharp as a slap.

Vansen turned to see that Gyir was still upright, though his guards had prostrated themselves. Everything in the Storm Lantern's featureless face showed in his eyes alone, wide with excitement and fear, but also hot with rage. Just beyond Gyir, Prince Barrick swayed as if in a high wind, scarcely able to balance even on his knees, his face a pale, sickly mask in the flickering light. For a moment Vansen could see the sister's handsome features in the brother's, and suddenly he felt his almost-forgotten promise stab at him like a dagger. He could not surrender while there was breath in him—he had an obligation. Despair was a luxury.

Prayers to the Trigon brothers seemed pointless on the very doorstep of the Earthfather's house. Unbidden, another prayer wafted into his thoughts like a fleck of ash floating on an updraft, a gentler prayer to a gentler deity—an invocation of Zoria, Mistress of the Doves. But although his lips moved, he could not make his clenched throat pass the words. *Zoria, virgin daughter, give me . . . give to me . . .*

A moment later the Zorian prayer, Zoria herself, even his own name, all blew out of Ferras Vansen's mind like leaves in a freezing wind as Jikuyin stopped in front of them and leaned down. His face was so huge it seemed the cratered moon had dropped from the sky.

"A gift to you." The demigod's voice shook Vansen's bones; his breath smelled like the fumes from a smelter's furnace, hot and metallic. *"You will witness my supreme moment—and even participate."* The curtain of dangling heads swayed stared sightlessly, shriveled lips helplessly grinning.

I'll be joining them soon, Vansen thought. How would the gods judge him? He had done his best, but he had still failed.

Jikuyin's great, bearded head swiveled to inspect Vansen and his companions, and Vansen had to look away—the god's eye big as a cannonball, the power of that squinting, reddened stare, were simply too much to bear. *"Your blood will unseal Immon's Gate,"* Jikuyin rumbled, *"open the way to the throne room of the Dirtlord himself, that piss-drinking King of Worms who took my eye. And when Earthstar is mine, when his great throne is mine, when I wear his mask of yellowed bone, then even if the gods find their way back I will be the greatest of their number!"*

You are mad, said Gyir wonderingly. Many in the room heard his silent words: a moan of fear rose up, as though the slaves who could understand him expected to share his punishment.

"There is no madness among gods!" Jikuyin laughed. *"How will I be called mad when I can shape everything to my own thoughts? Soon the gate will open, the blood will flow, and then what I speak . . . will be."*

My blood will dry to powder, to choking dust, before I let you spill so much as a drop in pursuit of this madness.

Jikuyin reached out a giant hand, fingers spreading as though he would crush Gyir to jelly. Instead, he only flicked at him, knocking the Qar warrior into a mass of shrieking prisoners. After those who could escape had scrambled away, the Storm Lantern lay unmoving where he had fallen, his featureless face in the dust.

"Who said it was your blood I wanted, you little whelp of Breeze?" Jikuyin laughed again, a booming roar of satisfaction that threatened to bring down the cavern roof. His hand reached out again, knocking Vansen to the ground, then it folded around Barrick, who let out a thin shriek of surprise and terror before the breath was squeezed out of him. Jikuyin dropped the limp prince among the guards. *"Him—the mortal child. I can smell the Fireflower in him. His blood will do nicely."*

Vansen struggled helplessly against the heavy shackles as the guards dragged Barrick toward the looming gate, but they were too tight to slip, too heavy to break. Ferras Vansen let out a howl of grief. Whatever happened, he would certainly die too, but the imminent death of the prince seemed a greater failure, a more horrifying finality.

Something grabbed at his arm. Vansen kicked out and one of the stinking, shaggy guards fell back, but got up immediately and came toward him again. Fighting the inevitable, Vansen managed to land another kick (to even less effect) before he saw that something was strange about the creature's expression. The apelike face was slack, and the eyes wandered lazily, fixed on nothing, as though the guard were blind. It was also holding a key in its clumsy, clawed hand.

If they want me unshackled before they kill me then it only means I'll take some of them with me. But why would they want to take that risk? As the creature fumbled roughly with the shackles, he suddenly realized he had seen that befuddled expression before on the creatures Gyir had controlled. Vansen looked to the fairy. The Storm Lantern was staring up into nothingness, squinting so hard in concentration that his eyes were little more than creases. Another guard stood behind Gyir, doing something with his bonds as well, but even if the fairy was controlling them both, time was running out.

The guards had dragged Prince Barrick to a spot just before the mighty doors which stretched above them higher and wider than the front of the great temple in Southmarch. Ueni'ssoh, the terrible, cadaverous gray man, walked slowly up to stand beside them and raised his skeletal hands in the air.

"O Fire-Eyed, White-Winged, hear us through the empty places!" he intoned in his harsh, unfeeling voice, "O Pale Question, grant us audience!"

Vansen could understand every word, but the tongue was nothing he had ever heard before, as inhuman as the sawing of a cricket: the sound of the gray man's fluid speech was in Vansen's ears, all tick and slur, but the meaning was in his head.

"O Emperor of Worms, see us through all darknesses!" Ueni'ssoh sang, "O Empty Box, grant us audience!"

The gray man's voice now rose, or gained some other power, because it seemed to fill Ferras Vansen's head like water poured splashing into a bowl, louder and louder until he could scarcely think, although the actual tones seemed as measured and unhurried as before. This was no song of Kerneia that he had ever heard, but Vansen thought he recognized a few words here and there, the ancient words of mourning his grandfather had sung at his grandmother's grave in the hills, but the gray man's terrible, flat voice made Ferras Vansen see pictures in his head that had nothing to do with his long-dead grandmother or his father's burial plot. A crimson-lit world of scuttling shadows filled his thoughts, an end to all things so final and so terrible that it lay on his heart like an immense weight.

The fairy-spelled guard still scrabbled at his shackles. Vansen was not free yet—he could not let the voice overwhelm him. He could not fail.

> *"See now where the darkness twists in us like a river*
> *It is time to get up and go to the land of the Red Sunlight*
> *The land where the sun sets and does not rise.*
>
> *"O Burned Foot, let us shelter in your hard folds of shadow*
> *Where we can still see the dying sun until the last day.*
> *Crowfather*
> *Wearer of the Iron Gloves*
> *Husband to the Knot that cannot be Untied*
> *We are frightened, O King. Open the gate!"*

At first, in his terror and confusion, Ferras Vansen thought the massive stone portal was beginning to fade, or to melt away like ice. But no, he realized a moment later, something much stranger was happening: the great doors were swinging inward into shadow, the darkness beyond so absolute that it could smother the stars themselves. Vansen's heart quailed. His body felt suddenly boneless, limp as an empty sack.

Ferras Vansen, do not despair! The words came like a whisper from the other side of the world, but they gave him back a little of himself. It was Gyir speaking, Gyir in his head, but only faintly. He could feel the fairy's powers stretched to their utmost as they touched Vansen, Barrick, the guards working at their bonds, and many others Vansen could not even name—Gyir's will spreading among them in an invisible spiderweb of influence, although the web quivered and sagged now, near its breaking-point. The Storm Lantern's strength was astonishing, far beyond anything Vansen could have dreamed.

Fight! Gyir demanded. *Fight for the boy—fight for your home! I need more time.*

Time? Why? It did not seem as though even the fairy's heroic efforts would make much difference. Whether they were shackled or not, the world was ending right now, here in the darkness beneath the ground. Whatever was behind that door would swallow them all . . .

But even now, when nothing mattered, Ferras Vansen could not forget his oath to Barrick's sister. It was almost the only thing he *could* remember: his own name and history, all that had happened to him before this moment, were fading swiftly, swallowed in the gray man's sonorous words.

> *"O Silver Beak, Send your flying ones before us*
> *O Ravens' Prince, Make a trail in the sky*
> *Show us the way to the gate, the gate of your servant."*

The gray man's incantation now filled the cavern like the noise of a rising storm, harsh and booming, but it was also as intimate as if he whispered in Vansen's ear. Surely no human throat could sound like that . . . !

> *"The ocean of mud where the breathless sleep*
> *Pass it by!*
> *The dreaming tree that lifts mountains with its crushing roots*
> *Pass it by!*
> *The forest of the beating heart*
> *Where the flutes of the lost play in the shadows beside the path*
> *Pass it by!*

The Storm of Tears
With rain that wounds the faces of pilgrims like arrows
Pass it by!"

The gate was completely open, a hole into absolute blackness, but a blackness that was still somehow, inexplicably *alive*—Vansen could almost hear it breathing, and his heart seemed to swell in his breast until he thought it would push up into his throat and choke off the last of his air.

"Skull Eater, destroy our enemies hiding beside the road;
Roots of the Immortal Pine, fill our nostrils so we do not smell demons!
Shepherd of the Mummies, lead us safely among the unquiet dead;
Black Bones, hold us tightly in the icy winds!
Cloak of Singing Dust, show us only to the stars!

The gray man gestured. Two huge, hairy guards pulled Barrick up onto his knees in front of Ueni'ssoh, who was still chanting, then one of them yanked Barrick's head back so that the boy's chin jutted out toward Vansen and the others watching. The other guard unsheathed a strange, terrible knife with a jagged blade half as wide as it was long, and set it almost tenderly against the white flesh of the prince's throat. Frenzied, Vansen tried to struggle to his feet, and just at that moment he felt the creature behind give a last wrench at the shackles and they tumbled off his arms. Knives of pain stabbed in his joints as he raised his arms and staggered toward Barrick and the guards.

"O Narrowing Way, open the gate!"

The chanting words of the Dreamless filled every part of the world, every part of Vansen's thoughts. They were heavy as stones, dropping on him, crushing him—or was that the thunder of Jikuyin laughing? The prince, the guards, and the gray man were washed by torchlight but framed against absolute darkness as if the gods themselves had forgotten to provide a world for them to inhabit.

Ueni'ssoh's voice surged in triumph.

> *"O Spiral Shell, lead us to the center!*
> *O Cauldron Lord, give us back our names!*
> *Grass Chieftain, open the gate!*
> *Earthlord, open the gate!*
> *Black Earth! Black Earth! Open the gate between Why and Why*
> *Not . . . !"*

Something was in the black space of the door now, something invisible but so all-pervasive and life-crushing that Vansen shrieked in terror like a child even as he threw himself at the shaggy guard who held the knife to Barrick's throat. A shadowy recollection of Donal Murroy's teachings came to him as if from another person's life: he grabbed, braced, and snapped the guard's elbow against its own hinge, so that the creature howled with pain and dropped the queer blade. Vansen snatched it up and whirled to look for Ueni'ssoh, but the gray man seemed lost in some kind of trance, so Vansen lunged at the other guard instead, knocking Prince Barrick free from the creature's grasp as he did so and sending the shaggy beast skidding face first across the rocky floor. Vansen snatched up a stone from the floor and began pounding on the lock of the prince's shackles, intent on freeing him, ignoring Barrick's cries of agony as the boy's crippled arm was rattled in its socket.

A moment longer, something whispered in his head. Ferras Vansen's own thoughts were so tangled and diminished that for a long instant he could not understand who was talking to him, and even when he could, he could not understand it. *Keep fighting a moment longer . . . !*

The lock broke and the prince's shackles fell away just as the other guard attacked him. It was all Vansen could do to shove Barrick aside, then use the knife to dig at the guard's stinking, hairy body. Vansen and the guard stood, locked in a helpless clinch, gasping into each other's faces, each with a free hand gripping the other's weapon, both weapons shuddering in front of an enemy's wide, terror-staring eye. Vansen could see the monstrous open gateway past his attacker's shoulder, the blackness roiling and bubbling with invisible forces that squeezed Vansen's bones and guts until he thought his heart would stop.

Vansen had a moment to wonder if Gyir really had made a plan, but that everything beyond getting the shackles off had simply failed to happen. Then the second guard hit him in the back, forcing him to let go of the other creature's killing hand. He swung his weight and ducked to avoid the stabbing blow to his face and he and the two guards became tangled. Locked in a straining, gasping knot, the three of them hobbled a few steps, then stumbled together over the threshold of the god's door and fell into darkness.

Black.

Frozen.

Nothing.

The apelike guards spun away and vanished into the void as they all plummeted downward; within a heartbeat their wordless screams had faded. His own voice was gone. He could feel his lungs shoving out a scream of absolute terror but he heard no sound except the almost silent whistle of his fall.

Ferras Vansen hurtled down and down. Within moments he was far beyond the point where he could survive the impact, but still he fell. At last his wits flew away in the emptiness and wind.

35

Blessings

Of all the rebel gods who had survived the battle against the Trigon, only a few were spared. One of them was Kupilas, son of Zmeos, because the Artificer proclaimed his allegiance to his uncles and promised he could bring many useful things to the three godly brothers and their heavenly city. And thus it proved to be. He taught them healing and other crafts, and even the making of wine, so that mortals could make offerings of drink to the gods as well as meat and blood.

—from *The Beginnings of Things*
The Book of the Trigon

Utta stared at her reflection. Even looking in a mirror was an unusual experience, since Zorian sisters were generally given neither opportunity nor encouragement to contemplate their own reflections. "I cannot help it," she said. "I look like something in a mummer's play."

"You do not," said Merolanna, invisible for a moment in a cloud of powder as her little maid Eilis vigorously applied the brush to Utta's face. "You look extremely handsome—like a highborn gentleman."

"I am not supposed to be a gentleman, even in this ridiculous imposture, but an ordinary servant. In fact, though, I am neither of those. I am an old woman, Your Grace. What am I doing got up in such a semblance?"

"You must trust me," the duchess replied, waving away the last of the powder. The maid began to cough, so Merolanna sent the girl out of the room. "I simply cannot do what must be done," she said when they were alone in the bedchamber, "since I am bound to be at the blessing ceremony, especially with Duke Caradon coming to Southmarch. The Tollys are swarming, so we Eddons must make a show. I have to go. That is why you must do your part, my dear."

But I'm not an Eddon. Utta looked at the duchess with what she hoped was a certain sternness. She thought Merolanna had grown a bit careless about this matter of her lost son, her plans getting stranger and more wild, as though the steps they were contemplating now really were nothing more dangerous than a mum-show. She also clearly felt that Utta had become some kind of foot soldier in the cause, bound to obey all orders.

"I can understand how you feel about the child . . ." she began.

"No, you can't, Sister," said the duchess with unconvincing good cheer. "Only a mother can. So let's just get on with this, shall we?"

Utta sighed.

When she was finished, with all the unfamiliar ties and buckles done up, Utta took one last look at the dour creature in the glass—an aged, effeminate servant dressed in dun-colored robes and a shapeless hat. It seemed scandalous to be showing so much hose-covered leg, but that was what men did every day. She squinted.

"You know, all the men's clothes in the world cannot make a woman truly look like one. A man, I mean. Our faces just are not the right shape." She traced the line of her own too-delicate jaw with her finger.

"That is why we will wrap this close around you," Merolanna said briskly, winding the tails of the hat around Utta's chin and neck like a scarf. "It is a cold day—no one will take much notice. Especially not today."

"But is it wise, this plan?" She felt fairly certain it was not, but was torn between her good sense and her loyalty to Merolanna.

"To be honest with you, Utta, I don't care." The duchess clapped her hands together, which brought the little maid back into the chamber. "Help me with my jewels, Eilis, will you?" Merolanna turned toward back toward Utta. "Now you had best be on your way. We have only a few hours left—it is still winter, and dark so early."

Utta wasn't certain that hurrying off because the danger would be worse in a few hours made sense, especially when she hadn't agreed that the plan was warranted in the first place, but she had long since learned that Merolanna could not be opposed with anything less than a wholehearted and extremely patient effort.

"Very well," she said. "I will meet you afterward as we arranged, then."

"Thank you, dear," said Merolanna, remaining statue-still as her maid struggled to close the hasp on a necklace that looked as heavy as a silver harbor chain. "You're very kind."

Each time he looked at her Matt Tinwright had to look away after only a few moments. He felt certain that his guilt as well as his longing must shine from his face like the light of the brazier burning on the altar.

Only once had Elan M'Cory looked up to meet his gaze across the vastness of the Trigon Temple, but even from half a hundred paces away he felt the touch of her eyes with so great a force he nearly gasped aloud. Even in the midst of this nominally festive occasion she wore black clothes and a half-veil, as though she were the only person in Southmarch castle who still mourned the death of Gailon Tolly—as she might very well be. Tinwright had never been able to learn what Gailon had been to Elan, whether a secret lover, her hope for a good marriage, or something even harder to understand, but it confirmed him in his belief that nothing was less knowable than a woman's heart.

Hendon, the dead duke's youngest brother, stood beside Elan dressed in an elegant outfit of dove gray with black accents, his sleeves so deeply slashed that his arms seemed thicker than his legs. Elan M'Cory might be the most important person in the room for Matt Tinwright, but it was the woman on the other side who was clearly of the most interest to Hendon Tolly: Southmarch's guardian did not even look at Elan, let alone talk to her, but spent much of the blessing ceremony whispering to Queen Anissa. It was the queen's first day out in public since the baby had been born. She looked pale but happy, and quite willing to receive the attentions of the current guardian of Southmarch.

The nurse beside her held the infant prince; as Tinwright looked at the tiny, pink face he could not help marveling at what a strange life this child had been born into. Just a few months ago little Olin Alessandros would have been the youngest in a good-sized family, the happy child of a healthy, reigning monarch in time of peace, with nothing ahead to trouble his horizons except the business of being part of the most powerful family in the March Kingdoms. Now he was almost alone in the world, two brothers and a sister gone, his father imprisoned. If Matt Tinwright could have felt sorry for something as unformed as a baby (and Tinwright was beginning to feel he actually could)—well, then young Prince Olin was a good candidate for pity, despite having been born with everything the poet would most have liked to have himself.

Well, almost everything. There was one thing that even having been born royal would not have given him, and at this moment the lack of it burned in Tinwright's heart so that he could barely stand still. And tonight . . . the awful thing he must do tonight . . . !

He looked at Elan's pale face again but her eyes were cast down. If she could only understand! But she couldn't, as had been made all too clear. She had invited Death into her heart. She wanted no other suitor.

Hierarch Sisel finished the invocation of Madi Surazem, thanking the goddess for protecting the child and his mother during the birth. Tinwright thought the hierarch looked drawn and unsettled—but then, who did not? The shadow of the Twilight People hung over the castle like a shroud, chilling the hearts of even those who pretended not to feel it. It was having its effect in other ways, too, with fewer ships coming into the harbor and, because of all the refugees from the mainland city and villages, many more mouths to feed even as many of the kingdom's farms lay deserted and untended. Little as he knew about such things, even Matt Tinwright realized that when spring came and no crops were planted it could mark the beginning of the end for Southmarch.

Hierarch Sisel stood behind a small altar that had been erected just for this ceremony so that the ceremonial fire could be placed atop the large stone altar. The flames billowed behind him as cold air swirled in the high places of the temple. "Who brings this child before the gods?" he asked.

"I do," said Anissa in a small voice.

Sisel nodded. "Then bring him forward."

To Tinwright's surprise, the queen didn't carry the child to the altar herself, but nodded for the nurse holding the baby to follow her. When they stood before the altar, Sisel threw back the child's blanket.

"With the living earth of Kernios," he proclaimed, rubbing the bottoms of the child's feet with dark dust. "With the strong arm of Perin,"—he lifted the tau cross called the Hammer and held it over the child's head for a brief moment before setting it down—"and with the singing waters of Erivor, patron of your forefathers, guardian of your family's house . . ." He dipped his fingers into a bowl and spattered the child on the top of the head. The baby began to cry. Sisel grimaced ever so slightly, then made the sign of the Three. "In the sight of the Trigon and all the gods of Heaven, and soliciting the wise protection of all their oracles on this, the prophets' own day, I grant you the name Olin Alessandros Benediktos Eddon. May the blessings of heaven sustain you." The hierarch looked up. "Who stands for the father?"

"I will, Eminence," said Hendon Tolly. Anissa gazed at him with grateful pleasure, just as if he had really *been* the child's father, and in that moment Tinwright felt he saw it all plain: of course Tolly did not want Elan—he had bigger plans. If Olin did not come back his wife and son would need another man in their lives. And who would be better than the handsome young lord who was already the infant prince's guardian?

Hendon Tolly took the baby from the nurse's arms and walked slowly around the altar, symbolically introducing young Olin to the household. Any other family, even a rich one, would have performed this ceremony in their own home, and before this day even the Eddons themselves had blessed their new children in the homely confines of the Erivor chapel, not in a vast barn like the Trigon Temple. Tinwright could not help wondering whose idea it had been to perform the blessing here in front of so many people. He had thought they were holding the Carrying ceremony ahead of Duke Caradon's arrival because to wait a day—to hold it at the beginning of the Kerneia—would be bad luck. Now he decided that Hendon simply did not want his older brother present to steal any of the attention he commanded as guardian of the castle.

The second time around the altar Hendon Tolly lifted the infant above his head. The crowd, which had sat respectfully, now began to clap and cheer, with Durstin Crowel and Tolly's other closest supporters making the most noise, although Tinwright could see expressions of poorly-hidden disgust on some of the older nobles—those few who had actually attended. He wondered what kind of excuses Avin Brone and the others had made to stay away—even if he were a man of power himself, Tinwright would not want to risk offending Hendon Tolly.

A moment later, as Hierarch Sisel completed the final blessing, Matt Tinwright realized the madness of his own thoughts. He was frightened of refusing an invitation from Tolly to a child blessing, but he was smuggling poison to Tolly's mistress.

It is like a disease, he thought as the crowd began to break up, some pushing forward toward Anissa and the high nobility, others hastening out into the cold winds that swirled through Market Square. In all respects it looked like an ordinary, festive occasion, but Tinwright and everyone else knew that just across the bay a dreadful, silent enemy was watching them. *A fever of disordered thinking rules the place, and I have it as badly as anyone here. We are not a city anymore, we are a plague hospital.*

To his shock, Hendon Tolly actually noticed him as he tried to slip past.

"Ah, poet." The guardian of Southmarch fixed him with an amused stare, leaning away from a conversation with Tirnan Havemore. Elan, who stood beside Hendon, did her best not to meet Tinwright's eye. "You skulk, sir," Tolly accused him. "Does this mean you will not have your poem ready for us at tomorrow's feast? Or are you merely fearful of its quality?"

"It will be ready, my lord." He had been staying up until long past midnight for almost a tennight, burning oil and candles at a prodigious rate (much to the disgust of Puzzle, who had an old man's love for going to bed just after sundown and for pinching coppers until they squeaked). "I only hope it will please you."

"Oh, as do I, Tinwright." Tolly grinned like a fox finding an unguarded bird's nest. "As do I."

The master of Southmarch said a few more quiet words to Havemore, then turned to go, tugging Elan M'Cory after him as though she were a dog or a cloak. When she didn't move quickly enough, Hendon Tolly turned back and grabbed at her shoulder, but wound up pinching the pale flesh of her bosom instead. She winced and let out a little moan.

"When I say step lively," he told her in a quiet, measured voice, "then you must jump, slut, and quickly. If there are any tricks like that in front of my brother I will make you dance as you have never danced before. Now come."

Havemore and the others standing nearby did not even appear to have noticed, and for a mad moment Tinwright could almost believe he had imagined it. Elan silently followed Hendon out, a patch of angry scarlet blooming on the white of her breast.

It was strange to step out this way, her lower limbs moving so freely. In truth, Utta felt disturbingly naked—the shape of her own legs was something she usually saw only when she bathed or prepared herself for sleep, not striding down a street with nothing between them and the world but a thin layer of worsted woolen hose.

Sister Utta had done her best not to nag at Princess Briony when the girl had become fixed on wearing boy's clothing, although in her heart Utta had felt it was the sign of something unbalanced in the child, perhaps a reaction to all the sadness around her. But suddenly she could understand a little of what Briony had meant when she had spoken of "the freedoms men take for granted." Was it truly the gods themselves who had made women the weaker sex, or was it something as simple as differences of dress and custom?

But they are stronger than us, Utta thought. *Any woman who has been despoiled or brutalized by a man no taller than she knows that only too well.*

Still, strength alone was not enough to make superiority, she reflected, otherwise oxen and growling lions would command empires. Instead, men hobbled oxen so they could not move faster than a walk. Was it true, as Briony had complained, that men hobbled their women as well?

Or do we hobble ourselves? But if so, why would we do such a thing?

Of course, women would not be the first or only slaves to aid their captors.

Listen to me—slaves! Captors! It is these times in which we live—they turn everything downside up and make us question all. But meanwhile, I am not watching what I am doing and will probably walk myself into the lagoon and drown!

Utta looked up. She hadn't actually reached the lagoon yet, and was in fact only halfway down Tin Street, near the Onir Kyma temple—still outside the Skimmer neighborhoods. She was glad of the temple tower and the few other landmarks she recognized: she had never been this far from the castle except on the main road to the causeway when she and her Zorian sisters went to the mainland for the spring fair.

A group of men lolled in the road ahead of her, all but blocking the narrow way. As she drew closer she saw they were ordinary men, not Skimmers—laborers by the look of them, unshaven and wearing work-stained clothes. To her surprise, they did not make way as she approached but remained where they were, watching her with sullen interest.

I am used to being a woman, she thought—*and a priestess at that. People step aside for me, or even ask blessing. Is this the way it is for all men? Or is there some reason they are blocking the road?*

"Here now," one of the smallest of the men said. He had a lazy, self-satisfied tone that suggested he was their leader, size notwithstanding. He pushed himself away from the wall and stood before her, blocking her path. "What do you want, little fellow?"

It was all that an outraged Utta could do not to argue: among women she was considered tall, and she was nearly the same height as this fellow, although vastly more slender. "I have business ahead," she said in her gruffest voice. "Please let me by."

"Oh, business in Skimmertown, have you?" He raised his voice as though she had said something shameful and he meant everyone to know. "Looking for a little fish-face girl, eh, fellow?"

For a moment Utta could only stare. "Nothing of the sort. Business," she said, and then realized she might sound too haughty. "My master's business."

"Ah," said the one who had been questioning her. "Your master, is it? And what business does *he* have down in Scummer Town? Hiring fishy-men for cheap, I'll warrant, taking work away from proper fellows. Ah, see the look on his chops now, boys!" The small man brayed a laugh. "Been caught out, he has." He took a step nearer, looked Utta up and down. "Look at you, soft as marrow jelly. Are you a phebe, then? One of those?"

"Let me go." She tried to keep her voice from shaking but didn't entirely succeed.

"Oh, do you think we should?" The man leaned closer. He stank of wine. "Do you?"

"Yes," said a new voice. "Let him go."

Both Utta and her persecutor looked up in surprise. A hairless man had come into the alley from a side-passage—a Skimmer, Utta realized, with a scar down his face that pulled one eyelid out of shape. The crowd of men blocking the alley stirred with an animal shiver of hatred Utta could feel.

"Hoy, Fish-face," said her antagonist. "What are you doing out of your pond? This part of town belongs to pureblood folk."

The Skimmer stared back with a face stiff as a wax effigy. He was not small, and for a Skimmer he was solidly built, but he was hugely outnumbered. Several of the men moved so that he was more nearly surrounded. He smiled—his injured eye squinted shut as he did so—then he raised his head and made a froggy, chirruping noise. Within moments half a dozen more young Skimmer men began to drift into the alley, one holding a baling hook in his fist, another tapping a long wooden club against his leg, grinning toothlessly.

"Merciful Zoria," Utta breathed. *They're going to kill each other.*

"You lot shouldn't be past Barge Street," said the man who had accosted her. He was grinning, too, and he and the first Skimmer had begun to circle each other, one lazy step at a time. "You shouldn't be here. This is ours, this is." He spoke slowly, like an invocation—he was summoning the powerful mystery of violence, Utta realized, with as much careful method as a priest used to call the attention of a god. She could not help staring at the circling pair, her skin fever-chilled.

"Get out," someone said from just behind her—one of the other Skimmers. She felt strong hands take her and pull her away, then another hand shoved her in the small of the back. She took a few stumbling steps away from the center of the now-crowded alley, slipping and tumbling into the mud. She looked back, half-expecting one of the men who had accosted her to try to stop her, or one of the Skimmers to shout at her to run away, but she was out of the center of the violence-spell now and she might as well have ceased to exist. The two main antagonists were feinting gently and almost lovingly at each other with knives she had not seen before. Their comrades were silently facing off, ready to throw themselves at their opposites when the first blow was struck.

Slipping in the wet street, clumsy as a newborn calf, Utta struggled upright and hurried away even as someone let out a shout of pain and fury behind her. A larger roar went up, many voices shouting, and people began to step out of the tiny, close-quartered houses to see what was the matter.

The child who opened the oval door was so small and so wide-eyed that at first, despite herself, Sister Utta could nearly believe the Skimmers were indeed a different kind of creature entirely. She was still shaking badly, and not just because of her encounter with the street bullies. Everything was so strange here, the smells, the look of things, even the shapes of the doors and windows. Now she stood at the end of a swaying gangplank on the edge of the castle's largest lagoon, waiting to be admitted to a floating houseboat. How odd her life had become!

There were no Skimmers left in the Vuttish Isles of Utta Fornsdodir's childhood, but they still featured heavily in local stories, although those in the stories were far more magical than those who lived here beside the lagoon. Still, they were strange-looking folk, and Utta realized she had spent almost twenty years in Southmarch Castle without ever really speaking to one of them, let alone knowing them as neighbors or friends.

"H—hello," she said to the child. "I've come to see Rafe."

The urchin looked back at her. Because the child had no eyebrows, hair pulled back (as was the habit for both male and female Skimmers) and a face still in the androgynous roundness of childhood, Utta had no idea whether it was a boy or a girl. At last the little one turned and scuttled back inside, but left the door open. Utta could only guess that was an invitation of sorts, so she stepped up onto the deck and into the boat's cabin.

The ceilings were so low she had to bend over. As she followed the child up the stairs she guessed that the cabin had at least three stories. It definitely seemed bigger inside than outside, full of nooks and narrow passages, with tiny stairwells scarcely as wide as her shoulders leading away both up and down from the first landing. Her guide was not the only child, either—she passed at least half a dozen others who looked back at her with no sign of either fear or favor. None of them wore much, and the youngest was naked although the day outside was cold even for Dimene and the houseboat did not seem to be heated. This smallest one was dragging a ragged doll by the ankle, a toy that had obviously once belonged to some very different child since it had long, golden tresses. None of the Skimmers Utta had ever seen were fair-haired, although their skins could be as pale as any of her own family back in the northern islands.

The first child led her up one more narrow staircase and then down another before stepping out onto the deck on what she guessed must be the lagoon side of the houseboat. Utta could not help thinking they seemed to have reached it by the most round-about way possible.

The young Skimmer man looked up from the rope he was splicing. The little one, apparently now relieved of responsibility, skipped back into the boat's ramshackle cabin. The youth looked up at her briefly, then returned his attention to the rope. "Who are you?" he asked in the throaty way of his folk.

"Utta—Sister Utta. I come with a message for you. Are you Rafe?"

He nodded, still watching the splice. "Sister Utta? I thought you smelled a bit unmanly, even for *that* place." He meant the Inner Keep, she guessed, but he said it as though he were talking about a prison or a forest full of unpleasant wild beasts. "Did someone tell you we'd be after any woman, no matter how old?"

I am old, she reminded herself. *Surely I can't take offense.* She looked at him; he carefully did not look back. He was as young or younger than any of the Skimmers who had come into the alley, and his arms seemed long even by the standards of his folk. He had slender, artful fingers, and a firm, good jaw.

"I was sent by the Duchess Merolanna of Southmarch," she said. "She was given your name as someone who might help us. We need a boatsman."

"Given?" He raised a hairless eyebrow. "Someone's been free. Given by whom?"

"Turley Longfingers."

He snorted. "Would be. He'd be happy to see me get myself killed on some drylander errand, wouldn't he? He knows Ena and I will be hanging the nets come springtime and she'll be old enough then he can't stop us." He stared at Sister Utta now with something like curiosity. "Does it pay well, still, this errand?"

"I think so. The duchess is no pinchpurse."

"Then tell me what she wants done and what she'll pay, Vuttswoman."

"How did you know?"

"That you're Vuttish?" He laughed. "You *smell* Vuttish, don't you? Still, you're better than most. Compared to a Syannese or Jellon-man, you're spring seafoam and pink thrift-blossoms. Jellon-folk eat no fish, lots of pig, don't they? You can smell one a mile distant. Now, if we've finished talking on how folks smell, let's speak of silver."

36

The False Woman

Suya wandered long in the wilderness and suffered many hardships until at last she came to the dragon gate of the palace of Xergal, and there fell down at the verge of death. But Xergal the Earthlord coveted her beauty, and instead of accepting her into his kingdom of the dead he forced her to reign beside him as his queen. She never after spoke a word.

—from *The Revelations of Nushash*, Book One

THERE WERE SKULLS FOR SALE in all the market-places of Syan, some baked of honey-glazed bread, others painstakingly carved from pine boughs, and even a few shaped out of beautiful, polished marble for nobles and rich merchants to put on their tables or in their family shrines. Sprigs of white aspholdel were set out on tables to be bought and then pinned to a collar or a bodice. Kerneia was coming.

Briony realized with astonishment that she had been traveling with the players for a full month now, which was nearly as strange as what she found herself doing most days—namely, acting the part of the goddess Zoria, Perin's daughter. In truth, it was stranger than that: as a character in Finn's play, Briony was a girl pretending to be a boy pretending to be a goddess pretending to be a boy, an array of nested masks so confusing she could not concentrate on it long enough to waste much time thinking about it.

Makewell's Men had not yet performed the whole of Teodoros' rewritten play about Zoria's abduction, but they had worked up most of the main scenes and tried them out on the rural population of northern Syan as the company moved from place to place. It had been strange enough for Briony to speak the goddess' words (or at least such words as Finn Teodoros had given her) in the muddy courtyard of some tiny village inn. Now the players had begun to follow the green course of the Esterian River and the towns were getting bigger as they traveled south. Audiences were growing, too.

"But there are so many words to remember," Briony complained early one evening to Teodoros as the others trooped back from their afternoon's sightseeing. "And I have memorized only half the play!"

"You are doing very well," the playwright assured her. "You are a cunning child and would have done most professions proud, I'll warrant. Besides, most of your speeches are in the parts of the play we have performed already, so there is not much left for you to learn."

"But still, it seems so much. What if I forget? I almost did the other night but Feival whispered the words to me."

"And he will again if you need him to. But you know the story, my girl—ah, I mean, my boy." He grinned. "If you forget, say something to the point. Hewney and Makewell and the rest are experienced mummers. They will come to your aid and put you back on the track."

It was the sort of thing old Steffens Nynor had always said to her about court protocols, and as with the castellan's instructions about the intricate details of the Smoke Ceremony she had been forced to learn for the Demia's Candle holidays, she suspected it wasn't going to be quite as easy as everyone was telling her.

The Esterian river valley was perhaps the most fertile part of all Eion, a vast swath of black soil stretched between rolling hills that extended from the northern tip of Lake Strivothol where the city of Tessis spread wide, up the hundred-mile length of the river to the mountains northeast of the Heartwood. Briony remembered her father saying that he guessed as many as a quarter of the people in all of Eion lived in that one stretch of land, and certainly now that she saw the farms covering nearly every hillside, and the towns (many of them as large as any city in the March Kingdoms outside Southmarch itself) butting against each other on either side of the wide, cobbled thoroughfare and along the river's eastern shore as well, she found it easy to believe.

Ugenion, once a great trading city, now much reduced, Onir Diotrodos with its famous water temple, Doros Kallida—the company's wagons passed through them all, sometimes traveling only a few hours down the Royal Highway (still called King Karal's Road in some parts) before they stopped again in another prosperous village or town. Syan was at the same time so much like and unlike what Briony had known most of her life that it made her even more homesick than usual. The people spoke the common tongue with a slurring accent she sometimes found hard to understand (although it had been their tongue first, Finn Teodoros enjoyed pointing out, so by rights Briony was the one speaking with an accent). Some of the folk who came to see the players even made fun of how Makewell and the others spoke, loudly repeating their words with an emphasis on what they clearly felt was the harsh, chopping March Kingdoms way of talking. But the Syannese also seemed to enjoy the diversion, and Nevin Hewney told her one day it was because they were more used to such things than were the rustic folk of the March Kingdoms, or even many of the city dwellers of Southmarch.

"*This* is where playmaking grew," Hewney explained. His broad gesture took in the whole of the surrounding valley, which in this unusually empty spot looked like a place that had scarcely seen a farm croft, let alone a theater. As always when he had downed a few drinks, the infamous poet was enjoying his own discourse. Seeing Briony's confusion, he scowled in a broadly beleaguered way. "No, not *here* by this particular oak tree, but in the land of Syan. The festival plays of Hierosol—dry tales not of the gods but of pious mortals, most of them, the *oniri* and other martyrs—here became the mummeries of Greater and Little Zosimia and the Wildsong Night comedies. They have had plays, playmakers, and players here for a thousand years."

"And never once paid any of them what they're worth," growled Pedder Makewell.

"It's only because there are so many of them around," said Feival. "Too many cobblers drives down the price of shoes, as everyone knows."

"So then why did we . . . did you, I mean . . . come here?" asked Briony. "Would there not be places to go where players would be a rare and greatly appreciated thing?"

Hewney looked at her, his eyes narrowing. "You speak very well for a servant girl, our Tim. How did you learn to turn a phrase so nimbly?"

Finn Teodoros cleared his throat loudly. "Are you boring the child again with your history of stagecraft, Nevin? Suffice it to say that the Syannese love our art, and there is a sufficiency of people here who will be glad to see us. And now we have something new to show them, as well!"

She frowned. "What?"

"You. Our dear, sweet little goddess. The groundlings will water at the mouth when they see you."

"You're a pig, Finn!" Feival Ulian laughed, but also seemed a little hurt—he was the company's stage beauty, after all. "Don't mock her."

"Oh, but Tim here is special," said Teodoros. "Trust me."

Half the time I don't understand what these people are talking about, Briony thought. *The other half the time, I'm too tired to care.*

★

The town of Ardos Perinous sat on a hilltop. It had once been a nobleman's fortress, but the castle was now occupied by no one more exalted than a demi-hierarch of the church, a distaff relative of the Syannese king, Enander. Briony's ears had pricked up when she heard that—Enander was the man whom Shaso had thought might help her, if only for a price.

"What's he like, the king of Syan?" Briony asked Teodoros, who was walking beside the wagon for once, sparing the horse having to carry his weight up the steep road. She had never met King Enander or any of his family except a few of the more distant nephews and nieces—the lord of Syan would never send his own children to a place as backward and remote as Southmarch, of course—but she knew of him by reputation. Her father had a grudging respect for Enander, and no one disputed the Syannese king's many deeds of bravery, but most of what she had heard were tales from his younger days. He must now be past sixty winters of age.

The playwright shrugged. "He is a well-liked monarch, I believe. A warrior but no great lover of war, and not so crazed by the gods that he beggars the people to build new temples, either. But now that he is old I have heard that some say he is disinterested in anything except his mistress, a rather infamous Jellonian baroness named Ananka—a castoff of King Hesper's, it is said, who somehow found an even better perch for herself." His forehead wrinkled as he thought about it. "There is a play in that, if one could only keep one's head on one's neck after performing it— *The Cuckoo Bride,* perhaps . . ."

Briony had to struggle to concentrate on what Finn was saying—she had been distracted by the mention of Hesper of Jellon, the traitor-king who had sold her father to Ludis Drakava. He was another one she wanted desperately to have at the point of a sword, begging for mercy . . .

"And there is the heir, too—Eneas, a rather delicious young man, if a bit mature and hearty for my tastes." Teodoros showed his best wicked grin. "He waits patiently. They say he is a good man, too, pious and brave. Of course, they say that about every prince, even those who prove to be monsters the instant their fundaments touch the throne."

Briony certainly knew about Eneas. He was another young man on whom her girlish fancies had once fixed when she had been only seven or eight. She had never actually seen him, not even a portrait, but one of the girls who watched over her had been Syannese (one of Enander's disregarded nieces) and had told her what a kind and handsome youth Eneas was. For months Briony had dreamed that someday he would come to visit her father, take one look at her, and declare that he could have no other bride. Briony had little doubt she would look on him differently now.

They were nearing the top of the hill. The walls of the castle loomed over them like the shell of some huge ancient creature left behind by retreating tides. It was a strange day: although the weather was winter-cold, the sun was clear and sharp overhead, yet the sky just above the river valley was shrouded with thick clouds. "How long until we reach Tessis?"

Teodoros waved his hand. He was breathing heavily, unused to such exercise. "There," he gasped.

"What do you mean?" she said, staring up at the stone walls she had thought belonged to the keep of Ardos Perinous. "Are you saying *that's* Tessis?" It seemed impossible—it was far smaller than even Southmarch Castle, whose growing populace had spilled over onto the mainland centuries earlier.

"No," said the playwright, still fighting to get his breath back. "Turn . . . around, fool child. Look . . . behind you."

She did, and gasped. They had climbed up above the treeline and now she could see what had been blocked by the bend of the river. Only a few miles ahead the valley opened out into a bowl so wide she could not see its farthest reach. Everywhere she looked there were houses and more—walls, towers, steeples, and thousands of chimneys, the latter all puffing trails of smoke into the sky so that the entire valley lay under a pall of gray, like a fog that only began a hundred feet in the air. Channels led out from the Esterian River in all directions and crisscrossed the valley floor, the water reflecting in the late light so that the city seemed caught in a web of silver.

"Merciful Zoria," she said quietly. "It's huge!"

"Some say Hierosol is bigger," Teodoros replied, wiping at his streaming forehead and cheeks. "But I think that is not true anymore." He smiled. "I forgot, you haven't seen Tessis before, have you?"

Briony shook her head, unable to think of anything to say. She felt very small. How could she ever have felt that Southmarch was so important—an equal sister to nations like Syan? Any thought of revealing herself to the Syannese and asking for help suddenly seemed foolish. They would laugh at her, or ignore her.

"None other like it," Teodoros said. " *'Fair white walls on which the gods themselves did smile, and towers that stirred the clouds,'* as the poet Vanderin put it. Once the entire world was theirs."

"It . . . it looks as though they still own a good share," said Briony.

By all the gods, she thought as they rolled down the wide thoroughfare, jostled and surrounded by dozens of other wagons and hundreds of other foot travelers, *Finn says this is not even the biggest street in Tessis—that Lantern Broad is twice the size—but it's still wider across than Market Square!*

She had never before in her life felt so much like—what had Finn called her that first day? *"A straw-covered bumpkin just off the channel boat from Connord."* Well, she might have been annoyed at the time, but it had turned out to be a fair assessment, because here she was gaping at everything like the ripest peasant at his first fair. They were still at least a mile from the city gates—she could see the crowned guard towers looming ahead like armored giants out of legend—but they were already passing through a thriving metropolis bigger and busier than the heart of Southmarch.

"Where are we going to stay?" she asked Teodoros, who was happily ensconced in the wagon again, watching it all pass by.

"An agreeable inn just in the shadow of the eastern gate," he called down. "We have stayed there before. I have made the arrangements for a tennight's stay, which will give us plenty of time to smooth the wrinkles out of *Zoria* before we go looking for a spot closer to the center of town."

Feival Ulian wandered back. "You know, Finn, I know the fellow who built the Zosimion Theater near Hierarch's College Bridge. I heard that he's having trouble finding anyone to mount some work—a feud with the Royal Master of Revels or some such. I'll wager it's free."

"Good. Perhaps we shall move there after the inn."

"It might be free now . . ."

"No!" Teodoros seemed to realize that he'd been a bit harsh in his refusal. "No, I've just . . . I've made the arrangements, already, good Feival. At the inn in Chakki's Hole. We would not get our money back."

Feival shrugged. "Certainly. But should I see if I can find out, for later . . . ?"

"By all means." Teodoros smiled and nodded, as if trying to make up for his earlier loud refusal.

Briony was a little puzzled by Finn's vehemence, but she had other things on her mind. She was merely floating, she realized— letting herself be swept along this road and through this foreign land like a leaf on a stream. In fact, she had been swept along ever since meeting the demigoddess Lisiya—only some three dozens day ago, yet already it seemed like a dream from her distant child-hood. She reached into her shirt and patted the charm Lisiya had given her, stroked the small, smooth bird skull. What should she do now? The demigoddess had only pointed her toward the players, but had told her nothing of what she should do or where she should go next. Briony suspected Lisiya wanted her to make her own decisions, that in some way she was being tested—wasn't that what gods did to mortals?

But why? No one ever explained that curious whim. *Why should the gods care whether mortals are worthy of anything?* It was a bit like a person walking around in a stable, testing all the animals to see which were pure of heart or particularly clever, so they could be rewarded and the other beasts punished. She supposed people might do that to find which were the most *obedient* animals—was that the gods' reasoning?

See, here I am, drifting again, she chided herself. *What is Briony Eddon going to do now, that's the question. What's next?* Before his death in the fire, Shaso had talked about raising an army, or at least enough men in arms to protect her when she revealed herself, a force to defend her from the Tollys' treachery. He had talked of appealing to the Syannese king for troops and here she was in Syan. Most of all she wanted to go to Hierosol where her father was prisoner—she ached to see his face, to hear his voice—but she knew it was a foolish idea, that at best she would only join him in captivity. Shaso would tell her to cast her dice here, among old allies.

But would that be a good suggestion, or would it simply be Shaso, the old soldier, thinking as old soldiers did—no other way to reclaim a kingdom except by force of arms?

Thinking of the old man scalded her heart, the terrible injustice she and her brother had done him, caging him like an animal for months and months . . . *And now he is dead. Because of me. Because of my foolishness, my headstrong mistakes, my . . . my . . .*

"Tim? Tim, what's wrong?" It was Feival, his handsome face full of surprised concern. "Why are you weeping, pet?"

Briony wiped angrily at her cheeks. Could it be possible to act more like a girl? It was a good thing all the players knew her secret. "Just . . . just thinking of something. Of someone."

Feival nodded wisely and turned away.

The tavern called The False Woman—a somewhat ill-omened name, Briony couldn't help feeling, considering her own nested impostures—crouched in the corner of an old, beaten-down market in the northeastern part of the city, a neighborhood known as Chakki's Hole after the Chakkai people from the mountains of south Perikal who had come to the city as laborers and made this maze of dark streets their new home. The Hole, as inhabitants often called it, was so close to the high city walls that even just past noon on a clear day the winter sun was blocked and the whole neighborhood in shade. One of the city's dozens of canals neatly separated it from the rest of the Perikalese district.

The sign hanging above the tavern doorway showed a woman with two faces, one fair and one foul, and a pointed hat of a type that hadn't been worn in a century or more. The taverner, a stout, mustached fellow named Bedoyas, ushered them through into the innyard with the air of a man forced to stable someone else's animals in his own bedroom. "Here. I'll send my boy around for the horses. You will drive not a single nail into my wood without my permission, understood?"

"Understood, good host," said Finn. "And if anyone is asking for us, send them to me. My name is Teodoros."

When Bedoyas had stumped off to see to other guests (not that he seemed to be overwhelmed with custom this winter) Briony helped the company begin setting up a stage—the most permanent they had built since she had been with them, because they would now be at least a tennight in one place. Several of the men were in truth more carpenters than performers, and at least three of the shareholding players, Dowan Birch, Feival, and Pedder Makewell himself, had worked in the building trades.

Hewney claimed he had as well, but Finn Teodoros loudly suggested otherwise.

"What rubbish are you spouting, fat man?" Hewney was helping Feival and two of the others lash together the barrels that would be pillars for the stage. They did not bother to bring their own, since most inns had more than a few empties to spare, and The False Woman was no exception. "I have built more houses than you've eaten hot suppers!"

"You must have set up Tessis by yourself, then," said Pedder Makewell. "Look at the size of our Finn!"

"It would be a more telling jest, Master Makewell," Teodoros replied a touch primly, "if your own greatly swollen sack of guts were not falling over your belt. As it is, the nightsoil digger is suggesting that the saltpeter man stinks."

Briony did not know why she found that so funny, but she did; she nearly fell over laughing despite (or perhaps because of) Estir

Makewell's sour look. She and Makewell's sister were shoveling sand into the barrels to make them stronger supports under the middle of the stage. Estir still did not really like the person she thought of as "Tim"—she would never like adding another hungry mouth to the troop, which reduced the income of the shareholdings—but she had softened toward Briony a bit.

"Leave it to a child," said Estir, rolling her eyes, "to find such a jest so laughable." She scowled at the others. "And you men are just as bad. You would think you were all still babies, soiling your smallclothes, to see you get such pleasure out of dribble, fart, and ordure."

This started Briony laughing all over again—it was the same thing her prim and squeamish brother Barrick had often said about her, although her twin had obviously never blamed it on her being a child.

It was cold out and her hands were chapped and aching already from the rough handle on the shovel, but Briony felt oddly content. She was almost happy, she realized—for the first time in too long to remember: the miseries that dogged her thoughts were not by any means gone, but for the moment she could live with them, as if she and they were old enemies grown too weary to contend.

The men brought out the pieces of the stage and joined them together in one large rectangle, then set it on top of the barrels and lashed the whole thing together. Briony herself, as one of the lightest, was sent to stand on top of it to test its resilience. When she had bounced up and down on it vigorously enough to assure everyone, they continued preparing the rest of their makeshift theater. The smaller of the two wagons was rolled into place at the back of the stage where it would serve as a tiring-room for entrances, exits, and quick changes, as well as a wall on which to hang painted backdrops. They lifted up the hinged top of the wagon, folding it upward so that it could serve as a kind of wall or tower-top from which actors could speak their lines or, as gods, meddle in the lives of callow mortals from on high. Briony could see the persimmon-colored sunlight of fading afternoon on the uppermost peaks of the mountains southeast of Tessis and wondered if the gods were truly up there as she had been taught, watching her and all the other petty mortals.

But Lisiya said they were . . . what? Sleeping? They can hear us, she said—but can they still see us?

It was strange to think of the gods being blind and only faintly aware of the existence of Briony's kind, like vastly aged grandparents snoring in their chairs, barely moving from the beginning of one day to its end.

No wonder they long to come back to the world again, as Lisiya said. She was immediately chilled, although she could not quite say why. She bent and returned to bracing the wagon wheels with stones.

The morning meal, a surprisingly hearty fish stew the tavern-keeper Bedoyas had served them in a big iron pot, with a spicy tang that Finn told her came from things called *marashis,* was not lying quietly in her stomach. It was no fault of the tavern's cook, though: Briony was fretful. The tavern yard was already starting to fill, even though the play would not begin until the temple bells rang in Blessed Lady of Night to call the end of afternoon prayers, which was most of an hour away. She had never performed in front of more than a few dozen people in any of the villages or towns along the way, but there were twice that many here already and the yard was still half empty.

What are you frightened of, girl? she asked herself. *You have fought a demon, not to mention escaped a usurper. You have stood before many times this number and acted the queen in truth—or at least the reigning princess—a far more taxing role. Players don't lose their heads when they fail to convince, as I almost lost mine.* She thought of Hendon Tolly and a little shudder of rage passed through her. *Oh, but I would glory to have his head on a chopping block. I would take up the ax myself.* Briony, who although rough and boyish in some ways, as her maids and family had never ceased pointing out, was not or blood-thirsty, but she wanted fiercely to see Tolly humiliated and punished.

I owe it to Shaso's memory, if nothing else, she thought. *I can't make amends for imprisoning him, but I can avenge him.*

Shaso had been innocent of her brother's murder, but she still did not know who exactly was guilty, beyond the obvious. Who had been the guiding hand behind a murder by witchcraft? Hendon Tolly, however dark his heart and bloody his hands, had seemed genuinely surprised at Anissa's maid's horrific transformation—but if the Tollys had not had her brother murdered, then who was to blame? It was impossible to believe the witch-maid had conceived and executed such a scheme on her own. Could it have been one of Olin's rival kings? Or the distant autarch? Perhaps even the fairy folk, reaching out somehow from their shadowy land, a first blow before their attack? In truth, the lives of the Eddon family had been completely shaken to pieces in a matter of months by magic and monsters. Why had *any* of this happened?

"Hoy, Tim." Feival was already pulling his shirt over his head as he squeezed into the cramped wagon. "You look stuck—do you need help with your dress?" As the company's principal boy he was more familiar with putting on a gown than Briony herself, who had always been assisted by her maids.

She shook her head, almost relieved. The workaday had returned to push out other things, no matter their importance. "No, but thank you. I was just thinking."

"Good house today," he said, stepping out of his tights with the indifference of a veteran player. Briony turned away, still not used to seeing naked men, although it had not been an infrequent experience since she had been traveling with the troop. Feival in particular was lithe and well-muscled, and it was interesting to realize that she could enjoy looking at him without wanting anything more.

Maybe I really am boyish, as Barrick used to say. Maybe I'm just fickle of eye and heart, like a man. There was no question, though, that she wanted more in her life than simply a handsome man at her side. She could feel it some nights, different from the yearning she felt for her lost brothers and her father: she did not want a particular person, she wanted *somebody,* a man who would hold her only when she wanted, who would be warm and strong.

But sometimes when she had such thoughts, she saw a face that surprised her—the commoner, the failed guardian, Ferras Vansen. It was exasperating. If there was a less appropriate person in the world for her to think about, she could scarcely imagine it. Who knew if he was even alive?

No, she told herself quickly, *he must be alive. He must be fit and well and protecting my brother.*

It was odd, though, that Vansen's not-so-handsome face kept drifting into her thoughts, his nose that bore the signs of having been broken, his eyes that scarcely ever looked at her, hiding always behind lowered lids as he stared at the ground or at the sky, as though her very gaze was a fire that would burn him . . .

She stopped, gasped in a short breath. Could it be?

"Are you well?"

"No—I mean yes, Feival, I'm well enough. I just . . . I just poked myself with something sharp."

It was madness to think this way. Worse, it was meaningless madness: if Vansen lived, he was lost—lost with her brother. The whole of that life was gone, as if it had happened to another person, and unless she could somehow find help for herself and Southmarch, nothing like it would ever come again. Her task now was to be a player, at least for today—not a shareholder, even, but an assistant to the principal boy, working for meals in a tavern yard in Tessis. That was all. She knew she must learn to accept that.

"We are not in the March Kingdoms any more, so speak your parts loudly and broadly," said Pedder Makewell, as if any of them did not know that already. "Now, where is Pilney?"

The players were all crammed into a little high-walled alley behind the tavern because there was not room for them all in the tiring-room and the yard was filled by their audience, a large group of city folk finished with work and eager for the start of the Kerneia revels. One end of the alley was bricked off, the other sealed with a huge pile of building rubble, so the spot was fairly private, but a few people in the buildings that backed on the alley leaned out of their windows to stare at the crowd of actors in their colorful costumes. "Where is Pilney?" Makewell asked again.

Pilney, younger even than Feival Ulian but far more shy and not half so pretty, raised his hand. The heavyset, red-faced youth was playing the part of the moon god Khors, and although this had thrown him much together with Briony, he had scarcely spoken a word to her that Teodoros had not written.

"Right," Makewell said to him sternly. "You have spattered me quite roundly with blood the last two performances, boy, and you have spoiled my costume both times, not to mention my curtain call. When you die today, do me the kindness of facing a little away before you burst your bladder, or next time you'll die from a real clubbing instead of a few taps with a sham."

Pilney, wide-eyed, nodded his head rapidly.

"If you have finished terrifying the young fellow, Pedder," said Finn Teodoros, "perhaps I might essay a few truly important points?"

"It is an expensive costume!" said Estir Makewell, defending her brother.

"Yes, the rest of us, in our rags, have all noticed."

"Whose name is on the troop, I ask you?" Pedder demanded. "Who do they come to see?"

"Oh, you, of course." Finn made a droll face. "And you are right to warn the boy. Otherwise, tavern gossip all over Syan would whisper that in the play about the death of gods, Pedder Makewell, at the end of the particularly bloody slaughter of his archenemy, was seen to have blood on him! Who would pay to witness such a ludicrous farce?"

"You mock me. Very well. *You* may launder Perin's fine armor, then."

"Or better yet, Makewell," called Nevin Hewney, "we could dress you in a butcher's smock, which would suit both your sword-play *and* your acting!"

"Quiet!" shouted Teodoros over the bellows of outrage and

amusement, "I would like to get on with our notices, please. Also, I have a few changes.

"Feival, in the first act, where Zosim comes to Perin to describe the fortifications of Khors' castle, instead of 'Covered in shining crystals of ice,' could you say, 'In shining ice crystals covered,'? It suits the foot better. Yes, and lordly Perin, the word is 'plenilune,' not 'pantaloon'—'My foeman smite, and cleave the plenilune'—it means full moon, and, needless to say, gives the speech quite a different import."

Over laughter, Makewell said with returning good nature, "Plenilune, plenilune—I trow he has invented the word just to trouble me. The fat ink-dauber has choked many an actor in his day."

"Yes, good, good," said Teodoros, staring at the rag of paper on which he had scratched his reminders. "All three brothers must turn together toward the Moon Castle when we hear the trumpets, we spoke of that. Certes." He turned the bit of paper over. "Ah, yes, in the second act, we must see Khors truly grab at Zoria when she flees him. Pilney, you have already seized her and dragged her to your castle. Now you must clutch at her as though you mean to keep her, not as though she has dropped something in the street and you have retrieved it." As Pilney blushed and mumbled, Teodoros turned to Briony. "And you, young Tim. Do not shake him off when he grabs you, no matter how whey-faced his manhandling. You are a virgin goddess, not a street bravo."

Now it was her turn to blush. Shaso had taught her too well: when a hand encircled her arm she threw it off without thinking. The first time they played the scene she had pinched Pilney's wrist hard enough to make him gasp. She suspected it was one of the reasons he had kept his distance.

"And where is Master Birch? Dowan, I know your knees pain you, but when Volios is struck down by Zmeos, the earth shakes—that is what the stories tell. You cannot let yourself down so carefully."

The giant frowned, but nodded. Briony felt sorry for him.

Perhaps she could find some spare cloth and make him thicker pads for his large, bony knees.

Teodoros went on to change much of the blocking at the beginning of the siege to obscure the fact that Feival and Hewney had to scramble out of their Zuriyal and Zmeos costumes and into armor, then appear from the tiring-room to portray the gods and demigods Perin was leading against the moon god's fortress. He changed a few of Feival's lines in the fourth act when the youth portrayed Zuriyal, the goddess who was Zoria's jailer while her brothers Zmeos and Khors fought against Perin and the besiegers.

Teodoros was also making a few changes to shift the balance in Khors' death scene away from Pilney, who had a tendency to grow quietest when he should be loudest, and to give most of the speech to Hewney (who would "milk it as 'twere a Marrinswalk heifer," as Teodoros put it) when the tavernkeeper Bedoyas stuck his head out into the alley and inquired whether they were actually going to perform their miserable play, or had they just concocted a complex but novel way to rob him?

"Zosim, Kupilas, and Devona of the Harp, gladden the hearts of those who will watch us," said Teodoros as he always did, his hands on his chest. "And off we go!"

Things went smoothly enough in the first three acts. The tavern yard was very full but the day was gray and cold, and the torches burning brightly on either side of the stage made it hard for Briony to make out much more of the crowd than dim faces watching from under hoods and hats. From what she could see, they seemed to be a slightly more prosperous group than the company had drawn at other stops, but they were still mostly laboring folk, not lords and ladies. A few companies of youths (prentices of some sort enjoying a drunken afternoon's roistering) had set themselves up in the front row, where they whistled loudly and shouted rude remarks at Feival, Briony, and anyone else dressed as a woman. The fact that these were holy goddesses they were eyeing so lasciviously did not seem to trouble them much.

Briony herself was doing better than she had feared she would.

It was not as hard to remember the lines as she once had thought—simply speaking them over and over, day after day, made them as familiar as the names of people she saw often, and the lattice of other player's parts helped to hold her together during the few times her memory slipped. And the story itself was exciting—you could see it in the crowd's reaction, their groans of worry and cheers of pleasure as the action turned first this way, then that. When Perin led his forces against Khors' great castle—the wagon serving not just as a dressing-room, but as the moon siege itself, with Pilney standing atop it shouting defiance—the audience whooped, and a few seemed as though they were considering climbing onto the stage and joining in the assault. When Perin's son Volios was killed by Khors, and Dowan Birch toppled as heavily as the tree for which he was named, blood running down his belly from between his clasped hands, Briony thought she actually heard a few sobs.

It was in the fourth act, as the virgin goddess stole away from the distracted Zuriyal and escaped the castle, only to become lost in a whirling snowstorm (with fluttering rags on sticks and the moan of the wind-wheel standing in for Nature) that things suddenly went wrong. One moment Briony was speaking her lines,

> *"The snow! It bites like Zmeos' cruel bees,*
> *And shrinks to pebbled hide my uncloaked skin!*
> *I shall don these clothes the serving boy left.*
> *They shame my maidenhood, source of my woes,*
> *But will keep me quick when cold would kill me . . ."*

The next instant she found herself staring into a diminishing tunnel of light, the torches and the overcast sky all swirling together as the blackness rushed in from the sides. She swayed, then managed to get her feet under her, and although the world still sparkled queerly, as though fireflies surrounded her, she managed to finish her speech.

> *" . . . But warmer though I be, still lost am I,*
> *And without food, then—cold or warm,—will die."*

A few moments later, when she should have gently sunk to her knees, she found herself instead doing what Finn had asked of Dowan Birch, crashing to the stage with a thump. Again the world darkened. She could hear nothing, not even the spinning, burlap-covered drum that made the noise of wind, could feel nothing but an overwhelming sensation of being close to Barrick—an awareness more alive than any mere scent or sound, a sense of actually being *inside* her brother's frightened, confused thoughts.

Out of the darkness crept a terrible shape, a starvation-thin shadow with a gray, corpselike face. At first, in her frightened baf-flement, she thought that it was death itself coming for her. Then she realized she must be seeing something through her twin brother's eyes—an emotionless mask with glowing moonstone gaze, gliding nearer and nearer. It was not Death, but she knew it was something just as final and much less merciful.

She tried to scream her brother's name, but as in a hundred nightmares she could not make any real sound. The ghastly gray face came closer, so terrifying that the blackness collapsed on her again.

"Zoria!" said a loud voice in her ear. "Here she lies, my virtu-ous cousin! Are you dead, sweet daughter of the Skyfather? Who has done this terrible thing to you?"

It was Feival, she realized, standing over her and improvising lines, trying to give her time to get up. She opened her eyes to see the young player's concerned features. What had happened to her? That deathly, nightmare face . . . !

"Can you walk, Cousin?" Feival asked, trying to get an arm beneath her so he could lift her. "Shall I help you?" With his mouth close to her ear, he whispered, *"What are you playing at, girl?"*

She shook off his hand and clambered unsteadily to her feet. She could feel the tension that had fallen over the company and audience alike; the latter were not certain yet that something was wrong, but they were beginning to suspect. She couldn't think about Barrick. Not right now. This was like her life back at home, something she knew: she must put on her mask.

"Well, noble . . ." She swayed, took an uneven breath. "Well, noble cousin, kind Zosim," she began again. "I can walk now that . . . that you are here to guide me out from these unfriendly winds."

She could hear Finn Teodoros sigh with relief at the back of the stage, half a dozen yards away.

The last few bystanders were milling about in the tavern yard, finishing their food and drink. A handful of drunken prentices talked in overloud voices about which goddess they would rather kiss. Estir and Pedder Makewell had gone inside with Bedoyas the tavern keeper to sort out the afternoon's take, while Teodoros, Hewney, and the rest celebrated the success of the afternoon's production with a few pitchers of ale. Briony still felt shaky. She sat by herself on the edge of the stage, holding a mug without drinking and staring at her shoes. What had happened to her? It had been like nothing she had ever felt before—not even like seeing Barrick in the mirror that time, but like *being* Barrick. And who or what was that ghastly gray . . . *thing?*

She felt bile climb into her throat. What could she do about it, in any case? Nothing! She didn't even know where he was. It was like a curse—she could do nothing to help her own brother! Nothing, nothing, nothing . . .

"Well, my lady, I see you took my advice after all."

For an instant she only stared—the voice was familiar, but although she knew the dark-skinned face, she could not at first recall . . .

"Dawet!" She slid off the stage, almost spilling her ale. For a moment it was such a surprise to see someone she knew that she nearly threw her arms around him. Then she remembered that they had met because Dawet dan-Faar had come as an envoy from Ludis, to negotiate on behalf of her father's kidnapper.

He smiled, perhaps at her visible confusion. "So you remember me. Then you may also remember that I suggested you see something of the world, my lady. I did not think you would take my advice quite so much to heart. You have become a stage-player now?"

She suddenly realized others were watching, not all of them from her troupe. "Quiet," she whispered. "I am not supposed to be a girl, let alone a princess."

"Passing as a boy?" he murmured. "Oh, I hardly think anyone would believe that. But what *are* you doing here in such unlikely guise and company?"

She stared at him, suddenly mistrustful. "I will ask the same of you. Why are you not in Hierosol? Have you left Ludis Drakava's service?"

He shook his head. "No, my lady, although many wiser than me have already done so . . ." He looked up and past her, his eyes narrowing. "But what is this?"

The tavern keeper Bedoyas and both Makewells were coming across the tavern yard toward the company, but it was their escort—a dozen guardsmen wearing the crests of city reeves—that had caught Dawet's eye. For a moment Briony only stared, then realized that she of all of them had the most to lose if captured or arrested for some reason. She eyed the nearest ways out of the yard but it was hopeless: the guards had already surrounded them.

A heavy-faced soldier wearing an officer's sash across his tunic stepped forward. "You of the players' company known as Makewell's Men, you are remanded in arrest to His Majesty the king's custody." The captain saw Dawet and scowled. "Ah. You, too, fellow. I was told to look for a southern darkling, and here you are."

"You would be wise to watch your tongue, sir," said Dawet with smooth venom, but he made no move to resist.

"Arrested?" Finn Teodoros' voice had an anxious squeak to it. "Under what charge?"

"Spying, as you well know," said the captain. "Now you will be introduced to His Majesty's hospitality, which I think will be a little less to your liking than that of Master Bedoyas. And entertain no thoughts of daring escape, you players—this is no play. I have half a pentecount more of soldiers waiting outside."

"Spying?" Briony turned to Dawet. "What are they talking about?" she whispered.

"Say *nothing*," he told her under his breath. "No matter what happens or what they tell you. They will try to trick you."

She put her head down and let herself be herded with the others. Estir Makewell and young Pilney were both weeping. Others might have been, but it was hard to tell, because rain had started to fall.

"I'm afraid I cannot go with you," Dawet said loudly.

Briony turned, thinking he spoke to her. He had drawn himself back against a wall of the courtyard, a knife suddenly twinkling in his gloved fingers. "What are you doing?" she demanded, but Dawet did not even look at her.

"Enough of your nonsense, black," said the captain. "Were you Hiliometes himself you could not overcome so many."

"I swear on the fiery head of Zosim Salamandros that you have the wrong man," said Dawet. One of the guards stepped toward him, but the Tuani man had the blade up and cocked for throwing so quickly the soldier froze as if snake-addled.

The captain sighed. "Swear by the Salamander, do you?" He stared at Dawet dan-Faar like a householder trying to decide whether to buy a lump of expensive meat that was only going in the stew, anyway. "You two, you heard him," he said, gesturing to a pair of guards standing nearby, short spears at the ready. "Deal with him. I have better things to do than waste any more time here."

The two heavily-armored men lunged forward and Briony let out a muffled shriek of alarm. Dawet, handicapped by the much shorter reach of his dagger, feinted as if to throw it, then turned, leaped, and scrambled over the courtyard wall. The two guards hesitated only a moment, then hurried out through the yard's back entrance. A few other soldiers moved as if to follow, but the captain waved them back.

"Those two are canny fellows," he told his men. "Don't worry, they will deal with that Xandy fool."

"Unless the darkling can fly like Strivos himself, you're right to call him foolish," the tavernkeeper Bedoyas chuckled. "That alley's a dead end." Briony wanted to hit the man in his fat face.

But to her surprise, the guards appeared a moment later without Dawet. They were smiling nervously, as if pleased by their own failure. "He's gone, sir. Got clean away."

"He did, did he?" The commander nodded grimly. "We'll talk about this later."

The rest of the guards shoved Briony and the other players back into line again and led them out of the inn, marching them toward the stronghold in the great palace at the city's center. Bad enough to have lost a throne, but now even her humble, counterfeit life as a player was in ruins. Briony's eyes blurred with tears, though she tried hard to wipe them away. As they crossed the first bridge it seemed she walked through some place even stranger than the capital of a foreign land.

37
Silence

Thunder and his brothers at last found Pale Daughter wandering lost in the wilderness without her name or her memory. His honor satisfied, Thunder did not think any more upon her, but his brother Black Earth was unhappy with his wife, Evening Light, and their music had strayed out of sympathy. He sent her away and took Pale Daughter to be his wife. He gave her a new name, Dawn, that she might not remember what had gone before. She was ever after silent, sitting beside him in the dark chambers beneath the ground, and if she remembered her child Crooked or her husband Silvergleam, she did not say.

—from *One Hundred Considerations*
out of the Qar's *Book of Regret*

WHILE MATT TINWRIGHT PAUSED for breath and mopped his brow, Puzzle played a refrain on the lute. The tune was a little more sprightly than Tinwright would have liked, considering the seriousness of the subject matter, but he had finished his poem so late that the two had found little time to practice.

He nodded to the old jester, ready to begin again. Most of the courtiers, although not all, politely lowered their voices once more.

"*At last Surazem came to birthing bed,*" Tinwright declaimed, half-singing in the Syannese style now expected at court entertainments,
> "*As the Four Winds hovered to cool her brow,*
> *Her sister, her semblance, stood at her head*
> *Dark Onyena, bound by a sacred vow*
> *Like oxen traced unwilling to the plow.*
> *On high Sarissa her own infant son*
> *Lay coldly dead 'neath the pine's snowy bough*
> *Because Sveros cruelly had decreed that none*
> *Should midwife one twin but the other one . . .*"

For long moments Tinwright could almost forget what was really happening—that almost no one was listening to the words he declaimed, that the rumble of talk and drunken laughter made it hard for even those few who wanted to hear, and that in any case there were darker, grimmer matters to think about than even the fall of gods—and could revel in the fact that for this moment, at least, he was presenting his verse before the entire royal court of Southmarch. His own verse!

> "*But now as Perin's infant head appeared*
> *Surazem's dark twin saw her time, and thieved*
> *From out her sister's belly, blood-besmeared,*
> *That essence which the world has so long grieved*
> *For Onyena with it three more conceived,*

> *Repaying cruelly the death of her own,*
> *A fated tapestry which first she weaved*
> *As her sister in childbirth's pain did groan*
> *And thus were the seeds of the gods' war sown . . . "*

One of the few people paying attention was the man who had commissioned the poem, Hendon Tolly himself, who frightened Tinwright in ways he had never even imagined possible. Another was the young woman Elan M'Cory, the object of Tinwright's own painful affection, to whom he had promised to bring poison tonight.

A strange audience, at best, he admitted to himself.

One of those most obviously *not* paying attention was Hendon's brother, the new Duke of Summerfield. Caradon Tolly was more like the dead brother Gailon than like Hendon, jut-jawed and big across the shoulders. His square face reflected little of what went on behind it—Tinwright thought he seemed more statue than man—but he was known to be heavy-handed and ruthless, though perhaps lacking his younger sibling's flair for cruelty. Just now Duke Caradon was staring openly at the Southmarch nobles gathered in the banquet hall, as if making a list of who would serve the Tollys well and who would not. The objects of his gaze looked almost uniformly discomforted.

Looking at this cold, powerful man, Matt Tinwright felt sick at his stomach. *What am I thinking, meddling in the Tollys' affairs? I am far out of my depth—they could kill me in an instant!* Remembering how certain he had been only a few days ago that he would be executed, he almost lost his place in the poem. He had to swallow down this sudden fright and force himself back into his words, spreading his arms as he declaimed,

> *" . . . But those three treacherous siblings, theft-bred,*
> *Plotted long Perin's heritage to steal*
> *When Sveros, fearsome sire of all, was dead.*
> *'Til then, they'd follow meekly at the heel*
> *And by soft words and smiles their lies conceal*
> *While Zmeos, their chief, banked his envious fires . . . "*

A few courtiers shifted restlessly. Matt Tinwright, sliding back and forth between terror of death and the nearly equal terror of having his work ridiculed, could not help wondering if he had made the beginning of the poem too long. After all, every child raised in the Trigonate faith heard the tale of the three brothers and their infamous step-siblings at almost every religious festival. But Hendon Tolly wanted legitimacy, and so he had wanted as much in the poem as possible about the selfless purity of Madi Surazem and the perfidy of old Sveros, Lord of Twilight—the better to prop his own family's claim to virtue, Tinwright supposed.

He did feel a little ashamed to be trumpeting the self-serving nonsense of such a serpent as Hendon Tolly, but he consoled himself with the thought that no one in Southmarch would ever actually *believe* such things: Olin Eddon had been one of the best-loved kings in memory, a bold warrior in his youth, fair and wise in his age. He was no Sveros.

Also, Tinwright was a poet, and he told himself that poets could not fight the powers of the world, at least not with anything but words—and even with words, they had to be careful. *We worshipers of the Harmonies are easy to kill,* he thought. *The hoi polloi might weep after we are gone, when they realize what they've lost, but that does us no good if we're already dead.*

In any case, only Hendon Tolly appeared to be following the words with anything more than perfunctory interest. Now that his brother Caradon was no longer surveying the crowd, and had turned to stare disinterestedly at the banquet hall hangings, the rest of the courtiers were free to watch the duke and whisper behind their hands. Almost all of them had been out in the cold wind that morning when Caradon Tolly and his entourage had disembarked from their ship and paraded into Southmarch at the head of four pentecounts of fully armed men wearing the Tolly's boar and spears on their shields. Something in the soldiers' grim faces had made it clear to even the most heedless castle-folk that the Tollys were not just making a show, but making a claim.

As Tinwright declaimed the verses in which the Trigon brothers finally defeated their ferocious father, Caradon continued to tap his fingers absently and stare at nothing, but his brother Hendon leaned forward, eyes unnaturally bright and a smile playing across his lips. By contrast, Elan M'Cory seemed to shrink deeper and deeper into herself, so that even though Tinwright could see her eyes, they seemed as cold and lifeless as one of the eerie pictures in the portrait hall, the dead nobility that watched upstart poets with disapproving gazes. Matt Tinwright's longing and dread were too great to look at her for more than a moment.

As with all the stories of the immortals, he had discovered he could only make an ending happy by a careful choice of stopping point. This was a poem in honor of a child-blessing, after all—he could not very well go on to describe the hatred that grew between the Onyenai and Perin's Surazemai. Tinwright did not think even Hendon Tolly expected him to celebrate young Olin Alessandros' naming day with a poem about one set of royal brothers destroying the children of another royal wife. If Olin or one of the twins ever regained the throne, that would be the kind of thing remembered at treason trials.

Treason. As he raised his voice to begin the last stanzas, Tinwright felt cold sweat prickle his forehead again. Let Zosim, god of poets, stand beside him now! Why was he worrying about something as far away as a treason trial? He was planning to do something tonight that could get him beheaded without any trial at all!

He faltered for a moment, just as Perin was about to throw down his cruel, drunken father. Ordinarily Tinwright didn't think much about the actual gods except as almost inexhaustible subjects for poetry, but there were moments like this when his childhood terror of them came sweeping back, moments when he stood again in their long cold shadow and knew that someday he must face their judgment.

> "Great Sveros, Twilight Lord, roared in his rage,
> 'How, shall sons spit into their father's face?
> My curse shall rain like blood on all this age

And pursue each whelp of my cursed race
Until Time doth all who now live erase.'
They bound him then in chains Kernios made
And cast him into dusky vaults of space
To drift unfleshed in sempiternal shade
'Til thought and feeling both should frameless fade . . ."

His legs shaky, as much from misgiving as from being so long on his feet, he spoke the final lines and Puzzle gave a last flourish on the lute. Tinwright bowed. As the courtiers lazily followed Hendon Tolly's lead, applauding and calling a few words of praise, Elan M'Cory rose from her seat beside the guardian of Southmarch and made to go. For a moment Tinwright caught a flick of her eyes beneath the veil, then Hendon Tolly extended a hand and stopped her.

"But where are you off to, dear sister-in-law? The poet has labored hard to deliver this work to us. Surely you have a few words of praise for him."

"Let her go," growled Caradon Tolly. "Let them all go. You and I have things to talk about, brother."

"But our poor poet, swooning for want of kind words from fair ladies . . ." prompted Hendon, grinning.

Elan swayed, and Tinwright had a sudden terror she would crumple, that she would faint and be surrounded by lady's maids, the physician would be called, and all Tinwright's careful plans to free her from her misery would be upset. "Of course, my dear brother-in-law," she said wearily. "I extend my praise and gratitude to the poet. It is always instructive to hear of the lives of the gods, that we mortals can learn to comport ourselves properly." She gave a half a courtesy, then reached out a trembling hand, letting one of her maids support her arm as she made her way slowly out of the room. The murmur of conversation, which had dropped almost to silence, now rose again.

"Thank all the gods my wife is not such a frail flower," Caradon said with his lip curled. "Little Elan has always been the doleful one of that family."

Hendon Tolly beckoned Tinwright forward. He produced a bag that clinked and put it in Tinwright's hands.

"Thank you, Lord Tolly." He tucked it away quickly, without testing the weight—to receive anything other than a blow from this man was a gift in itself. "You are too kind. I am glad my words . . ."

"Yes, yes. It amused me, and there is little that does so these days. Did you see old Brone squirming when you spoke the part about 'Ever must the blood of tyrants water That free and sovereign soil of our fair honor'? It was very funny."

"I . . . I didn't notice, my lord."

Tolly shrugged. "Still, it is like spearing fish in a soup bowl. I miss the Syannese court. They are sharp as daggers, there. A good jest is appreciated. Not like here, or in my family's house, which is like dining with the local deacon in some Helmingsea village."

"Enough, Hendon," said Caradon sharply. "Send this warbling phebe away—we have men's talk to talk and your childish festivities have wasted enough of my time."

Tinwright thought the look Hendon gave his brother the duke was one of the strangest he had ever seen, a combination of amusement and deadly loathing. "By all means, elder brother. You may withdraw, poet."

Tinwright, sickened, could tell that Hendon planned to murder his brother someday. He had also seen in that same moment that Caradon himself knew it very well, and that the duke probably planned the same for his younger brother. The two of them scarcely bothered to conceal their feelings, even in front of a stranger. How could one family breed such hatred? No wonder Elan wanted to escape them into death.

"Of course," Tinwright said as he quickly backed away. "Going now. Thank you, my lords."

He at least had the small satisfaction of seeing that Erlon Meaher, another court poet who thought much of himself, had been watching his conversation with the two Tollys. Meaher's face was twisted in an unhidden grimace of envy and dislike.

"Get yourself some wine, Tinwright," Hendon Tolly called after him. "I'm sure reciting poetry is almost as thirsty work as killing—if not quite as enjoyable."

It was the hardest hour of waiting he had ever experienced. He knocked on her door while the bells were still chiming the end of evening prayers.

Elan M'Cory opened it herself, shrouded in a heavy black robe. She had sent away her servants to protect him, Tinwright realized, and he was surprised again by the intensity of feeling she aroused in him.

It was a touch of lover's madness, surely—the very thing he had written about so many times. He had always felt secretly superior to the sort of lovesick people found in poems, almost contemptuous, but in these last days, as he had come to realize that he could not sleep, eat, drink, stand, sit, or talk without thinking about Elan M'Cory, matters had begun to seem very different. For one thing, although he had alluded in many a poem to the "happy pain" or even the "sweet agony" of love, he had not understood that the agony could be worse than any other sort of agony—worse than any actual pain of the limbs or organs, worse even than the way his head felt after a night out with Hewney and Teodoros, which he had previously thought could not be outdone for misery. And there was no way to separate a wounded heart from the body it tormented—no way except death.

He was terrified to realize he now understood Elan's pain very well, although hers had quite a different cause.

He reached out to take her hand but she would not let him. "Let me beg you one last time, my lady—please do not do this." He felt oddly flat. He knew what her response would be, and in fact, he could think of no other way forward at this point except to let the grim machinery turn, but he had to say it.

"You have been a loyal, kind friend, Matt, and I wish nothing more than it could be another way, but there is no escape for me. Hendon will never loose his claws. He savors my pain too much, and he would kill you in an instant if he thought I cared for you. I could not bear that." She hung her head. "Soon Queen Anissa will be his, too, if she is not already—he pays court to her as though she were already widowed. Nobody knows the depths of that man's evil." Elan took a deep breath, then undid the tie of her robe and threw it off, revealing a brilliant blaze that startled him like lightning. She was dressed all in white, like a bride or a phantom.

"Do you have it?" she said. She was anxious, but happy, too, like a woman on her wedding day. "Do you have that which will save me, sweet Matty?"

He swallowed. "I do." He reached into his pocket and found the swaddled flask. He had replaced the kelp leaf in which it had been wrapped with a square of velvet he had stolen from Puzzle, but it still smelled of the sea.

She wrinkled her nose. "What is it?"

"It does not matter. It is what you wished, my lady. My Elan." He himself was as fretful as the most callow bridegroom. She looked so beautiful in her white nightgown, even though he could scarcely see her through his tears. "I will administer it for you. I will hold your head."

She had been staring at the tiny flask with horrified fascination, but now she looked up, confused. "Why?"

He had not thought about this, and for a moment he was flustered. "So that it does not stain your gown, my lady. So your beauty is not . . . is not spoiled . . ." He gasped, a sob stuck in his gorge that was so big he feared he would not breathe again.

"Bless you, Matt, you are so sweet to me. I know I am . . . I know I am not fit for you or any other gods-fearing man . . . but . . . but you may love me, if you wish." She saw that he did not understand. "Make love to me. It will make no difference where I'm bound, and it would be sweet to have such love from you before . . . before . . ." A single tear rolled down her cheek, but she smiled and wiped it away. She was the bravest thing Tinwright had ever seen.

His heart squeezed him. "I cannot, Lady. Oh, gods, my beloved Elan! I would like nothing . . . have thought of . . . I . . ." He paused and wiped his forehead, sweaty despite the evening chill. "I cannot.

Not this way." He swallowed. "I hope one day you will understand why and forgive me."

She shook her head, her smile so sadly sweet it was like a knife in his chest. "You do not have to explain, dear Matthias. It was selfish of me. I had only hoped . . ."

"You will never know the depth of my feelings, Elan. Please. Let's not speak of it anymore. It is too hard." He squinted, wiped fiercely at his eyes. "Just . . . let me hold your head. Here, lie against me." As she nestled against him, her back against his belly, her head against his shoulder, he could feel every place she touched him, through both her clothes and his, like a hot nail through a blacksmith's glove. "Lean back," he whispered, feeling as though he were a monster worse even than Hendon Tolly. "Lean back. Close your eyes and open your mouth."

She shut her eyes. He marveled at her long lashes, which cast shadows on her cheeks in the candlelight. "Oh, but first I must pray!" she said in a small voice. "It is never too late for that, surely? Zoria will hear me, even if she decides to spurn my request. I must try."

"Of course," he said.

Her lips moved silently for a while. Tinwright stared. "I am done," she said quietly, her eyes still tight shut.

He leaned forward then, letting her breath swirl gently against his face, then kissed her. She flinched, expecting something else, then her lips softened and for a moment that seemed like an hour he let himself vanish into the astonishing truth of what he had dreamed so often. At last he pulled back, but not before one of his tears splashed on her cheek. So sweet, so trusting, so sad!

"Oh, Elan," he whispered, "forgive me for this—for all of this."

She did not speak again, but lay with her mouth open like a child who waited, fearful but bravely patient, for some terrifying physic. He used his sleeve to pull the stopper from the flask, then used the needle ever so carefully to lift a single drop and let it fall into her mouth.

Elan M'Cory gave a little gasp of surprise, then swallowed. "It does not taste like so much," she said. "Bitter, but not painfully so."

Tinwright could not speak.

"I could have loved you well," she said, and a smile played around her lips. "Ah, what a strange sensation! I cannot feel my tongue. I think . . ."

She fell silent. Her breath slowed until he could not perceive it any longer.

One moment Ferras Vansen was there and the next moment the guard captain was gone, tumbled into nothingness without even crying out, torn away so quickly that, like a man whose leg had been blasted off by a cannonball, Barrick Eddon had only perceived the shock but not the loss itself.

The demigod Jikuyin was bellowing with both his voice and his thoughts, making the air of the cavern shudder and Barrick's bones throb inside his flesh. *"OH! OH, THEY ARE FREE, THE CURSED LITTLE TRICKSTERS!"* The giant swung his shaggy head toward Barrick, who crouched panting at the base of the massive doorway, dropped by his guards as they fought Vansen. The demigod's great eye narrowed and he turned to his lieutenant, the gray man; even the Dreamless seemed to have been caught by surprise. *"Ueni'ssoh!"* Although he spoke less harshly, the demigod's words still rattled Barrick's skull. *"Carry on, you bloodless fool!"* For the first time, Barrick could hear the actual words Jikuyin spoke, a rumbling, spiky tongue that bore no relation to what he heard in his head. *"The gate is still open! Finish the invocation!"*

Ueni'ssoh glided toward him and Barrick stumbled to his feet, but three more guards had fallen in behind the Dreamless, two of them armed with jagged-bladed axes, and he knew it was only a matter of moments until they would have him bleeding like a hung pig all over the threshold of the god's gate. But his shackles were gone, he realized in wonder: somehow Vansen had struck them off before the darkness took him.

Down! The warning in his head seemed so close, so powerful, that for an instant he thought it must be the voice of the demigod himself pounding in his skull. *Get down! Now!*

Barrick looked around in confusion. Gyir was free of his shackles, too. The fairy-warrior stood on the top of a small rise of stone with half a dozen dead guards sprawled at his feet and something burning brightly in his hand—a flaming skull . . . ?

If you want to live another moment, boy, the fairy's voice trumpeted through his thoughts, *THEN LIE DOWN!*

Barrick threw himself toward the ground even as Gyir's arm swept forward and what seemed a tiny comet hurtled across the cavern. For a moment everything seemed to stop—the faces of guards and prisoners lifted and turned like sunflowers as they followed the path of the blazing thing—then a blast of heat and light crashed across the cavern and rolled Barrick violently before dropping him again. He lay in a vibrating silence, unable to get up, as if lightning had struck only a short distance away.

The rush of ideas into his head was so violent that at first Barrick could make no sense of the demigod's angry burst of words and thoughts—he felt only a huge hammer of noise pounding at his ears and mind until he felt sure his head would collapse like an eggshell.

" . . . *HOW DID THAT MONGREL CREATURE, THAT FACELESS SLUG, GET HIS HANDS ON MY PRECIOUS FIREPOWDER . . . ?*"

Stunned and limp, Barrick thought it might be easiest simply to lie here on his back and let the world end, but a small, nagging voice in the back of his mind kept suggesting that perhaps a prince should meet his death sitting up. He rolled over, trying to get his legs under him.

Another thunderous crack, farther away this time and followed not by ringing silence but by hoarse screams, proved that at least there was still sound and direction and distance. Barrick sat up and brushed something wet off his arm—a rag of bloody skin, but not his own. The rest of the shaggy guard and his two companions, victims of the first of the flaming things Gyir had thrown, were scattered across several yards of cavern floor. Even in such chaos,

Barrick was glad the lights were dim: it was madly strange to see things that were so small and yet obviously part of a person who had been alive only moments before.

Gyir, who had been surrounded by guards and prisoners, now stood alone in a widening circle as creatures scrambled away from him in all directions. The fairy held a dirt-smeared death's head in each hand, and Barrick wondered what strange magic the faceless warrior had summoned.

Get up and run, Barrick Eddon. Gyir's words echoed in his head and he clambered to his feet almost without realizing. *I will keep them back as long as my fireballs last.*

Barrick could not frame the words, but Gyir must have sensed his confusion.

Exploding devices. I had those I could command pack skulls with gunflour, seal them with mud, and leave them here for me. This way Jikuyin's victims will get at least a little revenge! Gyir's thoughts billowed like windblown flame—he was laughing! For the first time Barrick could feel that the fairy had truly been raised in battle, that it was his element in a way it would never be Barrick's. *Now go, while I hold them at bay! Strike for the surface!*

But Vansen . . . !

Is gone, likely dead. All that is certain is that he is lost to us now. You must go. Do you yet have the thing I gave you?

Barrick had forgotten the mirror. His hand crept to his shirt. *Yes.*

Think of it no more. Flee! I will do what I can here.

But you have to come with me . . . !

It is more important that at least one of us escapes, Barrick Eddon. Take it to the king in the House of the People. Now go.

But . . . !

"ENOUGH!" The demigod Jikuyin rose up above a screeching herd of prisoners with flames running in their fur or their ragged clothes. The ogre seemed to grow like a ship's bellying sail until his head threatened to bump the roof of the cavern. "*YOU HAVE WASTED ENOUGH OF MY TIME, STORM LANTERN. THE DOOR TO THE EARTHLORD'S HOME IS*

OPEN. NO LAW, NOT EVEN THE BOOK OF THE FIRE OF THE VOID *ITSELF, SAYS I CANNOT SEAL THE CHARM BY SQUEEZING THE BLOOD OUT OF THIS MORTAL CHILD LIKE WATER FROM A BAG OF WHEY!"* Jikuyin took a stride toward Barrick, but Gyir bent and lit another muddied skull from the torch by his feet, then straightened and flung the fizzing, sparking ball toward the towering shape. It spat a great gout of fire and hot air as it flared at the giant's feet and knocked him staggering, but it flung Barrick back onto his knees as well.

Run, said Gyir in a small, insistent voice, and then he lit two more skulls and flung them at Jikuyin. Before they had even struck, the fairy was running toward the roaring demigod with a spear he must have taken from one of the guards. Then the giant and Gyir both disappeared in the double-crash of light and sound: Barrick could feel the skin on his cheeks blistering in the heat.

Barrick got up again, dizzy, with head throbbing and eyes blurred by stinging tears. He was almost blind, anyway—the cavern was full of billowing dust. He stumbled toward what he hoped was the way out, stepping over bodies that squirmed slowly, like dying insects. One of the hairy guards, its face nearly burned away, clutched weakly at his shin with charred fingers. Barrick crushed the creature's skull with his booted foot, then pulled an ax out of its clawed grip, a weapon he could wield with his one good hand. He half climbed, half stumbled up the slope toward the doorway leading out of the great cavern. All the other prisoners and guards who could do so seemed to have fled through it already: nothing blocked his way but corpses and whimpering near-corpses.

When he reached the opening, Barrick turned back to see the demigod Jikuyin outlined by the flames in which he stood, grinning and roaring so that his cracked face seemed about to split open, with Gyir clutched in his great hand. The fairy, who should have been crushed by that awesome grip, instead stabbed and stabbed at the giant's chest with his spear, each thrust followed by a spurt of black blood, each spurt only seeming to make Jikuyin laugh louder.

"YOU CANNOT HURT ME!" the giant shouted. *"THE ICHOR OF SVEROS HIMSELF RUNS IN MY VEINS! I COULD DROWN YOUR ENTIRE RACE IN MY BLOOD AND STILL SURVIVE!"*

Gyir jabbed silently, not just at Jikuyin's chest and face, but at his massive hand, too, struggling to keep the giant from throttling out his life.

"I WILL FIND YOUR LITTLE SUNLANDER BOY LIKE A CAT FINDS A LIMPING MOUSE," Jikuyin chortled. *"THEN I WILL RIDE HIS BLOOD TO THE VERY SEAT OF THE GODS!"*

Barrick knew he should run—should take advantage of Gyir's sacrifice, however hopeless—but now something new distracted him. The light of a torch had bloomed in the cavern's entrance. Several Drows, the twisted creatures that looked like Funderlings, had pushed a huge corpse-wagon into the cavern doorway. This one was not loaded with the bodies of dead prisoners but with barrels, and the barrels were surrounded by dry straw.

A bearded Drow sat atop the barrels. He seemed oblivious to the bizarre, apocalyptic events in the cavern below him, his eyes fixed instead on something in the middle of the air. He might have been an old man beside a busy road, content to wait until his passage would be perfectly safe.

"AND WHEN I HAVE THE EARTHLORD'S POWER," Jikuyin was gloating, oblivious to the thick, shining blood that oozed down his front, heedless of the dozen new wounds on his face and neck, *"I WILL PAINT YOUR PEOPLE'S EPITAPH WITH THE JUICES I WRING FROM YOUR CORPSES! AND DO YOU KNOW WHAT THAT EPITAPH WILL BE?"*

I know what yours will be. Gyir's thought was so quiet that Barrick could barely understand it, although he stood only a few dozen yards away. *It will be, "He was not good at thinking ahead."*

The fairy's arm shot out. His spear jabbed so hard it pushed all the way through the demigod's neck and out the nape. Jikuyin bellowed in anger, but did not seem any more crippled by this blow than by the others. Gyir leaped onto the giant's neck and used the shaft of the protruding spear as an anchor so he could wrap his arms and legs tightly around Jikuyin's head. The ogre's cries of rage now as loud as the earlier explosions, he staggered out into the middle of the track that ran down from the doorway to the cleared space in front of the earth god's black gateway.

The driver atop the wagon full of barrels raised the torch and waved it. The little men massed behind him shoved the cart out onto the downslope.

As the cart picked up speed, bouncing down the track faster than a horse could run, the driver made no attempt to dismount. Instead he dropped the torch into the straw piled around his feet. The flames flared high around the barrels, so that within a few more moments a great billowing blaze surrounded the little man and filled the back of the wagon. At the base of the track the unheeding giant still tore blindly at the small shape on his back, the faceless gnat who so annoyingly refused to die.

Jikuyin finally yanked Gyir free, pulling the fairy's arm loose in its socket so that it dangled helplessly and the spear dropped from his nerveless fingers. As Jikuyin bellowed in triumph, ignoring the wagon, Barrick realized what was in the barrels.

"I WILL EAT YOU, INSECT!" the demigod roared.

You will choke on me. The skin of Gyir's outer face had been torn away, and his strange small mouth twisted in what might have been a bloody smile. *Look.*

For the merest instant Barrick saw Jikuyin's face and the way it changed, then the blazing cart crashed into the demigod and the entire cavern vanished in a howling, crackling storm of fire. Barrick felt the Storm Lantern's last thought, a joyous curse on his defeated enemy, then the prince was flung away up the slope, skidding and rolling, and he felt the fairy's presence in his thoughts wink out like a snuffed candle.

Barrick came to a stop in the doorway amid the shrieking Drows who had brought the wagon, awakened by Gyir's death into this incomprehensible chaos. The stupefying concussion of the gun-flour, still echoing, was followed a moment later by the cracking, scraping sound of the cavern's stone roof collapsing. Solid rock jumped and boomed like Heaven's own drums. Several of the creatures who had unwittingly engineered this monstrous event scrambled over Barrick like rats in their haste to flee the doomed cavern. The prince could only cover his head and hold his breath as the impacts lifted and dropped him.

A millionweight of stone came tumbling down, burying demigod and mortals alike, sealing the open gateway to the gods' realm for the next thousand years and more.

38

Beneath the Burning Eye

Even the gods weep when they speak of the Theomachy, the war between the clan of the three heavenly brothers and the dark clan of Zmeos the Horned One. Many of the brightest fell, and their like will never be seen again, but their deeds live on, that men may understand honor and proper love of the gods.

—from *The Beginnings of Things*
The Book of the Trigon

PELAYA HAD NEVER SEEN anything like it. Even in her worst childhood nightmares, chased by some hungry monster like Brabinayos Boots-of-Stone out of her nurse's stories, she had not felt a terror and hopelessness like this.

The sky above Hierosol was black as if with a terrible storm, but it was smoke, not clouds, that had hidden the sun for three days now. On either side of the citadel much of the Crab Bay and Fountain districts were in flame. Pelaya could see the flames in particularly bright relief from the window of the family house near Landsman's Market, a horrible and fascinating sight, as if beautiful, glowing flowers were sprouting all across the city. In the districts along the seawalls the sickly smoke of the sulfur rafts had crept over the houses in a poisonous yellow fog. She had heard her father telling one of the servants that the autarch's burning sulfur had emptied most of the Nektarian Harbor district, that even the seaport end of the Lantern Broad was as silent as a tomb but for hurrying files of soldiers moving from one endangered part of the wall to another. Surely this must be the end of the world—the sort of thing the ragged would-be prophets in the smaller church squares were always shrieking about. Who could have guessed that those dirty, smelly men would be right after all?

"Come away from there, Pelaya!" her sister Teloni cried. "You will let in the poison smoke and kill us all!"

Startled, she let the window shutter go, almost losing her fingers as it crashed down. She turned in fury but the angry reply never came out of her mouth. Teloni looked helpless and terrified, her face was as white as one of the family's ancestor masks.

"The smoke is far away, down by the sea walls," Pelaya told her, "and the wind is pushing the other direction. We are in no danger from the poison."

"Then why are you looking? Why do you want to see . . . *that?*" Her sister pointed at the shutter as though what lay beyond were nothing but some unfortunate person—a deformed tramp, perhaps, or some other grotesque who could be ignored until he gave up and went away again.

"Because we are *at war!*" Pelaya could not understand her sister or her mother. They both skulked about the house as though this astonishing, dreadful thing was not happening. At least little Kiril was waving his wooden sword, pretending to slaughter Xixian soldiers. "Do you not care?"

"Of course we care." Teloni's eyes filled with tears. "But there is nothing we can do about it. What good does it do to . . . to stare at it?"

Pelaya got her shoulder against the shutter and lifted it again, pushing so hard that she almost fell out as it began to open. Teloni gasped and Pelaya felt her own heart speed—the cobbled courtyard was three floors below, quite far enough to break her bones.

Her sister grabbed Pelaya's arm. "Be careful!"

"I'm fine, Teli. Look, come here, I'll show you what Babba's doing."

"You don't know. You're just a girl—you're younger than me!"

"Yes, but I pay attention when he talks." She got the shutter all the way open and propped it with the thick wooden rod so she'd have her hand free to point. "There, by the Gate of the Fountain, do you see? That's the place where the autarch's cannons are trying to knock down the wall, but Babba is too clever. As soon as he realized what they were doing, he sent men to build a new wall behind it."

"A new wall? But they'll just knock that down too, won't they?"

"Perhaps. But by the time they do, he'll have built another . . . and another . . . and so on. He will not let them break through."

"Truly?" Teloni looked a little relieved. "But won't they dig under the wall? I heard Kiril say the autarch's men would dig tunnels under the walls here by Memnos or Salamander where there's no ocean—that they could come up in our garden if they wanted to!"

Pelaya rolled her eyes. "You don't listen to me, but you listen to Kiril? By all the gods, Teli, he's only seven years old."

"But isn't what he says true?"

"Do you see those?" She pointed to the strange shape by the nearest section of the citadel wall. "That's a sling engine—a kind of stone-throwing machine. It throws stones almost as heavy as the ones that come out of the autarch's big cannon. Whenever Babba and his men see someone digging a tunnel, they throw big stones at them and crush it."

"With the autarch's soldiers still inside?"

Pelaya snorted. Was she going to weep about the enemy who was trying to kill them? "Of course."

"Good. I'm glad." Teloni stared, eyes wide. "How do you know these things, Pelaya?"

"I told you—I listen. And speaking of listening, that's how they find the tunnels if they ever come close to the walls. Or they use the peas."

"What are you talking about?"

"Dried peas. Papa and his men dig special drums into the ground all along the walls and put dried peas on the drum heads. That way, if anyone is digging deep down in the ground under them, the peas jump and rattle and we know. Then we can drop stones and burning oil down on them."

"But they have so many soldiers!"

"It does not matter. We have our walls. Hierosol has never been conquered by force—that's what Babba says. Even Ludis Drakava could never have taken the citadel if the old emperor had an heir. Everyone knows that. The Council of Twenty-Seven was afraid of the autarch, so they opened the gates to Drakava instead."

"What if they do that for the autarch now? What if he offers them some bargain to let him in?"

Pelaya shook her head. "The council may be cruel old men, but they aren't fools. The autarch never keeps promises. He would execute them all and chew on their bones." Her childhood dreams abruptly came back to her again—the giant Boots-of-Stone with blood spattered in his beard, his jaws grinding and grinding. It didn't matter what she told her sister, the world was still going to end. She freed the wooden rod and let the window shutter down. "Let's go help Mama. I don't want to look anymore."

"No! Don't close it yet! I want to see some of the Xixians crushed or burned!" Teloni's eyes were bright.

It was only when she was saying her midday prayers that Pelaya suddenly realized that although the plumes of foul smoke, missiles of burning pitch, and the incessant fall of hot cannonballs from the autarch's ships might have driven the Lord Protector Ludis and his advisers out of the palace and into the safer lodgings of the great Treasury Hall in Magnate's Square, nobody had said anything about evacuating the rest of the palace's inhabitants. Which meant that King Olin of Southmarch might still be there, trapped in his cell.

None of the servants knew where her father had gone, and her mother was so worried about the count's safety she practically burst into tears when Pelaya asked her, but she didn't know either. Pelaya paced back and forth in the entry hall, trying to think of something, growing more certain by the moment that nobody else had even remembered Olin Eddon. She returned to her mother, but Ayona Akuanis had gone to comfort the baby, who had been fretful all night, and together they had fallen into exhausted sleep.

Pelaya looked at her mother's face, so young and beautiful again now that sleep had for a moment soothed her fearful heart. She could not bear to wake her. She went to her mother's desk instead and wrote a letter in such a careful hand that Sister Lyris would have been proud of the execution, if not the purpose. She closed it with wax and her mother's seal.

She found Eril with three of the lower servants, trying to make order of the chaotic pantry. The Akuanis family never moved into the Landmarket house this early in the year and the household had not been prepared for their sudden arrival.

"I want you to take this letter up to the stronghold," she told him. "I want you to bring someone back here."

Eril looked at her with the full amount of hauteur he could afford to show to the daughter of his master. "To the stronghold, *Kuraion?* I don't think so. It is not safe. What do you want so badly? We packed up everything."

"I didn't say some*thing,* I said some*one.* He is a king, an important man, and the lord protector has left him in the stronghold to die."

"That is not a task for such as me—not unless your father himself asks me," he said with the firmness of an aging servant who had been cajoled and tricked over the years in every way young girls could devise.

"But you must!"

"Really? Shall we go and see what *Kura* Ayona has to say about it, then?"

"She's sleeping and can't be disturbed." Pelaya scowled. "Please, Eril! Babba knows this man and would want him saved."

The servant draped his fingers across his forehead in the manner of one of the *onirai* ignoring his persecutors while communing with the gods. "You wish me to risk my life for some foreign prisoner? You are very cruel to me, *Kuraion*. Wait until your father returns and we will see what the master's wishes are."

She stared at him for long moments, hating him. She knew that even if she somehow forced Eril to go, there was no promise he would do what he was told, anyway—he was as stubborn as only a venerable family retainer could be. The citadel hill was in chaos and he could easily claim he had been prevented somehow.

Her heart was hammering—each crash of cannonfire might be the one that brought the stronghold roof down on poor Olin Eddon. She would have to go herself, but even in good times it would have been scandalous as well as dangerous to cross the city alone. She needed some kind of armed escort.

"Very well," she said at last, then turned and stalked away. She had a plan, and in fact was rather shocked with herself for even thinking of it, let alone putting it into action, but if she hadn't balked at forging a letter from her mother then she certainly wasn't going to let herself be frustrated by one difficult servant.

At the bottom of the road she stopped at the front gate of their neighbors, a wealthy family named Palakastros. A group of beggars stood outside, as usual. Unlike Pelaya's thrifty mother, the mistress of the Palakastrai was a rich old widow who worried about what would happen to her after she died, and so she made a practice of sending food out from her table nearly every day. This assured that there was almost always a crowd of the aged and infirm outside her gate, much to the annoyance of Ayona Akuanis and other householders on the long, wide street. Because of the siege there were two or three times as many as usual today and they quickly surrounded Pelaya.

Anxious at being hemmed in by so many strangers, especially dirty strangers, she picked one who looked extremely old and frail and thus less likely to try any tricks. She pulled him aside, leaving the others grumbling, and handed him a small copper coin with a crab on it. "Go to that household," she pointed back up the road toward the broad eaves of her family's house, "and ask for Eril the steward. Speak to him *only*. Tell him Pelaya says he is to meet her at the Sivedan Temple on Good Zakkas Road, and that he must bring his sword. If you do this properly, I will bring you two more of these tomorrow, right here. Understand?"

The old beggar gummed the coin reflectively, then nodded. "Temple of Siveda," he said.

"Good. Oh, and tell Eril that if he brings my mother or anyone else I don't want to see, I will hide and they will never find me, and it will all be his fault. Can you remember all that?"

"For three copper crabs? Half a seahorse?" The old man laughed and coughed, or it might have been the other way around—it was hard to tell the difference. "*Kura,* I'd sing the Trigoniad from stem to stern for three coppers. I've ate nothing but grass for days."

She frowned, wondering if he was making fun of her. How could an old, toothless beggar know the Trigoniad? But it didn't matter. All that mattered was getting King Olin to safety.

In fact, Pelaya thought, if this worked, Olin Eddon would almost certainly invite her to his own court someday out of gratitude. She could tell her family, "Oh, yes, the king of the Marchlands wishes me to come for a visit. You remember King Olin—he and I are old friends, you know."

She set off for Good Zakkas Road, half a mile away in the Theogonian Forum district. She had thought of bringing a knife herself, but hadn't known how to get one without risking her plan being discovered, so she had decided to do without. That was why she needed Eril and his sword. It had been years since he had fought in her father's troop, but he was big enough and relatively young enough that no one would try to rob her in his company, at least not in daylight. Still, robbery might be the least of the dangers.

Am I mad? The streets were full of soldiers, but most of the rest of the citizens had returned from their scuttling morning errands and were locked in now, terrified of the cannons, of the foul smoke and fire that fell from the sky. *What am I doing?*

Doing good, Pelaya told herself, and then remembered the Zorian injunction against self-importance. *Trying to do good.*

The rag had slipped from his mouth down to his chin and the dust was getting in again. Count Perivos spit out a mouthful of grit and then pulled the cloth back into place, but he had to lay down his shovel to tie it. He cursed through ash and dirt. When you had forty pentecounts of men at your disposal, you didn't expect to be wielding a tool yourself.

"Smoke!" the lookout shouted.

"Down, down!" Perivos Akuanis bellowed as he threw himself to the ground, but there was little need: most of the men were down before him, bellies and faces pressed against the earth. The terrible moment was on them, the long instant of whistling near-silence. Then the massive cannonball hit the citadel wall with a bone-rattling crunch that shook the ground and smashed more stone loose from the wall's inner side.

After waiting a few moments to be certain the debris had stopped flying, Count Perivos opened his eyes. A new cloud of stone dust hung in the air and had coated everything on the ground; as the count and his workmen began to clamber to their feet he could not help thinking they looked like some sort of ghastly mass rising of the recent dead.

One of his master masons was already on his way back from examining the wall, which had been pounded over these last days by a hundred mighty stone cannonballs or more.

"She'll take a few more, *Kurs,* but not many," the man reported. "We'll be lucky if it's still standing tomorrow."

"Then we must finish this wall today." The count turned and shouted for the foreman, Irinnis. "What do we have left to do?" he demanded when the man staggered up. "The outwall can only take a few more shots from those monstrous bombards of theirs." Count Perivos had learned to trust Irinnis, a small, sweaty man from Krace with an excellent head for organization, who had fought—or at least built—for generals on both continents.

Scratching his sagging chin, Irinnis looked around the court-yard—one of the citadel's finest parks only a tennight ago, now a wreckage of gouged soil and broken stone. The replacement wall being built in a bowl-shaped curve behind the battered outwall was all but finished. "I'd like the time to paint it, *Kurs*," he said, squinting.

"*Paint* it?" Akuanis leaned toward him, uncertain he had heard correctly: his ears were still ringing from the impact of the last thousandweight of stone cannonball. "You didn't say 'paint it,' did you? While the whole citadel is coming down around our ears?"

Irinnis frowned—not the frown of someone taking offense, but more the face of an engineer astonished to discover that civilians, even those gifted and experienced in warfare like Count Perivos, could not understand plain Hierosoline speech. "Of course, Lord, paint it with ashes or black mud. So the Xixies will not see it."

"So that . . ." Perivos Akuanis shook his head. All across the park the men who had not been injured in the last blast, and even those whose injuries were only minor, were scrambling back to work. "I confess, you have lost me."

"What good are our arrow slits, *Kurs*," said Irinnis, pointing to the shooting positions built into the curving sides of the new wall, "if the autarch's landing force does not try to come through the breach their cannon has made? And if they see the new wall too quickly, they will not come through the breach and die like proper Xixian dogs."

"Ah. So we paint . . ."

"Just splash on a little mud if that's all we can find—something dark. Throw a little dirt onto it at the bottom. Then they will not see the trap until we've feathered half of the dog-eating bastards . . ."

The foreman's cheerful recitation was interrupted by the

sudden appearance of Count Perivos' factor, who had been over-seeing the evacuation of the palace, but now came running across the yard as if pursued by sawtooth cats. *"Kurs!"* he shouted. "The lord protector has given the foreign king to the Xixians!"

It took Perivos Akuanis a moment to make sense of that. "King Olin, do you mean? Are you saying that Ludis has given Olin of Southmarch to the autarch? How can that be?"

His factor had to pause for a moment, hands on knees, to catch his breath. "As to how, my lord, I couldn't say, but Drakava's Rams came for him before I could finish moving him and the other pris-oners, *Kurs*. I'm sorry. I've failed you."

"No, the fault is not yours." Akuanis shook his head. "But why are you sure they meant to take Olin to the autarch and not just to Ludis?"

"Because the chief of the Rams had a warrant, with the lord protector's seal on it. It said precisely what they were to do with him—take him from his cell and take him to the Nektarian harbor seagate where he would be given to the Xixians in return for 'such considerations as have been agreed upon,' or something like."

Count Perivos smelled something distinctly unsavory. Why would Ludis trade such a valuable pawn as Olin, unless it were to end the siege? But Sulepis would surely never give up the siege for the single lowly prize of a foreign king, especially the master of a small kingdom like Olin's, which hadn't even managed to ransom him from Ludis after nearly a year. None of it made sense.

Still, there was no good to be gained wasting time trying to understand it. Count Perivos handed his sheaf of plans to the factor, then turned to the foreman. "Irinnis, keep the men work-ing hard—that outwall won't last the night. And don't forget that the wall near the Fountain Gate needs shoring up, too—half of it came down."

The count hurried away across the wreckage of what had once been Empress Thallo's Garden, a haven for quiet thought and sweet birdsong for hundreds of years. Now with every other step he had to dodge around outcrops of shattered stone knocked loose from the gate or smoking gorges clawed into the earth by cannonballs: the place looked like something that the death-god Kernios had ground beneath his heel.

With twenty full pentecounts of the city's fiercest fighters surrounding his temporary headquarters in the pillared marble Treasury Hall, it would have been reasonable to suspect that Ludis Drakava, Lord Protector of Hierosol, feared an uprising from his own people more than he feared the massive army of the autarch outside his city walls.

Perivos Akuanis looked bitterly at the huge encampment as he walked swiftly between the rows of soldiers. *We have nearly had two breakthroughs along the northern wall since the last sunrise. Neither of them would have happened if these men hadn't been held back*—a thousand out of the seven or eight thousand trained soldiers in the entire city, all they had to counter the autarch's quarter of a million. The Council of the Twenty-Seven Families had surrendered the throne to Ludis so that a strong man would stand against the Autarch of Xis, whatever the loss of their own power, but it was beginning to look as though they would have neither.

If the outside looked like a fortress, the inside of the treasury looked more like the great temple of the Three Brothers: half a dozen black-robed, long-bearded Trigonate priests surrounded the transplanted Jade Chair like roosting crows, and like crows they seemed more interested in hopping and squawking than doing anything useful. Count Perivos, who had never liked or trusted Ludis, had lately come to loathe Hierosol's lord protector with a fierce, hot anger unlike any he had ever felt. He hated Ludis even more than he hated the Autarch of Xis, because Sulepis was only a name, but he had to stare into Ludis Drakava's square, heavy-browed face every single day and swallow bile.

The lord protector stood, flapping his arms at the priests as though they truly were crows. "Get out, you screeching old women! And tell your hierarch that if he wants to talk to me he can come himself, but I will use the temples as I see fit. We are at war!"

The Trigonate minions seemed unwilling to depart even after so clear an order, but none of them was above the rank of deacon.

Grumbling and pulling at their whiskers, they migrated toward the door. Scowling, Ludis dropped back onto the throne. He caught sight of Count Perivos. "I suppose I should count my blessings the Trigonarch was kidnapped by the Syannese all those years ago," Ludis growled, "or I'd have *him* whining at me, too." He narrowed his eyes. "And what kind of stinking news do you bring, Akuanis?"

"I think you know about what brings me, although it was fresh to me only a half-hour gone. What is this I hear about Olin Eddon?"

Ludis put on the innocent look of a child—particularly bizarre on a brawny, bearded man covered with scars. "What do you hear?"

"Please, Lord Protector, do not treat me as a fool. Are you telling me that nothing unusual has happened to King Olin? That he has not been hustled out of his cell? I am told he is being traded to the autarch for ... something. I do not know what."

"No, you don't know. And I won't tell you." The lord protector crossed his heavy arms on his chest and glowered.

There was something wrong with the way Ludis was behaving. Drakava was a surprisingly complex man, but Akuanis had never seen him show the least remorse for anything he'd done, let alone act like this—childishly petulant, as though expecting to be scolded and punished. This from the man who had declared an innocent priest (who also happened to have the only legitimate claim to the Hierosoline throne) a warlock and had him dragged from his temple and pulled apart by horses? Why should Ludis Drakava have become squeamish now?

"So it's true, then. Is there time to stop it? Where is King Olin now?"

Ludis looked up, actually surprised. "By Hiliometes' beard, why should we stop it? What can a milk-skinned northerner like that mean to you?"

"He is a king! Not to mention that he is an honorable man. Pity I cannot say the same of Hierosol's ruler."

Ludis stared at him malevolently. Count Perivos was suddenly aware of the fact that he was surrounded by troops who owed him no personal loyalty, but who received their pay in the lord protector's name each month. "You climb far out on a thin branch," Ludis said at last.

"But what do you gain by this? Why give an innocent man over to the cruelties of that . . . that monster, Sulepis?"

Ludis laughed harshly but turned away, as though still not entirely comfortable meeting the count's eyes. "Who wears the crown here, Akuanis? Your reputation as a siege engineer gives you no right to question me. I protect what I must protect . . ."

He broke off at the sound of shouting. A soldier wearing the crest of the Esterian Home Guard shoved his way through Drakava's Golden Enomote and threw himself down on the mosaic in front of the throne. "Lord Protector," he cried, "the Xixies have come over the wall below Fountain Gate! We're holding them in the temple yard at the foot of Citadel Hill, but we have only a small troop and won't be able to hold them long. Lord Kelofas begs you to send help."

Akuanis strode forward, all thoughts of Olin Eddon blasted from his mind. The temple yard was only a couple of miles from the townhouse where his wife and children waited in what they thought was safety—they and thousands more innocents would be overrun in a matter of hours if the Fountain Gate defenses collapsed. "Give me some of these men," he demanded. "Let me go and hit Sulepis in the teeth now—this moment! You have a thousand around this building, but they will be like straws in a gale if we don't keep the autarch out."

For a moment Drakava hesitated, but then an odd look stole across his face. "Yes, take them," he said. "Leave me two pente-counts to defend the treasury and the throne."

After all the harsh words, Count Perivos was astonished that the lord protector would give up his troops so easily, but he had no time to wonder. He dropped to his knee and touched his head to the floor—bowing not to Ludis, he told himself, but to all the Hierosoline kings and queens, emperors and empresses, who had sat on the great green throne before him—then rose and hurried off to the *taksiarch* of the men encamped around the treasury. He could only pray that the engineers and workers he had left behind in the Empress Gardens had almost finished the wall, or holding the wall at Fountain Gate would mean nothing.

"Make us proud, Count Perivos," shouted Ludis as Akuanis and the taksiarch got the men into fast-march formation. The lord protector almost sounded as though he were enjoying some theatrical spectacle. "All of Hierosol will be watching you!"

Eril was so furious with his young mistress that at first he wouldn't even speak to her, but only followed with his sword nearly dragging in the dust as they set out from the Sivedan temple toward the Citadel Hill. As they climbed upward on the spiraling road, breasting a great tide of folk hurrying the opposite way, he finally found his tongue.

"You have no right to do this, *Kuraion!* We will be killed. Just because I am a servant doesn't mean I should die for nothing."

She was surprised by his vehemence and his selfishness. "I couldn't do it unless someone came with me." That seemed obvious to her and it should have to him as well, now that he'd been given time to digest it. What did he want, an apology? "The poor king needs our help—he's a *king,* Eril."

The servant gave her a look that in different circumstances she would have reported to her mother. Pelaya was shocked—old Eril, silly old Eril, acting as though he hated her!

"Anyway," she said, a little flustered. "It won't take long. We'll be back before supper. And you'll be able to tell the gods you did a good deed when you say your prayers tonight."

Judging by the noise he made in reply, Eril did not seem to find much consolation in the thought.

Although there were still many people on the grounds of the palace and in the stronghold, mostly servants and soldiers, it quickly became clear to Pelaya that Olin Eddon wasn't one of them. His cell was empty, the door standing open.

"But where is he?" she asked. She had come so far and taken so many risks for nothing!

"Gone, Mistress," said one of the soldiers who had gathered to watch this unusual performance. "The lord protector had him moved somewhere."

"Where? Tell me, please!" She brandished her forged letter. "My father is Count Perivos!"

"We know, Mistress," said the soldier. "But we still can't tell you because we don't know. The lord protector's Rams took him somewhere. You'll have to find out from him."

"You talk too much," another soldier told him. "She shouldn't be here—it's dangerous. Can you imagine anything happens? It'll be our heads on the block, won't it?"

She led Eril out of the stronghold and across Echoing Mall toward Kossope House, ignoring his complaints. If the servants were still in their dormitories, especially the dark-haired laundry girl, perhaps they'd know where Olin was. Servants, Pelaya had discovered, usually knew everything important that happened in a great house.

As the echoes of distant cannon echoed along the colonnade, Pelaya saw that whether the laundry women were here or not, many other servants had remained, although they did not look very happy. In fact, many of them seemed to glare at her as though it were somehow her fault they'd been left behind. She was glad Eril had his sword. Pelaya could almost imagine these abandoned servants, if left here long enough, turning entirely wild, like the dogs that roamed the city midden heaps and cemeteries after dark.

"The one I want to talk to is in here," Pelaya said, pointing toward the large building on the far side of the palace complex. "Poor thing, she has such a long way to walk each day."

Eril muttered something but Pelaya could not make it out.

When they reached the dormitory they found that the residents were guarding it themselves: three strong-looking young women with laundry-poles stood before the door, and they gave Eril a very stern look before letting him accompany Pelaya inside.

To her delight and relief they found the laundry girl almost immediately, sitting morosely on her bed as though waiting for a cannonball to crash through the roof and kill her. To Pelaya's shock, the dark-haired girl not only wasn't pleased to have a highborn visitor, she seemed frightened of Eril.

"Follows me!" she said, pointing. "He follows!"

Eril scowled. "She never saw me, *Kuraion*. I'm sure she didn't. Someone told her."

"He followed you because I needed to know where you lived," Pelaya said gently. "He's my servant. I had to find you quietly, when King Olin wanted to speak to you. Now, where *is* Olin? Do you know? He's been taken out of the stronghold."

The girl looked at her in blank misery, as if Olin's whereabouts were of no particular interest compared to her own problems, whatever those might be. Pelaya scowled. How could she converse usefully with a laundry maid who could barely speak her language? "I need to find him. *Find him*. I'm looking for him."

The girl's face changed—something like hope flowered. "Help find?"

"Yes!" Finally, sense had been made. "Yes, help find."

The girl jumped up and took Pelaya's hand, shocking the count's daughter more than a little, but before she could protest she was being dragged across the dormitory. It was not Olin that the brown-haired girl led Pelaya to, but another laundrywoman, a friendly, round-featured girl named Yazi who seemed meant to translate. The new girl's command of Hierosoline was not much better, but after many stops and starts it finally became clear that the brown-haired girl hadn't agreed to help find Olin, she herself wanted help finding her mute brother, who had been missing since the middle of the night.

"He *not go*," she said over and over, but clearly he had.

"No, we have to find Olin, King Olin," Pelaya told her. "I'll ask my father to send someone to help you find your brother."

The Xandian girl looked shocked, as though she could not have imagined anyone would say no to her request.

"Haven't we had enough of this, *Kuraion?*" said Eril. "You have dragged me across the city for nothing, risking both our lives. Are we now going to have to search for a runaway child as well?"

"No, of course not, but . . ." Before Pelaya could finish, someone else joined the small crowd of women that had gathered around the brown-haired girl and her round friend. This new arrival was considerably older than the others, her face disfigured by what looked like a bad burn.

"Oh, thank the Great Mother!" this old woman said when she saw them all, then leaned against the wall, gasping hoarsely for breath. "I . . . I . . . was frightened I wouldn't . . . find you." She looked at Pelaya, surprised. "Your Ladyship. Forgive me."

Pelaya just barely nodded a greeting, irritated by yet another interruption. Eril was right—they needed to get back to Landsman's Market.

"What is it, Losa?" asked the round-faced girl, Yazi.

"The boy who can't talk, the little brother! He is up in the counting house tower and very . . ." She waved her hands, trying to find the words. "Angry, sad, I don't know. He won't come down."

"Pigeon?" Qinnitan sat forward. "He not . . . hurt?"

"I don't think hurt, no," said Losa. "He is just hiding in that tower, the old broken one near the seawall. I think the . . . cannons? I think the cannons scare him. He wants his sister."

"We'll come, too," said Yazi. "He likes me."

"No!" said Losa. "He is very scared, the boy. He almost falls when I come. Up very high. If he sees people he doesn't know so well . . ." She shook her head, unable or unwilling to come up with the words for such a dire prospect. "Just his sister."

The dark-haired laundry girl did not appear to grasp everything said, but she smiled—it did little to hide the anxiousness in her face—and said something in her own tongue to the girl Yazi. For a moment Pelaya wondered if she should go with them to help—Olin had taken an interest in this girl, after all—but she could think of too many reasons why she should not let herself get further involved.

After the old, scarred woman had led the brown-haired girl out,

Pelaya began to move toward the front of Kossope House. "It's good she's found her brother," she said, smiling at the other laundry women. "Family is so important. Now I must go back to mine. May the gods protect you all."

The faces of the servants turned toward her as she reached the door. They watched her, silent as cats.

"I'm sure everything will be well," Pelaya called to them, then had to hurry to catch up with Eril, who was already striding off in a determined way in the general direction of Landsman's Market.

Old Losa led Qinnitan across the courtyard into a section of the palace deserted days earlier by the clerks who had worked there. It was strange to move freely through rooms she had only tiptoed through before, terrified she might break someone's concentration and earn a whipping.

"Why would he run away like this?" Qinnitan asked, falling back into Xixian now that the young noblewoman and her servant had been left behind. "And how did you happen to find him?"

The old woman spread her palms. "I think the cannons frightened him, poor little lad. I heard him calling and found him where he was hiding, but he wouldn't come with me."

"Calling?" Qinnitan said, suddenly fearful again. "But he can't speak. Are you sure it was him? My Pigeon?"

Losa shook her head in disgust. "There you go. I don't know whether I'm coming or going, all this has me in such a muddle. I heard him crying—moaning, that's the word I meant. Here, go down this passage."

"But you said he was in the old countinghouse tower—isn't it that way?"

"You see? I can't think straight at all." Losa pointed a dirty finger at the low bulk of the almshouse where it hugged the inside of the seawall, the arched doorway of its single squat tower showing dark among the vines like a missing tooth in a bearded mouth.

"Not the countinghouse tower but the *almshouse* tower, the old almshouse. There. He's there, I promise you."

Losa guided her into the shadowed antechamber of the building, which had been abandoned and all its poor relocated a few years before the siege. The mosaics on the floor were chipped and scratched so that other than the hammer-shaped object in one's hands, it was impossible to tell which of the Trigon brothers was which. Qinnitan suddenly had the awful feeling that the old woman had tricked her for some reason, but then she saw Pigeon staring back at her from the shadows of the stairwell with his eyes wide. Her heart seemed to swell and grow light again. She rushed toward him but he did not move, although she saw his jaw pumping as though he would have much to say if given his tongue back.

"Pigeon?" Something was wrong, or at least odd: she couldn't see his arms. As she moved closer she saw that they were behind him, as though he had something hidden for her there. A few more steps and she could see that they were tied at the wrists, and the cord looped through the latch of the heavy stairwell door. She reached him, felt him trembling with terror beneath her hands, and turned toward Losa. "What . . . ?"

The old woman was pulling off her face.

As Qinnitan stared in terror, Losa scraped the skin off her cheeks, peeling it away in long, knubbled strips. She had straightened up, and now seemed a head taller and a great deal more solid. She wasn't old. She wasn't even a woman.

Qinnitan was so shocked that she lost control of her bladder; a trickle of urine ran down her legs. "Who . . . what . . . ?"

"Who doesn't matter," the man said in perfect Xixian. Underneath the waxy remnants of false flesh his skin was nearly as pale as King Olin's had been, but unlike Olin, this man had not a flicker of kindness in his eyes, nor a flicker of anything else: for all the expression he wore, his face might have been carved on a statue. "The autarch sent me." He straightened up, shredding the shapeless dress he had worn to reveal man's clothing beneath. "Don't scream or I'll slit the child's throat. By the way, if you decide to sacrifice the boy and make a run for it, you should know that I can hit a rabbit with *this,*" —he lifted his hand and a long, sharp dagger appeared in it like a conjuror's trick—"from a hundred paces away. I can put it in the back of your knee and you'll never walk without a crutch, or I can put it between two of your chines and you'll never walk again at all. But I would prefer not to carry you all the way to the Golden One, so if you do as I ask, you'll keep your health." He kicked away the remnants of the dress, then used the knife blade to cut away a sack he had tied to his waist with rags to give him an old woman's sagging belly.

Qinnitan wrapped her arms around Pigeon, tried to stop him shivering. "But . . ." Faced with this empty, emotionless man, she could think of nothing to say. Somehow she had known this day would come—she had only hoped it would take longer than this brief couple of months. "You won't hurt the boy?"

"I won't hurt him if he does nothing stupid. But he is the autarch's property, so he goes back, too."

"He's not property, he's a child! He did nothing wrong."

The merest hint of a smile stole across the stranger's cold face, as if he had finally heard something worth his getting out of bed that morning. "Sit down and put your legs out."

She started to argue, but he had closed the distance between them in an astonishingly swift step or two, and now stood over her, the knife only inches from her eye. She sat back on the stairs and extended her feet. He put the end of the knife gently against her throat and held it there with his thumb on the other side of her windpipe, then looped a piece of cord around one ankle. When he had tied the other end, a length of the cord about the distance from her wrist to elbow stretched between her two legs, leaving her neatly hobbled. He took a long dress out of the sack—it was something she had seen some of the chambermaids wearing—and dropped it over her head, then yanked her to her feet. When she stood, the hem of the dress almost touched the dusty tiles, hiding the cord completely.

"Does the boy understand speech?"

Qinnitan nodded, dully, hopelessly. Even if the others went

looking for her, she had just realized, it would be to the counting-house tower on the other side of the palace grounds.

The pale man turned to the boy. "If you try to run away, I will cut off her nose, do you understand? The autarch won't care."

Pigeon looked at the man with narrowed eyes. If he was a dog, he would have growled, or more likely, simply bit without making a noise. At last he nodded.

"Well, come along then." The man landed a single kick that made the boy whimper wordlessly and scramble awkwardly onto his feet so his bonds could be cut. Pigeon rubbed his wrists, unable to look at Qinnitan for the shame of having been part of her capture. "No tricks," the man said. "It would waste time if I have to kill or cripple either of you, but it wouldn't change anything important. Move along now." He pointed to the doorway. "We don't want to keep your master waiting. He's much less patient than I am, and much less kind."

Qinnitan stepped out into the light of the deserted courtyard, the cord chafing her ankles at each constrained step. She was too shocked and empty even to cry. The space of a few heartbeats had changed everything. Only a few dozen yards away in Kossope House she had friends, a life, all the things she had wanted so badly, but they were all lost now. Instead, she belonged to that madman again—the terrifying, utterly heartless Living God on Earth.

39

City of the Red Sun

*So Habbili, son of Nushash, found himself alone in the
world after he had been crippled by cruel Argal. He took
himself on a journey into the far west, my children, of
which only legends speak and where men have never
traveled. There it is said he spoke with his father at one end
of Nushash's mighty voyage, and afterward returned to the
lands we know.*

*To his lordly father he said that one day he would throw
down the children of Mother Shusayem, and so he did.*

—from *The Revelations of Nushash*, Book One

FOR A LONG TIME THE MAN wandered without a name through a forest of black poplar trees and tall cypresses that swayed in an unfelt, unheard wind. A dark stream wandered near the path, but its course veered away and vanished into the mists again as he went forward. Willows curtained it, drooping and shivering like crying women, their branches dangling just above the silent waters.

The man had no strength to wonder where he was, or how he had come to this land of mist and shadow. For a long time he could think of nothing to do but walk. The sun was utterly absent, the sky a gleaming emptiness that was neither dark nor light. He thought that he had been in such a place before, a country of perpetual evening, but he also felt certain he had never been in this gloomy country. The only other thing he knew was a quiet fear that if he did not keep moving he would become as still and hopeless as the black poplars that surrounded him—might even sink into the muddy, squelching soil and become one of the trees himself.

The man wished someone were with him, a voice to sing, or speak, or even weep, anything that would pierce the unending stillness. He tried to do it himself but he had lost the knack of making words and noises just as he had lost his name. It was very quiet in this country. A few black birds walked on the branches above his head, or fluttered from tree to tree, but they were as silent as the trees and the wind and the water.

He walked on.

He had been seeing moving shadows on the far side of the stream for some time, misty figures with the shapes of men and women. Now he saw something else on that far shore which made him pause in wonderment, but he was still uncertain. He wished again he had a voice so he could ask for help from those shadow-folk, for he could see no way to cross the water, and although it seemed to move slowly he did not trust its opaque quiet.

But what do I have to lose even if the water swallows me? He had no immediate answer, but he felt that somehow he did possess something, a truth of some kind he did not wish to surrender, but which the waters of the stream might wash away.

How can I cross, then?

You cannot. Or if you do, you will never return from that other shore.

A small, naked child of three or four years old stood beside him, her pale hair fluttering slowly. His first thought was to feel sorry for her, so tiny and so unprotected from the wind. Then he looked into those eyes like molten gold flecked with particles of amber and knew she was no child, or at least no mortal child.

Who are you? he asked.

Her voice was not that of a child either, or at least not of one as small as she appeared. Each word was as measured and golden as her gaze. *One who remains after the others have gone. One of the elder guardians of this place—no, "guardians" is not correct. "Guides" would be better. And clearly you need guidance, little lost one.*

But I want to cross the river. I need to. I . . . I think I see someone there that I know.

All the more reason to fear it. That is the way most of your kind lose their way in our land, by following someone they know, or think they know. You are not ready. Your time comes soon—all your kind are only a blink away at most—but it has not come yet.

He did not know what any of this meant. How could he, when he did not even know his own name? But that did not change the things he felt, the pull of the farther side.

Please. He reached out then, tried to take the child's hand, but it was as though she stood at the bottom of a stream that bent the light deceptively. Wherever he reached, she was not there. *Please. I never told him . . . I did not . . .*

Her face at first was tranquil as a marble mask, but it changed as something like pity stole across it. *Then you take it upon yourself,* she said at last. *It is only because you have come here by mischance that it is even possible. You may cross—you may see both how things are and how things were—but you will have to be lucky as well as strong to cross the dark water a second time and come out again.*

He lowered his head, humbled by his greed for something he could not even name, could not quite understand. *You are kind.*

Kindness is not part of these laws, especially once you are beyond my hand. The child-face was solemn. *There, rules are like the paths of the stars through the great vault, fixed and remorseless. You must not eat any food or accept any gift. And you must not forget your name.*

But . . . but I can't remember it. He looked around at the endless grove of poplars, the trunks marching away in all directions. It seemed his name was almost within reach but he still could not summon it no matter how he tried.

The child shook her head. *Already? Then you are all the more a fool for taking such a risk. Only the strongest hearts can enter the city and yet live.* She lifted her tiny, pale arm and a boat slid up to the bank, a thing of rusty nails and gray, weathered boards. *Very well, this is the last thing I can do. I do it in memory of one like you, long ago, who also put his life in my hands. Your name is Ferras Vansen. You are a living man. Now go.*

And in the next moment he was upon the river. Both banks had disappeared and there was nothing but mist everywhere.

He was a long time on the black water. Vast shapes moved just below the surface, and sometimes the boat rocked as they passed beneath it; once or twice the things even broke water and he could see their wet hides, black and shiny as polished metal. They did not touch him or threaten him in any way, but he was very glad he was in a boat and not floundering in the dark, cold current with those huge shapes swimming beneath him, drawn to his warmth and movement.

Ferras Vansen. That is my name, he reminded himself—here on the river he could almost feel it slipping away again as the mists streamed past. It had seemed so clear when the child said it, so true, and yet he knew he could lose it again as easily he had forgotten it in the forest of black trees.

How did I come to these lands? But that memory was even more lost than his name had been. He knew only that the child had said he did not come the way most men came—*mischance,* she had named it—and that was enough, somehow, to comfort him.

Something felt strange beneath his hands, under his feet. He looked down and saw that the boat was no longer made of gray wood, but of snakes—hundreds of dully shining shapes woven together like the twig mats old women made so their husbands and sons and grandsons could wipe the mud of the fields off their boots. But these were *not* twigs, they were serpents, alive and writhing. He lifted his feet and hands but it was no good: the entire boat was made of snakes and there was nowhere to go to escape them.

Even as he stared in horrified surprise, the snake-boat began to unravel, those at the top and along the rails slithering free of their weave and dropping like heavy ropes into the dark, quiet water. They kept peeling away, first in ones and twos and then more swiftly, until the water was coming in on all sides and he rode on nothing more solid than a blanket of cold, thrashing shapes.

He looked up, staring helplessly into the mists ahead in search of the far bank, a stone in the river, anything that might save him. The snakes fell away. The boat fell away. He tried to remember the names of the gods so he could pray but even those had been taken from him.

Vansen. I am Ferras Vansen. I am a soldier. I love a woman who does not love me, and could not if she would. I am Ferras Vansen!

And then he tumbled into the cold swells and swallowed all the blackness.

He was not in the river or on the shore, but in a twilight street. The lamps had been lit above the cobbles. They burned as fitfully as witchfire, glowing without much illuminating the ramshackle houses. It was not yet full dark but the streets seemed utterly empty.

What place is this? He thought he wondered silently, but someone heard him.

It is the City of the Sleepers. The voice of the girl-child who had given him back his name was faint, as if she stood on the far side of the river he could no longer see. *There is only one way through, Ferras Vansen, and that is always forward. Remember . . . !*

And that was the last he heard of her. After that he could scarcely even recall how she looked, how she sounded. He stepped forward and his footsteps made no sound, though he could hear the noise of water dripping and a quiet wind rustling and whispering along the rooftops.

Most of the windows were dark, but a few were lit. When he

looked inside he saw people. They were all asleep, even those who stood or moved about, their eyes closed, their movements slow and aimless. Some merely sat on stools or chairs or leaned against the walls of their drab, dusty chambers, motionless as stones or swaying like blind beggars. Some tried to stir pots under which no flame burned. Others tended children who lay like cloth dolls, limbs a-flop as their sleeping parents dressed or undressed them, small heads lolling, mouths gaping while their parents fed them with empty spoons.

After a while he stopped looking into the houses.

As he came to the center of town the streets began to fill with people, although these too moved like weary swimmers, staring into the bruised gray sky with unseeing eyes. Blind sleepers drove carts piled with shrouded bundles, and even the horses that drew the wagons slept, long jaws grinding as they chewed at nothing. The crowds slowly drifted to and fro like fish at the bottom of a winter lake, standing rapt before spectacles they could not see, buying things they could not taste or use. Slumbering musicians played dust-caked instruments, making unheard melodies, while sleeping clowns danced slow as snowmelt and did halting somersaults in the dirt, coming up smeared and draggled.

As he stared around him in fearful wonder, a young woman wandered toward him out of the crowd. She was pretty, or should have been. Her face was bloodlessly pale, with only the barest sliver of her eyes visible under her long lashes, but her mouth sagged like an idiot's, though she tried to curl her lips in a fetching smile. She lifted her hand to him, offering him a withered flower, a reddish streak running the length of the white petals like a vein of blood. *Asphodel,* he remembered, *the god's flower,* although he did not know what god he meant.

Am I fair? she asked. Her lips did not seem to move enough for him to hear her voice so clearly.

Yes, he said, trying to be kind. He could see that she had been fair once, and might be again, in some other place, under some bolder light.

You are sweet. Here, have my flower. She squeezed her lips together as if to keep them from trembling. *It is very long since I have spoken to someone like you. It is lonely here.*

Pitying her, he reached out his hand, but just before his fingers closed on the waxy stem he remembered another young woman, high and fair, to whom he owed something. His hand paused, and then he remembered what someone had told him so long ago: *Accept no gift!*

I cannot, he said. *I am sorry.*

Her face changed then, from that of a mortal woman into something older and much more hungry. Her body twisted and lengthened into a feral shape with achingly scrawny limbs and reaching claws. It snapped and fluttered before him like a scorched insect, writhed until his eyes blurred watching it, then smeared away into the twilight, leaving nothing behind but a thin shriek of misery and rage.

Shaken and sad, he walked on.

On the outskirts of the city, among the midden heaps and bone-yards, where a few ragged sleepers huddled around flickering, smoky fires, he at last found the one he had glimpsed across the river, although that now seemed an entire lifetime ago. This sleeper was an old man, with hands that had been large and powerful now knotted with age, and shoulders that had been wide and a back that had been straight now coarsely bent, so that he had the shape of a bird huddling in its own feathers against the cold. Ferras Vansen could see the pale, slow shimmer of the fires through the man's substance, as if the old fellow were no more tangible than mist.

Father, he said, but he was suddenly unsure. *Tati,* he asked like a child, *is it really you? Do you know me?*

The old man looked at him, or at least turned blind eyes in the direction of the questions. His face was not merely translucent, it shifted like oil on rippling water.

I am no one. How could I know you?

No. You are Pedar Vansen. I am your son, Ferras.

The old man shook his head. *No. I am Perinos Eio, the great planet. I died and lay four days in a stone casket surrounded by darkness and distant stars. Then I awoke again into the light of what is true.* He sighed and a tear escaped his tight-shut eye. *But I have forgotten it all again, and now I am lost . . .*

You died in your own bed, Tati. I didn't have the chance to say farewell. For a moment Ferras Vansen could feel tears stinging painfully in his own eyes, as if in this place to cry was to pierce the flesh and let out blood, not water. *There was no stone coffin. We were poor people, and I did not come back in time to pay for even a wooden box, although I would have done so gladly. You were buried in a winding sheet.* He hung his head. *I am sorry, Tati. I was far away . . .*

Help me. The old man reached out a hand, but where it touched him it was no more substantial than a tongue of fog, cool and slightly damp. *Help me to find my way back, to learn the answers again so that I can pass on.*

Anything. And in that moment, he meant it. This was a man whose impossible needs had pressed down on Ferras Vansen's childhood like the lid of the stone coffin he was prattling about, but the love was still stronger than any fear, any comfort. To do what his Tati asked he would break even those fading commandments, *Eat no food, Accept no gifts, Remember your name!* He would flaunt the gods themselves before their thrones.

But the gods are asleep, too, he remembered, or thought he did. *Who told me that?*

Come, he told the faded ghost of his father. *Come. I'll take you where you need to go.*

Beyond the city they passed into a shadowy wood and then walked down a hillside covered with black ivy and gray birches into a silent valley. They crossed a blood-colored river at the bottom of the valley on rocks that stood up through the flood like teeth. They walked on, the sky as bleak as stone, the light never brighter than a faint reddish glow in the far west, like a bloodstain that would not wash out of an old shirt.

Time passed, or would have in a different place. Vansen's father sang as he walked, senseless ritual ditties about dividing his body in pieces, endless loving verses that described the divestiture of flesh and memory, but otherwise the old man said little and seemed to recall nothing of his former life. There were moments Vansen thought he had been terribly wrong, that he had seized some old man who was not his father, but then an angle of his companion's insubstantial face, an expression flitting across the thin mouth like a fish in a shallow pool, would convince him he had been right after all.

They crossed four more streams, one of moving ice, one of water that boiled and bubbled with heat, one so full of green growing things that it seemed motionless, although the streambed squirmed between the roots with tiny, chittering, splashing shapes, and last a torrent of which they could see nothing but moving fog in a deep crevasse, although they heard sounds coming up from it that no fog ever made, and across which they had to leap, Vansen clutching at the misty shape that marked where the old man's hand should have been.

Eventually all distinctions became one, each step the same step, each song the old man sang the same song. Shadows approached them, some of them fearful to look at, but Vansen told them his name and the old man's name and they retreated into the twilight once more. Other times the shadows came in fairer shapes with offers of hospitality—sumptuous meals, soft beds, or even more intimate comforts—but Vansen learned to refuse these just as firmly, and those shapes retreated, too.

Finally they came to a wide, empty land where the dust blew always and the wind was fierce, a place where they could walk no faster than a dying man could crawl. At times in that place his father faltered and Vansen had to pull him along through the stinging, smothering dust. Once, when even the twilight was blotted out by thick clouds and they trudged forward in complete darkness, the old man fell and could not get up. As he lay, croaking a song about white bracelets and hearts of smoke, Ferras Vansen crouched beside him in despair. He knew that he could rise and walk away and the old man would not see him go, would never even realize he was gone. Instead he staggered to his feet, then bent and lifted the old man onto his back. Pedar Vansen's body had no more substance than a woman's veil, but somehow he was also heavier than a great stone, and Vansen could walk only a few steps each time before he had to stop to catch his breath.

At last the dust storms subsided. They were still in the empty land, the gray expanses, but for the first time he saw something on the horizon other than more nothingness. It was a house—a hut, really, a crude thing made of sticks and unworked stones, its crevices mortared with what looked like centuries of dust, so it seemed the mound of some tremendous and slovenly insect. A man stood in front of it, leaning on his long staff like one of the Kertish herders who had sometimes come to live in Ferras Vansen's dales when driven out by a tribal feud back home.

There! It was a triumphant moment, overshadowing even the sight of another being in this endless, dust-choked void. He had remembered something new: *I am Ferras Vansen—a man of the dales.*

The stranger wore the kind of ragged cloth around his belly that the ancients had worn, but was otherwise without ornament. His long beard was gray as cobweb beside his mouth, but dust had turned the rest of it yellow. He did not move but only watched them approach, and Vansen and his father's ghost had almost reached him before Ferras Vansen realized this bearded apparition was the first being he had seen in these lands for as long as he could remember whose eyes were open—the first who was not asleep.

Who are you? Vansen said to him. *Or is it forbidden to ask?*

The man's eyes seemed bright as stars beneath his bristling brows. He smiled, but there was no kindness in it, or malice either. *You stand before the last river, but the place you wish to go does not exist in this Age of Sleep. You must cross instead to another side, one in which those great ones you wish to see are still in their houses to be seen.*

I don't understand, Vansen told the bearded man. As they spoke, his father sat down in the dust and began singing to himself.

You do not need to understand. You need only do what you must. Whether you come through again afterward is in the hands of greater powers than mine. The dusty old man shifted his bare feet, the spread, leathery toes of someone who had never worn shoes. Unlike Vansen's father, he was as real as could be—Ferras Vansen could see every inch of his coppery skin with great clarity, every scar, every hair.

You will not tell me who you are, Master?

The bearded man shook his head. *Not a master—certainly not yours. A shape, an idea, perhaps even a word. That is all. Now step through the door. You will find water there. Both of you must wash yourselves.*

And without knowing how it happened, Ferras Vansen found himself on the inside of the small wooden hut, but here for the first time they had left the twilight behind: what he could see through the cracks in the walls was velvet black sky and the gleam of stars. He stepped closer to the walls and peered through one of the openings. The entire hut was surrounded by stars, innumerable white sparks flickering like the candles of all the gods in heaven—stars above, beside, and even below them, as though the hut floated untethered through the night sky. Dizzied by the enthralling, terrifying view, he turned to see his father already washing himself with the water from a simple wooden tub as crude as the hut itself.

Vansen joined him, and for long moments lost himself in the glory of water running down his skin. He had forgotten he even *had* a body, and this was a wonderful way to be reminded. Even his father's phantom, no more substantial than if he were made of spiderwebs, seemed to have come close to something like happiness.

I should have come home, Vansen said. *I feared you, Tati. I feared your suffering. And I hated you, at least a little. Because you did not make it easy for me, when you could have.*

His father broke off his singing and for a long time did not say anything. He stood up straight and let the water slide off him like rain dripping down a window.

I was a prisoner of my own understanding, Pedar Vansen said at last. *At least that is what I imagine. In truth, I cannot remember—it is all gone, drifted away like smoke . . .*

And then, before Vansen could hear any more of these words that came to him like food to a starving man, they were out of the hut again, returned to the twilight and dust. The bearded man stood leaning on his long staff, a length of wood as gnarled and knobbed as the ancient man himself. *There,* the bearded man said, pointing at a pile of dull, red-orange stones lying in the dust. *Crumble them and rub yourself with it so you may cross into the last sunset light and still retain something of yourself. Both of you. There is no difference now between living and dead in this house—all are subject to the same laws.*

Vansen rubbed the red rocks together, scraping them into blood-colored powder, rubbing that powder onto his clean skin. Instead of rubbing dirt onto himself, it seemed instead as though he rubbed himself with light. When he finished, he gleamed, and even his father's phantom shimmered beneath its layer of dust and seemed more substantial.

This ocher gives life to the unloving, said the old, bearded man. *And it protects the living from the dead in the place you go to now, who would otherwise cover you like flies on honey. Go.*

What waits for us? Vansen called back to the ancient as he and his father walked forward.

What has always waited for you. What always will wait for you and for me, and for everything. The end of all.

And then the bearded man was gone, lost in the dust which had begun to swirl around them once more, billowing, choking. Vansen held in his breath, then a time came when he could not hold it any longer. He breathed and the river of dust entered him. He became the dust. He passed through.

And now they entered the true city, the metropolis beside which the City of Sleepers was no more than a village.

The oracles say that this greatest and most awful of habitations fills the earth from pole to pole, so that everywhere living men walk, beneath their feet lie the streets of the City of the Red Sun. Nobody laughs in that city, the oracles also claim, and nobody cries except in thin, almost silent sobs, or sings above a whisper.

As Ferras Vansen and his father entered, a hush lay upon the place like dust lay in the streets. The sleepers all had open eyes, and every face stared hopelessly into eternity. Each step forward felt as though he lifted a hundredweight of stone. Each street seemed as bleak and empty and comfortless as the one before.

Always, though, he and his father's shade moved toward the great, dark lodestone at the heart of the city, the palace of the Earthlord himself. Thousands of other phantoms moved with them toward the mighty black gate, shadow-people of every kind and every shape. Few wore more than rags, and many were naked, but even in their nakedness some were clothed in feathers or dully gleaming scales, so that they did not look quite like people. Vansen and his father were swept along in this silent crowd like bits of bark on a slow-moving river, the gate and the wall and the palace growing always larger before them.

Ferras Vansen looked at his father, who of all the dead throng still had closed eyes, and saw that although the old man's features were still indistinct as smoke, his father had retained something of the glow of the ocher, a red gleam like fire reflected on silver. Then he saw that the other spirits had it too, and that the glow did not come from the dead themselves but from the great palace, whose every window spilled sunset-red light.

The House of the Ultimate West, his father whispered, but as though he recited a prayer instead of explaining something. *Raven's Nest. The Castle of Everything-Falls-Apart. The Great Pine Tree . . .*

But first, someone whispered, *we must pass the Gate of the Pig.* These words traveled through the crowd like a fire through dry grass, the whisper becoming a hissing murmur. *The Gate. The Gate.* They were groaning the words, some of them, although one laughed uproariously as he said it over and over, as though it were the first jest ever to be told in the grim, blood-colored city. After a while his laugh turned to a choked sob. *The Pig's snout will sniff out every lie, every cheat, and then we will be swallowed down . . .*

As the voices rose around him the darkness rose too, like a pall of smoke, until Ferras Vansen could see nothing. Even his father's shade was gone. He was lost in black emptiness, and the voices of the crowding dead had become animal noises, braying, snorting, barking, as if the ghosts of men had become the ghosts of beasts. It was a terrible din, harsh, desperate, and full of terror. He could not help thinking of the farm creatures he had driven to the slaughterer. The darkness seemed infinite, empty but for himself and a choir of horrifying echoes.

But that is truly me, he thought suddenly. *Herding the animals with a switch. Walking down the road to Little Stell. That is a memory of me, of my life.*

I am Ferras Vansen, he told the void. *I have a name. I am a living man.*

Something came nearer to him then—he could feel its approach, slow and ominous as a thundercloud. It seemed bigger than the darkness itself, and it stank. It also seemed . . . amused?

Living man.

They were not words, not even thoughts, really, but something larger, like shifts in the weather, but somehow he could understand them. He was in the grip of something so much larger than himself that he could scarcely think. He was beyond fear—he was not significant enough to be fearful.

At last it spoke, or the weather changed, or the stars revolved in their black firmanent around Ferras Vansen.

Pass. I will speak for you and He will decide. You will die, or you will live . . . at least for a little longer.

And then he was in the midst of the strangest place yet—a festive hall that was also a monstrous pit, a solemnly beautiful throne room whose ceiling was the vault of black and endless night. It was the crumbling root-raddled ground, a silver fantasy of towers, the slow-beating heart of all sad music, it was all those things and none of those things. He was alone, his father's phantom gone, but a million shadows swirled around the great throne at the center, on which sat the greatest shadow of all.

The voice he had heard before spoke to him.

The master of this place says you do not belong in his dream.

I am Ferras Vansen, he said humbly. Of course he did not belong, here at the end of all things. *I am a living man. I only wanted to help my father.*

The voice of the Gatekeeper spoke again, slow as the slide of glaciers and just as deadeningly chill.

You cannot. It is impertinence to try. His fate is between him and the gods—which is to say, between him and his own heart. And that is why you must go. You are a hindrance, however small, to What Should Be.

Vansen quailed at the anger in that titan voice. *I meant no harm!* But he felt ashamed of himself for his fear. Even if it meant he must live here forever, eating clay and drinking dust with these sad shadows, he still did not need to crawl. *I tried to help. Surely even the gods themselves cannot condemn that?*

There was a pause before the Gatekeeper spoke again. He did not seem to have heard what Vansen had said.

Be grateful you did not hear the Earthfather's voice. Even the murmur of his sleeping thought would send you mad. Instead, he permits you to leave—if you can cross the rivers and come safe out of this land once more. If not, then you will become one of his subjects earlier than you might have otherwise—but it is only a short time to lose, after all, the butterfly-life of your kind.

But why can you speak to me? Why aren't you asleep, like the Earthfather?

Make no mistake. I also sleep, said the Gatekeeper. *In fact, it could be that you and all these dead, and even the Earthfather himself, are part of **my** dream.*

The voice laughed then, and the world shook.

Go now—return to the land of the living, if you can. You will not receive such a gift a second time.

And then the great hall of madness, of sleep and earth and the deep song of the globe itself, was gone. The Gatekeeper was gone. Nothing remained in all the cosmos but Ferras Vansen, it seemed, standing in sudden alarm on an achingly narrow arc that stretched above a massive nothingness, a white stripe over an abyss. He could not see an end to the slender bridge in either direction, and the span was scarcely as wide as his own shoulders. There was nowhere to go but forward into the unknown or backward into quiet, undemanding death. His father's shade was gone, left behind in the sunset city to face its own fate, and the living could mean nothing to Pedar Vansen anymore. His son had not been able either to save the old man or forgive him, but something had changed and his heart was lighter than it had been.

"I am Ferras Vansen," he called as loudly as he could. There was no reply, not even an echo, but that did not matter: he was not speaking to anyone except himself. "I am a soldier. I love Briony Eddon, although she can never love me. I'm tired of being lost and I'm tired of dying, so I'm going to try something different this time."

He began to walk.

40

Offered to Nushash

Crooked labored long for Moisture's children, shaping their kingdom in all its greatest glory, making things of great craft for those who had destroyed his family—palaces and towers, Thunder's irresistible hammer, Harvest's basket that was always full, the deadly spear of Black Earth, and more.

But in his heart he had become as crooked as his name, his song not just somber but sour. He plotted and he dreamed, but could see no way he could equal the power of the brothers, whose songs were at their mightiest. Then one day he thought of his grandmother Void, the only creature whose emptiness was like his own, and he went to her and learned all her craft. He learned to walk her roads, which no one else could see but which stretched anywhere and everywhere. He learned many other things, too, but for long he kept them hidden, waiting for his moment.

—from *One Hundred Considerations,*
out of the Qar's *Book of Regret*

THE STRANGER WHO HAD CAPTURED HER was working very hard to open the rusted lock, his bland face intent as he probed the slot in the gate with the strip of metal he had produced from the sleeve of his shirt. A little sweat had beaded on his lip. Qinnitan turned away as casually as she could, trying not to look directly at the troop of guards moving rubble at the base of the wall a hundred yards away. She and Pigeon and the stranger were crouched in the shadows of an aqueduct near the base of Citadel Hill.

"You're wondering whether you could call to those guards and get help," said the stranger in his weirdly perfect Xixian, although he had not looked up from the lock. "Where I grew up in Sailmaker's Row, near the docks, the fishermen could take an oyster out of its shell with their knives, flick it up in the air, then catch it on the blade, all with just one hand." He opened the fingers of his free hand to slow her a small, curved blade nestled there. "If you move, I will show you the trick—but I will use the boy's eye."

Pigeon clutched Qinnitan's hand even more tightly.

"You grew up in Xis?" If she could get the man talking some good might come of it. "How could that be? You look like a northerner."

He still did not look up, and this time his only answer was the rasp and click of the metal strip as he at last defeated the lock. The gate swung open and they passed under the stone arch, then the stranger dragged them to their feet and hurried them down a ramshackle stone staircase which hugged the side of the steep Citadel Hill. Qinnitan was tripped several times by the cord around her ankles. The air on the seaward side of them was dark with what she thought at first was fog, but then realized was smoke. In the distance cannons rumbled, but it seemed like thunder from far away, the bad weather of another country.

The Harbor of Nektarios was in ruins, the water choked with floating wreckage from burned and shattered ships. Half the warehouse district was on fire and blazing uncontrollably, but just enough soldiers had been spared to fight the blaze to keep it from spreading upslope on either side to the temple complex atop Demian Grove or the wealthy houses on Sparrow Hill. Overwhelmed by their struggle with the flames, none of them paid much attention to the stranger and what doubtless seemed to be his two children. One smoke-stained guardsman hurrying past, the golden sea urchin on his tunic marking him part of the naval guard, shouted something to them Qinnitan couldn't understand, but when their captor calmly waved his hand in acknowledgement the guard seemed satisfied and trotted on.

Cannonfire crashed out from the seawall and was returned from the ocean beyond. Qinnitan could actually see one of the autarch's massive dromons sliding past the mouth of the harbor, kept out only by a hundred yards of massive chain thicker than Qinnitan's body, sagging across the mouth of the harbor that Magnate Nektarios had so famously and expensively built.

They passed the entrance to Oniri Daneya Street, a wide thoroughfare lined with shops and markets and warehouses that led out from the harbor and ran east across the center of the old city. The famous street had been blocked off here at its harbor end with deserted wagons and the rubble of the bombardment, and seeing the usually thriving place so ruined and empty washed Qinnitan with a new wave of despair. No one would help them, she was increasingly certain—not with the city on fire and the autarch's troops almost inside the walls. She reached down and took the boy's hand. She had survived before, but this time she had Pigeon to care for, too.

"We will go fast now," the man said. "No talking. Follow me."

"Do you really have to bring the boy, too . . . ?" Qinnitan began. A moment later she was on her knees, eyes full of tears, her face stinging. He had hit her so swiftly she had not even seen it.

"I said *no talking*. Next time, there will be blood—that is, more blood than this." The man's hand shot out like a serpent's strike.

Pigeon shrieked in a way Qinnitan had never heard, a rasping yelp that made her want to vomit. The child grabbed at his face and his hands came away covered in blood. His ear had been sliced halfway through; part of it hung down like a rotting tapestry.

"Bandage him." The man threw her a rag from his pocket—the remnants of the old woman's scarf he had worn as part of his disguise. "And don't think either of you are safe just because I have to deliver you to the autarch. There are ways I can hurt you that even the Golden One's surgeons won't discover. Play another trick on me and I will show you some of my own—tricks that you'll remember even when the best torturers of the Orchard Palace are hard at work on you." He gestured for them to move forward along the length of the harbor front.

Qinnitan held the bandage tight against Pigeon's ear until he could hold it for himself. She walked when the man indicated, stopped when he stopped. Her heart, which had been beating so swiftly only a moment ago, now seemed as sluggish as a frog sitting in summer mud. There would be no escape for either of them.

Near to the end of the long row of boats lay a set of narrow slips where smaller craft were tied next to each other like leaves on a tree branch. Here their captor found what he was seeking, a small rowboat with a tiny awning just big enough to keep the sun off one large person or two small ones. He had her lie down next to Pigeon under the awning, then rowed them out between bits of charred wreckage, ignoring the cries of the harbor guards as they headed for the open sea, where cannons rumbled like thunder and smoke drifted like evening fog. She watched the man as he rowed, the only strain to be seen the tense and release of the muscles in his pale neck.

"What is the autarch giving you to do this?" she asked at last, risking another blow. "To kidnap two children who have never done you any harm?"

He looked over his shoulder at her. "My life." The corner of his mouth twitched, as though he had almost smiled. "It's not much, but I've some use for it still."

The man would not be lured into speaking anymore. Qinnitan lay back and put her arm around Pigeon to comfort him, but she could not help thinking what it would feel like to roll over the water into the cool embrace of the ocean and a comparatively simple and swift death by drowning. If it had not been for the shivering child beside her she would have gone without hesitation. Anything would be better than looking into the autarch's mad gaze again, feeling his gold-netted fingers scrape her flesh. Anything except the knowledge that she had left poor, mute Pigeon behind. But what if she wrapped the boy in her arms so they could go down into the peaceful green depths together? She could hold him while he struggled, then take a gulp to fill her own lungs. No, Pigeon wouldn't struggle. He would understand . . .

The man released the oars, letting them dangle in the oarlocks while he looped a length of cord around the bench on which they sat and tied one end to each of their ankles.

"You shouldn't think with your eyes, girl." In the distance behind him she could see the stony strip of hills called the Finger and its occupied forts jutting from the water, silhouetted against the reddened evening sky, surrounded by ships bearing the autarch's Flaming Eye of Nushash—an all too vivid reminder of what it was to face Sulepis' own burning stare. "But it's a bit late to learn now."

Vash did not want to go on another voyage. He had barely recovered from the last. What good was it to reach a venerable age and be one of the most powerful men in the world if you still could not stay choose to stay on dry land?

He swallowed his irritation, since it would do no good, and steadied himself against the rocking of the anchored ship before stepping out of the passage into the autarch's great cabin, a hall of wooden beams a hundred paces long that ran half the length of the ship and most of its width, and was hung with fine carpets to keep in the warmth even during the coldest sea storm. At its center, seated upon a smaller version of the Falcon Throne (tethered to the deck to protect the Golden One's dignity during times of unsettled seas) was the man who could make Pinimmon Vash do such uncomfortable things.

"Ah, Vash, there you are." The autarch extended a lazy hand, gold glinting on his fingertips. Other than jewelry, Sulepis wore nothing but a linen kilt and a massive belt of woven gold. "You are just in time. That fat Favored whose name I never remember . . ." He waited so long that it was plain he wished the name supplied.

"Bazilis, Golden One?" Outside, on the cliffs above them, one of the great crocodile-cannons boomed and the ship's timbers creaked. Vash tried not to flinch.

"Yes, Bazilis. He is bringing me my gift from Ludis. The god-on-earth is a happy god today, old man." But Sulepis did not look happy: in fact, he appeared even more feverish and intent than usual, the muscles in his jaw twitching like those of a hound anticipating a meal. "We have waited and worked a long time for this."

"Yes, Golden One, we have. A very long time."

The autarch frowned. "Have you, too? Have you really, Vash? And have you gone without sleep for weeks on end to read the ancient texts? Have you wrestled with . . . *things* that live in darkness? Have you wagered your godhead against your success, knowing that simply hearing of the torments that await you if you fail would kill an ordinary man? Have you truly worked and waited as I have, Vash?"

"N–no, no, of course not, my astonishing master! I did not mean 'we' in that way, not truly . . ." He could feel sweat budding on his old skin. "I meant that the rest of us, your servants, have waited anxiously for your success, but that success, that . . . mastery . . . will of course be all yours." He cursed himself for a fool. An entire year serving this poisonous youth and he still had not learned to ponder every word before it left his mouth! "Please, Golden One, I meant nothing disrespectful . . . !"

"Of course you didn't, Vash. You are my trusted servant." The autarch smiled suddenly, a flash of white as bereft of kindness as the bite-grimace of a canal shark. "You worry too much, old fellow. My gaze is everywhere. I am aware of how loyal my subjects are, and *especially* of what my closest servants do and think."

Vash swayed a little—too little to notice, he prayed—and wished he could sit down. The autarch was hinting at something again, surely. Was it the remark the new Leopard captain Marukh had made? But Vash had not agreed with him—in fact, surely he had upbraided the man! But it was also true that he had not gone straight to the autarch to report the man's treasonous impertinence.

If I denounced every man who chafes under our new autarch's rule, he thought desperately, *the autarch's strangler would die of overwork and the Orchard Palace would be empty of anything except ghosts by year's end.*

He bowed his head, waiting to find out if he would live another hour.

The autarch lifted his hands before his eyes, frowned again as he examined his finger-stalls. "I am wondering if I should wear the ones made in the shape of a falcon's talons," he said. "In honor of the upcoming fall of Hierosol. What do you think, Vash?"

The paramount minister let out a silent sigh of relief. Another hour, at least. "I think it would be a suitable honor to your ancestors, especially . . ." He paused, determined not to say anything troublesome, but could see no problem. ". . . Especially your great ancestor Xarpedon, who carried the Falcon all across Xand."

"Ah, Xarpedon. The greatest of us all—until now." He looked up as a servant stepped silently through the curtained doorway and stood, head lowered, waiting to be recognized. "Yes?"

"Favored Bazilis is here, Golden One."

"Good! You may step aside, Vash."

The paramount minister moved through the ring of attendants toward the cabin wall, and wound up standing next to the golden litter of the scotarch, a gilded conveyance only slightly smaller than the autarch's own. Crippled Prusus peered out of the litter's window like an anxious hermit crab. Vash nodded to him—a formality only, since everyone knew the scotarch was simpleminded and did not notice such things.

Leaning back against his throne, Sulepis waved for the eunuch to be sent in. Bazilis entered a moment later, grave and immense in his robes; it took him some time and a great deal of rustling of fabric to abase himself at the autarch's feet.

"O Master of the Great Tent, blessed of Nushash . . ." he began, but was silenced by the stamp of Sulepis' sandaled foot.

"Shut your mouth. Where is he? Where is the prisoner?"

"Out . . . outside, Golden One. I thought you would wish to hear of my . . ."

The autarch kicked out. The eunuch whimpered and fell back. He crouched and looked up at his master in fear, his hand rising to his face where blood already welled from his lip. "Get him," the autarch said. "I am waiting for *him,* you fool, not you."

"Y—yes, Golden One, of course." Bazilis backed out of the massive cabin, still on his hands and knees, his brightly-robed bottom waving in the air.

Sulepis turned to Vash with the slightly prim expression of a tutor. "Out of courtesy to our guest, we will speak Hierosoline in his presence. How is yours, Vash?"

"Good, good, Golden One, although I have not used it much of late . . ."

"Then this will be an excellent chance for you to practice." The autarch smiled like a kindly old uncle, although the man he was smiling at was more than three times his age. "After all, you never know when you might be called on to administer a continent where Hierosoline is the chief tongue!"

While Vash pondered what sounded like a bizarre promise of advancement to viceroy of all Eion, the prisoner appeared.

Vash could not help noticing that the man the eunuch and the guards marched into the cabin seemed like another kind of animal entirely in comparison to their master the autarch. Where Sulepis was young and tall and handsome, with golden, close-shaved skin and a high-boned, hawklike face, the northern king was startlingly ordinary, his brownish beard thick and not very well tended, his dark-ringed eyes emphasizing the pallor of his confinement. Only the way he stared back at the autarch betrayed that he was anything other than some petty merchant or craftsman: it was a calm, thoughtful gaze, measured and measuring. The only person Vash had ever seen look so unmoved in the autarch's presence had been the murderous soldier, Daikonas Vo, but a smile that would never have been on Vo's face flickered around the northern king's eyes and lips. The more he thought about it, the more astonished Vash became that Olin's expression of contemptuous amusement, subtle as it was, hadn't driven the autarch into one of his sudden rages. Instead, Sulepis laughed.

"There you are! My fellow monarch!" He raised an imperious finger. "Bring a seat for His Majesty." Two servants scuttled across the great cabin, then hurried back, carrying a chair between them. "I have waited so long to meet you, King Olin. I have heard so much about you, I feel as if I know you already."

Olin sat down. "How interesting you should say so. I feel very much the same."

"Oh ho!" The autarch laughed again; he sounded as though he were genuinely enjoying himself. "And what you think you know you do not like, do you? A good joke. We will be friends. In fact, we *must* be friends! If we insist on formal protocol, our conversations will be so long and so dreary—and we will be having so many conversations in the days ahead. I look forward to it!"

Olin folded his hands carefully on his lap. "So you will not kill me yet?"

"Kill you? Why would I do such a thing? You are a prize, Olin Eddon—worth more than gold or ambergris—worth more than the famed rubies of Sirkot! I have been doing my best to lay hands on you for the longest time!"

"What are you talking about?"

Vash could not help cringing at the northerner's tone of

voice—one simply did not talk to the Golden One that way, not if one wished to keep one's skin stretched over one's meat. But instead of calling for Mokori, his favorite strangler, the autarch only chuckled again. "But of course," he said gleefully. "You could not know. In fact, I wonder if, with all your learning, you will understand even when I explain to you."

Olin regarded the monarch of all Xand with a combination of interest and growing discomfort. Vash was oddly reassured—he had begun to wonder if his master was truly as mad as he seemed, or if he, Pinimmon Vash, were simply losing perspective, so he was glad to see he was not the only one who found Sulepis puzzling. "It does sound as though you do not intend to kill me today."

"But I already told you that!" Sulepis feigned astonishment. "You and I have much to do, see, and speak about. First, though, we really must get you cleaned up. Ludis has taken shocking care of you."

The northern king inclined his head. "May I ask what price you paid for me? Or was I a gift to you from Ludis—a sort of welcome present?"

"Ah, Olin—you do not mind if I call you Olin, do you? You may call me Golden One, or even . . . yes, you may call me Great Falcon."

"You are too kind."

"Ah, we will get along splendidly. You have a sense of humor!" The autarch leaned back in his throne, flicked his hand at the servants. "Take King Olin and let him bathe, then feed him. Give him one of my tasters so that he can dine with a peaceful heart. We will speak again later, Olin—we have much to discuss. Together we will remake the world!"

"You seem very certain that I will agree to help you with this . . . grand project." Olin tilted his head, examining his captor; Vash could not help admiring the poor, doomed savage.

"Oh, your agreement is not necessary for my success," the autarch told him with a sympathetic little frown. "And, sadly, you will not live to see its fruits. But you may rejoice in knowing that you were indispensable—that without you, the world would have remained lost in shadow instead of gaining the salvation of the great light of Nushash—or of *Nushasha Sulepis,* to be precise, for that is who it will be *this* time." Now he favored the foreign king with the lazy smile of a predator too full to eat but not too stuffed to terrify a few lesser animals. "As I said, we will speak later, Olin Eddon—oh, we will speak of many things! We will be something like friends, don't you think? For a little while, anyway. Now, go enjoy your bath and your supper."

The man who had kidnapped Qinnitan had only to produce a few parchments from an oilskin envelope—documents with the seal of the autarch himself prominently displayed—and the sailors and soldiers on the great flagship *Flame of Nushash* scuttled to do his bidding. Just when she wanted life to slow down to the slowest crawl the immense Xixian bureaucracy could provide, everybody around her seemed to be swarming as busily and industriously as ants. The three of them were escorted up the gangplank by soldiers—some, she could not help noticing, in the same Leopard helmet that Jeddin had worn, the architect of her current misery. Why had she not denounced him the moment he had begun his mad talk of loving her? Because she had been flattered? Or because she had pitied him, glimpsing the fretful child she had once known inside the hard-muscled body of the soldier? Whatever the case, he had doomed her with his love as certainly as if he had drawn his dagger across her throat: this trip up the gangplank was only the ending of something that had been inevitable from the first moment of his foolish treachery and her equally foolish silence.

At a murmured aside from their captor Pigeon was taken in hand by one of the Favored. She was about to protest, then realized that although the boy was desperate to stay with her, being separated from her was his best hope.

"Ssshhh," she said, and then told him an awful lie. "I'll be back. Everything will be fine. Just go with them and do what they say."

He was not fooled. As he was led away he wore the shocked, disappointed look of a dog tied to a tree and left behind by its master.

The Leopard officer who had now taken charge of Qinnitan and her captor asked if he wished to make either himself or his "gift" ready to be received.

"I was told to bring her to the Golden One with all speed," the hunter said. "I am sure he will forgive me if I take him at his word."

The officer and one of the more important of the Favored looked at each other apprehensively, but the courtier bowed. "Of course, sir. As you say."

Qinnitan took a shaky breath as they were led down the long, surprisingly wide hallway of the rocking ship. She felt nothing, or at least nothing she could recognize. If she had fallen into the water this moment, as she had imagined doing earlier, she knew she would sink straight down. She felt cold and hard and dead as stone.

They paused outside the doorway of the ship's central cabin while the Leopard officer discreetly and almost apologetically searched the man who had caught her. The chief of the Favored did the same for Qinnitan. The eunuch's breath smelled of mint and something sharper and fouler, the stench of a rotting tooth, perhaps; at any other time she would have been revolted by his touch, but now she just stood and let herself be handled like a corpse readied for burial. There was no point in feeling anything. No use caring.

The Favored led them through the door and across the broad cabin toward the tall man seated on a plain chair at the center, legs spread, booted feet planted firmly on the ground, examining the documents Qinnitan's captor had given to the courtiers.

It was not the autarch.

"All hail High Polemarch Ikelis Johar, Overseer of the Armies!" said the Favored, striking his staff three times on the cabin's wooden floor.

The general looked up, his heavy-browed face turning from

Qinnitan to her captor. "Vo, is it? Daikonas Vo. I think I have heard the name before—your father was a White Hound, too, am I right?"

So the empty-faced man who had taken her had a name, Qinnitan realized—not that it mattered. Soon she would be beyond remembering any name, even her own.

"Yes, Polemarch." The man seemed a little taken aback, although his face was still stony and indifferent. "Forgive me, Lord, but can you tell me when I may see the autarch? I was given very specific orders . . ."

"Yes, yes." The general waved his calloused hand. "And you have done well to come here swiftly and without waiting. But as it happens, you have missed the Golden One by a matter of half a day."

"What?" Vo seemed, for the first time, quite mortal. "I don't understand . . ."

"He has gone in one of his swiftest ships, *The Bright Falcon,* leaving me behind to watch over the rest of the siege." The polemarch grinned. "And leaving me as governor over Hierosol when it falls, as well. I shall have my hands full trying to keep the men—especially your comrades in the Hounds—from burning the place to the ground. They are fierce and hungry, and have waited a long time for this."

Qinnitan was stunned. She'd done her best to prepare herself to see the autarch's terrifying smile and she felt as though she had stepped off a cliff where she had expected to set her foot on hot coals. She didn't know what to think, except that her torment would go on a little longer, her death would be a little delayed, and she had no idea what she felt about that.

The Overseer of the Armies slapped his hands on his knees and stood up. He was tall, and looked half again as heavy as Daikonas Vo. "Well, then, if you just pass the girl over to my servants we will keep her most safe until the autarch returns."

"No."

The polemarch, who had begun to turn away, pivoted slowly on his heel, surprised. "No? Did I hear you say no to me, soldier?"

"You did, Lord. Because the Golden One himself commanded me to bring him the girl with all dispatch—me and no one else. I will need your fastest ship."

The high overseer looked from Vo to the rest of the courtiers and soldiers standing in the room. His mouth curled, but the smile did not hide his annoyance. "My fastest ship, eh? You are insolent, even for one of the Hounds."

Vo had recovered his equilibrium. He stared back. "There is nothing insolent in serving the Golden One just as he commands—in every word. Our master was most insistent."

The older man looked at Vo, and Qinnitan could almost believe they were staring at each other over a game board, a fierce bout of Shanat, perhaps, like the old men played in the marketplace, everyone talking except the two competing. At last Ikelis Johar shook his head.

"Very well," he said. "We will find you a ship. You will tell the autarch, when you find him, that this was your own idea."

"I will certainly do that, High Polemarch." Vo turned. "I would like some food and drink while I wait for the new ship to be readied."

The polemarch frowned heavily, but at last sat down in his chair again. "The servants will see to it. Now you will excuse me, Vo—I have some little work to do, after all."

"Yes. One last question, Polemarch." Vo almost seemed to be doing it on purpose now, poking Johar to see if he could make one of the world's most powerful men lose his temper. "How long ago did the autarch leave for Xis?"

"Xis?" Now the polemarch regained his good humor. "Who said anything about Xis? Your journey will not be so easy. The Golden One is bound north on our fastest ship, following the coast."

"North?" Daikonas Vo, Qinnitan saw, was not feigning surprise: he was genuinely astonished. "But where is he going?"

"To a small, backwater country few have ever heard about, let alone cared to visit," the polemarch said, signaling for one of the servants to bring him something to drink. "It is so small he is only taking a few hundred soldiers, although they are all fine, fierce troops—your Hounds among them. And we are sending three more ships full of soldiers after him, too, as well as one of the Royal Crocodiles on a barge—one of the big cannon."

"Taking them where?" said Vo, confused. "What country? Why?"

"Why? Who knows?" Johar took his goblet and downed a long swallow. "The autarch wills it and so it happens. As to where, it is some insignificant place called Southmarch. Now take your runaway whore and let me get back to the business of destroying a real city."

41

Kinswoman to Death

The gods have reigned in justice and strength ever after,
defending the heavens and the earth from all who would
harm them. The fathers of mankind have prospered under
the gods' fair leadership. Those who follow the teachings of
the three brothers and their oracles and do them proper
fealty find a welcome place in Heaven after their own
deaths.

—from *The Beginnings of Things*
The Book of the Trigon

A GULLBOAT JUST IN FROM JAEL, which had received its news from other ships newly arrived from Devonis, had brought word to Southmarch that the Autarch of Xis had sent a huge war fleet to Hierosol. The gullboat had left southern waters before collecting any further news, but no one in Southmarch Castle doubted that holy, ancient Hierosol was even now surrounded and besieged.

The doings of those aboveground only seldom stirred the inhabitants of Funderling Town, but they had already heard a great deal of bad news this year—the king imprisoned, the older prince murdered, the royal twins gone and perhaps dead. Many of the small folk wondered whether the final days had truly come, whether the Lord of the Hot Wet Stone had lost his patience with mortals entirely and would soon lay waste to all they had built. There was little work, anyway, nor much to eat or enjoy, so the most pious Funderlings spent their days praying and insisting that the rest of their people join them.

Today, two of the Metamorphic Brothers were standing just inside the gates of Funderling Town, scolding all who passed for trafficking with the sinful upgrounders. Chert turned his head away from them, ashamed but also angry. *As if I had any choice.*

"We see you, Brother Blue Quartz!" one of them called as he hurried past. "And the Earth Elders see you too! You of all men must immediately foreswear and repent your wicked deed and evil companions."

He choked back a bitter reply, seized by a sudden, superstitious pang. Perhaps they were right. These were ominous times, no doubt, and it seemed he was squarely in the middle of every bad omen.

Protect me, O Lord of the Hot Wet Stone, he prayed. *Protect your straying servant. I have done only what seemed best for my friends and family!*

His god did not send any reply that would make him feel better, only the echo of the Metamorphic Brothers shouting after him, ordering him to repent and come back to the faithful.

The castle above was in chaos. Soldiers were everywhere, and the narrow streets were so crowded that he needed twice as long as he'd expected to make his way through the Outer Keep. Chert began sincerely to repent one thing, at least—agreeing to return to Brother Okros.

Those few big folk who even noticed him stared as though he were some unclean animal that had slipped into a house when the door had been left open. Several bumped hard against him in the most crowded passages and almost knocked him over, and the men driving ox-wagons did not even bother to slow when they saw him, forcing him to dodge for his life in the muddy street among wheels taller than he was.

What madness is this? Why such hatred? Are we Funderlings to blame for the fairy folk across the bay? Or for the autarch trying to conquer Hierosol? But anger, he knew, would do him no good; better simply to keep his eyes open and avoid confrontation wherever possible.

To add to Chert's miseries, the soldiers at the Raven's Gate also seemed inclined to give him a difficult time. He had to wait, furious but silent, as they mocked his size and made doubting remarks about his errand to Brother Okros. He heard the bells of the great temple begin to toll the noon hour and his heart sank: he was now late to a summons from the Royal Physician. His fortunes improved a moment later with the arrival of a wagon driver looking to enter the Inner Keep with his huge, overloaded cart of wine barrels and no proper authorization. While the soldiers gleefully began to confiscate the shrieking driver's cargo, Chert slipped past them into the heart of the castle.

Why could Okros not have met me in the Observatory as he did last time? Chert thought bitterly to himself. *That is only a few hundred steps from the gate to Funderling Town. I would have been there already and not had to stand and be mocked by the gate guards.* But the summons had said Chert must come to the castellan's chambers, where Chert supposed Okros must be involved in other business. *Does that mean he has carried the mirror all the way across the castle?*

Chaven Makaros had been delighted to see the summons from his treacherous onetime friend. *"Praise all the gods,"* he had cried, *"that means Okros still has not solved it yet!"* The physician had actually trembled with relief as he read. *"Of course you must go to him again, Chert. I will give you various paths to offer him that will lead him astray for weeks!"*

Remembering, Chert made a noise of disgust. So he must tramp all the way across Southmarch and bear several kinds of indignity because two half-mad physicians were determined to play tug-of-war over a mirror! Of course, he reminded himself, it was not a good idea to turn down a summons bearing the royal crest of Southmarch, either.

Chert Blue Quartz had not entered the exalted premises of the royal residence since he had worked on a large crew under the older Hornblende some ten years earlier, excavating a cellar to make a new buttery under the great kitchens. It had been a hard job, and now that he thought of it, a queer one: the king had set out very precise limitations on where they could dig, and as a result the new buttery had been a thing of strange angles, crooked as a dog's hind leg. Still, he remembered the job fondly—it had been one of his first as a foreman in his own right—and still remembered the pride he had felt to be working in the king's residence.

Today, though, he was cursedly late, and Chert's heart sank even further when he saw a group of soldiers lounging in front of the residence gatehouse. Chert knew as well as he knew how to spot a shear in a basalt facing that dealing with this number of guards would hold him up even longer. His experiences going in and out of Southmarch in the old days so he could explore the hills near the Shadowline had taught him that one guard had little to prove, and two would have generally made accommodation between themselves not to work too hard, but soldiers in larger groups often decided to prove themselves to their fellows, or to show off—either way, disastrous for a man Chert's size who was also in a hurry.

He ducked behind a hedge as tall as he was and hurried out into the garden on the residence's western side, bypassing the front gate in search of an easier entrance. He found it along the wall behind a row of tangled, skeletal bushes, a window leading into one of the ground floor rooms. It was too small for an ordinary man, and a tight fit even for Chert, which might have explained why it had been left unlatched. He wriggled through it and hung wincing from the frame until his eyes adjusted to the darkness and he could see how far it was to the floor. The room seemed to be an annex to the pantry, full of barrels and jars but blessedly empty of people. He dropped down, then hurried across it and out into the passage.

Now came the difficult part, trying to find his way across the residence to the castellan's chambers without anyone noticing him (or at least without anyone realizing he had bypassed the gatehouse). He sighed as he reached the end of the first long hall. Half the hour must be gone now. Okros would be very angry.

After several false turnings, one of which led him into a parlor where a surprised group of young women sat sewing—he bowed repeatedly as he backed out—Chert found the inner gardens and made his way across the nearest one to the center of the residence, then back down the main corridor to the offices and official chambers near the front entrance. *I would have been better off to let the guards abuse me,* he thought in disgust. *I have wasted twice as much time this way.* Still, he had finally reached the section of the residence to which he had been summoned, so he no longer needed to hide himself whenever he heard footsteps. With the help of a slightly suspicious page he discovered the hallway to the castellan's chambers, and was about to rap on the beautifully carved and polished oak door when something stung his hand.

Chert cursed and swatted, but his attacker was no hornet or horsefly: instead, something like a long, slender thorn hung from the flesh of his hand. He brushed at it in irritation but it did not come out, and when he at last plucked it painfully from his skin, he discovered to his astonishment that it was a tiny arrow only half the length of his finger, fletched with tiny strips of butterfly wing.

For a moment he could only stare at it, completely befuddled, but when he looked up and saw a little manlike shape clinging to a tapestry just across the hall, Chert finally realized what had happened. But why should the Rooftoppers want to hurt him? Wasn't he their ally—hadn't he and Beetledown been something like friends?

The minuscule assassin did not try to escape, but waited as Chert strode toward him. For a moment he was tempted to reach up and, like some terrible giant, simply pluck the little creature from the hanging and throw him down on the floor, perhaps even step on him. But even at the end of a bad morning, late to an appointment and with his hand throbbing, Chert was not the kind of man to hurt another without good cause, and he did not understand yet what had happened.

He leaned his face close. It was a young Rooftopper male, but not one he recognized. At least his attacker looked suitably frightened. "What are you after?" Chert growled.

The little man was hanging from a thread like a mountaineer on a rope. He waved one of his hands and piped, "Quiet, now! Be tha Chert, Beetledown's companion?"

"Yes, I be bloody Chert. Why did you arrow me?"

"Beetledown—un sent me to say tha beest in danger! Go not inside!" The little man looked terrified now, and Chert considered how he must look to the fellow, a mountain with a frowning face. He leaned a little ways back.

"What do you mean?"

"No time—hide 'ee!" The Rooftopper, as though seeing something Chert could not see, scuttled up the thread to the top of the tapestry and disappeared behind it.

Before Chert could do more than blink, the door of the castellan's chamber across the hall rattled as the bolt was pulled back. Hide? Why? He had been summoned, hadn't he? He had every right to be here!

But why would Beetledown send someone to shoot an arrow at me just to get my attention if I wasn't truly in danger?

Suddenly his hackles were up and his skin was tingling. It must be some misunderstanding—but if it wasn't . . . ?

There was no room to slip behind the tapestry, but a marble statue of Erivor stood in a little alcove shrine only a few steps down the passage on the same side as the door. Chert bolted for it. The statue rocked as he pushed his way behind it, and he barely had time to steady it before the door creaked open.

"He knows, curse him," said a voice that he recognized—Okros. "I should have simply had your men take him, Havemore."

"It would have been better not to alarm the little diggers, and if he had come of his own accord they would have been none the wiser," said the other man. "But now the soldiers will have to search for him."

"Yes, send them at once and search his house. The more I think, the more I believe he knows where Chaven is. That question I told you of, what he asked about the mirror—that was too close to the mark." Okros' voice seemed hard and hot at the same time, like iron being shaped. Chert, with growing horror, could no longer pretend they were talking about someone else. They were sending soldiers to his house!

"Come with me, Brother," said the milder voice of the man called Havemore. "You will have to accompany the soldiers yourself because they may not recognize what is important."

"I will go, and gladly," Okros said. "And if we *do* find Chaven Makaros, I ask you only for a few hours alone with him before we inform our lord Hendon. It might . . . benefit us both."

The two men walked quickly down the corridor, followed by several soldiers. They had been waiting for him! If Beetledown hadn't sent the little man with the arrow, Chert would have been arrested and dragged off to the Earth Elders only knew what end—imprisonment at the least, more likely torture.

And they're on their way to Funderling Town! To my house! Opal and the boy were in terrible danger—Chaven too if he was not hidden. Chert knew he had to get them all into hiding, but how? Cursed Okros and the man Havemore were already on their way down with armed soldiers!

He looked to make sure the hall was empty, then quickly extricated himself from the alcove shrine. He tugged gently on the tapestry and hissed for the little man.

"Help me, please! Can you get a message to Funderling Town quickly?"

After a moment the little man appeared again at the top of the tapestry and shimmied down on his thread. "No, can't, sir. Take too very long. P'raps if someone by bird went, but cote's all the way t'other side o' the Great Peak. Couldn't get to Fundertown fast enough ourselves, which be why Master Scout Beetledown sent me here to find 'ee." His tiny chest puffed up a little. "Travel faster, me, than nigh any other."

Chert sank to the floor in despair. It was hopeless. Even if he could somehow sneak out of the residence and through the Raven Gate, running as fast as he could, Okros and the soldiers would still get there before him. All this because of Chaven and his damned, blasted mirror! *Ruined by his cursed secrets . . . !*

Then he remembered the passage underneath Chaven's observatory. That would get him to the outskirts of Funderling Town in only moments, perhaps while Okros and the soldiers were still trying to find their way through the confusing stone warren of dark streets to locate his house—he doubted any Funderling would give the big folk much help. Nothing made Chert's neighbors more resentful than people from aboveground throwing their weight around, especially in the little folk's own domain.

It's barely a chance, but it's better than naught, he told himself. He jumped to his feet and put his head close to the Rooftopper.

"Thank you, and tell Beetledown I thank him, too," Chert whispered. "I will ask the Earth Elders to lead him to great blessings—but now I must go save my family."

Chert ran off down the passage, leaving his tiny savior spinning on his thread like a startled spider.

The last two days had brought Matt Tinwright attention that at any other time would have delighted him, but just now was wretchedly inconvenient. Because he had been invited to read a poem by Hendon Tolly himself, and in front of Hendon's brother Duke Caradon, many of those at court had decided Tinwright was becoming a pet of the Tollys and therefore someone whose acquaintance was worth cultivating. People who had never bothered to speak to him before now seemed to sidle up to him wherever he went, desiring a love poem written for them or a good word spoken about them to the new masters of Southmarch.

Today he had finally found a chance to slip off on his own.

Most of the castle's inhabitants and refugees were in Market Square at the festival celebrating the third day of Kerneia, so the corridors, courtyards, and wintry gardens of the inner keep were largely empty as Tinwright made his way out of the residence and into the warren of cramped streets that lay in the shadow of the old walls behind the residence.

When he reached the two-story cottage at the end of a row of flimsy, weatherbeaten houses not far from the massive base of the Summer Tower, he went up the stairs quietly—not because he thought anyone would hear him (the street's inhabitants were no doubt all drinking free ale in Market Square) but more because the magnitude of his crime seemed to demand a certain respect best shown by silence and slow movements. Brigid opened the door. The barmaid was dressed for the tavern, her bodice pushing up her breasts like biscuits overflowing a pan, but that was the only thing welcoming about her.

"Tinwright, you miserable lizard, you were supposed to be here an hour gone! I'll lose my position—or worse, I'll have to turn my tail to Conary again to keep it. I should go right to your Hendon Tolly and tell him all about you."

His guts turned to water. "Don't even joke, Brigid."

"Who's joking?" She scowled, then turned to look back at the pale figure lying on the bed. "I'll say this for you, she's pretty enough . . . for a dead girl, that is."

Tinwright swayed a little and had to grab the doorframe. "I told you, don't joke! Please, let me in—I don't want anyone to see me." He edged past her and stopped. "Brigid, love, really truly, I'm grateful. I treated you badly and you've been more kind than I had any right to hope."

"If you think that you can honey-talk me instead of paying me . . ."

"No, no! Here it is." He pulled out the coin and put it in her hand. "I'll never be able to thank you properly . . ."

"No, you won't. Ah, well, the wee thing is all yours now, right and proper." Brigid smirked. "I always knew you were a bit of an idiot, Matty, but this goes beyond anything I'd guessed."

"Has she showed any signs of waking?"

"Some. A bit of moaning and tossing, like having a bad dream." She threw her shawl over her shoulders. "Must go now. Conary will be furious, but maybe I çan sweeten him up by working late. I'm never swiving with that old mackerel again if I can help it."

"You are a true friend," he said.

"And you're an idiot, but I think I said that already." She stepped out into the misty afternoon and pulled the door closed behind her.

The noise of Elan's quiet breath did not change much, but somehow he knew that she was awake. He put down the book of sonnets and hurried to the side of the bed. Her eyes were moving, her face slackly puzzled.

"Where . . . where am I?" It was scarcely more than a whisper. "Is this some . . . some waiting-place?" She saw him moving and her eyes turned toward him, but for long moments they could not fix on him. "Who are you?"

He could only pray that the tanglewife's potion had not injured her mind. "Matt Tinwright, my lady."

For a moment she did not understand, perhaps did not even recognize the name, then her face twisted into anguish. "Oh, Matt. Did you take the poison, too? You sweet boy. You were meant to live."

He took a breath, then another. "I . . . I did not take poison. You did not either, or at least not enough to die. You are alive."

She shook her head and her eyes sagged closed again.

He had told her. She hadn't heard him. Did that mean he was allowed to run away into the night and never look back? Not that he dared desert her, but the gods knew that almost anything would be preferable to standing before this woman and telling her he'd betrayed her trust . . .

"What?" Her eyes opened again, far more alert this time, but wide and frightened like those of a trapped animal. "What did you say?"

The moment to escape, if there had ever truly been such a

moment, was gone. Tinwright wondered if a real man should offer to take real poison to make up for his crime. Perhaps, he reminded himself, but he wasn't a real man—not that kind, anyway. "I said you're not dead, my lady. Elan. You're alive."

She tried to lift her head, but could not. Her gaze jumped fearfully from side to side. "What . . . ? Where am I? Oh, no, surely you are lying. You are some demon of the lands before the gate, and this is a test."

He was surprised to discover that he felt even lower than he had thought he would. "No, Lady Elan, no. You are alive. I could not bear to see you die." He dropped to his knees and took her hand, still cold as death. "You are in a safe place. I had confederates." He shook his head. "I make it too grand. A woman I know, one who has been kind enough to tend you, and to help especially with . . . with your privacies . . ." He felt himself blushing and was disgusted. Matt Tinwright, man of the world! But something about this woman reduced him to childish embarrassments. "She and I stole you out of the residence." He could not quite bear to tell her yet that they had dragged her to this place in a laundry basket.

Her eyes were now shut again. "Hendon . . ."

"He thinks you have run away. He seemed amused, to be honest. He is a bad man, Lady Elan . . ."

"Oh, the gods have mercy, he will find me. Matt Tinwright, you are a fool!"

"So everyone tells me."

She tried to rise again, but was far too weak. "I trusted you and you betrayed me."

"No! I . . . I love you. I couldn't bear to . . . to . . ."

"Then you are twice a fool. You loved a dead woman. If I could not let myself love you then, how could I now, when you've denied me the one release I could hope for?" Tears ran down her cheeks but she did not, or perhaps could not, lift her hands to dry them. Tinwright moved forward with his own kerchief, but as he began dabbing at her face she turned away. "Leave me alone."

"But, my lady . . . !"

"I hate you, Tinwright. You are a boy, a foolish boy, and in your childishness you have doomed me to horror and misery. Now get out of my sight. Is there no chance the poison might yet kill me?"

He hung his head. "You have been asleep almost three days. You will regain your strength soon."

"Good." She opened her eyes as if to fix his face one last time in her memory, then squeezed them shut again. "At least then I'll be able to take my own life and do it properly. All gods curse me for a coward, seeking to do the deed with womanish, weak poisons!"

"But . . ."

"Go! If you do not leave me alone, you craven, I shall scream until someone comes. I think I have the strength for that."

He stood on the stairs for a long time, uncertain of where to go, let alone what to do. The rains had begun again, turning the muddy alley into a swamp and the Summer Tower into an unlit beacon on a storm-battered coast.

Can't go back, can't go forward. He hung his head, felt the cold rain dribble down the back of his neck. *Zosim, you nasty godling, you have put me in another trap and I'm sure you're laughing. Why did I ever think you and your heavenly kind might have changed their minds about me?*

"Opal!" Chert shouted, then a fit of coughing snatched what little remained of his breath. He bent over in the doorway, gasping as if he had cut into a bed of dry gypsum. "Opal, get the boy," he called when he had recovered a little. "We have to hide." But it was strange she had not come to him already.

He staggered into the back room. It was empty, with no sign of his wife or Flint. His heart, already put to a cruel test with his dash across the Inner Keep and just beginning to slow, instead started to race once more. Where could she be? There were at least a dozen possible places, but Brother Okros and those soldiers could only be a short way behind him and he did not have time to rush around searching blindly.

He went out into Wedge Road and began beating on doors, but succeeded only in frightening their neighbor Agate Celadon half to death. She didn't know where Opal had gone, nor did anyone else. Chert sent a desperate prayer to the Earth Elders as he sprinted toward the guildhall as fast as his weary legs could take him.

There seemed to be more people around the venerable building than usual, he saw as he hobbled up the front steps, important and unimportant folk milling about on the landing before the front door. The inner chamber was equally crowded. Several of the men called to him, but when he only demanded to know whether they'd seen Opal or the boy, they shrugged and shook their heads, surprised that he did not want to hear what they had to say.

Chert almost ran into Chaven in the anteroom of the Council Chamber. The physician caught him, then waited patiently while the exhausted Funderling slowly filled his lungs back up with air.

"I am longing to hear your news," Chaven said, "but I have been called with some urgency by some of your friends on the Guild Council. It seems a stranger—one of the big folk as you call us, one of my kind—has stumbled into the Council room. Everyone is quite upset about it."

"By the Lord of the Hot, Wet Stone, don't go in there!" Chert reached up and grabbed Chaven's sleeve as tightly as he could. "That's what I've come ... come to tell you about. It must be one of Brother Okros' soldiers—maybe even Okros himself!"

"Okros? What are you talking about?" Now Chert had the physician's full attention.

"I'll tell you, but ... but if they are already in the guildhall, I fear my news is too late." Chert slumped to the floor, panting. "I'll just c–catch my breath, then I ha–have to find Opal."

"Tell me first," Chaven said. "The keepers of this hall told me it is only one man. Perhaps we can take him prisoner before his fellows realize where he has gone." He stood and waved some of the other Funderlings over, then squatted by Chert once more. "Tell me all."

"It does not matter," Chert moaned. "I have lost my family and

I can't find them. Soon the soldiers will be everywhere. There's nothing we can do, Chaven."

"Perhaps." For the first time in a while, the physician seemed his old, confident self. "But that does not mean I will give in to that traitorous thief Okros without a fight." Chaven turned to the other Funderlings who were beginning to gather around them. "Some of you men must have weapons, or at least picks and stone-axes. Go get them. We'll capture the one lurking in the Council Chamber first, then make him tell us where his fellows are."

So now the Funderlings were to follow a paunchy scholar into battle against Hendon Tolly and all the giant soldiers of Southmarch? If Chert had not been so close to weeping, he might even have enjoyed the bleak joke of it, but all he could think was that his people's world was ending and it was mostly his fault.

"By all the oracles, it is bitter out here!" Merolanna said for perhaps the fifth or sixth time. "I should have brought more furs. Is there nothing in this boat to keep an old woman from freezing to death?"

The young Skimmer Rafe didn't even look up from his oars. "It's not a pleasure barge, is it? Fishing boat, that's what it is. Might be a sealskin in that bag, still."

The duchess waited for Sister Utta to volunteer her services; then, when Utta did no such thing, she began with evident reluctance to poke among the articles wedged under the bench, sighing loudly. Utta, who was determined not be moved, looked away.

She returned to her inspection of Rafe, their boatman and (at least as long as they were on the water) their guide in unfamiliar territory. It was not just the long Skimmer arms that marked him out, although those were very much in evidence as he plied the oars against the choppy swells of Brenn's Bay. Some of the other differences were hidden now that he had put on a thin shirt, seemingly more as a sop to convention than as actual protection against the chill bay winds: like his arms, his neck seemed longer than with most folk, and it made a bit of a hump where it joined his back between the shoulder blades.

His head seemed canted forward, too, as if the point of connection was higher on the back of the skull, but most interesting and disturbing of all was the confirmation of what Utta had thought only a rumor, but now knew as truth: Rafe's fingers and toes were webbed, although most of the time it did not show.

Could all the childhood stories be true, then? Were the Skimmers a different race entirely, like the Rooftoppers surely must be?

"What do your people say?" Utta asked him suddenly, then realized she was speaking thoughts aloud that he couldn't possibly understand. "About where they came from, I mean?"

He looked up at her, wrinkling the skin of his brow in distrust. "Why do you ask?"

"I am curious, I suppose. I grew up in the Vuttish Isles, and none of your folk still live there, although there are stories that they did . . ."

"Stories?" he said bitterly. "I'll trow there were."

"What do you mean?"

"That were all ours once, your Vuttland."

"It was?"

He snorted. "Wasn't it? Didn't our kings rule there, with the Great Moot? Didn't the Golden Shoal come to rest there, at the rock of Egye-Var?"

She had no idea what he was talking about. "Then why did they leave?"

"Should ask T'chayan Redhand, shouldn't you?"

"Who is that?"

His eyes widened. He was not pretending—he was truly astonished. "Don't know T'chayan the Killer? The man who murdered most all my kind in the islands, women and spawn, too, drove our people out of our home and hunted us wherever we went with his dogs and his arrows?"

She blinked, surprised. "Do you mean King Tane the White?" Utta was better read than most of her fellow Vuttlanders, especially because she had gone away, first to the women's remove at Connord, then to the Eastmarch convent to complete her Zorian novitiate. In fact, she knew more of history than most men, but what the Skimmer youth said was new to her. "Tane is not so well known to us now. I may have heard his name once or twice when I was a girl. When Connord conquered the isles and converted the Vuttish Isles to the Trigonate faith, much of our old history was lost."

"Your people do not remember T'chayan Redhand?" The Skimmer youth shook his head in stunned horror. "Sure, you're lying to tease me, then. Your people don't repent his bloody deeds, or at least celebrate them?"

"What *are* the two of you going on about?" demanded Merolanna, poking her head out from the hood she had made of the sealskin.

Sister Utta shook her head. "I'm sorry," she told Rafe. "Truly, I am. My people have forgotten, I suppose, but that doesn't mean we should have."

He shut his mouth with an almost audible snap and refused to talk anymore, or even look at Utta, as though she herself had just returned from the long task of eradicating all memory of the wrongs done to his forebears.

The day was cold and cloudy, with intermittent rain. The fog that lingered in the mainland city seemed weirdly heavy to Utta, like clouds that lay on the ocean instead of hanging in the sky. She could make out a few landmarks jutting through the murk, the market flagpoles and all the temple spires, but the mists made them seem something else, perhaps the skeletal ribs of ancient monsters.

Rafe moved the boat ably through the high waves as they got closer to land; Merolanna alternately clutched the side of the boat and Utta. At times they actually lifted off the benches, then slammed down hard in the next trough. For the first time, Utta wished she had changed back into women's clothes, since they would have offered more protection for her rapidly bruising fundament.

At last they were through and into the shallows. Rafe grounded the boat on a sandbar. "If you walk up that way, won't get your feet too wet," he said.

"Aren't you coming with us?"

"For one silver urchin? You'll want a bodyguard or a troop of soldiers, and you won't get them for one merely urchin, will you? I said I'd bring you here and take you back. Means I'll sit and wait, not go in 'mongst the Old Ones. Their kind don't like my kind."

Utta helped Merolanna out, but despite the duchess' best efforts, the hems of her long skirts still dragged in the water. "Why don't they like you?"

"Us?" Rafe laughed. His face changed when he did it, looked both more and less like an ordinary man's. "Because we stayed behind, didn't we?"

Utta did not get to ask any more questions because just at that moment Merolanna slipped and fell. As the older woman floundered in the shallow water, Utta struggled to lift her until Rafe jumped lightly out of the boat to help. Together the two of them managed to get the dowager duchess upright again.

"Merciful Zoria, look at me!" Merolanna groaned. "I am soaking wet! I'll catch my death of something, that's sure."

"Here, wait," said the young Skimmer, then splashed back to the boat. He returned with the sealskin. "Wrap this around you."

"Thank you," said Merolanna with a certain amount of ceremony—certainly more than this isolated cove had seen in some time, Utta could not help thinking. "You are very kind."

"Still not going with you, though." Rafe waded back to the boat.

"Your Grace, I suspected this was not a good idea before. Now I am certain of it." Sister Utta was trying her best not to peer at the empty houses on either side of the Port Road because they didn't really *seem* empty: the black holes of their windows seemed something more sinister, the eye sockets of skulls or the mouths of dragon caves. Even here on the outskirts of town, where the

houses were low and the winds brisk, the fog still hung in cob-
webby tendrils and it was hard to see more than a few dozen paces
ahead. "I think we should go back to the castle."

"Do not try to change my mind, Sister. I have come all the way
here and I will speak to the fairy folk. They can kill me if they
want, but I will at least ask them what became of my son."

But if they kill you, why would they let me go? Utta did not speak
this thought aloud, not out of any desire to spare Merolanna's feelings, but because in her growing hopelessness, suspended in this
foggy dreamworld as if they were ghosts roaming aimlessly in the
realms of Kernios, she did not think it would make any difference.
Utta knew she had cast her sticks, as the old gambler's saying went,
and now she must shake out her coppers.

They walked slowly up a steep road, Merolanna dripping with
every step, into the open, rain-sprinkled cobbles of Blossom
Market Square—not a place to buy flowers, but the venerable
home of the mainland fish market, whose famous stink had been
jestingly memorialized in its name. Other than the still-pungent
memories of market days past, the square seemed empty now, the
awnings and tents gone, the people all fled to the castle or to cities
further south, but Utta could not rid herself of the sense of being
watched. If anything, it grew stronger as she walked with the
duchess across the open space, so that each step seemed slower and
more difficult, as though the mist was getting into her very bones,
making them sodden and heavy. It was almost a relief when a
figure stepped out of a shadowed arch at the edge of the market
and stood waiting for them.

Utta had prepared herself for virtually anything, her imagination fueled by the books in the castle library and the tales of her
Vuttish grandmother. She was ready for giants, or monsters, or
even beautiful, godlike creatures. She was not as well prepared for
an ordinary mortal man in a simple, homespun robe.

"Good afternoon to you," he said. Utta thought he must be one
of the few who had stayed behind, although it seemed impossible
he should have come unhurt and unchanged through the Twilight
folk's conquest of the city. She could see now that there *was*

something strange about him, something not quite right, and as he approached she found herself shying back.

"No need to fear me." He turned and bowed to Merolanna. "You are the duchess, are you not? I have seen you once or twice in the castle after I was released."

"Released?" said Merolanna. Utta stared—there *was* something familiar about him, although by most standards he had one of the least noteworthy faces she had ever seen. "Who are you, sir?"

"I was known for many years by the name of Gil, and had no other. Now I am called Kayyin . . . again. My story might interest you—in fact, it might interest me, too, if I could remember it all—but for now I am only to be your escort. Please, let me take you to her."

"To whom?" Merolanna asked. Utta was suddenly too fearful to speak. The sun was sinking behind the great seawall and the city was all shadows. "What are you talking about, man?"

"To the mistress of this city. You are commanded to come to her."

"Commanded?" Merolanna bristled a little.

"Oh, yes, Your Grace. She can command anyone—she is greater than any mere queen." He stepped nimbly between them and took each woman by an elbow. "Even the gods must fear her. You see, she is kinswoman to death itself."

"You certainly are an impertinent man," Merolanna said. "Why do you speak so strangely? How did you come to be here?"

"I speak strangely because I am no man," he told her. "Nor am I one of the Qar—not anymore, not after I lived so long as one of your kind, forgetting I was anything else. I am unique, I think—no longer one or the other."

Utta was uncomfortably aware of shapes appearing from the shadows and falling silently into place behind them like an army of cats. She looked back. There were at least three dozen of the tall, slender warriors, eyes gleaming in the depths of their hoods and helmets. Chilled, heart speeding, she said nothing. If Merolanna did not know, let her enjoy her last moments of security.

The duchess certainly seemed to be doing her best to remain

ignorant. "Are you not shamed to speak so?" she asked their odd guide. "I must say I do not think very highly of someone who is such thin milk as to say, 'I am not one or the other'—especially when our two peoples are at war!"

"If you cut out the gills of a fish, Duchess, would you then blame him when he said he did not belong in the water? And yet, he still would not be a man, either." As they reached the far end of the foggy square their guide stopped and raised his hand. "We are here."

Before them lay the bulky stone towers of the Council House where the city's leaders had met, a second seat of power in Southmarch that had on occasion, during times of weak rulers and strong councils, set itself on a nearly equal footing with the throne itself. Its square central tower still loomed above the surrounding buildings, a blocky shape like the chimney of some immense, underground mansion, but the rest of the ancient Council House looked different. It took Utta a moment to realize that what had softened its contours and shadowed its façade was a lattice of woody, dark vines that shrouded most of the building. The vines had not been there the last time she had been in Blossom Market Square, she was certain, but they looked like the product of centuries.

The three dozen or so Qar walking silently behind them had now grown to hundreds, a true army, which filled the square on either side of them, a forest of dimly glittering eyes and pale, hostile faces. Some did not even come close to resembling mortal men. Utta made the sign of the Three and fought against an urge to pull away from their guide and run. She turned to whisper something to the duchess, but she could see by Merolanna's face that the older woman already knew what was happening and had only been pretending she didn't. It was not obliviousness, but a sort of bravery.

More Qar stepped out in front of them, leaving only a narrow aisle between their ranks, leading to the steps of the Council House.

Zoria, forgive me for my selfish thoughts and my pride. Utta put her head down, then lifted it as proudly as she could, like a prisoner going to the gallows. They climbed the wide stairs behind the man who did not know what he was.

It took a moment for her eyes to make sense of the gloom inside the main hall, and when she did she was surprised to see how many of the Twilight folk were here, too: they truly were quiet as cats, these Qar, as they seemed to call themselves. In fact, it was almost exactly like disturbing some congregation of alley-lurkers: the faces swung up, oddly shining eyes fixed on the newcomers, but the faces showed nothing. Some of them were so disturbing to look at that she could not bear to see them for more than an instant. When one of them curled a lip and snarled at her, showing teeth sharp as needles, Utta had to stop, unable to walk for fear she would stumble and fall.

"Just a little farther," said Kayyin kindly, taking her arm again. "She waits right there—can you see her? She is beautiful, isn't she?"

Utta let herself be led forward to the empty center of the room, which contained only one unprepossessing chair and two figures, one sitting, one standing. The one standing behind the chair was female, dressed in plain robes, but her eyes gleamed like fogged mirrors.

The woman in the chair was less obviously unusual, except for her size. She appeared to be as tall as a good-sized man, although achingly thin, but the spikiness of her dark, unreflecting armor made it hard to gauge anything to a certainty. She had the single most unfeeling face Utta had ever seen, one that made the famously stern statue of Kernios in Market Square seem like a child's favorite uncle. Her high, slitted eyes and her wide, pale-lipped mouth might have been carved from stone. Utta felt her legs begin to tremble again. What had the odd man called her— Death's kinswoman? *Merciful Zoria and all the gods of heaven, she looks like Death itself!*

Merolanna too seemed to have lost her courage: they both had to be urged forward by Kayyin, each step heavier than the last, until at last they both slumped to their knees a few paces from the foot of the throne.

"This is Duchess Merolanna Eddon, a member of the royal family of Southmarch," Kayyin said as if he were the herald at a court ball. If he truly had lived in the castle once, Utta decided, it was not surprising that he knew Merolanna's name. But then he added, "And this is Utta Fornsdodir, a Zorian sister. They wish an audience with you, Lady Yasammez."

The woman in black armor looked slowly from Merolanna to Utta, her stare like the touch of an icy finger. A moment later she turned away as if the women were no more substantial than air. "Your japes bring me no pleasure, Kayyin." Her voice was as chill as her gaze; she spoke with a strange, archaic lilt. "Take them away." She spread her long white fingers, said something in a low mutter, then spoke aloud again in a language Utta and Merolanna could understand. "Kill them."

"Hold a moment!" Merolanna's voice trembled, but the duchess clambered up onto her feet even as Utta began to pray, certain that her last moments were upon her. "I have come to you not as an enemy, but as a mother—a mother wronged. I come to you seeking a boon and you would kill me?"

Yasammez stared at her, a black, unreadable stare. "But I am no mother," the fairy woman said. "Not anymore. What seek you?"

"My child. My son. I am told he was taken by the Twilight . . . by the Qar. Your people. I wish to know what happened to him." She gained strength as she spoke. Utta could not help admiring her: whatever her other foibles, Merolanna was no coward.

"Do you hear?" said Kayyin suddenly. "She is appealing to you as one woman to another. As one parent to another." There was something oddly barbed in his tone. "Surely you will not harden your heart to her—will you, Mother?"

Yasammez shot him a look of venom unlike anything Utta had ever seen. If it had been directed at her, she felt sure she would have shriveled and burned like a dry leaf fallen into a fire. A stream of the sharp-edged yet strangely fluid speech rushed out of the woman in the black armor. Kayyin smiled, but it was the miserable smile of someone who had, with great effort, cut off his own nose to spite his face.

Death's kinswoman swiveled around to stare at Utta and Merolanna—this time, Utta could not meet her fierce gaze. "You come to me on a day when I have learned of the death of my treasured Gyir, when I have *felt him die*—the one who should have been my son instead of this changeling traitor. And with Gyir the Storm Lantern dead, the Pact of the Glass must be ended, because the Glass itself will never reach the House of the People." The armored woman slammed her hand down on the arm of the rough chair and the wood snapped into flinders, but she did not seem to notice. "I will now wage war again on your people until the place you call Southmarch is mine, and if I must kill every sunlander man, woman, and child within its walls, I will do so without a qualm." She stared again. Her anger faded and her expression hardened as though ice covered it. "It could be, though, that you will be more use to me as messengers, so I will not kill you yet. But speak no more to me of your child, sunlander bitch. I could not care if my people stole an entire litter of human whelps from you." She waved. Several guards stepped forward and took possession of Utta and Merolanna, although the duchess seemed to have fainted. Utta could make no sense out of what was happening, only that they had stumbled into something more dreadful than her worst fears.

"It will be a joy to hear again the screams of your kind," the monstrous woman said to Utta, then waved the prisoners away.

42

The Raven's Friend

So it is that the true gods have reigned in peace ever since, thanks to Habbili and the wisdom of Nushash. After they die, those who bow their heads and do them homage will find themselves serving at the right hand of the mighty in the ultimate west. So say the prophets. So says the god of fire. It is truth, my children, it is true.

—from *The Revelations of Nushash*, Book One

BRIONY'S MALE DISGUISE, which had already been compromised by her stage costume representing the goddess Zoria, had not survived a search for weapons by the Syannese soldiers who had arrested her and the other players.

(Feival Ulian, who had left the stage as Zuriyal, wife of the rebel god black Zmeos, had also been led off to the palace in a gown. It was an open question as to which of them, he or Briony, felt more comfortably dressed.)

Briony and Estir Makewell had been shoved into a room that

wasn't quite a dungeon cell, but was no chamber for honored guests, either: dank and windowless, it smelled of mold and sweat and urine, and contained no furniture but a single crude bench; the sound of the outside bar being lowered had a distressing thump of finality.

"Should have known there was more to you than a chance meeting," Estir sneered. "That old mare Teodoros, up to his same old tricks. Did he bring you along to get into someone's bed, then, winkle out secrets that way? Now we're all for the headsman's block, thanks to you two."

"What are you talking about? I'm not a spy—I had nothing to do with any of this!"

"Oh, that's likely." Estir Makewell sat back with her arms folded across her dirty dress, but Briony could see that the woman was shaking with fear, and her own anger turned to something like pity.

"Truly, I knew nothing about this. I was running away from . . . from my home when I fell in with you." Estir sniffed in an unconvinced manner. "What do you mean, same old tricks?" Briony asked. "Has he done something like this before?"

The woman glared at her. "Don't pretend with me, girl. I saw you talking to that black fellow like he was an old friend—that Xixian. How would you know someone like that if you weren't one of Finn's coneys?"

Briony shook her head. At least Dawet had escaped, not that it would do Briony any good. "I know him a little, but it's nothing to do with Finn. I had met him before, in Southmarch. But I swear on . . . on the honor of Zoria herself," she thumped her fist against her chest, bleakly amused to be swearing on herself, or at least her costumed self, "that I knew *nothing* about any spying." She suddenly looked at the closed door. "Do you think they're listening?" she asked in a quieter voice. "Did we say anything we shouldn't have?"

"What do you care if you've nothing to hide?" sniffed Estir, but she seemed a little less angry. "You're right, though. We should keep our mouths closed. If that fat know-it-all's got himself in trouble, it won't be the first time. That's all I'll say, except to curse him for dragging us all into it this time."

Briony looked at the walls, so damp they seemed to be sweating. They had trudged for the better part of an hour to reach this place, which she assumed must be in the royal palace, but they were several floors below the main body of the castle. *I could disappear here very easily,* she thought. *Executed as a spy, and that would be the last of me. King Enander would be doing Hendon Tolly's work for him without even knowing it. Unless they're already in league . . . ?* It was hard to believe—Southmarch had never been a threat or even a real rival to Syan. What could Tolly offer to the more powerful Syannese monarchy except the uncomfortable possibility of dynastic upheavals? What king would want to encourage that unless it benefited him personally?

But what had Finn Teodoros been up to? Was it a coincidence Dawet had come to the innyard?

Briony fell into a frowning, miserable silence, trying to understand what had happened and decide what she could do about it. *Me,* she thought, *it's down to me. Keep drifting or stand up.* At last she went to the door of the room in which they were prisoned and rapped on it hard, with both hands.

"Tell your captain or whoever is in charge that I want to talk to him. I want to make a deal."

"What are you doing, girl?" Estir demanded, but Briony ignored her.

After a moment the door swung open. Two guards stood in the doorway, only a little less bored than when they had thrown the two women into the room. "What do you want? Make it fast," said one.

"I want to make a bargain. Tell your commanding officer that if you'll bring me the man called Finn Teodoros and let me speak to him, I swear on the gods themselves that afterward I'll tell you something that will make even the king of Syan sit up and take notice."

Estir was watching her with her mouth open. "You traitorous bitch," she said at last. "Trying to buy yourself out? You will get us all killed!"

"And take this woman out," Briony said. "She knows nothing. Let her go or put her somewhere else, it makes no difference to me."

The soldiers, actually interested now, exchanged a brief glance with each other, then closed the door and tramped away up the corridor.

"How dare you!" Estir Makewell said, striding forward to stand over her. Wearily, Briony stared up at her, hoping she wouldn't have to fight the woman. "How dare you tell them what to do with me?"

Briony rolled her eyes, then grabbed the woman's arm roughly, silencing her. "Stop—I'm trying to help you." Estir stared at her, frightened. She had her mask on now, Briony realized, the Eddon mask that none of the players had seen. She made her voice hard. "If you keep your mouth shut, you and the others may walk away from this happy and healthy. If you cause a fuss, I can't promise anything."

Estir Makewell's eyes grew wide at the change in Briony's tone. She retreated to the other side of the room and stayed there until the guards came and led her out.

Finn Teodoros had some bruises around his eyes and a bleeding weal on his bald head. He gave Briony a shamefaced look as the guards led him in and sat him down on the bench beside her.

"Well, Tim, my young darling," he said, "it seems as if your disguise has been penetrated by these crude folk from outside the theatrical fraternity." He touched his swollen cheek and winced. "I swear I didn't tell them."

"They found out when they searched me. It doesn't matter anyway." Briony took a breath. The very fact that the guards had left the two of them alone in the room meant they were almost certainly listening to everything that was being said. "I need your help," she told Teodoros. "I need you to tell me the truth."

He gave her a look that contained a mixture of caution and amusement. "And who in this wretched old world can actually say what *that* is, dear girl?"

She nodded, conceding the point. "As much truth as you know," she said, then looked significantly around the room. "As much as you can tell."

He sighed. "I am truly sorry you were caught up in this. I have tried to tell them that you had nothing to do with it."

"Don't worry about me. I am less innocent than you think, Finn. Just tell me one thing—were you working for Hendon Tolly?"

He stared at her, clearly calculating. "Tolly?"

"I may be able to protect you, but you must tell me the truth about that. I *must know*."

"You, protect me? Girl, you are not Zoria in truth, you merely aped her on the boards!" He smiled, but it was little more than a fearful twitch. He swallowed, leaned close to her. "I . . . I do not know," he said in a voice that was scarcely even a whisper. "I was given a . . . a task . . . by someone else. Someone high in the government of Southmarch."

She hazarded a guess. "Was it Lord Brone? Avin Brone?"

His eyebrows rose. "How would you know of such things?"

"If I can save us, I will, and then you will learn more. Were you to meet with Dawet dan-Faar on Brone's behalf? Drakava's man?"

This time Finn Teodoros could say nothing, but in his surprise could only nod.

Briony stood up, walked to the door. "I wish to talk to the guard captain, please," she called, "or anyone in authority. I have something to say that the king himself will want to know."

This time there was a much longer wait before the door opened. Several guards came through, followed a moment later by a well-dressed man in the high collar of a court grandee. He had gray in his pointed beard, but did not otherwise seem very old, and he moved with the grace of a young man. He reminded her a little bit of Hendon Tolly, an unpleasant association. "Do not rise," the noble said with perfectly pitched courtesy. "I am the Marquis of Athnia, the king's secretary. I understand you believe you have something to say that is worth my listening. I'm sure it goes without saying that there is a very unpleasant penalty for wasting my time."

Briony sat up straighter. She had heard of Athnia—he was a member of the old and wealthy Jino family and one of the most important men in Syan. Apparently the guards had taken what she said seriously. On the bench Finn Teodoros swayed, almost fainting with apprehension at the appearance of such a powerful figure.

"I do." She stood up. "I can do no good to anyone by proceeding with this counterfeit. I am not an actor. I am not a spy. I do not believe this man here or any of the other actors are spies, either—at least they meant no harm to Syan or King Enander."

"And why should we believe anything *you* say?" the marquis asked her. "Why should we not take you down to the brandy cellars and let the men there extract the truth from all of you?"

She took a breath. Now that the moment had come, it was surprisingly difficult to put off the cloak of anonymity. "Because you would be torturing the daughter of one of your best and oldest allies, Lord Jino," she said, straightening her spine, trying to will herself taller and more imposing. "My name is Briony te Meriel te Krisanthe M'Connord Eddon, daughter of King Olin of Southmarch, and I am the rightful princess regent of all the March Kingdoms."

It's my dream, he thought. *I'm trapped in my own nightmare!*

Shouts and screams surrounded him like strange music. The corridors were full of fire and smoke and some of the running, horribly charred shapes were as black and faceless as the men in his dream.

Is that what it meant, then? He staggered to a stop in a wide place at the junction of several tunnels and crouched beside an overturned ore cart. Every bone and sinew in his body had been battered until he could hardly walk, and his crippled arm felt like the bones were grinding together each time it moved. *Was my dream telling me that this is where I die?*

A small, clumsy shape staggered past him, keening in a shrill, mad voice. Barrick tried to rise, but couldn't. His heart was shuddering and tripping like a bird's, and his legs felt as though they would not support a sparrow, let alone his own weight. He let his head sag and tried to breathe.

I don't want to die here. I won't die here! But what was the sense of such foolish statements? Gyir hadn't wanted to die here either but that hadn't saved him—Barrick had *felt* the fairy's dying moment. Ferras Vansen hadn't wanted to die here either, yet he had still fallen down to certain destruction in the stony black depths. What made Barrick think he would be any different? He was lost in the deeps of an old, bad place, trapped in the dark, surrounded by enemies . . .

But I have to try. Must. I promised . . . !

He wasn't even sure any more what he had promised or to whom: three faces hovered before his eyes, shifting and merging, dissolving and reforming—his sister with her fair hair and loving looks, the fairy-woman with her stony, ageless face, and the dark-haired girl from his dreams. The last was an utter stranger, perhaps not even real, and yet in some ways, at this moment, she seemed more real and familiar than the others.

Push against it, she had told him on that bridge between two nowheres. *Escape it. Change it.*

He had not understood—had not wanted to understand—but she had insisted he not give up, not surrender to pain.

This is what you have, she had told him, eyes wide and serious. *All of it. You have to fight.*

Fight. If he was going to fight, he supposed he'd have to get up. Didn't any of them understand he had a right to be bitter—to be more than bitter? He hadn't asked for any of this—not the terrible injury to his arm or the curse of his father's blood, not the war with the fairies or the attentions of an insane demigod. Didn't all the women who were demanding he do this or that—go on a mission, come home safe, fight against despair—didn't they know he had a right to all that misery?

But they just wouldn't leave him alone.

Barrick sighed, coughed until he doubled over and spat out blood and ash, then climbed back onto his feet.

★

Many of the tunnels started out with an upward slant, but soon tilted back down again. The only certain way to know that he was climbing was to find stairs. But Barrick Eddon was not the only one with that idea: half the lost, shrieking creatures in the smoky depths of Greatdeeps seemed to be looking for a way to the surface. The others, for reasons he could not imagine, seemed equally determined on rushing down toward the place where Gyir and the one-eyed demigod had died, a cavern that had already collapsed in fire and black fumes when Barrick had crawled away from it perhaps an hour ago. Sometimes he actually had to wade through a tide of maddered shapes, some of them as big as himself, all hurrying as fast as they could down toward what must be certain death. He had lost the ax when the ceiling fell; now he found a spadelike digging tool that someone had dropped, and used it the next time the tunnel became frighteningly cramped, clearing his way with it, hitting out when he needed to against the claws or teeth of frightened refugees.

As he climbed higher through the mine the stairwells opened onto rooms and scenes of which he could make no sense whatsoever. In one broad cavern which he had to traverse to reach the bottom of the next stairwell, dozens of slender, winged creatures were savaging a single squat one, their voices a shrill buzz of angry joy—their victim might have been one of the small Followers like those that had attacked Gyir in the forest, but it was hard to tell: the silent creature was too covered with blood and earth to be certain. Barrick hurried past with his head down. It reminded him of his own vulnerability, and when he saw the dull glow of a blade lying on the stairs where its owner had dropped it, presumably in panicked flight, he dropped the digging tool and picked this up instead. It was a strange thing, half ax, half poniard, but much sharper than the spade.

A couple of floors up the stairwell suddenly filled with small, pale skittering things which seemed to care little whether they were upside down or right side up; just as many of them raced across the ceiling and walls as along the floor. Their bodies were bone-hard, round and featureless as dinner bowls, but they had little splay-toed feet like mice. The scrabbling, clinging touch of those tiny claws disturbed Barrick so much that after the first one landed on him he hurriedly brushed off all others.

Barrick Eddon was staggeringly weary. He had climbed several staircases, some taller than anything back home in Southmarch, and also two high, terrifyingly rickety ladders, yet he still seemed no closer to the surface: the air was still as dank, hot, and choking as before, the other slaves and workers just as confused as they had been a half dozen levels lower. He was lost, and now even the strength that terror had brought him was beginning to fade. Things fluttered past in the dark tunnels and shadowy figures slid across his path before vanishing down side passages, but more and more he seemed to be alone. That was bad: to be alone was to be obvious. The monstrous demigod might be dead but that didn't mean Jikuyin's surviving minions would just let Barrick go.

He grabbed at the first creature he found that was smaller than himself, a strange, hairless thing with goggling eyes like a two-legged salamander, the last of a pack that slithered past him in a stairwell. It let out a thin shriek, then before he could even find out if it spoke his language it fell into pieces. Arms, legs—everything he tried to grab dropped off the torso and the whole slippery, strange mess tumbled from his grasp and then hopped and slith-ered away down the stairs after its fellows. Barrick was so startled that he stood staring as the hairless creatures (trailed by the one he had captured, still in its constituent parts) hurried down and out of his sight, then was almost crushed by a large, hairy shape chasing after them.

The hairy thing was on him and then past him so quickly that he only knew it was one of the apelike guards by its foul smell and by the scratch of its fur as it forced its way past him down the narrow stairwell. He stood for a moment after it was gone, gasping, grateful that it seemed more interested in the hairless things than in him.

Maybe they're good to eat, he thought miserably. Barrick wasn't only aching and tired, he was famished—the guards hadn't bothered to feed them before dragging them off to the gate. *I'll be killing and eating the horrid things myself before long, and glad to have them* . . .

Just as he reached a landing, lit fitfully by a pair of guttering torches, a small shape dashed out of one of the side passages. The little, manlike creature took one look at Barrick and turned to run back the way he'd come, but Barrick lunged forward—surprising himself almost as much as the newcomer—and gripped the creature's knotted, oily hair with the fingers of his good hand.

"Stop or I'll kill you," he said. "Do you speak my tongue?"

It was a Drow like the one which had ridden the burning wagon, tiny and gnarled, with bristling brows, a wide, onion-shaped nose and a ragged beard that covered much of its face. It was strong for its size, but the more it struggled the tighter Barrick held. He drew it toward him and laid his found blade against its face so it could not fail to notice. He struggled not to show the creature how much it hurt him just to hold the blade with his bad arm.

"Nae hort," it cried, the voice both gruff and high-pitched. "Nae hort!"

It took a moment. "Don't . . . don't hurt you?" He leaned closer, glaring. "Don't think to trick me, creature. I want to go out, but I can't find the surface—the light. Where is the light?"

The little man stared at him for a long moment, then nodded. "Yow beyst in Rootsman's Nayste—ouren Drowhame. High in mountain, beyst, wuth caves and caves, ken? Wrong way to day-burn."

If he listened carefully, he could make sense of it. So he was climbing inside the mountain itself—no wonder he couldn't find the surface! He was relieved, but if the creature considered the weak light of the shadowlands worthy of being called "dayburn," he hoped it never found itself in the true light of day on the other side of the Shadowline.

"How do I get out. Out to . . . to dayburn?"

"Thic way." The Drow squirmed gently until Barrick loosened his grip. It turned and pointed with a stubby, crack-nailed finger. "Yon."

Barrick gratefully transferred his blade to his good hand. "Very well. Lead me."

"Willae set a free?"

"If you lead me to the dayburn, yes, I'll free you. But if you try to run away from me before we get there, I'll stick you with this!" He was sick of blood and killing, but he didn't want to spend the rest of a short, miserable life in these caverns, either.

Barrick didn't know if it was a good or bad sign that the farther the creature led him, the more deserted the corridors became. They moved mostly horizontally at first, through rooms that clearly had some kind of function, mostly as storehouses stacked with bent and broken digging tools, battered, empty ore buckets, broken wagons awaiting repair, ropes and other supplies, or with less comprehensible things—piles of what looked like fired clay chips covered with incised marks, leaking bags and barrels of different colored powders, even one chamber so misty and chill that at first he thought they had stepped out of the mines at last and into the midst of a terrible winter storm. He was several paces into this last cavern before he realized they were still deep under the earth, and that the tooth-chattering cold was because the room was piled high with blocks of snow or ice. But why? And where could such things come from?

The answer to the second came a few moments later, as he began to see what was stacked along the walls, largely hidden by the mist. Corpses, although of what it was hard to tell, because they had been quartered as if by expert butchers. His already cringing spirits plummeted even farther. What was the reason for such madness? In a trembling voice, he asked the Drow, but the creature only shrugged its ignorance.

Was it meat? But certainly none of the prisoners had been fed any, and there hadn't seemed enough guards to need such a monstrous supply: the frost-blanketed carcasses were stacked like kindling all around the huge room. And where did the ice itself come from? It had been cold outside, rainy and often miserable, but there had been nothing like snow, let alone such vast quantities of ice.

Unless all this was meant just to feed Jikuyin, he thought, and his stomach lurched with horror. He shoved the little Drow to make him trot faster. Barrick could not get out of the icy cavern fast enough.

They passed through another large storehouse cavern, this one lit only by a single small torch, and Barrick was grateful that the Drow could move more easily in the dark than he could, since he could barely see anything. As to what the piles of cloth-covered bundles in the room might be, he couldn't tell and did not particularly want to investigate, but a stream ran through the middle of the room—he could hear its whispering progress more clearly than he could see it, since it was set in a deep crevice in the floor—and dozens of tiny, pale creatures fluttered about the room. It was only when one of them landed on his shoulder, startling him so badly he almost cut himself with his own blade trying to knock it off, that he saw the little flyers were winged white salamanders, blind gliders that came up out of the crevice in the floor like bats heeding the call of sunset. Now he could see that the pale creatures were clinging everywhere on the roof and walls of the chamber, as placid as if they basked on a hot rock in the summer sun instead of in a dark chamber deep in a mountain.

As they came out of the salamander cavern and onto a downward sloping path, he caught at the Drow and demanded to know why they were heading back down into the depths. The bearded, pop-eyed creature looked understandably frightened of the blade at his throat, but not, as far as Barrick could tell, guilty of any wrongdoing.

"Canna go out lest go down from Rootsman's Nayste," his guide explained. "Nayste is riddlin', full o' holes, all different roads up, down—f'Rootsman, see?"

After wearily puzzling over this for a little while, Barrick finally decided that the little man was telling him they had to descend from something called Rootsman's Nayste—or maybe Nest?—because he had climbed up in it too high to go straight to the gate that led out of the mines. If it was true, the little bearded man was playing him fair and he might actually soon be out in the air again.

Even as hope surged, he could not help thinking of his lost companions. There were many times he had felt sure he would die in these tunnels, and he was still far from certain he would survive, but he had never once imagined the possibility of getting away without the other two. Now, even if he managed to escape the mines, he would still be alone in a murderous, bizarrely unfamiliar place.

He pushed the thought away, knowing that if he didn't the last bit of his strength would leak away and he would tumble to the ground and never get up.

As they crossed a wide chamber lit with a thousand small tapers, which burned on the walls and ceiling like the light of the stars themselves, the little bearded man slowed and stopped. "Here beyst," he said breathlessly, his voice hoarse with fear. "See. Fore yow beyst the dayburn."

Barrick stared. At the far end of the chamber there was a glimmer of light—a crack at the bottom of a door leading to freedom, perhaps—or might it be merely an illusion? "That?"

"Ayah." The creature stirred nervously in Barrick's grip, but it was quite possible the Drow's fretfulness signified only that he did not know whether or not Barrick would prove trustworthy and release him as promised.

"Let's go ahead, then, and see if it opens." Barrick laughed, although he did not know why. He was light-headed at the thought of getting out, but half-certain the little man was trying to trick him. "We'll do it together."

Joy washed over him as he drew closer and could see that it truly was the great front doors of wood and metal, the light spilling in where they had been left a little way open, perhaps by deserting guards. With the surprisingly strong arms of the Drow helping him he managed to tug them wider, until he thought the space was big enough for him to slip through. At another time he might have been interested in the figures and runes that had been cast in the black metal and carved into the dark wood, but now he was overwhelmed by the light of day spread before him, sumptuous as a meal.

It was day only in the most basic sense, of course—the gray, sunless day of the shadowlands—but after his imprisonment in the depths it felt like the brassy blaze of a Heptamene afternoon.

So much light was also far too much for the Drow, who stepped back from the doorway waving his hands before his face and hissing like a serpent. Easing himself sideways into the gap, Barrick ignored the creature—the Drow had fulfilled his bargain, after all—but a moment later the little man staggered back into view and tumbled at Barrick's feet, three feathered arrowshafts quivering in his back and the wounds already soaking his ragged, dirty shirt. The little creature was not dead yet, but judging by his harsh, whistling breath, he had only moments.

"You are perfectly framed in the doorway," a stony voice declared, stirring up echoes. "If you do anything but move slowly back toward me, my guards will shoot you. You will not die as fast as your small friend, however."

Barrick knew that even if he could force himself through in one try, the invisible archers would have plenty of time for an unimpeded shot. Even if he got out, he had no strength left to outrun anyone, let alone evade the arrows of trained bowmen. Barrick slowly eased himself out of the doorway and stepped back into the cavern. Standing before him, at the front of a mixed pack of apish guards and bony, quietly gabbling Longskulls, several of whom held longbows, stood the cadaverous figure of Ueni'ssoh, his eyes gleaming like blue fires.

"You were Jikuyin's," the gray man said in his cold, uninflected voice. "But now you are mine. We will dig out the gateway chamber once more. Nothing has changed except who will own the god's treasures."

"I'd rather die," Barrick said, then turned and leaped toward the doorway, but something hit him in the leg like a club and he tumbled to the floor, half in and half out of the room with an arrow through his boot and a searing pain across his calf. Despite the queer, breathless ache of the wound he could feel the cool, gray light of the outside world on him like a balm, smell the sweetness of the air. Only now did he realize how foul were the stenches he had been living in so long, the smoke and blood and filth.

So this was the ending. After all that he had done, after all the people he had tried to please . . . well, he had told them he wasn't up to it, hadn't he? He had told them he would fail—or if he hadn't actually told them, they should have known.

The gray man stood over him now, the bright eyes watching Barrick intently. Ueni'ssoh's tongue flicked out, lizardlike, to touch his dry lips. "There is *something* . . . Yes, you have something. I feel it now. Something . . . *powerful*. Things begin to make more sense."

Barrick snarled at him, but it was hard to make words, at least any words that mattered. Then he remembered.

The mirror. Gyir's mirror, the sacred trust of Lady Yasammez! Barrick could feel it against his breast in the pocket of his shirt. He could not let this hairless, corpselike thing take it. "I don't know what you're talking about . . ."

"Silence." The gray man reached out a bony hand that paused just above Barrick's chest. The Longskulls and hairy-pelted guards crowded around their master, staring down like the demons in a temple fresco. "Give it to me."

Barrick tried to deny him again, but although the gray man was not touching him, he could feel a force tugging at the mirror under his shirt. An intense agony blossomed in his chest, as though the mirror had sunk roots into his skin and bones, as though it would not be pulled away without tearing the greater part of Barrick away as well. He shrieked, but the gray man did not even flinch; except for those moonstone eyes, Ueni'ssoh might have been carved stone.

Barrick gripped the mirror through his shirt, but a curious weakness was already starting to spread through him. What use resisting? This creature, this gray demon, was stronger than he could ever hope to be—*so much stronger* . . .

"No!" He knew that voice in his head. It was not his own but the gray man's. "I won't . . .!"

A smile curved the stony lips. The pull on the mirror seemed as though it would yank Barrick's entire body inside out. Ueni'ssoh was kneeling above him, hand held a foot above Barrick's breast. "But you will, sunlander—of course you will. And when I have this secret thing in my hand, I will know why One-Eye was so interested in you . . ."

"You can't . . . !" But they were nothing but gasped words. He could not resist the gray man's power. He would lose the mirror and lose everything.

"Stop fighting," said the Dreamless. His teeth were clenched, and Barrick suddenly realized that beads of sweat had formed on Ueni'ssoh's ashy forehead.

But I'm not fighting, Barrick thought. *I wouldn't know how, not against something like him.* Still, something was resisting the gray man's power—something was holding the Dreamless at bay.

A great heat suddenly filled Barrick. It was the mirror itself, blossoming with power even as Ueni'ssoh tried to make it his. A light flared around them, warm and almost as brilliant as the sun itself, so strong that Barrick himself screamed out, though it caused him no pain. As the light burst forth all the guards screeched and fell back, waving their clawed hands before their eyes. A moment later the light fell back on itself, but Barrick could still feel it even so, a tingling like sparks all over his skin. Someone else was howling now, too. Like a spider that had caught a huge, murderous wasp in its fragile web, it was now Ueni'ssoh who was trying to break contact—Barrick could feel the gray man's mounting terror, could almost smell it, or hear it like a shrill noise—but the mirror or whatever empowered it would not let the Dreamless go.

"No!" the gray man shrieked and tried to stand up, but something invisible had clutched him and he contorted and thrashed like a living fish dropped on a hot stone. His eyes bulged, and his muscles writhed beneath the parchment skin, knotting and coiling. A moment later great black flowers of blood appeared on his face and neck and hands. The bestial guards, still howling in pain at the light that had blinded them, began stumbling away in all directions, tearing at each other in their haste to escape the growing incandescence that pulsated between Barrick's breast and Ueni'ssoh's still outstretched hand.

Then the gray man caught fire.

Ueni'ssoh jerked upright, shrieking and jigging, as the glow spread up his arm and into his chest. His eyes began to burn out of their sockets. His gaping mouth vomited flame. The guards fled barking out of the wide anteroom, back into the darkened corridors of the mine.

When Barrick looked again the gray man was nothing but a hissing, twitching, blackening shape. The boy turned away in horror and disgust, crawling over the arrow-riddled corpse of his Drow guide in his desperation to get out into the daylight.

Outside, he looked down the narrow valley beyond the base of the steps, bewildered. Was he really free? What had happened? Had *he* destroyed the gray man somehow? He didn't think so—it had been the mirror, defending itself. But it had done nothing until the gray man had tried to take it. Would it have let Barrick be killed if the gray man had left the mirror itself alone? He didn't know, and he certainly didn't want to do anything to find out.

He broke off the protruding arrowhead and pulled the arrow out of his boot, which was slippery from the blood of his slashed ankle, then he limped down the steps and onto the open ground—the end of the long road they had traveled as prisoners to come to this terrible place, however many days or even months ago that had been. Only a little more walking, however painful, and he would be out of reach of the mine's guardians, if any were minded to follow him.

Feeble as it was, the half-light still seemed strong to him after his days in underground darkness, and so at first Barrick did not notice the trembling of some of the huge statues in front of him until one of them swayed and then fell over, landing with a shuddering crash that almost knocked him off his feet. Two more statues toppled as the soil erupted before him in great crumbling chunks. A massive shape thrust itself up out of the earth and into the daylight.

At first Barrick thought in weary horror that it was some unimaginably large spider from the depths, all hair and malformed, corpse-colored limbs and gleaming, dripping fluids. But its appendages stuck out in unexpected directions, some shattered and peeling, all smoking and oozing like melted candlewax, as though the thing were some terrible combination of sea urchin or jellyfish and butchered animal. Then he finally saw the raw face hanging between two of the limbs, oozing with the glowing golden ichor that ran through it instead of blood. The horror that had cut off his escape still had a few tendrils of singed beard around the broken-toothed maw, and that single huge, mad eye.

"You wretched little ball of shit." The demigod's lower jaw was shattered, drooling a liquid that looked like molten metal, and so Jikuyin's physical voice was an unrecognizable gurgle. The words were only in his head, but so powerful despite the demigod's countless injuries that Barrick stumbled and almost sank to his knees. *"Thought I was dead, didn't you? But we immortals aren't so easy to kill . . . !"*

Barrick staggered to one side, praying he could dodge around the huge, crippled thing, but despite all his terrible wounds the demigod moved with devastating speed, scuttling crablike on his broken limbs to block the boy's escape.

"Not so fast, man-child. Your blood will open the god's house and I will be made whole again. This is only an inconvenience."

Barrick's head seemed too heavy to hold up any longer. He could not get past the thing and he certainly couldn't outfight it. He could not go back, either. He was done.

Unless . . .

Barrick Eddon reached into his shirt and pulled out the mirror. For a moment he felt it warm in his hand, felt its power begin to bloom again as it had when the gray man had tried to take it, but Jikuyin held up a splayed, shattered hand—Barrick thought it must be a hand—and the burgeoning flare of light suddenly died.

"Whatever it is," Jikuyin told him, *"it is a lesser power than mine, mortal boy."* His single, bloodshot eye no longer had the means to show expression—the meat of his face was too ravaged for that—but Barrick could tell the demigod was pleased and even amused. Barrick knew also that what Jikuyin said was true—the mirror was now cold and inert. *"After all, the blood of the great gods runs in my veins . . . !"*

Something dropped down out of the sky, covering the demigod's face for a moment like a living black shadow. Jikuyin let out a screech of startled pain that ripped through Barrick's brain and knocked him to his knees. When he managed to climb back onto his feet, Barrick saw that the black shape was gone and that the spidery demigod was moaning and rubbing at his face. When he took his limbs away, the place where Jikuyin's single remaining eye had been was now a welling crater of radiant gold.

Blind . . . ! He's blind! Barrick knew he had only one chance: while the monster shrieked and thrashed his tattered arms in fury, Barrick put his head down and ran at stumbling speed straight toward him, then veered wide, diving and rolling just beneath the grasping talons of a gold-dripping hand the size of a wagon wheel.

The giant sensed that he had missed his quarry and let out a rasping, wordless bellow that shook the very hills around them, so that stones came tumbling down out of the heights. Barrick did not stop to look, but ran as fast as his exhausted muscles could carry him, gasping for breath with every step. The god's cries of rage dwindled behind until at last they were only a distant noise like thunder.

He had finally staggered far enough to feel safe. He dropped onto his hands and knees, straining for breath. A black shape plummeted down out of the air, its wide wings brushing him as it landed. It took a few hopping steps and then leaped up onto a rock to regard him with a bright eye. Barrick had never thought he would be so pleased to see the horrid creature.

"Skurn—is that you?"

"Where be my other master?"

It took a moment for Barrick to realize what the bird was asking. "Vansen. He . . . he fell. Down in the mine. He's not coming out."

The raven regarded him carefully. "Saved you, I did. Poked that big one's eye right through, did. Was that Jack Chain?"

Barrick nodded, too tired to speak.

"Then I be the mightiest raven what ever lived, be'nt I?" The bird appeared to consider this, walking back and forth along the top of the stone, clucking a bit. "Skurn the Mighty. Pecked out a god's eye."

"Demigod." Barrick rolled onto his back. He had better be far enough away now, because he couldn't move another step.

Skurn leaned back his head. His throat pumped, swallowing. "Mmmm," he said. "God's eye. Slurpsome. Wishet I'd got the whole thing."

Barrick stared at the bird for a moment, then began to laugh, a ragged, painful bray that went on and on until he began to choke.

When the boy had his breath again and was sitting up, a thought came to him. "Tell me, you horrible creature, do you know where Qul-na-Qar is? The House of the People?"

The raven regarded him. "What be in this plan for me? Didn't save me like my master did—fact be, *I* saved *you.*" He preened. "Fact. Skurn the Mighty."

"If you'll help me take this . . . if you'll help me get to Qul-na-Qar, I'll make sure you never have to hunt for food the rest of your life. In fact, I'll bring you fresh kills on a plate, every day."

"True?" The raven hopped a few times, fluttered up, and settled. "Bargain, then. If you be trustworthy."

Despite feeling as empty as a forgotten scarecrow, Barrick could still muster a little irritated pride. "I am a prince—the son of a king."

Skurn made a snorting noise. "Oh, aye, *that* makes a difference." He thought, blinking his dark eyes slowly. "But you were my master's friend. So—partners."

"Partners. By the gods, who would have thought?" Barrick crawled into the bushes, not caring where he lay his head. "Let me know if anyone comes to kill me, will you?"

He did not wait to hear the raven's reply, because sleep was already pulling him down into dark places deeper than any mineshaft.

Vansen kept on because there was nothing else he could do, putting one foot in front of the other, trudging forward along the endless pale span through black nothing. There were times that he paused to rest, but he never did it for long, because each time he would begin to worry that he might somehow get himself turned around, that he would confuse the two indistinguishable directions and by accident set off back in the direction he had come.

At other times he entertained the amusing notion that instead of a curving span across an abyss, he was walking on the outside of a great ring floating in darkness, that it had no beginning or end, and that he, Ferras Vansen, sentenced for crimes about which he was not quite certain (although he could judge himself guilty of much) would walk it forever, undying, an endless sentence.

But could the gods really be so cruel? And even if they were, why did he still feel tired, as a living man might feel?

And what was it about the gods that pricked at him? Why were they weighing so heavily on his thoughts? Every time he tried to remember how he had come to this place, what had seemed solid fell apart in his grasp, like fog. He could not remember where he had been before this—in fact, he could remember almost nothing that had happened since he threw himself against the guards in the demigod's underground fortress. He seemed to recall a city, and something about his father, but surely those were dreams, since his father had been dead for years.

But if those had been dreams, then what was this place? Where was he? Who or what had set him on this unending track?

What if he just stepped off this pointless, endless bridge, he wondered, and let himself fall? Could whatever happened—death or an equally pointless, endless plunge—really be so much worse? It was something to keep in reserve, he decided—a door. It might turn out to be the only door that could lead him out of this dreadful emptiness.

Ferras Vansen had no answers, but being able to ask questions at least kept him from going mad.

★

It was as though he had blinked, but the moment of his eyes being shut had lasted for a year instead of an instant. When he noticed what had happened, everything had changed.

The abyss was gone, the infinite, eternal black faded in some strange way to a much more tangible darkness, that of ordinary shadow. Something that felt like stone still lay beneath his feet, but flat, not curved, and he had the distinct sense of being surrounded by something other than the dreadfully familiar void.

He stopped, surprised and more than a little frightened—after so long, any change was terrifying. He dropped to his knees and sniffed the cold stone, pressed his forehead against it. It felt real. It felt *different,* which was even more important.

He stood up and to his immense surprise the darkness itself began to recede, or rather the light came and dissolved it: brightness flooded in, the light of actual, homely torches, and he could see walls around him, stone walls that had been decorously carved. He followed the lines of the ceiling up and discovered, to his horror, an immense shape looking back down at him, black and ominous. But it was only a statue, a huge image of Kernios, and although Vansen was startled when he looked down and saw the same statue staring up at him from beneath his feet, he grasped a moment later that he stood on some kind of looking-glass stone, a vast mirror which reflected the pit so intricately carved in the ceiling overhead, as well as great Kernios looking down, or up, from its depths.

Staring up and then down made him dizzy. Vansen almost fell, but caught himself. Where was he? Was this some deep place in the earth beneath the demigod's mine? He had fallen through the god's open gateway—was this the heart of the god's sanctuary? But it seemed too . . . ordinary, somehow. The carving was beautiful, the statue of Kernios awe-inspiring, but they did not seem other-worldly.

He caught himself when he almost toppled again, forced himself to breathe. He was weary beyond belief. He was alive. The one was proof of the other, and the solid room around him was more proof that he had survived, no matter where he might be. Across from him was a massive doorway. He went to it and tested it. Despite its heaviness, it swung open at a touch.

The room on the other side was full of small figures—waiting for him, Vansen thought at first, but when he saw the startled look on the little men's faces he knew that was not true. Servants of Kernios, perhaps? But there had also been tiny men like this in Jikuyin's mines. Vansen held up his hands, wondering if they could speak any language he knew. "Can ... you ... understand ... me?"

"What in the name of the Earth Elders were you doing in the Council Chamber, stranger?" one of the little men asked him, frowning. "You're not allowed in there." His eyes grew wide with alarm and he turned and scuttled out the far door. The rest of the little men followed him, looking back fearfully as they fled, as though Vansen were some kind of dangerous beast.

He stared after them and a chill traversed his spine from tail-bone to skull and back. Not only was it his tongue the little man had spoken, it had been a perfect Southmarch accent. What was happening? What kind of trick was being played on him?

Vansen stood for a long time letting his heart slow, staring around the wide room and trying to make sense of what had happened to him, but almost afraid to find out. At last the door of the large chamber opened and a group of the little men, this time carrying shovels and picks and other weapons, came cautiously toward him across the shiny stone floor. Vansen lifted his hands to show he was unarmed, but his attention was caught by the stout man who came with them—a normal man, someone Vansen's own height. There was something oddly familiar about his face ...

"I know you, sir," he said as the big man and his child-sized army approached. "You are ... gods save me, you are Chaven, the royal family's physician."

"So you say," the man said. He did not look the type to be leading any armed band, even one this size. "But I do not admit it. You are trespassing here, you know. What are you doing in the Funderling's guildhall?"

"Funderlings? Guildhall?" Vansen could only stare at the man. "What madness is this? Where am I?"

"By all the gods," Chaven said, and stopped. He put out his arms to hold back the nearest Funderlings, or perhaps to support himself—he looked as though he had been struck a blow. "I know this man, but he was lost in the battle against the Twilight People. Are you not Captain Vansen, sir? Are you not the captain of the royal guard?"

"I am. But where am I?"

"Don't you know?" The physician shook his head slowly. "You are in Funderling Town, of course, underneath Southmarch Castle."

"Southmarch . . . ?" Ferras Vansen looked around the chamber again in stunned amazement, then took a staggering step toward Chaven and the Funderlings, causing some of the little men to raise their weapons in alarm. Vansen fell to his knees, raising his arms in the air to praise all the gods, then the crowd of Funderlings watched with worried faces him as he threw himself down on the floor, laughing and weeping, and pressed his face against the blessed solidity of the stone.

Appendix

PEOPLE

Aduan—former king of March Kingdoms, husband of Ealga, and builder of M'Helan's Rock lodge

Aesi'uah—Yasammez' chief eremite, of Dreamless blood

Aislin—a Skimmer tanglewife

Alessandros—Anissa's father, grand viscount of Devonis

Ananka—baroness, former mistress of King Hespter, now Enander's.

Angelos—an envoy from Jellon to Southmarch

Anglin—Connordic chieftain, awarded March Kingdom after Coldgray Moor

Anglin III—king of Southmarch, great-grandfather of Briony and Barrick

Anissa—queen of Southmarch, Olin's second wife

Annon—a demigod, son of Kernios, killed by Jikuyin

Argal—Xandian name for Perin

Argal the Dark One—Xixian god, enemy of Nushash

Arimone—the autarch's paramount wife

Arjamele—one of Qinnitan's neighbors at her childhood home

Ashretan—Qinnitan's sister

Autarch—Sulepis Bishakh am-Xis III, monarch of Xis, most powerful nation on the southern continent of Xand

Avin Brone—count of Landsend, the castle's lord constable

Axamis Dorza—a Xixian ship's captain

Ayona, Countess—wife of Perivos Akuanis

Azinor of the Onyenai—a god, one of Zmeos' sons by Zuriyal

Baddara—an innkeeper in Lander's Port

Barrick Eddon—a prince of Southmarch

Barrow—a royal guard

Barumbanogatir—a demigod, child of Sveros

Baz'u Jev—a Zandian poet

Bazilis, Favored—envoy for autarch

Beetledown—a Rooftopper

Berkan Hood—the Tollys' lord constable

Birin, Lord of the Evening Mist—a god, one of Perin's sons, killed in the God War

Bloodstone Smoke Quartz—magister of Smoke Quartz family

Brabinayos Boots-of-Stone—Hierosoline name for Barumbanogatir

Brigid—a serving woman at the Quiller's Mint

Briony Eddon—a princess of Southmarch

Brother Lysas—Pelaya's and Teloni's tutor

Caprock Gneiss, Highwarden—important Funderling of the Fire Stone House

Captrosophist Order—school of mirror-lore, founded in Tessis

Caradon Tolly, Duke of Summerfield—second oldest Tolly brother

Caylor—a legendary knight and prince

Celebrants of Mother Night—Qar order/subspecies/cult

Chakkai—a people of the southern Perikalese mountains

Chaven—physician and astrologer to the Eddon family

Chert Blue Quartz—a Funderling, Opal's husband

Cheryazi—Qinnitan's sister

Children of the Emerald Fire—a Qar tribe

Cinnabar—a Funderling magister

Collum Dyer—one of Vansen's soldiers

Conary—proprietor of the Quiller's Mint

Conoric, Sivonnic, and Iellic tribes—"primitive" tribes who lived on Eion before conquest by the southern continent of Xand

Crooked—Qar name for Kupilas

Daikonas Vo—a Perikalese White Hound

Dandelon—a character in Hewney's *King Nikolos*

Dawet dan-Faar—envoy from Hierosol

Dawtrey—a legendary knight, sometimes called "Elf-spelled"

Devona—a goddess, aka "Devona of the Harp"

Devonai kings—ancient line of Hiersoline royalty

Dimakos Heavyhand—one of the last chieftains of the Gray Companies

Doirrean—young Prince Olin's nursemaid

Donal Murroy—onetime captain of the Southmarch royal guard

Dowan Birch—a player in Makewell's Men

Dreamless—also known as "Night Men"

Drows—a race behind the Shadowline, related to Funderlings

Durstin Crowel—baron of Graylock

Ealga Flaxen-Hair—former queen of March Kingdoms, wife of King Aduan

Earth Elders—Funderling guardian spirits

Effir dan-Mozan—a Tuani merchant

Eilis—Merolanna's maid

Elan M'Cory—sister-in-law of Caradon Tolly

Ena—a young Skimmer girl, Back-on-Sunset-Tide clan

Enander II—king of Syan

Eneas—son of Enander, prince of Syan and heir to throne

Erasmios Jino—Marquis of Athnia, aide to King Enander of Syan

Eri—Chaven's oldest brother

Eril—an Akuanis family servant

Erilo—god of harvest

Erivor—god of waters

Erlon Meaher—a court poet in Southmarch, rival of Tinwright

Eshervat—Xixian name for Erivor

Estir Makewell—sister of Pedder Makewell

Fanu—a relative of Idite

Febis—cousin of the autarch

Feival Ulian—a player in Makewell's Men

Ferras Vansen—captain of the Southmarch royal guard

Finn Teodoros—a writer

Four Sunsets—the fairy who owned Dragonfly

Funderlings—sometimes known as "delvers," small people who specialize in stonecraft

Gailon Tolly, Duke of Summerfield—an Eddon family cousin

Geral Kelty—one of the Southmarch guards lost behind the Shadowline

Gil—a potboy at the Quiller's Mint

Grandfather Sulfur—a Funderling elder of the Metamorphic Brothers

Gray Companies—mercenaries and landless men turned bandits in wake of the Great Death

Great Mother—goddess worshipped in Tuan

Gregor—a laundry worker

Gregor of Syan—a famous bard

Guard of Elementals—a tribe of the Qar

Gyir—a Qar, Yasammez' captain, aka "Gyir the Storm Lantern"

Habbili—a god, the crippled son of Nushash

Harsar—Ynnir's counselor

Hendon Tolly—youngest of the Tolly brothers, Guardian of Southmarch

Hesper—King of Jellon, betrayer of King Olin

Hijam Marukh, aka "Stoneheart"—captain of the autarch's Leopard guards

Hiliometes—a legendary demigod and hero

Idite—Effir dan-Mozan's wife

Ikelis Johar—High Polemarch (chief general) of Xis

Iomer M'Sivon—Baron of Landers Port

Irinnis—foreman of military engineers, Hierosol

Jacinth Malachite—a female magister

Jeddin—chief of the autarch's Leopard guards

Karal—king of Syan killed by Qar at Coldgray Moor

Kaspar Dyelos—Chaven's mentor, aka "Warlock of Krace"

Kayyin—"real" name of Gil the potboy

Kearn Tinwright—Matt Tinwright's father, a tutor.

Kellick Eddon—great-grandnephew of Anglin, first of Eddon family March Kings

Kelofas—a Hierosoline noble

Kendrick Eddon—prince regent of Southmarch, eldest son of King Olin

Kernios—god of earth and death, one of the Trigon brothers

King Nikolos—Syan monarch who moved the Trigon out of Hierosol

Kiril—Pelaya's brother

Krisanthe—Queen Meriel's mother, the twins' grandmother

Kupilas—god of healing, also known as "Habbili" and "Crooked"

Lady Simeon—a lady-in-waiting during the twins' youth

Lander III—son of Karal, king of Syan, aka "Lander the Good," "Lander Elfbane"

Lawren—the old Earl of Marrinscrest

Lida—Elan M'Cory's maid

Lisiya Melana of the Silver Glade—demigoddess, one of the nine daughters of Birgya and Volios

Lord of the Peak—a Rooftopper deity

Lorick Eddon—Olin's older brother, who died young

Losa—a laundry worker

Ludis Drakava—Lord Protector of Hierosol

Madi Surazem—goddess of childbirth

Magister Scoria of the Gneiss family

Makaros ("the Makari")—Chaven's family name

Matthias Tinwright—a poet, aka "Matty"

Meriel—Olin's first wife, daughter of "a powerful Brennish duke"

Merolanna—the twins' great-aunt, originally of Fael, widow of Daman Eddon

Mesiya—moon goddess

Metamorphic Brothers—a Funderling religious order

Milios, Bandit-King of Torvio—character from a play

Moina Hartsbrook—a young Helmingsea noblewoman, one of Briony's ladies-in-waiting

Mokori—one of the autarch's stranglers

Muziren Chah—the autarch's regent in Xis

Nenizu—Xandian name for Mesiya the moon goddess

Nevin Hewney—a playwright and player in Makewell's Men

Nikos—Dorza's Hierosoline son

Niram—Chaven's older brother

Nodule—Chert's brother, aka "Magister Blue Quartz"

Nushash—Xixian god of fire and chief god of Xis, patron god of the autarchs, Xandian name for Zmeos

Nynor—Steffens Nynor, Count of Redtree, lord castellan of Southmarch Castle

Okros Dioketian—Brother Okros' full name

Olin Alessandros Benediktos Eddon—son of King Olin and Queen Anissa

On. Iaris—an oracle of the Trigonate Church

On. Zakkas (known as "the Ragged")—an oracle of the Trigonate Church

Onir Kyma—an oracle with a temple in Southmarch

Onir Soteros—"Dreamer Soteros," an oracle of the Trigonate Church

Opal—A funderling, Chert's wife

Palakastros—neighbors of the Akuanis family

Pale Daughter—Qar name for Zoria

Panhyssir—Xixian high priest of Nushash

Parnad—father of current autarch, Sulepis, sometimes known as "the Unsleeping"

Pedar Vansen—Ferras Vansen's father

Pedder Makewell—actor, sponsor, of troop of players

Pelaya—daughter of Count Perivos

Perin—sky god, called "Thane of Lightnings"

Perivos Akuanis, Count—steward of the Hierosoline citadel

Petris Kopayis—famous Kracian siege tactician

Phelsas—Hierosoline philosopher, founder of School of Phelsas, postulator of Many Worlds idea

Pilney—a young player

Pinimmon Vash—Paramount Minister of Xis

Prusus—scotarch of Xis, sometimes called "Prusus the Cripple"

Puzzle—court jester to the Eddon family

Pyarin Ky'vos—Skimmer name for Perin

Qar—race of nonhumans who once occupied much of Eion

Qinnitan—an acolyte of the Hive in Xis, later a bride in the autarch's Seclusion

Quicklime Pewter, Highwarden—important Funderling of the Metal House

Quicksilver—important Funderling family

Rabbit—a laundry worker

Rafe—Ena's friend, Hull-Scraped-the-Sand clan

Red Stag—the Qar name for the god Honnos

Robben Hulligan—a musician, friend of Puzzle

Rooftoppers—little-known residents of Southmarch Castle

Rorick Longarren, Earl of Daler's Troth—an Eddon cousin of Brennish ancestry, related to Meriel

Rose Trelling—one of Briony's ladies-in-waiting, a niece of Avin Brone

Rud—a god, son of Zo and Sva, aka "Golden Arrow"

Rugan—the high priestess of the Hive

Salamandros—one of Zosim's holy names

Sanasu—widow of Kellick Eddon, known as "Weeping Queen"

Saqri (of the Ancient Song)—queen of the People, Ynnir's wife, aka "The Sleeping Queen"

Sard Smaragdine, Highwarden—important Funderling of the Crystal House

Sawamat—Xixian name for Great Mother, a goddess

Selia—Anissa's maid, also from Devonis

Shaso dan-Heza—Southmarch master of arms

Shoshem—Xandian name for Zosim

Shusayem—Xandian name for Madi Surazem

Silas of Perikal—semilegendary knight

Sisel—Hierarch of Southmarch, chief religious figure in March Kingdoms

Sister (or "Sor"), Lyris—Pelaya's tutor

Siveda—goddess of night

Skimmers—a people who make their living on and around water

Soryaza—mistress of the laundry, former Hive acolyte

Surigali—Xixian goddess

Suya—Xandian name for Zoria

Sveros—old god of the night sky, father of Trigon gods

Talibo—Effir's nephew

Tane, King—ancient Vuttish king known as Tane the White and T'chayan Redhand

Tedora—Axamis Dorza's Hierosoline wife

Teloni—Pelaya's sister

Thallo—a Heiosoline queen from the imperial period

Timoid, Father—Eddon family mantis (priest)

Tirnan, Havemore—Brone's former factor, later castellan of Southmarch

Travertine, Highwarden—important Funderling of Water Stone House

Trigon—priesthoods of Perin, Erivor, and Kernios acting in concert

Trigonarch—Head of Trigonate Church, chief religious figure in Eion

Turley Longfingers—a Skimmer fisherman, Back-on-Sunset-Tide clan

Twelve Families—governing body of old Hierosol

Twilight People—another name for the Qar

Tyne Aldritch, Earl of Blueshore—an ally of Southmarch, killed by Qar

Ueni'ssoh—Jikuyin's adviser, one of the Dreamless

Umdi Onajena—the Xixian name for Madi Onyena

Upsteeplebat, Queen—monarch of the Rooftoppers

Urekh—a god, wore wolf-armor

Urrigijag the Thousand-Eyed—Funderling name for Immon

Ustin—King Olin's father

Utta—aka "Sister Utta" or "*Sor* Utta," a priestess of Zoria and Briony's tutor—full name: Utta Fornsdodir

Uvis White-Hand—a god, wounded by Kernios

Vanderin—a Syannese poet

Vermilion Cinnabar—wife of Quicksilver magister

Volios of the Measureless Grip—a son of Perin, god of war

Waterman—a player

Whispering Mothers—a Qar tribe

White Daughter—a name for Zoria

Widowmakers—Jikuyin's troop in ancient days

Willow—a young woman

Xarpedon—name of several autarchs of Xand

Xergal—Xandian name for Kernios

Ximander—a mantis, "writer" of a famous book

Xosh—Xandian name for Khors

Yaridoras—a Perikalese White Hound

Yarnos of the Snows—a god

Yasammez—Qar noblewoman, aka "Lady Porcupine"

Yazi—a laundry girl from Ellamish border country

Yirrud—a god, son of Rud and Onyena

Yisti—Sanian metalworkers of Funderling blood

Ynnir the Blind King—lord of the Qar, "Ynnir din'at sen-Qin, Guardian of the Fireflower, Lord of Winds and Thought," aka "Son of the First Stone"

Zamira—Chaven's sister

Zmeos—a god, Perin's nemesis

Zoria—goddess of wisdom

Zosim—son of Erilo, god of playwrights and drunkards

Zsan-san-sis—chieftain of the Children of the Emerald Glow

PLACES

Akaris—an island between Xand and Eion

Aldritch Stead—castle of Tyne Aldritch, late earl of Blueshore

Ardos Perinous—a mountain town in Syan

Badger's Boots—a Southmarch inn

Basilisk Gate—main gate of Southmarch Castle

Blessed Lady of Night—a temple of Siveda, in Tessis

Brenland—small country south of the March Kingdoms

Brenn's Bay—named after legendary hero

Cat's Eye Street—a street in Xis

Chakki's Hole—a district in the northestern corner of central Tessis

Citadel Hill—small palatine hill of Hierosol

Coast Road—a road in Marrinswalk

Coiner's Point—a pramantony of Landsend

Coldgray Moor—legendary battleground, from a Qar word, "Qul Girah"

Creedy's Inn—tavern in Greater Stell

Dagardar—trading port of Tuan, also a famous siege by the troops of the old autarch Parnad

Daneya Street—a waterfront street in Hierosol, haunt of prostitutes

Dawnwood—site of a battle between Qar and demigod

Deep Library—a place in Qual-na-Qar

Doros Kallida—Syannese town

Ealingsbarrow—human settlement now ruined behind the Shadowline

Eastmarch Academy—university, originally in old Eastmarch, relocated to Southmarch at the time of the last war with the Qar

Eion—the northern continent

Ellamish—border country to Xis

Emberstone Reach—in the Funderling Depths

Esterian River Valley—in Syan, most populous place in Eion

Falopetris—capitol of Ulos, home of Chaven

Firstford—main city of Silverside

Funderling Town—underground city of Funderlings, in Southmarch

Great Gable—Rooftopper sacred spot

Great Kertish Road—a road between Silverside and Kertewall

Hakka—islands off the coast of Xand

Hallia Fair—a town in Kertewall

Harbor of Kalkas—Hierosolian harbor

Harbor of Nektarios—Hierosolian harbor

Hierosol—once the reigning empire of the world, now much reduced; its symbol is the golden snail shell

Hive—a temple in Xis, home of the sacred bees of Nushash

Holy Wainscoting—Rooftopper sacred spot

Iyar—country in Xand

J'ezh'kral Pit—a place out of Funderling myth

Jellon—kingdom, once part of Syannic Empire

Karalsway—a road in Marrinswalk

Kertewall—one of the March Kingdoms

Kinemarket—a town in Marrinswalk

Kolkan's Field—manorial farm outside Southmarch, site of the last Qar/human battle

Krace—a collection of city-states, once part of Hierosoline Empire

Kulloan Strait

Lake Strivothos—a large lake (really a bay) at the center of Southern Eion

Lander's Port—a Marrinswalk fighing town

Landsend—part of Southmarch, Brone's fief, colors red and gold

Landsman's Market—a district in Hierosol with a famous market

Lantern Broad—widest street in Tessis

Lily Gate—gate leading out of the Seclusion into the city of Xis

Little Stell—Daler's Troth town

Mandrake Court—inner court of the Orchard Palace in Xis

Marash—a Xandian province where peppers are grown

March Kingdoms—originally Northmarch, Southmarch, Eastmarch and Westmarch, but after the war with the Qar constituted by Southmarch and the Nine Nations (which include Summerfield and Blueshore)

Market Road—one of Southmarch's main roads

Market Square—main public space in Southmarch

Marrinswalk—one of the March Kingdoms

Meadows of the Moon—pastures for the horses of the Qar

Mihan—a nation in Xand

Mount, The, aka Midlan's Mount—rock in Brenn's Bay upon which Southmarch is built

Mount Sarissa—mountain in southern Eion ("lance")—visible from Hierosol, has "neighbors"

Mount Xandos—mythical giant mountain that stood where Xand now lies

Northmarch Road—the old road between Southmarch and the north

Nyoru—chief city of Tuan

Observatory House—Chaven's residence

Odeion—a theater

Onir Diotrodos—Syannese town

Onir Soteros—a district in Hierosol

Onsilpia's Veil—a large city in Silverside

Oscastle—a city in Marrinswalk

Pomegranate Court—an outer court of the Orchard Palace

Port Road—a main road running along the mainland Southmarch seafront

Qirush-a-Ghat—cavern towns of the Qar; name means "Firstdeeps"

Quarry Square—a meeting-place in Funderling Town

Qul-na-Qar—ancient home of the Qar or Twilight People

Raven's Gate—entrance to Southmarch Castle's inner keep

Reheq-s'lai—Wanderwind Mountains

Rimetrail—a magical river that separates Everfrost from Xandos

Royal Highway—sometimes called King Karal's Road, in Syan, leading all the way to Tessis

Sailmaker's Row—a street near the docks in Great Xis

Salt Pool—underground sea-pool in Funderling Town

Sandy Head

Sania—a country in Xand

Sessio—an island kingdom in the south of Eion

Settesyard—capitol of Settland

Settland—small, mountainous country southwest of the March Kingdoms; ally of Southmarch

Shadowline—line of demarcation between lands of Qar and human lands

Shehen—"Weeping," Qar name for Yasammez' house

Shivering Plain—site of a great Qar battle

Siege of Always-Winter—a mythical castle

Silent Hill—a place behind the Shadowline

Siris—Akuanis family county in northeastern Hierosol

Sirkot—legendary city in the southernmost part of Xand

Skimmer's Lagoon—body of water inside Southmarch walls, connected to Brenn's Bay

Sleep—the city of the Dreamless

Smoking Islands—an archipelago in the sea, far southwest of the Kracian Peninsula

Southmarch—seat of the March Kings, sometimes called "Shadowmarch"

Square of Three Gods—town square in mainland Southmarch

Stoneless Spaces—from Funderling myth, a place of banishment

Sublime Canal—the main canal in Xis, which runs through the Orchard Palace

Summerfield Court—ducal seat of Gailon and the Tolly family

Syan—once dominant empire, still a powerful kingdom in center of Eion

Tessis—capitol city of Syan

Theogonian Gate—a city gate in Hierosol

Torvio—an island nation between Eion and Xand

Tuan—native country of Shaso and Dawet

Tyrosbridge—a principality near the northern Syannese border

Ugenion—Syannese town

Wedge Road—Chert and Opal's street

Wharfside—a district of mainland Southmarch

Whitewood—a forest on the border between Silverside and Marrinswalk

Willowburn—Elan M'Cory's family home

Wolfstooth Spire—tallest tower of Southmarch Castle

Xand—the southern continent

Xis—largest kingdom of Xand; its master is the autarch (adjective, "Xixian")

Zan-Ahmia—country in Xand

Zan-Kartuum—country in Xand

THINGS

Adelfa—head of a Zorian sisterhood

Arrow Count—a Qar ceremony

Astion—a Funderling symbol of authority

Bandit-King of Torvio, The—a play

Black Wrack—a Skimmer wine

Blueroot—favorite Funderling tea-herb

Book of Regret—a semi-mythical Qar artifact/text

Book of the Fire in the Void—"the source of the music that governs even the gods"

Book of the Trigon, The—a late-era adaptation of original texts about all three gods

Council of the Twenty-Seven Families—the leaders of Hierosol

D'shinna—Tuani word for fairies

Demia's Candle—a holiday

Dragonfly—a Shadowline horse

Earthstar—spear of Kernios

Eddon Wolf—the symbol of the Eddon family (silver wolf and stars on black field)

Ever-Wounded Maid—a famous story

False Woman, The—a tavern in Tessis

Fireflower—immortality among the Qar's ruling family

Firmament, The—a theater in Southmarch

Four Sisters Courtyard—a large courtyard in the Hierosoline palace

Gestrimadi—religious festival in March Kingdoms

Golden Enomote—an enomote (about two dozen) soldiers who guard the ruler of Hierosol

Great Zosimia—a holiday, known for religious drama

Hierosoline—the language of Hierosol, found in many religious services and scientific books, etc., and the root to the common speech of Eion

Hours of Refusal—a Zorian prayer Kerneia—a holiday

Kori-doll—effigy thrown onto Eril's Night bonfire

Kossope—a constellation

Kossope House—a dormitory for servants working in the Hierosoline citadel

Kulikos or Kulikos Stone—a reputedly magical object

Life and Death of King Nikolos, The—a play

Little Zosimia—a holiday, known for religious drama

Mantis—a priest, usually of the Trigon

Mihanni—object from Mihan

Morning Star of Kirous—Jeddin's ship

Mossbrew—a strong Funderling drink

Oak Tree—Perin's hammer

Onir Kyma—a temple

Orphan Boy in Heaven, The—a play

Outcrop—the ceremonial center of the Funderling Stone Cutter's guild-hall

Pentecount—a troop, numbering fifty

Perin's Forgiveness—a common religious ritual

Perinos Eio—largest planet in the skies

Polemarch—a general of Xis of Hierosol

Prophet's Day—the day before Kerneia

Quiller's Mint—a tavern

Raging Beast—a monster defeated by Hiliometes in a famous story

Salute of the Bone Knife—Qar ceremony

Seal of War—a Qar gem, object of great importance

Shanat—a popular Xandian game

Shining Man—center of the Funderling Mysteries

Shivering Plain—a famous Qar battleground

Shouma—a drink with strange properties

Silver Thing—part of the Rooftopper's crown jewels

Silverbeam—sword of Khors

Smoke Sacrifice—a Trigonate ritual

Song of the Owl's Eye—Qar ceremony

Soso—Aislin's rescued gull

Sun's Blood—an elixir prepared by the priest of Nushash

Taksiarch—a military rank of Xis of Hierosol

Trigon—the religious power of Eion, a triumvirate of priesthoods (Perin, Erivor, Kernios)

Umeyana—the "blood-kiss"

War-Stone—a weapon of the Whispering Mothers

Whitefire—the sword of Yasammez

Wickeril—a Skimmer liquor

Wildson Night—a festive winter holiday

Wildsong Night—a holiday evening, also known as Winter's Eve

Xandian Federation

Xarpedon—an autarch of Xis

Ximander's Book—selections from the *Book of Regret*

Xol-priest—one who can manipulate the autarch's parasite

Years of Blood—when the Qar fought against the last demigods and monsters

Zoria, Tragedy of a Virgin Goddess—a play

Zosimion Theater—a theater in Tessis

Days of the Week: in the Eionic calendar, there are three ten-day periods in each month, called "tennights." Therefore, the twenty-first day of August in our calendar would be more or less the third Firstday of Oktamene. See the explanation under "Months" for more information.

Firstday
Sunday
Moonsday
Skyday
Windsday
Stonesday
Fireday
Watersday
Godsday
Lastday

Months: each Eion month is thirty days long, divided into three ten-days, with five intercalary days between the end of the year—Orphan's Day—and the first day of the new year, also known as Firstday or Year Day—thus month/month correspondents are liable to differ by a few days: the first day of Trimene in Southmarch is not the exact same day as March 1st on our calendar.

Eimene—January
Dimene—February
Trimene—March
Tetramene—April
Pentamene—May
Hexamene—June
Heptamene—July
Oktamene—August
Ennamene—September
Dekamene—October
Endekamene—November
Dodekamene—December

About the Author

Tad Williams has held more jobs than any sane person should admit to – singing in a band, selling shoes, managing a financial institution, throwing newspapers and designing military manuals, to name just a few. He has also hosted a syndicated radio show for ten years, worked in theatre and television production, taught, and worked in multimedia for a major computer firm. He is co-founder of an interactive television company and is currently writing comic books and film and television scripts. Tad and his family live in the San Francisco Bay Area.

For more information go to www.tadwilliams.co.uk

Find out more about Tad Williams and other Orbit authors by registering for the free monthly newsletter at www.orbitbooks.net.

Introducing

THE DRAGONBONE CHAIR

The first volume of Tad Williams' classic
Memory, Sorrow and Thorn series

THE SICKLE DESCENDED AND BREYUGAR sagged forward. Purplish blood pumped from his throat, spattering down onto the coffin. For a moment the Lord Constable twitched violently beneath the priest's hand, then went limp as an eel; the dark flow continued to drizzle on the black lid. Enmeshed in the bizarre intermixture of thought, Simon helplessly experienced Pryrates' panicky exhilaration. Behind that he felt the *something-else* – a cold, dark, horribly vast thing. Its ancient thoughts sang with obscene joy.

One of the soldiers was throwing up; but for the flabby numbness that unmanned and silenced him, Simon would have done the same.

Pryrates pushed the count's body aside; Breyugar tumbled in a disordered heap, oyster-pale fingers curled toward the sky. The blood smoked on the dark box, and the blue light flickered more brightly. The line it described around the edge became more pronounced. Slowly, dreadfully, the lid began to open, as if forced up from within.

Holy Usires Who loves me, Holy Usires Who loves me – Simon's thoughts were a rush, a panicked tangle – *help me, help me help it's the Devil in that box, he's coming out help save me oh help . . .*

We have done it, we have done it! – other thoughts, foreign, not his – *Too late to turn back. Too late.*

The first step – the coldest, most terrible thoughts of all – *How they will pay and pay and pay . . .*

As the lid tilted up the light within burst forth, throbbing indigo touched with smoky gray and sullen purple, a terrible bruised light that pulsed and glared. The lid fell open, and the wind tightened its pitch as if frightened, as if sickened by the radiance of the long black box. At last what was inside could be seen.

Jingizu, a voice whispered in Simon's head. *Jingizu . . .*

It was a sword. It lay inside the box, deadly as an adder; it might have been black, but a floating sheen mottled the blackness, a crawling gray like oil on dark water. The wind shrieked.

It beats like a heart – the heart of all sorrow . . .

Calling, it sang inside Simon's head, a voice both horrible and beautiful, seductive as claws gently scraping his skin.

'Take it, Highness!' Pryrates urged through the hiss of the wind. Enthralled, helpless, Simon suddenly wished he had the strength to take it himself. Could he not? Power was singing to him, singing of the thrones of the mighty, the rapture of desire fulfilled.

Elias took a dragging step forward. One by one the soldiers around him stumbled back, turning to run sobbing or praying down the hill, lurching into the darkness of the girdling trees. Within moments only Elias, Pryrates, and hidden Simon remained on the hilltop with the hooded ones and their sword. Elias took another step; now he stood over the box. His eyes were wide with fear; he seemed stricken by wrenching doubt, his lips working soundlessly. The unseen fingers of the wind plucked at his cloak, and the hill grasses twined about his ankles.

'You must take it!' Pryrates said again, and Elias stared at him as though seeing the alchemist for the first time. 'Take it!' Pryrates' words danced frantically through Simon's head like rats in a burning house.

The king bent, reaching out his hand. Simon's lust turned to sudden horror at the wild, empty nothingness of the sword's dark song.

It's wrong! Can't he feel it?! Wrong!

As Elias' hand neared the sword, the wail of the wind subsided. The four hooded figures stood motionless before the wagon, the fifth seemed to sink into deeper shadow. Silence fell on the hilltop like a palpable thing.

Elias grasped the hilt, lifting the blade out of the coffin in one smooth movement. As he held it before him the fear was suddenly wiped from his face, and his lips parted in a helpless, idiot smile. He lifted the sword high; a blue shimmer played along the edge, marking it out from the blackness of the sky. Elias' voice was almost a whimper of pleasure.

'I . . . will take the master's gift. I will . . . honor our pact.' Slowly, the blade held before him, he sank to one knee. *'Hail to Ineluki Storm King!'*

The wind sprang up anew, shrieking. Simon reeled back from the flapping, whirling hill-fire as the four robed figures lifted their white arms, chanting: *'Ineluki, aí! Ineluki, aí!'*

No! Simon's thoughts flurried, *the king . . . all is lost! Run, Josua! Sorrow . . . Sorrow on all the land . . .*

The fifth hooded shape began to writhe atop the wagon. The black robe fell away, and a shape of fire-crimson light was revealed, flapping like a burning sail. A ghastly, heart-gnawing fear beat outward from the thing as it began to grow before Simon's terror-fixed eyes – bodiless and billowing, larger and larger until the empty, wind-snapping bulk of it loomed over all, a creature of howling air and glowing redness.

The Devil is here! Sorrow, his name is sorrow . . .! The king has brought the Devil! Morgenes, Holy Usires, save me save me save me!!

He ran mindlessly down through black night, away from the red thing and the exulting *something-else.* The sound of his flight was lost in the screaming wind. Branches tore at his arms and hair and face like claws . . .

The icy claw of the North . . . the ruins of Asu'a.

And when he fell at last, tumbling, and his spirit fled from such horror, fled away into deeper darkness, it seemed that in the final instant he could hear the very stones of the earth moaning in their beds beneath him.